Acclaim for David Anthony Durham's

Pride of Carthage

"Terrific. . . . Durham has a gift for locating with unfailing precision the humanity of his characters. . . . I have rarely encountered in fiction a hero as three-dimensional and vivid as the Hannibal who appears in these pages."   —*The News and Observer* (Raleigh)

"An extraordinary achievement: Durham puts flesh on the bones of Carthage in a way that no novelist has done since Flaubert wrote *Salammbô.*"   —Tom Holland, author of
Rubicon: The Last Years of the Roman Republic

"Not since *I, Claudius* has a book so successfully portrayed an alien world yet made it seem so contemporary. . . . It's not just historical drama but a story of manhood and consequences."
—*San Diego Pages*

"Compelling. . . . At once a sweeping saga, an intimate portrait of an individual, a military history, and a tale about love, devotion, and loyalty."   —*Bookmarks Magazine*

"Sweeping. . . . Brimming with historic details."   —*Tucson Citizen*

"Heady, richly textured. . . . Durham weaves abundant psychological, military and political detail into this vivid account of one of the most romanticized periods of history."
—*Journal Gazette* (Fort Wayne)

"A brilliantly executed and movingly written historical novel—the best of its kind I've ever read."
—Paule Marshall, author of *Brown Girls, Brownstones*

David Anthony Durham

PRIDE OF CARTHAGE

David Anthony Durham earned an MFA from the University of Maryland and is the author of two widely praised novels, *Gabriel's Story* and *Walk Through Darkness*. Durham lives in Massachusetts with his wife and children.

PRIDE OF CARTHAGE

PRIDE OF CARTHAGE

A NOVEL OF HANNIBAL

DAVID ANTHONY DURHAM

ANCHOR BOOKS
A DIVISION OF RANDOM HOUSE, INC.
NEW YORK

FIRST ANCHOR BOOKS EDITION, JANUARY 2006

The Library of Congress has cataloged the Doubleday edition as follows:
Durham, David Anthony, 1969–
Pride of Carthage: a novel of Hannibal / David Anthony Durham.
p. cm.
1. Punic War, 2nd, 218–201 B.C.—Fiction. 2. Hannibal, 247–182 B.C.—Fiction.
3. Carthage (Extinct City)—Fiction. 4. Generals—Fiction. I. Title.
PS3554.U677P75 2005
813'.6—dc22
2004045532

Anchor ISBN-10: 0-385-72249-4
Anchor ISBN-13: 978-0-385-72249-0

Book design by Michael Collica

Map designed by David Cain

www.anchorbooks.com

Printed in the United States of America
10 9 8 7 6 5 4 3 2 1

To my son, Sage
May you be as wise as your name
and may your life be one of peace,
free from the madness of these pages.

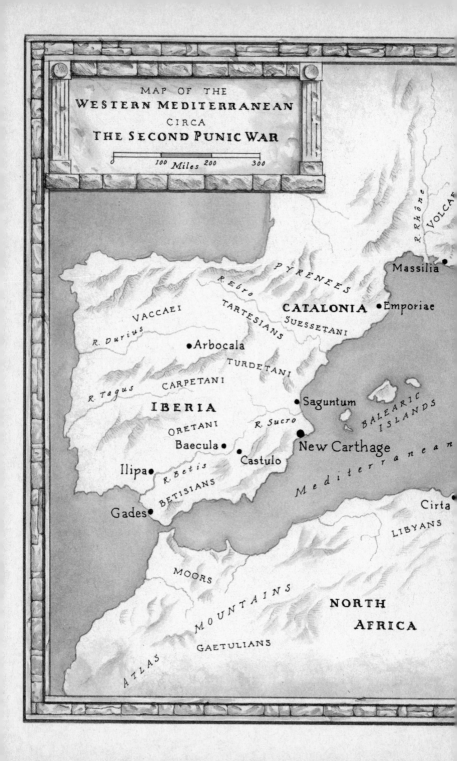

PRIDE OF CARTHAGE

I mco Vaca was a slim figure, barely sixteen, with a sparse beard
and lips that some joked had a feminine pout. His head might
have been better suited to a poet than a warrior, but the young
man knew his only aptitude with words was in quick jest, banter, and
trivial things. He believed poets to be of a more serious bent.
Though he was a citizen of Carthage, his family had long ago fallen
into poverty, affairs ill managed and Fortune never kindly toward
them. As the sole son among five children, he feared that the fates
awaiting his sisters were shameful. Thus his tenure in the Carthaginian army in Iberia was not the answer to a calling but an attempt to
secure a wage. And, as his father said, armed conflict provided the
chance to distinguish oneself and better the family prosperity. Much
to the young man's surprise, that is just what happened on the last
day of the siege of Arbocala.

His division was posted near the most likely breach. As the battering ram worked its methodic destruction, Imco stood with his
shield held over his head, catching arrows shot down from above.
His eyes bounced around so quickly they scarcely registered the
things around him except in glimpses of single objects: the braid of

1

hair down the back of the man in front of him, the tattoo on the shoulder of another, the crook of his own arm and the throbbing artery in the soft spot there. The other soldiers jostled for position, each seeking the best point from which to gain the wall. Imco had no such interests. He might even have retreated, but the crush of bodies behind him would not allow it.

When the wall crumbled, the bulk of it fell inward, all save one great block that hung for a moment teetering on the still-standing portion of the wall. Imco fixed his gaze on it, sure that he recognized his own demise. But when the block fell it shifted to one side and squashed the flank of soldiers just to his left. Seeing the damage done to their comrades, the other soldiers roared. The sound was so fierce that it buffeted Imco forward, one step and then another, around the block and over the next. He scrambled up the slope of debris, then hoisted himself onto a wide slab of rock and found that there was nothing else to climb. He caught a momentary glimpse of the city below him and realized where he was. The defenders huddled there, dusty-armored, eyes upraised, weapons gripped before them, a prickle of spearheads like the back of a sea urchin. Archers behind them let their missiles fly. Imco had no desire to proceed, but if he was going to, he at least wished for company. He raised a hand to signal the ease of his route to those behind him. An ill-fated move.

An arrow struck him in the flat of the palm. The force of it snapped his arm back, throwing him off balance. He tumbled down the slope amid the legs of the men who had been following him. The next few moments of his life saw him trodden upon and kicked and tripped over. Someone stepped on the arrow, wrenching it about in his flesh and sending slivers of pain down as far as his toes. Another broke two of his ribs by planting the shaft of his spear in his chest as he climbed over him. But after all this, the young man struggled to his feet and looked up from the rubble to behold a conquered city.

Later he discovered that he held the honor of being the first soldier on the crumbled wall of Arbocala. The officer who told him this was aware of a certain comic element to the award, but it was his nonetheless. That night he drank wine from the city itself and feasted on strips of venison and bread from the Iberian ovens. The captain of his company sent a young woman to him in his tent. She straddled his battered body and lowered herself onto him and received his climax a few moments later. She had large eyes that stared into his, unflinching and with no emotion. With a trembling voice he asked her name. But she was already finished with her work and had no desire to have anything more to do with him. She had scarcely slipped out of the tent when another visitor entered.

He wore the snug breastplate of an infantryman, with a dark tunic beneath it. He was bare-armed and square across the shoulders, brown-faced and black-eyed and handsome in a way that has nothing of feminine beauty in it. Imco had never seen him before but he knew at first glance that he was an officer. The soldier flushed and rearranged his bedding, afraid that he might greet this visitor with a view of more than the man was interested in. His heart beat like a bird's. He thought himself an absurd impostor and was sure that the man would see him as such.

"So you're the honored one?" the man asked. "So hungry for the blood of Arbocala? I might not have guessed it to look upon you, but it is what's inside a man that matters. Why have I not heard your name before?"

Imco answered, as honestly as he could, this and the following questions. He spoke about the origins of his family name, about the length of time he had been away from Africa, about where and under whom he received his training, about how he missed his father and sisters and hoped his soldier's pay was easing their burdens. Five minutes into the conversation, Imco had almost managed to forget the importance of his guest and think him a field lieutenant who must often talk with foot soldiers. The man listened with his eyes and with more empathy than the soldier had felt since he left home. And so he was not offended when the officer interrupted him.

"Forgive me, but are yours a humble people?"

The young man said, "Iberian rats eat better than my family."

"No longer. My secretary will come and take down your family's details. In honor of your bravery, I will send them a small package, with it a portion of land outside of Carthage, a hundred field slaves to work it, house servants as well. Will that ease their burdens?"

The soldier had lost his speech, but he managed to nod.

The other man smiled and said, "This day you helped put one task behind us to clear the way for the great things to come. You will fight as bravely for me during the next campaign?"

Imco nodded, although his head was spinning and shocked. He could not fully comprehend anything except that he had been asked a question and that it behooved him to answer positively.

"Good. There are many paths to our fates, but none so direct as war. Remember that. All of our lives lead to death, Imco Vaca. The gods leave us no say in this. But we've at least some influence on how we shape our living moments, and we are sometimes prompted to achievements beyond our early reckoning. This is something you should consider."

The officer turned away, pushed open the tent flap with an arm, and paused a moment, taking in the night. He said, "Fate does not move walls for us without reason."

With that, the man slipped from the tent and was gone. Only as the quiet moments progressed did Imco order the meaning of the conversation. The complete understanding of whom he had just spoken to did not so much dawn on him as slowly fill him. He had never before been close enough to look his commander in the face, but now he had. His commander, a man who held the power of life and death over so many, with a fortune endless in its riches, a soldier who although not yet thirty years old had a genius for war that some said he harbored inside his body, in a compartment just beside his heart. Hannibal Barca.

Realizing this, the young man called for the servant assigned to him. He begged him bring a bucket or bowl or something, quickly. This day had heaped one amazement on another and this last was just too much for him. He was going to be sick.

ONE

Prelude

The delegation arrived in the capital of the Roman Republic during the waning days of the Mediterranean autumn. They had traveled from the city of Saguntum in eastern Iberia to beg an audience before the Senate. Once they were granted it, a man named Gramini spoke for them. He looked about the chamber with a clear-eyed visage, voice strong but somewhat lispy. The Romans had to crane forward on their benches and watch his lips to understand him, some with hands cupped to their ears, a few with grimaces and whispers that the man's Latin was unintelligible. But in the end all understood the substance of his words, and that was this: The Saguntines were afraid. They feared for their very existence. They were a jewel embedded in a rough land, rife with tribal conflict and turmoil. They were sheep living with a mighty wolf at their back. The creature's name was not new to them, for it was the ever hungry Hannibal Barca of Carthage, the son of Hamilcar, avowed enemy of Rome.

The delegate explained that Rome had neglected Iberia to the Republic's detriment. The African power had taken advantage of this to build an empire there. It had grown into a stronger foe than

5

it had ever been during their earlier wars. He wondered aloud whether Romans had forgotten the lessons of history. Did they not remember the damage Hamilcar Barca had inflicted upon them during the last war between Rome and Carthage? Did they deny that he had gone undefeated and that the conflict had been decided by the flaws of others beyond his control? Did they remember that after this reversal Hamilcar had not only prevailed over the mercenary revolt in his own country but had also begun carving into Iberian soil? Because of him, the Carthaginians grew even richer on a harvest of silver and slaves and timber, a fortune that flowed daily into the coffers of their homeland.

By the benevolent will of the gods, Hamilcar had been dead some years now, but his son-in-law, Hasdrubal the Handsome, had stretched their domain farther and built a fortress-city at New Carthage. Now he, too, was dead: Thankfully, an assassin's knife had found his throat as he slept. But Hamilcar had been resurrected in his son Hannibal. He had set about completing their mission. Altogether, the three Carthaginians had defeated the Olcades and destroyed their city of Althaea, punished the Vaccaei and captured Salmantica, and made unrelenting war on the tribes of the Baetis and Tagus and even the Durius, peoples wilder and farther removed than those of Saguntum. Even now, Hannibal was off on a new campaign against Arbocala. If this proved successful—as the emissaries feared it might have already—most of Iberia would lie under the Carthaginian heel. There was only one great city left, and that was Saguntum. And was Saguntum not an ally to Rome? A friend to be called upon in ill times and likewise aided in Rome's own moments of calamity? That is why he was here before them, to ask for Rome's full commitment of support should Hannibal set his sights next on them.

The senator Gaius Flaminius rose to respond. A tall man among Romans, Gaius was self-assured beneath a bristle of short black hair that stood straight up from his forehead as if plastered there with egg whites. He joked that the Saguntines could not be mistaken for sheep. They were a mighty people in their own right. Their fortress was strong and their resilience in battle well known. He also added, a bit more dryly, that there was one wolf of the Mediterranean and it resided not in Iberia but upon the Tiber. He did not answer the Iberians' questions directly but thanked them for their faith and urged patience. The Senate would consider the matter.

Gramini bowed at this answer but showed with his upraised hand that he was not yet finished. He wanted it understood that the danger Saguntum was in related to its allegiance with Rome. Should that allegiance prove to be of no substance, then a grave injustice would have been committed against a blameless people. Saguntum had every intention of staying loyal to Rome. He hoped that Rome would likewise honor its commitment, for there were some who claimed Saguntum was foolish to put so much faith in a Latin alliance. He ended by asking, "Can we have your word, then, of direct military assistance?"

"You have yet to be attacked," Flaminius said. "It would be unwise to conclude a course of action prior to understanding the nature of the conflict." He assured the Iberian that in any event the Saguntines should return to Iberia in good spirits. No nation had ever regretted, or would ever regret, making a friend of Rome.

Having received this answer, Gramini retired and was soon making the arrangements for his return voyage. The Senate, for their part, did engage with the questions the Iberian had posed, in depth, in heated debate, that afternoon and all of the next. They agreed to send a messenger to this Carthaginian, Hannibal Barca. Let his cage get a good rattling. Let him remember the power of Rome and act accordingly. Beyond this, however, they could come to no firm consensus. They had other foreign issues to deal with, in Gaul and Illyria. The resolution of this affair with Carthage would have to wait.

Each afternoon since arriving in Iberia two weeks earlier, the youngest of the Barca brothers, Mago, had taken a long, vigorous ride through the countryside. On returning each afternoon he paused at the same vantage point and stared at the physical manifestation of his family's legacy. New Carthage was breathtaking. It sat at the far end of a long isthmus, like an island tacked to the continent by an arm of the land that refused to let go. From a distance its walls rose straight up out of the water on three sides, only that narrow stretch of earth connecting it to the continent. The harbor carved an almost perfect circle around the city, with fingers of jutting rock that all but closed its mouth. Two thirds of its water sank into a blue-black no different from the deep water offshore; the other third, on the south side of the city, shone a wonderful turquoise blue, lit from below by a shallow bed of rock and coral that caught the sun like the inside of an oyster shell.

The fifteenth time he took in this view, he knew something had changed. It was a minute detail and he took a moment to spot it: The flag normally flapping above the citadel had been pulled in. No longer did the red standard of campaign snap in the breeze. Now, even as he watched, a new flag climbed into position. It shivered, curled, trembled, and never stood out clearly, but he knew what it was: the Lion of Carthage. His family's symbol. It meant his brothers had returned from the insurrection they had gone to put down in the north. Messengers had brought word of the army's approach earlier in the week, but they must have made better time than anticipated.

A rider sent out to find him met him near the southern gates to the fortress. Hannibal asked that he come without hesitation, the messenger said. When Mago dismounted and headed toward the palace the man said, "Not there. Please follow me."

The walk took a further few minutes. The messenger led him at a trot across the main courtyard, down several flights of marble stairs, through a series of tunnels, and then up a sloping ramp onto the wall itself. Beyond it, Mago caught sight of the returning army, coming in from the northern approach. His steps slowed as he took it in.

The long, wide column flowed over the rolling landscape, receding into the distance and still visible on the farthest ridge of the horizon. The infantry marched in loose formation, in their respective companies and tribal affiliations. The cavalry rode out to either side of the army. They circled and wheeled and galloped in short bursts, as if they were herdsmen at work with a great flock. The elephants strode in a similar deployment but spaced at larger intervals. He could see the nearest of them in detail. They were of the African breed, so their drivers straddled them just behind their ears. The riders' heads and torsos swayed with the slow rhythm of the creatures' strides. They talked to their mounts and smacked them with rods, but these seemed automatic gestures, for the creatures saw the fortress and could already smell the feed waiting for them.

Mago turned and sped off behind the messenger, pushing his way through a growing, joyous crowd. He had to move quickly to slip between them. By the time the messenger slowed his pace and looked back at Mago, they had again dropped down to the base level of the city. They walked down a dark hallway. It was rank with moisture, cooler than the exposed air. Old hay had been swept out and piled along one side of the corridor. The acidic bite of urine made Mago walk with his head turned to one side. He was about to ask the messenger which this was—a joke or a mistake—but then caught sight of a head glancing out from a room toward the end of the hallway. A body emerged after it: his older brother, Hanno, the second after Hannibal. Mago pushed past the messenger and jogged toward him, arms upraised for the greeting he expected.

Hanno shot one arm out. His fingers clamped around his brother's bicep and squeezed a momentary greeting. But then that was done with. He pulled Mago's eyes to his own and fixed his lips in a stern line. "Romans," he said. "They arrived just before us. Not the homecoming we expected. Hannibal is just about to speak with them. Come."

Hanno motioned for his brother to enter the room behind him. Though swept clean of straw and filth, the room was simply a corridor, lined along one wall with stalls. It was lit by a mixture of torchlight and the slanting gray daylight from a passage that opened onto the horse-training fields. Several soldiers of the Sacred Band lined the walls. These were guards sworn to protect the nation's generals. Each was clean-shaven on the cheeks and upper lip, a carefully trimmed knob of whiskers at the base of his chin. They stood one before each stall, arms folded and gazes fixed forward.

In the center of the space, a chair had been set, by itself, straight-backed and tall, with wings coming out from either side that hid the profile of whoever resided in it. Which is what it did for the man now seated in it. His arms rested dead upon the armrests, the knuckles of his hands large and calloused, the brown skin stained still darker by some substance long dried and caked against it. Several figures bent close to him, speaking in hushed tones. One of them—half hidden behind the body of the chair and visible only as a portion of the head and shoulder—Mago recognized. When this person looked up he saw the bulky, square-jawed face and the thickly ridged forehead, topped with a mass of wavy black hair. Though his face was grim, the man flashed a smile upon seeing the newcomers. It was Hasdrubal, the third of the Barca sons. As Mago had known from the start, the seated man was his eldest brother, Hannibal.

Mago stepped toward them, but Hanno caught him by the arm. He nodded toward the mouth of the passageway. Five men had appeared in the space. They seemed to stand considering the corridor, looking one to another and sharing thoughts on it. One of them shook his head and spat on the ground. Another made as if to stride away. But yet another stayed them all with a calming gesture of his hand. He pulled the crested helmet from his head and tucked it under his arm, then stepped forward into the passageway. The others fell in a few paces behind him, five silhouettes against the daylight.

"You and I will take a position to the right of him," Hanno whispered, "Hasdrubal and the translator to the left. This is a strange greeting, yes, but we want you to stand as one of us."

The two of them slipped into position. Mago still could not see his eldest brother's face, but Hasdrubal nodded at Mago and whispered something that he did not catch. Then they all turned toward the Romans in silence, still-faced and as empty of expression as possible.

The leader of the embassy halted a few strides from the chair and stood with his legs planted wide. Though he wore no sword, he was otherwise dressed for war. His skin tone was only a shade lighter than the Carthaginians', yet there was no mistaking the differences in their origins. He was half a head shorter than most Carthaginians, bulky in the shoulders and thick down through the torso. One edge of his lips twisted, an old scar, perhaps, a wound slow in healing and left imperfect. His eyes jumped from one to the other of the brothers, studying each and finally settling on the figure enclosed by the chair.

"Hannibal Barca," he said, "commander of the army of Carthage in Iberia: My name is Terentius Varro. I bring you a message from the Republic of Rome, by order of the Senate of that Republic."

He paused and glanced over his shoulder. One of the men behind him cleared his throat and began to translate Varro's Latin into Carthaginian. He was cut short by a single, small motion that drew all their eyes. Hannibal had raised a finger from its grip on the armchair. His wrist twisted in a motion that was at first unclear, until the digit settled into place, a pointer directed toward one of the men standing behind him, his own translator, a young man dressed in a simple cloak that covered him entirely save for his head and hands. He conveyed the introduction.

"Welcome, Terentius Varro," Hannibal said, via his translator. "Let us hear it, then."

"You will have me speak here, in a stable?" Varro looked around. One of the men behind him exhaled an exasperated breath and checked the bottoms of his sandals for fouling. "Let me say again, Hannibal Barca—"

"It's just that I was told you were anxious to speak to me," Hannibal said, breaking in with his Carthaginian. "I've just returned from the siege of Arbocala this very hour, you see. I am tired, unwashed. I still have blood under my fingernails. All this and yet I've paused here to listen to your urgent message. Once you've given it you can mount and take my answer back to Rome. And do not worry about your sandals. We can provide you new ones if you like."

The commander pointed to a soldier in the far corner and motioned him out of the room. The young man seemed confused, but hurried out anyway. "You'll like our sandals," Hannibal said. "There are none better for comfort."

The Roman turned and shared a dour expression with his translator, as if asking him to make some official note of all of this. He turned back to the commander. "It's come to the Senate's attention that some of our allies here in Iberia are dismayed by Carthaginian actions."

Hannibal made a sound low in his throat, a rumbling acknowledgment.

The Roman took no note of it. Saguntum, he reminded the commander, was a friend of Rome and would be protected as such.

Rome had been generous with Carthage so far, not curtailing its ventures in Iberia since the time of Hamilcar, through Hasdrubal the Handsome. Now Rome was still acting with restraint in her dealings with Hannibal. But this should not suggest that Romans had forgotten the details of previous treaties. They still honored the agreement with Hasdrubal that limited the Carthaginian sphere of influence to south of the Ebro. They acknowledged that the familial and tribal ties of some of Carthage's Iberian allies approached that border, and for that reason they had so far looked the other way in the face of these minor violations. But Rome would not remain inactive if Saguntum were threatened. And she would allow no activity whatsoever beyond the Ebro. None. She wanted this understood by the young commander, in the event that his predecessor's untimely death had left him with any questions.

As the translator finished this, Varro glanced over his shoulder at his colleague, a knowing look that suggested he was just now getting to the crux of his speech. "Rome therefore demands that Hannibal limit his dealings around Saguntum to peaceful transactions among existing allies, establishing no settlements there and mediating no disputes in the region. Rome demands that no Carthaginian or Carthaginian ally cross the Ebro for any reason whatsoever. Furthermore, Rome demands—"

"Enough!" Hannibal said in Latin. He had not spoken loudly, but the word clipped the Roman to silence. He leaned forward, for the first time bringing his profile into Mago's view. His deep-set eyes remained in shadow, recessed beneath prominent eyebrows and beside a sharp blade of a nose. Like the men of the Sacred Band, he wore a trimmed bulb of hair on his chin. He touched it with his fingertips and seemed to pluck his words out like single strands. "I'll have no more furthermores. You have made your case. Will you have my response?"

Varro gathered his composure. More than startled by the interruption, he seemed ill at ease speaking directly to the Carthaginian in Latin. He had to clear his throat before responding. "As I have been interrupted, I would not say that I have made my case completely."

"Be that as it may . . ."

Hannibal stood and stepped forward, a head taller than the Roman. His arms were bare from the shoulder. He flexed his triceps, rolled his shoulder joints, and tilted his chin in a way that audibly cracked his jaw. There was something in his appearance that surprised Mago, though it was not a difference in his actual physique. He had always been fit and disciplined beyond the norm, but now his movements had a new focus and deliberateness. Even as he appeared to be somewhat weary of the discourse, there was still a thoughtful tension behind his eyes. He paced the floor before the envoy, glancing at various objects around the stable: the dirt floor, the wood of the stalls, the insignia on the shield of one of the Sacred Band. He touched for a moment on Mago and registered his arrival with his eyes.

"Whence comes this history of kinship between Rome and Saguntum?" he asked, speaking once more in Carthaginian. His translator kept time just after him. "Where is the treaty written? It seems to me that this city is a new friend to Rome, perhaps a friend in name only, for a purpose only. Be true and speak to the source of your passions. Rome is troubled to see Carthage flourish. You thought us a defeated people but find instead that we blossom. We came to this wild place and tamed it and now manage the riches that flow out of it. This is what you covet. Rome has always hated the way silver coins appear between the fingers of Carthaginian hands as if by sorcery. Speak truthfully and admit that you stand here before me because of greed and envy, not for the protection of a single city. This matter of Saguntum is just an excuse for opening hostilities with us."

Hannibal paused. When the translator halted a moment later, the Roman answered promptly. "A treaty of alliance between Saguntum and Rome is held by the record keepers of the Senate. It is a well-known friendship that is not in question here."

"Fine, fine," Hannibal said, breaking in before the translation was finished. "Let us move on, then."

Instead of doing so he approached one of the stalls. As he neared it, a horse's head emerged from the shadows, a solid black muzzle, lean until it flared at the nostrils. Hannibal clicked his tongue in greeting and reached out to stroke the creature. He lost himself in examining the horse's mane and ears and brushing his hand across its eyelashes. When he spoke he almost seemed to do so absently.

"My second point of dispute is with your interference within our realm of influence," he said. "Saguntum is surrounded on all sides by many who are loyal to Carthage. But the Saguntines have interfered in the well-being of our allies the Turdetani. Just this year past the headmen of three clans were put to death. And for what? How did these small tribal powers so threaten Saguntum—or Rome, for that matter? What did they do that they deserved crucifixion? I ask, but I do not pause to hear your answer because you do not have one, not a true one."

He spun from the horse and set his eyes back on the Roman. "What did you say your name was?"

"Terentius Varro."

"Let me tell you something, Terentius Varro, which you may not know of Carthage. We aid those who have been wronged. With our strength we defend our friends from tyrants. That is my only grievance against Saguntum. I ask that they make amends for the wrongs they have done. And yet you come here as though I had entered the city and taken their leaders by force and nailed them to crosses. This is rubbish and you know it. Go back to Rome and tell your masters so. Go back to Rome and tell them that I heard your message and give them this response . . ."

Hannibal inhaled deeply and let a moment of silence pass into another. Then he exhaled a long, petulant sigh through loose lips that blubbered as the air escaped. A similar sound came from one of the stalls in answer. One of the Sacred Band chuckled, then caught himself and went stone-faced.

"What was that?" the Roman asked.

"You can make that sound, can you not? Something like a stallion bored with chewing grass. Take that back to Rome and stand before the Senate and in your best and most distinguished voice, say . . ." Again he made the sound, longer this time and even more equestrian.

Varro stared at him. His official haughtiness slipped from his features. "Do you really want conflict with us?"

"What I want is not the important thing," Hannibal said. "The important thing is what will be. In deciding this, Hannibal is only one of a million minds, only a single man among a host of gods. We've done nothing to violate our word. That is all the answer I need give you. I've spoken to you simply. Flippantly, yes, but my message is clear. I do have disputes with Saguntum. These may, Baal willing, be resolved peacefully, but do understand that they will be resolved one way or the other. Pray to your gods that there is no conflict in this. Good-bye, and fair journey to you."

The meeting was concluded. Hannibal spun on his heel and fell into instant conversation with Hasdrubal and the others around him, speaking of the things yet to be done that afternoon, the care the returning animals would require, and the provisions he was ordering released for the men to celebrate their victorious return. The Romans looked uncomfortably at each other. They milled about briefly, exchanging glances and a few whispers. Varro seemed on the verge of calling out to the commander, but one of his advisers touched him on the elbow. The group reluctantly retired, five silhouettes again traversing the long stretch of the stable, out into the ashen gray of the winter day.

As soon as the Romans were gone Hasdrubal clapped his brother on the back. Hannibal shook his head and laughed. "Was it imprudent of me to snort so? Do you think he will take my message to the Senate?"

Hasdrubal said, "I would love to see their faces if he does. But Hannibal, look, the other young lion has returned." He nodded toward Mago.

Hannibal followed his gesture and was in motion even before he had actually spotted him. "By the gods, he has! And he will now get a proper greeting." He pushed through his advisers, reached Mago in a few steps, and clapped his arms around him. Mago recognized the smell of him, a scent that was stale and sharp and yet sweet all at once. He felt the curly locks of his brother's hair beside his face and the prickle of his chin hairs against his shoulder blades, and he almost gasped at the pressure of the embrace. It seemed to last for some time, but he realized this was because his brother was silently mouthing his thanks to Baal.

"Mago, you do not know how it fills my heart to see you," Hannibal said, still continuing the embrace, his voice just above a whisper but full of emotion. "It has been too long. I pray that your education was worth these years of absence. I know Father wanted you to build upon the gifts of your intellect, but many times I've wished for you by my side."

As Hannibal released him, Hasdrubal stepped forward, throwing a slow punch at his chin. The motion then became a quick jab toward his ribs and a moment later was an embrace. Speaking over his brother's shoulder, Mago said, "I came to serve you, brother, but I did not expect to find a Roman in the stables."

"Neither did I," Hannibal said, "but let us remember that all such occurrences are the will of Baal. There are great things whistling in the air around us, possibilities, the shouts of the gods to action. So unexpected happenings should be expected. But listen . . ." He spread his arms and spun in a gesture that encompassed them all. "Is this not an amazing moment? After years of separation, Hamilcar's sons are finally all together. Tomorrow will bring many great things for us and for Carthage, for Hamilcar's memory . . ."

Just then the soldier who had been sent away for sandals stepped into the room sheepishly, his burden pressed to his chest. Hannibal broke into laughter. "We let our guests leave without their footwear! The pity of it. Bring me a pair, then. My feet have been well abused in the north. And give one to my brother, the first of many welcome presents."

He took a pair of the sandals and smacked them to Mago's chest. "I must attend to my returning army," he said. "They've labored incredibly, so they deserve their rewards. But tonight . . . tonight we'll praise the gods. We'll let the people celebrate. And soon I'll reveal all the many things I have planned for us."

By dusk all the work that was going to be done had been. An hour later, the officers and chieftains and dignitaries, the courtesans and entertainers began to turn up in the main banquet hall, an enormous, high-ceilinged affair with walls painted the rich red of an African sunset, across which roamed lions in black silhouette. The guests walked into air alive with the beating of hand drums, the tinkling of cymbals, and the dry rhythms of palm fiber rattles. Tables crouched low to the ground. Cushions functioned as backrests. Thick rugs were layered throughout for comfort. Wine was the drink of choice, and it was easy to come by. Boys younger than twelve moved among the guests with jugs of the ruby liquid. They had been told to fill all goblets whether asked to or not. This duty they fulfilled with youthful enthusiasm.

The chefs sent out the feast in waves. The servants all moved in unison, by some signal in the music, perhaps, though the onlookers could not follow it. On each table they set a great fish with a gaping mouth before the guests. They slit the fish open in one smooth slice the length of its belly. They slipped their fingers inside and helped the fish to birth yet another, a red-skinned creature, which likewise housed another fish, which contained a roasted eel, from which they drew a long, slim procession of miniature octopuses, infant creatures the size of large grapes that were likewise tossed into the mouth. In the space of a few moments the single fish had become a bouquet of the ocean's splendor, each with its own distinctive seasonings, each cooked in a different manner before being sewn inside the next one's belly.

Naked men carried boars in on spits balanced on their shoulders. The beasts, in their charred grandeur, were set above slow coals, massive, coarse-haired things that even in such a reduced state looked like beasts set upon the earth by a twisted god. The guests took chunks out of them with their knives and stood, greasy-lipped, awed by the taste of the meat, for it had somehow been infused with a smoky, sweet, succulent flavor that left the lingering taste of citrus on the palate. Amid all this, small dishes bloomed, fruit plates and grilled vegetables and bowls of various olives and vials of virgin oil.

Such was the banquet for the officers and allied chieftains and particular soldiers who had distinguished themselves during the campaign. It was well known that the commander himself partook of few such delicacies. The excesses he did have were mainly those that the military world called virtues: a clear conscience in the face of pain, torture, death; an absurdity of discipline; a cool head though his command was of life and death over thousands. He exercised his body even while at leisure. He paced when he could have been still, stood while writing letters or reading them, walked with weights sewn into his sandals, held his breath for long intervals while training—this last a habit largely unnoticed, but it assured him endurance beyond all others. His brother Hasdrubal was a physical specimen of similar craftsmanship, but his exercises were done in public, and his love of mirth well known. The full length of Hannibal's exertions could only be guessed at. His temperance was better documented. He never drank more than a half-goblet of wine. He never ate till satiated, never slept beyond the first wakeful moments of any morn, and rose always to take in the dawn and measure the day ahead. He preferred lean meat to fat, simple clothing to elaborate, the hardness of the ground to the luxury of his palace bed. And he favored his wife over all other women, a true aberration in a man who ruled with complete power over slave girls and servants and prostitutes, the wives and daughters of the adoring, or ambitious. He might have had his pick of thousands of beauties captured from vanquished tribes. He did not. Instead he saved himself for the things he believed mattered.

As everyone knew this, few bothered to protest when the commander retired. He did so quietly, leaving his brothers to share among themselves his portion of pleasure, which took on a more carnal tone after his departure. Later that evening, Hannibal stood on the balcony of his bedroom overlooking the city, watching the play of light from the many fires, listening to the muffled shouts of revelry in the streets. He took it all in with a silent stillness at his center that was neither joy nor contentment nor pride but something for which he had no name. Though the night was chill, he was clothed only in a robe. The silken fabric draped over his shoulders and fell the entire length of him, brushing the polished stones beneath his feet.

Behind him, his chamber glowed brightly. It was a luxurious museum of carved mahogany and eastern fabrics, low couches and narrow-legged tables that seemed to produce fruit and drink of their own accord, never empty, never wilting. The architects of this deception hid in the shadows and corners of the room. These slim servants were ever present, but so vacant of face and so secretive in their work that one could stand rimmed by them and feel completely alone. A single fireplace heated the room, so large that a stallion could have walked upright into the flames. Like that of the banquet he had so recently escaped, none of the opulence behind him was of his own design, none of it close to his heart. It corresponded to a role he must fill. And it was a gift to her who had granted him immortality.

Though his robe was too luxurious for his tastes, he was thankful for the thinness of it. With his eyes closed, he concentrated on the heat at his back and the chill night air on his face and the sensation of movement as heat rushed from the room and fled into the sky above. There was something intoxicating about it, as if he might himself fly up with the warmth, overcome the night, and look down upon his city from the sky, might for a moment glimpse the world from a god's perspective. He even saw this in his mind's eye, a strange swirling view that no man had ever had. He looked down upon the curve of creation from a distance so great that the creatures below moved without sound or identity, without the passions and petty desires so apparent from up close.

He opened his eyes and all was as before, the city around him, his marble balcony open to the night sky. The blue light of the moon fell upon him and the stone and even the glimmering sea with the same pale tint. How strange it was that at moments of celebration he was struck with bouts of melancholy. Part of his mind glowed with the knowledge of another success and looked forward to the quiet moments he would soon be able to share with his brothers. But another part of him already viewed the conquest of Arbocala as a distant event, lackluster, a mediocre episode from the past. Some men would have taken such a victory and spent the rest of their lives reminding others of it, accomplishing only the exercise of their tongues in their own praise. Perhaps he was a battleground upon which two gods contested an issue he had no inkling of. Why else would he strive and strive and then feel empty . . . ?

A voice broke through his thoughts. "Hannibal? Come and welcome your beloved."

He turned to see his wife approaching, arms cradled around a sleeping infant. "You have made us wait long enough," she said. Her Carthaginian was smooth and measured, though her pronunciation had a rough edge to it, an indelicacy of her native tongue that made her voice somewhat masculine as compared with the fine artistry of her features. She was, after all, a native of Iberia, daughter of Ilapan, a chieftain of the Baetis people. Her marriage had thrown her completely into the arms of a foreign culture, and yet she had adapted quickly, gracefully. Hannibal had even come to believe the apparent affection between them to be real. At times, this gave him great joy; at others, it concerned him more than indifference would have.

Imilce stopped some distance from the balcony. "Come out of the cold. Your son is here, inside, where you should be as well."

Hannibal did as requested. He moved slowly, taking the woman in with his eyes, a wary look as if he was studying her for signs that she was not who she claimed. Hers was a thin-lined beauty, eyebrows of faint brown that seemed drawn each with the single stroke of a quill, lips with no pout at all but rather a wavering, serpentine elegance. Her features were held together with a brittle energy, as if she were a vessel that contained within it the spirit of a petulant, well-loved child, a glimmering intelligence that had been, in fact, the first thing that drew his eyes to her. He slid a hand to the small of her back, pulled her close, and touched his lips to the smooth olive skin of her forehead. He inhaled her hair. The scent was as he remembered, faintly flowered, faintly peppered. She was just the same.

Though she was the same as before, his son most certainly was not. Five months seemed to have doubled his size. No longer was he a seed of child that Hannibal could hold completely within his upheld palms. No longer was he pale and wrinkled and bald. His complexion had ripened. He was thick around the wrists, and his clenched fists already seemed mallets to be contended with. The father saw himself in the child's full lips and this pleased him. He took the boy awkwardly from his mother. The child's head lolled back. Hannibal righted it and cautiously lowered himself to a stool.

"You're just like your older sister," Imilce said. "Kind as she has been to me, Sapanibal, too, tries to wake him through clumsiness. Always wants to see his gray eyes, she says. But it will not work this time. He's full of his mother's milk and content, drunk with all the food he asks of all the world."

Hannibal raised his eyes to study her. "Enjoy it, Mother, for soon this one will look up and see a world beyond your breasts. Then he'll be all mine."

"Never," Imilce said. She made as if to take the child, but did not. "So how do you feel in victory, husband?"

"As ever, Imilce. I feel the nagging of neglect."

"Hungry already?"

"There is always some portion of me left unfilled."

"What can you tell me of the campaign?"

The commander shrugged and sighed and cleared his throat. He said there was little to tell. But she waited, and he found first one thing and then another to mention. The three brothers had returned in good health, each unscathed. Arbocala was theirs, not that this was a great gain, for the city was a sadder collection of hovels than Mastia had been before Hasdrubal the Handsome built New Carthage upon it. The Arbocalians had been not only defiant but also arrogant and disrespectful and treacherous. They murdered a party sent inside the city to present surrender terms. They flung the decapitated bodies out with catapults and had their heads mounted on posts above the city's walls. This insult Hannibal felt keenly, for he had almost sent Hasdrubal in with the delegation. They were so stubborn a people that the only good he could see in the whole venture was the possibility of making them into soldiers for Carthage. If they had the sense to see this, they would find themselves richer than they had ever imagined. But he doubted it would be an easy thing to convince them of. He imagined that even now they were bubbling with hatred and anxious for some way to break the treaties and be free again.

"It will never be an easy task to hold this domain together," he said. "You Iberians are a troublesome lot, like wild dogs mastered by neither force nor friendship."

The baby grimaced, cocked his head, and strained against his father's arms. Imilce reached for him.

"He's got the blood of those wild dogs in his veins, you know," she said. "Do not anger him. We should let him sleep in peace now. You'll have your fill of him tomorrow."

She walked to the edge of the room and handed the child to a servant who stood waiting. She whispered to her and the girl withdrew, moving backward and bowing and cradling the baby all at once. Imilce spoke then to the room, two sharp words in her native tongue. She was answered by rustling in the shadows along the wall, the slight sound of movement, servants slipping from the room through several different exits, never seen except in glimpses.

A moment later they were all gone, and Imilce turned back to her husband. Her face already looked different, as if her cheeks had flushed and her eyes grown more sensual. As she walked toward him she pulled the pins from her tightly bound hair. The dark strands fell loose and draped around her shoulders. It seemed the mother in her had left the room with the child, and here was a different sort of creature.

"Now we are alone," she said. "So show me."

The commander smiled and stood for this custom of theirs. He released the belt of his gown and slid the material off his shoulders and let it drop to the ground. He stood naked before her, hands held out beside his hips, palms upward so that she could see the parts of his body. The long muscles of his legs stood out each in its layered place; his calves seemed smooth river stones slipped beneath his flesh, the cords of his inner thigh like ribbons stretched taut. His sex nestled in its place somewhat shyly, and above it the ridged compartments of his torso swept up into the bulk of his chest and the wide stretch of his shoulders.

"As you can see," he said, "there's no new mark upon me, neither nick nor bruise."

The woman's eyes dipped down toward his groin. "Nothing lopped off?"

Hannibal smiled. "No, I am still complete. They did not touch me."

"But you touched them?" she asked.

"Surely. There are many now who regret their actions, some that do so from the afterworld."

"But yourself, you have nothing to regret?"

He followed her with his eyes as she circled him. "Baal was beside me in this venture. I was simply the humble servant of his will."

From behind him, she said, "Is that so? Hannibal bends to another's will?"

"If that other is my god, yes."

Imilce placed a finger at the base of his neck and traced the line of his spine, pulling away just above his buttocks. "I see," she said. "And what's this?"

"What?" Hannibal craned his neck around to see, but before he had done so Imilce showed her teeth and nipped the flesh of his shoulder. He spun away from her and then swept back and pressed her to his chest and carried her toward the bed, feet dangling above the floor.

Later that evening, Hannibal lay upon blankets thrown across the floor. He spread out on his chest, eyes intent on nothing except the folds on the fabric just before him, the ridges and swells of it, the range of peaks that he had plucked up with his fingers and now studied like objects made of stone. Imilce slipped quietly back into the room. She paused to watch him from a dim place against the wall, and then she let her gown drop again. She dipped her fingers into a bowl of flavored water and swept them across her swollen nipples. She moved forward into the lamplight. She climbed on her husband's back and settled with her spine cradled in his, her shoulders resting on the stretch of his back, his buttocks molded into the hollow above hers. Neither spoke for some time, but when Imilce did it was clear enough of what she spoke.

"So, you are going to do it, are you not? You will attack Rome?"

"The time is near and I am ready."

"Of course you are ready. When were you ever not ready? But Hannibal, I do think you push things too quickly. I will not try to convince you of this. I know your mind is your own, but tell me, love, where will this course lead?"

"To glory."

Imilce stared up at the ceiling as she thought about this. One of the lamps had begun to smoke and a ribbon of black haze floated across the plaster like an eel seeking a home. "Is that all?" she asked. "Glory?"

"And justice as well. Freedom. And yes, you might ask— vengeance." Hannibal exhaled a long breath and spoke with a curtness to his words. "I will not have this discussion with you. Imilce, your husband is no normal man. I was born for this. That is all there is to it. I love you too much to be vexed with you; so stop."

Imilce rolled over and nestled under his arm. He adjusted to suit her and pulled her in close. "Do you know what I thought when I first saw you?" Imilce asked. "It wasn't on our wedding day, as you may think. I spied on you before that. I hid once in the curtains along the walls in my father's court when he was entertaining you. I slit the fabric just enough to look out at you."

"You're father would've skinned you alive for that," Hannibal said.

"Perhaps, but he was desperate to wed himself to the Barcas. He was not so powerful as you believed."

"I know. The Baetis are of little importance now. Perhaps I should throw you to the side and find another bride."

Imilce pressed her teeth against the flesh of his shoulder, but otherwise ignored his comment. "I was afraid of you," she said. "Resting on the couches you looked like a lion so confident in his strength he has only to lie down and stretch to make others tremble. I feared that you would devour me. I thought for a moment that I should step out from behind that curtain and disgrace myself and ruin the marriage plans."

"But you did not do that."

"No, because as much as I trembled at the thought of you, you pulled me toward you. I felt, perhaps, like an insect so attracted to the light of the torch that it flies into the flame. Do you understand what I am telling you?"

Hannibal nodded. "At Arbocala I met a young soldier who'd behaved bravely," he said. "In honor of this I bestowed upon his humble family a plantation outside of Carthage. I gave his people slaves and a small fortune in silver and in the space of a few moments changed their lives forever. That is the power I have because of the things I accomplish. And if I can give all of that to a boy soldier, what is a suitable present for my wife? Not simply treasure. Not more servants. These things are not enough. In two years, you will be able to look from the balcony of this or any other palace you choose and know that all the Mediterranean world is yours to shape. How many men can say that to their wives and mean it? Would you like that to be so?"

Imilce squeezed herself further under him, until he rose up and she could wrap her legs around him. She looked at him frankly, long, as if she might disclose some secret to him. But then she smiled and stretched up toward him and brushed her lips across his and touched him gently with her tongue.

Hanno Barca began the day with clearer eyes than most. Though he had reveled with the rest, he rose before the dawn and busied himself at self-assigned tasks. Mounted on one of Hannibal's stallions, he rode bareback through the city streets. The quiet lanes were awash with debris, bits and pieces of material without form in the morning light, metal fragments that might have once been armor but which had been torn apart during some segment of the evening's ritual. Hanno might have questioned this waste of military hardware, but there was little use in that. Such was the army of Carthage that it gathered soldiers from any and all the strange corners of its empire. Who knew all of their customs? And what did it matter, anyway? Somehow, Hannibal welded them into a whole, and that whole had made a custom of success.

The fountain in the main square had been drunk dry. The bowl overflowed with limp bodies: persons clothed and unclothed and in all states between, stained the ruddy brown of spilled wine, greasy with leftover food, bits of bone still clenched in some hands, grease yet moist on mouths thrown open to the chill morning air. The fires had died down from their raging heights, but they still smoldered, giving the whole scene a surreal aspect. It seemed Hanno was looking not upon a festive city but at a conquered one. Strange, he thought, that the two opposites had so much in common to the unprejudiced eye. Missing were only the wretched of the war trains, poor folk who would have been picking through the bodies for what small treasure they could find among the dead. Even such as these must have had their fill the night before.

In the stables he kicked grooms from their drunken slumbers and prodded them to work. The horses in their care needed them despite their hangovers. Then he called on the priests of Baal. Rites of thanks and propitiation had been going on since the army's return. Hanno had made offerings to the gods as appropriate the previous afternoon, but he was anxious lest more be in order. He dismounted and approached the temple holding his sandals in his hands and feeling the chill slap of his feet on the marble stairway leading up to the main entrance. He moved slowly, out of reverence, but also because he had no choice. The steps were set at a shallow angle that made it hard to mount them quickly. One had to place each foot carefully, a process that heightened the sense of awe and foreboding at approaching the god's sanctuary.

At the mouth of the temple, however, Hanno learned that the head priest, Mandarbal, would not see him. He was engaged in high matters and could not break off at that moment. Nor was his present ceremony one for outsiders to observe. Hanno was forced to withdraw, stepping backward down the god's steps, uneasy, for in this snub he felt a rebuke he did not deserve. After all, he was the most devout of all the brothers, the one most mindful of the gods, the first to call on them for aid, the one who praised them for every success. He had even confessed to Mandarbal once that he might have joined the priesthood if he had not been born Hamilcar Barca's son. To this, the priest had just grunted.

A few hours later, Hanno stood on the terrace overlooking the exercise ground reserved for the elephants. He watched the trainers tending the animals for some time, moving about beneath the beasts, talking to them with short calls and taps of their sticks. He thought several times that he would descend and walk among the creatures and run his hands over their coarse hairs and wrinkled flesh. He liked talking to the mahouts, appreciated the way they had only one job but knew it so well. But he was stayed by other thoughts, memories that he had no use for but that seemed intent on troubling him. They pushed into the central portion of his mind, that place separate from sight or hearing or bodily movements, the part that takes a person over even as he continues to occupy the physical world.

He thought of the child he had once been and the brother he was blessed, or cursed, to be second to. Hannibal's never-ending campaigns were tests that always ended in his success. What pained Hanno even now was that their father had known that only Hannibal among them had this gift. Hamilcar had told him as much in a thousand ways, on a thousand different occasions. Hanno had watched throughout his adolescence as Hannibal excelled first at youthful games, then into a physicality that bloomed like a weed into manhood. He had watched as his brother, just two years his senior, went from the verge of the council circle to the circle itself, and soon to the center. He was a young upstart in some ways, but all the men seemed to see the great commander perpetuated in his firstborn. It was not that Hanno showed any obvious lack: he was tall, strong limbed, and skilled enough with all the weapons of combat. He had studied the same manuals, trained with the same veterans, learned the history of warfare from the same tutors. But there was room for only a single star in their father's eyes, and Hanno had never been it. Hamilcar had rarely given him command of any force larger than a unit of a hundred soldiers. The first time he did proved tragic.

He was to lead a patrol from a conquered capital of the Betisians, up the Betis River toward Castulo, branching off before he reached that town and following a tributary south to New Carthage. His orders were to march the troops home by a prominent route, feeding the Iberians' sense that they were inevitably surrounded by a more organized foe. It was a routine procedure, usually done in pacified territory, meant mostly as a show of force to natives of ever-doubtful allegiance. Hamilcar gave him a company of two thousand Oretani soldiers, Iberians who, though not completely loyal, were believed to be tamed at least.

The mission started unremarkably, but three days into the march a scout brought his guide information that changed their course: The Betisians were planning an offensive to retake the recently captured city. Their troops had not all surrendered. In fact, many had been held in reserve and were hidden in a valley stronghold in the Silver Mountains, waiting for the Carthaginian force to diminish. With Hanno's group on the march via a northerly route and Hasdrubal on the southerly, they saw their opportunity to attack Hamilcar's dispersed forces.

Hanno heard this information with a calm façade, though his heart hammered out a more frantic reception. He began to give orders to turn back, but the scout suggested something different. Why not send a warning to Hamilcar? Hanno's was still a strong enough force to contend with the rebellion, so long as they were forewarned. With a messenger dispatched, Hanno himself could march on the Betisians and rout their unprotected stronghold. Their camp, not marked on any map that the Carthaginians held, was hidden away in a narrow defile easily accessible only from either end. The scout assured him that it was a valuable settlement and that taking it would do much to disrupt the tribe. The Betisians would have nothing to return to and would thus truly be ready to come to terms with the Carthaginians.

Hanno tried to imagine what his father would have him do, or what Hannibal would have done faced with the same circumstances. His information was reliable, he believed, for the messenger was of Castulo blood and they had been faithful allies for almost two years now. Should he not seize the opportunity? He could turn a routine mission into a small victory, and then return home to casually present his father with details of a blank spot on their map. It was a risk, yes, and it was beyond his orders, but had not the Barca sons always been instructed to think on their feet? He imagined the dour look his father might turn on him if he went home with the news of this opportunity offered and passed upon. And that he could not face.

He turned the column for the defile and entered it two days later. The guide moved forward to scout with an advance party of cavalry. The route largely followed the course of a narrow stream, hemmed in on both sides by trees. It was narrow enough that the line thinned, first to four abreast and then to three. It broke down even further as the men jumped from rock to rock or splashed through small pools. It was a fair day, warm enough that the soldiers drank handfuls of the cool water and talked rapidly in their native tongue. Hanno led the company from horseback, he and a group of twenty of the Sacred Band at the front of the line. There was a nervous energy among them, the Band looking one to another, whispering that the guide should have returned by now, or they should have caught up with him. But still they came on no settlement, nor were there many signs that an armed force had passed this way recently. Hanno took note of this and yet, inexplicably even in his own reckoning, he did not halt the march. The column moved on into slightly easier territory, although steeper on both sides and still tree-lined.

They had all but cleared the rise at the far end of the ravine when it happened. He knew he had been led into a trap when he heard the first arrow sink into the soil a few feet from him. It was almost silent, a muted thwack that only in its wake carried the whistle of its falling and only in its quivering shaft betrayed the speed with which it had appeared. For a few moments Hanno was frozen. He saw and felt the world in surreal detail: the feathers of the arrow gray and imperfect, the breeze on his skin as if it were a gale across a fresh wound, a single bird clipping its song and rising, rising up from the ground and away. Then another arrow struck home, not into the soil this time but through the collarbone of an infantryman a few feet behind him.

Hanno spun to give his orders—exactly what they would be, he had not yet formulated—but it did not matter. The din and confusion were beyond his control already. The arrows fell in a hail, glancing off armor and some finding their homes in flesh. The soldiers ducked beneath their shields and sought to see from beneath them. The Betisians crashed down through the trees, tumbling at an impossible speed and angle, more falling than running. Some tripped and whirled head over heels, others slid on their backsides. All screamed a war chant at the top of their lungs, a song they each sang the same but not at the same time. Two ragged walls of Iberians smashed into the thin column from either side, instantly shredding any semblance of order. Before the battle had even progressed beyond this chaos, a new wave of war cries fell upon them. The archers had put down their bows and were now running to join the others, swords in hand.

A lieutenant tugged on Hanno's arm. "We must go," he said. "Those men are lost."

"Then I, too, am lost." He tried to spin his horse but the Sacred Band drew up close around him. One snatched his reins from him and another prodded his horse and all of them moved forward, forming one body. Hanno cursed them and lashed out and even moved to draw his sword. But it was no use. A moment later they were over the rise and all was downward motion. They were soon met by a contingent of Numidian cavalry and with these in their rear they kept up a running fight for the rest of the afternoon and sporadically over the next two days. But the Betisians chased them halfheartedly; they had more than achieved their goal. Hanno was not sure if they were hunting him or simply driving him forward.

Over the space of several days after his arrival at New Carthage it all became clear. There had been no attack on Hamilcar's forces. The only attack was the one upon Hanno's. And as that had proved successful, the whole territory was thrown into confusion once more. Hanno did not see his father till they met on the field a month later. But if the old soldier had forgotten his anger during that space of time, it did not show. He found Hanno in his tent. He strode in unannounced, in full battle armor, helmet clenched in one hand. The other, his left, he swung up like a rock and slammed across the bridge of his son's nose. Hanno's nose poured blood instantly, the stuff thick in his mouth, running freely from his chin down onto his tunic.

"Why must you always disappoint me?" Hamilcar asked. His voice was even, but cast low and scornful. "Next time you lead two thousand men to their deaths, stay with them yourself. Have at least that dignity. In my father's time you would have been crucified for this. Be glad we live in a gentler moment." Having uttered this and thrown his blow, the old warrior spun and pushed through the tent flap.

That night Hanno sought no treatment for his nose but slept wrapped around it. The next morning his physician threw up his hands. It would no longer be the envy of the women, he said, but perhaps now he would look more like a warrior. Hanno walked out to take his place beside his father with his nose swollen, his eyes black and puffy. Within a fortnight Hannibal led a force against the Betisians and met them in an open field. By the end of the afternoon he had their headman's skull on a javelin tip. By the end of the week he had their main settlement, and their allegiance ever after. Such was the difference between his brother and him. Hanno never forgot it.

Hanno roused himself. He realized he had been standing above the pen for some time, watching the handlers at their work but not actually seeing them. He turned and walked off. The elephants did not need his inspection. They were well tended. Of course they were.

———

More so than any of his brothers, Hasdrubal Barca lived his life astride a pendulum swinging between extremes. By day, he honed his body to the functions of war; at night he sank up to the ears in all the pleasures of consumption available to him. Hannibal had once questioned the structure of his days and whether his habits were suitable for a Barca, suggesting that Hasdrubal's pleasure-seeking indicated a flaw that might weaken him with the passing years. Hasdrubal laughed. He proposed instead that his devotion to the body was the greater discipline. The fact was, he said, that he could rise from an all-night romp and still train with a smile on his face. Perhaps this was a sign of stamina that Hannibal had never himself mastered. As for indications of decay or weakness, at twenty-one his body was a chiseled monument surpassing even his eldest brother's. So, for the time being, he passed his days and nights as he saw fit.

During the winter, he kept to a strict training routine. Three days after his return from Arbocala he began the regimen again, already ill at ease after a few days of uninterrupted leisure, the celebration of victory almost too much even for his own resources. He slept naked, always in his own bed, always completing the night alone, no matter whose pleasures he had shared earlier in the evening. His squire, Noba, woke him just as the sun cleared the horizon line and rose up in spherical completion. Together they bathed in the chilly waters of the private bath on Hasdrubal's balcony. Noba once had to break the skin of ice upon the water before they could enter, an unwelcome task for an Ethiopian. Hasdrubal found this ritual dunking to be the surest cure for the fatigue caused by the previous evening's debauchery.

He broke his fast with a small meal of something dense and meaty—cattle liver topped with eggs, venison on a bed of onions, stewed chunks of goat—and then it was on to the gymnasium. Hasdrubal and Noba had received the same instruction in hand-to-hand combat, but Noba carried with him earlier knowledge, the wisdom of the martial arts of his southern people. The two men merged these tactics and pressed beyond them. They wrestled each other into awkward positions and then talked through the most ef-

ficient, deadliest way to free themselves, the quickest way to deal
a deathblow. They made killing a game, a physical and mental exercise that they joked their way through, lighthearted, companion-
able. Yet they both learned their lessons well and on more than
one occasion credited their survival to tactics first thought up during these sessions. From wrestling, the two moved on to weapons
practice. They sparred with thrusting sword or sweeping falcata,
Spartan spear or javelin. When Hasdrubal tired of those, they ex-
perimented with using different shields as weapons, fighting with
broken swords, with the shafts of blunted spears, or with the spearheads minus the shafts.

Before his afternoon meal, Hasdrubal walked stairs in the gymnasium with an ash beam balanced on his shoulders. He stripped
down to nothing for the exercise, grabbed the straps that aided his
grip, and hefted the beam with the full exertion of his body, slowly
finding the balance point, sliding his body underneath the weight,
and coming to peace with it. He took each step deliberately, pressing his foot down into the stone and thereby lifting himself and the
weight carried like outstretched wings. It was a slow ordeal, a hundred steps up, a slow turning, and then a hundred steps down, another turning, and on again.

Groups of young noblewomen sometimes gathered to watch him.
They whispered among themselves and pointed and laughed and
sometimes called out to him, asking him whether he ought not exercise that third leg, for it was limp and lifeless compared with the
two others. Hasdrubal kept on at his work, giving them little more
than a smile or shake of his head. Instead of being bothered by their
teasing, he was amused, flattered, encouraged, reminded that pleasure was never that far away. He slipped out from under the beam
only when his legs were useless, rubbery things that wiggled beneath him and disobeyed the instructions his mind gave them.

The rest of the day was spent in training of a less overtly physical
sort: honing his horsecraft, practicing the tribal languages, studying
accounts of earlier campaigns, learning from the mistakes or triumphs of others, and fulfilling whatever obligations Hannibal had
assigned him. A week after their return from campaign and the appearance of the surprise envoy from Rome, Hannibal called a meet-

ing of his brothers and all his senior generals. Mago met Hasdrubal in the gymnasium baths. They had agreed to attend the meeting together so that Hasdrubal could fill his younger brother in on any details that eluded him. The elder brother stood naked before Mago as Noba pounded out a massage on the wings of his back. The squire's dark face was calm and somewhat vacant, his body lean and tall, perfect in a manner unique to his people. The muscles of his arms popped and contracted at their work.

"You should train with me," Hasdrubal said. "Carthage will make a man soft. Too much palm wine and too many Nubian servant girls to rub you with oil. You need a good thrashing and then for Noba here to beat the fatigue out of you."

The Ethiopian patted his master on the back and stepped away from him, indicating that he was finished. Hasdrubal rolled his head on his shoulders and stretched his torso at several angles, as if he were testing that the parts still functioned as they should. Then he began to dress.

"So," Mago said, sitting on a stone bench and looking into the yellowish water of the baths, "is it a certainty, then? We attack Saguntum in the spring?"

Hasdrubal slipped on his undertunic and tugged it into place. "It's a certainty that we'll be at war with someone. Hannibal will spend the winter securing the goodwill of our new allies. He will succeed, in part, but never completely. Men who have just been soundly beaten and humiliated are slow to grow into true friends. If it were my decision we would not attack Saguntum next year. You know I like a fight, but there's enough fight left in the rest of Iberia to keep me occupied. Our brother, I believe, has long wanted to chastise the Saguntines. That Roman envoy only succeeded in making the prospect irresistible."

"Perhaps that is why it's a sound move to attack Saguntum," Mago said. "To show our new allies that we can share common enemies. It will take their humiliation and heap it onto another people."

Hasdrubal glanced up for a moment and took his brother in frankly. He sat down beside him and laced up his sandals. "Perhaps," he said. "In any event, Hannibal rides before the vanguard of reason. He leaves it to the rest of us to catch up. By the way, watch yourself or you'll find you have been betrothed to some chieftain's daughter. That is a sure way to secure their goodwill—to make them family."

"You make that sound unpleasant. Hannibal has done so himself."

"True, but not every man's daughter is an Imilce. Truth be known, brother, I like this country. I am more at home here than in Carthage. The Celtiberians make good allies and amusing enemies. And I've even grown to appreciate their women, pale things that they are. Mago, you would not believe this creature I've been screwing lately. She's beautiful, yes? Silver eyes and a gentle voice and a mouth that always seems in a pucker, you know? She thinks up things that would make an Egyptian blush. She does a trick with a string of beads . . ." Hasdrubal's eyes rolled upward into a flutter. He leaned back against the stone wall, momentarily lost in contemplation. "I won't even describe it. I don't know what you'd think of me."

"Is this love or just passion?" Mago asked.

"It is the love of passion, my brother. The love of passion."

The two brothers were among the first to climb the winding stone staircase to the top of the citadel, where the meeting of the generals was to take place. The tower was open to the air, a round platform ringed by a waist-high stone wall. It offered a view of both the fortress and the turquoise sea stretching out to the horizon. A wind whipped and buffeted the brothers, cold and mischievous. It made talking a challenge, but what Hannibal had to discuss he did not mind shouting out. And they were far from prying ears anyway.

Most of the officers were still settling in after the Arbocala campaign. If they were surprised to be called to a meeting so soon, they did not show it. They mounted the platform, shadowed by their squires, with a variety of characters reflected on their faces, as different in temperament as in the shades of their skin.

Maharbal, the captain of the Numidian cavalry, stepped onto the platform with a stern demeanor throughout his entire body. He wore his hair long. The thick, wiry strands gathered at the back, secured with a strip of leather. His dark skin had a reddish hue, as if baked by the sun and ripened to a rough, thick coat. His nose was slim and sharp; his chin protruded as if his face were a hatchet meant to slice the wind. Indeed this was just what he was famous for, the speed and precision of his riding.

"He is new to leadership," Hasdrubal said, "sent by King Gaia of the Massylii. He knows his men and their horses and commands a devotion that almost rivals their admiration of Hannibal himself. He has almost too much power, but he has thus far proved true to us. We would be legless without Numidian horsemen."

Adherbal, the chief engineer, also arrived early, dressed in a flowing Carthaginian tunic. He set his palms upon the stone wall and gazed out over the city he had helped create. His eyes moved with a singular intelligence, as if the wheels of his thoughts spun behind them, figuring calculations and making measurements even as he smiled and spoke and listened. Recently, his skills at building and knowledge of the laws of physics had been used to destroy cities rather than create them.

"If we lay siege to the Saguntines it'll be his machines that win it for us," Hasdrubal said.

Just before the meeting, the others arrived in quick succession. Young Carthalo commanded the light cavalry under Maharbal. Bostar and Bomilcar: the first Hannibal's secretary and the second a favored general. Synhalus, the oldest man of the group, had served as the Barcas' surgeon since Hamilcar's time. He was the slimmest of them all, fine-featured and intelligent, of Egyptian blood. He had quiet eyes and full lips and a face not given to showing emotion or betraying any thoughts whatsoever. A man named Vandicar stood beside him, the chief mahout, a native of the distant land of the Indians. His complexion was a touch darker than the Carthaginians', but his closely cropped black hair was absolutely straight, oily and dense. Behind each of the primary players stood their squires and assistants, quiet shadows like Noba who heard all with blank faces, trusted aides and friends, battle-hardened soldiers in their own right, some free, some bound by slavery.

Most of these men Hasdrubal knew both from the rigors of campaign and from the pleasures provided by leisure moments. He greeted them with nods and an easy grin. There was in his movements and posture the swagger of a young lion confident with his place among his peers. So he seemed until the first sighting of the crown of one man's black mane. This man was Monomachus. He took the company in with a disdainful glance that touched on everyone but moved on quickly, as if none of those he saw proved to be of sufficient interest. His eyes were intense and bulbous, seemingly too large for his face. Or perhaps they only seemed so because of his shrunken cheeks and the withered, dry pucker of his mouth.

Hasdrubal's glib expression vanished. He whispered to his brother, a little lower than previously, his eyes not upon the man in question but looking off at nothing in particular. "There stands a more ancient form of man than most."

"I remember him," Mago said. "He's Monomachus. He created the Lion's Way, did not he?"

Hasdrubal nodded. "And he's no saner now than he was then. He's devoted his works to Moloch, the Eater of Children. He leaves very few of his opponents alive. At least he fights for us. Of this be thankful."

When Hannibal appeared he swept up onto the platform in a flourish of purposeful energy. He wore the leather corselet he sometimes sparred in. Its polished blackness was as impressively sculpted as hammered iron. He wore a red cloak that fell almost to the ground, but beneath this his arms were bare, as were his legs below the thigh. He gave the impression that he had just come from training, still flushed and warm from it. When his eyes touched on Hasdrubal, the young man felt a warm flush on his face despite himself. His brother's gaze in joy was like the sun bursting from behind a cloud.

Hanno appeared just after him. He nodded at his younger siblings, then crossed his arms and waited.

When he began, Hannibal's voice rang loud and clear, despite the wind trying to spirit his words away. "Remember with me for a moment the grandeur of our nation and the work we've accomplished here in Iberia," he said. "We who were beaten through treachery have here carved one of the world's great empires. We who should be poor are rich. We who should be defeated know only victory after victory. We've much to be proud of. Be so in the name of my father, Hamilcar, and my brother by marriage, Hasdrubal the Handsome, for they made this possible. Their work was well begun, but it's not yet complete. As they have passed on to Baal, it passes to us to make real the world they both envisioned. We still have an enemy, a single foe, but a foe like none other. You know of whom I speak. . . . Not the Greeks whom we fought so often in times past. Not those Celts still defiant in the north of this very country. Not even the Saguntines, to whom I will direct your attention in a moment. I speak now of that den of thieves and pirates that they call Rome. Need I recount their crimes against us?"

The group murmured that these crimes were well known to them all.

Hannibal said the names anyway, slowly, each word broken into its separate syllables. "Sicily. Sardinia. Corsica. All taken from us. Our wealth. Blood. Possessions. All taken from us. The enormous cost of a war we did not start . . . Heaped upon us to pay for far into the years to come. Our navy destroyed. A people who were above all seamen now limited to a few vessels, cursed to walk instead of follow the wind. These losses are too great for a proud people to bear. And we are proud, are we not?"

All agreed that they were. Monomachus grunted low in his throat.

"Now, friends, the wolf's nose is sniffing even here in Iberia. Again the Romans are on the verge of ignoring honor. They wait not for right but only for opportunity. Some back in Carthage call themselves the Peace Party. They would have us avoid all conflict with Rome—would have us bow and bow again. They argue that we should accept the rule of our betters and profit from what commerce we can, like street peddlers scrounging for business in back alleyways. But what do these peaceable sorts know of the things we have created here? They know only that wealth pours from us to them, and that is as it should be. They need know little else, because it is we here on this citadel who determine the future of our nation. Make no mistake—we are Carthage, the heart and arm of it both. We are a small group here, but each of you is key to this army. Each of you makes Carthage great through your work. Each of you owns some portion of this empire. And what we've built thus far is but the foundation for something larger.

"I will speak to you plainly, so that you'll understand me the same way. We will move against Saguntum in the spring. Either the Romans will come to the Saguntines' aid, or the city will fall to us. If it falls, then the Romans will know what we think of them and they'll have to respond. So, either way, Saguntum is the opening thrust in an attack upon Rome itself. The Romans will be slow to recognize this completely. My sources say that they are now more concerned about events in Illyria than they are about us here. They will move more like tortoises than wolves. By the time they know we are their enemy, we'll be on their soil, with our swords at their necks. So . . . Saguntum this summer. Rome the next. Do any question me?"

Only the wind did, smacking hard across the citadel with three strong gusts. Hasdrubal had known this was coming, but the simple statement of it stunned him. The words seemed to come so easily to his brother's lips. They seemed so reasonable, despite the fact that they introduced the first official mention of a massive endeavor. He wondered if any would object, but from the generals and advisers all was silence until Monomachus said, "None question you."

Hannibal nodded and said, "This goal is for our closed council only. The mass of men need not know my intentions; neither should the spies of Rome be given warning. But I will not keep secrets from you. This coming year we are still the Carthaginian army of Iberia. Next year they will be calling us the Army of Italy. Come, let's begin. There is everything to do."

The Numidian spent the last of his silver on the passage to Iberia at the Pillars of Hercules. He traveled solitary, aligned with no city or king or general. Though a horseman by birth, he stood and walked on his own two legs. His head was shaved clean, with skin the color of oiled mahogany. He dressed simply in an earth-colored tunic, with a leopard skin flung across his shoulder and secured before him, a garment and blanket and bedding all in one. His arms bore tattoos, fine lines that were not words but were intelligible to those who knew how to read them. He had a strong hook of a nose and thin facial hair that clung in small curls just under his chin. His eyes were as clear now as they had been in his youth, though at twenty-nine he had seen things that meant the better portion of his life was behind him and now only dimly remembered. His name was Tusselo.

On disembarking in Iberia he began to search. The many signs were not hard to follow. The land had been trodden thin by the feet of so many thousands of men. It was scarred by horse hooves, flattened by the round, padded footfalls of elephants, cut by the wheels of carts and by the myriad other objects that seemed to have been dragged or pushed or somehow conveyed along the ground in a manner that left deep gouges. The farmland to either side had been stripped of its summer harvest. Many of those he passed still smarted from the inconveniences of the earlier horde and by no means was this lone traveler looked upon kindly. He was barred from settled places often, whether city or town or village it did not seem to matter. An old woman in Acra Leuce spat at him in the street and cursed his gods as weaklings. A man in an unnamed town cut him with an Iberian dagger, a clean slash across his forehead that bled profusely but was no real threat. It was a strange encounter, for having cut the Numidian the man just stood back and watched him walk away without further molestation. He was once followed by a band of young avengers who would have punished him for other men's crimes. They came upon him late at night, but he was ready for them and was more a man than they and left them smarting with the awareness of this. He carried a spear for a reason, and he explained this to them at close quarters.

Nor was nature disposed to aid him. The sun burned daylong in unclouded skies. Shade was thin and hard to come by and the landscape filled with hulking shapes in the distance. Once he traveled a barren stretch of land cut by dry rivers, some of enormous girth that might have funneled torrents but now lay parched beneath the summer sun. Later, he traversed a wide, shallow sea, the liquid so potent that it crystallized on his feet and coated them with a crust. Around him little thrived save for thin, delicately pink birds, creatures that stood on one leg and then the other and gestured with their curved beaks as if engaged in some courtly dance. On occasion his passage disturbed them; and the birds rose in great waves, thousands upon thousands of them, like giant sheets whipped by the breeze and lifted into the air. He never forgot the sight of them.

Nor of the opal sea in the morning. Nor of a stretch of white beach as smooth as polished marble. Nor the white-winged butterfly that awoke him with a kiss upon his forehead.

He began to despair that he would succumb to some mishap before reaching his goal, but then he crossed the river Sucro and knew that he was close. He spent the night in a village by the sea and found that the people were not unkind to him, stranger though he was. He would always remember eating roasted fish on the beach, served up by an old man with whom he could not communicate in words but who seemed a friend nonetheless. The two sat on the sand near each other and scooped up the flaky white fish with their bare fingers. Tusselo tried to pay the man, but he refused, his hands raised before him and vertical so that no object could be placed upon them. In parting, Tusselo walked away a short distance and then turned to wave a good-bye. But the old man had turned his back to him and was kicking the sand to cover the spot upon which they had sat. Tusselo found something disquieting in this.

A week later he caught sight of scavenging parties sent out to supply the army. He avoided them for a day, but the next afternoon a lone horseman spotted him. The rider sat a rise a little distance away, contemplated him, and then rode forward into a dip. When he emerged Tusselo knew him for what he was, Massylii, slim and dark and so at one with his mount that he rode bareback and without reins. Tusselo raised his hand in greeting, knowing that his solitary travel was over. The rider stopped a short distance away and asked the stranger his business.

Knowing the man's warm tongue, Tusselo responded in kind. He came bearing knowledge the commander might find valuable, he explained. He had come to serve. He had come to fight for Hannibal.

The siege of Saguntum began early in the spring of the year following the defeat of Arbocala. It went on unabated, week after week, as spring gave way to summer. The city perched on the edge of a rocky plateau, high enough to afford a view of the surrounding hills and out toward the sea. It was well fortified, walled completely, in differing heights and thicknesses as suited the varying landscape. There were towers spaced along the walls at intervals, of such stout proportions that one might have thought the city perfectly defended. Hannibal was intent on proving this belief mistaken.

Under his direction a mass of men blanketed the ground all around the city, working in a hundred ways to break through the skin of the place and climb inside. One section of wall collapsed during the first weeks in a chaos of dust and debris and falling bodies, creating a great wound in the city's defenses that extended the whole length from one tower to the next. The Saguntines stanched it before the invaders could pour in, building a new shell from the rubble, working ruined homes into the fabric of the wall, throwing up barricades in all gaps, and using whatever materials came readily to hand. Some fought to keep the invaders at bay even as others ran between the defenders, working in stone and wood and earth. The wound remained, scabbed over and livid, yet the city had protection for another day.

The Saguntines received Hannibal's terms each time he offered them, but they refused to accept them. He knew the source of their resolve was threefold. There was simple loathing of defeat and the indignities it entailed. The stubborn bravado natural to all the Iberians he had yet encountered. And, of course, the Saguntines looked daily to the sea-horizon for salvation. From spies, Hannibal knew of three envoys who had escaped the city to renew their entreaties for Roman aid. He might have intercepted them with ease, but it suited him that they reach their goal and state their case in the Senate. He wanted the Romans to roil and fume. If they stirred to action against him, so too would he against them.

But despite all his planning, the siege threatened to carry on indefinitely. That was why, one sweltering morning in mid-June, Hannibal decided something must be done. He knew as well as any other that his actions verged on foolhardy, but he awoke to the knowledge that a lethargy had taken hold of his men. The heat of the summer day threatened to stew them slowly and would perhaps turn them upon themselves in surly frustration. He could not allow this to happen. Although he could not break through walls by himself, a lone man can inspire a mass to greatness beyond the power of an individual. His father would have done so, and as he was gone the responsibility fell to the first son.

He mounted the stallion that had of late become his favorite and rode out onto the debris-laden field between the city's walls and the mass of his fatigued, bored men. He shouted them to action. They looked up at him from the dust and grime. They saw his figure through the wavering haze cast by the heat and thought him a madman or an annoyance. Then they realized who he was and began to make sense of his words. Those who spoke no Carthaginian understood him only when he spoke in Greek, or in Celtiberian or Numidian. Some spoke still other languages and received his message through translation or by inference. He began simply anyway.

Get up and be men, he told them. Get off your lazy backsides and follow me through the walls of this city and through to the orgy of a lifetime. He told them they had everything they needed to storm the city that very hour. All the manpower and the machinery, the weapons and the opportunity. They needed only the balls to make it happen. They had been spurned and spurned again by the smug gluttons of Saguntum. Right now they were being laughed at and humiliated. Even the women and children of the city must think them pathetic, worth neither friendship nor obedience nor even a fuck.

He rode into a corps of Celtiberians, the big horse unwary of stepping on them. The soldiers jumped up and peeled back to allow his progress. They were pale of complexion, some with dustings of gold in their hair. Many of them were seeing their leader close up for the first time and they stared at him with slack jaws.

"Saguntum," he said, voice not nearly loud enough to carry to them all but reaching many. "Does this task seem daunting, my friends? Does it tax you and strain your patience and will? So it should. This is a great city, whose foundations run deep, whose walls are thick, and whose inhabitants are thickheaded and vain. These months of work have pained us all—me as well as you—and yet we are here for a goal of undeniable worth. We came here at the bidding of our friends the Turdetani, those good people who suffered beneath the repression of the city behind me."

A shout went up, which must have been the Turdetani responding to the mention of their name. Hannibal acknowledged them with a nod and spurred his horse in their direction. "There are issues of right and wrong to be discussed," he said, "a dispute best handled by an impartial party. That is why I offered to be a judge in the matter. But rather than discourse like honorable men, these Saguntines called upon Rome to clap its mighty palm down on us. This before we'd chosen sides and taken up arms. Romans came to my fortress and stood before me and told me, Hannibal, what I could do and what I could not do. They told me that I was a child and all of you my bandy-legged playmates. Is that how you see yourselves?"

Hannibal kicked his horse into a gallop that sent infantrymen diving out of his path. The translation took a moment. As the various precincts understood his question, the answer rolled back like claps of thunder during a storm, some loud and some far and some near at hand, some sharp and others grumbling, in increasingly angry tones as if this insult was more than they could bear, something they had not considered before but which touched them sorely. In many languages, the men replied in the negative. They were not playmates; Hannibal was no child.

When the commander spoke again he did so from deep within a host of Libyan mercenaries. The soldiers reached up and touched his legs as he passed. They were copper-skinned men, noses and chins like features carved in granite and left rough-edged. In many ways they were the core of his army, battle-hardened veterans whose families had fought for Carthage for several generations. The relationship between the two peoples was not a formal alliance; Carthage was not sworn to protect the Libyans, nor was their king, Syphax, bound to her. But Syphax had continued the long-standing tradition of allowing his men to hire themselves out as mercenaries in the Carthaginian army, especially as a portion of their pay went to him in one form or another. The Libyans around Hannibal did not speak as he passed, but each stomped one foot in a throbbing rhythm.

"Who are the Saguntines to call another our master? Does that sound like the action of a people to be pitied? Nor shall they be pitied. Not for the injustice that began this conflict, nor for the months of labor they have caused, nor for your brothers who have been sent on to the next world. Just in the last few days I detailed to them through one of their citizens my terms for their surrender. Even at this date Hannibal conceded the possibility of mercy. But I went spurned."

He paused at the edge of the Libyans, facing a company of mounted Massylii Numidians, these men easy on their horses, dark and tattooed as was their custom, with matted ropes of hair brushing their shoulders, eyes that sat deep and moved heavily. These men were also paid for their services, but they had been offered to the Carthaginian army by their king, Gaia, who made it clear he longed for an official, lasting union with Carthage.

When the various translations ceased and the crowd hushed, Hannibal spoke in rhythm with the throbbing beat still kept by the Libyans. "So let this now be known: That city, when it falls, goes to the men who capture it! What booty may be found there, in gold, in coins and jewels and weapons. In men and children. In women. Hannibal claims none of it. We will send some tribute to Carthage, so that the people may understand our work, and portion some to fund this great army. But beyond that Hannibal gives it all to those brave enough to take it, to do with it what they please. This siege has gone on long enough, my friends—let us now raze this place and be done with it!"

He did not have to await translation to get the men's roar of approval. Those who understood his Carthaginian shouted their immediate pleasure. Others joined in, perhaps not understanding completely but knowing that something unusual was being offered to them and willing to express joy and get the details later. They fell on Saguntum that day with an enthusiasm that must have rocked the defenders. The motley soldiers of Carthage threw their bodies at the walls as if they could claw through the stone itself. The Saguntines in return hurled down their spears and stones. Bodies were impaled and burned, skulls shattered and limbs snapped. But each man that fell was stepped upon by another willing to climb over his body and get for himself a portion of the city's riches. And perhaps each man was aware that the body he climbed over made one fewer to divide the treasure with.

Nor were the soldiers without a model of bravery. Hannibal was among them. Later all the men would claim to have labored beside him at some point during the day. He dragged back the battering ram and ran forward yelling his fury into the base of the wall. He scaled the lower portion of a ladder and only just jumped to safety when a log was set rolling from the wall above, peeling off the men before and below him and leaving them shattered and broken. He landed awkwardly from his leap and limped so markedly that Mago convinced him to mount again. He did so, and rode exhorting the men. It was atop that churning mass of muscle that the hand of another's fate touched him in a way it had never before.

In all the movement and action, his mouth open and yelling, horse swirling beneath him, men rushing about him, he did not notice the falarica let loose from a tower high on the wall. He did not see the fingers that released it or hear the prayer on the lips of that person. The spearhead itself was four feet long, followed by a compartment smeared with pitch and set aflame, behind which stretched ten feet of shaft that gave the weapon a deadly weight in falling. It cut a fiery, indirect path toward its target, first up into the air, then arching, arching, losing upward speed, but gaining from gravity's pull as it returned to the earth. In the time this missile was in the air Hannibal and his mount circled and pranced and galloped a short distance and pulled up. He and the horse might easily have been yards from the spear when it struck the earth. This fact would haunt him afterward though he would never voice his questions about what this meant for the will of the gods or the intentions of the fates.

A guard next to him shouted a warning, too late and unheard anyway. The point of the falarica slammed into Hannibal's leg and through his flesh and muscle and past him into the leather of his saddle and farther still into the back of the horse. It broke two of the mount's ribs and lodged so deeply inside it that the wound was mortal. The horse was dead on its feet. Hannibal batted at the flaming pitch along the shaft as if he might right the matter with the fury of his palms. Then he felt the horse start to buckle and knew that he might be crushed beneath it. So he did what he had to.

As the horse fell to one side, he wrenched himself the other way. The sharp prongs of the spearhead ripped sideways through his leg, pausing for a moment against a thin ribbon of reluctant flesh, then tearing free. Hannibal landed on top of the horse. He tried to spring away, but as one leg was useless, he ended up with his chest on the horse's rump. In one of its last acts on this earth the creature kicked, and Hannibal was made aware of three things. The air was knocked completely out of his chest so that his lungs were momentarily flat and useless. He realized in midair that the force of the blow had sent him over the heads and beyond the first few who had come to aid him. And as he rolled and scraped across the ground and settled in an undignified jumble, he understood that he would never be able to stand before Imilce as he had in the past. He was no longer perfect. This thought stunned him even more than the pain, even more than the proximity of death, the few inches that placed the spearhead in one portion of his body and not another.

When the messenger found him, Mago was at the far edge of the camp, surveying the quantity and abundance of lumber recently hewn for siege engines. He left directly. He cut through sections of the camp he had never explored before: the tent neighborhoods of the various tribes, wherein each people kept to its way and lived by its customs. He passed the hovels of camp followers—squat dwellings of animal skins, others woven of plant matter, and some built of bricks of mud and feces; he passed through open-air markets, carcasses hanging to air, fly-spotted, the ground below them splattered with offal, the air rife with the scent of slaughtered flesh, with the stench of fish guts. Beyond the confusion created by the mass of nationalities there were women in abundance, cooks and prostitutes and maids, wives and sisters and even daughters, especially from the Celtiberian tribes who were not so far from home. There were children among them, the same urchins who made their lives in the alleys of cities, quick and nimble and somehow thriving beneath the feet of warriors. The lanes were even patrolled by the requisite stray dogs, thin-limbed and shorthaired and none of them of any particular breed. Like the children, they managed to eke out an existence in and around the machinery of war. There was little order to it, except for the knowledge that each and every soul within miles knew the name Hannibal Barca.

But few of them recognized the Barca striding past them behind the messenger, which suited him well as yet. Mago had been face-to-face with his responsibilities as never before. He kept a daily record of all notable developments, organized the notes and engineering reports from Adherbal, kept track of morale in the various contingents, settled disputes in Hannibal's name when the weary soldiers turned their frustrations against each other. He was even left in charge of requisitioning supplies for Vandicar, the chief mahout, whose elephants were as sorely taxed as any soldier by the siege work.

In his attempt to fulfill all the tasks set for him, Mago found himself down among the soldiers, examining the machines and learning about strategy from those who would answer his questions. At first he was hesitant in dealing with men older than he, more experienced than he, with scowling faces and opinions they did not mind spouting at the least provocation. But each evening as he completed his work he catalogued the day's interactions and noted where he had been lacking.

One morning Mago yanked the young cavalry general, Carthalo, from his horse and held him pinned beneath his foot. The horseman's infraction had come the day before, a matter concerning his disregard for an order he saw as beneath his men, but Mago had needed the evening to devise his response. It came as a surprise to many—Carthalo included—but went unnoticed by few. The youngest Barca was growing to fill the promise of his family name quite quickly.

Mago nodded to the guards posted outside Hannibal's tent. He slipped quietly past them and into a gloomy haze of incense, the close, moist smell of sweat and exhaustion, of blood and vinegar. As his eyes grew accustomed to the light the room came slowly into relief, its sparse furnishings ordering themselves before his eyes. A single wooden table stood at the center, cluttered with maps and other papers and surrounded by stools pushed back a little distance. Just beyond the table, lining the far wall, Hannibal lay on a small bed. He was propped up on one elbow and from that position watched his physician, Synhalus, who worked beneath the lamp glow provided by his assistant.

"Welcome, brother," Hannibal said, his tone surprisingly light. "Sorry to call you away, but I need your services as scribe. The sickly creature who last had the post died most unpleasantly. My surgeon here says it was the cost of his sexual habits, consumed from the loins up into his abdomen. I would prefer a death in battle, to be sure."

The Egyptian physician glanced over his shoulder and seemed to consider the interruption for a moment. He exhaled and pushed himself to his feet and spoke a few words to the commander. As he did so, Mago was provided a view of his work. His brother's leg was bare, punctured at mid-thigh in a circle of jagged flesh that cut deep into the muscle. The surgeon draped a wet cloth over the wound. The white material flushed on contact and then, gradually, deepened to a red and on toward brown.

"Don't think me too infirm," Hannibal said. "They pierced the skin and muscle of me, Mago, but not the bone, not even the main artery, and certainly not my heart or resolve. I don't doubt I am the victim of some stable boy who snatched up a javelin when he saw his chance for glory. It does vex me, mostly because my foolishness broke our momentum and the siege carries on. Come in and sit. Synhalus is leaving me now but he will soon return. He has all manner of tortures planned for me this afternoon, but he thinks he can keep this leg from becoming the death of me."

Hannibal grasped the surgeon by the wrist in a parting gesture. Synhalus nodded and left the room without making eye contact with Mago. His assistant took the lamp with him and for a moment after their departure the room dropped into shadow.

Mago navigated through the stools and sat as instructed. He found it hard to look directly at his brother, for his eyes wanted only to stare at the wound. "I would take your place if I could," he said. "I'd accept the foul weapon into my own flesh to see you whole again."

The smile on the commander's face dropped away. Though the air in the tent was a comfortable temperature, beads of sweat dotted his nose and temples. These were the only indication of the pain his leg must have been causing him. He shifted position and said, "You would never have been as foolish as I. There are many reasons for me to risk my life for our goals; impatience isn't one of them. Are the men greatly disturbed?"

"None can remember seeing you injured," Mago said. "It has been a shock. Rumors spread faster than fever in times like this."

Hannibal shifted as if he were about to rise, but understanding his thoughts Mago stayed him with a hand. "We're dealing with it, brother. I made sure that the priest who sacrificed this morning found the signs positive. Also, I instructed the generals to speak not of your frailty but of your courage, to remind all men that you have as much to lose in this battle as they and yet you do not shrink from it. I tell them that, but be more careful in future, brother. It's not true that you have as much to lose as they; you have very much more."

"Wise counsel," Hannibal said. "Sometimes I think you are more like me than any of our father's children."

"You speak too highly of me."

Hannibal did not smile, but there was something ironic in his expression. "I don't think so. You are the most like what I would be if I could be other than I am. Hasdrubal takes joy from life in a light way that I never could. Hanno lives well, but carries a weight around his neck that hinders him. Some doubt was planted in him young, and he's never grown beyond it. You, Mago, have a balance that I envy. One day I will show you the depths of my admiration, but let us first take care of what we must. I called you here because again the Romans have sent envoys to chastise us. I've kept them waiting along the shore, stewing, I hope, and blistering under the sun. I might have received them previously, but not in this state. I am sure that in a day or two they'll sail from here directly to Carthage. But let us forewarn the Council. Better they hear from me first. You'll find writing materials there behind you."

He waited as Mago got his supplies ready. He started to adjust his position, but his leg stopped him. He gave up on the effort. Instead he swiped at the flies that had settled on his bandage. They scattered, only to circle and return a moment later. When his brother looked up at him, he began.

"Transcribe my words exactly. Have you any question, stop me and ask it. We can have no errors in such a correspondence. Write this . . . Honored and venerated Council of Carthage, beloved of Baal, descendants of Elissa, Hannibal hails you. I write to you on a matter of grave importance, which I ask you to consider the very day you receive this. As you know, I serve you humbly in Iberia. I carry on the work of my father, Hamilcar, who through sheer force of will wrested Iberia from the waste of tribal bickering. He built of it a fine holding, rich in silver and timber and other resources. My father filled your coffers, aiding as no other could in the rebuilding of Carthage's depleted fortunes. He died in these efforts, sacrificing even his life to the country he loved."

Hannibal paused to allow Mago to catch up. He was surprised to find that his brother stopped writing only a moment later. "So fast as that? They have taught you well. Perhaps I need not have sent for that Greek to keep a record of events for me." He proceeded, speaking a little more rapidly.

"In the time after my father's death, my brother-in-law, Hasdrubal the Handsome, ably managed Iberia. On his death I took his burdens upon myself, not solely of my own wish but at the request of all who cared for Carthage's glory. Since then I've all but completed the conquest of Iberia. I did not call on Carthage for resources then, but at my own expense gained domination over the tribes of the Tagus, and captured Salmantica and Arbocala. Carthage favors generals who win and generals who enrich the city of their birth. This being so, you can have no complaint about Hannibal or the legacy of the Barcas.

"I remind you of all this so that it will be fresh in your mind when you receive the embassy of the Romans. They will come to you condemning me, spinning truths into lies and lies into truths, as is their way. You know the mission that I am on, so remember two things, that Saguntum is south of the Ebro, and that we've no obligation to honor Roman commands concerning a city within our realm of influence. I believe that my actions in taking Saguntum do not violate existing agreements. Even if they did, you have the authority to reject those agreements, as they did not come directly from yourselves. What I ask of you is simple. Send those Romans home like the disobedient dogs they are. I will complete this business soon, and I assure you Carthage will benefit handsomely from it. And know also that, should Rome challenge us with force, Carthage can count on Hannibal and his army to meet any threat before it reaches African soil."

Hannibal motioned for his brother to hold the scroll up for him to see. "You have a fine hand," he said, his tone conversational. "They are indeed precious, these Romans. They call me barbaric, when they are the masters of treachery and the breakers of treaties. They present themselves here like children shocked at the harsh world all around them. But even these Saguntines shall one day attest that Hannibal is both just and strong."

"Shall they?" Mago asked. "That would surprise me. I mean, that they would admit as much."

"They cannot say I failed to offer them a choice. Think of it like this: When you come upon a great tree that blocks your path, do you stand against it and challenge it to battle? When you are out walking in the night and hear behind you the growls of a lion, do you turn and fight it lest it inconvenience you? No. You walk around the tree. You quicken your pace away from the lion and find shelter. I present the Saguntines with a force beyond their capacity to defeat. They must adapt to it. If they had the wisdom to acknowledge this, we would not be fighting now. When they rejected me, they asked for my wrath instead of my friendship. So their fate has been decided by their own actions. This is no perversity of my own. The world is cruel. One must take on a portion of that cruelty to live in it. That is all I've done."

Hannibal paused and tilted his head to listen to some shouts outside, and then continued. "But, some might ask, Is Hannibal propelled by the breeze or does he shape the breeze? To which I admit that the behavior of the Saguntines suits me perfectly. I knew how they would react, and how Rome will react. Though I might have thought we would capture them sooner, I am glad this is proving a challenge for my men."

Mago nodded, though he found himself resisting Hannibal's

logic. Questions popped to mind fully formed; facts occurred to him that he might have pointed out to undermine the general's assertions. It could not be denied that the Saguntines were fighting bravely for their very lives, to protect their women and keep their children from being sold into slavery. At night, when he heard them calling out curses from the walls, he could hear the brave desperation in the voices. The poet in him was struck by this. Perhaps it was the *Iliad* haunting him once more, recalling the fate of Priam and his Troy. He had always been disappointed by that aspect of the great tales. All that heroic grandeur resulted in rape and pillage and the utter destruction of a people. But Mago had never voiced such thoughts to anyone and he held his peace.

"In any event, the Council will know my mind and they will be swayed by it," Hannibal continued. "Though I've been away from home too many years, I still know my people. My message will, by the gods' grace, fly past the Roman envoy and find a home in the hearts of our countrymen. That's my will. Let us see it fulfilled." So saying, he placed his stamp upon the scroll. Mago rolled and wrapped it safely and passed it on to a messenger, who was waiting at the mouth of the tent.

It seemed that Hannibal was on the verge of dismissing Mago, but he delayed him a little longer. He ran a hand down the ridge of his nose, and opened his fingers across his lower face as if he would capture the heat of his breath. "Mago, write me another letter. As with everything that passes between us, this correspondence is not to be spoken of. Perhaps this woman is my weakness, brother, and if that is so I would have none but yourself know it."

He hesitated for a moment after Mago was ready, and there was some reluctance in his voice when he spoke again. "Dearest Imilce . . ."

Sapanibal was as much a Barca as any of her brothers. She had Hannibal's deep-set eyes, Hanno's stature and wide forehead, Hasdrubal's shapely mouth, and Mago's sensitive mind. Like all her siblings, her younger sister Sophonisba included, she had been raised to serve the family's interests. Her marriage to Hasdrubal the

Handsome had done just that, creating a bond stronger than mere pledges and promises. In this her sacrifice was as earnest as if she had dedicated her life to war; Sapanibal had endured her task with the same dedication expected of her brothers. Perhaps this was why she had been out of sorts of late. What was required of her was no longer certain. Her husband had been dead some years now and therefore no longer a tool through which to exert influence. None of the children he had planted in her had lived more than a few months inside her, so she could not focus herself on motherhood. Her brothers were always busy with warcraft, in which she could take no official role. And then there was Imilce, who now commanded Hannibal's attention in a way that Sapanibal felt was gradually, inevitably, replacing the influence she might once have exerted.

A late summer morning found her walking the meandering path into the woodland of New Carthage, a small square of dense trees, aged giants trapped within the city's granite walls. The same architecture that protected these chosen few had grown wealthy at the expense of the miles and miles of forest once thick outside the gates. With the price of fine lumber rising, the wood standing in New Carthage was a great luxury, which had been protected during the governance of her husband. It was rumored that his forbearance sprang not from an interest in nature, but to please a concubine of whom he was particularly enamored. For this it was called the Whore's Wood, a name Sapanibal was quite fond of. She had long ago ceased to take offense at Hasdrubal's infidelities. He had been a man, and men showed their prime weakness in giving in to the hungers of the groin. Anyway, the whore in question had been sharing Hasdrubal's bed on the night he was assassinated. She died in Sapanibal's place, her chest and abdomen speckled with stab wounds, just like her lover's. Baal had a sense of humor after all.

She found a certain peace and calm beneath the cloak of interwoven branches, inhaling the dampness of the place. Who could help but stand in awe of the towering columns of oak and spruce, with ferns thick around the legs and the leaves above stirred by breezes little felt upon the ground? Though she never spoke of it to anyone, she had occasionally slept in the woods. Stretching her body out on the mossy floor, eyes closed, she had listened as the natural world shifted around her. It was a rare, private pleasure, the only time she felt truly herself because it was the only time she truly forgot herself.

She spotted Imilce, her maid, and their guard before they were aware of her, waiting as had been arranged by messenger a few hours earlier. She slowed her pace and watched them a moment. Sitting on stools that servants must have placed for them, they were dwarfed by the trees, both the many standing and one great beast that had fallen two years before. It was thicker than either woman was tall. It ran behind them like a wall thrown down by the forest itself. Strange, Sapanibal thought, that a race of creatures who built such enormous structures could themselves look like insects before the mute girth of nature.

"Good Imilce," she called as she walked into the clearing, "forgive me for asking to meet you here. It's just that I never begin a day without a walk in the forest, and I thought how pleasant it would be for you to share it with me. Come walk with me a little. I will be your guide to the Whore's Wood."

Imilce rose and nodded to her maid; they fell in step with her sister-in-law. Imilce's body had a lithe, supple quality that contrasted sharply with Sapanibal's stride. Though Sapanibal was well dressed, her hair neatly woven into braids, and her ears adorned with silver loops, still she was a goose leading a swan and she knew it. She felt it keenly despite herself and hid it through banter. The wood was full of life and she told Imilce all about it as they walked.

The ear-piercing calls of tropical birds—flamboyant creatures of bright greens and reds, some of solid white, big-beaked and absurd by design—cut the air in cacophonic waves. They were not native to the forest but were replenished each year, kept in place by clipped wings and the barren stretch of treeless land around the city. The parrots were not the only foreigners. A troop of monkeys lived within the forest. They had been imported from Africa, tiny-faced and long-limbed and so agile as to defy possibility. They called to each other and threw insults down upon the intruders. Sapanibal pulled dates from a pouch attached to her waist chain and hurled them one by one into the trees. This brought more cries. The monkeys jumped from limb to limb and snatched the fruit out of midair. They shadowed the women until they reached the edge of the wood and stepped out onto the close-cropped field that ran away a short distance to the city's wall.

Sapanibal lowered herself and sat with her legs crossed before her, straight-backed. "We are a strange people," she said, pointing to a small group of creatures near a crook in the wall. From a distance they looked like horses, but there was something different in their movements and colorings. Zebras. "There are some who would make New Carthage a pen for all things exotic, people or jewels or animals. In truth, it sometimes seems to me that my brother succeeds not because of Carthage but despite it. This extravagance will be our downfall if anything is. Did you know, Imilce, that once a merchant named Sastanu traveled from Carthage with two fully grown giraffes? He called them wedding presents for Hasdrubal and me. One died of fever; the other bit a guard in the backside and found the artery in her throat sliced by his sword."

Imilce was still considering the prospect of settling down on the grass. Eventually, reluctantly, she did so. "I had not heard that before. I'd quite like to see a giraffe. Are they really so tall as they say?"

Sapanibal, though she had opened the topic, grew impatient with it. "Yes, you could walk upright beneath the belly of one with room to spare. But I've not come to talk of such things. I bring you a message, sister-in-law, from my brother."

"My husband?"

Sapanibal reached inside the loose folds of her gown and produced a small, tightly rolled scroll. "It seems the siege goes on, slow as the summer and not nearly as pleasant."

"You have read the letter?"

Sapanibal looked at her dryly. "I've not read it, sister. Much mail comes through me, and this I thought I'd deliver to you rather than hand it off to another."

Imilce took the scroll and held it awkwardly. Her fingers caressed the string that bound it. A moment passed in silence until finally she thanked Sapanibal and seemed on the verge of taking her leave.

But Sapanibal said casually, "I'll read it for you, if you like."

This stopped Imilce. She began by shaking her head, but turned the gesture into a one-shoulder shrug instead. "I would not want to trouble you," she said.

Sapanibal opened her palm. "It's no trouble. A small thing that I am happy to do for you."

Imilce handed back the scroll and waited as Sapanibal removed the string, unrolled it, and pressed it flat with her fingers. " 'Dearest Imilce,' " she read. " 'May this find you as when I last saw you, the model of health and beauty. I pray the summer has not been too oppressive in New Carthage. I heard early reports of a fever in the region, but later I was told this was not so. Please speak of this when you next write me. This business here is slow. Our adversary is a more tenacious one than I expected, as you warned me. You know these people better than I. Perhaps next time you will remind me of this occasion and force your counsel upon me. But the siege will be concluded before the warring season ends. I assure you of that, and then you will find me in your presence once more.' "

Sapanibal paused and cleared her throat and brushed away a fly that had settled on her arm.

" 'How is young Hamilcar? It is one of my sorest trials that I cannot see him daily growing. I hope you are whispering to him as we spoke of in the spring, speaking close so that his tiny ears might hear of his father and recognize me upon my return. I was told recently that since I departed you have daily offered sacrifice on my behalf. I thank you for this. May the gods smile on you and pass your wisdom on to our son. Imilce, you may also have heard that I've been injured. There is nothing in this rumor; I am in fine health, as ever. From your husband, who loves you. Hannibal.' "

Imilce was silent for a long moment, and then said, "He's lying, isn't he? He's been hurt. I should go to him."

"You should not," Sapanibal said. "If my brother says he's in fine health, then you must believe him. And if he was injured, then it's a matter for a surgeon, not a wife."

"So you, too, think he is hurt?"

Sapanibal ignored this. "He must know that you are here and well and lovingly unconcerned. Even this letter is too much of an indulgence. He is the commander of an army, Imilce. His mind should be at ease and focused solely on his goal. The lives of many people and the fate of our nation depend on it. If you like, I can help you write a response, a cheery letter that reminds him his son is healthy and his wife loving. That is what he needs. Do you understand?"

Imilce lifted her gaze and watched the zebras in the distance. "You make it quite clear, sister."

"Good," Sapanibal said. "The best hope Hannibal has for recovery is full focus on it."

Imilce snapped her head around and stared at Sapanibal, exasperated. "So you do believe he's been injured! Or do you know it from another source? Tell me, please. You have spies everywhere, don't you? Nothing passes Sapanibal. Only I am kept ignorant."

"You slight us both and in neither case do you speak truly. Nobody would ever suggest Imilce is ignorant, or that I've any power whatsoever. I only offer you my counsel as one who has been a soldier's wife. You know as well as I that Hannibal has been provoking Rome. If he engages with the Romans fully it will be a war like none the world has yet seen. It'll be no summer campaign but a far longer struggle. You should consider how best to aid our cause in this."

"Perhaps I will accompany him," Imilce offered.

Sapanibal pursed her lips—at the world at large, for Imilce had lowered her gaze to her lap. "Some wives have done that, yes," she said. "And there are always women among the camp followers. But you know as well as I that is a foolish notion for you, with the baby certainly. On the contrary, I believe you should return with me to Carthage and wait out the war there."

"You would have me leave Iberia?"

"It would be for the best. You are married to Carthage, after all. You might as well see it, learn the language properly, meet my mother, Didobal, and my sister, Sophonisba."

"I will ask my husband."

"You can do that, but know that I've already spoken with him on this matter, and he agrees with me."

Imilce looked askance at Sapanibal as she considered this news. "I will ask him myself." She rose and patted bits of debris from her gown. "I will sacrifice to Baal this evening and I will have a letter composed, cheerful as you say. Thank you, sister, for your counsel."

Sapanibal watched Imilce move away. Despite the young beauty's deferential words, Sapanibal did not trust her, was not yet confident that she would not somehow corrupt the course of events to come, intentionally or otherwise. She was, after all, the daughter of a conquered chieftain. Though others did not yet realize this, Sapanibal knew that Imilce formed her own opinions. This much, at least, she could see behind the elegant façade.

Just as Hannibal hoped, the Carthaginian Council had time to consider his letter before the Roman envoy called on them. They turned him away casually, citing the arguments elucidated to them in the letter. Unfortunately, the same messenger who brought this news back to Hannibal also brought word of a rebellion among the Carpetani, in central Iberia. The commander left Saguntum to deal with it personally. He might have delegated this task to a trusted general, but he deemed it grave enough to require his personal attention. If left unchecked, these unruly tribes might inspire more discontent with Carthaginian authority. This was impermissible.

In his absence he left Hanno at the helm, with instructions to bring the siege to a conclusion if it all possible. But almost before Hannibal's silhouette disappeared over the Saguntine hills, the men's enthusiasm drained from their weary bodies. Hanno saw this. Perhaps even more significantly, he felt it as well. He had no inspired speeches to energize his sweat-soaked, reeking, insect-plagued men, but he believed that no city could stand forever against dogged persistence. He had the men build ever larger siege engines, towers taller than the walls, that could be pushed forward on the level areas. From these they hurled volleys of arrows and spears and darts as cover for those working beneath them. In other areas, they built sheltered pathways so that workers could go forward in safety and chip away at the foundation of the city in relative safety. Adherbal, the chief engineer, reported that the blocks at the base of the walls were fitted and sealed with clay. These blocks he had pulled away in great numbers, weakening the fortress at its very base. Occasionally the massive walls shifted and adjusted to the intrusion, groaned against it as if calling out for help.

This was normal enough—to be expected as the battering rams

shook the barriers deep down into their foundations—but Hanno woke one stiflingly hot late-summer morning, feeling something in the air, something amiss. When a messenger brought him news of a strange occurrence he almost felt like he had been expecting it. A corner section of the city's sloping northern bulwark had shifted suddenly, crushing the corps of workers undermining it, burying them in an instant mass grave, one great noise and then complete silence, no cries or moaning or calls for help. As the dust slowly cleared it revealed the strangest of architectural adjustments. The wall had not collapsed at all but simply sunk about ten feet, completely intact, no weaker for the change, no more easily breached.

Inspecting the sight, Hanno felt a sudden, gnawing doubt wrap around his gut. What force had lifted its massive boot and pressed it down upon those fifty men, blotting them from the earth without a trace? It was too odd an occurrence to go unconsidered. There might well be a portent in it of things to come. Perhaps the Saguntines had called upon the power of a god whose devotion to them outweighed Baal's commitment to the Carthaginians. If that were so, not even Hannibal's skills could hope to further their cause. Hanno ordered a halt to similar work and called upon the chief priest for guidance.

Mandarbal was a taciturn man with a disfigured face. His upper lip attached directly to the lower portion of his nose, leaving his mouth ever open, his large yellow foreteeth jutting out. It was rumored that he had been born with hands like the flippers of a sea creature, fingers all attached to each other with a webbing of skin that a clerical surgeon sliced away on the day they accepted the orphaned boy into their order. For this reason the priest always wore leather gloves, as he did that afternoon as he invoked the presence of the gods and their wisdom and guidance in the question before them. The animal to be offered was a she-goat that had spent some time in a blessed state, waiting to be called upon. Mandarbal's black-cloaked assistants led her into the dusty courtyard of the command tent, chanting sacred words, the meanings of which were known only to themselves. The goat eyed them warily, skittish and ornery, pulling against the rope that bound her. The priests had difficulty maintaining the appropriate solemnity while controlling her.

Mago, who stood beside his brother, nudged him in the ribs. "Seems she knows what's coming," he said. "Our future written on the inside of her. Strange how the gods speak to us."

The animal's struggles turned out to be short-lived. Mandarbal knew his work well and went to it without delay. With the help of his assistants, he straddled the goat across the shoulders and jabbed her in the neck with a long, thin spike. An artery spurted a few quick streams of blood and then eased into a steady flow that slowly blackened the goat's neck and dripped down to the parched earth. The priest stretched out his hand for the next tool, a knife with a convexly curved blade and a handle said to have been made from the backbone of a sea monster. The motion he used to cut the creature's throat was awkward, but so fast that the goat barely noticed it. She had dropped to her knees before she realized new damage had been done to her. This much of the ceremony was public, but as the priests bent to the surgery they closed in around the victim and worked silently.

Mago began to whisper something to his brother, but paused to watch a man stride up to the edge of the group. He was a short man, thin around the chest, with slender arms like those of an adolescent boy. His head seemed somewhat larger than the norm, squared across the back and covered in a mass of curly black hair. But for all his seeming frailty he was tanned a leathery brown and strode up with a massive pack balanced on his shoulders, the legs supporting him sinewy and nimble. He tossed his burden down in the dust and introduced himself, speaking first in Greek, then a little more in Latin, and finally, eloquently, in Carthaginian. He was Silenus, the Greek who was to take over as Hannibal's official historian and chronicler. He said that he had come from afar to immortalize this colossal undertaking in words that would make the ancient poets jealous. He needed little more than wine to wet his pen.

Mago warmed to him immediately, but Hanno said, "You have arrived at an inconvenient time. We expected you several weeks ago."

"I know it, sir. I've been held up by too many things to recount in brief. I will bend your ear if you ask me to, but it is a tale better told at leisure."

Hanno considered this prospect for a moment before answering.

"It can wait," he said. "Search out the camp quartermaster. He'll get you settled and show you the layout of the camp. You'll explain your lateness to me this evening."

"At dinner," Mago said. "Explain it to me as well. Tell the tale in leisure, as you suggest."

Hanno looked at his brother but did not contradict him. He turned his attention back to the divination, although he was still aware that some moments passed before the Greek hefted his load and moved away.

Mandarbal finally rose, the bloody liver cradled in his gloved hands. The goat lay on its side, abdomen slit open and viscera strewn from the wound and freckled with pale dirt, already swarming with flies. The priest placed the sacred organ carefully upon the ceremonial table and bent close to it, his attendants on either side of him, shoulder to shoulder, head to head so that the two brothers saw nothing of the signs written on the liver itself. Mandarbal stood erect above the scene for a moment, then turned and walked toward the brothers. As he left the circle of priests, the space he vacated closed behind him. Hanno only caught a momentary glimpse of the mutilated flesh.

"The signs are uncertain," Mandarbal said, his voice high and lisping. "The offshoot of the liver is abnormally large, which suggests a reversal of the natural order. The right compartment is healthy and fine, but the left bears a black mark shaped like a young frog."

"How do you read that?" Hanno asked.

"It is uncertain. We are favored by the gods in some aspects, and yet there are divine forces aligned against us."

"Is that all you can see?"

Mandarbal considered this. He looked back over his shoulders. An insect landed on his lip but flew away instantly. He said, "Perhaps you have offended a single deity and may yet suffer for it."

Hanno pressed his tongue against his teeth for a moment. "I would look upon the organ myself," he said. "Might I—"

The priest stopped him with his hand. His fingertips spotted Hanno's breastplate with blood. "You cannot see the sacred parts. This is forbidden to your eyes. You would profane the rites. I've told you more than enough. Trust when I tell you that the future is not certain. Sacrifice to Baal and to Anath. I will ask El for guidance. Perhaps the aged one will speak to us. And Moloch, also—give praise to death."

Mandarbal made as if to return to his attendants, but noting the expression on Hanno's face, he paused. "Events will unfold by the will of the gods," he said. "To know their desire is not always our fortune; to have a part in it, regardless, is the blessing and curse of our lives. Be at ease with it. A thrashing man will always drown; a passive one may sometimes float."

With that, the priest turned and showed the Barcas his back.

Mago shrugged, pursed his lips, and patted his brother on the shoulder. "What did you expect?" he asked. "They are priests. It is against their creed to speak clearly."

Hanno took the sacred ceremonies much more seriously than his brother, but he could not deny the simple truth Mago referred to. The priests always left one more ill at ease than before, more uncertain, more troubled by the numerous possibilities. It was a strange art, theirs, but one he could never turn his back on.

Had he had only his own inclinations to consider, he would not have joined his brother for the evening meal but would have retired early to privacy. But, as so often since Hannibal's departure, his presence seemed an official necessity. In honor of the Greek, the officers dined in a style he was familiar with, lounging on low couches in Mago's tent, sampling cheeses and fish, vegetables and goat meat with their fingers. The day was still stiflingly warm. One wall of the large tent was folded back to encourage the first stirrings of an evening breeze. Silenus spoke Carthaginian with a Syracusan accent. He entertained the weary soldiers with tales of his voyage from Carthage to Sicily, from there up to the Greek town of Emporiae in northeastern Iberia, from which he sailed along the coast aboard a trading vessel that dropped him at Saguntum. It was hard to know just where fact met fantasy in the man's story, for his odyssey seemed calculated to outdo the poem sung by Homer. He spoke of pirates off the Aegates, of sighting a leviathan longer than the quinquereme in which he sailed, and of a lightning bolt that darted down out of a clear sky and struck the surface of the water.

"It sounds as though we are lucky to lay our eyes on you," Mago said. He motioned for a servant to refill the Greek's wine bowl, a task attended by a slim-shouldered Arbocalan.

"That you are," the Greek agreed. "If I had known that I would miss the commander, I might not have rushed."

"Better that you delayed no longer," Hanno said. Without his meaning to reveal it, his voice bore an edge of threat. There was something about the scribe that annoyed him, more so because he chided himself for showing it in the face of a company that seemed kindly inclined toward the man. In a more controlled tone, he said, "There's a great deal you'll have to learn about what we require of you."

"Of course that is so," Silenus said. He bowed his head and left it at that.

One officer, Bomilcar, seemed particularly amused by Silenus. Though a giant of a man, perfectly proportioned but at a scale rarely witnessed, Bomilcar was neither a terribly disciplined nor especially intelligent officer. His muscular bulk made him a leader of men regardless. His family was an old one in Carthage, but they had maintained a remarkable purity of Phoenician blood, evidenced by the curved blade of his nose, his sharp chin, and the bushy prominence of his eyebrows.

"Greek," he said, "let me ask you, how did your gimp god Hephaestus secure Aphrodite as a wife? Why not Ares instead? Why not Zeus himself? Or that one from the sea?"

"The blacksmith has got poor legs," Silenus said, "but his other limbs function quite well. He spends his days pounding iron—"

"And his nights pounding something else!" Bomilcar was laughing at his own joke before he had even completed it.

Silenus smiled. "Yes, but Hephaestus is known as a kind god, as well. Perhaps Aphrodite finds this a virtue. This may come as a surprise to you, Bomilcar, but I am not personally acquainted with the Olympians. I've invoked their presence more than once, I assure you, but as yet they've spurned me. Artemis, Hera, Aphrodite—I've asked them all to dine but they've ignored me. I caught a glimpse of Dionysus once, but my head was a bit foggy at the time. No, the gods are largely silent as concerns young Silenus."

"Are you a Skeptic, then?" Mago asked.

"Not at all," Silenus said. "I've seen Ares in a man's eyes and sampled Aphrodite's handiwork and every day one sees Apollo's labors. I've simply been shunned, and I am bitter."

Hanno said, "Greeks are strange creatures. They claim to revere their gods above all others and yet at the same time they pretend to believe in nothing. Have you no fear of the insult you may cause and of the punishment brought down on you?"

"Insult to the gods?" Silenus asked. He held his wine goblet beneath his nose for a moment, thinking. "I am too small a man to accomplish that. You see these arms, this misshapen head? What god could reasonably take offense at anything I utter?"

"You toy with questions instead of answering them," Hanno said. "We Carthaginians fear our gods. We ask daily, hourly, each minute that their wrath be directed at our enemies instead of at ourselves. We never know what will displease them, so we are ever respectful."

"How unfortunate," Silenus said. He seemed to have more to say but left it at that.

"Let's not talk of our faiths," Mago said. "We all honor Baal. That is never in question among this company, Greeks included. But tell us something more useful, Silenus. You have actually been to Rome, haven't you? Tell us of the Romans."

Silenus picked up on the topic happily enough. "The Romans are an uncultured lot. It is not so long ago that Rome was a flea-infested sewer of no consequence at all. They've no literature to speak of. They appease the gods when it suits them, but they make a muddle of it. They've actually just borrowed our Greek deities and renamed them. One wonders whom they think they are fooling. Not the gods themselves, surely. I imagine that when they decide they need a literature of their own they'll take it from Greece. Take Homer and rename him Pomponius or something similarly absurd and change all the names in the *Iliad*. They are shameless, I assure you. This could well happen."

"If they aren't humbled first," Bomilcar said. "Which they shall be by Baal's grace and Hannibal's cunning. I wish he were here to meet you, Greek. Then you'd see the face of the future. He'll squash these Romans beneath his heel soon. Hannibal puts steel in all his men's backbones. Rome is no foe to be feared."

"I am no warrior," Silenus said, "but I might argue there's a thing even more powerful than steel."

"And what's that?" Bomilcar asked. "Surely not pen and ink? Are you of that school?"

"No," Silenus said dryly, looking almost saddened by the admission. "I'm not such an idealist that I believe that. What I'm referring to is not easily explained. I don't have the word for it just yet, but . . . Have you heard of Cincinnatus? During the early forging of the Republic, the Romans battled with their neighbors constantly. In the instance I am speaking of, the Roman army was pinned down by the Aequi, in a dire situation, trapped with dwindling food and water and outnumbered. As things seemed hopeless, Rome looked to the priests for direction, and in answer they were instructed to call upon Cincinnatus, a veteran soldier some years retired into a quiet life. They found him working in his field, plow in hand, sweating, squinting at the sun, I'd imagine, wife and children and some pigs about the place. You can picture it. But still they called him up and bestowed upon him the powers of dictator. He left the plow where it rested and raised a new army from the fields and farms around him. He marched on the Aequi within a few weeks and defeated them soundly. Quite a feat for a humble farmer, would not you say?"

"But Cincinnatus was no humble farmer," Hanno said. "He was a veteran. Retired, but still a warrior. What point do you wish to extract from this tale?"

"I assert that he was a warrior and also a simple farmer. He was both, and not more one than the other. That is my point. Romans believe themselves to be simple farmers. But they believe that hand in hand with this goes the requirement that they also be their nations' soldiers. Plow one minute, sword the next, depending on the call of the country. After his victory Cincinnatus laid down the title of dictator and walked away from the rule of Rome and returned to his farm. He picked up his plow where it lay and carried on with his real work of choice."

Mago doubted that the man's plow had stood untouched in the fields and said so. Silenus waved this away as superficial. "That is a detail of the storyteller. It enhances the tale's symmetry, but should not distract from the truth of it. Still, my point—"

"I understand your point," Hanno said, "but no army of farmers can stand against an army of trained soldiers, men who have chosen war above other paths. A soldier who has just stepped from the field cannot hope to defeat one who has been drilled and drilled again, one who knows nothing but the life of the sword and scorns men who would break their backs trying to grow plants from the dry earth. Our army succeeds not despite the absence of civilians, but because of it. No man in the Carthaginian Council could last a day in battle beside my brother or me. I'd wager that the same is true of Roman senators. I think this Cincinnatus is just a fiction, a detail from an earlier storyteller, to use your words."

Silenus shrugged. He lifted his bowl and realized it was empty. Holding it up to be refilled, he said, "But if I understand the possible plans this conversation has suggested to me, then your brother would consider attacking the Romans on their own soil. Men fight differently with their wives and children at their backs. The Saguntines demonstrate it at this very moment."

Hanno studied the Greek through narrowed eyes. "One wonders if you are suited to the job required of you." Without awaiting a response, he rose, bade them fair evening, and turned to leave.

"Hanno," Bomilcar called. "You haven't said whether we resume in force tomorrow. I know the signs were troubling . . . but my men are ready to push the assault. Adherbal says—"

"I know," Hanno snapped, "but architects do not give orders. They follow them. And I've not made up my mind. I must think on it more." He stepped out into the summer night and stood for a moment with his eyes closed, feeling the movement of the evening air across his face. The scent of cooking meat floated to him. Beyond that came the flavor of incense and the musty rankness of horses, and, behind it all, the dry smoke of a thousand small fires. He heard bits of conversation, a yell in a language he did not recognize, laughter like that of children at play, and a prayer spoken loud to Shalem, the god who most loved to contemplate the setting sun.

He moved off toward the cottage he had been staying in of late. It was somewhat farther up the slope, set back on a flat shelf and abutted by a stony outcropping. It had been a retreat for one of Saguntum's wealthy leaders, just far enough from the city to provide some quiet, high enough up for the air to be better than that found near the sewers of the city, with a view that one could contemplate indefinitely. Hannibal would not have approved—rather a simple tent or the bare ground, like the men who served them—but the commander was away. Hanno was no stranger to the trials of camp, but when opportunity allowed he preferred solid walls around him and comfort in his bed and the privacy to share it as he saw fit.

While he ascended the hill, the sky bloomed in magnificent color. The horizon glowed radiantly auburn, as if the air itself took on the warmth of the sun and hummed with it. Even the smoke rising from the city caught the crimson heat. Highlights swirled into the billowing gray and black. Hanno remembered the earlier mention of Hephaestus. The sky around his volcano-forge would look much like this. . . . He shook his head to clear it of Greek thoughts. There was only one aspect of Silenus' stories that he cared for: the notion that the Romans read the prophecies correctly when they sought out Cincinnatus. Would that he had such wisdom himself, for he was more puzzled about how to proceed than ever. Was he the drowning man Mandarbal referred to? He felt this to be so, but how did one float in a sea as tumultuous as the one he found himself in?

As he reached his cottage, a figure rose from the ground before it, no soldier or guard but one of the young men who cared for the horses in the hills beyond the camp. He was perhaps fifteen, bare-chested and lithe, a Celt with hair touched by the sun and large black eyes that he kept lowered as the general approached. Hanno did not pause to address the boy, but he was warmed by his presence and thankful for the silent company he was to offer. He walked past him without a gesture or greeting. The boy waited a moment. His eyes rose enough to take in the scene of the city before him, and then he turned and stepped through the threshold.

Hannibal met Hasdrubal en route from New Carthage, and the two brothers rode together at the head of a force of almost twenty thousand. In the week they spent riding inland Hannibal kept his brother tethered to his side, discussing tactics with him, testing his knowledge of the country, quizzing him on the various chieftains, their characters, flaws, and virtues. He needed to know that this young one was capable of the things that were to be asked of him, and the time left for training diminished daily. The army was a mixed company made up partly of the veterans stationed at New Carthage, with some Iberians from the southern tribes, completed by new Libyan recruits and a unit of Moorish mercenaries, and augmented by a company of elephants fresh from North Africa. They had never fought together as one body, but at least they knew the commands as given by the trumpet. Even more important, Hannibal trusted the generals overseeing them to carry out his will.

The farther inland they marched the hotter it grew, dry and unrelenting through the day and a slow bake at night. When they looked back on the column, the army faded rank after rank into a thickening cloud of dust. Hasdrubal once commented that the men were like individual licks of a great fire—a fitting image, Hannibal thought.

Though he spoke of it to no one, Hannibal's wound troubled him constantly. It had half healed into a ragged, fearsome-looking scar, and the leg was just barely sound enough for him to walk and ride. Synhalus had opposed this excursion, and Hannibal soon acknowledged the physician's wisdom—if only to himself—as days in the saddle took their toll on him. At night the pain of the wound gnawed at his leg with such convulsive ardor that he once dreamed a miniature fox had been sewn alive into the wound. He awoke drenched in sweat and angry at himself. A man should control his pain and not the other way around. His father had exemplified such strength during the last decade of his life, and Hannibal was determined to be no different. To prove it he brought his fist down upon his thigh as if to punish the creature within it, to beat it into submission. This proved largely impossible, however. He was glad when battle came, for during it he truly forgot the pain and had no purpose save one.

The Massylii scouts had brought back partial reports earlier in the day. Therefore Hannibal knew as he approached the river Tagus that the Carpetani were near at hand. But it was not until the full force of the barbarians blocked their path that the situation became completely clear. They stood on the near bank of the river, thousands upon thousands of them, a force larger than any they had yet mustered. Hannibal knew at a glance that this horde represented not a single tribe but the confederation of several. They outnumbered the Carthaginians by at least three to one. Moving forward in a semi-ordered mob, they shouted out in their various dialects and blew their horns and bashed their spears and swords against their shields.

The Barca brothers watched this from atop anxious horses. Hasdrubal cursed that they had no choice but to engage fully, but Hannibal shook his head. It was late afternoon already; the sun was slipping behind the hills to the west. He gave orders for the army to back and fight, back and fight. He engaged chosen units briefly and then withdrew them, inflicting what damage he could with pikemen and with the quick spears of the Moorish skirmishers. The elephants wreaked some havoc among the Carpetani but even these he held at close rein.

The afternoon passed into evening, and it appeared—not solely to the Carpetani but also to many among the Carthaginians themselves—that the Iberians had bested Hannibal's men for the day. As the sun set, the Carthaginians turned from warfare to architecture, building the fortifications to protect them till the morrow. Hannibal instructed them to make a great show of it, with plenty of noise, to make it clear that they were settling in for a prolonged fight the next day.

Toward the end of the night's first quarter, Hannibal and a group of scouts led the infantry and most of the cavalry on a five-mile hike upstream. They traveled silently, through what cover of trees as they could. They cut through a narrow pass in the hills and dropped down to the river level and forded it, blessed for most of the crossing with moonlight so bright above them that it lit the river rocks and the hillsides in pale, ghostly gray and etched ribbons of white into the dark water. The march back down toward the enemy army was carried out in the black hours after moonset and before the dawn. The next morning the tribes woke to find their enemy largely behind them, somehow transported to the other side of the river. This threw them into confusion, into quick consultations, arguments, and impromptu councils.

"Watch them," Hannibal said to his brother. "Just watch them."

Whatever debate the tribal leaders had, it seemed to lead to no organized action. They collected at the waterfront, shouting insults across at the Carthaginians, calling them cowards, women, dogs. Hannibal held his men, silent, watching, waiting. Something about this calm enraged the Carpetani further. A single soldier stepped nearer than the others and sent his spear across the river. It fell short. The point bounced off a rock and the spear skittered across the ground and rolled to rest at the foot of a Libyan. The infantry-man picked it up and considered it, weighed it and tested its grip. Then he tossed it down as useless.

Whether this single action served as a catalyst for the mob to move or not was uncertain, but move they did. One flank of Iberian soldiers waded into the water far off at the downstream edge of the river. Others, seeing their boldness, marched in also. Soon a waver-ing, ragged line of soldiers reached midstream, up to their waists in the current. Hannibal remained silent until some of the enemy crossed the midpoint and began to emerge from the deeper portion of the river. Then he called the Moorish javelin throwers to the ready. A moment more passed and he had them heft their weapons. As the first Iberians stumbled into knee-deep water, he gave the call. The trumpets blew the quick, deafening blast that signaled the spearmen, and a thousand javelins took to the air. The Iberians were ill prepared for the volley, their shields held at awkward angles or up over their heads or caught in the current and tugging them off balance. The missiles pierced their simple tunics and leather breast-plates, drove into the bones of men's skulls, and tore through shoul-der joints, or thrust through the water to find thighs and groins. Another volley followed and after that the javelin throwers hurled at will so that the air was a whir of missiles finding targets picked out at the spearmen's discretion.

Hannibal, speaking to nobody in particular but within earshot of his brother, said, "I need a greater foe than this."

The Iberians kept coming until finally, through sheer numbers, they pushed the battle to ground on the Carthaginians' shore. The two sides engaged in earnest. Though the Carpetani were full of rage, they were also sodden and tired. They found the Libyans savage opponents, burly-armed and black-eyed demons who fought in their own version of a phalanx, shields locked tight, their heavy spears forming a living being with thousands of iron-tipped arms. Hannibal rode his stallion into the fray and hacked from horseback with his sword, yelling confidence into his men. Hasdrubal shadowed him and saved his life by sinking a spear into the neck of a Carpetani just about to do the same to the commander. But the two brothers were not long in the thick of battle. Hannibal galloped out again and shouted his next order to his signalers.

The resulting call sounded from the trumpets and when the answer came it did so not from the field of battle itself but from behind the tribal force. The elephants, their mahouts riding just behind their heads, roared out of the old camp and toward the unorganized backside of the enemy. Upon turning to see these great beasts hurtling toward them, the Carpetani realized the complete misery of their coming fate.

Hannibal's stallion spun and snapped his neck from side to side, seeming to be looking for something to sink his teeth into. The commander cuffed him about the ears and yelled to his brother over the din of slaughter: "Do you understand this? Do you see the truth here before you? These people will always be beneath us. They never look upon the past to create something new. They only take what is given to them and perpetuate it. They've never fought a man like me, and they will always be as they are and will never change except by dying into something new. That time has come. This will be your work, Hasdrubal. When I march on Rome, I will leave Iberia in your hands. Next year you'll not only rule over these people, you'll also bring them into our world and mold them into soldiers for Carthage. Today we slay them; tomorrow we resurrect them in our image. Do this, Hasdrubal, and the world is ours to shape."

The next morning Hannibal rode for Saguntum. He left his brother to bring home the full weight of the victory to the cities and towns that had so foolishly sent their men out to slaughter. The commander's leg pained him terribly after the efforts of the previous day. He rode with a small corps of the Sacred Band and seemed intent on punishing himself throughout the journey, driving on as the pain grew, sometimes slapping his thigh in defiance of it. He thought often of Imilce and that was another stab of frustration, which left him little joy from his recent victory. Now behind him a day or two, the Tagus was like a distant memory from another man's tale.

Nor did his return to Saguntum improve his mood. Though he arrived in the dead of night he soon learned that the siege was no further along. For all the labor done in the weeks of his absence, the scene viewed under the moonlight appeared just as before he had departed. He found Hanno in his cottage and called him out. An anger came upon him quickly and with a fury he did not often show outside of battle. He addressed it to his brother, his face inches from Hanno's. What had Hanno been doing with his command? How had three weeks passed with nothing to show for them?

Hanno did not answer the questions directly but stood in his loose sleeping garments, reciting a chronology of the things they had accomplished. If he was taken aback by his brother's outburst he did not show it. Nor did he react when Hannibal waved him to silence and said, "Hanno, what a gift you would have given me if I'd returned to dine inside those walls. Instead you've worked on at a snail's pace, taking your pleasures in your summer home. How would this please our father to see?"

He sat down on a stool and closed his eyes to the view of the city and tried to shut out the pain of his leg. "They tell me you have been troubled by omens and signs," he said, almost too quietly for Hanno to hear. "Did not our father teach you that these signs are way markers for our path forward? If you displease the gods, it's not through your actions but through your delays. We will destroy them, Hanno. That's how we honor the gods, by victory in their names. We will end this within a week. Everything we have, we throw at them now. Saguntum loses all except the memory of my name and the knowledge that the will of Baal acts through me. That is how this ends, and on the day I name."

When he saw the city was finally falling, Imco Vaca chose to enter via a different route than on the last such occasion. He scrambled up the giant wooden stairs of a siege tower, following on the heels of one man, feeling the claws of another behind him. He moved frantically, his whole body alive with purpose. Before he knew it, he had reached the top of the structure and found himself spat out as if by a great mouth. He landed on the top of the wall itself, but he and the man before him both stepped right off the wall and fell free through the air some twenty feet down to a lower landing. Imco thought surely this would end him, but again providence aided him. The man before him took the impact and cushioned Imco's fall. Afoot again, Imco fell in with the stampede of invaders as if he had followed a precisely chosen course to that moment.

The mass of Carthaginians hit the waiting defenders with a force that rocked both groups. Weapons were useless and they stood eye to eye. Then that moment was gone and Imco was hacking with his sword, thrusting, ducking, spinning. He took a Saguntine down by slicing his leg through the knee joint. He missed another with a downward blow, but caught him under the chin with an upward jerk. The point of his falcata slit the man's windpipe. He heard the soldier's breath escape the wound in a rasp. Another thrust a spear at him, but it glanced off his helmet and the Libyan beside him put his spear inside the Iberian at the armpit. Imco's helmet had twisted sideways. He fought without correcting it, a little blind to the left side but no worse for it because he fought to the right. For some time he struggled within a mixed company of friend and foe. But soon his singular progress took him away from his comrades and he knew that he would not die that day. It was like a billow of air blown into him, the knowledge that some god favored him. The defenders recognized this as well as he. They gave way before him as his sweeping blows became wider.

He was soon running through the streets with the others, kicking in doors and hunting down small groups of men. Hannibal's orders were clear and simple. They were to kill all men. That was their only charge. Soldiers disappeared into homes and did not return again. They screamed and tossed over furniture and searched for inhabitants, men to kill and women to rape and children to enslave. Others came out laden with booty, jewels and ornaments, iron cookware and silver cutlery, dragging prisoners by fistfuls of hair. He saw a group of young men driven into a market, weaponless. The Carthaginian men behind them slashed and thrust and kept them moving. One of the

Saguntines pleaded for mercy, argued his innocence and friendship, and pointed at others and named their crimes against Carthage. He might have gone on like this, but one of his number punched him squarely in the jaw and left him spitting blood.

By midday, Imco had seen his full share of human suffering. He stepped into a small house at the end of a lane, not expecting to find anything left, but wondering if he might pass a few moments in solitude. He stood for a long moment looking about the room. Indeed, the house had been pillaged and no single object stood upright, no vase was unbroken. He was numb and blood-splattered and very tired. The stillness of the room closed about him, the strangeness of being in somebody else's home. Shame dropped like a shawl about his shoulders. He thought he heard something, but as he listened he realized the sound was within him. A bone-weary cry wrung itself from inside him, a howl not of words but something earlier and more honest, emotions at battle within him. He was unable to order them. He just needed to stand still for a moment, just had to push emotion from him, for there was no place for it.

A muffled cough interrupted his thoughts. He followed the sound and spotted a foot dangling from the chimney above the cooking fire. He set down his booty and yanked the person free: a girl of eleven or so, soot-covered and tearful, hair so long it must never have been trimmed. Her eyes shone in white relief against her sooty face. They were full of terror. She reached for Imco's eyes and would have ripped them out. But he slapped her hands down and pinned her arms to her side. He shushed her violently and yelled that he had something to tell her. When she finally fell silent he did also, though his grip did not loosen.

"Are you the last?" he asked. "Did you have family?" He stopped himself and answered his own question. "Of course you did. We all have family, conquered and conquerors both." The girl stared into his face, searching for meaning but knowing nothing of his language.

From outside came a new yelling. Soldiers kicked an old man from his house into the street, accusing him of having daughters and demanding that he betray them before he died, threatening to rape him with the shaft of their spears if he did not speak. Imco could not make out his response, but it did not satisfy his tormentors. He and the girl both listened, neither moving until the man's ordeal ended and the soldiers moved on.

"I want you to sit down," Imco said. He reached out with his foot and righted a stool. Adjusting his grip on the girl, he set her down upon it and slid his hands away. He stood back and studied her.

She was pretty. He could tell this despite her grimy face. Her chin was a little weak, one eye lower than the other, but she was pretty nonetheless. Her body was still boyish, but this was not a flaw. She was not too young to be taken, nor to be sold, nor to be rented out. He walked around her and stood behind her for some time. He had to think about this. He was aware as never before how much suffering this girl's life now offered her. Her shoulders were so thin, but their frailty would please many. Her skin was a translucent covering over her frame. She must have been hungry these past months, but that too would make some men want her. Her hair fell over her shoulder and he could see the pulse of the artery in her neck. He reached out and touched it with his fingertips. The girl moved slightly, but he whispered her to stillness. Her pulse was strong, warm. It seemed irregular in its beating and at first he did not question why. Someone would profit from her suffering. Before the end of the month she would have been used by hundreds of men. She would be diseased and battered. She would rot from the inside out, both body and soul. But right now she was sound. In sorrow, yes. In mourning, surely. But her nightmare had not yet begun in full. He—by whatever divine hand—had been given her life to shape. Some men would have thought this a great gift, so why did it pain him so?

Just after the question formed in his mind he realized why her pulse seemed strange. He snapped his fingers away from her neck and struck the same spot with a slicing sweep of his sword. She dropped from the stool, and he darted outside a moment later, striding away, putting the tiny house behind him. He would forever remember the moment when he realized that the girl's irregular heartbeat was actually a mixture of his pulse with hers, both of them captured there on his fingertips for the few moments they were connected. He might have become a soldier in the last few years, but he was still a brother, still a child who loved his sisters, still soft in some portion of his heart. He prayed that the girl might understand his action as he had meant it: as a twisted, merciful gift.

When word of the sack of Saguntum reached the assembled Roman Senate several senators rose to their feet with calls for an immediate declaration of war. Valerius Flaccus stood with these, finding in the moment so much enthusiasm that he blurted out an entire plan of attack, so complete it had obviously been thought out ahead of time. Another senator pointed out that they should have dealt with Carthage much earlier. Hannibal had gone this far only because certain individuals put their personal interests in Gaul ahead of those of the people. Some cheered and echoed his complaint, but others tried to refocus the debate on the issue at hand: Rome had an enemy. There should be no mudslinging among senators.

From some of the most respected men came some of the most cautious words. One proposed another envoy: Let one of their number journey directly to Carthage and ask once and for all whether Hannibal's actions were indeed Carthage's actions as well. If the Carthaginians failed to answer satisfactorily, then the matter of war would be decided. Let no one say that Rome went to war without due consideration. Roman justice should first be reasoned; then, when necessary, as swift as a falcon. Despite heated debate, this plan was adopted before the close of the day, and Fabius Maximus the elder was chosen as the message bearer.

The envoy sailed in surprisingly good weather, nothing ominous in the sky or upon the sea itself. It did not seem that nature was aware of the import of the debate to come. Fabius suffered from arthritis on damp days, and his eyesight was not what it used to be. One shoulder sat a bit higher than the other—the result of damage to his left leg years before—but he hid this well when not within the confines of his own home. The black hair of his youth had gone prematurely gray. After a few years of fighting it, he now wore this badge of maturity proudly. It was his age that gave depth to his authority. It was one of many reasons that he was chosen to head the embassy, charged with the responsibility of asking one question and responding to it as appropriate.

They were met by the Carthaginians and offered the city's hospitalities with all courtesy. These Fabius turned down, asking only for an audience with the Council. Fabius wasted little time. He moved carefully to the center of the chamber, which was a dimmer space than the Roman equivalent, lit not by the sun but by large torches jutting out of the walls. It was damp and fragrant from bubbling vats of herbs and sticks of incense. With his fading vision, Fabius could barely make out the men he was to address, and the smells assaulted his nose. But he stood straight-backed and feigned the most direct of gazes. He asked whether Hannibal had acted upon his own folly in attacking Saguntum, or whether he was a true representative of the will of Carthage.

Cries went up from several quarters, not in answer to the question but with questions and assertions of their own. Fabius waited.

One Imago Messano quieted the others and rose to speak. He responded politely: The question was not so much whether Hannibal had acted upon state orders or upon his own whims. Rather, it was one of law and precedent. Saguntum had not been in alliance with Rome when the treaty between Rome and Carthage was made. And later, the agreement made with Hasdrubal the Handsome could not truly be considered binding because it was concluded at a distance from the Council and therefore had no official sanction. This being so, Carthage had no responsibility to bow to Rome's wishes.

"This matter with Saguntum," Imago said, smiling, "is an internal affair and should be respected as such. That is our position."

Fabius chose to proceed simply. He clasped a fold of his toga in his fist and looked about at the stern faces surrounding him and made sure that all saw his gesture. He gripped so firmly that his knuckles went white with pressure. "In this hand I hold war or peace," he said. "I offer either as a present to the Carthaginian people, but it is up to you to decide which you would rather receive."

Imago, gazing about him for his fellows' approval, answered with a shrug. "We accept whichever your Roman heart prefers to give."

And so Fabius opened his hand and released the folds of his toga in a manner that made it clear which the Roman heart preferred. As he spun to leave, the Carthaginians spoke in one voice, declaring their acceptance of the gift and their devotion to fight it to the end. Thus was the second war between Carthage and Rome agreed upon by cordial means.

During the winter following the siege of Saguntum, Hannibal released his Iberian troops to enjoy their families for the season, with the order to return in the spring to embark upon a journey to immortal fame. But for the commander himself and those who served him most intimately, there was little rest. To his family, it sometimes seemed that Hannibal had not returned from campaign at all. He was gone on exercises for days or sometimes weeks. When he was at home his time was filled morning to night with meetings and counsels, with planning sessions, with dictating letters to foreign leaders and collecting information from spies. The project he now had before him was a massive puzzle of matters military, geographical, cultural, monetary, issues as diverse as supply trains and political ramifications, topics as varied as naval routes and the physical constitution of elephants.

He drilled his Libyan veterans beyond any of the soldiers' expectations. They were up before the winter dawns, sent on far-ranging marches in full gear, with food and animals and siege weapons. They prowled the high mountains, going so high as to press through knee-deep snow, scaling rock faces, and rigging rope systems to aid the pack animals, coating their bare limbs with grease and marveling at the way their breath made ghosts before their mouths. He had new supplies of elephants shipped across from Carthage, mostly the native variety from the wooded hills of North Africa. They were not so large as the specimens found farther south, nor even did they stand as tall as the Asian variety, but each was a four-legged juggernaut. With a skilled mahout behind their ears they could mow down the enemy. Just the sight of them might clear a path through the barbarians who stood between them and Rome. Hannibal also called up new corps of Balearic slingers, for he had come to admire the pinpoint accuracy of their strikes, the way they turned the tiniest of stones into missiles that flew at blurred speed. He made arrangements to transfer some of his Iberian troops to defend Carthage, while bringing Africans over to protect Iberia in his absence. He hoped to assure their loyalty by keeping each group far from their homes, away from the enticement to desert, and dependent on their Carthaginian masters. And he sent emissaries to the tribes whose territories they would have to cross, rough Gaelic and Celtic peoples with whom he preferred friendship to war.

In the days just before the Mediterranean winter loosed its grip on New Carthage, Hannibal received his most detailed map yet of the territory through which his route to Rome lay. Alone in his chambers, he spread it out across his table and bent to study it. On the map the Alps were little more than a single jagged line of peaks, like a strange scar across the land. The document suggested routes through several different passes, but it provided no details, no indication of height or terrain or forage. There was little here from which he could choose a course. What to make of tales of peaks that pierced the sky, of yearlong ice and earthquakes wherein snow and rock flowed in torrents that were like water one moment, then set like cement the next? He wondered how the elephants would fare in those conditions. Some sources suggested that elephants would perish in the cold. Others argued that their thick hides would protect them. He had heard of the bones of mighty pachyderms found trapped in the ice of northern places. Giants, they said these were. If those creatures grew so large there, perhaps the climate would suit his elephants more than people knew.

If this were not confusion enough, the names of the tribes stood out among the depiction of the natural features: Volcae, Cavares, Allobroges, Triscastinii, Taurini, Cenomani . . . What peoples were these? Some of them were known to him; some channels of communication had long been open. Some of the tribes, like the Insubres and Boii, were actively hostile to Rome and interested in his plans. But others were only names shrouded in rumor and speculation. Blond creatures who lived in regions so frigid as to change their natural skin color, making them pale as marble statues, taller than normal men, and fierce as wolves. They drank the blood of slain heroes and made ornaments from bones and teeth and adorned their hovels with the bleached skulls of their foes. They fought with a wild abandon that had no order to it save the desire for personal glory. He understood they went into battle naked or nearly so, and that they often went clothed only in trousers that covered their legs like a second skin. Such a strange notion: to rarely see the muscles and flesh and hair of one's own thighs. It was hard to know just how accurate these tales were, and yet he did not doubt that any errors were deviations from even stranger truths.

Standing over the chart he felt a flush of blood tint his face. For all the information, the map was terribly inadequate, the detail etched by a man's pen, pushed by a single hand and mind. It was not the real world but only a vague, incomplete outline of it. The day would come when these mountains and these people were real before him, when he would feel the sharp rocks through his sandals and look upon the barricade of mountains receding before him in solid fact, when he would see these peoples' eyes and smell their breath and grasp their hands in friendship or spill their blood in enmity. Strange that thousands of lives depended on the plans he made now, pulled from the air in calm solitude. He wished his father were beside him so that they could share this, but he pushed the thought from his mind with a resolve long practiced. Uncertainty was the shackle that constrained normal men.

As he bent staring at the map, his sister appeared in the corridor opening. Sapanibal stood a moment in silence, then stepped through the threshold, nodding to the door servant as she did so. The slave bowed his head and slipped from the room, leaving the two siblings alone for the first time in nearly a year.

"My brother," Sapanibal said, "I trust I am not disturbing you."

Hannibal looked up from the chart. Seeing her, his face went through a quick transformation. At first he met her with the stern visage of a general. This faded almost to the half-grin of a brother, and fast behind this came the honest, tired expression with which he addressed few people in the world.

"Many things disturb me, sister, but you are a welcome visitor."

"I come, actually, as an emissary of your beloved. She is worried about you. Thinks you're sure to catch a consumptive illness with this winter training."

Hannibal smiled and shook his head. "She is afraid for me now, while I'm simply practicing for war? You women are strange. Happy to send me off into battle, but fearful that a cold might fell me."

"Small things are sometimes the death of great men. I do not think Imilce is alone in fearing that you tax yourself."

"Tax myself?" Hannibal asked. "If only you knew, sister. To see this coming war into being requires an unending vigilance. This is just the calm; come and see the makings of the storm." He waved her closer to the table. "For all its art, this map is a crude thing, filled with empty spaces, dotted with deaths yet to be written. You know my plans?"

"No one has invited me to council," Sapanibal said. "The things I've heard I dismiss as speculation only."

Hannibal doubted her knowledge was so limited, but he said, "A land attack. Since the Romans destroyed our navy during our last war, they've believed themselves safe in their own land. The physical barriers have always seemed insurmountable. An army cannot swim the sea. Nor can an army climb the heights of mountains like the Alps and Pyrenees. So the Romans believe, at least. Our spies report they think they'll fight this war on their own terms. They expect me to entrench here in Iberia and wait to defend myself. On this they are mistaken."

He paused for a moment and studied the map. Sapanibal, dryly, asked, "Has the commander changed the map of the world to suit him?"

"The map can remain as it is," Hannibal said. "We will march along the Mediterranean coast this spring, cross the Pyrenees in early summer and the Rhône at midsummer, and traverse the Alps before the autumn. This will be a long and difficult march, but I do not accept that it is impossible. It only means that we will be the first. Think of the things Alexander achieved by again and again attempting the unimaginable. What do you think of this?"

Sapanibal laughed. "Hannibal asks a woman's advice on matters of war?"

Hannibal watched her and did not answer but awaited hers. She was the eldest of Hamilcar's offspring and though she was a woman she was easily Hannibal's equal in wisdom: they both knew it. She had made sure he knew it from his earliest memories of her. There was a time, in fact, when she was his physical superior. Her strong, long-legged form had thrown his often during the wrestling matches of their youth. A twelve-year-old girl, in the quick bloom of early womanhood, is in no way inferior to her nine-year-old brother. Hannibal had never forgotten this. It hung behind all discourse between them. So yes, he would ask a woman's advice, and he knew she would give it.

"Your plan is the best possible one," she said. "Father would be proud. And what of the rest of us? What fates have you assigned your siblings?"

Hannibal stepped back from the desk and rolled his shoulders for a moment, as if his day's training had just caught up with him. He sat down on a nearby stool and rotated his head to ease some tension in his vertebrae. The bones made an audible crack, but judging by the commander's grimace this provided no relief.

"Everyone has a part to play," he said, "though I've yet to settle everyone's role exactly. I will do so soon. But for your part, I ask—"

"I will escort your wife to Carthage," Sapanibal said, "and introduce her to our mother and Sophonisba and bring her more fully into our country's ways." After a short pause she added, "If that is your wish, brother."

"You have learned no fondness for my wife, have you?"

"What has that to do with it?" Sapanibal asked, with her usual flat frankness. She stood and circled her brother and pushed his hand from his neck with her palm. She stood a moment with her fingers on the firm wings of his shoulder muscles, then she squeezed and released, squeezed and released. "I respect her," she said. "That is what matters. I understand the value of your union with her here in Iberia. She is beloved of her people, and this is a good thing for Carthage. And, too, brother, I acknowledge your passion for her."

Sapanibal pressed her thumbs into Hannibal's back with a force that surprised him, as if the two digits were formed on gnarled tree roots. He almost turned around to check, but her hands held him.

"If the marriage had been mine to arrange," she continued, "I might have found you an equally useful, yet somewhat more homely bride. A man should value the bond with his wife and honor her accordingly, but a commander should not mix duty with ardor. Better to respect your wife and stick your penis in some pretty camp follower."

Again Hannibal almost turned, for it seemed to him that his sister was speaking with doubled significance about her own marriage. But she stopped any movement with an admonishing click of her tongue.

"Do you truly mean that?" Hannibal asked. "Father was not so with Mother. . . ."

"Yes, but her strength equaled his. You are a man, Hannibal. You can have no idea of the sacrifices required of women. Mother was the foundation from which Hamilcar Barca launched himself at the world. But she was never, never a source of weakness to him. This is something you cannot know, but believe your older sister."

"So you think my wife is not such a foundation?"

"I've never said a sour word against Imilce. I'm just voicing my thoughts on a subject, and on the virtues of our mother. Of any wife of yours . . . She should be handled strictly, so as to cause the least distraction."

Hannibal heard this with pursed lips, a frown tugging at one corner but not completely allowed. It faded with a few moments of silence. "Sister, we should have spoken more often. Your counsel is wise where I am shortsighted. It would have been good for us to debate the matters of life more fully."

"Why do you say 'should' and 'would'? Are we not at council now? You speak as if we've no future before us."

Just then, both siblings caught movement at the mouth of the corridor. Imilce stepped in. She met the two with her gaze, cleared her throat, and placed a hand upon her delicate collarbones.

Hannibal placed a hand on his sister's fingers. She withdrew them. As he rose and approached his wife he said, softly and—though his eyes were on Imilce—to Sapanibal alone, "We've a war before us. Beyond that very little is certain."

How the child escaped his governess's care none could say, but he was a lively boy, recently emboldened by his mastery of two-legged travel, and such children have their own, secret devices. He progressed unnoticed through several long corridors, through a room set off with a long dining table under which he walked, out onto a balcony into the winter afternoon, and then back into the warmth by another entrance. He stepped flat-footed, bowed at the legs, his fat feet slapping against the smooth stones, chubby legs rotating from the hips so that his cloth-bound behind served as the pivot from which he wiggled himself forward. He pushed through a curtain partition and into a room filled with male voices. These drew him, for among them was the timbre and cadence that he recognized as his father's. It was only there, standing at the edge of the room, looking shyly toward the table and the large men around it, that he was recognized.

Hannibal's expression had been serious, his hand massaging the ball of his chin-beard in thought. But his eyes brightened on spotting the child. "Little Hammer!" he said, cutting off one of his guests in mid-sentence. "Excuse me, friends, but we're being spied upon." The commander rose from his place at the table and strode toward the child. He snatched him up and held him above his head a moment, the boy convulsing with sudden glee. "What are you doing here, Hamilcar?"

"He's come to learn of matters political and martial," Bomilcar said.

Bostar, to explain to the guests, spoke in Greek. "Hannibal's son," he said, "named in honor of his grandfather, of course. He keeps the maids on their toes, but this time he's escaped them."

The three Macedonians nodded at this. None seemed offended by the interruption. Instead, one commented on the boy's healthy looks; another offered that perhaps it was not maids the boy needed but young soldiers to keep up with him.

Lysenthus, head of the Greek party and therefore seated at the center, asked to see Hamilcar up close. He wore a dark leather breastplate on which ridged abdominal and chest muscles had been outlined in silver studs. He was a solid man, scarred across the cheek and nicked on the eyebrow in a raised welt. His straight brown hair hung in somewhat greasy strands around his face. But for all his warrior's appearance he had about him the look of a sensualist, an easy manner and smirking mouth. He reached for young Hamilcar and propped him up on the table before him.

Hannibal stood nearby for a moment, but as the child seemed fascinated by the Macedonian he returned to his seat. Lysenthus uttered a string of nonsense words to the boy, neither Greek nor Carthaginian but the babble so often spoken to children. Hannibal felt Bostar's gaze and knew he was being invited to mirth at the sight of Lysenthus—warrior of Macedon, personal envoy of Philip the Fifth—reduced to using nonsense words by a small boy. For the first time in the several hours they had been talking, Hannibal noticed that Lysenthus was missing a finger from his left hand. Not an unusual wound by any means, but it surprised him that he only noticed now, when the absence of the digits so stood out on hands cupped around his son's back.

"I've made a few like this myself," Lysenthus said. "More than I can count, actually. Will he wield a sword like his father?"

Hannibal tilted his head and spoke careful Greek, perhaps more pure in his pronunciation than the Macedonians themselves. "If he lives to see that day, by Baal's grace . . . I believe his fate in life was chosen by powers other than my own."

"The child of a lion is a lion, yes?"

The other visitors agreed with solemn nods, but Bostar was not so sure. "I heard a tale from the land of Chad that might dispute that. It's said that once, not too many years ago, a lioness gave birth to an antelope and raised her with affection."

"You're mad!" Bomilcar said, speaking in Carthaginian. "Did I hear you right? A lion give birth to an antelope?"

"That is what I've heard," Bostar said, keeping to Greek. "The Ethiopians swear such things have happened more than once and each time foretells a shift in the world's fortunes."

Bomilcar frowned at this and looked about for a translation. His Greek sufficed for giving military orders, but was not up to casual conversation.

Hannibal said, "I know not the order of things beyond the great desert. One certainly hears tales, but this child is born of my blood—a cub from a lion. Perhaps he will exceed me in time."

Hamilcar, as if in answer, reached for the dagger sheathed

beneath Lysenthus' arm. The Macedonian moved the boy out to arm's length and laughingly asked, "Has he ever held a blade?"

Hannibal shook his head, lips in a tight line now and forehead creased uneasily.

Lysenthus held the boy by one hand and with the other pulled the short dagger from its holder. He held it before the child a moment, watching the fascination in his eyes, rotating the blade so that it reflected glimmers of light on Hamilcar's face. The boy reached for it, delicately, as if he knew that he must show care if he was to be allowed the object. Lysenthus, looking only at the boy now, slid his fingers onto the blade and offered the child the handle. The young Hamilcar took the weapon and held it before him, clasped in two hands, upright and as large as a sword to a man. He was all stillness for a long moment, and the party watched in a hush that suggested awe, as if they were witnessing something prophetic. But then the young one remembered he was a child. He let out a babbling gurgle and jerked the knife up and down, suddenly wild. Lysenthus snapped his head back, an instant too late. The tip of the blade sliced a tiny nick in his nose that dripped red instantly. Just as Hannibal snapped to his feet the Macedonian's hand fell over the child's and pried the blade away.

"A warrior indeed!" he called, laughing and trying to sheath the weapon. "A year old only, and he has already cut the flesh of a warrior. Were you so young as this when you first drew blood, Hannibal?"

The tension in Hannibal's body was slow to uncoil. Eventually, he smiled, pulled a cloth from inside his tunic, and tossed it to Lysenthus. "I do not remember the first time I drew blood," he said. "And neither will he."

Hannibal hefted his son and set him down on the floor. He motioned for Bostar to amuse the boy, a task the officer went at awkwardly, but well enough to permit the meeting to go on. They had already been through the long, gradual introductions to their respective positions and plans for the future. Hannibal had offered a pact of friendship with Macedon and found the king's ambassadors as receptive as he could have hoped. But the matter to which he had turned just before Hamilcar's entry was more delicate. Lysenthus returned to it in a roundabout way.

"Philip has no love for Rome," he said. "On the contrary, he loathes the manner in which they interfere in Adriatic matters that should not concern them. He will watch your progress with interest, but Commander, he is not yet ready to join you in war against Rome."

Bomilcar somehow managed to follow this well enough to form a response. "Philip would have us do all the work first—is that what you're saying? Then he'd join in the victory celebrations."

Lysenthus dabbed at the cut on his nose. "Philip would take an active part in any victory over the Romans," he said. "You might well find you need our formidable aid in achieving it, but events will have to unfold somewhat before that time comes. You have fought admirably against the barbarians of Iberia, but Rome will be an altogether different test. They will come at you, and quickly."

"Not quickly enough," Hannibal said. "I know much of what transpires in Roman councils. They plan a two-pronged attack: one consul and his army attacking Carthage itself, the other aimed at us here in Iberia. This is a reasonable plan, but they will find things progress in a way they cannot imagine."

Lysenthus thought about this a moment, glanced at his aides, and then looked back at Hannibal, a new understanding etched on his features. "You're going to attack them first, on their own soil? How? You have no navy . . . no way to reach them."

Hannibal glanced at Bostar, who seemed anxious to rise from the floor and say something, if Hamilcar had not been climbing over his knees and attempting to unlace his sandals.

"You'll forgive me, Lysenthus," the commander continued, "if I do not reveal all the details. But do make sure that Philip watches these opening moves with close attention. He'll see what we are made of and what we can accomplish—we hope with his friendship and aid. At the very least, let us continue to correspond."

Lysenthus assured him that this was possible and that the message would reach the king as soon as he did. With that, the meeting drew to a close. The two officers escorted the Macedonians away and off to an afternoon hunt, their last before preparing for the hazardous sea voyage back to Macedon.

Hannibal sat a moment, watching his son at play with the balls of wadded paper Bostar had improvised as toys while the men spoke.

It was a joyful image, yet quick behind the joy came a tension low in his gut, almost like the anxiety of battle. He had lied in answering Lysenthus' question: In truth, he did remember the first time he drew blood. The memory was seared into his consciousness, one of his earliest, from before he came to Iberia.

He was still living in Carthage, at the family's palace on the hill of Byrsa. His father had roused him from sleep. His face was ragged and coated with sweat and filth. He smelled foul and he still wore the soiled armor of battle. "Come, I would show you something," Hamilcar said.

The boy Hannibal's heart thumped in his chest; not only from the abruptness of his awakening, but he had not even known his father had returned from the war. Mercenaries had turned on the city and besieged it. The conflict had been brutal beyond recent memory, but under Hamilcar's leadership the Carthaginian nobles had finally driven the mercenaries out into the desert, where the traitors made their last stand. What exactly had transpired, the boy had no idea.

Nor did Hamilcar open his lips as he led Hannibal through the dark palace and out onto the grounds. They passed through several courtyards and down into the stables. A torch burned at the far end of the corridor. They moved toward it through the shadows. The horses snorted and shifted nervously, watching their progress; they seemed as aware as Hannibal that something profound was to happen.

But it was not until they had actually halted that Hannibal saw the figure to whom they were drawn. A man had been nailed to wood supports by the wrist, his body drooping, head down upon his chest. He was covered in crusted fluids and dust and had been hanging for long enough that the blood dripping from his impaled wrists had congealed into black globules. Hamilcar grasped a handful of the man's hair and yanked his head upright. The man's eyes opened, rolled up, and then veered off into semiconsciousness.

"This man betrayed Carthage," Hamilcar said, his voice a dry rasp that he could not shake, though he cleared his throat several times. "Do you understand that? This man conspired to open the gates of our city to the mercenaries. He did it for money, for power, out of a sheer hatred that he hid behind the mask of a countryman.

He almost succeeded. Had this man the power, he would yank you up by the ankles and bash your skull against the stones beneath us. He would nail me to a cross and leave me to die slowly. He'd see me a rotting, maggot-filled corpse, and he would laugh at the sight. He would slit your brother's necks and rape your mother and have her sold into slavery. He would live in our house and eat our food and rule over our servants. This is the man before you. Do you know his name?"

Hannibal shook his head, his eyes pinned to the stones and not moving even as he answered.

"His name is Tamar. Some call him the Blessed, others the Foul. Some call him friend. Some father. Some lover. Do you understand? He has other names also: Alexander. Cyrus. Achilles. Khufu. Yahweh or Ares or Osiris. He is Sumerian, Persian, Spartan. He is the thief in the street, the councillor who sits beside you, the man who covets your wife. You choose his name, for he has many, as many names as there are men born to women. His name is Rome. His name is mankind. This is the world we live in, and you'll find it full of men like this."

Hamilcar released the man's head and placed his hands on his son's shoulders. He pulled him close and let the boy rest his forehead against his cheek. Hannibal did this willingly, for he did not want to look at the man about whom they spoke. "Son," he said, "there was a noose around our neck and to cut it I had to kill many men most horribly. You are a child, but the world you were born into is no kind place. This is why I teach you now that creation is full of wolves aligned against us. To live in it without falling into madness, you must make of yourself more than a single man. You love with all your heart as a father and son and husband. You wrap your arms around your mother and know the goodness of women. You find beauty in the world and cherish it. But never waver from strength. Never run from battle. When the time comes to act, do so, with iron in your hand and your loins and your heart. Unreservedly love those who love you, and protect them without remorse. Will you always do that?"

Against his father's chest, the boy nodded.

"Then I am proud to call you my firstborn son," Hamilcar said.

He pulled away and stood up straight and yanked a dagger from the sheath on his ankle and pressed the handle into his son's hand. "Now kill this man."

Hannibal stared at the blade in his small hand, a dagger nearly as large as the toy swords he practiced with. He closed his fingers around the handle slowly, felt the worn leather, the rough weave of it and the solidity of the iron beneath it. He raised his eyes and moved toward the man and did as his father ordered. He did not lift the man's head, but he slipped the blade under his chin and cut a ragged, sloppy line that yanked free of his flesh just under the ear. He fell against the dead man's body for a moment. Though he sprang back, the touch still stained his nightclothes with the man's newly flowing blood. He was just eight years old that night. Of course he had not forgotten that moment. Nor would he. It would be with him on his deathbed, if the moment of his passing allowed for reflection.

Both he and young Hamilcar were roused from their thoughts by the chatter of maids in the hall. Beyond them the sharp urgency of Imilce's voice betrayed her concern. Hannibal rose, snatched his son up, and held him high, staring at him as the boy struggled and reached out to pat his father's face, not sure now whether to play or call for his mother. The child's eyes were indeed a striking gray, hair touched with some of Imilce's fairness. But his nose and mouth and stocky build were nothing if not Barca. He had such smoothness of skin, no blemish upon it, with a fragrance that was like nothing, for few things are as pure. His lower front teeth stood perfectly straight, close-fitted like a tiny phalanx of four warriors. Drool escaped the infant's lips and collected on his chin, bunching in preparation for a fall. Hannibal, in one quick gesture, licked the spittle clean.

"By the gods," he said, "you are the sum of me, of all that came before. You are all that ever I can be."

He placed the boy on the stone floor and watched as he spun away and tottered off, first randomly, then toward the sound of his mother's voice, just outside in the corridor now.

Watching him, full of love, the father whispered, "Our lives are torture."

Camped outside New Carthage for the winter, Tusselo had time to look back on the two periods of his life now concluded and to consider the new one just dawning. As a child he had been on horseback from as early as he could remember. He had been one of many in his village, from a large family, all speaking the same language, tied to the same gods, and living by the same customs. He had thought himself master of his young world and faced his coming manhood with eagerness.

But one evening he went to bed a free person, a Massylii Numidian, a horseman; when he awoke, the curved blade of a Libyan knife at his throat was whispering that all of that was done. Dawn found him shuffling along in chains, driven by slavers who cared not that his blood was much like theirs. Within a week, they reached the shore. There a Roman captain bought him and carried him for the first time out into open sea. He had just reached an age when his thoughts turned kindly toward the girls of his clan, but on the first day at sail these thoughts had been forever made a punishment by his captor. With the quick slice of a knife, his immortality vanished. Tusselo doubled over, clutching at his groin, awed and pained beyond all reckoning, amazed to hear the laughter of the man who had emasculated him and listening, despite himself, to the man's jokes that he might now play the woman on occasion but would never again inflict his manhood on any other. It was an absolutely unimaginable act, a change in fortune so profound that he refused to believe it even as he writhed across the deck in a puddle of his own blood. Unfortunately, he was to live through many days thereafter that made it clear human cruelty was never to be underestimated, always to be believed in, much more constant then the favor of any god.

He spent twelve years as a slave to Rome, sold from one master to another three times before finding a permanent place with a traveling merchant of middling wealth. In those twelve years he had lived a lifetime that almost negated the years before. Almost, but not quite. That was why he grasped for freedom several times, finally achieving it one night not far from Brundisium. He had escaped with a pouch full of coins that the drunken man foolishly left resting in his open palm. He used them to pay for a single, extortionately priced passage to Africa.

In his homeland nothing was the same, neither in the sights he saw nor in him, who perceived them. There was no one left to call family. Tusselo found a miserable cluster of hovels more like a leper colony than the thriving town of his birth. He sat down on a hill facing north and looked out on the grassy plains and ragged woodland that flowed toward the sea. It was a beautiful country. It had a largeness different from the land of his enslavement. It pained him that he had to think of that place so often, and yet he could not stop. Every memory his homeland brought to mind had at its back the shadow of how slavery had destroyed it. He had hoped that his hard-won freedom would end some portion of his suffering, but this was not the case. He had been robbed of so many things—how completely, he understood only as he gazed out across a land that pained him with memories and offered no solace. He was an exile in his own country: that was why he had left it to join Hannibal. And it only seemed right that the journey he embarked on should aim back to Italy.

On the day that Tusselo spotted that lone rider near Saguntum—after tracking Hannibal's army on foot—he had not been atop a horse in thirteen years. Nor had he immediately remedied this. He spent months at Saguntum as little more than a laborer, accepting whatever task fell to him. He worked with a more reverent obedience than he had ever shown a master, and he kept always in the company of his countrymen, remembering their ways. He stayed with the victorious army when it returned to New Carthage, and he made sure his desire to mount and fight again was well known.

It had been his master's custom to keep all of his slaves' heads shaven. As he was a slave no longer, Tusselo freed his hair to run its course. He did not remember when he stopped dragging the honed edge of his knife over his scalp, but his hair soon grew long enough that he could take fingerfuls of the curly stuff and twirl them into matted locks. He rarely caught sight of his own reflection—it had never before mattered to him—but now he took to pausing and studying himself in still pools of water, in the circlets of pounded metal shields, or in the dull reflection on the flat of his knife. He took some joy in what he saw. It was a different self than he had known for some time, an earlier incarnation. His hair was black, thick. It sprang from his head with pent-up aggression, as unruly as Medusa's crown of snakes and no less impressive. It framed his face and gave his features a new completion, a solidity, a strong African-ness that he welcomed. Perhaps that was why his master had shaved him, to deprive him of these things and to leave him ever a stranger to his own reflection, so that he would forget himself and remember only the slave. No longer. He had his hair back, and in midwinter he also regained his identity as a horseman.

The day he was assigned a mount he stood weak-kneed, his throat tight and fingertips tingling. The army horses were Iberian mostly, pulled in from a variety of tribes and regions of the country, schooled by different techniques from African mounts, and all with varying perceptions of their role in relation to man. They were somewhat larger than the fleet-footed creatures of North Africa, in a myriad of colors and temperaments, with a wild energy that flared up as Massylii riders cut individuals from the herd to examine them more closely. It was a wonder to watch and Tusselo, having lived many of his years away from his homeland, was struck with awe at the horsecraft he had been born into.

The Numidians cinched their legs around their horses' backs and spoke to them. They sent signals through touch, sometimes with a stick, but often with their fingers. They shifted their body weight accordingly and flapped their arms from their shoulders as if this motion translated into speed in the horses' hooves and called sudden, surprise maneuvers. The mounts seemed to understand them completely and to take joy at slicing through the Iberian horses, dividing them and circling and dizzying them till the Iberians stood dazzled. Tusselo remembered it now, but he had seen no such skill during the years he spent in exile. It almost shamed him to have gotten so used to how Romans handled horses, with no art, no joy but simply mastery of man over beast.

When his turn came to receive a mount he did not hesitate to take it. He had to move with confidence, he knew, for these men would spot any awkwardness as a lioness sees weakness in her prey. He approached the horse from the side, one arm flat against him and the other raised just slightly, fingertips extended as if he were brushing them across stalks of tall grass. And yet there was no guile in his approach, no stealth. He walked toward the horse as if to do so were the most natural thing in the world. He spoke words of encouragement to her, not shy, but like one friend to another on meeting again.

Before she knew it, he was beside her. And as she cocked her head to follow him he leaped, a smooth motion that somehow draped him over her back as a blanket might fall. He wrapped his arms around her and spread his weight across her and continued his string of words. He had thought that gladness was a thing of the past for him, and perhaps this was so, but there was something stirring in him now and it was not the slow simmering he had carried for so many years. He knew already that he could be nearly his whole self with this horse. Astride her, he could again learn to ride like a whirlwind. He could again belong to a people and fight with a purpose. This horse would never question his manhood, would never taunt him for the damage done to him by his old master. And that was a great blessing. In return he would be kind to her, and feed her well, and not ride her too hard, and lead her only into sensible battle. Together they would see wondrous things. No portion of the earth would hold either of them in bondage. These were some of the things he told her, and, Iberian though she was, she soon calmed to listen.

As his mare was not versed in the Massylii manner of riding, the headman of the cavalry gave Tusselo leave to train her, to care for her as his own. He had seen all he needed to in Tusselo's actions to confirm he belonged among them. Tusselo rode up into the hills beyond New Carthage that very evening, the horse powerful beneath him, her hooves pounding the earth and tearing up divots, the speed of it intoxicating to one so long cursed to the pace of his own legs.

He stopped the horse on a hill. Behind him, New Carthage smoldered, as cities always do, cloaked in a blanket of haze. To the south the sea swelled and receded against the land. To the west and the north the land rolled away to the horizon. None of it seemed beyond him. He was free for the first real time since his boyhood.

And—if the gods had finally chosen to smile upon him—he would soon return to business unfinished in Rome, not alone this time, but with an army.

There are some men whom the gods curse by birth into times of war; there are others for whom this is a blessing. There are some who crave nothing more than chaos, who eat their pain and revel in that of others. Such a man was Monomachus, and such was the gift bestowed upon him that he could daily take the base materials of life and open them to air and search out the root of human emotion and twist it into knots of anguish. It was no secret that he had devoted his military labors to Moloch, the Devourer, but many speculated that he communed with even earlier deities. Some said that he was of Egyptian origins and that he walked the modern world as an incarnation of the lost gods of that aged place. Others said the source of his barbarism could be found within the span of his singular life, if one were bold enough to search for it. Still others refused to speak of him or even utter his name. And a few were loyal to him as to no other and served only under him.

Hannibal chose this man to lead the delegation that would introduce Carthage to the Gauls. A strange choice, perhaps, but the commander wished to make certain things clear to those coarse men from the start. Monomachus stood before the Gauls like the seething pulse of enmity. His cheekbones were high and feline, so prominent that the rest of his face hung shadowed beneath them. He was so devoid of fat that his body seemed little more than a skeleton wrapped in striated cords of muscle. When the Gauls beheld him they knew that even by their own standards this was a creature not wisely crossed. Most of them were glad they did not have to cross him. For, despite the simmering intensity in his stare, he offered friendship. He lavished presents of gold and silver on the chieftains. He unsheathed finely crafted Iberian swords and offered them up, blade held between his fingers. He talked of the power of Carthage and the benefits of friendship. And he said that he had been sent only to guarantee safe passage through their lands as the forces of Carthage marched toward Rome. Should the Gauls choose to join in the great war, they would be welcome as comrades, with the bounty of Italy shared among them all. He found most tribes eventually proved amenable.

But when he reached the Volcae things changed somewhat. These were an even rougher sort of barbarian tribe than most, warlike and primitive, caring little for the outside world. Monomachus found his translator having difficulty communicating with them. They took the gifts readily enough, but they saw no need to bow to these foreigners' wishes. There were only a few of them, after all, and the Volcae were a numerous people. The Carthaginians presented their gifts and called councils, and all the while more of the Volcae slunk out of the foothills in seemingly endless small bands. Their camp grew around the envoys, and the Carthaginians sensed the whispered malice multiplying minute by minute.

The group spent one sleepless night in these people's company. It was a frigid winter and none of the warm-blooded Africans fared well in it. They heard movement around them all through the night; by morning it seemed their host had doubled in size yet again. The party of twenty-five stood steaming in the morning air, talking among themselves in whispers that crystallized before their faces. One man whispered to another that they would not leave this place alive, but Monomachus punched the young man and told them what he had learned in the night, for he had not been idle. Their interpreter had managed to gain this information through bribes: this day would indeed be their last. The chieftain was to invite them to his hut to receive more presents, but once inside they would be seized. Then the masses outside would attack the rest of the contingent. They would be killed by various tortures. Their heads would be cut from their bodies and used for sport. Their skulls would later adorn the entrances to Volcae homes, or roll upon the floor as toys for children.

"At least," Monomachus said, "this is how they would have things." But he had a different idea and his men bent willing ears to it.

They went to the chieftain bearing no arms of their own, but with a gift of swords, one carried by each of the five who would enter the hut. There was some debate about this, but, in the end, prudence gave way to greed, for the Gauls desired the fine swords. Inside was smoky and dark and close. The five stood before the chieftain and explained their proposals. They felt the armed guards pressing at their backs, but Monomachus spoke easily, describing the war to come and the part they might play in it, actively if they chose, or passively by allowing the army to pass unmolested. Either suited Hannibal. They waited as the translator did his work.

When the response came, it was as the Carthaginians expected. The chief would promise nothing until he had seen the gifts they offered. And these gifts had better be magnificent, for he was not inclined to allow a foreign force to pass beneath his nose. Who was this Hannibal, anyway? Why had he not come himself? If he was so powerful, why did he send such a small delegation? Why try to bribe his way through a territory, if his army was all that they claimed? He asked again to see the gifts. He might talk more after that.

Monomachus heard this calmly. He stared at the bulbous nose of the Gaul, at the blue eyes and the red, creviced skin. He held the curved sword before him, like nothing the Gaul had seen before, glinting even in the dim firelight. He said this: They would pass. They would, with his blessing or not, beneath his nose or no. In fact, he would take his nose to Hannibal and let the commander decide the matter. Before the translator had completed the Gallic version, Monomachus slammed his head forward, mouth open, teeth bared. He clamped down on the chieftain's nose and shook his head from side to side with all the fury of a lion at the kill. He broke away with a chunk of the man's flesh in his mouth. The Gaul's face was a bloody mess, but that was soon to be the least of his problems.

Monomachus stepped back and put the gift-sword to use. He struck low and sliced the Gaul clean through both legs just below the knee. The man fell as his shins slipped away from him, but a moment later he was upright, fighting for balance on the bloody stumps that were now his legs. This could not last long, but the Carthaginians did not wait to see him fall again. In a blur of stabbing and slashing they dispatched the rest of the Gauls, who scarcely had the time or the space to swing their swords into motion.

The small party flew out of the shelter and into the arms of a massed army. The rest of the group, who had been waiting outside, had drawn their swords at the first sounds of confusion from within the hovel. The moment Monomachus joined them they hit the wall of blond chests with a shocking, immediate fury, a scream rising from their leader and stirring the other men into a frenzy of hacking, thrusting progress. Though they started at twenty-five before the meeting they were seventeen by the time they reached their horses, and eleven when they could finally look behind them without fear. Two others died of their injuries in the days to come. One was dispatched at his own request.

And so it was a ragged band of eight that finally returned to New Carthage. Monomachus went straight to Hannibal, unwashed and still crusted in blood he chose not to wash from his armor. He said things had gone quite well in Gaul. They had many friends. They would not find that their passage along the Rhône need be made through entirely hostile peoples. "There were a few tribes that might prove troublesome," he said, "but they will find themselves overmatched."

Entering his chambers at a brisk walk, Hannibal spotted the servant before she noticed him. She lay prone across his bed, the curve of her hips betrayed through the thin fabric of her shift, her legs stretching bare beyond these. The sole of one foot caressed the toes of the other. She seemed completely absorbed with something just beside her, out of view. Hannibal cleared his throat and the young woman's head snapped around. She gasped and sprang to her feet, head bowed and arms pinned at her sides. Only then was it clear that she had been cuddling with the child, Hamilcar. The boy, also as if caught in some clandestine moment, rolled from back to belly. He paused on all fours and stared at his father, unsure why he had caused such alarm in his maid. After a moment of apparent thought, he offered a babble of greeting.

"Would you seduce my son already?" Hannibal asked. The maid began a hurried response, but he shushed her silent and moved forward, tossing his cloak across a chair. "Where is my wife?"

"She should be here in a moment," the maid said. "She . . . sent me with the young lord to await her, and you, on the hour." Her eyes darted up just quickly enough to stress this, pointing out—

whether she intended to or not—that Hannibal had arrived early for his planned meeting with his wife. She had an attractive face, full and fleshy-featured. Though she was shorter than Imilce, her body was more languidly curved. Her breasts, wide-spaced and full, pressed against her shift, staining the garment with moisture from her nipples.

Noticing this, Hannibal asked, "Do you feed my son as well as sport with him?"

"Yes, my lord. But only on occasion. Your wife feeds him well."

"You must have a child of your own, then?"

"A girl."

"And how does she fare? Does she not want for your milk?"

The maid seemed uncomfortable with the line of questioning, but she answered, "No, lord: As I give milk to your son, so another gives hers to mine."

Hannibal almost asked about that woman's child, but he had already shared more words with her than he usually did with servants. At some point, he knew, somebody's child might well perish so that his son was fed richly. He did not want to linger too long on this thought. He dismissed the maid with a motion of his head. "I will care for the boy," he said.

When Imilce entered the room, father and child were seated on the floor. Hannibal was trying to position marble soldiers in a particular formation, but Hamilcar kept interrupting him, picking up first one soldier and then another, bringing them to his mouth as if he were a giant who would solve the dispute by chewing off their heads. Imilce paused a moment, taking the scene in, and then walked in without expressing whatever thought she entertained about them.

"A strange thing happened this morning," she said, motioning with her fingers that she would not sit on the stone floor. Hannibal rose and cast himself onto the bed. Imilce joined him, continuing with her story. Apparently, the cook preparing the afternoon meal in honor of the small delegation from the Insubrian Gauls had been blinded in one eye. It was the oddest of accidents: He had simply plunged a ladle into a vat of boiling oil to test its consistency. But at the touch of the utensil, the oil spat up a single droplet. It hit the cook's open eye and sent him stumbling away in pain. On hearing of this, Hanno was quite upset. He had called for Mandarbal but he had been informed that the seer was ill with a fever and could not attend him. "This distressed him even more," Imilce said, "for it seemed a doubly ominous warning."

Hannibal listened with little interest, commenting that his brother was too inclined to find ill omens in the simplest of things. "One should be attentive to the gods," he said, "but not paralyzed in all matters. A drop of oil is hardly a sign from Baal. I trust the man can cook with a single eye just as well as with two."

As he spoke he moved closer to his wife, caressing first the smooth skin on the back of her hands and then the joint of her knee and then the pale stretch of her inner thigh. "I've decided a position for Hanno in this conflict," he said. "I will inform him of it soon, though I've no doubt he will find something of ill-fortune in my decision."

"And what of your family?" Imilce slipped her hand over Hannibal's, simultaneously caressing it and slowing its upward progress. "What fate have you assigned us?"

"The best and only course for you is that which is safest," Hannibal said. "So, you, my love, will finally see my homeland. Sapanibal will escort you and introduce you to my mother and my younger sister and to Carthage itself. I am sure you will find them all most welcoming. You'll wait out this war in the embrace of more luxury than you've yet tasted."

"If that is your wish," Imilce said. "But I had held some hope that I might go with you."

Hamilcar rose to his feet and pulled a bowl of olives from the serving table. Imilce half-rose to attend him, but was stayed by her husband's arm. She watched the child spill the fruit and roll it beneath his palms.

"You would ride with me into battle?" Hannibal asked, squinting as if the thought of this bewildered him. "I knew not that you were of the Amazon race."

"Do not joke at my expense. I wish to travel with you, so that I might see you at times and so that your son need not forget you. I am not so feeble as to be a burden. Hasdrubal schooled me well in riding last year."

"Did he teach you to hurl a javelin as well? Did he teach you of the parts inside a man's body and how best to destroy them?" Imilce began to respond, but Hannibal continued, his voice edged. "Life on campaign would ill suit you. What would become of you should I die? Should the Romans lay their hands on you they would dishonor you. They might well form a train behind you and each of them—hundreds of them—push their seed inside you and so punish me as well. This is no idle threat but the way of war, the nature of hatred. What if they captured my son? What might they do with him? The thought is unimaginable."

"You misunderstand me," Imilce said, though her voice was chastened and had lost its playful timbre. "I meant only that we be near. You might capture a city early and we might come to it and live in safety, in a fortress you thought of as a home within their—"

Hannibal pushed her caressing hand away, kicked his legs off the bed, and rose. "And when word got out that Hannibal's beloved wife dwelled in that city? It would soon become a target. If I were at the gates of Rome with my hands upon the ram and word came to me that you were in danger, what would you have me do? No, the very idea is absurd. You would create in me a weakness where there need not be one."

"If it came to that, I would die before—"

"You would be fortunate to be allowed death," Hannibal said. "No. That is my answer. You go to Carthage with all that is precious to me. Let us talk of it no more."

Though her eyes were cast aside and her visage tight with things unsaid, Imilce nodded. She rose and scooped up her son and started to move away.

"What are you doing?"

In answer, Imilce clicked her tongue twice on the roof of her mouth. The boy's maid appeared, took the boy, and slipped away with him. Imilce turned back toward her husband. Reaching to loosen her hair, she said, "Perhaps the commander would like a second child. If so, we should not waste time."

The men gathered for the meeting with a nervous, expectant air. Hannibal was finally to set all the pieces of his plan before them and each would learn his own position within it. Though they had attended councils throughout the winter and most had even spoken privately with the commander, this meeting marked a new stage, the moment at which preparation met the bridge into action. They sat on cushions around a low table, at ease for the moment but not slouching or leaning back as they might while at leisure. Mago and Hasdrubal, Bostar and Bomilcar, Maharbal and Carthalo, Monomachus and Vandicar: all men of importance in the campaign to come, each a representative of components of the army serving under them. Hannibal disdained clutter at meetings such as these. Instead he trusted in the generals beneath him to hear his desires and to carry them through.

Hanno, taciturn as ever, took a seat at the edge of the low table, his cushion pushed back a little way so that those next to him had to look almost over their shoulders to address him. He had long dreaded this meeting. He felt the fear now in the pulsing of the arteries in his hands. Whether he clenched them into fists or held them loose or laid them flat on his thighs, in each position his heart seemed to be contained within them and to thump, thump, thump. It was most distracting, all the more because he had to concentrate to think past it, to brace himself for the role he would soon be assigned. Which would be worse, a position of prominence from which to err yet again in decision-making, or a demotion to some lesser role that would indicate to all that Hannibal found him wanting?

The arrival of the historian roused Hanno from his thoughts. Silenus entered laden with the writing supplies with which he would keep a record of all of Hannibal's accomplishments. He took a seat near Hanno, greeting him with a smile that the Barca returned coldly. He had grown no fonder of the Greek than when they first met. Silenus was silent enough as he prepared his writing utensils, but once readied he looked about the group and immediately found a jumping-off point in some quadrant of the conversation. He said, "Which puts me in the mind of the story of Titus Manlius and his son. Has anyone heard of this?"

He addressed his question to the room rather than to anyone in particular and it might have passed unnoticed, except that Bomilcar threw up his hands. "He speaks! Our resident historian and Roman expert! Silenus, if you were as productive in bed as you are in producing tales you would have created your own nation by now."

"You may have something there," Silenus said, "but for better or worse the gods have not so endowed me. I pleasure in bed like any man, but of issue . . . As yet I am the father only of tales. This one I am assured is true, however. You might find it instructive of the Roman character."

Before Hanno could find the words to discourage him, Mago did the opposite.

"We await patiently," he said.

"The consul Titus Manlius," Silenus began, "once gave orders to his entire legion that they were not that day to engage the enemy."

"What enemy?" Hasdrubal asked.

"Not relevant to the story," Silenus said. "It was a clear enough order and easily obeyed, one would think. But Titus had an impetuous son with other—"

Silenus cut off his words at the entry of the commander. All rose to greet him, but Hannibal squelched any formality with a gesture. He must have had his hair trimmed that very afternoon, for it was shorter than it had been the day before, cut close around the ears and with a straight line across the base of the neck. His face was fresh, and clean-shaven save for his chin beard, which had only been snipped for shape, not shortened. He sat down heavily and took the scrolls handed to him by an assistant. While he stretched them out across the low table, he nodded that the Greek could carry on.

"Titus Manlius had a son," Silenus resumed, "a brave youth who that very day had an encounter with the enemy. The latter had called the young Titus out to single combat and Titus could not restrain himself. The two did battle and young Titus came away the victor. He slew a distinguished opponent," Silenus said, "robbed the enemy of a leader, and . . ."

"Disobeyed his father," Bostar said.

"Exactly. Manlius summoned the young man and called for an

assembly to be sounded. Once all were in attendance he gave a speech, the words of which escape me in exact—"

"No!" Bomilcar said. "Surely you were there and can quote him word for word."

Silenus let this sit and looked sadly around at the company, his eyes alone conveying a humorous disdain for the large Carthaginian. "As I understand it, he spoke of the need for discipline. His son's actions were in contradiction to his order, and his order was a stitch in the fabric that held Roman arms together. If the young Titus was allowed to snap this thread, then the cloak of Roman arms might well fray and come apart at the seams."

"Sounds like a quote to me," Hasdrubal said. Bomilcar seconded the notion.

"The consul summoned a lictor," Silenus continued, "and had his son grappled and bound to a stake and beheaded before the view of all the company, without any further debate. Such is the nature of Roman discipline and the lengths they'll go to in ensuring it, whether justly or not."

Monomachus said that whether the punishment was just was not the issue. He was sure, on the other hand, that it had proved effective in keeping discipline thereafter. "That, surely, is the point Silenus is making."

Bostar said, "You all assume too much of the fatherly bond. Perhaps the old man had no love for his issue. Perhaps he was glad to be rid of him."

"No father can help but love his son," Hannibal said, absently, only through his words showing that he was listening at all.

"So you would not have acted as Manlius did?" Silenus asked.

"My son wouldn't have disobeyed me. Just as I never disobeyed my father."

"But if by chance . . ."

Hannibal finally looked up from his charts. "That's not a decision I would have to face. If it's impossible for me, it deserves no comment from me. Silenus, you are needed here as a scribe and chronicler, not as a storyteller. Keep notes of what passes now. The things we will speak of today are known in part to all of you. But I will state the order of things again so that none misunderstand.

"This spring the army of Carthaginian Iberia marches for Rome. Hasdrubal, to you goes command here in Iberia, with all the duties that entails. It will be no easy task to fend off Roman parties while also keeping a tight grasp upon the Celtiberian tribes. It will require all of your skills, and Noba's as well. Vandicar, you and your elephants will sail as far up the coast as possible in transport ships, but by the Pyrenees the creatures will need to be afoot. The rest of us will all march from here in a month's time. We will suffer considerable losses before ever touching down in Italy. No one can say how many, for no one has attempted this before. But we can minimize our losses by carefully managing the march. We must find the best guides for each portion: one pass could lead to death, the next to Rome. We must choose correctly. And we must be stern with the mountain Gauls. We'll send an advance guard two days ahead of the column. They can welcome us as friends and see us provisioned, and they can even join our cause if it is close to their hearts' desires. If they oppose us we'll leave their houses aflame, their men dead, and their women weeping. It's as simple as that."

Though Hannibal seemed to be ready to move on to the next point, Monomachus signaled with an upraised finger that he would like to speak. "These Gauls will be a thorn in our side each day of our journey," he said. "I've no doubt that we will kill many of them. But why waste the dead? From the early days of the march, the army should be fed a daily ration of enemy flesh."

Cries of disgust went up from Hasdrubal and Bostar. Bomilcar slapped his hand down upon the tabletop. Mago blurted, "Is he mad?"

Monomachus spoke calmly over the din. "This way we'll put their very flesh to use. We'll harden the men to the practice and later, should we need to fall back on it in times of famine, the men will find it easier to bear. And also, there are some people who believe one grows stronger by eating the flesh of conquered warriors. Perhaps some essence lives on in the tissue."

"Hannibal, must we discuss this?" Mago asked.

The commander considered for a moment before answering. "Monomachus, I pray we never become enemies," he said. "I understand that there is a measure of dark logic in your proposal. An army that not only kills but that dines on its enemies would be an awesome force, preying on the minds and courage of their opponents. But, to be truthful, the idea turns my stomach. And I would not force my men to a practice I will not take part in myself. We will make do as we always have."

"There are tales of—"

"Let us not think too much on tales. The answer is no. We will make our way through the Alps and smoke the Romans from their den. I will not fail to lead us there through lack of willpower. But we will not become eaters of flesh. Let us move on."

It was clear that Monomachus had more to say, but Hannibal's voice was firm. Monomachus sucked his cheeks in and stared at a space on the far wall of the chamber.

"Hanno, you will stay with a company guarding the mountain passes. This is our only road to Italy and, once secured, it must be kept open for reinforcements. This is a most important post, for without an artery connecting our army to Iberia we will be cut off within the belly of our enemy."

Hannibal carried on with his speech, but for a moment Hanno heard nothing save a repetition of the words previously uttered, his fate. What did this mean? A company guarding mountain passes? Was it an insult, to be left on some rocky outcrop among barbarians, a banishment to a snowy wasteland? Or was there some importance to the role and the command—small though it might be—that he would exercise? It was too much to think over quickly, not while he sat among this company, wanting to present an expressionless face, to act as if he had known all along his post and even had some hand in planning it. He felt again the pulsing in his palms. He slid his hands from his thighs, down and out of view.

"Mago will attend me," Hannibal was saying. "He will be the left arm twinned beside my right. Bostar, Bomilcar, so, too, will you test yourselves on Italian soil. Maharbal, the hooves beneath you will resound in valleys and hills around Rome. This, at least, is the order of the first prong of this attack. Next year we will spend the cold months in the land of the Gauls, where the Boii and Insubres are ready to unite with our cause. The spring of that year we attack, with a larger army than has ever before threatened Italy. Once we have them in a defensive posture, Hasdrubal can follow with another army. Should Baal and the fates favor us, by autumn of the second year hence we will dine within Roman halls, as guests or conquerors, depending on what peace terms the situation dictates."

"And if we meet Romans while still in Catalonia?" Maharbal asked.

After getting Hannibal's approving glance, Bostar answered. "That could be to our advantage. We know that the Romans will divide their consular armies: one for Iberia, another for Africa. If they do land an army in Iberia, it will certainly be in the north, nearer to their Greek allies in Massilia. It would do us no harm to fight there, far from New Carthage. With our victory, they'll recall the second consular force from threatening Africa."

"Either course of events suits us," Hannibal said, "although we cannot count on Rome to do our bidding. We must imagine a plan wherein our actions carry us through."

"Then why not besiege Rome itself?" Bomilcar asked. "We've made no preparations to take siege engines. This must be reconsidered."

"Siege will not be our first resort. The engines would be too burdensome to journey with us by land. They might reach us by ship, but our navy is too small. We might build the machines once in Italy, but in any case I believe a siege might be an error. Rome is too well fortified."

"No city can hold out forever," Bomilcar said.

"Neither can a small army survive indefinitely on hostile lands," Hannibal answered. "No, we must meet them on the field of battle and beat them resoundingly. We wound them first and then follow until weakness betrays them. We show their Latin allies not the city of a strong friend under threat, but proof that their masters have a superior on the field. A winner never lacks for friends. Said simply: We march to Italy, we defeat the Romans in battle, we break the old alliances with their neighbors, and then—only then—we press upon Rome itself. I've spoken to each of you fully about these matters. This is how we will proceed. Through the rest of the early spring you will each school yourselves in all the matters important to your roles.

"Now," he said, leaning over the charts and smoothing them with his hands, "let us examine all these points in more detail."

Hanno, bending forward with the others, watched his brother's profile: his hair, wavy and dark, forehead ridged with the thoughts he sought to convey, eyebrows like two ridges of black basalt, full, shapely mouth. For the first time he gave a word to the feeling he had for his brother, the sentiment that lingered just beyond his love, at the backside of admiration and adoration, fast behind the awareness that they shared blood and features and a scent so similar even hounds could not tell them apart. In a place further back than all these things, a seed planted in his infancy, there resided an emotion, named now for the first time. It humbled him just to form the word in his head and hear it sound within him.

Hate.

Hasdrubal awoke knowing that he had dreamed of the day of his father's death. He did not remember the particulars of the vision. It faded into the vapors of the unconscious world even as he opened his eyes upon the earthly one. He was left with something equally disturbing—the memory of the actual events, the part he had played in them, and the frightening world in which his childhood was a narrow sliver of his life, maturity demanded even before his body began the change toward manhood.

The second youngest male Barca had emerged into awareness while his homeland was in the depths of defeat. One of the first things he knew of his country was that they had lost a war to a great power called Rome. Lands and property and pride had been taken from them. They had staggered beneath a war indemnity and, further, the city itself had been besieged by its own mercenaries. The outcome of that conflict had been no sure matter. It was only by the belated will of the gods that his father, Hamilcar, had finally managed to raise the siege and drive the mercenaries out into the desert and slaughter forty thousand of them in a trap of epic proportions, leaving a mass grave almost beyond imagination—though Hasdrubal's youthful mind created images of it often.

This was the Carthage into which the boy Hasdrubal came of age.

As some children run up dark stairs for fear of the imaginary beast behind them, Hasdrubal ran through his early years pursued by massed armies of the dead waiting to sweep away all he knew in a whirlwind of violence. He might have grown into a shy adult had not his father modeled such complete, military confidence. Hamilcar set out to change this world, with Iberia as his stepping-stone, with his sons nipping at his heels like cubs. With a foothold on the river Betis, he carved his way into Iberia through brute force, constant war, prevailing by the sheer might of Barca will.

The year of Hamilcar's death it was the city of Ilici that put up the fiercest resistance. Hamilcar's siege of the city had dragged through late summer, through autumn, and on into winter. The quarrelsome people showed no signs of surrender. In their resolve, they even tossed the bodies of the old and infirm over the walls, men and women with their throats cut, a message that they preferred death to starvation: better to be corpses than to be the slaves of the Carthaginians. Patient but resolved, Hamilcar released some of his army for the winter and kept up the siege with a reduced force. He believed that patience would assure them victory. They had recourse to resupply while the suffering Ilicians did not. His position was strong. It was simply a matter of time, and the two sons attending him—Hannibal and Hasdrubal—would benefit from the lesson of patience.

When Orissus, a tribal king from just north of the city, approached them under the banner of peace it seemed reasonable enough. The man had been on favorable terms with them for some time. It was likely he wanted to better his position to exploit the Ilicians' misfortune. He offered Hamilcar entertainment in his stronghold, a reprieve from the siege, and the opportunity to consider an allegiance between them. He spoke with no guile on his face, offering simple truths and promises kind to the ears of battle-weary men.

In private council to consider the offer, Hamilcar asked his sons their opinion. Hannibal, long his father's confidant, warned against accepting. He argued that they should bear out the cold and see the siege through. Let rest come when the work was completed, not before. For his part, Hasdrubal was not yet accustomed to being asked his opinion. He fumbled for an answer, trying to disguise his own eagerness with logic. "We have no reason to doubt Orissus," he said. "He's been a friend thus far. And there is your health to consider, Father. Cold is sometimes the death of great men."

Hamilcar heard them both out, standing with his arms folded, the bunched muscles of his arms prickled with cold bumps, his breathing phlegmy and difficult. He pointedly did not comment on the question of his health, but he did overrule Hannibal. It was not simply a matter of pleasure, he explained, but an opportunity to build political alliances.

They set out with a mounted company two hundred strong, leaving some behind to maintain the siege. Hamilcar rode at the side of the Iberian, sharing a skin of warmed, spiced wine between them. He honestly seemed to enjoy the other man's company, although Hamilcar was such a statesman that it was hard to say for sure. The sky was slate-gray and so thick that one could not sight the orb of sun in it. It rained steadily, as it had done all week long, not freezing on the ground and yet so unrelenting as to chill one to the bowels. Hasdrubal, following the muddy flanks of his father's horse, wished only that they would move faster. He had notions of native girls in his head, of wine and warmth and all the tastes he had developed a liking for. Silly things to think on, he knew, not worthy of his consideration. Glancing to his side he saw his brother and knew from his focused, stern face that no such desires clouded his thoughts. Hasdrubal remembered thinking an ill thought of his brother at that moment. It was something he might well have forgotten, but it was welded into his consciousness by the actions that interrupted it.

A Massylii scout came galloping in from the rear and beckoned anxiously for Hamilcar's council. He said something in his own tongue that got the commander's complete attention. He pulled up and moved off to hear the scout. What the Massylii said was this: A mixed company of Iberian infantry and cavalry had dropped into the valley behind them, cutting them off from Ilici and trailing behind them. What number? The Numidian was not sure for the visibility was poor, but he estimated a thousand, perhaps half that again concealed by tree cover. He believed they had seen him and would be fast behind.

"What people?" Hamilcar asked.

The Numidian, without raising his gaze but using only his chin, indicated those he believed responsible.

Hamilcar snapped his gaze around at Orissus. Meeting his eyes was all the confirmation he needed. The Iberian recognized this. He yanked his horse into motion, followed at once by the rest of his company. Hamilcar barked an order. Monomachus and a small contingent of cavalry went off in pursuit. But before Hamilcar could speak another command—with divots of mud thrown high from horse hooves still falling around them—the ambushing army breached the far horizon.

It was not even a battle or a running skirmish but simply pure flight after that. There was no time to consult maps save the internal one that Hamilcar had etched inside his skull. They rode west at a dead run, vaulting over the bodies of Orissus and his men, not even pausing to comment on their betrayers. The opening of a valley to the north brought with it yet another band of attackers. The Carthaginians raced past and forded the river without a pause. They emerged on the other side under a barrage of arrows, some hitting their targets, most skittering across the stones. They were at this for the better portion of the winter afternoon.

By the time they reached the impassable river the horses were lathered beyond all health. Before them churned an unnamed river that would have been easily crossed in summer. But now it was in full spate, high enough to cover the base of trees and churn brown water through branches usually the home of birds and squirrels, not fish. His father gave a command then, the only one of his that Hasdrubal wished he had disobeyed.

"You two," he said, "ride south with the Sacred Band. Go now, at all speed. Meet me in a week's time in Acra Leuce."

With that, Hamilcar spun his horse and rode, yelling to the rest of the soldiers to follow him. Hasdrubal glanced at his brother and for a moment saw the same concern on his face. To go upriver was madness. With the Iberians fast behind him, Hamilcar would have no escape route, for the river in its higher sections would surely be a tumbling torrent. Hasdrubal wanted to cry out for his father to stop, to halt, to reach forward and grasp the great man by the hair and stop him. He wanted all this, but turning once more to his brother he found Hannibal's face had changed. The visage now directed at him was set in stone, unkind and pitiless.

"You heard," Hannibal said. "Turn and ride as ordered. Wipe the questions from your face."

And so he had. He could no more disobey his brother than he could his father.

It was in a warm chamber in Acra Leuce that Monomachus brought them the news. Hamilcar Barca was no more. Drowned in crossing the upper reaches of that mad river. He and his horse flung and battered until lifeless, pushed and shoved and tossed by the muscle of water around the bone of stone. His father died so that his sons might live, for surely Hamilcar had chosen his route in full awareness of the risks. He had led the pursuers on and thereby sacrificed his own life.

Hasdrubal refused to look at Hannibal, though they heard the news together. He felt a hot anger toward him like nothing he had felt before or since, but it lasted only until he felt his brother's hands on his shoulders, then his arms around him. With that the anger went unmasked and betrayed what it truly was, the shocked sorrow of one who is suddenly an incomplete link in a chain, an orphan not yet ready to lose his father because he has not yet become completely a man of his own. Neither a child nor a father but a brother still. For some reason it was this last realization that set him to tears.

These memories did not leave him until late in the morning, when the preparations for Hannibal's address to the mass of returning soldiers took precedence. Hasdrubal, attending his brother in the last moments before his speech, could hear the gathering crowd outside the city walls: the entire army, some ninety thousand strong, brought together to hear Hannibal's plan for the upcoming campaign. Certainly the men knew whom they were going to war with, and knew that they would take the battle to Rome, but only now, on this morning, would the commander reveal the entirety of the plans to them.

Hannibal dressed with more care than he usually allowed, more attention to luxurious detail. He even accepted suggestions from his vain younger brother. He wore a breastplate with an image of Elissa—Carthage's founder—at its center. The woman's face was beautiful and ferocious and vacant all at once. Beneath this, his tunic was pure white, sewn with red thread and embroidered along the shoulders in gold. Even his sandals were carefully chosen, fine leather tanned to near black, adorned with silver studs. Hasdrubal had never seen him look finer, but Hannibal's mind was on other things.

"At the end of that corridor I will look out across a vast and well-trained army," Hannibal said. "But can I tell them what the future holds? No, because I do not have that power unless they give it to me. In fact, I'll propose a future, and they'll tell me if I've imagined correctly. And then over this, Fate will sit in judgment."

"Brother, they would follow you anywhere," Hasdrubal said.

"Perhaps. The Persian kings believed their troops to be nothing but instruments of their will, yet their numbers were no match for the anger of free men. No, when I step onto that platform I am posing a question. It is they who answer."

Hasdrubal heard this in silence and nodded his eventual acceptance of it. Still watching the empty corridor, he asked, "May I ask you one last thing?"

"Of course."

"I don't know whether it's been asked, and I would hear your answer. Is there no other course than war with the Romans? Some say that if we ignored them we could enjoy the empire we've built here. We could expand further, equals to the Romans and alongside them. I don't run from battle. You know that. I am your student in all things. I question you only because I would understand completely. Do we hate them so much?"

Hannibal watched his brother's downturned face. "Do you remember when, as boys, we used to chase the shadows of clouds across the land? Mounted, we would outrace the wind and smite whole legions of foes made of nothing but white vapor."

Hasdrubal nodded. Hannibal smiled and left the thought; he did not pick it up again or explain its significance.

"You ask an honest question, and in answer to it I will speak of two points. Yes, I do hate them. I had the joy of spending more years with our father than any of his sons. He burned with a hatred for the Romans. They have robbed us of so much. They are treacherous and remorseless and cunning. I believe our father to have been among the wisest of men. He hated Rome; I do as well."

Mago and Bostar appeared from the corridor leading to the landing. They indicated with nods that all was ready. The men were waiting. Hannibal nodded and motioned them back along the corridor.

"But I'm no fool," Hannibal said. "Hatred is to harness, not to be harnessed by. I wouldn't attack Rome simply out of hate. The truth is we've no choice. The Romans have a hunger different from any the world has yet seen. I have many spies among them. They bring me the pieces of a puzzle I've been fitting together for some time now. I have enough of it clear before me to know that Rome will never let us be. Perhaps they'd allow us five years of peace, perhaps ten or fifteen, but soon they'd come for us again. They grow stronger yearly, Hasdrubal. If we don't fight them now, on our terms, we will fight them later, on theirs. Father knew this as well and schooled me in it while young. Nothing he said on this matter has proved mistaken. We all want power, yes. Riches, yes. Slaves to satisfy us. Carthage is no different. But in their secret hearts the Romans desire more than just these things. They dream of being masters of the entire world. Masters of something intangible, beyond mere power or riches. They'll settle for nothing less. In such a dream, you and I would be but slaves."

He let this declaration sit a moment, then continued, inhaling a breath and gathering himself up. "So my answer is twofold. I hate Rome, yes, but I accept this war because I have no choice. We'll be fighting for nothing less than the world, my brother. Nothing less than everything there is. We chase clouds no longer. We couldn't, even if we wished to."

The commander rose and placed a hand on his brother's shoulder and squeezed the bunched muscle there. Without another word he moved away, across the room and into the corridor. His sandals scraped across the grainy stone. The sound of them faded and Hasdrubal listened on. He knew the moment Hannibal stepped out onto the platform above the waiting army. The roar that greeted him was deafening.

TWO

The Thunder of Baal

I n her own way Aradna had been born to war. To be a follower of war, that is. One of the ragged many who trailed behind the machinery of carnage, scavenging a life from dead bodies and burning villages and the strewn chaos of spent battlefields. She never knew her mother, but her father had been almost good to her. With the help of a single mule, he had driven a cart laden with found objects for sale, trinkets so inconsequential that soldiers in the passion of battle failed to strip them from the bodies of the slain: silver rings, shot pellets for the slingers, sandals, strips of leather, healing ointments, talismans from various countries, figures of gods significant only to the faithful of certain sects. He was a gruff man, a Greek, big-shouldered and well known among the horde. He was famous for having punched a Bythian mercenary so hard during an argument that the man was left literally speechless—he who had been a loudmouthed creature could no longer form words with his unwieldly tongue. Aradna's father might have been a warrior in his own right, but he chose to live by exploiting other men's follies, not joining them.

While he lived, Aradna's childhood was one of relative safety. He might not have known kindness and how to show it, but in his way he was soft on her. He spoke quietly at night, told her of her mother, of the small village they had fled from years ago, of the great wrong done to them that pushed them from the island he loved dearly and so wanted to return to. All this wandering was nothing, he told her. These were simply the trials he must face as an actor in the drama that was his life. He wanted only to return to Greece. He prayed daily that the writer of his story would provide the means, would make his tale a saga but not a tragedy. He watched her in the morning so that sometimes she awoke to his gaze above her and was comforted by it.

He was taken by an illness that came upon him quickly and simply killed him. She was twelve and was first raped that evening by the very man who had helped her bury him, her father's friend of many years. It was payment, the man said, and if so the bill was a large one, for he claimed her as his own and traveled with her tied to the back of the cart that had been her father's. He took her nightly, calling out another woman's name as he came and always angry with her afterward. She did not mourn when he died, taken slowly by a pinprick wound that started in his foot and ate up his leg to the center of him.

She was in farm country south of Castulo and found temporary peace in a village. She worked for an elderly man who loved to look at her but could do no more. He spoke to her as he said he could not to his own daughters. It was hard work, farming, but a far cry from the life she had thus far lived. She felt in the daily work some distant familiarity, an ancestral memory. She might have stayed on there after the old man's death but his daughters ran her from the property, fearful that their husbands would be drawn to her. She might have asked those two to think of her as a sister but she knew they could not. They were not kin, and they saw nothing in her except their own lacks.

She was fourteen then and became a scavenger once more. She left childhood behind and quickly grew hard in her woman's body. She became lean with muscle, and thick-skinned. Her mind had a sharpness of purpose that never rested, for neither did the carnivores sniffing around her. She was not the only female on the battlefields, but her face was prettier than most and her slim, androgynous form attracted men's stares. Her eyes were the color and quality of opal. Set against her tanned skin and even features they were two curses from behind which she viewed the world.

She walked from Gades to the Tagus and traversed the spine of the Silver Mountains and the whole coastline of Iberia as far as New Carthage. She was present at the fall of Arbocala and witnessed firsthand the cruel power of the Carthaginians. Everywhere she found men the same, their desires as predictable as her need to repel them. They came at her in the night and during the day and during sunrise and dusk: she fought them equally. She permanently damaged one man's sight by dragging a jagged fingernail across his eye; another she stabbed in the abdomen with a spearhead; still another she bit in the cheek and half-pulled the flesh away. For this last she was beaten insensible and raped with a retributory violence.

But for all these trials she was not defeated but tempered, fired to new strength. She was the victim, yes, but she saw within men's behavior a frailty that made them weak. Men might have been the stronger sex, but when they were filled with lust they were the more vulnerable, too. To sate themselves they must bear their naked, upraised clubs before them. Perhaps this was the final thing that defeated many women, seeing that member engorged, one-eyed and hooded like the evil serpent that it was. She had this thought during her waking hours but it came to her again while dreaming. A dead woman spoke to her and said that serpents—no matter how venomous—could be squashed beneath a well-placed heel.

When Aradna joined the train behind Hannibal's army she did so with little interest in the war's outcome. She walked behind the men but not out of devotion to them. This was simply the next campaign: either side might provide her the things she sought. She kept a treasure in a bag around her neck. She wore it like a talisman, and indeed it did contain within it the bones of an eagle taken from the egg, cloves of garlic often replaced to keep the scent strong, a single lock of hair said to have been snipped from Clytemnestra's murdered body so many years before, a tiny statue of Artemis carved from whalebone. But also within were several gold coins, the beginning, she hoped, of the small fortune she would need to buy herself a plot of land in that faraway country she had never seen but from which she had sprung. She followed Hannibal's army, but she was concerned with no destiny save her own.

Publius Scipio was much like any other young noble at the start of the war with Hannibal. He was of medium build, not bulky of musculature, but well sculpted and fit from training. His face was cut close to the bones that formed it, topped with light brown hair. Indeed, his friends often joked with him that his profile was fine enough to be minted on a coin, though why anybody would want to do that none of them could imagine. His father had already arranged for his marriage to the daughter of a prominent senator, Aemilius Paullus, a sure sign that his future shone brightly. He had every intention of honoring the distinguished family from which he sprang—through service in the Senate, through the acquisition and generous sharing of wealth, through noble comportment, and through distinguished conduct in war. He was, considering all this, quite receptive to the news of a coming conflict with Carthage. He had been schooled since boyhood that only through arduous struggle could a man truly make a name for himself. Struggle, therefore, was something to be sought out.

Publius believed—as much as is possible in a vibrant young man sniffing out his own view of the world—that his father was superior to other men in all matters of importance. Cornelius Scipio had been elected consul in a moment when the Roman Senate anticipated war. Thereby the people themselves had demonstrated their confidence in him. When the elder Scipio laid out his plans for a two-pronged attack—himself sailing for Iberia while the other consul, Sempronius Longus, aimed at Carthage itself—the young soldier believed it could not fail. Even when the threatened uprising among the Boii and Insubres detained them in the region of the Padus, Publius did not doubt that the delay was of little significance. The barbarians' pretensions needed to be checked. All knew that not that far back in the history of Rome the likes of them had sacked the city itself. But those were different days. A different Rome. And the Gauls needed to be reminded of it by occasional demonstrations of force.

They burned villages and seized property, fought skirmishes with the wild creatures, and watched dry-eyed as the particularly recalcitrant hung to their suffocating deaths upon wooden crosses. They suffered some casualties, felt seething animosity behind all those blue eyes, but never truly met the anticipated armed, organized resistance. The younger Scipio was later to recall that a Gallic woman he bedded for a casual evening's entertainment had uttered Hannibal's name as she crept from his tent. This made little sense at the time and was soon forgotten, only to be remembered later with the significance of a curse belatedly understood.

Confident that the would-be rebellion had been squelched before it began, Cornelius and his legions sailed for Massilia, on the coast just west of the Alps. The consul was fighting with the latter stages of a cold, felt feverish, and complained that his feet had never recovered from the rot of a wet spring. He sent his son to meet in council with the city's magistrates, and then retired to the comfort of his chambers. It was there that Publius found him that evening, relaxing in his brother's company.

Cornelius sat on a low couch, his toga drawn up high on his thighs, bare legs propped up on a wooden stool. Even in repose the consul had about him an air of authority. He was lean, his face the model for his son's sculpted features. A teenage boy knelt before him, with one of the man's feet clasped in both hands. The young man held the foot just before his face, as if smelling it. His energy was concentrated in his fingers, in the balls of his thumb and the kneading they were administering to the consul's insole and toe pad.

Cornelius, noticing his son, said, "Do not think me turning into some vile old soldier. These feet will be the death of me. They were spoiled in years past, and spring campaigns are ill to them. This boy has fine hands and he soothes them. I take some pleasure in it, though I am not yet a Greek."

Publius nodded a greeting at his uncle, who stood near the far wall, contemplating the world through a tiny window, holding a goblet of wine just under his nose. Gnaeus was of medium height, but thick in the legs and torso, with long, powerful arms some compared to a blacksmith's. He bore little resemblance to his elder brother except in speech: the brothers' voices were nearly identical even to ears accustomed to them both.

"I've nothing ill to say against Greeks," Publius said.

"That is true. I forget you associate with a fair number of them when at leisure. Perhaps it is your decency we should be concerned with. You bring me news, don't you?"

"I bring you a report," Publius said. "It's news if it is reliable, but that I'm not sure of. Apparently some of the Volcae claim that Hannibal has crossed the Pyrenees and is approaching the Rhône."

Gnaeus jerked his head toward his nephew, spilling a few drops of wine on his toga. "That can't be!"

Cornelius received the news more calmly, with little expression save for the skeptical wrinkling of his lips. "What does Marius make of this claim?"

"The governor credits it. He heard this from a trusted informer, with the blessing of tribal leaders of importance. He says they have no reason to lead us astray. Since he's been posted in Massilia, they have caused no real trouble. And the Volcae seem to need no convincing of Hannibal's threat. They have their own reasons to hate Carthage, it seems. Also, this is in keeping with reports from Catalonia."

"Catalonia is not the Rhône valley," Gnaeus said. "How is this in keeping with such reports?"

"It's possible, I mean. He may have been able to cross the Pyrenees—"

"True enough," Cornelius said, "but why would he? Our spies have confirmed that he means to fight within Iberia, where he is strong. I understood him to have planned an Iberian war in detail. Why change his plans now?"

"Perhaps our spies were not worth the gold we paid them," Gnaeus said.

Cornelius tugged his foot away from the servant, who parted his hands and knelt immobile, waiting instruction. The consul set his feet on the ground and pushed himself upright. He was a tall man among Romans, a brow's height above his son, not an old man although in the later years of his military service. Though he was no longer in his physical prime one could forget this at moments when he gathered his stature around him. He did so just then, shooing the servant away and placing an arm on his son's shoulder to walk him toward Gnaeus.

"Why would the brute cross the Pyrenees?" Cornelius asked again. "Easy enough to believe he would make a grab for all of Iberia up to the Pyrenees, but into the land of the Volcae? Too much at once, and too close to our interests. He would have to know that we would not allow it. Why stretch himself so when he knows we are preparing to attack him? Sempronius queried me in writing whether I feared Hannibal intended to cross the Alps. The idea gave me pause, but I had to dismiss it. It would be absurd, and—impetuous though Barcas are—Hannibal is no madman. So what then . . . ?"

The consul let the question hang. Some might have found it an invitation to answer, but Publius knew it was not meant for him. He took a goblet of wine, swirled it beneath his nose, and awaited the continuation of his father's musings.

"Perhaps it is a ruse," Gnaeus offered.

Cornelius tipped a few droplets into his brother's goblet, drank a long draft from his own, and then nodded agreement. "It may well be a trick to keep us occupied here instead of focused on a direct attack of New Carthage. He knows he overstepped himself, but he is bold. He has decided to pull back by pushing forward, if you understand me. If he keeps our attention here, he may yet save his city. He might, at the end of the year, withdraw into Iberia and so end the year retreating, but with more gained than lost. This is why I am still resolved to press on into Iberia. Gnaeus will land at Emporiae to prepare the way. I'll follow with the bulk of the army. Let Hannibal get word that his own city is besieged, and that Sempronius is sailing for his homeland. He will see then that ruses are nothing against determined might. Don't you agree?"

Publius nodded, but he had another thought and knew he had finally been given leave to speak. "But—for the sake of thoroughness—what if he *is* mad?"

"What?"

"What if his target is Rome?"

Cornelius studied his son a moment, head cocked, squinting, as if he was not sure he recognized the young man. "For the sake of thoroughness . . . If Italy is his target he must surely stick near the coast and confront us. He would not attempt the inland mountains. The casualties he would suffer would make that a daily battle in and of itself. He might have overreaching hubris, but still he would not waste his army fighting snow and ice and Gauls. If he reached Italy at all it would be as a band of starving beggars. No, if he wants Rome he must first come through us, and I would welcome such a meeting."

His tone, once more, suggested that further discussion was not an option. He refilled Publius' goblet and offered it to him. He said, "All considered, I think we can continue our preparations with little fear."

None could call the journey to the Rhône uneventful for the Carthaginians. They expanded their dominion to the farthest extent it had ever known, through strong-worded negotiation, at times through open war or siege or ambush. Hannibal knew he must keep control of the lands between him and New Carthage. The army traveled in three war columns, separated by miles, each with its own trials to face and each led by a Barca. They sent before them emissaries of peace, but it was hard for any people to look upon this massed power and not grasp for sword or spear. The small, sturdy Balearic Islanders marched in the fore, their slings held at the ready, able in an instant to send a stone whirling through the air at blinding speed; beside them strode the strange gray beasts ridden by men whose nation could only be guessed at. The gray beasts were big-eared and massive, with a nose as flexible and strong as any limb. Behind them came rank after rank of soldiers, marching in their various companies and in tribal groups and followed by horsemen; in the wake of it all, a baggage train that fed the beast of war. Carthage's army churned the spring ground into a wide wasteland. The land to either side of them was stripped clean as if by a swarm of locusts, and behind them came wolves and foxes, buzzards and ravens and swarms of flies.

They came to an agreement to pass through the territory of the Ruscino, but there were other tribes and factions of tribes to contend with. No leader could govern each and every member of a people. Although no Carthaginian head rested easy at night, toward the end of the summer they could claim a tenuous dominion over all of Catalonia. No Roman legion had appeared on the horizon, so Hannibal left Hanno in command of the tribes washing right up to the foothills of the Pyrenees. He then marched the army over the mountains and came down into the plain leading toward the Rhône.

At that river, the Volcae massed to make their stand. Standing on the west bank, Hannibal got his first glimpse of the wild creatures whom Monomachus had barely escaped on his earlier expedition. They were longhaired and half-clothed, pale as pine flesh, some painted in shades of blue and green. Their calls carried across the flat, slick expanse of steady current, taunts spoken in the strangest gibberish, a guttural dialect totally foreign to an African's ear. And yet the meaning behind the words was clear enough when twinned with their gestures. They gesticulated with their arms and fingers, exposed their buttocks and grabbed at their crotches, stuck out their tongues and waved their long swords in the air above them. Clearly, they were not a people open to negotiation.

Mago, standing beside his brother, said, "Those people are out of their minds."

Hannibal took it all in with an impassive face. "Insane or no," he said, "they are in our way."

And so he constructed a plan to remove them. To fulfill it, Mago marched out just after dark, a contingent of the Sacred Band close around him. Behind them came the bulk of the war party, Iberians chosen for their comfort in the water, several with Gallic horns tied to their backs and protruding above them as if long-necked birds were growing out of their flesh. They followed the lead of two Gallic guides, who risked their lives and their family's freedom if they led the soldiers astray. They progressed not in ordered ranks but weaving through the trees, ducking low branches and jumping across creek beds, into shadow and out. They followed the Rhône for some time. Then they left the Rhône to climb into a hilly area, from which they sometimes caught glimpses of the distant river, a black snake across the landscape, save where the light of the moon touched upon it in gleaming silver. They camped for the day in a high pine wood, careful to move little and to keep fires small. Mago found the bedding of needles almost luxurious. He pinched the needles between his forefinger and thumb and snapped them, one after another, for some time. There was something comforting in the action.

When they dropped down to the river again the next evening, the guides led them to the area they wished for. It was as promised: A tree-covered island split the current. The riverbed out to it was shallow enough that the men waded most of the distance across and lost their footing for only a few moments, though frantic ones for those who could not swim. Mago's heart pounded in his chest the moment his feet slipped free of the bottom. His chin dipped under the water. He spat and gagged and tilted his head so far back that he looked straight up at the sky and felt it moving above him and had the momentary sensation that each pinprick of light was an eye looking down on him. But then his foot brushed a stone. One, then another, then a large one that clipped both his legs and sent him tumbling. After that it grew shallower. He made it to the island in no worse shape than the others.

But that was only half the crossing; the far side was deeper and swifter. They set to work hewing pines, chopping the branches from them, and lashing them together into rafts. It was hard work in only the moonlight, but they completed it before the moon dipped and cast them into deeper darkness. They pushed off onto the swaying, hard-to-steer rafts, paddling toward the dark woodland on the far bank.

They were barely ashore when the light of day grew on them. They pulled the rafts up into the trees and gathered together in a narrow valley to warm themselves before fires and be fed. Mago posted guards, but most of the men spent the day at rest, falling asleep as they hit the ground. The Barca was not so quick to fall into slumber. He lay staring up at the thick canopy of trees above them, the myriad branches layering and crosshatching across each other. His eyes sought out patterns in the lines and shadows but there was none to be found. Something in this troubled him, for it seemed that nature so rarely displayed order in the chaos of the earth. Why was this so? Why were no two branches the same, no two leaves true replicas of each other? He did sleep eventually, but it was not a restful slumber.

Few stirred until the late afternoon. Hunger awoke them and consciousness reminded them of the task before them. The third night was devoted to the march back downstream, a difficult venture as they feared being discovered. They moved with such stealth that the head of the party stumbled upon a group of deer caught unawares. The buck of the group stood at the crest of a bare hill, feeding on the low shrubs growing up in the scar of a fire a few years old. Around him were five does and two young males, all heads down and content in their nighttime dining. The two Gauls spotted them first. One flung an arm out to stop the other. The sudden motion was enough in the tense night to send a shock wave back through the group and man after man froze in his tracks. This must have been a stranger sound than that of their motion, for the buck looked up, lifted his nose, and studied on the silence. He grunted a warning and bolted, leaving the does momentarily at a loss. Then they, too, found motion. They bounded up the hillside and out of view, backsides taunting in their spring, somehow deceptive as compared to the speed of the creatures. In the empty stillness after this the two Gauls looked long at each other. They began mumbling at the profundity of such a sighting and might have carried on for some time had Mago not hissed them into silence.

The trip was uneventful after that. They were in place as planned on the morning of the fourth day. Mago had the signal fire kindled and the agreed message went up into the air in billows of white smoke. Watching the plumes rise, he whispered a prayer to Baal, beseeching his attention and blessing on the venture just before him. This done, he signaled the men forward.

Though Imco Vaca knew that Mago had led a small band out on some mission, a few days before, the plan had not been explained to him. It was with considerable trepidation that he pushed off from the shore and began the crossing. The Volcae's numbers had increased over the last few days. It was hard to count them, for they lined the shore from horizon to horizon. Many camped right on the stony edge of the river, others among the trees and into the hills behind them. When they saw that the Carthaginians were finally beginning their crossing they hooted with joy. They drummed their swords against their shields and blew on their great upcurving horns, instruments not musical at all but like the bellowing of an elk caught in a bog. They seemed to think the Carthaginians were floating to the slaughter.

During the early half of the journey, Imco would not have disputed this. He was on one of the large barges that pushed off from far upstream. He manned a pole for the first portion of the journey, heaving it up from the bottom and starting again. They tried to gain the greatest momentum they could before the river deepened, but by the time they switched to their makeshift paddles it seemed they moved more with the current than across. Nor were they alone. Spread out into the distance along the river below them were innumerable vessels of every description. Barges of full-grown trees lashed together with bark ropes, rafts that rode so low their occupants stood ankle deep in river water. A few vessels flew simple sails to aid them; some dragged behind tethered ponies. Some men even bestrode sections of log, legs in the water on either side, weapons strapped to their backs, paddling forward with their hands. Only the Iberians were truly comfortable in the water. Many of them disdained the vessels altogether. They swam with their shields snug to their chests and their clothing and gear in leather sacks upon their backs. It was a motley flotilla.

Halfway across the first of the Gallic missiles began to fall, zipping into the water with little more sound than a pebble tossed from the shore. But they were not pebbles, as the man beside Imco soon learned. The young soldier heard the man's speech cut short. He recognized the squelching, muted thud of the impact. But he did not know where the man had been hit until he grasped him by the shoulder and yanked him around. The other had caught the arrow in his open mouth. It pinned his tongue against his palate and pierced the voicebox. The man's eyes betrayed no alarm at this, only incredulity. This must have changed with deeper realization of his situation, but Imco did not notice.

He turned away, grabbing his shield and ducking beneath it. He knew with complete certainty that joining this campaign was the biggest error of his young life. Nothing had gone right for him since the march began. The first week out, he had stepped barefoot on a fishing barb at the edge of a stream. The wound was a tiny one in the eyes of the warriors around him, but it caused him no end of pain as he marched. Dirt and grime had entered with the barb and made the whole area into a swollen pad of pus-filled agony. Somewhere before the Pyrenees, Imco had picked up an infestation of savage pubic lice. They terrorized his groin, biting him with such vigor that he sometimes jolted to a wincing halt in the middle of the war column.

Now he was sure his miserable life was about to end, body left floating like so much debris in the current. He imagined the ravages of nature upon his corpse, focused particularly on the genitals: a hungry turtle clamping down on his limp penis, fish nibbling the wrinkled sacs of his manhood, his asshole—an area he had never allowed violation of in life—prodded by bald, long-necked buzzards. What a fool he was! He should have quit the army and sailed home to Carthage to take some pleasure in his family's newfound wealth. He had no business in this strange land. His war successes had thus far been gifts from the gods. Now he had overreached their benevolence by thinking himself a true warrior, imagining he could march beside Hannibal on this mad mission.

Thinking thus, he was slow to notice the change in the course of events. It was only when a soldier near him prodded him with a jest about his courage that he peeked over the rim of his shield at the far shore. The Gauls were in chaos. They were shouting, but not out over the water: They were yelling to one another now. Some had their backs turned to the approaching watercraft. The rain of arrows had nearly stopped. There seemed to be a great confusion behind them, which they only increased with their clamor. The air filled with smoke, not of campfires but of destruction. And then came the horns. They were no different really from the horns the Volcae had been blowing on only moments before, but they came from the wrong direction and were blown inexpertly. They spluttered and cut off short and rose and fell in volume. Their discordance sent the Gauls into further confusion. Then Imco caught sight of them: Mago's small band.

Mago's force would have been hopelessly outnumbered, except that by this time the first of the watercraft were reaching the shore. A few Iberians jumped into the river, swords in hand, and lashed out. Cavalrymen mounted their horses, cut them free, and urged them through the water. Some began to hurl their javelins from the barges, catching the Gauls in the backs and flanks. The man beside Imco—not wanting to waste one of his preferred weapons—hurled an ax toward the shore. It cut an awkward, tumbling arch in the sky and hit a Gaul flat on the top of his skull. Though it did not pierce him with the blade portion at all, the impact was enough to liquefy the man's legs and drive him to the ground. The ax thrower sent up a howl of bestial pleasure at this. The scream pulled chill bumps up across Imco's entire body, and yet a moment later he was joining in. It was clear already that this engagement was to be a rout.

By the time Imco could see the stones in the knee-deep water where the barge grounded, he had forgotten the fear that had huddled him beneath his shield. The bloodlust on the underside of cowardice is a powerful thing. Imco felt it in the completeness of his being. He jumped ashore and his first strike was into the calf of a young man in full, frantic flight, for some reason running along the shore instead of away from it. The Gaul went down and spun around and looked up through a mass of dirty blond locks. For some reason that was not entirely clear to him, Imco aimed his next thrust directly between the man's grayish blue eyes.

By the fifth day of the crossing the army was over, save for the elephants and their keepers. These last had been preparing since they first arrived on the banks. A few rafts had been sent into the current with single pachyderms aboard, but more than one of the beasts panicked and dove headlong into the water. Two made their way back to the near shore; another two managed to progress all the way to the far side, the spine of their backs, the crests of their skulls, and their trunks jutting out of the water. It seemed to the watchers that the elephants had somehow found shallow portions of the riverbed just perfect for their crossing. One of the mahouts swore that the elephants had swum, and that he had known them to swim even farther in his eastern homeland, but he was shouted down as mad.

The small rafts were deemed too risky, and so they decided upon another method. Vandicar ordered the elephant handlers to build a jetty far out into the water. Beyond this they constructed rafts of stout trees, some as thick around as a man, lashed together with great quantities of rope. They shoveled earth onto the rafts and set tufts of grass atop the dirt; they even secured leafy trees in upright postures. Even greater stretches of rope were purchased from far and wide up and down the river. The ropes were tied together and secured to the raft and rowed across to the far shore, where it took a whole corps of men to hold the rope steady against the bowed pressure of the river.

Loading the beasts onto the floating islands was no easy task. Cow elephants led the way, calmer than bulls and more inclined to faith in humans. Behind them a few bulls followed nervously, testing the ground and finding it questionable and expressing as much with loud bellows and flapping ears. Vandicar cursed them in his Indian tongue. The chief mahout seemed to have no fear of the beasts whatsoever. He smacked them on the bottoms and yanked on their tusks and even seemed to spit in their eyes when he was truly angry.

These actions went uncommented upon for a while, but then one of the young males took exception to it. He cocked his head. It was not an angry motion, but it was swift enough to catch Vandicar off guard. The elephant's tusk nudged him in the shoulder. One of the man's feet got tangled in the other. He reached out for support from a sapling that had no roots and therefore was no support. A moment later he landed in the river: flat-backed, arms out to either side, mouth an oval of surprise. This seemed to confirm the suspicions the young bull had. He pivoted and bolted back onto solid ground, bringing in his wake the rest of the elephants, male and female alike. When it came down to it none completely trusted the mad fellow, certainly not now that he was climbing out of the water looking much like a drenched rat.

Eventually though, the creatures were brought across—some afloat and some swimming—and the army departed again. They kept the Rhône to their left and followed it northward. Hannibal knew that at some point it would curve up into the Alps and that in being farther from the coast they were farther from the Romans. Though he had been tempted to engage with Scipio's legion, he preferred to gain Italian soil, then do battle in the Romans' own country, where any victories could be quickly followed up. Also, they were nearing the greatest natural challenge of the journey. Already he sensed the growing buzz of anxiety in the army. They had put more than a normal season's trials behind them, but it was the unknown test of stone and ice that now kept the men awake at night, murmuring around the campfires. Hannibal saw all this, for his eyes were quick and his fingers touched each segment of his host like those of a physician who probes a patient's body in places far removed from the perceived point of illness.

Thus it was no oversight but a conscious decision not to enforce his expulsion of the camp followers. It would have been hard to implement the order in any event, but also Hannibal knew that a portion of his fighting men would slip away with the expelled. Among them a few of the officers hid slaves and concubines. Even some of the paid foot soldiers employed the followers, to carry out their foraging duties, to secure food and comforts. Many, of course, answered sexual needs. Men in a conquering force are rarely without some spoils, coins or weapons or jewelry; the camp followers provided entertainments on which to spend these trinkets. A few among the Libyan veterans had acquired slaves from among the Gauls. As Hannibal knew these men took seriously their right to the spoils of war, he said nothing about this. Perhaps, also, even the many with no direct stake in the camp followers were encouraged by the normality they suggested. If women could journey into these wildlands, along with thin-armed children and men older than battle age and even goats and pigs . . . then surely men in the prime of health were suited to it. Hannibal knew this line of thinking and allowed it for the time being, though he also knew it for a delusion. None but the strongest had any true place in this venture.

He was surprised, in fact, that the noncombatants held on as well as they did. The marching had never been easy, and now they were crossing territory with no roads worthy of the name. They forced their way through forest and over ridges and across rivers with all the order they could muster in the broken terrain. And this was not much. It was not winter yet, but already the chill hours just before dawn were hard on those from warm climes. Increasingly, they awoke to damp mornings and a low mist that was cool to the touch and hung among them a little longer each day. Stepping out of his tent one hushed morning, Hannibal looked over a camp dusted with frost, sparkling in the pure, early light. The thin threads of ice melted quickly, but all the army recognized them as harbingers of the coming season.

Hannibal paused the march long enough in the region of the Cavares to hear a dispute between two brothers, each of whom laid claim to the chieftaincy of their clan. Occupied with their own turmoil, they showed the Carthaginians no hostility. Instead, they asked for Hannibal—as a foreigner with no personal stake in the affair—to judge. They agreed that they would honor his decision. Hannibal wasted no time. He heard them out and promptly deduced that the matter was one of the younger brother's might overthrowing the elder's right. He sided with the elder brother, as age is the determining factor in such matters. In pronouncing his decision, he cited the precedent of thousands of years of history.

The Carthaginians marched out with no inkling of whether the decision would hold, but serving as arbitrator had served their cause well enough. The older brother provisioned the army handsomely from their autumn supplies. He sent them off with an escort force that flanked them through a rolling landscape that began to give way to ever higher vistas, all the way into the foothills of the Alps.

The Cavares turned back at the Druentia River, a vicious, multi-channeled torrent, rock-strewn and swirling. It was a nasty, frigid confusion and an ordeal to cross. It was now—as they were left friendless at the foot of the mountains, bunched up against the banks of these spiteful waters—that the men's grumbling grew truly audible. None carried his complaints directly to the commander, but Hannibal heard enough through his generals. The men wondered whether this mountain crossing was truly possible, especially so late in the season. Did the commander not see, as they did, the decrepit huts of the straw-haired peasants? The shriveled cattle, the sheep shivering with cold, rivers tumbling and frothing? This was no land for civilized men. Did Hannibal wish to be famous for marching an entire army up into white oblivion? Delegations of soldiers proposed new plans to their officers: they should winter where they were; they should attack Massilia; they should retreat to Iberia with the considerable booty of the long campaign.

Hannibal heard all these complaints but answered them, for the time being, with silence. He was personally among the first to succeed in crossing the Druentia, visible to many as he balanced on the slippery back of a hewn pine. He wrenched his way through the branches, jumped from the trunk to a boulder, and then dove, flat-bellied, into a stretch of moving water. He finally emerged on the other side, dripping and frigid. He looked back at the waiting army with an accusation etched in his stare. The others, grumbling, could not help but follow his example.

Soon after, a delegation arrived from the tribe into whose lands they were about to enter, the Allobroges. It was a small group, five elders, each with a few warriors in support of him. Monomachus— trusting no people as little as he did Gauls—escorted them into camp personally, his handpicked corps flanking the party, strong armed Libyans who shared their general's lust for carnage. Hannibal granted the Allobroges an audience before his tent. He sat on the plain three-legged stool he always brought with him on campaign. It had been his father's, as he explained to the delegates through his translators. After exchanging the customary pleasantries and accepting the gifts the Gauls offered—most notably, the enormous gilded skull of a stag—he asked them their business.

The leader of the delegation, Visotrex, stepped forward to speak for them. A screen of unkempt hair hid his face; the dull silver strands must have once been blond. His words came out with a rasping deepness that made them completely beyond Hannibal's comprehension, so that for once he had to rely entirely on his translator. Visotrex claimed that his tribe had heard all they needed to of Hannibal and the powerful army he led; they had no wish to clash in arms. He came to offer free passage through their lands, guides even, for the routes were difficult and only a local's knowledge would see them through without grave loss.

Hannibal asked the man to pull his hair back from his face. Visotrex did so. His visage was one of caved depressions, his eyes so deep-set they huddled in shadow, his cheeks receding beneath his facial bones, his mouth a pucker sucked back against his teeth. There was a growth on his neck that might have accounted for the strange constriction of his speech; it bulged as if the man had swallowed a lime whole and carried it stuffed to one side of his throat. For all this, the Gaul's face was unreadable, a fact that Hannibal noted well.

"You speak for all your people in making this offer?"

Visotrex said that he did, looking to his companions for verification. They nodded and spoke in their tongue until Hannibal waved them to silence.

"And are you a chieftain, or simply a messenger?"

The Gaul said that he was a chieftain, as his father before him had been, and that his son would lead his people after his death. Saying this, Visotrex indicated the young man standing behind his left shoulder. Hannibal took him in. He was a head taller than his father, wide-shouldered, with little in his well-formed face to connect him with his sire.

"This one is your son?" Hannibal asked. "He looks to be blessed by the gods."

Visotrex, for the first time, showed an emotion. Pride. He said, "In him I see the future of my people. This is a fine thing."

"Yes, it is," Hannibal said. "You are wise to come to me like this, as a friend, with no suspicion, no hostility. As you have been told, we've no quarrel with you. Our enemy is Rome alone. But the path to them takes us through your lands. If you're true to your word, you will find our passage no great burden. You may profit from it, in fact. I ask only that you travel at my side while we're in your country. If I may offer you our hospitalities even as you offer us yours . . ."

Visotrex, who had followed the speech with one ear tilted toward the translator, stiffened at the last suggestion. He seemed unsure of how to answer it, even glancing to the others for some direction. Finally, he gestured with spread hands: This was not possible. A chieftain had many duties. There were ceremonies he must preside over, so what the commander suggested could not be—

"Then I will have your son," Hannibal cut in, "as my guest. I will show him the same courtesy I would show you. The son of the chief is the future of the people, yes? I'd be honored to have him as my escort. Thank you for your wise counsel. My generals will speak with you of our route."

Without awaiting a reply, Hannibal rose from his stool and retreated into his tent. He stood there a moment, just inside the flap, listening to the short, confused conversation that followed. Visotrex, once he fully understood the commander's words, tried vainly to dispute them: A mistake had been made; for many reasons, he could not agree to leave his son. But, just as he would have instructed them, Hannibal heard Bostar and Bomilcar close down the discussion and move the party away.

As they receded, Mago and Monomachus entered the tent. Hannibal saw the questions on their faces, but spoke as if they had simply come to hear his instructions. "Tomorrow morning we'll call the men to full dress and have them march in battle order," he said. "Tell them it is meant as a display and that the grander the spectacle they make, the less trouble we'll have with these Allobroges. I will speak to the assembly then. And when we march, I want the chief's son always at my side."

"You do not take the Gauls at their word, do you?" Mago asked.

"No, you should not," Monomachus said. "I fear there is treachery in this. I would slice the man's throat and listen for what truth escapes without his tongue to first twist it."

"I hear you both," Hannibal said, "but we cannot deny that these people offer us much. Baal knows that we will all benefit if they are true to their word." He parted the tent flaps with the wedge of his hand and watched the receding backs of the Gauls and the escort that flanked them. "But do not think me misled in this. We can trust them no more than one does a captive wolf. We must hold close to our swords that which the chief values most highly. His heir; his people's future."

That evening Hannibal lay staring up at the fabric of the tent above him. He had to quash the whispered fears eating at his army's morale, and he had to do so in a single speech. He would offer encouragement to his men every step of the way, but he could not be seen to be fighting a losing battle, like a mother imploring her children to behave. He tried to compose in his mind the words he would say on the morrow, but each time he began, his thoughts ordered themselves differently and looped off in varying directions. He pushed all such thoughts from his head toward the middle hours of the night. He knew what his men needed to hear, what his father would have said. Best simply to stand before them and speak the truth as it came from his heart.

Having dismissed the subject, he worked his way through a catalog of other difficulties. He searched in his short conversation with Visotrex for signs of deception. He reviewed his knowledge of the names and histories of Gallic tribes, but could retrieve no memory of having heard of Visotrex. He did believe, however, that the young man he called his son was indeed his offspring. Fatherly pride is easy to spot and hard to hide. Hannibal knew the threat implicit in his securing the young man as hostage, but whether Visotrex would eschew any treachery to preserve his son's life he could not measure. He put the issue in its place and moved on.

He would press Visotrex for extra supplies as soon as he could: skins and furs, dried meats that were easily carried, footwear suited to ice and snow, grease for the men to cover their bare skin with. He would demand more than they could spare and therefore get somewhat more than they would like to give. He wondered if he should paint the elephants with a mixture of animal fat and herbs, as some had suggested. Vandicar was against it, but even he could not say what would become of the beasts. Hannibal needed them alive and impressive, especially for the descent into the Padus valley. His men would be weakened, half-starved, frostbitten, feverish by the time they emerged. The army he would speak to tomorrow bore little resemblance to the one that would stumble into Italy in several weeks' time, even as the current army was diminished from the one he had left Iberia with months ago. But if the elephants still walked upright they might distract the Carthaginians' enemies from their army's other weaknesses. Yes, they should be covered in animal fat, he decided. It could do them no harm, and he could not afford to neglect them.

He went once more through the mental map he had of the distribution of the Gallic tribes in the Padus valley, deciding on the best entry point, the preferred route by which to reach the Insubres and the Boii, the two tribes who were already in revolt against Rome. And he decided to issue a new warning to the camp followers: if they chose to follow farther, they would be tolerated only so long as they were not a burden. The first sign of delay or weakness and they would be dispatched and left unburied, unburned, unmourned, food for wolves. They should abandon this journey and make their way home as well as they could. He would say this, but he already knew it was too late. Cut off from the army, the camp followers would be pounced upon by marauding Gauls before an hour had passed. This issue decided, he went through others yet waiting for his attention. This list was long. Only when he felt sleep truly weighing heavy on his lids did he let his mind wander to Imilce, and that only for a few moments. More was hard to bear.

The next morning Hannibal stood on a rise before the gathering army. The ground was nowhere truly flat, but on the rolling, tree-dotted landscape the ranks of soldiers before him seemed to blanket all the habitable earth. Behind him, a slab of gray granite jutted up from the trees and stretched toward the sky—impressive, yes, but also a sign to his men that he would not be cowed by the scale of the mountains awaiting them. The Gallic envoy stood beside him. Together they watched the men march into position, first one contingent and then another, the various nationalities, differing in race and custom, in armor and preferred weaponry and artistry of shield and helmet. It might have looked like a conglomeration of brutes. It *was* a conglomeration of brutes. But there was order in it. The various parts made an unlikely whole.

Hannibal waited until the hush had settled and grown into an energy of its own. Sixty thousand men in silence, horses and elephants quiet as well, beyond them along the outskirts the camp followers, silent wraiths, seldom seen but always seeing. The commander held the silence still longer, listened to it build. Then, motioning so that the translators knew to begin, he turned and addressed Visotrex.

"What have our visitors to say to this?" he asked. "Does my army offend the eye, or is it a thing of wonder?"

Visotrex consulted with the others in his party. He answered that before him was the greatest army he had ever seen. "Truly," he said, "the world is Hannibal's to shape as he sees fit."

After waiting for the Gaul's response to reach the masses in their different tongues Hannibal asked, "Do you hear that? The elders of the Allobroges look upon you in fear. These old men who themselves live in this country you find so harsh . . . They see you as a mighty army, engaged in a quest like none the world has ever known. They see the greatness in you and have come to offer us safe passage through their lands. They wish to escort us through, just like the Cavares who led us this far. But what am I to say to them, when among you there is talk of fear? Talk of these mountains ahead of us. Of the Romans waiting to meet us on the other side. What do I say to these men who see before them an undefeatable army? Would you have me tell them of your doubts?"

He paused and let the various translations flow through the army. Visotrex said something to the Gallic translator, an Iberian trader Hannibal had employed since the Pyrenees. The man did not speak. He would not look Visotrex in the face but stared only at the ground below him. The Gaul nudged him angrily. Without meeting his gaze, the translator trudged away a short distance, turned, and set his gaze on the commander, completely ignoring the Allobroges.

Hannibal did not acknowledge the exchange. These words were meant for his army, not for Visotrex. When he began again, he spoke while on the move, slowly, with natural pauses so that the translations never lagged too far behind him. He walked close to the troops, strolling the various lines of them in easy appraisal, something humorous indicated in his gait. "Tell me truthfully, what's this I hear of fear in your hearts? I believed myself to be in the company of the heroes who carved up Iberia, who strode across the Pyrenees and hacked a path through tribe after tribe of barbarians. Is there not a man among your number named Harpolon, who slew the champion of the Volcae with one swing that loosed his head from the body that supported it?"

A confused murmur ran through the group, until one man held

his spear aloft and shouted that he answered to that name and that deed.

Hannibal stood for a moment on the balls of his feet to seek out the hero, then proceeded with his walk. "When pressed hard by the barbarians in the Pyrenees, did not a man named Trasis save his whole company by mounting a riderless stallion and singing them to re-form? Among us, is there not a young soldier named Vaca who was first over the wall of Arbocala? I believe that these are men to be praised, honors draped around them that they can carry all their days. But honors are nothing unless a man sees them through with further action. Would men still sing of Alexander the Great if he had retired from war and lived to be a hundred, fat and rich and fearful of the glories of his youth? No! The truth is that here in our company we have heroes awaiting a poet to immortalize them. But there are no poets to be found at the foot of the Alps. Nor in retreat across the Rhône. Not even in New Carthage itself. If you would have someone write your tale, you must first seat yourself in a Roman palace. From there call forth the best writers of the world. Call forth Greeks, who weave words so well. Dictate to them the deeds that will make you immortal. This is all within your power if you are men enough. If you are men enough . . ."

The commander repeated the last phrase slowly, questioning it, prodding them with it and with his gaze, which moved around, pausing on individuals and probing each as if he asked the question of him in particular. As the murmurs of the translators faded away Hannibal looked up and caught Bostar's eye; Bostar in turn motioned for a young squire. The boy ran forward, leading Hannibal's most recent mount, a stallion with a rusty brown coat so dark it neared black. Hannibal clucked his tongue in greeting. He took the reins from the squire, but instead of mounting he set the reins back over the horse's head and walked on, continuing his discourse. The horse followed of its own accord.

"As for those among you who care little for words to be spoken in later ages: Think, then, of riches. Think of bloody joy. The booty of conquest. Do you see the men of this mountain country? Even Gauls such as these once sacked Rome. They came home laden with all the riches their new slaves could carry, lingering joy written on their faces, dicks exhausted, hanging beneath them, dripping. . . . Why should they pleasure so and not us? Think about it. Are there any riders in the world equal to the Massylii? Any soldiers who can stand face-to-face with Libyans? Any race as determined as the Iberians? Any people as wildly brave as our Gallic allies? What do you think the Alps are, anyway? Are they anything more than rock and snow? Higher than the Pyrenees, yes, but what of it? The fact is this: No part of the earth reaches the roof of the sky; no height is insurmountable by determined men. We do not need to soar on wings to cross these mountains. We have our feet and our courage. That is all we need."

Hannibal, without waiting for a response, snapped around and strode toward his horse. He mounted and let the horse kick up into a short gallop. He paused a moment after the translations had straggled to a halt, then spread his arms. "Perhaps, my friends, you have forgotten whose army you fight in. Am I not Hannibal Barca? The child of a thunderbolt. Blessed of Baal and the seed of Hamilcar. If you forget your own courage, study mine. If you forget honor, look to me for its definition. If you doubt your destiny, know that I've never doubted mine. Imagine, my men, the view from the heights down upon the rich land of Italy. Let us end this story in a way that pleases the gods, on Mars Field, between the Tiber and the walls of Rome."

There followed the pause during which his words were passed from one dialect to another and absorbed. Hannibal knew that during the mumbling, multilingual hush thousands of eyes would stay fixed on him. He kept his arms aloft, fingers loose and open. With the pressure of his legs he directed his horse to move him before the troops. It was in that swaying, wings-spread posture that he heard his army's response.

The shouts of approval came first from the Carthaginians, as he had known they would: Bomilcar's booming voice; a call that he recognized as Mago's even though it had a strangely falsetto quality; Monomachus yelling the names of the gods best invoked in combat preparation. This was as he expected, but he knew the true reception of his speech when the Libyans answered him. From the central, African heart of the army came the deep-chested chorus of the heavy infantry. After that came a volley of shouts from the Balearic troops, their voices projected in bursts just as their missiles were in battle. Next the Numidians' voices rose in jackal-like ululations. And then the entire army bloomed into a ruckus of echoing, reverberating proportions. If there was doubt in any man's mind it was pummeled to silence by the cacophony of an army remembering itself, declaring its rebirth in a theater framed by granite.

Hannibal lowered his arms. He moved away, past the bewildered Allobroges and toward his quarters. This discourse completed successfully, he put it out of his mind and thought about the things to come, the dying that this alpine crossing was to be.

Carthage sprawled atop a craggy landscape that looked out onto curving stretches of pale beach. Many of its buildings were bleached as white as eggshells. Between them thronged such a variety of shapes and objects as to make a puzzle of urbanity, a confusion on the eye, a maze punctuated by obelisks and stout-columned temples. Here and there plumes of palms and spires of pines sprouted above the skyline, suggesting cool springs beneath, bubbling waters, a lushness Imilce had not expected. A city of almost a million people, all secured behind battlements that dwarfed those of New Carthage, higher by twice the measure, visibly stout, as if the architects wished to advertise the thickness of the walls. And beyond this throng of humanity, a cultivated landscape stretched farther than the eye could see, field upon field of wheat and barley, vineyards, orchards of dates and plums and olives.

Standing on the docks, Imilce could barely keep her balance. Nausea swelled in her and she had to fight back the urge to double over and grasp her abdomen. The world was supposed to be steady, her feet back on firm ground, but instead the dead stillness of the stone beneath her was a misery worse than the rocking of the boat. And worse still was the fact that only she seemed to notice this. People surged past her on all sides, men hefting urns, pulling sledges, loading packs atop mules. An elephant—far too near at hand for her comfort—dragged behind it a massive piece of furniture, exactly what she was not even sure. She was aware simultaneously of wealth and of poverty, of fragrant perfumes in one breath and the sweating stench of labor in the next. Though she looked from one thing to the next the sights cluttered her mind instead of resulting in order. She touched on forms without registering the meaning behind them. She had to reach out to steady herself and was surprised to realize she had grasped Sapanibal's arm. The older woman looked askance at her, not sharply but with her usual air of silent criticism.

"Come," she said, "there will be a carriage waiting."

Imilce swallowed down the taste from her belly and walked. She realized that many of those moving around her were attending them and the stores of gifts and personal items they had brought with them. Her maid was at her other elbow, and Little Hammer clung to her, his eyes wide and hungry for this new world. Inside the small carriage, Imilce sat stiff as her maid placed Hamilcar on her lap. She placed a hand over his knees, hoping that the boy would hold still and let her think. But he would not. Even this cramped enclosure offered many things of interest: the polished wood frame around them, the gold buttons sewn into the padded fabric abutting the women's knees, the view of the passing world through the carriage door. Imilce reached up and tugged a curtain across the opening. A moment later Hamilcar grabbed the material in two fists and buried his face in it, finding in this act an unreasoned joy that translated throughout his body. The mother had a sudden desire to squeeze him tightly, two-handed across his belly. But instead she pulled him back and pinned him to her chest. She kept her eyes lowered for the rest of the jolting ride, taking no comfort in it, enjoying no luxury despite the soft fabric and the cushion beneath her.

Sapanibal glanced at her several times throughout the ride but said nothing.

By the time she entered the Chamber of the Palms at her mother-in-law's palace, Imilce walked on unsteady legs. Her insides moved and shifted of their own accord, threatening to spill up and out of her in waves that came without rhythm but often. It was good, at least, to be out of the sun, away from the heat and bustle of the streets. She listened to the wooden door as it swung shut behind them, heard the bolt driven into place. She moved forward behind Sapanibal into a reception area as cool as an ancient forest. Granite pillars grew up from the stone slabs like the trunks of giant trees. The ceiling must have been wooden, but it was planed smooth and painted a dark crimson. The walls were not really so far away, the room not really that large, but the rows of pillars several deep gave the space a feeling of cramped grandeur. Something about it even stilled young Hamilcar. He went limp in his nurse's arms, tilted his head back, and stared, openmouthed, at the ceiling.

Sapanibal halted in the central area of the room, a greater space as one pillar was missing. There were chairs and low sofas nearby, but they did not sit down. Sapanibal stood with her hands clasped before her and was silent for a time. Then she said, "We'll wait here."

A few moments later, a door at the far end of the chamber swung open, pushed on its wooden hinges by two adolescent boys, each bent to the task. Behind the swinging barricade came Didobal, widow of Hamilcar Barca, mother of the pride of lions now at war with Rome. Attendants framed her on either side and from behind, young and old women in colorful dress. A boy walked at her side, his head a platform on which she rested her left hand.

Imilce had conjured absolutely no image of this woman ahead of time and therefore her appearance was always to have been a revelation. And indeed it was that. Imilce knew that Didobal's mother was of native stock, from the Theveste people who lived south of Carthage, but she was still surprised at the richness of Didobal's skin, darker than any of her sons'. Her eyes sat widely spaced and her cheekbones were high, rounded, and regal. Her hair, woven into an intricate crosshatching of tight braids, was black, thick. From her first glimpse of the Barca matriarch, Imilce knew that she was not a woman easily deceived. Though she did not exactly know why, this realization troubled her.

Sapanibal greeted her mother with a formality Imilce had never seen in her. She touched one knee to the floor, bowed her head, and pressed her hands to her forehead, ready to receive her mother's blessing. Didobal stepped up close to her, studying her as if she might not positively recognize her. Sapanibal whispered a prayer of greeting, speaking reverently, admitting her debt to this woman for her very creation and invoking the blessings of Tanit, the mother goddess of Carthage.

Didobal heard all this indifferently. "Rise, dear," she said. "I know what you owe, and I know that you know it as well."

Sapanibal released the woman's hand and straightened. She stood with her arms stiff at her sides, chin upraised in a posture wholly out of character.

"You have not aged well," Didobal said. "There was always too much of your father's mother in you, too much of the East. But I have made peace with that long ago. You are distinguished in your own way, and you are welcome here. It will give your sister joy to see you. Tell me of this other one now, daughter."

Released from scrutiny by that simple sentence, Sapanibal resumed herself. She half turned toward Imilce and said, "Mother, this is Hannibal's beloved, Imilce, daughter of a chief of the Baetis named Ilapan. She is known as a beauty and is fertile as well, for she has borne us a son, the first male of his generation."

Didobal would have known all of this already, but she rested her gaze on Imilce and nodded as her daughter spoke. Imilce knew something of how to greet Carthaginian women, but still she felt completely unprepared for this encounter and wondered how she had ever gotten to this point without thinking more of this moment. When Sapanibal paused, Imilce imitated her formal greeting, her hands outstretched from her forehead, head parallel to the ground, one knee against the cool stone beneath her. It seemed to take forever for the woman to acknowledge her with a touch. Fleeting and brief though it was, Didobal's fingers left a scent on hers, a perfume carried in an oily lotion that Imilce was to smell for days after. She heard the woman bid her rise.

"You have a delicate face," Didobal said.

"Thank you," Imilce murmured. She tried to look at Didobal directly but this was no easy thing. The woman's eyes were not hers alone but were also those of her son, deep-set, of a similar color, and with the same simmering intelligence. Strange that the quality of the mind behind the eyes can be conveyed through them. Imilce knew she would never be able to look at Didobal without seeing her husband. What she did not know yet was whether this was going to be a blessing or a curse.

"If my son married for beauty alone, then he chose well," Didobal said, "but old ones such as me know that counts for little. There is more to a woman than her face and bosom. More even than her abundance in childbearing. I told my son this in writing and he assured me more substance was to be found within you. He asked of me the patience to see you slowly. I will grant him that. But, daughter, I have no love for your country. It's a mistress that has kept my men from me for too many years. This is hard to forgive. . . . But now, before we take our leisure, let me see my son's child."

Imilce motioned to her maid, who offered her Little Hammer. She held him awkwardly on her hip. The child was surprisingly still, his fists clamped tight around folds of his mother's gown.

Didobal frowned: The view was not sufficient. She slipped her dark hands around the boy and pried him away from his mother. Hamilcar seemed ready to protest, but he paused before doing so, unsure how such an action would be dealt with. Didobal took a few steps away and studied him in a shaft of light that cut down diagonally from a window high on the wall.

Imilce wished she had answered more strongly. She should have said that Carthage was her country now and it was war that was their men's mistress, not any particular nation. She should have said that she too regretted that her husband was always away, always in danger. She should have said many things, she thought, but they were already dead inside her. Silent, she glanced up at the ceiling. Her eyes were first attracted by the flight of a tiny bird, but then lingered up there because of the sudden suspicion that the ceiling was not solid at all but was a dark liquid threatening to drop down on them in a sudden deluge. It was hard to pull her eyes away from it.

Didobal turned around. Her façade was composed and calm as before, but her eyes tinged a watery red. She handed the boy back, not to Imilce but to the maid. She half turned away, but paused long enough to say, "Come. You are welcome in my house."

Imilce searched the woman's profile for any sign of the emotions behind it. But there was nothing to betray her thoughts. Viewed from the side and heavy-lidded, her eye was flat and without perspective, a single dimension and therefore harder to read.

The interview over, Didobal withdrew. The two women waited a moment as the matriarch's servants escorted her out, like insects buzzing protectively around their queen.

Though Didobal did not speak directly to Imilce again that day, she formally introduced her to the aristocracy of Carthage. The women greeted her as if modeling themselves on the matriarch: aloof, distant, grandiose, indicating in their words and gestures that she had yet to prove herself to them. The men were a little kinder, but clearly, however, this was not a measure of true respect but of an irreverent flirtation. They commented upon Hannibal's good fortune in winning her, upon his epicurean eye. They alluded to the women the commander could have chosen from, the others he must have sampled prior to her, the attentions she could, in turn, wring from the besotted hearts of other men.

Despite even these flatteries, the essence conveyed throughout the afternoon was that she was not very important. Her presence was of note for two reasons: her link to her long-absent husband, and the role she filled as mother to another generation of Barcas. They asked again and again about her son, and told her again and again about her husband, as if she did not actually know the man but was in need of education by these Carthaginians, people who, despite their distance from him in space and time, seemed to believe they knew him better than she. She felt increasingly ill at ease throughout the afternoon. Her stomach still churned and protested within her. Cramps racked her from low in the pelvis, radiating up.

In a lull before the evening's activities, Imilce excused herself to go to her bath chambers. There, as she squatted to relieve herself, she discovered the reason for her physical symptoms. They were not borne of the day's stresses alone, but were the long forgotten symptoms of her monthly bleeding, which she had not had since the blessed month she became pregnant with Little Hammer. How many moons had passed since last this flow issued from her? How many years? She had hoped that Hannibal's seed would somehow take hold in her again—even before she knew that her cycle had resumed—but clearly this had not happened.

Still squatting, she let herself lean back against the stone wall. She grasped her head in her hands and squeezed; she did not know why. She thought of Hannibal—wherever he might be at that moment—and she silently chastised him for leaving her alone with all of this.

Sophonisba appeared like an answer to prayers Imilce had not even uttered. Hannibal's youngest sibling approached Imilce in the garden of the palace in the early evening light. She carried two small goblets, one of which she offered up. They had met earlier in the afternoon but had exchanged only nods and the routines of greeting.

"Have you tried this?" Sophonisba asked. "It's a wine made from the fruit of palm trees. It's a poor person's drink, but Mother is fond of it and always has a little on hand. We should drink discreetly, though. Come, talk with me by the fish ponds."

Sophonisba could not have been more than twelve or thirteen, just budding with the first indications of the woman she was to become. But she walked this line between childhood and maturity nimbly, with a confidence that touched Imilce with shame. And it only took her a few glances to realize that Sophonisba was at the verge of a monumental beauty. She was her mother's daughter, in her forehead and the character of her cheekbones and in her nose, but her skin tone was the lightest of all her siblings' and her mouth was narrower, a soft, full oval. Imilce felt her own appearance wanting beside this girl. Fortunately, Sophonisba did not agree.

"You're the most graceful woman in Carthage," she said. "The others will be jealous, so pay them no mind. One would think you were carved by an artist instead of born from between a woman's legs. And your baby . . . Mother was beside herself. You cannot tell it to look at her now, but this afternoon she went to her chambers and cried, thinking about him. She hasn't done that since she learned of my father's death."

Imilce held the palm wine without lifting it. "Did the child so disappoint her?"

"Disappoint?" Sophonisba asked. She ridged her forehead in a manner that temporarily rendered her surprisingly unattractive. Then she dropped the expression and all was as before. "She was moved to tears of joy. She beheld her firstborn grandson for the first time today. She saw her son in his face and in that is her husband's face made immortal. No, she was not disappointed. What she felt was . . . It was rapture."

Imilce stared at her for a moment.

Noting the look, Sophonisba stepped closer. She said, "Though I am just a girl, I think perhaps we can be friends. Would you like that?"

Imilce nodded. "Very much."

"Good. As my service to you, I will tell you everything there is to know about Carthage. Everything important, at least. But first, you must speak to me. Tell me of my brothers. I've not seen any of them save Mago in years. Truthfully, sister, I do not remember my other brothers at all. Tell me about them, and then about other young men. The noble ones. I am as yet unmarried. There is a boy here, a Massylii prince named Masinissa, who is quite taken with me. He says he will have me for his wife someday. Have you heard of him?"

"No," Imilce answered.

A ripple of disappointment passed over the girl's face. "Well . . . You will in years to come. I might have him as a husband, but not without knowing something of real men, men of action. Masinissa is handsome, but he is as yet a boy. So, tell me. Talk. I will hold my tongue while you do."

Though the girl did hold her tongue, Imilce began slowly. She wanted to convey how much Sophonisba had just done for her, how she was awash in relief and affection. How only this girl among all those whom Imilce had so far met had spoken to her with an open face. But she had not been asked this, so instead she cleared her throat, sipped the palm wine, and answered all of Sophonisba's questions as completely as she could. Though she carried on bleeding, silently, secretly, she knew she could bear this world a little longer.

When he first heard about the Roman legions' arrival in northern Iberia, Hanno desperately wished that he possessed his eldest brother's brilliance, or Mago's intelligence, or Hasdrubal's boldness. But he also remembered that he had left them all months before, with farewells given through gritted teeth. The last time he spoke with Hannibal, the words between them had boiled almost to violence. It was the nearest Hanno had come since they were adolescents to lashing out physically at his brother. There had been a time when they often fought each other to the ground and came away bruised and bloody. But as they both became more adept at warcraft they seemed to recognize a tendril of threat that they dared not touch. Still, when Hannibal ordered him to stay south of the Pyrenees Hanno suffered through a few moments of wanting to swing for his brother's head with something heavy and sharp. It was not just the order. It was the timing as well, the evening he received it, and the host of things it suggested his brother knew of and thought about him.

He had begun the night drinking the local wine with Mago, Bostar, Adherbal, and Silenus. Adherbal spoke of a correspondence he had received from Archimedes, the Syracusan mathematician, detailing theories he thought applicable to military defenses. Silenus remarked that he had once dined with Archimedes—raw oysters, if he remembered correctly, eaten on a patio abutting the sea rocks, from which they watched boys pull their meal directly out of the water. A short while later, Silenus interrupted Bostar midsentence. The secretary had just mentioned the suggestion that new coins be struck bearing Hannibal's likeness on one side, with words naming him conqueror of Italy on the obverse. Silenus found this premature.

"One cannot count a victory accomplished in advance," he said. "Consider the Aetolians just a few years ago. They were certain that their siege of Medion was soon to prove victorious. So much so, that as they neared the date for their annual elections the retiring leaders argued that they should have a say in distributing the spoils and receive credit for the victory by having their names engraved on commemorative shields. The soon-to-be-elected objected. If the siege succeeded on the first day they were in office, well, so be it. Must be the will of the gods! And so only their names should go on the shields. Of course, neither party could accede to an agreement that gave the other the honor, so they resolved that whoever was leading them when the siege succeeded they would all share the spoils with their predecessors. Very high-minded of them, don't you think? Very egalitarian, to use a word you may not be familiar with. They even worked out the inscription they were to engrave on their shields to commemorate the victory."

"And your point?" Bostar asked.

"I am just now reaching it. Demetrius of Macedon had hired himself to help the Medionians. His contingent of five thousand Illyrians landed on the very evening after this resolution was passed. They met the surprised Aetolians the next morning, dislodged them from their positions, and trounced them. So much for their sure victory. On the day following, the Medionians and Illyrians met to discuss the issue of the shields and how they should be inscribed. They chose to use the same structure the Aetolians had decided upon, inscribing both the names of the present Aetolian commanders and those of the favored candidates for the following year. They made one change, however. Instead of writing that the city was won by the Aetolian commander, they wrote that it had been won *from* the same commander. Clever, yes? A single word altered and yet with such significance."

Silenus leaned back and hefted his goblet. "Do not count your cause prematurely victorious. That is my point. And do not put your hubris in writing, for some quick mind will surely find fault with it."

The Carthaginians answered this with the usual guffaws and good-humored jesting. All except for Hanno. He had never been fond of Silenus, but of late it seemed that the Greek irritated him every time he parted his lips. His mouth even had an insolent shape. It was too narrow, too full toward the middle, pursed slightly, as if Silenus were always on the verge of blowing a kiss. The others did not seem to notice it, but the Greek's smugness was unbearable.

Later, when he found himself walking toward his tent with the verbose Greek beside him, he listened just to see how long Silenus would rattle on before he realized that his words were falling on deaf ears. When Silenus stepped inside Hanno's tent unbidden Hanno still believed he was on the verge of strangling him. And yet that is not exactly what transpired.

Seating himself on a low couch that had recently belonged to a tribal leader, Silenus unplugged another vase of wine. He kicked his wiry legs up beside him and tugged his short tunic into place with his free hand. As he poured, he said, "You're a hard nut to crack, Hanno. Do not take that amiss. What I mean is that I've been watching you. Watching you watch others, myself included. An interesting study, I promise you. But it is the way you look at your brother that I've yet to figure out. You sometimes look upon Hannibal with . . . What's the word I mean?"

"Like all men who know him," Hanno said, "I trust my brother's wisdom."

"But you are not 'all men.' He is your brother, for one thing."

"Yes, we are fingers of a hand," Hanno said.

Silenus smiled at this, pursed his lips, and then smiled again. He seemed to have a response, which at first he waved away, but then could not help but speak. "Who is the long pointer of this hand, then? Who is the thumb, and who the little runt on the end? Tell me truthfully, Hannibal wears heavy on you at times, yes? His eyes are ever judging. He sees weaknesses less observant men miss."

Hanno formed a casual rebuttal to all of this, words expressing nothing but disdain for the topic. About to deliver it, he caught the spark of amusement in the Greek's eyes and knew that his re-hearsed words would sound dead even as they left his tongue. Instead, he snapped, "It is not my fault that my brother disapproves of my inclinations."

"Of course it isn't. Who meets Hannibal's standards but Hannibal himself?"

Hanno took the wooden cup Silenus proffered and brought it to his mouth immediately, feeling the bite of the wine against his chapped lips. He found, without either realizing it or being surprised by it, that he was inclined to speak, to fill the Greek's unusual silence with confessions.

"Do I feel his eyes always upon me?" he asked. "Yes. Even when his back is turned toward me. If I take one moment of luxury, one pleasure, he looks askance at me. This from a man richer than most who have ever lived, from a family and a people who love wealth and fine things. He seems to think I am weak just for being true to my people."

"Does he see the same weakness in Hasdrubal? That one certainly takes his pleasure unsparingly."

Hanno realized his palms were sweaty and his chest tingled as if he were approaching an enemy to do battle. Just a few moments had passed, but he had no idea why he had spoken as he just had. "This is no business of yours," he said. "As usual, you forget yourself."

"I apologize," Silenus said, "but, Barca, you are a difficult script to read. Have you ever wondered what your life would have been if you'd been the firstborn of your mother?"

"The same as it is now."

"How do you mean? Would you have been the leader of the army then? Hanno, the Supreme Commander of the Army of Carthage . . . Or would that title have gone to your brother, as it does now, but somehow skipping over the eldest? I mean, in which way would it have been the same?"

"It is a foolish question," Hanno said. "A philosopher's trick. You may speak circles around me, but the world is as it is. No other way. This talk bores me, Silenus. You bore me."

"Are you sure of that?" Silenus asked. He dropped a leg down from the couch, exposing his inner thigh for a moment. "Sometimes it seems to me that what you feel for me is not boredom, not distaste at all, but rather a certain hunger. We Greeks understand this hunger better than any. I possess the tools for this training in abundance, my friend. In abundance. Perhaps you should have me school you in it."

"Perhaps," Hanno finally said.

Silenus, his face quite near the other man's, grumbled an affirmative, a sound from low in his throat, stretched out. "Yes," he said. "Perhaps . . ."

The Greek let the word and the possibilities presented by it linger in the air between them. Again, Hanno felt the overwhelming desire to lash out. But he knew the feeling was not simple anger at all. It was, as Silenus said, a certain hunger. He wanted to press his mouth to the Greek's and silence him with the force of his lips and tongue. He wanted to lift him bodily and throw him down and teach him that they were equal in body if not in wit. He had never considered that he harbored such passion for this one, with his thin frame and bowed legs and his too-large head and the arrogance that bound it all together. He was no warrior. No specimen of manly beauty. And yet Hanno wanted him with an urgency that punched him low in the abdomen. He wanted brutal, intimate violence, and he had never understood this fully until that moment.

A call from outside his tent interrupted his revelation. Hanno answered hoarsely, and a messenger said that Hannibal wished to see him. "The commander apologizes for the late council," the voice said, "but he would speak to you presently in his tent."

Silenus raised a single eyebrow and finished the sentence he had started ages ago: ". . . and perhaps not," he said. "In any event, not just now." He drew himself up and looked around as if to gather his things.

Hanno did not move anything except his eyes, which followed as Silenus rose and made his way toward the tent flap.

The Greek glanced back briefly before departing. "Give my best to your brother."

A few moments later, Hanno wove his way through camp. Somewhere a lone musician worked out a melody on a bone whistle. Campfires illumed various quadrants with a low glow, as if a thick, moisture-laden blanket hovered somewhere just above the height of a man's head and allowed no light to rise above it. As he passed a tethered horse the creature let flow with a stream of urine. The splash was so loud and abrupt that Hanno started. He slid half a step to the side, steadied himself, and glanced around. Nobody was in sight. He cursed the horse under his breath.

Hannibal's tent flap was open to the night. The commander sat on his three-legged stool, studying a scroll on the table before him. He did not rise to greet Hanno, but took in his attire with a long look. Having seen enough, he bent his head back to the tablet. "I've called you from leisure, have I?"

Hanno had no wish to name the activity he had been called from. "I thought I might find you the same," he said. "The men are at pleasure. . . . Will you never stop to savor your victories, brother?"

Hannibal answered without looking up. "At the end of a day, do you praise yourself for having lived through it? Do you not know that after the night comes the dawn of a new day? When you exhale a breath in one moment, do you believe you have accomplished greatness? Or do you remember that the very next moment you must draw another breath and begin again? A thousand different forces would love to see me fail. I cannot abandon my vigilance for a moment. That is what it means to command. Perhaps you will understand this fully someday. Come closer and sit down, if it pleases you."

Hanno took a few steps forward, just two bites of the distance between them, no more.

"Hanno, I know that you've not been happy with my decision about your role, but I've thought it through and my mind is unchanged. You will stay on here and watch over the Suessetani. They'll need a strong hand to keep them subdued. I am sure you understand the importance of this. See Bostar in the morning. He is preparing written details for you: names and familial affiliations of these people, geography and accounts of resources. You should learn more of the local tongue as well. We'll get you a tutor. I would only ask that you keep your pleasures in check. Remember, the knife that killed our brother-in-law found him in his bed."

The interview was over. Hanno, like any common officer, had been dismissed. He flushed hot, felt a leaden pressure behind his eyes. Though he told himself to turn and throw open the tent flap and stride away he did not do so. He could not make his feet move.

"Am I so worthless to you?" he asked.

Hannibal, without looking up or changing his posture or tone, said, "You are my brother and I need a trusted commander here."

"Have you never considered that I, too, want to kick open the gates of Rome?"

This brought up the other's gaze. "I've never had to consider it. The answer can be assumed by the blood within your veins. But why do you question me? This post is no punishment. It is my will. You'll adhere to it. If I am ever to ask great things of you I must know that you will serve me unquestioningly. You have not always achieved that in the past. Consider this a new opportunity."

Again, Hannibal bent his head and signaled the discourse was concluded. But again Hanno spoke ahead of himself. "In one breath you say that this assignment is not a slight," he said. "In the next you name my faults. But what's true? Speak plainly to me! You owe me that much."

"I did not know that I was in your debt," Hannibal said. "I thought perhaps you were in mine."

Hanno—watching his brother's brow, the artery that beat high on it, the eyes running over the words—knew that it was within him to kill his brother. It was a quiet thought, really. There was something comforting in it. An escape he had not imagined before. No matter what might come afterward, it was within the realm of possibility that he could murder; that Hannibal could die. On this ultimate of things they were equally balanced. With that thought in his mind, Hanno spun and trudged from his brother's tent. He avoided him in the following days and parted from him as if they were enemies and not siblings at all. He pushed thoughts of Silenus from his mind. He had never before felt shame at his desires, but there was something different about the scribe and the depth of the turmoil he fueled inside him.

Now, two months later, a lieutenant brought him the news he feared. A legion under Gnaeus Scipio had landed at Emporiae, a Greek settlement that had refused a Carthaginian alliance. The Romans had been welcomed joyously. They numbered easily twice the ten thousand soldiers Hanno controlled and made it no secret that their aim was to hunt down Hanno, and quickly.

"We must send word to Hasdrubal," Hanno said during a meeting of his officers. "We don't have the numbers to meet them."

A lieutenant, though junior to Hanno in both rank and age, shook his head. "There can be no reinforcements. Hasdrubal is south of New Carthage. A message has already been dispatched to him, but we must act independently."

"Decisively," another added.

Hanno pressed the flat of his palms over his eyes and dug his fingers into his flesh. An unusual gesture for a general, but he ignored the nervous shuffling of the officers. His bowels twisted and pulled knots and his chest felt constricted, as if with each released breath a strap pulled tighter across his chest so that he was denied a full inhalation of air. Should he act decisively? Of course he should. It could do him no good to wait. The Romans might land more troops. They might forge alliances with the Iberians and learn the features of the land and find ways to gain advantage. They would only become stronger with passing days. And Hasdrubal might still not reach him. But Hanno had no plan. What could he do to make their numbers more equal? Why did he have to struggle with this question? He should have had more men. It was Hannibal's misjudgment that had created this situation. He left him here to manage the Iberians, but not truly prepared to fight a Roman legion. Still, still, he had to act! Perhaps he could catch the Romans off guard with a full frontal attack, before they had even settled in. They would never expect such boldness. Surely, this was the way to proceed. And if his gamble rebounded on him? Well, at least Hannibal could not chastise him for hesitation as he had at Saguntum.

Hanno finally peeled his fingers from his forehead. He looked around at the junior officers and gave them his decision. It was a choice for which he was to suffer terribly.

The first boulder announced itself with a tremor, a rumble that came from no specific direction but was transmitted through the bones of the earth itself. Mago felt it in the soles of his feet. When he saw it—a chunk of stone as large as an elephant, gray just like those beasts, first sliding down a sheer section of cliff at near free fall, then striking the slope and churning, end over slow end, snapping and pushing trees out of its path—he thought the commotion of the army had loosened it. The boulder landed on the ravine floor a short distance away, crushing under it a mule and the two men driving it. Then the whole scene flooded with a dusty confusion and a rain of smaller stones. And that was just the beginning.

The army had made steady progress in the days leading up to this one, but they spent the bulk of the fourth day winding into a narrow defile. They had to travel a few abreast, for the rock walls closed in on either side, sometimes rising up vertically around them. Mago rode near the vanguard, with the bulk of the cavalry and the two Allobroge guides, while Hannibal brought up the rear with corps of infantry. They progressed awkwardly, negotiating the stream that wound in front of them at each step, climbing over rocks, managing the horses, convincing the elephants that nothing was amiss. The line must have stretched for miles; the front of the column could not see the rear, and communication between them was difficult. It was a perfect trap.

A chorus of shouts went up from high above, followed by spears thrown down in a coordinated hail. The bulk of a freshly hewn tree careened to earth in a spray of pine needles. More boulders fell, and smaller stones, and more trees. The damage they did was amplified by fright. Pack ponies made easy targets and when wounded began to scream in pain. A few bolted and this maddened others. They looked wide-eyed around them and kicked out at the men trying to steady them. They bared their teeth, for they were not sure who was causing this alarm and believed it to be anyone who sought to control them. Mounts steady and calm in battle were caught off guard by this, and more than one threw its rider. And the elephants . . . They had been spread along the lead of the column and this was fortunate. Mago watched a single creature, maddened by three darts in the back, as it roared down the narrow passageway, trying to flee, knocking over carts, trampling men, and butting horses out of its path.

"General," Maharbal called, "what is your command?"

Mago spun and called out, asking the question he already knew the answer to. "The Gallic guides—where were they? Somebody grapple them," he said, but his order was unanswered in the chaos, and the Gauls were nowhere to be seen. He scanned the heights for some way to dislodge the attackers, but there was no clear route. And, it now seemed, there were too many of them up there to deal with quickly even if they could gain the heights. It was clear the head of the column was outside of the main danger, but any sense of relief this provided was short-lived.

Gauls poured out of a ravine a short distance ahead of Mago's position. In an instant they cut the army in half and inflicted terrible damage on the confused Iberian unit they met. They worked under a protective cover of spears thrown down from a knob on the cliffside that offered a view up and down the ravine. It was clear that this was the center of the ambushers' operations. Mago noted as much. He was to the rear of the Iberian soldiers, but rushed forward to direct their charge. A few moments' observation changed his mind. Stones of all sizes fell among them, denting helmets and knocking them at strange angles on the wearers' heads, battering shields more forcefully than the blows of any sword. He saw one man impaled through the foot by a spear, pinning the limb to the ground. The man threw his head back in a howl of pain that Mago could not hear for the other noises. It was short-lived anyway. Stationary target that the man now was, two other spears pierced him. One slammed through his lower back and out his pelvis. A death wound if ever there was one.

Mago called for an ordered retreat, which was easier requested than accomplished. A sliver of rock sheared from high above fell among them. It was as tall as a man and twice as thick. It impaled the path like a spearhead. The men around it stood back in horror. When it stayed upright, however, they dismissed the threat of it and moved around either side of it like water around an obstacle. There seemed no end to the confusion. No end to the objects hurled down on them. Mago was kicked in the flat of his upraised palm by a frenzied stallion. The blow spun him with a force he thought might have shattered the bones of his fingers. But his hand was only bruised, and it tingled the rest of the day.

He did not reach Hannibal's council until after dark, traveling in stealth with a small contingent of guards. He found the officers huddled around a fire in the cover of a lean-to, talking in low voices that betrayed their fatigue and dejection. As he stepped into the circle of firelight, Bomilcar rose and grasped him in a quick, painful embrace. The big man tended to be both ferocious and affectionate after battles. "You are sound?" he asked.

"Yes, but only by the whim of the gods. Monomachus was right," Mago said, nodding at the taciturn general. "This was treachery planned thoroughly. How did you fare back—"

He did not complete the question. His eyes were drawn to one among the group and this silenced him. Visotrex' son sat among them, leaning back against a pack, still as one contemplating the fire. Mago stood gaping at him. Though he had just witnessed a day of carnage, something in the young man's presence beside the fire seemed even more horrific. His jaw hung open and his eyes stared straight before him. The damage to him was not obvious, and yet it was clear that he had been dead several hours now, his skin a pale greenish blue.

Hannibal had looked up long enough to study his brother, to inventory his body parts and verify his health. Then he lowered his gaze and watched the fire. Bostar answered Mago's unfinished question. They had suffered badly, he explained. Four hundred dead among the Libyans, for example. If they had not placed their best infantrymen to their rear the army might have been wholly lost. They had faced about at a moment's notice and fought with a resolution that would have impressed even Spartans. Bomilcar asked Mago his news and he confirmed what they had already been told. The army was cut in half, spread thin, its entire length overseen by hostiles who held all the high ground. This information given, the council fell silent, awaiting the direction of their commander.

When Hannibal spoke his voice betrayed a melancholy unusual to him. He did not look at Mago directly, but it was clear he was answering his brother's unasked questions about the Gaul. "Just before it started I had been talking to him of his people's customs and of his family. Do you know that he is the father of two children, twins? Two girls? I had, for a moment, convinced myself that he was being true with me. That his people were to be true to their word."

"They nearly destroyed us, Hannibal," Bomilcar said. His deep voice made the statement hard to refute.

"I know. I know. It was my sword that slit his belly. It does confound me, though, that men should be so foolish. This Gaul need not be walking in his underworld right now. Nor should my men have suffered so."

Bomilcar spoke louder, as if his commander's hearing was in question. "Had they destroyed us they would be the richest tribe in these accursed mountains. That's all the reason they needed."

Hannibal studied the fire a moment longer. "Quite so," he eventually said. "Mago, just before you arrived I realized something. When the first rocks rolled down and the cries of alarm went up, this Gaul jumped back as if to draw his weapon. I beat him to it and sank my own into his belly. Such was the bargain his father traded him into. But what seemed odd to me then was the look of astonishment he fixed on me. It was an honest look, the face of a man just realizing he'd been deceived. Do you know what I am saying?"

Mago thought that he did. "Visotrex had not told him of the planned ambush. His own son . . ."

"What kind of man would do that? It is right for a father to die for the sake of his son, but not the other way around. Not like this. What is the honorable means of burial for these Gauls?"

They all looked to Bostar. He shrugged at first, but then offered, "I believe they make elevated platforms, wrap the body tight in skins, and post mourners to keep away the wild beasts."

Hannibal nodded. "Let that be done. I will not see his body defiled more than it already has been by his father's avarice. Who will carry out this rite?"

The group was silent. And the one who answered did so without speaking. Monomachus grunted a reproach to his fellows, strode forward, and grasped the Gaul around one thick ankle. He dragged him away by it, like a laborer resignedly accepting one last chore for the day.

When the sound of the body scraping across the ground faded and only the crackling of the fire could be heard, Hannibal said, "I can feel already the strains on my humanity." He inhaled, drew himself up, and retrieved his commander's voice. "Now, we've much to do tonight. Sit down with us, Mago. Remember that half of our army is separated from us. We've had no word as to how they manage. We must devise a method to unite with them. The way must be opened."

The younger Barca thought about this. "It can be. I will tell you how," he said.

Later that night under the cover of cloudy darkness, Mago led a small force out. They gained some height by shimmying behind a flake of granite that led to a hidden chamber, which provided access to a zigzagging route up a nearly sheer stone face. Several times Mago doubted he could find a route that would bring them up as high as the protrusion from which the Allobroges coordinated their attack. But his whispered prayers seemed to help them onward. They were in place a couple of hours before dawn. Mago, from hiding, studied on the Gauls' fires, caught occasional breaths of their

conversation. For a time he heard the sonorous rhythm of someone's snoring, so loud he sent a few scouts to investigate it. But the
offender could not be found near at hand.

At the first light of dawn they sprang. The Gauls, unprepared,
were slaughtered over their morning meal. Another rain of spears
fell, but this time it was the Gauls pinned to the ground beneath
them. The way was opened. The two arms of the Carthaginian force
joined again. Though the army could not command all the heights of
the ambush gorge, they did march through, suffering still more men
dead, climbing over bodies, following in the swath of fear the elephants cut through the barbarians. When the gorge widened they
gained some relief. They halted in a section of the valley open to the
blameless sky that did not toss down boulders or trees or darts.

The ground was flat and easily defended, snow-dusted, with an
enormous rock at one end, upon which lookouts were posted. If
the Allobroges were to attack here, they would have to fight as a
massed army. Fatigued and injured though they were, many among
Hannibal's troops welcomed such an encounter for the opportunity
to pay back the wrongs done to them. But there was no sign that the
enemy cared to pursue them further, except in small bands that attacked stragglers. Mago figured that the work of scavenging from
the dead in the gorge was enough to keep the Allobroges occupied
for a week. The army spent two uneventful days nursing wounds,
numbering the dead and the missing, taking stock of the injured animals and lost supplies, welcoming the stray soldiers and camp followers who trickled into camp, a testament to human resilience, to
the dumb, animal instinct for survival.

It seemed no time had passed at all when Hannibal had the horns
sounded early on the third morning. They were to march on. The
soldiers rose damp from their slumber, pulled their clothing tight
against the chill. They looked for the sun, but the sky hung low and
heavy with cloud. As they rose the roof of the world descended to
meet them. Snow. It began in mid-morning, first one giant flake and
then another. Many of the men had never seen the likes of it before.
The Tartesians pulled red ribbons from their bags and wrapped
them tight around their heads with ceremonial import. The Libyans

tried vainly to avoid the flakes, lest they be weapons of Gallic magic. They dodged and wove, so serious in their alarm that the northern Iberians fell to the ground in fits of laughter. Tribesmen from the center of Iberia simply stopped, dropped their loads, and stared about them, gape-mouthed and indignant. The Numidians watched this all with disdainful eyes. They murmured to each other from horseback and tried to appear calm, although few could help but swat the gathering flakes from their arms and shoulders, quick gestures as one might use to dislodge scorpions.

Mago himself felt a growing sense of dread, but before it could take hold of him completely Hannibal acted. The commander dismounted at a central spot among the men and chided them for fearing puffs of white less substantial than pigeon feathers. He tilted his head up and caught the flakes on his tongue, encouraging others to do the same. His beard had grown thick over the last few weeks, but there was no disguising the smile of mirth hidden beneath it. He scooped up snow in his hands, shaped it into a ball and hurled it at his brother. Mago stared in bewilderment, unmoving, as the ball exploded on his chest. A moment later Hannibal repeated the maneuver, this time splattering a Numidian's upraised arm. Soon the men caught on and balls of snow cut through the air in all directions, men shouting and laughing. In a matter of moments, the soldiers remembered themselves. They often looked spear and arrows in the eye—what had they to fear from snow? The light mood changed, however, when Balearics began to fling ice balls from their slings. The impact of these on their targets was too much like actual warfare. With effort, Hannibal reined the men in and ordered the march to proceed.

Within a few hours, the snow had lost its strange aura and become a commonplace annoyance. It fell even more steadily, the flakes smaller but vast in number. White blanketed the stones and earth around them. It hung on tree branches and gathered on the soldiers' shoulders, atop their heads and helmets. They fought the cold with their labor, trudging forward beneath their armor and packs and weapons, but the furnace within them was dim, and it faded as the day progressed. Their naked arms and legs turned blue, grew sluggish and unwieldy. Ice collected between exposed toes, and some men, walking on numb feet, stumbled and fell and were slow to rise.

In the higher reaches they came into a treeless landscape, seemingly devoid of life, with jagged stone raised like weapons against the underbelly of the sky. Mago found something appalling in the silent bulk of the peaks, in the way they rose one after another like an army of gathering giants, in the strange dividing line where the earth ended and the infinite sky began, and in the awesome spectacle of elephants kicking their way through snow. He was sure that the earth had not witnessed such a spectacle since long ago when the gods roamed the earth in physical form, hunting the great beasts whose bones still emerged from the ground on occasion. In those times, anything was possible.

As it was now, under Hannibal's leadership. He seemed to be everywhere at once, no visible sign of fatigue on him. Mago was asleep each evening upon throwing his body down, and it seemed that the sound of Hannibal's voice both led him into slumber and pulled him out of it. Throughout the morning he rode through the company, extolling all to work on, to persevere, spinning grand notions of the bounty awaiting them in Italy, telling them that their deeds would be written of by poets and sung at campfires in times far from this. Here was their chance to be immortal. Had the Ten Thousand faced more than this? Did this not rate next to Alexander's marches through the Persian mountains? They would be remembered just as those of old were, but no such honor comes easily. On the first night they slept on snow-covered ground Hannibal tossed a thin blanket down on the ice, pulled a cloak over himself, and fell into an instant, deep slumber. Men, hearing his snoring, shook their heads and grinned despite themselves. What army ever had a leader superior to this?

The next morning Hannibal rode down the line telling the men they were near the top of the final pass. His scouts were certain. They had only to struggle a little longer and Italy would be theirs. To falter now would be the greatest of tragedies. Failure here would anger the gods themselves, who rarely see men come so close to everlasting fame.

Mago, leaning hard on his spear as he rested beside Silenus, heard the scribe mumble the reply, "Why settle for Italy? Why not a conquest of the heavens? I think the gates are up here, just a ten-minute walk or so. . . . Don't look at me like that," Silenus said, although Mago had not yet glanced at him. "This was not my idea. Did anybody ask my views? Do you know that it is said these regions are not meant for men? The closer we get to the gods, the harder our own lives become. Tell me you cannot feel it. Even the very breath coming in and out of your lungs is a labor. Tell me you do not feel it."

Mago prepared a smile and searched for a quick rebuttal, but nothing came to him and the effort tired him. He rested a moment longer in silence. Just as they were about to move on, he noticed Bomilcar's familiar form approaching them. He nudged Silenus and the two watched the man's progress. He walked with his weapons and a full pack, as he had since the beginning of the climb. To be an example among his men, he had explained. He took each step deliberately. He planted one foot and gave it a moment to meld with the ground. He pushed his enormous frame up and then planted the next foot, pulled the tree up by its roots, and repeated the motion. Mago and Silenus watched him ascend toward them for some time. Though he did not look up, he seemed to know just as he was passing the two. He said, "What tale have you now, Greek?"

"I am yet composing it," Silenus said. "It will be a tale of winter madness. You'll have a part in it, my friend. Be sure of it: the Goliath of the peaks."

"Your tongue knows no fatigue," Bomilcar said. "If your limbs fail you, perhaps your tongue will sprout legs and run you up these peaks."

Silenus seemed to find the image amusing. He might have said more, but Bomilcar kept trudging on and was soon receding into the white expanse above them. The Greek whispered to Mago, "I'd wager he has been perfecting that line since the Rhône."

In the almost-warm hours of the midafternoon, they trudged their way ahead at the rear of a long line of men. Though not as heavily laden as Bomilcar, Mago also chose to walk, an offering of sweat and labor to the common soldiers around him. And it was quite an offering. The irregular snowfalls, the cool nights, and the strong sun of the clear days created layers of slush beneath the surface snow, divided by skins of ice that tricked one into thinking they provided adequate support. A foot would punch through the top layer, the man's weight driving him down through the slush till he found purchase. Carefully, he would take one step and then another, finding security in the movement, believing he would go no farther down. But then, on a sudden whim of the living ice, he would break through again, first sinking to ankle depth and then up toward the knee and eventually as high as the waist. The pack animals, struggling against the stuff, sometimes sank so deep that only their frantic heads thrust out above the snow.

Thanks to a slightly larger ration than the common soldier's, Mago could function better than most. At first he tugged at men and dug away the snow with his hands, cut the white flesh with the blade of his sword, and slapped the men and beasts back into movement. Later—his hands too numb to hold his sword properly, too frozen even to scoop the snow—he shouted encouragement, orders, curses to keep them moving. This went on for hours, unchanging moments passing one into the next, each step like the one before it. The face of one man merged with the face of the man before him. The half-buried body of any individual looked like all the others. The glazed eyes, the cracked lips, the mumbled entreaties, the stiff limbs jutting up from ice: it no longer had a beginning and seemed to have no end. It was just the way of the world, and the things that had been life before made no sense anymore.

He could not count the number of times he believed he had reached the summit only to discover that he had mounted a lump in the mountainside, a protrusion, a ledge, beyond which new heights stretched. It was maddening. He was sure the landscape altered itself with malignant intent. It sprouted higher and higher each time he looked away. And the foul thing of it was that the world never betrayed its trickery. It always sat still and impassive under his scrutiny, like a great beast with its shoulders hunched in innocence.

At some point that he did not recognize at the time or remember later Mago gave up on the others and moved past them in silence.

He lost Silenus, but such was this climb—now you passed a man; a little later, he passed you. That was just the way it had to be, he realized. Each had to just struggle on—he just like the others. His extra rations were not enough to set him apart. His body was feeding upon itself. He could feel the process draining him, dissolving the tissue beneath his skin, sucking the fluids from his muscles and leaving them leathery cords, striated bands stiff in movement and slow to answer the instructions he willed upon them.

He was on all fours—scraping them forward inch by inch—when a burst of air hit his face with a force that nearly shoved him back down the slope. The air was sure to have been cold, but he felt the force more than the chill. At first he cursed it and ducked beneath his elbow, thinking he had reached yet another rise, with yet another view up toward the insurmountable. He felt his breath rushing back from the bitter cold just before his face. There was no warmth in it, and he wondered if he had begun to go cold on the inside. First his feet and then his hands, his knees and forearms, perhaps now his chest itself: all the parts of him were slowly freezing solid and becoming one with the mountains. He found this a pleasant thought. He could lie motionless and no longer struggle. He could remember stillness. It was possible to stop laboring and rest. The Greek was right. Such heights as this were not meant for mortal men. Why fight this truth when one could sleep instead? It was not so hard to give up. It was only hard to carry on.

And so Mago might have stayed if the voice had not reached him. He lifted his head and, squinting into the wind, realized why it buffeted him so forcefully. There was nothing above him but sky. To the south, a patchwork of clouds drifted across a blue screen. Mago rose to his feet and stumbled forward. The ground beneath him was suddenly bare rock, marbled by windswept currents of snow. The mountains dropped all the way to the valley floor before them. He could almost make out the flat plain and its imagined lushness. He was at the summit!

A madman stood atop a boulder, no more than a stone's throw away. It was the madman's voice that stirred Mago: He pointed out and shouted to the passing soldiers that the goal was in sight. "Look," he said, "the rich land of Italy! See it here, the rewards for your labors. We've brushed our heads against the roof of the world and need go no higher. The way is down from here. The hard work is behind you! Carry on quickly and lay your head to sleep on flat ground!"

Mago hardly recognized the shouting figure. His beard bristled wildly about his face, grown uneven and unkempt, the hairs laden with ice, even as his forehead dripped with sweat. A crust of reddish black clung to his cheeks. The man pulled off his helmet and waved it above him in triumph, revealing a mass of woolen hair pressed to his scalp in a rough impression of the headgear. He was a wholly wild creature, garments flapping about him, like some mad prophet yelling into a gale. But Mago knew exactly upon whom he was gazing. He could hear him plainly now, and he saw in his brother's eyes a sparkling enthusiasm like none he had seen before. Mago drew close enough to reach up and grasp his foot.

Hannibal looked down and smiled, joy written in the creases of his forehead and curve of his mouth. He spoke so quietly that Mago had to read the words on his lips. "Rome will be ours," he said. "Rome will truly be ours."

Mago nodded an agreement he did not feel. He wanted to share Hannibal's enthusiasm, but nothing was yet complete. The way was indeed down, but it was not to be easy. In many ways, the worst of the mountain crossing awaited them. The altitude that it had taken them days and miles to climb to was to be descended in only a portion of the distance, making the route almost unnavigably steep. Looking down from beside Hannibal's boulder, Mago wondered if the Allobroges had not led them to the most terrible pass in the Alps. The bastards might yet defeat them.

Imco Vaca had known no joy since leaving northern Iberia. Not a moment of happiness. Not an instant of pleasure. He felt as if he had been transported here and dropped down in the mountains by some creatively spiteful being intent on seeing poor Imco suffer. It made no sense otherwise. Ice and snow? Ridge upon ridge of jagged rock teeth? The small finger on his left hand black and hard as a twig? This must be somebody's idea of a joke. The fact that he could remember every step of the way, from sunny Iberia, up through the Pyrenees, into the Rhône valley, and all the way across the Alps explained nothing. Nor did it matter that he passed within spitting distance of the commander. Yes, Hannibal spoke encouraging words, but he was such an insane-looking creature that Imco would have crossed the street to avoid him had they met in some civilized city of the world. He walked past him without a word, determined to get down from these heights and fast.

But he was somewhere in the middle of the line, and the trail the scouts found twisted and turned down the mountainside. The snow he had to walk along had been softened in the sun and then compressed beneath thousands of feet into a sheet of rutted, dirty ice. Each step had to be taken with the greatest of care, but this was not possible in such fatigue, at the edge of starvation, on frostbitten feet, laden with heavy packs. Imco saw several of the men below him lose their footing. They clutched and struggled for purchase as they began to slide down the slope. They called out for help, naming men and then gods, and then as they blurred into unimaginable speed their cries became sound alone, distorted and echoing through the mountains.

The sight of the elephants was constantly baffling. The paths seemed impossibly narrow, but somehow the creatures moved forward as steadily as the men. He once spied a cow elephant negotiating a tiny shelf of rock. She balanced in such a way that her feet fell in a nearly straight line. It was a dainty move, something fit for a circus of curiosities, but she pulled it off with a finesse that Imco wished he possessed.

Toward the end of the second day he had to traverse a path that bent at an angle about fifty yards in front of him. Beyond the corner, yet another precipice, empty space stepping off into nothing. He could see the signs of thousands of feet already gone past. Though the way was clear in front of him, he saw two men stumble near the bend, one taking out the knees of the other and then the pair clutching each other, lucky not to have slid over the edge. Be careful when you reach that area, Imco thought.

Just then, he spotted a garment on the snow a few steps away, discarded in someone's sliding haste earlier in the day. He decided to fetch it up and sling it around his neck and present it to some unfortunate later. He lifted a foot toward it, but knew in an instant that this move had been misguided. His other foot slipped out from him as if he were kicking a ball. He landed on his outstretched hands and the heels of his feet. For a moment he held still, but then, slowly, painfully, he felt the four points of his limbs slithering over the ice. He tried to dig his fingers in and slam the soles of his feet for purchase, but he slid on, speeding up. He tried to think himself lighter, to rise up off the ice with the power of his mind and find purchase on the air itself. When this did not work he flipped over and embraced the slope for all he was worth, feeling the contours slide beneath him, each footprint and divot and ripple. He was sure the surface would drop away from him at any moment. He yelled his anger and fear right into the ice, his teeth so close to the surface he could have bit it. He might have done so, but even in such a state he knew his teeth should be protected. They were one of his best features.

He was not sure why he stopped moving. He only realized it because his yelling became the only noise in a silent world. The two men he had seen stumble were gazing at him from a few strides away. He had slid all the way to the bend. The precipice yawned just beyond his feet. He looked at the men, shook his head, and conveyed by rolling his eyes the depths of his impatience with all this; then he rose, very slowly, and moved on. He did not reach for stray garments again.

The third day was even worse. He first understood this when a groan of exasperation flowed up the line. An avalanche had wiped out a portion of the path below. It was a particularly steep section, offering no alternative routes. They would have to clear the slide. This was bad enough, but then he learned that many of the boulders mixed in with the snow and ice were too large to be moved even with the help of the elephants. They would have to break them into smaller pieces. Someone—whose expertise on this matter Imco doubted—suggested that they build a great fire around the rocks in question, making them red hot so that they could then be drenched with water and vinegar. The change in temperature, this man said, would split the stones and make them more manageable. It sounded dubious.

Imco spent the day hewing trees and dragging them through the snow to the fire. It was absurdly difficult work, as dangerous as battle. Stuck up to the waist in snow, hacking at the base of a tree that was so hard it did more damage to his ax than the blade did to it, Imco found himself crying. This was not exactly out of fear. He was not sure what he had to be afraid of anymore. The tears were not quite the product of sadness, nor of fatigue, nor of anger: he had felt all these things long enough that they were just part of his being now.

Memories brought the tears, the recollection that he had once been the child of a mother, that there was a woman living in the world who had slapped his bottom and wiped his mouth when he was sick and fed him bread dipped in olive oil. Everything about this seemed impossibly tragic. So much so that he did not even cheer with the rest when the rocks exploded amid plumes of steam and flying debris. What a silly thing to find joyful, he thought. Cracked boulders. More hiking. More cold. How did these things compare to the embrace of the fat woman who had created you? He could not help thinking all these men were mad, not only the leader.

Then something unexpected happened. He awoke one frigid morning at the foot of the Alps, four days after they had begun the descent. Italian soil lay beneath him. The awareness that they had done the impossible dawned on him as gradually as the brightening day. The army that had left New Carthage numbered upward of a hundred thousand. Now, they were down to a dejected, battered, and emaciated remnant of that. Perhaps thirty thousand, perhaps fewer. They had lost thousands of horses. And the elephants, though all still lived, were gaunt versions of their former selves. The rich train of booty and the thriving community of camp followers were, as far as he could tell, no more.

But on that morning, even knowing all this, Imco peered out his tent flap and looked up at the clear white-blue Italian sky. They were here. Despite it all, they were not defeated. He swelled with a sudden, long-absent enthusiasm. Things might yet look up. There might still be rewards awaiting him, pleasures that his mother's image had no place beside. Once again, Imco remembered himself, the soldier he had become and the mission he was part of. They were a storm about to break over Italy. What army could possibly stop them now?

Aradna considered herself blessed to have found the dead man. Though she had seen many corpses in her time, she would never forget the way he sat upright with an arm stretched out before him, like a blind beggar beseeching pity from unseen passersby. Perhaps it was because of this posture that so many had ignored him. Aradna, however, could not help but notice him when a raven perched on his shoulder, looked about, pecked at the man's lip, and looked about again. His features were those of an Iberian Celt, and he was older than most warriors. His eyes were open, lips crusted and peeling, cheeks blackened by frostbite prior to his death.

But it was not enough to deter her from reaching out and touching the garment draped over his shoulders, a thick cloak of wolf fur that might well have been cured earlier on the march. She wondered for a moment that a man could freeze with such a garment on him, but then she noticed his other hand. It pressed against a brown stain on his tunic, fingers stuck either side of an arrow shaft. His death must have been slow, his upraised hand an entreaty for medical attention that never came. It was not exactly easy to pry the cloak off him, but Aradna managed it. She trudged away wrapped in it and renewed in her belief that Artemis looked kindly upon her.

Such thoughts were truly acts of faith considering the hardships of the past weeks. The soldiers complained of their lot, but they knew nothing of true privation. She walked the same ground they did, through the same ravines and over snowy passes and across rivers cold as liquid ice. But she got no rations. The people she marched with held few supplies in trust and each harbored a deep suspicion of any person's actions toward them, kind or cruel. They had been cut to ribbons in the gorge, their numbers halved in that single afternoon and dwindling ever since. The loose order that had bound them to the army vanished. Supplies were abandoned to the Allobroges. Men and women were cut down and robbed of their possessions, some captured alive and deprived of their very freedom.

One evening the stragglers' camp she slept in was raided by local brigands. She had jumped to her feet at the first sound of confusion, but a man grabbed her wrist and began to drag her away. She yanked so hard against him that her upper arm popped out of its joint. The strange sensation this gave her attacker provided her a quick moment of confusion. She bashed his foot beneath her heel and fled. Her loose arm blinded her with pain, but the movement of running shifted the joint home and the pain was gone in an instant.

For a time after that she traveled alone, mingling with the rear of the army, scavenging on the debris left in their wake. She took even more care to attract no attention. Like the others, she had not bathed in weeks now. But she made sure that she was filthier than most. She caked her face with dirt and grease. Her hair grew into thick knots, hung with twigs and bits of rubbish. She strung a dead mouse around her neck. She ran her fingers through the stink of her armpits and then pressed the scent onto all her garments. She considered the fumes that met her nose when she squatted and thought that she might smear this scent on her outer garments as well. It was a short-lived idea, however. One could never tell what might stir a man's loins. She had heard of stranger things.

But even filthy and disheveled and starving, Aradna was a beauty. Men could not help but notice. A Gaul stopped her one clear morning at the foot of a scree slope. He was upon her suddenly, long sword in hand. He stepped from behind a tree as if he had lain in wait for some time and had chosen this moment for the fineness of the crisp air and the quiet solitude they found themselves in. He indicated with a thrusting pelvis the activity he had in mind. She spat at him. He ignored this, calming her with his weaponless hand, patting toward her to indicate that it would not hurt. Just a small thing, he seemed to be saying. Just a moment of your time. He never lowered the upraised sword. She hissed at him and gestured with her hands that he should pleasure himself and leave her out of it. But behind the bold rejection, she knew the threat he posed. He was a strong man in his prime who would happily injure her to have her.

He might lop off an arm to punish her, or beat her senseless and carry her into slavery.

Aradna dropped to her knees in the scree, opened her mouth, and motioned that she would receive him with it. He was wary of this, but as she sucked air in and out of her lips he began to think again. His trousers were down to his knees the next moment. Aradna almost smiled. The weakness of men never failed to amaze her. As he shuffled forward he did not notice that she grasped a jagged stone in either hand. She drew her arms up and back and snapped them together with a motion like a bird flapping its wings to take off. Her two hands brought the stones together on his penis. She turned and fled, but not before blood splattered her face. She shook her head at the foolishness and at the curse of the beauty she had never asked for and could not dispose of.

By the time she reached the snowy plains the stragglers had so thinned that she walked alone. She inspected bodies for coins and valuables, cut flesh from frozen pack animals, added and subtracted clothing as new pieces were presented to her. Midway up the slope the gradient lessened briefly and Aradna came upon a strange pit alongside the path. It was a crater with sloping walls the height of several people in depth. The base of it showed the rocky frame of the mountain itself. In the center of this stood a lone, dejected donkey. The creature was completely still, head hung low, eyes fixed on nothing at all and seeking nothing at all. A urine stink seeped up from the pit, strong enough to make Aradna clamp a hand over her nose. She realized that the donkey had nothing to do with the shaping of the depression. It was simply a spot that man after man had chosen to urinate in, so melting the snow and ice and leaving a steaming pit behind. The donkey must either have stumbled into it, or else sought it out in a desire to touch his hooves to solid stone. Aradna watched him a moment, thinking. Then she slid-climbed down into the hole. Gifts like this should not be questioned, just received gratefully.

She and the donkey reached the saddle of the pass late in the afternoon. Without knowing that Hannibal had done so before her, she climbed onto the lookout rock and took in Italy from the same vantage point. The army trickled down before her like a slow-moving stain, a river of filth cutting its way through the white slopes. The descent would be brutal. The night fast approaching a challenge just to live through. She could see these things plainly. But it was pleasing to look down upon the army marching before her. This was good, she thought. Good. The land they now entered was nearer to the place of her birth than she had been since she left as a baby in her father's arms. She felt the weight of her treasure bag between her breasts, heavier now than before because she had never ceased her scavenging. One would have thought it strange to look upon her, but beneath the hard actions and filth, behind tolerance for human misery and her scavenger's callous heart, there resided a quiet child, who could yet imagine beauty and still conceive of a life lived with joy. She saw the pathway to that joy before her, and so proceeded.

Aradna kicked out her foot and slammed her heel into the ice, dragging the reluctant donkey behind her. She took one step and then another, urging the beast down into the rich land of Italy.

The autumn of his first year in sole command of southern Iberia marked the zenith of Hasdrubal's Dionysian debauchery. He ended the campaigning season as early as he could and returned to New Carthage. Away from the stern eyes of his brother, he submerged himself in excess. Each evening the Barca grounds of New Carthage became a labyrinth of festivities, games and music, carnal consumption. Servants stoked the fires high and pushed into them stones, which, once they were white-hot, were pulled from the fire with care and doused in water, making the rooms almost tropical, inducing sweat and thirst, turning garments damp against the skin so that they slipped from shoulders and were soon upon the floor in formless heaps. Though Hasdrubal was careful to acknowledge the beauties of aristocratic blood, he made sure the functions were attended by the finest-looking daughters of Iberian chieftains, by prostitutes, by servant girls. Nor was he envious of other men. To be a friend to Hasdrubal was a privilege all aspired to. The steamy rooms were replete with the seminude forms of young soldiers, bodies hardened by war and training. Mix into this an abundance of red wine, rich meat and sauces, fruits and their juices, and incense, and one had night after night of scenes that would have impressed even Alexander's Macedonians.

Considering all of this, Hasdrubal looked to his impending wedding day with some trepidation. On his own he would not have wed himself to any one woman just yet—or ever, in fact. And if he had to choose a wife, he would have picked one of the more debauched vixens in his entourage, someone who could keep up with him, someone who likewise craved sexual variety. But the choice was not his to make. In the early winter he received a letter from the Council of Elders. It was written with aged formality, so convoluted that it was almost incomprehensible. He deciphered it only with Noba's aid.

The elders were ordering him to wed a daughter of the Oretani chieftain Andobales. He had not known that the Council was in contact with Andobales, but those old ones had long fingers, as Hamilcar used to say. The union was of strategic importance. The Oretani had been on the ascendant over the last few years. They managed to exploit the Carthaginian presence in Iberia to their benefit, striking at first one tribal neighbor and then another while delicately avoiding stirring Carthaginian wrath. They even turned Hanno's debacle of a few years earlier—when he led two thousand of them right into the trap set by the Betisians—to their account. They never failed to mention it, to smart at the terrible blow to their manhood. Andobales had even protested Hannibal's union with Imilce, asking whether it indicated that the Betisians were Carthage's favorites. For all these reasons, the Council was resolute in its decision that a high-level marriage was necessary. To disregard the order would be treason. The elders made it clear that they had the leverage of withholding reinforcements and the power to replace him if he refused.

Hasdrubal chafed at this insult. When Hamilcar or Hannibal ruled Iberia, few such orders had issued from Carthage. He stormed about his chambers, calling down curses on them for meddling; he threatened disobedience or outright revolution. But in the end he saw no way to refuse them. The move made sense. Carthaginian authority had been difficult to maintain even during the height of

Hannibal's power. The Iberians around him seemed to buck against African domination. Hasdrubal had tried throughout the summer to make it clear that his authority was as real as his brother's, but the Iberians were ever restless, always inclined to see only the faults of their present situation, only the benefits of a change.

So, much sooner than he would have liked, Hasdrubal found himself hosting a wedding banquet. Andobales arrived in a swarm of confusion. His people were loud, inclined to laughter and consumption, to anger and deadly pride just as quickly. Andobales himself was a large man, a warrior all his life. He had fought with neighboring tribes—or with Carthaginians or with Romans—each year since his tenth birthday. He wore his strength as sheer, massed bulk that increased throughout his torso and up to his hunched shoulders. He was a massive boar of a man, with a face that seemed to have been pressed between two stones and elongated through the jaw and nose. Looking upon him, Hasdrubal could not help but wonder what sort of daughter he might have produced. He had never seen or spoken to the girl and had no idea by what reasoning she was chosen as his bride, for he knew Andobales had several unwed daughters.

In keeping with her people's customs, the bride entered surrounded by her female relatives and went veiled throughout the ceremony. Try as he might, Hasdrubal could get no idea of either her features or the shape of her body. The women around her varied in appearance, from young to old, dark-haired mostly and no less attractive than normal, but he took no comfort in this. Just what did that veil hide? It might conceal any manner of disease or disfigurement. For all he knew his new wife had the face of a hairless dog, of a cow, or of her father. She could be pockmarked, pimply, toothless. She might have ringworm or diarrhea, a body rash or—as he had discovered once in a prospective partner—she could well have insect larvae growing in her gums. The possibilities were endlessly gruesome.

The bride and groom sat on opposite sides of the room. They did not share a word, but instead listened as one man and then another rose to give the union their blessing. The Celtiberians spoke with bellicosity. They stressed the significance of the bond between the two peoples. Some suggested that with this union Andobales' people should find themselves favored above other tribes and should have some measure of autonomy in subjugating their neighbors. One man mentioned an aged dispute with the Betisians that Hasdrubal had been trying to ignore, having no wish to open debate about such matters.

Andobales, who sat just beside Hasdrubal, stood to make a toast of his own. First he praised the hereditary line of the Barcas, naming, randomly and with little attention to chronology, their accomplishments and virtues. He lingered somewhat longer than appropriate on Hannibal himself, as if he were actually the prospective son-in-law. Following fast on all of this, however, he detailed his own lineage, which he claimed went directly back to a union between an Iberian princess and the Greek god of war, Mars. He recounted the deeds of his grandfather, and of his father after him. Nor did he fail to mention his own exploits, everything from feats of warcraft to abundance in the distribution of his seed through many wives and more beyond that.

This last point drew Hasdrubal's attention, but then the chieftain surprised him by barking out, "Bayala! Bayala! Come over here, girl."

The veiled form rose and wove toward them through the crowded banquet hall. She knelt before them, close enough to touch. Still the fabric of her veil revealed nothing. Hasdrubal barely heard the transaction that followed but understood enough of such moments to know that the Iberian was giving him the girl formally. Andobales grasped each of them by the hand. Serving as a connection between them, he named them wed, declared the two families and the two nations joined for eternity.

And that was all there was to it. The shawled form nodded and withdrew to the nuptial chambers, Hasdrubal's eyes following until she had exited the room. The chieftain crashed down onto the cushion beside him. He lost his balance for a moment, and strained to pull himself upright, clenching his massive fingers around Hasdrubal's arm to do so. As he was so near him, Andobales took advantage of the moment to whisper to his new son-in-law. His breath was like liquid wine itself, mixed with the fouler scent that marked some decay in his teeth. "My daughter has been kept pure. Pure!

She is yours to pierce for the first time. Enjoy her, my new son, and fill her with many young. Make her the womb of a new army. The mother of men to slay Romans!"

Hasdrubal did not hear the news of his wife's purity with eagerness: He preferred his women soiled and debauched. But he kept this information to himself. Nor did the notion of merging sex with his wife and Roman conquest sit right with him either. He was sure he would never rid himself of the image of tiny, fully formed, armored soldiers stepping out from between the girl's legs, swords in hand, evil expressions on their faces. He tried to follow Andobales' example and drink himself toward oblivion.

Later that evening Hasdrubal stood in the hall beside the curtain that hung between him and his wife, leaning hard against the wall. The wine had been savage to his body, but seemed to have had little impact upon the clarity of his thoughts. He stared at the thick purple fabric, utterly powerless to push it out of the way and stride through. It was silly, childish, shameful even, but he was terrified to enter his bedchamber. He imagined turning and slipping away to the company of familiar women, of the young officers he was so comfortable with. He might say he had fulfilled his husbandly duties already and was out for further leisure. But he did not welcome the questions his comrades would pose, the jokes they would make, the way his lovers would sniff his groin for a scent of his wife. No, he could not bear that. Strange that he had ultimate power over so many, and yet now he felt suspended from a spider's web, stuck fast, afraid to flinch for awareness that his movement would be translated out through a hundred invisible threads, bringing untold horrors . . .

He paused in mid-thought. A feminine hand pushed through the curtain and drew it slowly to one side. There stood his wife, still hooded, though she had changed her garments to a thinner gown, a weave so loose it was nearly transparent. She had, he was pleased to note, breasts, a flat belly, hips with something of a curve. But still he could see nothing of her face, and something in this felt ominous indeed.

"Come, husband," she said in a quiet voice, soft and young. She grasped the fabric of his tunic and drew him into the room, letting the curtain fall closed behind him. Then, to his surprise, she dropped to her knees, slipped her hand up under his tunic, and grasped his flaccid sex.

"Forgive me," she said, "but I've heard such tales. I must see this tool for myself."

So saying, she lifted his tunic up and tucked it out of the way. She leaned close and adjusted her veil. After a moment of silent examination, she said, "The gods have blessed you. And me as well."

Hasdrubal had as yet found nothing exciting in this examination, but that changed quickly enough. Bayala began to knead his soft member, pulling on it and drawing it out, squeezing it between her fingers. She dipped her hands in a fragrant oil and the warm moisture of this did much to stiffen him. Hasdrubal looked down on her, amazed. There was a skill in her fingers that surpassed any former lover's. She worked him to full length, moving one hand and then the other in a choreographed, twisting, sliding dance.

Pinned as he was to the new center of his being, Hasdrubal was at a loss for what to do with the rest of his body. He reached out to either side as if to grab hold of something, but his hands just hung there, twitching. Even his toes flexed and strained and seemed to cry out. His breaths came sporadically, in gasps that corresponded with the touch of the young woman's hand. It seemed that she had taken complete control of him, even of his capacity to inhale and exhale. He could not deny that the fact that he had yet to see her face added to his excitement, but neither could he resist the need to set eyes on her. With great effort he lowered one arm and got a fold of the veil in his fingers. After waiting for a spasm to pass, he yanked the fabric back.

The subtle hands paused in their work. Bayala looked up. Her face was not beautiful. Her nose drew a thin line, just off-center. Her lips, likewise, were not as full as he usually favored. The bones of her cheeks sat high, giving a gaunt aspect to her face. But she was young, her eyes were gray and devious, her teeth reasonably straight, and her gums, presumably, larvae-free. Inadvertently, Hasdrubal raised his eyebrows and pursed his lips.

"Hello, wife," he said.

Bayala grinned wider, seeming to find the greeting perfectly appropriate to the situation. "Greetings, husband. Forgive my bold-ness, but I've never seen a monument like this one," she said, squeezing the feature in question. "I have heard tales, but now I know them to be true. I could hang on this pole and exercise my arms by lifting my weight."

Hasdrubal, unnerved by the suggestion and the seeming possi-bility that she might just attempt it, said, "True enough. But do not try that just now."

Bayala fluttered her eyelids. "Why do you look so surprised, husband?"

"Your father . . ."

"Does not know me as well as he thinks. I would not have arranged this wedding had my own tastes not matched yours." Say-ing this, Bayala set her upper teeth on the tip of his penis and slid her tongue out against his foreskin.

Hasdrubal knew then that he had much to learn about marriage. He realized that there was a suggestion of feminine hubris in her statement that he should treat firmly. But he forgot this as the suc-tion of her lips drew him. Marriage, despite his reservations, sud-denly seemed to be an institution blessed by the gods.

On learning that Hannibal was attempting an inland crossing of the Alps, Cornelius Scipio acted quickly. He sent a dispatch to Gnaeus, ordering him to carry on with the attack on Carthaginian Iberia. He and Publius, on the other hand, would return to Italy and take control of the army in Gaul. A consul deserting his army, leaving an unelected relative to a command in the pursuit of battle, and then heading off to raise a new army of his own accord was an unprecedented moment in Roman history. But so, it appeared, was the conflict facing them. Cornelius already knew that he had underestimated Hannibal. He was intent that the damage should go no further.

As father and son traveled—first by warship, then by foot and horseback, then by river barge—news reached them piece by trou-bling piece. Hannibal had descended from the heights into lands dominated by the Gauls of northern Italy. His army was half starved and ragged and weak, but this gave Cornelius comfort for only a few days, until he learned that Hannibal had attacked the capital of the Taurini. It was into their territory that his descent had brought him; as the Taurini were at war with the Insubres, and the Insubres were known to have allied with Hannibal, they refused the Carthaginians' requests for help. The African took the town in three days. He put every adult male to death and enslaved the entire population of women and children.

His Numidian horsemen rode on wide-ranging raids of other Gallic settlements—even settlements of the Insubres, his erstwhile allies—killing many and robbing them of winter supplies and showing their superiority in each encounter. They even went so far as to taunt the Roman garrison at Placentia, one of the few centers of Roman control in the area. The Numidians rode close to the soldiers, singly or in small groups, challenging them to battle. Inspired by this bravery and losing faith in their Roman overseers, five hundred Gallic allies rose in the night and deserted to Hannibal's cause. Many of them carried the heads of their Roman camp mates as a token of their sincerity.

Though the men around him cited this as proof of the Carthaginian's simple avarice and unreasoning cruelty, the consul recognized a deadly logic that chilled him. This was not simply a barbarian grasping for quick riches. Each thrust had a dual purpose. In one stroke, the capture of Taurin had replenished his depleted supplies, renewed his men's confidence, and rewarded them with food, treasure, sex, new clothes and weapons, and even slaves to serve them. The capture also made it plain to every other Gallic tribe that Hannibal's power could not be ignored. And it had robbed Cornelius of a potential base. The attacks on the Insubres? Cornelius knew this tribe would have intelligence of the Roman approach. With their fickle nature they had probably reneged on promises they had made to Hannibal. They would have preferred to wait a few weeks and side with the victor after the two forces had met. Hannibal's punishment of them may have come from anger, but, too, he was defining them as reliable allies or beaten foes, either being preferable to simple bystanders. There was no madness in this, only cold logic.

They disembarked from a river barge near Placentia, mounted the horses awaiting them, and rode with haste. They dismounted in the late afternoon at the edge of the field stretching to the outpost. Cornelius wanted to walk into the fort, to greet his troops and be greeted by them, to make immediate contact and win them to him. The sight from a distance was actually heartening: the fort perched high and solid-looking, the tents pitched about the fields near it, abutting the bustle of the late harvest. It was comforting to note that the crops had not been destroyed, for they would need these supplies in the coming weeks.

But as he strode nearer to the soldiers' tents a dread crept up into him. It grew even before he realized what had prompted it. There was nothing peculiar in the things he saw, but something in the quality of dejection betrayed by them. The fires burned low and smoky. The men huddled near the warmth, heads low and shoulders hunched forward, gathered as if in mourning. There was little conversation, no laughter; none were engaged in vigorous exercise. Even the fabric of the tents hung limp, as if the tents, too, had been emaciated by the difficult summer. He knew these soldiers were the last battered remnants of an army who had experienced a series of near-defeats at Gallic hands. Now, at the end of the warring season, they were exhausted and war-weary. They would have been made fearful by the news of Hannibal's doings. But what Cornelius saw on the soldiers' faces was an emotion surpassing even this. They wore the expressions of men who had just learned the prophecy of their deaths.

The consul might have proceeded straight through the grounds without making himself known, but before he could, an observant centurion recognized him. He shouted the consul's presence to the others. Men glanced up and took him in skeptically. They rose to their feet, but not smartly, not with the spirit and discipline he would have liked.

"Be at ease, men," Cornelius said. "Rest now. We will soon need your strong arms."

That evening the consul wrote new letters. Of the Senate, he asked that the other consul, Sempronius Longus, be recalled and at once. The army here was not adequate to the task before it. He had nothing to rely upon but battered and fatigued veterans and a host of raw recruits barely able to march in unison. They were no match for Hannibal, especially not if he could muster the Gauls into mischief. The plan to send Sempronius to attack Carthage was no longer tenable, not with a foreign invader already on Italian soil.

He sent a letter to Sempronius, too. He began it: "Dear Comrade, read this and fly to me. The thunder of Baal has descended upon us."

Inside the thick fabric of the tent was a world viewed through weak tea. A small fire burned in a pit in the earthen floor. The melancholy quality of the room reflected the heavy skies and the inactivity of the past week. The struggles of the crossing were forgotten, followed as they had been by the quick moves that introduced Hannibal's army to the people of this region. But even the capture of Taurin and the Gallic raids now seemed old memories. The foe they wanted was Roman, and him they had yet to lure into confrontation. Hannibal had even assembled the entire army near Placentia and offered battle formally, but they had stood in the field unanswered all afternoon. Now Scipio was a short ride away, camped on the far bank of the river Ticinus. But his proximity only increased his caution. He would have to be caught off guard. In the meantime, Hannibal stayed focused on the larger battles to come.

"Let us go over it again," Hannibal said. He tossed a dried fig into his mouth and chewed it viciously, as was necessary to soften the shriveled stone into something edible. The sound of Hannibal's jaw abusing the fig brought up Mago and Carthalo's gazes from their study of the diagram the commander had carved into the tabletop with a dagger. It was a surprisingly precise sketch, illustrating the makeup and usual deployment of the Roman army. Bostar stood a little distance away, preoccupied, while Bomilcar lay on the couch, his large frame cast as if at ease, although somehow betraying a tight-wound annoyance.

Hannibal had incubated a vicious cough for several days now, and with it a sore throat so painful that each time he swallowed, a dull, rusty dagger pierced his larynx. He felt alternately hot and then cold; his vision was sensitive to light; when he rose, the world shifted like a vessel at sea. His frailty disturbed his mind almost more than his body. Physical pains were nothing new; and these hardly deserved comment compared to the injuries of war. But the very fact that he had succumbed to this illness seemed a defeat, a refutation of his discipline. Throughout the mountain journey and in the days since, he had recalled his father's training, the wisdom he, in turn, had learned from Xanthippus, the Spartan who for a time commanded the Carthaginian army in the earlier war with Rome. Xanthippus taught that a soldier only needed to ignore the bitter weather to defeat it. It was a man's acknowledgment of discomfort that allowed malignant humors to enter his body. The gods looked favorably on the Stoic; likewise, they disdained the weak-willed. Such thinking had seemed right enough and had served Hannibal thus far. He had rarely been ill in his adult life and had never been bed-bound by fever. He had been uncomfortable before, but he had beaten back the elements, fatigue, and pain. He wielded a stick inside his mind and struck at any part of him that suggested weakness as one strikes at a rabid dog. And yet the creature had somehow found a soft spot and sunk its teeth in deep. He had a strange, unmanly wish for Imilce's company, but he pushed the image of her away each time it appeared.

He swallowed the fig and spoke firmly. "A legion is composed of four thousand soldiers," he said. "These are divided into maniples of four hundred men. Each maniple is three lines deep, positioned so that there is space between them to retreat or charge through the various lines. The velites precede the heavy infantry with javelins, small shield, and sword. They usually lack armor, as they are the poorest of citizens. The first line of the heavy infantry is the least experienced, the hastati. They are helmeted and lightly armored. They hurl their spears, which they call pila, in unison at a predetermined moment to catch their opponents by surprise and break their front ranks. If the enemy does not break, the hastati pull back through the spaces and the second line, of the principes, attacks, first with pilum and then with sword. They do not swing wildly but instead try to knock away their opponents' shields with their own, then offer one jab in an exposed place. No wasted energy, but just enough to kill. And then the third line, of veterans, the triarii, follows to finish the work, with the first and second lines both able to return to the fighting at a moment's notice. And they do most of this in near silence: no shouts or ululations or boasting. Just action, with direction coming from the consul, through six tribunes and thence to the centurions, some sixty in number. They always seek to engage and do so without apparent hesitation. This is how it has been described to me."

Bomilcar guffawed. " 'Always seek to engage' . . . You should run through the idiot who said that."

Hannibal stood erect, though his eyes stayed on the diagram. "Where is the weakness in this?"

Mago glanced at Carthalo. He raised his eyes and cocked his head to show that he would defer if Carthalo had an answer prepared. The cavalry lieutenant, however, just furrowed his brow and leaned to study the diagram. They had all been over this material before, many times, in fact, but they each knew—perhaps the commander knew better than any—that the tactics they had conceived to fight the legion were insufficient, at least on paper. The Roman formation was more versatile than the phalanx, more disciplined than hordes of barbarians, more a machine than a temperamental beast. Some argued that it was the development of this formation that led the Romans to break with the old custom of seasonal skirmishes and begin to subjugate their neighbors completely. They had conquered in an ever-widening circle around them, had defeated most of the Carthaginian commanders during the first war, and had even humbled Pyrrhus of Epirus, whose military machine many had thought unstoppable. Hannibal had always said he was confident that his Libyan veterans could stand toe to toe against any soldiers the world had ever known. But they were only part of the army, few in number compared with the newly trained Iberians and the untested Gauls.

"I was hoping you would tell us," Mago finally said. "I cannot find the fault in it."

"Neither can I," Hannibal said, coughing abruptly. He cleared his throat and ran his palm over his mouth, as if he were drawing the illness from it and depositing it elsewhere. "If the men are well trained I think this formation is nearly unbeatable. A phalanx may be a bristling bull in full armor, but these Romans have created a creature with numerous eyes and many limbs. It may be that we cannot defeat them on an open field, not if the circumstances favor them. But discipline can be a flaw as well as a virtue. They will react as they have been trained, to each circumstance they've come to expect. So we must always present them with the unexpected. We must make sure that we never engage except under conditions to our advantage. We must fight intelligently, unpredictably."

Bomilcar had been waiting for a pause in his commander's address. "This talk was fine last winter, back in New Carthage, but what good is such chatter now? How can we prevail against a foe that will not fight us? That is the trick I'd like to hear explained."

Bostar glanced between Hannibal and Bomilcar, uneasy. His face had suffered more than most from the cold. The tip of his nose and a portion of his cheeks still dripped raw from the damage of exposure. Synhalus had coated his face with one of his salves, but whether the Egyptian knew anything about frost-damaged skin was doubtful. "What would you have us do?" he asked.

"March for Rome!" Bomilcar said. "It is south of us, and to the south is warmth. Is not that what we came for? I've never known Hannibal to hesitate. I pray he will not do so now."

Hannibal fixed Bomilcar in his gaze, a dangerous look that was not anger but could easily become it. He had trimmed his beard recently, close enough that one could note the tense trembling around his mouth. "I'll consider your words," he said. "Now leave me—all of you. We all know the situation we're in, so let us ponder it separately. Leave me and attend to your business."

Alone in the smoky chamber, the commander sat down on his stool and pulled his tiny field desk toward him. Bomilcar was right, of course—at least in that they must force an engagement before hard winter set in. Their situation was not so different from what he had anticipated back in the warmth of New Carthage. He knew that the campaign had thus far been more successful than most men would have dreamed, despite the death toll of the mountain crossing. But in some childish area at the back of his mind he had harbored notions of a great, swift victory. He had believed—and still believed—that the Romans would suffer only a few defeats before pleading for peace. They had gained too much in recent years to risk it all with a death struggle.

He lifted a quill and dipped for ink and ran his hand through the pages Silenus had left until he found a blank one. He had no clear thought of why he searched out these tools. He had a vague notion that he would scribble a few lines to inspire himself, that through the pressure of the quill point on the papyrus he would scratch out the words to frame the actions to come. But when his hand moved— tremulous and large around the instrument and half-cramped even at the first stroke—he wrote something very different.

"Beloved Imilce."

He gazed at the name a moment, taking it in, remembering it.

"It gives me pleasure to write out the letters of your name, to form the sounds on my lips. Here in my warrior's tent, in frigid Gaul, your name is like a revelation. When I recall that you live in this world . . ."

He paused, feeling a flood of maudlin words pressing against his will. It was almost overpowering, the desire to unburden himself to her, as a man can only do to a woman, to someone so much a part of his life and yet wholly separate from his violent work. But he could not give in to this desire—for many reasons, chief among them that such soft thoughts did nothing to hone his military mind. So he wrote a different truth than he had first intended.

". . . I am reminded why I fight. I am nothing if not a warrior, but I do not love to be far from you. I do not covet victory so much that I forget the softer things of life. Believe me in this. Even Hannibal . . ."

He cupped his hand tightly over his mouth, coughed into it, and checked his palm for discharge. There was none. Looking over his words, he frowned at them. "Even Hannibal" what? His quill swayed over the words, undecided, half of a mind to strike them and begin again, reading them with one meaning and then, in- stantly, seeing another. It seemed foolish to pen a love note, but al- most sacrilegious not to. The words were true, and yet they were lies also. He could not pin them down. He searched for a way to ex- plain the progress of the campaign instead. He thought of writing that they had come through the mountains unscathed, but he could not write such a blatant falsehood. He thought to describe military matters but did not progress far on such lines. Details of distances traveled, of soldiers and supplies lost, of allegiances made and broken: it would sound like men's babble to her, just another nightmare of masculine misery. It would make no sense in the luxury of Carthage. Nor could he find the words to describe the war in brief. Nor did he want her mind tainted by things martial. Another line of thought came to him.

"How fares Little Hammer? Perhaps he speaks some words by now. This seems an impossible thing, but speech comes to all of us. Do not let him grow soft in my absence. He is just a boy, but he will be a man sooner than you can imagine. Have him tutored by a Greek. And also in swordplay and archery. Even very young boys can fashion bows in the African style. Remember that he is a child of Carthage and he should pay daily homage to Melkart and Baal, and to all the gods of my people. Teach him to temper his passions. Also . . ."

He impaled the point of the quill in the papyrus, cutting the flow of words. What was he doing? It had been less than a year since he left. Only a few months, one season fading into another and that into another. Why write of passions when his son was a tiny child? Why act as if he could raise his son from a distance, through words on a page?

Maharbal entered the tent just then. He moved as swiftly on foot as he did on horseback and spoke in character with his face: sharply, directly, like a hatchet blade. "Scipio is near! If we want him we can engage him today."

Hannibal asked for details. The cavalry commander explained that one of his horsemen had sighted the Romans on the move on this side of the Ticinus River. They were mostly cavalry, perhaps a large scouting force, followed by pikemen and some infantry. They were an easy ride away, although foot soldiers might fail to reach them if they decided to retreat across the pontoon bridge they had used to span the Ticinus.

Hannibal made his decisions so quickly that they followed Maharbal's report without a pause. They were to mount and ride that instant. No infantry, but all the cavalry they could call up on a moment's notice. "We must move swiftly," he said. "Let's stick the Romans and draw a taste of blood."

As he rose, Hannibal grasped up the unfinished letter, smashing the flat of his palm against it and then pinching his fingers together like talons. He tossed the crumpled note into the small fire. He watched long enough to assure that all of it wilted in the heat and burst into flame. It had been a mistake, anyway. The musings of a tired mind at a weak moment. But that was behind him already. He stepped out of his tent into the damp chill of the morning, calling out orders as he walked.

And so it was only a few hours later that he set eyes on the Roman contingent. For the first time Hannibal saw a Roman consul's standard on the field before him. He thanked the gods for allowing this moment, and then he set about to please them through action. He took in the land and knew in an instant how he would proceed.

Cornelius Scipio had seen many battles. He had always fought well and believed he would until the hour he died. But in the days after the skirmish beside the Ticinus he lay twinging, haunted by nightmares and struggling to understand just what had occurred and how. The battle had started too quickly, changed too suddenly, and been decided too rapidly. The mounted Carthaginians appeared before them; the velites hurled their missiles; the two forces met; a sword slipped into the soft spot beneath his upraised arm; the Africans fell upon them from the rear. As quickly as that, the battle became a wild scramble. Someone jerked him from his mount. He struggled in the mud as shapes moved above him and horse hooves fell from the sky and battered him. He took the blows in the face and chest, his upraised arms, and his skull. Three teeth were knocked clean out and the whole of his jaw became a drooping joint of pain. He had his surgeon wrap it tightly and refused to talk. He gave orders only in writing and by nods or shakes of the head.

Two days passed before he understood just how his life had been saved and whom he had to thank. Publius. The younger Scipio was fighting near his father when the wind of the battle shifted. He saw his father take the sword point and topple from his horse into the mêlée below him. The young man rode as near as he could, hacking at anyone remotely foreign looking. When he could go no nearer on horseback, he slid off and scrambled through the horses' churning legs. He stabbed an African straight through one eye and sliced deep into the hamstring of another. He stepped upon the man as he fell, pressing his heel to the back of the man's neck, aware of the moment the man's scream of rage was silenced with a mouthful of mud. An Iberian nearly took his head off with a sweep of his curved sword, but Publius shifted his feet so quickly that they came out from under him. He dropped straight down, the sword cleaving the air above him. He looked up for the following blow but the Iberian was gone in the confusion.

Publius was on his knees when he reached his father. He beat away a Roman horse that stood dangerously close to him and cradled the man's battered head in one crooked arm. He held his sword waving above him and shouted orders in the clipped, strong Latin that his father used in battle. A small band of soldiers heard the cries. Soon they had formed a ring around the fallen consul. Publius lifted his father onto his back and stumbled from the field, a ring of soldiers close around him. They made it back into Roman protection and away.

Such was the story conveyed to the consul. He was thankful for his life and proud that the rescue cast a ray of glory upon his son, but he hated to learn of events from others' mouths. In those first feverish days, he also listened as his generals tried to explain the events of the skirmish; their conflicting accounts further confused him. The first true clarity came from a scout who described the events as he had seen them from high in the hills to the west, whence he had been returning from a solitary patrol.

The two forces had met with equal vigor, he explained, though the Carthaginians greatly outnumbered the Roman party. After the initial chaos of the horsemen cutting into each other's ranks, they dismounted and fought among their horses' legs. Nothing seemed unusual until a group of Numidian cavalry near the rear of the enemy force turned from the field. They surged off toward the south as if abandoning the battle, but then veered back a moment later, riding to the west, in a thin line heading toward the Roman rear. The main mêlée raged on with little change, save that the Carthaginian forces stretched the line of battle by rolling out along the northern edge of the Roman forces, as if individual riders were attempting to flank on that side. The Roman line stretched to resist this, forming a bent, thin front.

Watching that desperate struggle, the scout temporarily forgot about the detached cavalry unit. When he turned to seek them again, they had ridden into a set of hills behind the Roman contingent. They weaved into the trees and bunched together near the ridgeline, gathering like a swell thrown up onto a shore. Then they roared down through the trees in a tight wedge that caught the unsuspecting Romans from behind.

A moment later the scout saw the consul's standard falter and disappear. After that, he had watched no more. He rode at a gallop down toward the field to be of what aid he could. He saw no more from that high vantage, but he did have more to tell. The scout had wondered why the flanking cavalry had gone unnoticed. It seemed a mystery, and he feared that the hand of a god had hidden them for those few important moments. Only on inspecting the field the following day did he realize that the Numidian riders had conducted their maneuver on the far side of the ridge. They had moved through a narrow depression just deep enough to hide them. The lay of the land could not have been designed any better for the ploy; nor could the enemy commander have recognized it and played it to his advantage any more precisely.

Cornelius broke camp in the dead of night and forced a march to Placentia, destroying the bridge over the Padus in the process. Hannibal followed, constructed a new pontoon bridge, and within a few days mustered his troops in the open field once again. He called the consul to battle, but Cornelius would have none of it. Not on that day, nor on the days that followed as he waited, writhing and uncomfortable, for his fellow consul and the aid he would surely bring. He did not have to wait long.

Sempronius Longus arrived in a gale of motion, panting from his forced march, claiming that he had already clashed with a company of Numidian cavalrymen and thoroughly routed them. He had seen nothing but the backside of the Africans' horses, fleeing, the so-called soldiers showing their true nature when confronted by a superior force. His men had cut down more than a few and left them as feed for wild beasts.

"Already we have the bastard on his back foot," Sempronius said. "Another thrust and we'll topple him."

Studying his face, Cornelius saw all the features he knew so well: the familiar black bristling of his hair, the eyes set close together, the jagged scar from a childhood injury across his chin. But these features were pushed out of place, jostled, by the indignant anger in his brow, by pride in the smirk of his lips. Most of all, naked ambition gleamed in Sempronius' eyes. Instead of the joy he had expected to feel in his colleague's arrival, Cornelius discovered another form of trepidation, which only grew with subsequent meetings.

News came to them in pieces and none of it was good. They learned that the Roman depot of Clastidium had accepted four hundred pieces of gold for its surrender, thereby making a gift to the Carthaginians of its well-stocked granary. Several more of the local Gallic tribes quit their wavering and went over to Hannibal. Then word came that a contingent from the Boii to the east had arrived, swelling the Carthaginian's force further. Sempronius fed on all of this as a hungry wolf chews leather.

Watching him, Cornelius barely recognized his old friend anymore. He sat up in his sickbed and preached patience to his fellow consul. He argued that the Gauls now flocking to Hannibal would desert him in midwinter. Rome's cause would suffer gravely from a defeat, but would not gain equally from a victory. "Let Hannibal fight the winter," he said. "We can drill the army into true readiness and meet him at advantage in the spring."

But Sempronius would have none of this. He sat tracing his facial scar with his fingers, unmoved by the injured man's reasoning. He even offered the opinion that Cornelius' judgment had been clouded by the mauling he had so recently received. Sempronius wanted action, swift retribution, before Hannibal truly found his footing. Each hour the African spent on the soil of their land was an insult to the gods of Rome. He argued that the only right course was the direct course. Such was, after all, the Roman way.

Throughout these debates, the army shifted camps and marched and jostled for position with the Carthaginians, who seemed to own the land now and rarely left them in peace. As was the custom when two consuls joined forces, they shared command by alternating ultimate authority from one day to the next. On Cornelius' days, he backed and showed caution; when Sempronius held command, he moved forward, eventually setting up a new camp along the river Trebia. It was there, one dawn, that he got the battle he believed would bring him glory.

Following the orders received directly from Hannibal the day before, Tusselo and the other Massylii rose in the hours before dawn. This was no easy feat, for the night was the coldest he had yet experienced in his life, worse even than in the mountains. The air was raw enough that a dusting of frost covered the earth, but it was also heavy with a wet chill that thickened the very texture of the ether. As quickly as he could, he found one of the camp's raging fires and huddled next to it. He feasted on strips of meat from a sheep slaughtered the night before. He rubbed his face and limbs with oil, as did all the rousing, expectant soldiers. A few minutes of this and the weather did not seem so bad.

Even more significantly, Hannibal roamed among them, spurring them on, loud and cheerful, joking that a fine day was dawning, just right for a slaughter. The reckless consul was to command the day, and he was finally so nearby, so impatient, that Hannibal believed their moment had come. The commander knew exactly the method to win them victory. But he said, it depended wholly on them for its execution.

Once, he walked around the perimeter of the fire Tusselo sat beside. He patted men's shoulders and slapped helmets into place and encouraged them in their preparations. He reminded the men that they were far from home, deep in an enemy's land. A day of judgment was now upon them. They could not run from it or skirt it.

Their very lives hung in the balance. But so, too, did their greater glory. All the riches they had imagined for themselves when they began this quest were within reach. Rome still lay to the south of them, a fat jewel staring anxiously north, watching and waiting to see what Hannibal's army was capable of.

Tusselo's stomach was full and warm when he mounted. He knew he might get a knot in it from riding, but Hannibal wanted them to face the frigid day with fires burning within them. He rode away to the sound of his commander's voice fading behind him, part of him wishing he could stay on and listen longer; he found—as did other men, he was sure—something fascinating in their leader's person. But he had work to do, and his devotion was best demonstrated through action.

He rode as one among a thousand, all dark-skinned and well fed and glistening, many thickly maned. They moved through the trees, their horses fast and thundering in the open stretches, nimble and tiny-footed when stepping over fallen limbs. At some point in the journey each rider snapped a dead branch from a tree or dismounted and picked up sticks from the ground. They carried these secured in their fists, clamped in the iron grip of their fingers, just as they carried their javelins.

In the clearing on the near bank of the Trebia, they found scouts dispatched even earlier than they, led by the general Bomilcar. He did not speak at all, but simply rose from his squatting position and pointed to the ford. The horsemen turned as bidden. The stones on the bank of the river wore ice helmets, crystal rings licked by the moving current. Tusselo tried to ignore this and speak confidently as he urged his horse into the water. He gritted his teeth when the chill touched his feet and exhaled a sharp curse when the water invaded his damaged genitals. He heard other men gasp and tried to believe he was not so different than they.

Soon they emerged on the far bank, hooves making clipped, muted sounds as they smacked against the stones. The horses were quivering, nervous now and wary, for this whole venture seemed a strange one. A short gallop brought them within sight of the Roman camp. They emerged from the trees in steaming, panting clouds of vapor. Before them stretched a field of tall grass, each blade bent into delicate arches by the weight of its icy garment. And beyond this stood the Roman camp: earthworks piled high, freshly hewn trees cut and bound into lookout towers, thousands of jagged points penetrating the sky, tilted outward like a great beast's teeth. The camp was largely quiet, sleeping, the fires low, the wisps of smoke from them rising thin and fading into the low, heavy sky. The Numidian riders beheld the scene in silence and stepped forward slowly, gradually moving to well within missile range.

The calm was short-lived. They were spotted. Shouts issued from the camp, followed soon after by a blast of horns to awaken the entire camp.

The Numidians waited for Maharbal's command, and on the first shout from his clipped, strong voice, they all began the verbal attack they had been instructed in. They shouted in heavily accented Latin, taunting the Romans to come out and make merry, calling them children and women and goat-fuckers, offering them sexual favors, candied assholes and open mouths, all the things they had heard Romans enjoyed. They threw sticks at them—not spears, not javelins, but the dry wood they had snatched up earlier. Not weapons at all, but branches best suited for kindling.

At first the Romans scurried about in preparation for an attack. But as the twigs and insults flew their alarm changed to surprise. Head after head peered above the battlements. They were close enough that Tusselo could make out their openmouthed bewilderment, the confusion and then disbelief and—just beyond this— anger. They gesticulated insults of their own. A few even hurled back the mock weapons, as if the affront could be so easily returned. They stood in clear view and motioned the Africans closer. Then they remembered their lethal potential and began to loose their weapons.

The rain of javelins picked up, interspersed with arrows. Men began to fall, impaled. One riderless horse caught a javelin in its flank and went down in screeching, writhing confusion. A mounted man very near Tusselo was struck full in the chest with a bolt shot from one of the Roman crossbows. The force of the impact yanked him from the creature's back and sprawled him out upon the frozen tangle of grass. The field had suddenly grown deadly, the pristine carpet of moments before already trampled and churned up and stained here and there with blood. Maharbal signaled for the men to pull back slightly, just enough to bait the trap.

Sempronius ruled the day, and his first waking thought was that he was going to use it somehow. When he heard of the Numidians' antics he decided that the insult was too much to bear. He ordered full battle readiness. He knew the soldiers had not eaten yet, that they had not truly shaken off the night, or prepared their weapons or clothed themselves as they might have liked. These facts were unfortunate, but the enemy was near and so was victory. They could complete this work in a morning and dine as owners of the enemy's camp. At least, so the consul yelled to his officers when they expressed reservations. When Cornelius summoned him he sent back a messenger explaining that he was busy. There was no time for chat. But, he said, his fellow consul could rest assured that by the close of the day Rome would be safe again.

When they marched out through the camp gate, the Numidians jumped onto their mounts, spun a few circles, called out a few more oaths, and showed the approaching Romans their rumps. Watching this, Sempronius believed even more assuredly that victory was near. Less than an hour later, he reached the banks of the Trebia. On the far side, the consul saw the growing mass of the enemy, waiting for them under the first drops of icy rain that soon became a steady sleet. The Numidians were nearest, milling about like the savages they were, trilling to each other and slapping their horses into short gallops and acting as if they had achieved some victory. Behind them Sempronius distinguished the components he had expected, units sectioned off by ethnicity and fighting style: Libyans and Gauls and Celtiberians. The elephant-beasts churned the ground fretfully near the front. They had about them a fearsome aspect, but he had already instructed his men to aim their missiles at the riders, whose loss would make the creatures of little use, randomly floating islands of damage to all, but an aid to neither side. The army was a confused polyglot monster, unnatural and ill-suited to this part of the world. Sempronius had expected as much. He even caught sight of Hannibal's standard. He picked out the tight contingent of guards around a central figure and knew that finally the villain was within his grasp. He ordered his men forward.

The legions strode steadily into the river. They pushed through grim-faced, teeth clenched against the cold, clumsy because of the current pressing against them and the uneven stones beneath them, fighting for balance even as they held their weapons up out of the water. By the middle of the crossing the men were in icy water up to their chests. More than one soldier lost his footing and knocked his neighbors loose as well. Some dropped their weapons as they fought for purchase and a few went under and came up sputtering, white-skinned and dazed. Most made it across and emerged sodden, feet numb and clumsy beneath them and weapons held awkwardly in their stiff fingers.

The first of the Romans fell as stones whirled through the air with an audible hiss, nearly invisible projectiles that smashed sudden dents in helmets and broke ribs, snapped forearms, and pierced skulls through the eyes and nose. This was the work of the Balearic slingers. They were short men, not armored at all but dressed only against the cold because they did their damage from a distance. They taunted the Romans and called out oaths and swirled their stones into blinding speed. Sempronius, who had crossed the river on horseback, shouted for calm in his men. He told them to scorn these womanish weapons and form up into ranks. The words were scarcely out of his mouth, however, when a stone smashed into his mount's skull, splattering his face with blood.

He was on his feet screaming for another mount when the second wave of attackers hit. Several thousand Carthaginian pikemen moved into striking range, their absurdly long spears at the ready. Sempronius called for his men to throw their javelins, but the response he got was feeble. He and his men realized all at once, in a silent moment, that most had used their missiles already, either trying to hit the Numidians, or, moments before, when they tried to answer the slingers, who even now sent stones whizzing over the heads of their allies and home to their targets.

The pikemen picked their prey individually, skewering them from outside sword range. Some came with their weapon held in two hands and drove it toward abdomen or groin. Others hefted the spear up and thrust it single-handed into face or chest. Lightly armored, they danced away as the soldiers charged them, waiting for openings into which to drive their spearheads home. They retreated only when the sheer numbers of soldiers on the shore pressed them back.

Sempronius called his men to order yet again. He gave the instructions to form up for battle and proceed. He was still focused and confident. He loathed the unmanly tactics of his enemy and shouted as much so that all would know his disdain. And yet some part of him felt that something was amiss. He tried not to acknowledge it. Tried to recover from each successive surprise and shape his men into the disciplined ranks he knew to be unbeatable. But when he heard the trumpeting of the pachyderms, saw the raging bulk, witnessed the power with which a single creature swatted four soldiers and left them broken pieces of men—then, for the first time, he felt a knot low in his abdomen, a ball of fear that pulsed with the possibility that events were not about to unfold as he wished.

Though he was pressed to the ground—still and chilled as he had been since the dark hours of the night—Mago's heart pounded in his chest as if he were already in the battle. He saw it all happening and wanted to believe that all was as it should be, but he kept reminding himself not to let his expectations get ahead of events. He waited as the first Romans fell on the riverside. Watching through plumes of his own breath, he saw the legions mass and engage his brother's main forces. He recognized their attempt at order, the way the velites came to the fore to throw their missiles. They staggered forward, some already weaponless, many dropping before the slingers' pellets. Those who could hurled their weapons with remarkable accuracy, but they never launched their single, massive volley. Mago could find no fault with their efforts. It was simply that, from the first moments, the battle proceeded on Hannibal's terms, not on theirs.

Soon the elephants churned through the ranks, trumpeting and bellowing as their drivers smacked their skulls and urged them on. In the confusion men were trampled and swatted into the air or impaled on tusks. The Romans feared these animals, as any sane men would, but they did not give way. They aimed their sword thrusts at their eyes, hacked at their trunks, and jabbed their blades into their flanks. More than one mahout was jerked from his post at the point of a spear.

Despite these stampeding boulders, despite the sleet and the spray kicked up from the ground, the Romans still managed to form and re-form their ranks. They still inflicted damage. Their style of battle was tight and organized. They leaned forward, closely guarded by their shields, and cut down the wildly swinging Gauls particularly well, jabbing their short swords into their unprotected abdomens and pulling back and then jabbing the next. They ate steadily through the Gallic center of the Carthaginian forces, fighting with surprising efficiency considering the circumstances. But still the pieces came together against them. The Numidian cavalry rode circles around their Roman counterparts and soon had them on the run, pushed clear of the legions' edges and leaving their flanks open.

This, Mago recognized, was where he came in. He nodded to the soldier beside him, who snapped himself to his feet and bellowed out the call to the rest. They peeled themselves from the ground, stiff from the long wait, many of them chilled beyond shivering. They hefted their swords and shields and began shouting out, grunting and chanting, each invoking his favored gods, whispering prayers to them. Mago strode forward. He did not look back but trusted that the rest were behind him. For the first few steps, he barely felt his legs working beneath him. He smacked his feet down as heavily as he could to ensure his footing, and soon warmed to the work. He heard the clink of their armor and the thump of their feet against the semi-frozen ground. Initially there was something ghostly in the noise, but as they drew closer to the battle the men found further voice. Their jaws loosened, bodies fired with sudden heat. The discordant tongues blended as they ran, and became a wild bellowing that was beyond words, rooted in something earlier and deeper in the brain than language. The distance they had to cover was considerable and in the running their fury grew. Individuals picked out their targets and envisioned the damage they were about to inflict.

Mago saw the infantryman he wanted from a hundred strides out and homed in on him. He took the man with a swinging blow that cut his neck to the spine. A warm spray of blood coated Mago's clenched fist at the sword hilt and splashed up his arm. The man never knew what hit him. Nor was he alone. Mago's group drove into the side of the legions like famished locusts, stepping over the bodies they had slain to get to more. The legionaries in the center could not yet have known what had happened, but they must have felt the shifting press of the men on both sides of them and with it the first hints of panic. Their forward progress ground to a halt. Instead of slicing through unarmored Gauls, the front ranks were now toe to toe with the spears of the Libyan veterans, soldiers fresh from the fires, well oiled and salivating for Roman blood and urged on by Bomilcar, whose voice boomed above the din.

For Mago, the battle lasted no more than a few blurred moments. His arms lashed and thrust, his legs stepped over bodies, his ankles stiffened to steady him on the earth or on the abdomens or backs or necks of those beneath him. He turned and ducked and screamed at the top of his lungs, all at a speed beyond thought. A primal fury took hold of him completely and rendered him, for a few moments, a furious agent of death. He would remember afterward that he sliced open the unprotected belly of a velite with a right-handed stroke. On some impulse previously unknown to him, he punched a fist into the man's abdomen and ripped out the warm, steaming loops of viscera. He flicked them from his fingers and pushed the man from his path and carried on. He would later find images like this troubling, but in the heat of those short moments he was his father's son and Hannibal's brother, gifted at death, fighting not with his deliberative mind but with pure instinct.

He was among the first to drive the Romans into the river. He felt the euphoria of blood but the work was no clear rout. The Romans managed some order in their retreat. He was ankle deep in the crimson water when he realized Hannibal had called the battle to a halt. He stood panting, watching the remnants of the legions retreat behind the screen of falling sleet, which was turning gradually to snow. When he turned and looked upon the carnage, it took his breath away, not in elation or even relief. He knelt as if to pray and, thus disguised, spat chunks of his breakfast into the river.

His first true battle was behind him.

Waiting in the dank cell in Emporiae, Hanno had hour after slow hour to think about the mistakes that had led to his capture. But he did not consider the tactical maneuvers that Gnaeus Scipio had so easily countered. Instead he could not shake the memory of his hands' trembling in the hours leading up to the battle. He had first felt it as he lay awake in the predawn hours. He knew something was wrong with his hands, although he could not tell what. They alternately felt as if they were being pricked by thousands of tiny needles, or as if they crawled with ants, or as if they had been submerged in icy water and had turned blue with cold. He slid them under his buttocks and stilled them with the weight and warmth of his body, but after he rose the tremble continued, gaining strength.

At his meeting with his generals he tried to disguise the trouble, but they clearly noticed that he did not reach for the charts offered him, that he had one of them draw out the lay of the land with a stick instead of doing it himself, that he sat with his hands wedged between his knees. After he dismissed them, he stayed inside his tent and banged his hands against the table before him. This changed nothing. He bashed them on the hard floor of his tent. He sat on them, his mind roiling with fury that his own body spurned him so. None of these methods changed anything, and as he rode out to battle he could only still his hands by making sure they were always clenched on something: his helmet, the creases of his breastplate, the hilt of his sword, which he prayed would be drenched with Roman blood before the day waned.

This, however, was not to be. He knew it from the moment he saw the Romans on the field before him. The battle was a blundering fiasco. He tried to push it from his mind, unsure how he could even learn from such a jumbled collage of images, none of them making any sense, none offering him any alternative to help him escape the outcome. It was as if he had looked over a game board and made the move of ordering his men forward, only to discover that he had already fallen into some classic mistake—recognized immediately by his opponent—and that nothing now could avert his failure. He lost his entire army of ten thousand. Most of them were killed. Many were captured. He could not even be sure how many, because he himself was seized. His guards fought to the death with the swarm of Romans that surrounded him. But when he tried to goad them into murdering him they would not. Instead they worked toward him slowly, in vast numbers, pressing in on him from behind their shields until he was so boxed in that he could not even move. They disarmed him and bound him and kicked him before them in stumbling indignity, a prisoner, a Barca in chains, denied even a mount, so that he eventually entered Emporiae as an amusement for the astonished faces of the Greek townspeople. He would so very much rather have died.

Instead he found himself shoved into a tiny subterranean room, dim and wet from groundwater and frequented by rats. Holes the size of a man's fist lined the upper wall along one side. Through them torchlight from the hallway shone into the cell, casting shadow and highlight across the aged wooden beams that supported the roof. This was all that illuminated the chamber, but Hanno's eyes quickly adjusted. The four walls were carved from a whitish stone, roughly, as if the chamber had been intended for storage, not human habitation. He felt the chalkiness of the stone in the back of his throat. The film of it stuck to his skin. The chill seeped into him slowly, as if the longer he sat the more he himself took on the quality, texture, and substance of the stone. Once deposited here, he was left alone, passing time that he could only estimate by the movements of the guards outside his door, their rotations of duty, and the occasional meals they slipped under the door for him. His hands no longer trembled. They were still, stiff, and aching. Whatever fear he had held in them plagued him no more. This galled him nearly as much as their shaking had.

What type of place was this to keep someone of his stature? He realized that he had no idea what to expect from these Romans. They might treat him with dignity if it suited them, as Hannibal instructed his generals to do with prisoners of note. They might make overtures to Carthage, using him as a negotiating point. But nothing in their behavior so far made dignified treatment seem likely. The Romans were likely ignorant of Hannibal's policies on dealing with prisoners. If they remembered anything, it would be the atrocities of the earlier war between the two nations, when barbarity had reached its zenith. In truth, there were no shared traditions that his captors were obliged to uphold. If they wished, they could peel the skin from his living body and douse him in vinegar and take pleasure commensurate with his pain. He simply could not predict the course ahead of him. Being hit by the full force of this reality, he recognized the truth beneath it: He had never had control of his own destiny; never had the future been certain. So in this piece of knowledge, at least, he exceeded Hannibal in wisdom.

For all of the foulness of the cell and the possible tortures awaiting him, what troubled him most was more mundane. There was no latrine in the cell, neither a hole nor a sewage channel nor any space designated for the purpose. For the first six days he would not squat to relieve himself. He ate nothing and drank water sparingly. He swore that he would not shit until the Romans offered him a proper toilet of their own accord. This they did not do. By the third day he had to clench his buttocks tight. On the fourth day he focused in on the muscles right around his anus and scrunched them to fight the rhythmic churning power of his bowels.

When his feces final escaped it was in a moment of weakness, while he was drowsy and dream-racked. He found himself squatting in a corner of the cell and felt his backside open up before he even knew what he was doing. As he felt the euphoric release of the stuff curving out of him he tried to convince himself that this was an act of defiance. He was shitting on Rome, throwing his waste in their faces, soiling them. But a moment later he balled up on the other side of the cell and watched helplessly as his eyes watered over and tears spilled from them. Strange that this one thing struck him as such an indignity, but it did. It made him feel like a child without even the control of his own bodily functions. Through the wavering, dim scene before him he prayed to Baal, to El and Anath, to Moloch. The names of the gods felt dead on his tongue, but still he called on them, promising that if he lived he would inflict all manner of mayhem in their names, trying to convince himself that he was still a man who could make such promises into realities.

After a full week of complete solitude, Hanno welcomed the moment the door swung open and a Roman stepped through. At least something was now to happen, whatever it might be. The man dressed as an officer, with a red cloak flowing down his back. He carried a lamp before him, the single flame of which cast highlights on the long, prominent muscles of his arms. He stood for a moment surveying the room, looking from Hanno around the cell, pausing on the pile of waste. Then he fixed his gaze on Hanno and spoke with haughty confidence, without pausing to ask whether the Carthaginian could understand his Latin.

"Do you know me? I am Gnaeus Scipio, the victor in our battle. You, Barca, are the first joyful piece of news for Rome since your brother began this madness. Your failure will light fires in the hearts of my people, flames that no rain can douse, no wind extinguish. How does it feel to know you so hearten your enemies?"

Gnaeus moved closer. He bent and studied Hanno's face. He had heavy eyebrows, bushy and chaotic, and a rounded nose that might have been broken in his youth. "I can see that you understand me, so don't feign ignorance of my language. I truly mean what I am saying. You have done me a great service. When I first saw events unfolding at Hannibal's direction I feared the worst. But when I met you on the field I was reassured. Barcas can be defeated. I know, because I've witnessed it. And now you know it, too. You understand that we will send you to Rome eventually, don't you? You are, and will continue to be, a prisoner of the Roman Republic, but before you journey to my capital I will use you for a purpose or two here in Iberia. I've already sent word to every Iberian tribe that called you an ally. I've invited them all here to see you, to look upon a captured Barca and see you for what you are. Imagine the effect on them when they see you live in a tiny room, alone except for your own filth."

Gnaeus straightened and stepped away. "When you do go to Rome, I cannot say how the Senate will dispose of you. To some extent that depends on yourself, and on your brothers. Think carefully on what may be possible, because your lot need not be so foul as you might fear. Hannibal will lose this war. You do not have to lose it with him. You might, actually, manage to find favor with us. You might aid us and subsequently find yourself elevated even as your brother is defeated. For example, should you choose to speak reason to the tribes and dissuade them from their allegiance to Carthage . . . Or if you open your mouth and tell us things valuable to our fight against Carthage here in Iberia . . . There are many ways you can be helpful. Need I detail them to you?"

Hanno, having grasped the thrust of the man's comments clearly enough, answered him. "I will never betray my family, or Carthage."

"Better men than you have done just that, and no one calls a man a fool if he succeeds while his brother perishes. How can you be sure your brothers would not sell you to save their own skins?"

"You know nothing of us."

The Roman considered the prisoner from a different angle, and then twisted his head away as if to indicate that he saw nothing new. "In any event, you have already betrayed your nation. Do your people not frown on failure as a man's greatest sin? Perhaps I should put you on a boat bound for Carthage and let them deal with you. It's crucifixion they favor, isn't it? Or is it impaling?"

Hanno spat on the ground and then covered the spot with his foot. "I curse you and your line, your brother and your sons. May you father only girls and may all of them be whores to your enemies."

Gnaeus smiled. He held his chin in his hand a moment and seemed to think bemusedly on the curse. "Is it by your own gods that you curse me? I do not fear them. And you, you should not trust them. Look at how they've abandoned you." He knocked on the door and waited for the guards to let him out. Once the door was cracked he paused and addressed himself once more to Hanno. "Whether you like it or not, we will ask you many questions. It would behoove you to answer them. If you do not, we will find which torture persuades you most forcefully. By the gods—yours or mine—I would not wish to be inside your skin in the weeks to come."

With that he pulled the door fast behind him, leaving Hanno alone with the man's words echoing in his head.

———

After the battle beside the Trebia, a howling blizzard blew in. Snow fell for two days straight. On the third a new cold crept down from the mountains. It stung exposed flesh so that men could only walk blindly, faces shrouded, stumbling toward whatever goal spurred them to move. There was little rejoicing among the men and no real mention was made of following after the ragged Roman survivors. Few even ventured out to scavenge on the battlefield. That grave-yard was left to the wolves and ravens and other creatures fond of human flesh and impervious to the weather. The elephants that had traveled so far and inflicted such great damage could not withstand the relentless cold. All but one of them died within the week; this last creature, called Cyrus, was looked after with care, for now he was Vandicar's sole ward. The chief mahout swore he would keep the creature alive to see the heat of an Italian summer.

Despite the hardships, Hannibal was pleased that they had won their first battle against Rome. Over the winter, he managed to re-ceive several reports from spies and what they told him of events in Rome brought him pure joy. News of the defeat had traveled quickly to the capital and rocked the population's confidence. Dur-ing his first meeting with the Senate, Sempronius minimized the full extent of the tragedy and his role as the author of it. They had suffered this setback for a variety of reasons, he claimed. The raw-ness of so many of the troops. The bitter weather that impeded their deployment. The morale boost that the Carthaginians had fed upon after the skirmish on the Ticinus. The Trebia battle was no major defeat, he said, just an unfortunate incident.

Cornelius, arriving somewhat later, described the situation as he recalled it. He responded to the senators' questions as flatly and simply as possible, but still each answer fell like dirt filling into his fellow consul's grave. Among other things, he provided the most ac-curate estimate of the dead—more than thirteen thousand killed outright, more dead of infection. Questioned as to whether Sem-pronius had acted with gross negligence, Cornelius, surprisingly, said that he did not believe so. The events that benefited Hannibal that morning were too numerous to explain. No man could orches-trate such a thing. Perhaps only the gods could.

Nor was he the only one to arrive at this conclusion. Soon after the news of the defeat, tales began to circulate of prodigies that should have warned of the gods' displeasure. In Sardinia, a cavalry officer's staff had burst into flames. Some soldiers on Sicily had been struck by lightning while at exercise. At Praeneste, the rat population doubled in just a few days, and at Antium reapers swore that their hay had left traces of blood upon their blades. In more than one place it rained red-hot stones large enough to crack the skulls of the unwary. And these were not mere rumors. In each case of such an unnatural occurrence, a witness journeyed to Rome and told the story to the Senate. The Board of Ten consulted the Divine Writings, and on their recommendation the city spent much of the winter making offerings to Jupiter, to Juno, and to Minerva, conducting rites and holding public banquets like the Strewing of Couches, sacrificing pigs in Saturn's honor.

Fine, Hannibal thought. Let them pray themselves into a frenzy.

The early spring brought the news that Servilius Geminus and Gaius Flaminius had been elected consuls. They were both charged to prosecute the war by extreme measures. They were to take control of all the routes through the Apennines and bar Hannibal's southward progress. There were now to be two legions with each consul, another two for Rome itself, two more for Sicily, and a further legion to protect Sardinia. The two legions in Iberia were to continue their efforts there. Flaminius—a new man in the Senate and the first in his family to attain consulship—especially burned for action. He announced his plans to leave the city and commence the campaign immediately, eschewing the traditional ceremonies that would have delayed him well into the spring.

This was equally pleasant news to Hannibal. Religious fervor on one hand, arrogant impatience on the other: What more could he ask for?

In the days just preceding the first tentative signs of spring, the commander met in council after council, studying charts and interviewing scouts and debating the course ahead of them. His goal lay to the south, toward Rome and her prominent allies, but just which route to take was not easy to decide. They could march toward the east coast, take or bypass Ariminum, and roar down the Via Flaminia directly toward Rome. Another way lay across the Apennines toward the Etruscan town of Faesulae, from where they could weave their way south through several different channels, not as direct as the Flaminia, but a reasonable course that might provide them just enough forage and geographic protection to fight their way to the peninsula's heart. Or they could attempt a crossing of the Ligurian range, difficult terrain that merited consideration only because of the possibility of resupply from the Carthaginian fleet along the Tyrrhenian coast.

As usual, the commander's generals came to him with differing opinions and expressed them freely. Bomilcar and Mago argued for a march on Ariminum, for direct engagement with Servilius, the consul in command there: All of Italy would be open to them if they defeated him. Maharbal and Carthalo preferred some variation on the central route, a way that would suit their swift and far-ranging riders and let them fight the skirmishes they excelled at. Only Bostar favored the difficult march toward the western coast and the benefits of meeting up with the fleet. Monomachus did not seem to think the route mattered that much; each of them led to Roman blood and that was sufficient for him.

None of the routes suited Hannibal perfectly. He wanted something more devious, more disconcerting, a way forward that would again throw the Romans into confusion. When he heard that among Maharbal's horsemen was a man who claimed to know of just such a course, he had him brought forward at once.

The man in question joined Hannibal, Mago, and Silenus in Hannibal's tent late on a pleasantly mild morning. He entered humbly behind Maharbal, head down, eyes fixed upon the earthen floor. He was gaunt in a way that indicated he had suffered from months of poor diet. He stood like a stick figure dressed to scare birds from a field. His clothes hung off him, a collection of skins and furs piled upon each other against the cold. His hair was wild, grown long and matted. It did not flow down his back but stood out around him like a lion's mane.

"He is called Tusselo," Maharbal said. "He has been with us since Saguntum. He is a good rider, though I cannot say how he comes to know this land."

"You are Massylii?" Hannibal asked.

Tusselo nodded.

"Why do you know Roman geography?"

Tusselo did not raise his eyes, but his voice was steady and calm when he spoke. "I was a slave to the Romans. I lived twelve years in this land. My master was a merchant. We traveled much. I learned the land through walking it. Many places and the ways between them are still clear in my mind."

"Do you find the land different when looked upon with free eyes?"

"Different, yes. And the same."

"It cannot be easy to return to the land that enslaved you, especially not for a Massylii. Your people were not put on the earth to be slaves. Do you return to seek revenge?"

The Numidian did not answer immediately. He cleared his throat and waited and made no sign that he would respond. But Hannibal let the silence linger.

"I cannot answer you with certainty," Tusselo eventually said. "I have much anger, yes. I was robbed of many things, but not physical things that I can reclaim as such. I do want revenge, Commander, but I also want things I do not have words to explain."

"I will not press you to find those words," Hannibal said, "so long as there is always conviction in your actions. What is this route south that you know of?"

Tusselo explained that there was a neglected and difficult road to the north of Arretium. He pointed it out on the chart the generals had been using in their debates. It ran just south of the Arno River, through a marshy, swampy land. There was little forage on this route, the ground being so constantly soaked that only water plants flourished there. Trees had been drowned long ago and stood bare and rotting. Grass would be difficult to find. This time of the year it would be a chilly wasteland, a wide swath of country knee deep in water. The route had a single thing to recommend it, and that was that nobody would imagine they would choose it. They could emerge well into the center of Italy, behind the armies sent to bar their passage.

"My master once took this route to avoid the debt collectors who were hunting him," Tusselo said. "It proved a good choice. But even in the height of summer it was a wetland. It will be wetter in the spring."

"You still call him your master?" Silenus asked.

Tusselo turned his gaze on him, took him in, and then looked back in Hannibal's general direction. "It is just a word, the easiest for me to use. The truth is something different."

Mago placed his fingers on the papyrus and turned it toward himself. "If these marshlands are as you describe they'll be as deadly as the mountain crossing."

"It is the least favorable route imaginable," Tusselo said, "but if we managed it the army might pass both consuls undiscovered. We'd appear to vanish from the world in one place—"

"—and later appear in another," Hannibal concluded.

Tusselo nodded. For the first time he looked directly into the commander's eyes. "Like witchcraft," he said.

There was a silence. After a moment, Hannibal dismissed the Numidian. To Maharbal he said, "Do you trust this man?"

"I don't know how he came to us," Maharbal said, "but he has never given me reason to doubt him. I believe he knows this land. And I believe he is no friend to the Romans."

"I see as much in his eyes," Hannibal said. "Sometimes I wonder at the workings of the gods. I would not have found this route without this man, and yet I feel a drum beating inside me. This is part of our destiny. I must believe the gods placed him among us to make us see that which we would not have seen."

"Or to lead us astray," Mago said. "Not all gods look kindly on us. Brother, I do not favor defeating our cause by a march. We cannot survive another victory like the mountain crossing. I fear this will cost us too heavily."

"At times our fate is presented to us through unlikely vessels," Hannibal said. "I believe this Numidian is such a vessel. Why else would he return to the land that enslaved him? Even he cannot answer that question. This route is like an arrow loosed in the dark. The Romans will neither hear nor see the missile's flight. They will simply feel the shaft as it runs deep into their chest."

To Maharbal he said, "Tell this Tusselo that he rides at my side on this march. If we succeed I will be the first to credit him. If anything goes awry . . . he will learn the wrath of a new master."

When the meeting concluded a little later, Hannibal asked Silenus to remain. Once they were alone, the commander stood and paced the room. He cleared his throat, then touched his neck with his fingers, took a fold of flesh between them, and tugged. "You are loyal to me, are you not?"

Silenus, uncomfortable with the tone of the question, rose and said, "I've no notion of what has been said against me, but my loyalty is complete. Has someone spoken ill of me?"

Hannibal stopped pacing. He lifted his head and turned it just enough to focus on the scribe. "No, no one has spoken ill of you. The truth is, I have something to ask of you. It is a mission far beyond our agreement, but I have need of your help. It regards my brother, Hanno. I've just learned that his troops were badly defeated by Gnaeus Scipio. He was captured and is being held at Emporiae. You know this place, don't you?"

Silenus lowered himself back onto his stool. Clearly, this news struck him with a heavy significance.

"He's been there for too long already," Hannibal said. "The news was slow in reaching me. When I imagine my brother a captive to them . . . at their mercy . . . it boils my blood as few things ever have. He must be freed. I curse myself for not learning of his capture earlier. I would offer to ransom him, but I've no faith the Romans would oblige me this. Do you?"

The Greek cleared his throat. "It would give them great pleasure to receive that request," he said. "But no, they would not free him. I'm surprised they haven't transported him to Rome already."

"He's more use to them in Iberia. They've been parading him before the various tribes, degrading him, winning my allies from me by showing them a captured, powerless Barca. Someone over there understands that the unified might of Iberia—if ever harnessed—could push New Carthage into the sea, and with it everything I've striven for. Even so, I must assume they will send him to Rome soon, to display him yet again, but to the people of Italy. That cannot happen. Do you know a magistrate in Emporiae named Diodorus?"

The Greek nodded. "He's my sister's husband." After a long moment, as the two of them contemplated this, Silenus asked, "What would you have me do?"

Sapanibal waited for Imago Messano in her private garden, a secluded spot at the far end of the familial palace. Her chambers were less lavish than they had been at the height of her marriage to Hasdrubal the Handsome, but they suited her tastes well enough. Her sitting room extended from inside to out with hardly a boundary between the two. She sat on a stone stool beneath the shade of several massive palm trees. Water trickled down from a high, hidden cistern and ran in a tiny stream to feed the pond just behind her, rich with reeds and water lilies, home to several species of fish and a water snake that had grown fat and lazy in such bounty.

She had requested a meeting with the councillor for three reasons. One, because she knew he would be fresh from the Council and he was her best source for the things discussed there. Two, because she knew him to be utterly loyal to her family. This was something not to be taken for granted among the Carthaginian aristocracy. And thirdly, because she found the widower's obvious reverence of her appealing. She had not had many suitors before the politically important marriage to her late husband. Nor had she seen much interest in the years since his death. She attributed this to her strength of character, to the peculiar position of her family, to the unmatchable reputation of her brothers. And, beyond all that, she was no beauty. In light of all these things, Imago's interest in her was interesting to her as well.

Sapanibal did not rise when Imago appeared. For a moment—watching him walk toward her across the polished granite, his garments loose about him, flowing, his face aged just enough so that the awkwardness of his youth had been transformed into a more suitable composure—Sapanibal felt her pulse quicken. Though she promised herself she would never show it to him, this man appealed to her as few others had. She had first admired him in her girlhood, and some spark of that early devotion lingered. He was not a warrior, but he had ridden out with her father to put down the mercenary rebellion. This was no small act. That war had been one of incredible brutality. He would have known that capture by that rabble would have meant a horrible death. He had been a young man, with a considerable future ahead of him. That he put his life in danger confirmed his valor, even if his inclinations since had been of a tamer nature. He had also proved himself more recently by answering Fabius Maximus with Carthage's acceptance of war.

"Imago Messano," she said, "welcome. Thank you for favoring me with your presence."

"It is nothing," he said, taking a seat on the stool she indicated. "I am always happy to answer the call of a Barca."

Sapanibal offered him food and refreshments. She made small talk for a few moments, asking after his health and that of his children, avoiding any mention of his late wife. But it was not long before she asked him for a report on the debate in the Council. Before he answered, Imago sipped the lime-flavored drink a servant offered him. He closed his eyes in enjoyment of it.

"I've a fondness for bitter things," he said. Opening his eyes, he met Sapanibal's gaze. "You know, of course, what befell your brother Hanno. The Council received the news of his defeat and capture gravely. It's no small thing to lose ten thousand men. It was quite a resounding failure, really, and it puts our hold on Iberia in grave jeopardy."

Sapanibal felt the hair at the back of her neck lift to attention. "My brother had no choice, as I understand it. The Romans had landed and were welcomed at Emporiae. What would you have had him do? He fought for our interests. If the Council cared for justice they'd be negotiating for his release. Why aren't they?"

Imago considered his answer carefully. His hands were heavily jeweled. Thrumming his fingers in thought, the rings seemed almost some sort of armor. "It's unlikely that the Romans would release a general just so that he could turn around and fight them on the morrow. That's the only reason we've not pursued it. Time will provide another way."

"No, Hannibal will provide another way. Once he's reinforced and sent new troops, he will once more be unconquerable. I've no doubt he'll free Hanno himself."

Imago inhaled in a way that suggested deep import. "Let us hope that proves so. I should tell you, though, that the Council has decided to continue sending reinforcements to Iberia, but not to Italy."

"Not to Hannibal?"

"When the situation in Iberia is stabilized, Hasdrubal will be released to join your eldest brother."

Sapanibal flicked her fingers up and showed Imago her palm. Like some snake charmer's trick, this single motion silenced him. "But surely our councillors are more farsighted than that. Our strength still lies in Hannibal! His success means the safety of Iberia. But he needs reinforcements. You will not deny him this."

"It is complicated, my dear," Imago said, smiling an invitation to leave the discussion at that.

"As am I. Tell me what you know and I will explain what you do not understand."

Imago considered this a moment, turned it over, finally deciding that such wit was just the thing he liked about this woman. "Many in the Council do not support your brother with their whole hearts," he said. "They fear that this war has put our interests in danger. Iberia was barely contained under your brother's firm hand. With him gone, the Iberians may yet rise against us. Or—as Hanno has demonstrated—the Romans may manage to replace us there. And also they fear for Carthage itself. No one wants to find the Romans knocking at the gates, should your brother fail."

"And yet Hannibal did not declare this war, did he? That oath was sworn here in Carthage, by the same tongue that speaks to me now."

"Well, yes, but . . . Ours are a conservative people, Sapanibal. We do not want the world. We are not like Hannibal in that. What the Council wants most is to regain the possessions that have been lost. Sicily, Sardinia, Corsica. To hold Iberia—"

"Which my family alone conquered," Sapanibal snapped.

Imago pursed his lips. "Just so. And in this lies the further problem. Few could stomach the return of a victorious Hannibal. Jealousy is stronger than reason at times. The Hannons plead peace, now as ever, but what they really fear is that your brother will achieve his goals. That result would make them rich beyond all reason—but it would make Hannibal's fame immortal. Greatness always makes enemies, Sapanibal. The Hannons, like Hadus, hate and fear Hannibal as much as they hated and feared Hamilcar before him. I say this so that you understand that those who love your family—as I do—must move carefully in such circles."

"I pray you are wrong," Sapanibal replied. "My brother is the pride of Carthage. Perhaps the councillors don't truly know him. He has been nothing but a name here for so many years. Remind them of his virtues; make them proud of him, not envious."

"I think that you and I have a different understanding of men's natures."

"Then speak directly to the Council of Elders, the One Hundred. Invoke the memory of Hamilcar—"

This time it was Imago's turn to silence Sapanibal with a gesture. "Your brother has few friends among the One Hundred," he said. "He too closely represents the glory of youth, and this is troubling to old men. Councillors are not like foot soldiers. They do not risk their lives for those they adore, nor must they put true faith in the men they elect leaders. They would rather have a hero-less victory, so that no glory shines on another. Believe me, no councillor wants to see Hannibal worshipped in such a great triumph. This they just cannot accept."

"And you, Imago? What can you accept?"

"I would happily adorn your brother's shoulders with flower petals. I would be the first to bow before him. I've always been a friend to your family. I was loyal to your father and supported him even when his success made him enemies."

Sapanibal lifted her fruit drink for the first time, sipped it, and then put it down, a slight tremor in her hands. "I know, Imago. My father told me of your friendship. I do not doubt you, but what you report troubles me. If our councillors are already prepared to abandon my brother—when he has had nothing but hard-fought success—what will they do should he really falter?"

"Pray that he does not falter," Imago said. He averted his eyes to signal a change of the subject. He asked after Didobal's health. Sapanibal was reluctant to let the conversation drift, but she had learned much and they were both aware of it. She answered that her mother was well, as ever. Asked about her younger sister, she said the same. At first she was surprised that he would ask after a girl, but then he betrayed his real interest.

"I understand she is fond of King Gaia's son, Masinissa," Imago said. "But your mother has not confirmed their engagement, has she?"

Sapanibal had, in fact, spoken to her mother on this subject just the day previous, but the whole discussion had made her uneasy. It reminded her too much of the machinations that had led to her own ill-fated marriage. True enough, a union with the Massylii would bring them that much further under Carthage's sway, ensuring that the king would always supply them with his gifted horsemen, but she did not wish to think of her sister being delivered to a man who could use or abuse her as he saw fit. Who can know what lies behind a man's smile? She responded that Didobal thought the two in question were still quite young. There was time yet, and Didobal hoped that her eldest son would be able to bless the union in person, when he returned.

Imago smiled through all of this but responded with some gravity edging his voice. "I pray she does not wait too long. Hannibal may not return soon enough for this matter. Masinissa is a fine young man. He's destined for great things. Many in the Council believe so. But there are many others who vie to wed their daughters to a son of the Massylii. Either to Masinissa, or to some other who might usurp his power. For this reason, your mother should concede promptly. We need stability along the seacoast, now more than ever. If Rome were ever to attack us here, we'd need our allies more than we like to admit. Certainly Sophonisba should stay away from the Libyan, Syphax."

"What has he to do with it?"

"Did you not hear about the banquet during his last visit? Your sister danced. Hers was a brief appearance, yes, but it left the king salivating. He spent the rest of the night trying to learn all he could about her. He's a lecher, but we can't pretend he's not important. I fear he'll be the cause of trouble soon. He is eyeing King Gaia's domain as we speak. It's hard to see how it will all unravel, but I'm sure there is no better union for Carthage than one between Masinissa and a Barca. The prophets say the boy has a role to play in Carthage's future. They are never wrong. Consider what I say and sound out your mother."

Imago lifted his stool and scooted it closer. He changed his tone yet again: business was concluded. "You are looking well, Sapanibal. I believe the sun agrees with you. Truly it is a blessing to have you so near . . ."

Never in his whole miserable life had Imco Vaca seen anything like the marshes of the Arno. He thought the mountains had been a hell of ice and rock, a horrible place worse than any other in creation. He had dreamed of those heights throughout the long winter, night-mares in which he had yet to complete the crossing. He would awake knowing that thousands of souls were trapped in the ice and might be there forever. He thanked the gods daily that he had lived through the ordeal, and he had no plans to ever relive it in his waking hours.

That is why it seemed particularly cruel—almost a personal af-front—that Hannibal chose to drive them through such sopping desolation. Imco had emerged into the spring as a sickly, paltry ver-sion of his former beauty. His body was not accustomed to months of snowy cold. He had watched in horror as a surgeon hacked off his frost-damaged finger with a serrated knife. The surgery, miracu-lously, did not lead to infection, but Imco believed the wound al-lowed malignant spirits easy entry to his body. How else did the fever creep into him? And what about the cough? Try as he might, he could not expel whatever was growing inside his chest. Nor could he stop the flow of green mucus that clogged his nasal passages. Some men managed to scavenge decent food, but Imco barely had the energy to search for sustenance. Though he ate meat cut from pack animals, he had not had a piece of fruit or a serving of anything remotely like a vegetable since the stores grabbed from Taurin.

By the spring he could see in his arms and abdomen that he had shrunk. His thighs and calves and forearms ached all day long, but not just from labor. His muscles pulsed with pain even at quiet mo-ments. His teeth jiggled in his gums and, he was sure, his hair was falling out at an unnatural rate. His vision seemed to be disturbed as well. He could see objects clearly enough, but he had difficulty translating what his eyes saw into meaningful messages. Thus, though he noticed the horse's rump, he did not fully comprehend how ill-placed he was behind it until the creature kicked him with a muddy hoof. Other times he misstepped and fell to his knees in the muck, not because he had not seen the object that tripped him up, but because it had not fully registered that he needed to consider its influence on his life.

By the end of the first day in the swamp, he had fully reconsidered his notions of suffering. Hell was not frozen and hard. It was wet, damp, soft. It was ankle-deep water. It was mud sucking at your feet. It was not even being able to sit down and take a moment's rest. He should have known that something horrific was in the making when he learned of the placement of troops in the line of march. The best infantry, the Libyans, strode in the front of the line, so that the ground held firm for the first few thousand of them. Behind them came the other African troops, including Imco. Then the Iberian allies pressed through the increasingly sticky churned-up mud. In the rear of all the infantry came the Gauls. By now thousands of feet and hooves had so churned up the swamp that the men were wading and slipping through deep muck, clawing at it with their hands, struggling vainly to keep their loads from becoming soiled.

Watching them, Imco paused long enough to thank the gods for birthing him an African, for the sorry lot of the pale ones was nothing to wish for. Such was the Gauls' misery that they would probably have deserted, each and every one of them, except that Mago and Bomilcar followed them up with the Numidian cavalry. They rode through the swamp like ill-tempered, heavily armed herdsmen, pushing the army forward no matter what. Hannibal provided no one a choice in the matter.

It was a forlorn land; the only plants were thick, leathery grasses and reedlike tufts. Insects rose from the water and danced in swarms as big around as elephants. These seemed to appear spontaneously, deviously, so that if he glanced away for a moment Imco was likely to find himself spun in a confusion of the creatures, inhaling them and catching them in the corners of his eyes and his nose hairs. The white skeletons of long-dead trees dotted the landscape, some reaching for the sky, others lying as if they had finally given up and collapsed from fatigue. Imco had been told they were following a road. Looking through the haze of insects and mist, he saw no sign of such a thing. He had thought it before and now he could not help thinking it again: Hannibal was mad, a raving demon in a warrior's body, a despot who reveled in the misery of those around him. He did not go so far as to share this assessment with anyone, but silently he spoke a tirade against the man.

They could not stop to camp for the night, and so they kept up a squelching, dripping progress straight through and into the dawn. By the time the sun rose again all semblance of organized marching had evaporated. Fever coursed through innumerable men. The ill and dying, the ranting and pitiful were so close around him that sometimes maneuvering through them was like navigating a rough landscape. Imco—again thinking of spirits, as he had begun to do daily—thought he could see the contagion floating through the air from man to man, a diaphanous creature that touched the unwary with contaminated fingers. He ducked and shifted to avoid it, sometimes looking like a man swatting at bats that he could not see.

The only relatively dry spots were the corpses of pack animals. Men tried to catch moments of rest by perching on the flanks of mules and wrapping their arms around the necks of dead horses. Imco saw one man lying on two goats. It was a sorry enough sight in that there was no comfort in his posture, draped as he was across them, toes and fingers and buttocks each dipping into the muck. But it seemed even stranger when one of the goats lifted its head and stared at Imco piteously. It was not dead at all, just sunk up to its neck and disconsolate, its gaze a direct communication from beast to man. What is the point? it seemed to be asking. Imco had no answer. He just walked on. By that evening he was passing as many dead men as animals.

On the third day he caught sight of Hannibal in the distance. The commander rode behind the ears of the only living elephant. He was too far away for Imco to see his features, but others must have. Word spread that Hannibal had been infected by a fever. Some said that he had lost his sight, others that his hearing had gone as well.

Strangely, Imco found this news a prod to keep him moving. If it was true, then this journey had reached heights of absurdity that he never imagined possible. Would Hannibal the Blind and Deaf lead them to the gates of Rome? He was sure the commander would try, sitting atop his elephant, barking at them, devising clever ploys that he could neither hear nor see the result of. It was too much to imagine. The more reasonable possibility was that they would soon find themselves swimming amid sharks, leaderless and cut off from home or rescue. No other general could prosecute this war with Hannibal's determination. Without him, they would be pounced upon within a fortnight. The absurdity of this kept Imco going. He had to witness this farce played out. What a tale of woe he would have to tell in the underworld.

They had been four days and three nights in the dismal swamplands when Imco realized his feet were finding better purchase. In the afternoon of the fourth day he stepped out of the water and onto merely soggy ground. That evening he cast himself down and felt the earth's hard contours again. And the morning of the fifth day found him looking out over a land they said was called Etruria. This time, Imco had no difficulty translating what his eyes saw to what his mind understood: rolling farmland, pastures, a rich land in the full bloom of spring. With Hannibal's blessing they were about to plunder it to their heart's content.

Releasing the men to pillage was more than a simple reward for them, more even than a necessary measure to revive their physical strength and morale. In fact, Hannibal needed to keep them busy while he struggled with the curse he carried from the marshes. He was not yet blind, as rumor suggested. Not deaf. But he had emerged with a raging infection in his left eye. He had never felt so malignant a force at work inside his body before. It sought to gouge the organ out and leave the hole lifeless. It ate toward the center of him and left his very understanding of the world in disarray. Synhalus warned him that the infection could well spread, both to his other eye and beyond. The surgeon rinsed the eye often with fresh water, plastered it with salves, and nightly sprinkled it with precious drops of seawater to keep the orb moist and return it to its natural state. He had the commander drink herb teas specially designed to restore health and made him lie facedown so that the evil might loosen its grip and fall from him. But none of this curbed the infection.

As important as these clinical measures were Mandarbal's services. Hannibal knew the priest had been feeling slighted since the campaign began. Though he offered sacrifices at the beginning of each stage of the journey and read portents often among the Libyan and Numidian troops, Hannibal had not consulted him in military matters. Why ask for an opinion he might not wish to accept? With the mark of the divine to give them weight, the grim proclamations Mandarbal enjoyed making could hamper his efforts. And yet Hannibal did request that he intercede with the gods concerning his health. Mandarbal led sessions of prayer and sacrifice, calling upon the gods to drive the illness back whence it had sprung. He slit the necks of three goats, a young, unblemished calf, and a mature bull, offering them up to the deities he believed responsible. All to no effect.

In his own mind, Hannibal knew that there was no mystery concerning whence the illness had sprung. He had felt it leap up from the sodden ground beneath his mount's feet. A single drop of mud stuck to the edge of his eye. He had rubbed at it absently. A grain of the dirt bit into him, slipped around his eyeball and into cover, where it slowly went to work. He had not been the same since. The fluctuations in temperature had not helped. Nor had the constant moisture, the insects, the fevers, the smell of death in the air.

It was not that the march had been any worse than he had anticipated. He looked around at scenes he might have imagined beforehand. The death rate did not surprise him. The losses were at the extreme edge of what he thought possible, but Hannibal was rarely mistaken in his understanding of mortality. It was the fact that he had been personally struck that troubled him. He recalled that only a few years ago he had stood almost unblemished before Imilce, and he remembered once joking with Sapanibal that no simple cold, nothing so mundane, could ever harm him. Now the tissue of his leg bore the scars of that Saguntine spear; his body had failed to fight off the ill spirits transmitted through cold; his very eyes no longer perceived the world completely. He felt the bite of his own arrogance. Some, viewing his accomplishments from a distance, might think that he drove Fortune before him like a mule before the lash. It suited him that they thought this, of course, but he knew the dance between him and the Fates was more precarious than that.

The afternoon after emerging from the marshes he held a council. Throughout it, Mago stared at him in sullen amazement. He hardly uttered a word throughout the meeting, but as it closed he indicated that he would speak to his brother in private. Alone, he wasted no time in voicing his mind.

"How could this happen to you?" he asked. "You are nearly blinded! I can see even now that you only half perceive me. This is all the fault of that Numidian. We should take his eyes for the evil he has done you. Hannibal, surely we can reverse this. You must fight it more forcefully. Have you not heard Mandarbal's proposal? He believes a human sacrifice might appease the god who's afflicted you."

Noting the fear in his brother's face, Hannibal found his answer coming automatically. He knew how he should respond, and realizing it he also understood that he had been too long wrestling with the same doubts himself. He smiled. Unwittingly, Mago had prompted Hannibal to remember himself.

He said, "Our soldiers kill in our names daily. If a human sacrifice were the cure for this, then I would be immortal by now. No, it would seem that Hannibal cannot take his wounds as a commander should."

"But this is no wound! No spear did this to you! It is a curse brought down from—"

Hannibal shook his head. "Listen. You have heard of the general Bagora, yes? There is a tale Father told me about him. I've never heard it repeated, but Father believed it to be true. One of Bagora's captains, a brave fighter, was skilled with the spear and famous for his overhand thrust. He was a hero of the early wars with the Libyans, gifted in violence even before he'd taken a woman. But one day, while he worked his damage, he stepped over a man he believed to be dead. The man was not dead, though. He reached up and sliced the hero's spear hand clean off. The captain healed quickly enough, but without that hand he was no longer himself. He refused to resume his post, refused even to aid in training recruits. When summoned to explain himself to his general the young man complained that he was useless. He could not hold his spear! The gods had betrayed him, he who had only strived to honor them. Without another word, Bagora drew his sword and sliced off the soldier's other hand. The hero dropped to his knees and begged to understand. Do you know how Bagora answered?"

Mago shook his head.

"He said, 'You are useless to me now. But not because you lack one hand, nor because you lack two. You became useless the moment you called yourself useless, when you failed to realize that the gods despise self-pity.'"

Hannibal cleared his throat and raised his chin. After a moment of silence, he said, "Mago, I will not be despised by the gods. Let this be the last time I hear you bemoan damage to the body—mine or yours. There should be no such weakness in either of us. Thank you for reminding me of this."

The second morning in the dry lands of Etruria, scouts returned with word that the Roman forces under Flaminius were encamped near the city of Arretium. This meant that time was short. Word of the Carthaginian presence would reach the consul in days, if it had not already. As he pondered their next move, Hannibal thought of Tusselo. The Numidian had ridden beside him through the marshes. They had exchanged few words, for the route was as Tusselo had described and Hannibal's mind had been otherwise occupied, but now he felt a need to speak to him.

When Tusselo stepped through the open door of the tent, Hannibal acknowledged him by clearing his throat. He had just dabbed at the fluid oozing from his eye; his fingers were dripping with a pungent yellow liquid. He had seen all sorts of fluids emanate from men's bodies over the years. This substance, he knew, had no place issuing from the eyes. He wiped his fingers clean on his tunic.

"You have lost me half my vision," Hannibal said.

Tusselo did not dispute this. "If I could carve out my eye and give it you, I would."

"My surgeon is skilled, but not gifted enough for such a transaction. You make a tempting offer, though. My brother thinks I should have your eye as a tribute. I could wear it around my neck as a reminder that my powers of retribution are equal to whatever force did this to me."

Hannibal let the threat sit for a long time.

Tusselo finally said, "You may have my eye for that as well, if you choose."

"Hannibal does not inflict damage simply to sate his own vanity. The truth is, I thank you for the path you showed us. I am now where I wanted to be. Italy is before us, her armies behind—just as you said. Come, sit here and look on this map."

He motioned the Numidian to a stool on the other side of the small table before him. As directed, Tusselo gazed at the chart of Italy. His light brown eyes drifted over the lines and pictures for some time, but when he looked up his face showed little comprehension. "This is different from the land that lives in my mind," he said.

"Then shape the map in your mind into words and lay it before me. I wish to find a trap hidden in the land. Help me with this and you will make your life one I value."

The Numidian barely hesitated. He opened his mouth and began speaking. The words came out smooth and even, as if he had actually rehearsed them for this moment. Hannibal sat back and closed his eyes and realized that the view of the world thrown against the back of his eyelids was not dimmed by the infection. It was still possible to see clearly. He listened to the African speak for some time, learning the land in a way that all of his previous chart study had not approached.

That evening his physician came to him and after a long examination confirmed what Hannibal already knew: His eye was dead. Forever after, he would see the world through a single lens only. So be it, he thought. Knowing this, he felt there was no need to delay. Starting the next day, the army moved in a herd of flaming destruction. He turned them away from the Roman legions at Arretium and marched upon Faesulae, a fortified town which they took by the sword. They ravished it: the men killed, the women brutalized, the children kicked fleeing into the hills. They took what they could carry, torched the rest, and marched southward, repeating the pattern as they went. Their wake was a blackened wasteland of despair. On this march, Hannibal showed no mercy. It would take a hundred thousand deaths to end this war, so he might as well up the count daily. It was therefore up to the Romans to acknowledge his supremacy and call the bloodshed to a halt.

Passing Cortona, Hannibal's scouts brought him the news he had hoped for. Flaminius was behind him. His army pursued them at a headlong run, heedless that they were not chasing a quarry at all. They were being baited.

As he was nearer to the western coast than to the eastern, Silenus sailed from a nameless village port on the coast downstream from the city of Asculum. The entire journey was to take place clandestinely, with no mention of a Carthaginian cause and no use of an African vessel. The latter would make the journey time-consuming, but it was deemed best. The Romans, never sea-lovers, had as late gained some naval mastery. Silenus could not afford to be aboard a ship that might be targeted for attack.

Despite his secrecy he was stopped three times by random Roman patrols. The first time, Silenus claimed to be a merchant from Heraclea, plying his trade in leather goods along the Adriatic coast. Asked if this were not a risky undertaking, considering the war, he answered that he had complete confidence that Rome would vanquish the African foe soon enough, after which the fruits of his intrepid labor would richly reward him. When he produced samples of his wares and offered a sales pitch, he was soon released.

The second time, at the port of Syracuse, he named no concrete purpose to his life but simply wagged his tongue evasively during questioning. As he had grown to manhood in the city, he spoke with inflections that marked him as a native. The soldiers dismissed him for a nuisance, not a threat. Thereafter he stood for some time staring up at the city. It was—as ever—a wonder to look upon, an architectural marvel, a museum housing much of the world's knowledge and artwork. He longed to take a few hours away from his mission and climb up into the familiar environs, to look out over the views he loved and to search out old friends and share with them tales of the things he had seen in the last few years. He wanted the company of Greek men so much that he felt the desire for them deep inside his abdomen. Looking up at the accomplishments of Greek minds and labors, he wondered why he had so tied his life to the fortunes of another race. Maybe this was foolish.

As he stood thinking this, word came to him of a ship that would take him on to Emporiae, embarking that very afternoon. He turned to the man who brought him this news and asked how to find the vessel. He did not think the action through fully, but simply carried on with his mission. The prompting, defying all else, was of a personal nature. Though he had said nothing of it to Hannibal, the news of Hanno's capture had rocked him. To imagine any Barca in Roman custody was shocking enough, but this one he had a particular fondness for. It was hard for him to explain, even to himself, but he had always found something endearing in the traits others might call Hanno's faults. Hanno's taciturn nature brought Silenus a new pleasure in his own mirth. Hanno's superstitious fear of signs and symbols in the world made him smile at his own irreverence. Never had he met a person who took life so seriously, who stood so near to greatness and got less joy from it. Hanno was not impressive in the manly way of Hannibal, nor strikingly handsome like Hasdrubal, nor good-natured like Mago, but Silenus could not help himself. He liked the taciturn soldier best of all, and wished very much for a future in which they had the leisure to figure out the nature and depth of their relationship.

There could be no sight more offensive to Roman eyes than the horizon-wide view of farmland and villages burning under an invader's torch. Flaminius could scarcely believe the visions that assaulted his eyes as he pursued the Carthaginian army through Etruria. How had they appeared south of him, out of nowhere? The news sent him reeling with amazement. Somehow, Hannibal had already bested him. In his first move, he had slipped by without so much as a skirmish. Anger followed fast on shock, and Flaminius wasted no time in striking camp and setting the full two legions in pursuit.

And a strange pursuit it was. If Hannibal had been invisible a moment before, now he chose to leave signs of his passing in the sky and on the land and written on people's faces. Smoke billowed up into the sky from a thousand different fires. Even among the Roman officers there were whispers that this invader was blessed by some new gods and could not be stopped. It was foolish rumor, but a seed of doubt had sprouted within them. Flaminius decided to check this before it grew into outright fear.

One evening he had a great fire kindled. He stood with his back to it, stared into the red faces of his men, and harangued them at length. Could they not see that this invasion was a new version of the first barbarian wave? The first time Romans had come face-to-face with Gauls, they believed the brutes were divine warriors, sent to herald the end of the world as Rome knew it. Those yellow-haired monsters strode out of the north, a horde of giants, invincible, bone-crushing. The Romans who met them were so frightened they turned and ran. The Gauls found Rome an empty city, save for the Capitol, which a few soldiers held with their lives. They had plundered the land just as Hannibal was doing now, undisciplined, bestial.

"And yet here we are," Flaminius said, "generations later, rulers of all of Italy, branching out into the world. How is that possible? Because of the fortitude of a single man. A single citizen reversed the tide of Fate. That man was Camillus, as great a man as Cincinnatus. Camillus loathed these barbarians. He said, 'Look at them. They're not gods. Not demons. They're not harbingers of change. They're men like us, except beneath us. They have no discipline. They sleep in the open. They erect no fortifications. They gorge themselves on food and wine and women and collapse upon the ground.' Camillus saw them for what they truly were, and he taught the others how to vanquish them. With a corps of picked men he stole into their sprawling camp one night, walked quietly through their snoring masses until his men were everywhere among them. Then they fell upon the Gauls. They slit their throats and left them gasping, waking from their drunken dreams to see the face of hell."

Flaminius raised his hands out to either side, embracing the whole company before him, in silhouette with the fire bright behind him. "Never since that night has a Roman feared a barbarian. Let us not forget the teachings of our ancestors. We are Rome; we fear not the invaders now among us. We've only to remember ourselves to triumph."

At the morning meal the next day, scouts reported that Hannibal was heading toward Perusia, from which he would, presumably, make a dash for the south. Hearing this, Flaminius rejoiced. He could not have had better news. Little did Hannibal know that he would soon find himself trapped between two consular armies: Flaminius' own and that of Geminus, who even then was marching south in haste. It was perfect. The gods were with him. If he had his way, he would sever Hannibal's head from the body that bore it and carry it aloft on a spear. Rome would greet him with a triumphal welcome of unprecedented proportions.

In haste, both from impatience and also to demonstrate his determination to those around him, Flaminius left his breakfast half-eaten. He rose and hurried toward his horse, shouting out orders to the officers who scrambled to keep up with him. They must quicken the pace of march. At the same time, they would send word to Geminus and ask him for cavalry reinforcement. It just might be possible to pinch the enemy between the full weight of both their armies. "Then," he said, "by the gods we'll have them all."

Having spoken thus, he attempted to mount his horse with likewise conviction. He leaped directly from the ground. The move began sharply enough, with some of the grace of a mounted entertainer. Some of it, but not all. The horse skittered, backed, and then reared as the consul sought purchase. It spun in a tight circle and yanked the reins from the rider's hands. This flurry of motion ended in stillness: the horse standing a few paces away, calm and instantly undisturbed, the consul on his backside in the mud, gazing at his stained garments as if completely mystified by this outcome. It was an ill omen if ever there was one, but Flaminius swatted at the hands that offered him aid.

"Just a mishap!" he snapped. "Has no one ever fallen from a horse before me?"

Then, as if he had not already enough prods to rage, a report came that one of the standard-bearers could not pull his burden up from the ground. Before the gaze of astonished onlookers who were reluctant to touch the pole themselves, the young man strained and groaned and tired himself with the effort. True enough that the ground was damp, yielding stuff, but its grip on the shaft seemed unnatural to all onlookers, as if the earth itself wished to delay them in action.

Flaminius, however, tilted his gaze skyward and asked the heavens if ever a consul had led an army less inclined to action. He ordered the standard dug out of the ground and called for the march to begin. Omens be damned; the consul was determined to make contact with the enemy and bring him to a full test. And so he would, three days later, beside a lake called Trasimene.

A year ago, Aradna would not have imagined that she and her donkey would still be following the Carthaginians, but come the spring she had to set aside her plans of escape. Though she still had her treasure tied and snug between her breasts, it did not seem like enough. And also she had come together with the remnant band of camp followers over the long winter. They had aided each other by pooling their food and foraging in bands, although scavenging items of value was still a solitary, secretive pursuit. They were several groups—some composed entirely of Gallic women attending their husbands—of which hers was the smallest, fifteen in total. Even this modest number provided some measure of security above traveling alone. It was a mixed company of men and women, young and old. She managed to fend off the attentions of the men and live with them peaceably. And, better yet, she had come up with a proposal that had bettered their lot and won credit for it.

Like any army's livestock, the Carthaginians' had to be transported alive and afoot. There had once been a horde of slaves and servants and ambitious boys to attend to this, but their numbers had dwindled. Many of those still living were recruited as soldiers, now that every willing man—and some not willing—was needed. Why not let the followers aid in herding the beasts? Aradna passed this proposal to Hannibal's secretary through the large Celtiberian who thought himself their leader. The Carthaginian, Bostar she believed his name was, had agreed, and so the ragged followers became sheep and goat and cow herders. They got no pay for their labor except the poor portions of the slaughtered animals, but that was no small thing. And, of course, it placed them in a prime position to scavenge should a great battle soon reward them.

The evening that the army marched through the defile and down into the valley of the lake, Aradna believed that the time had come. No one thought to consult with or give directions to the followers, but they judged the signs for themselves and reacted to them. She and the others herded the few surviving goats and steers onto a high, grassy knoll. From it they had a vantage point that encompassed the entire valley below. The lower elevations were just slipping into shadow, but the air above seemed to suspend particles of the sun's amber vibrancy. The shore of the lake curved in a wide, irregular arch that slipped out of and then back into view. Beside it stretched a relatively flat expanse. This soon tilted and rose to a gradual, undulating slope dotted with trees and low vegetation. A little higher, the incline increased, leading up the rocky mountain ridge that hemmed in that side of the valley completely. The only easy access to the lakeside came from the narrow defile through which they had passed and from another similar gap at the far end. An army entering the field would have to march thinly through the pass, spread over a distance, with little room to move on either side until well down onto the flats.

The main contingent of Hannibal's infantry took up a position in the center of the far end of the plain, as if they were preparing to meet the Romans in a traditional combat on the morn. But the plain itself was not wide enough for the two armies to march toward each other in battle formation. Aradna recognized that the troop movements before her were made with guile. Units of cavalry took up positions near the mouth of the defile, on fairly open ground, but hidden behind the hills and ridges that marked that area. Slingers and light infantrymen were deployed in small groups along the whole length of the plain. They moved up toward the hills and slipped between the folds of earth there. Within a short time they had all but disappeared.

Aradna waited through the night, plagued by a nervous energy. She stared up at the stars, low-hung and gentle, near enough to touch if she had had the desire to disturb them. She wondered whether it was true that the lights floating up there were the souls of the departed. An old woman had told her so once, but she knew not whether this came from any particular doctrine. Her father might be up there. She tried to pick him out, but there were so many and they were so similar. If the old woman had spoken truly, then each night would see new stars born. The night would soon glow brighter than the day.

She did not intentionally drift to sleep, but upon waking she realized she had slept hard and she knew she had been awakened by something. She was damp with the night cool and felt the chill touch of a moist vapor slipping over her. The sky above was white with high cloud. The stars had retreated to wherever they passed the daylight hours. She took this in while still in the hold of a dreamy half-consciousness, but then she heard again the sound that had stirred her, a throbbing conducted through the earth beneath her. It took her a moment to place it—the rhythmic stamp of feet over the ground. She jumped up and, calling to the others, ran to the viewing point. The sight before her both surprised and exasperated her.

What had been a wide sweep of lakeside and a perfect view of the plains the day before was now hidden beneath a blanket of low fog. In the higher reaches, only stray bands of white vapor clung to a few hollows, but the rest of the valley was completely shrouded. She could, however, see the opening in the mountains through which the Roman army marched. They must have broken camp before the dawn to reach this point so early. They kept to a tight formation, moving in ordered lines, so disciplined that even their steps fell in unison. Looking toward the other end of the plain Aradna could just make out the movements of the main body of Hannibal's infantry. It was hard to know whether the Romans would have been able to see them. But whether they did or not, they marched on at full pace.

She watched the whole column until the straggling ends of the army slipped down into the mist.

Aradna could only guess at what followed from things she heard. She imagined the Carthaginian army silent and hiding, listening to the same tramp of Roman feet that had woken her. They waited, waited, waited. And then a scream broke the hush, from a single voice, two tones that hung in the air for a long moment. Next came a Gallic horn blast. Then the roar of thousands of voices merging in a similar purpose. She imagined the Carthaginians breaking from cover and sweeping down upon all sections of the Roman line. Though barely able to see, they must have run forward by whatever route they had chosen the previous evening. To the Romans their enemy would first have been a wall of sound, suddenly surging from a blank place that had moments before been silence. The Romans would not have had time to draw their weapons. Certainly not time to form ranks and receive instructions. When the Carthaginian forces materialized, they must have seemed like demons stepping out of the unknown, slashing and stabbing, sending missiles slicing through moist air.

"What god works here today?"

The voice that asked this question surprised Aradna. For a moment she had forgotten her companions, but then she recognized the voice as that of an older woman she had first met in the winter, one rarely impressed by anything. It was not a question meant to be answered, and no one tried. They kept their ears open to the valley below. Despite the yell of voices and clash of weapons and bellow of horns, the symphony of the combat was strangely muted. Aradna knew war as well as any soldier and therefore knew that the work of men slaughtering each other was punctuated as much by silence as by noise. Flesh makes no cry when it is pierced. Limbs lopped off and dropped to the ground barely make a thud. Men slipping in blood and tangled in entrails are unlikely to project any reasoned, measured complaint. A slung iron pellet squelches into flesh, a sound no louder than that of a pebble dropped into still water.

Because Aradna knew this, she listened with all of her being tuned to her ears. She listened for some indication that the Romans had managed to regroup, but there was nothing in the confusion to indicate this. According to her ears, the Romans were being carved to pieces. She could envision it no other way, even though her knowledge of the world whispered that this was not possible. Rome's soldiers were not supposed to die so easily. Hannibal had massacred them once already. But a second time in as many encounters?

She could not have guessed how much time passed like this. At some point, the very earth shook. The woman next to her grabbed her arm and the two of them waited it out together, both wondering if even that was something orchestrated by Hannibal, hearts beating faster for the possibility that he truly had some divine power working with him. When patches of the mist cleared, a wide stretch of the lake emerged, materializing with a sudden, disconcerting solidity. There was a disturbance in the water. It seemed that a great school of fish churned the surface at many places. As strange as the whole morning had been, Aradna half-believed that some creatures from the marine world were rising to comment on the battle, whether in praise or anger she knew not.

It took only a moment to understand the reality. It was the splash of soldiers rushing into the water, the slash of their arms and frantic kick of their legs. The Romans were fleeing. In their haste they threw off their helmets and flung away weapons and even tried to yank off armor that impeded them. Numidian and Celtiberian horsemen churned through the water behind them, slashing at the backs of men's heads, splitting them open like hard-shelled fruit, spearing them like fishermen. Eventually, even the most distant swimmers had to turn back. The far shore was beyond their reach, and few found the courage to drown themselves. As they neared the shore they were cut down one and all by the cavalry, creating a red stain so dark it blackened the whole shoreline of the lake. When the mist peeled away further, revealing the plain, Aradna caught her first full sight of the carnage. It was worse even than she had imagined.

Though she was no longer squeamish about violent death, Aradna turned her back on the scene and lowered herself to the turf. She had long ago learned something of the art of war, but of late she had found Hannibal a teacher of an altogether different sort. Sitting there, slowly taking in what she had seen, Aradna had a thought she had not previously considered. Hannibal just might do it. He just might win this war. Rome could not produce new soldiers for slaughter forever. They could not raise new generations of leaders overnight. They could not feed a thronging, hostile army on their own soil indefinitely. Through all her travels she had thought mostly of herself and her path back to her homeland. She had not really cared about or given much thought to the success of the war. Now, for the first time, she realized its outcome might well affect the course of her life, no matter in what quiet corner she searched for solace. This man, with his genius for death, just might change the world.

THREE

The End of War

E vents in Iberia had brought Hasdrubal little joy: neither the satisfaction of a single victory nor the hopes of any discernible change in the near future. All around him he felt whispers of discontent, vengeful scheming tended by the Romans like attentive men blowing on a kindling blaze. This Gnaeus Scipio, brother to the former consul, proved a surprising foe. Early in the spring, he ambushed Hasdrubal's entire navy while it was beached at the mouth of the Ebro. The Romans—surely with the advantage of some traitor's information—bore down on the sailors as they rose from slumber, driving in with the rising sun at their backs. It was no battle at all but a wild scramble, vessels rammed and stormed before they had even pushed out through the breakers. Boats not even afloat yet were grappled with hooks and towed into the water and set aflame.

On learning of the disaster, Hasdrubal imagined the far-off day when his brother would also get word of it. He beat his head with the flats of his hands so forcefully that his officers grabbed his arms to stop him. He wanted foremost to attack Emporiae and free Hanno, but Gnaeus kept him otherwise occupied. The Roman sailed south, stormed and sacked the allied town of Onusa, near New Carthage, then burned a village within sight of the city itself and destroyed crops meant for Carthaginian consumption. Hasdrubal had no choice but to retreat and protect the capital. And— as if the damage done by this single man had not been enough—the early autumn saw the arrival of his elder brother, Cornelius Scipio. Hasdrubal would have both of them to contend with from now on.

Despite these misfortunes, he did manage to hold most of the country together. He kept a firm grip on most of his Iberian allies, sending warnings sometimes veiled and sometimes graphically detailed. In many ways, he achieved the focus and breadth of vision that his brother asked of him, but he burned with the desire to be freed of this post and to carry out the next phase of Hannibal's plan. Not even the insatiable sexual appetite of his young bride distracted him from this for long. He felt that he was not truly helping to win the war and, increasingly, he considered pressing Carthage for leave to march for Italy. He had made this desire known to the Council, but had received no response.

So he greeted the news of the arrival of a delegation of Carthaginian ships with eagerness. Perhaps he was finally to receive the leave he wished for. He stood on the balcony of his chambers, watching the vessels drop their sails and row between the guard rocks at the mouth of the harbor. The fleet was an impressive sight, some thirty ships of varying sizes. Oars struck the water in unison, stirring foam with each stroke, shifting the ships forward in a motion that Hasdrubal always found odd to behold. The strange, buoyant agreement between the vessel and the water never ceased to amaze him. What made that surface both solid and fluid? Supportive to some objects, deadly to others, always threatening to consume at any moment, each swell in the surf like a hunger pain rippling across the belly of a beast. He could never have been a sea captain. Better death during a raging battle on land than from the bottomless suck of the sea.

Noba walked in swiftly, several loose scrolls clipped between his fingers. "They bring reinforcements," he said. "Four thousand of them. Scant, really, but at least they are Libyans."

Hasdrubal dipped one corner of his lip, and then righted it again.

He sat on a short stool, with his legs wide, hands resting on his knees. The shadow of a new beard added an unkempt aspect to his face. "And what else?"

"Ten elephants. Two hundred Massylii. And they have sent you a new general, Gisgo, son of Hannon. He is to serve as lieutenant governor. He is under your direction, but he will handle civil matters while you are on campaign and will be the main contact between Iberia and Carthage. This last is not good news, I think."

"No Hannon ever brings good news. Is there no further message for me from the Shophet or the Council?"

The squire shook his head.

"I must take them to task for that some day. How many have they sent to Italy?"

Noba stared at him for a moment. He cleared his throat and held up one of the scrolls and contemplated it for a moment. "They have not sent Hannibal reinforcements yet," he said.

Hasdrubal jerked his head upright, rose, and strode forward, hand out to snatch away the document. "Are you joking with me?"

"You know I have no sense of humor."

After a brief glance Hasdrubal tossed the scroll away. "Make me understand, Noba, because I see no reason in this."

"Perhaps their resources are not quite as great as we imagine," Noba offered.

"I can imagine much," Hasdrubal said, "but the wealth of Carthage is beyond even me. No, that is not the problem. They want him to fail, yes?"

"Think not of how those old men conspire. What matters is what we do here. Four thousand men is more than we had yesterday."

Hasdrubal caught sight of Bayala, who had entered at the far corner of the room. Seeing Noba, she lingered at a distance, running her hands over the fabric of a wall tapestry. Hasdrubal cut his jibe short and lowered his voice. "So why not give this Gisgo full control of New Carthage? He can have it. Write a dispatch to Carthage for me. Tell them I am going to my brother. I will take only a few thousand men—a portion of the number they should have sent Hannibal themselves."

Noba locked his arms across his chest. "The Council will not let you go. We both know that. Some would use the very fact that you made the request against you. One minute they'd say you are indispensable to Iberia; the next, they'd question your loyalty. They will reach their fingers into our business and strip away first this portion of your authority and then the next."

"Has Noba become all-knowing in the last few months? There was a time when you were loyal to me."

"Those loyal to you tell you when you are mistaken," Noba said. "This is a greater loyalty than feeding your moments of folly. You would see this if the gods had granted you wisdom as vast as your—"

Hasdrubal shot his hand out and snapped his fist closed before his squire's face, near enough that a simple thrust of his arm would have made the threat into a punch. "Finish that sentence and you will never know joy again."

Noba rolled his eyes to the ceiling. Then he seemed to reconsider and said, "Forgive me. I misspoke. Make whatever decision you must. I will go now and greet Gisgo for you. We should dine with him tonight."

As the sounds of the man's steps faded in the hallway Hasdrubal closed his eyes and exhaled a long breath. He heard Bayala approaching him. He opened his eyes. She circled him for a moment, looking at him coyly, the tip of her tongue peeking out from the grip of her front teeth. Her gray eyes squinted with the mischievous look she always fixed on him as an amorous invitation. Even though he felt his sex stir, he fixed his gaze on the far side of the room. He was in no humor for such distractions. She must have sensed this, for she surprised him when she spoke.

"Noba is right."

"He may be," Hasdrubal said, "but I did not ask your opinion."

"No, you did not. If you tell me to hold my tongue, I will, but there is no reason you should not speak with me about such things. He is a good man. You and your brothers are fortunate. You instill loyalty in those close to you. Few men achieve this as easily as Barcas."

Hasdrubal would not look at her. "What do you know of it? A woman's mind is poison to reasoned thought."

"In some countries women rule over men."

"This is not such a country."

Bayala creased her thin lips as if pressing this reality between them. Then she released it without comment. "Anyway, you are needed here in Iberia. I hear things, too, husband. Women talk as much as men and often of the same matters. Many tribes await the smallest excuse to leave you. Even my father may prove fickle. He would abandon you without a thought if Fortune deserts you. To get his power he killed his older brother, you know. Some say he had a stew made of his innards and had all the family eat of him, so that they all shared in his crime. I was not yet born, but I do not doubt this story."

A visual image of Andobales' bulk appeared in Hasdrubal's mind, the boarlike shape of his body, the jutting stretch of his jaw and nose. Hasdrubal did not like thinking about him, nor remembering that the object of so much of his desire sprang from him. But neither did it seem right for a daughter to tell disparaging tales of her creator.

"So you are now a woman who speaks against her father?" he asked. "I wonder what you will say of me behind my back?"

"Nothing that I would not say on my knees before you, husband."

Bayala slid a hand across his abdomen. Her fingers found a crease in the material and slipped through to caress his flesh. "You must stay here and protect your empire," she said. "You must protect your wife. I never feel safe out of your sight. Anyway, do you want so badly to leave me? Do I fail to give you pleasure?"

He almost said that there was more to life than the pursuit of pleasure, but the words died in him: first, because he wondered why she should feel endangered, and second, because he felt filled to overflowing with desire and doubted his assertion. Bayala did not seem to mind his silence. She pressed her body against his. He felt the soft weight of her breast held against his bicep. As she slid around toward his chest her breast swayed free. Something in the momentary, passing sensation of this sucked the air out of him.

"Do you like me, husband?" she asked.

Finally looking down at her—at the confident mirth in her eyes, the imperfect lines of her face, and the thin stretch of her lips— Hasdrubal knew that he liked her very much. More than he wished to tell her. He wondered whether any other Barca had ever felt such a weakness for a woman. A voice within him whispered that if he were not careful such emotion would be the death of him.

Imilce disliked sending Hannibal a letter written in another's hand, but she could not yet write with the grace she wished for. She had no choice but to speak her love aloud and watch it made manifest by the subtle fingers of a scribe a few years her junior. He never looked up at her, but kept his head inches above his work. She was thankful for this and spoke slowly so that he would have no need to interrupt her.

She began, "Hannibal, husband, beloved both of Baal and Imilce . . . I write you in longing and pride. I do not know where this will find you or what hardship you may be suffering at the moment you read this. I do not know, husband, if you will ever read this. But still I write in hope. The news here is that you have struck several blows at Rome, just as you said you would. This was met with great excitement, although not everyone in Carthage wishes you success. I will not put names in writing, but I now understand that beside each councillor singing your praises is another who grumbles that you are leading the nation to ruin. I would not have thought it possible for any to feel this way, but the people of Carthage surprise me in many ways.

"This city of your birth is beautiful, rich beyond my imaginings. And—for me, at least—it is stifling, confining, like a tomb. I do not wish you to think me ungrateful. Your mother and sisters have been very kind to me, but I am nothing here without you. None here save Sapanibal have seen me at your side. None see me as I would be seen. They are kind enough, but they make me feel like a jeweled necklace sitting in a box, without the neck for which it was crafted. Are you still convinced that I should not come to you in Italy? I would happily do so, especially now as you are winning fame for us all. . . .

"Have you got all that?" she asked the scribe.

Without looking up, he nodded that he did. He mumbled, "Fame for us all," as he finished writing.

Imilce picked up a date and tested the flesh of it against her teeth. She had seen Carthaginian women do this often, and—both consciously and not—she had adopted some of their mannerisms. On her young sister-in-law's recommendation, she had taken to wearing Carthaginian clothing. The garments were beautiful in their own right, but she never failed to be impressed by the effect they produced when combined with the voluptuous grace of African women. Didobal epitomized this and bore it with remarkable effect: her dark skin further enriched by the bright reds and oranges of her garments, by patterns and pictures stained into the cloth. Certainly, Carthaginian men looked kindly on her, but what did they matter? It was a women's world in which she found herself, and here she felt shockingly immature. Thinking of her mother-in-law, Imilce felt like an adolescent wrapped in adult garments, like a stick figure but not a true woman at all. Oh, she so very badly wished she could dig her fingernails into her husband's muscled back, direct his sex inside her, and know once more that he was real and that she was truly valued and that her future was assured. It was unfortunate that she had not become pregnant again. . . . But such thoughts were not for this scribe's ears. She tossed the date back into its bowl and carried on with another line of thought.

"I will tell you something now that struck me deeply," she resumed, "though I do not know what you will think of it. This afternoon I took the midday meal with your youngest sister, Sophonisba. I am sure you have not the slightest memory of her. She is just thirteen, but her beauty is blooming daily. Her eyes are so black and large, framed by eyelashes that seem to stroke the air itself with sensuality, as if each lash were a feather in an Egyptian dancer's fingers. How she can convey all this by simply blinking is beyond me, but the effect is quite real. It is frightening, really, how devastating she can be with that adolescent glare of hers. Grown men, soldiers and fathers and grandfathers even . . . They all crumble before her. Either that or they simper and flirt with her. She is barely more than a girl, but already the wolves are baying in the night.

"It is Sophonisba's mind that truly surprised me, however. She is a young woman of strong opinions. She is well informed and readily capable of discoursing on all manner of subject. She knows the details of the campaign, and she wishes she might herself take part.

She looked at me with all seriousness and said, 'Had I been born a man I would avenge the wrongs done us by Rome.' She asked, 'Do you not think that our women have bravery beyond that even of our men?'

"I answered her that if she was anything to go by, then that was undoubtedly true. But she would not be so easily flattered. She was looking for something more, but she was unsure of how to say it at first. I referred to her mother, and her mother's mother, and to all those who have bravely sent their men off to war and waited long years for their return. I did not mention myself, of course, but in listening to myself speak I did feel a certain pride at being as composed as I am in your long absence. Sophonisba did not dispute any of this, but she seemed saddened by it. She wished there were other ways to demonstrate her valor. She said, 'Imilce, I am not like most girls. I do not pray for childish things. I pray that I will somehow serve Carthage in a way that would honor the Barcas.'

"Can you imagine this? From a girl who should be dreaming simply of some foreign prince to wed . . ."

Imilce, for the first since beginning her letter, sat down on the intricate reclining chair in her sitting room. It was a piece of furniture she still did not care for. Despite its elegant shape and its tiny zebra-skinned cushion, it was an instrument of discomfort. If she had been confident of her position she would have replaced it by now. She sat silent for a moment, pressing her back into the perfectly straight length of mahogany, listening to the scribe's pen upon the papyrus.

She had reminded herself of Sophonisba's suitor, Masinissa, and considered mentioning him. She had first laid eyes on him a few days before as he returned from a lion hunt, an elite event in which he was participating for the first time. At Sophonisba's side, Imilce had stood on the wall near the city gates and watched the chariots thunder up the road. The afternoon was pleasantly cool, the surface of the road darkened by an early, light rain. Masinissa, being a Massylii, spurned the wheeled vehicles. Instead, he rode in the swarming confusion of horsemen. Sophonisba had no difficulty picking him out from the crowd.

"There he is," she had said. "The handsome one."

This was not, actually, a distinguishing feature among the throng of youthful warriors. Imilce nearly said as much. But then, to her surprise, she did spot a young man of more than usual grace. His dress was no different from the others', and his tack was simple. Yet as he circled and wheeled and trilled with his companions his face shone with a regal joy that separated him from the rest. Here was a boy at play with his friends; but here, too, was a monarch who knew his place among them and wore it comfortably. Word soon spread that the young prince had slain his first lion. He had made the kill from horseback, dancing around the beast, sinking three spears before it went down. That a young man so slender could slay a lion was difficult for Imilce to accept. She wondered whether the tale had not been exaggerated to feed the prince's pride. Though a woman, she knew as well as any man that a servant's deeds are often claimed by his master. But when she met Masinissa, saw his face and bearing from up close, felt his unusually calm confidence, the deferential smile and humility with which he received praise: considering all this, she believed the story.

She would have liked to share this and more with her husband, but she already felt she was rattling on too much, speaking of matters that were not particularly important and that Hannibal might find trivial when compared with the struggles in which he was engaged. And anyway, she never managed to convey her true heart in letters. Writing them made her doubt whether she knew her true heart.

"Perhaps your family shall have female heroes in the future," she dictated, "should your sisters be given a chance to shine like their brothers.

"All the love Baal permits between us, Your wife, Imilce."

When the scribe finished writing, she dismissed him, pointedly slipping the document from under his gaze so that he might not reread it to her, as he usually did. Alone a moment later, she studied the letter. She haltingly began to read it over, but then decided not to attempt the task. Though she could make some sense of the letters, she was never confident in her reading. Too many words escaped her, so that she always found her feelings incompletely rendered. The scribes never wrote one's exact words anyway; they abbreviated; they made intricate thoughts into simple, blocky senti-ments. If she let herself, she would call the scribe back and have him rewrite the thing several times. She had done this with previ-ous letters, but this time she disciplined the urge. Instead she did something else.

Once sure the ink was dry, she parted the fabric of her gown. She lifted the papyrus and pressed it against her naked flesh. She worked each section of it with her fingertips, feeling the damp of her sweat absorbed by the dry paper. She pressed from the skin of her belly up into the hollow that fused her ribs together, out over the soft give of her breasts. She held the papyrus there for several long breaths, imagining Hannibal receiving the document, believ-ing that he might sense her on it, might think the paper was her very flesh, might feel the longing behind the words and understand more things than she could say.

The massacre beside Lake Trasimene was unprecedented in Ro-man history. It was not a repeat of the Trebia disaster; it was worse. This time, fifteen thousand men were killed in the initial slaughter. Among them, the consul who had led them went down, run through by the spear of an Insubrian Gaul. Six thousand managed to escape the defile and flee to a nearby town, but they held out no longer than a day, giving up along with thousands of others. In addition, Geminus' cavalry had been met by Maharbal's superior force. The Numidians killed or captured all four thousand of them. If the last defeat had struck each Roman a blow to the chest, this one hit the collective soul of the people like a blacksmith's hammer. It left the citizens breathless, shocked, unsure what the limits of Hannibal's powers were, taking nothing for granted.

Soon, word came that some of the soldiers were straggling home. The people flocked to the gates of Rome, crowding the walls, wail-ing at the sight before them. Women ran forth, gripping the grimy, blood-caked soldiers, gazing into their faces, calling out the names of husbands, sons, brothers, beseeching the gods to bring their loved ones home. But the gods had turned away. Rome faced the possibility that Hannibal could not be beaten. Perhaps he had trapped Fortune and kept her caged and twisted her always to his advantage. Perhaps this man was more than just a man.

Great as the panic was, as lurid as the stories were, the Republic's leaders did not waste much time in hand-wringing. In the Senate, the faction dominated by the Fabian family and their allies called for the immediate naming of a dictator. It was a stunning proposal, one that nobody wished to believe was needed. With absolute power came grave danger, but if ever extreme measures were called for, this was such a moment. And somehow it was clear to all that the leader of the Fabians' own party was the only clear choice for the position. The gray-haired Fabius Maximus: former censor, twice consul, twice interrex, and once already named dictator, the very man who had declared war on Carthage by throwing out a fold of his toga. He was the embodiment of Roman virtue, steadfast, dogged, single-minded to a fault. He was neither fiery in speech nor quick to action, but he was vigorous once roused. He did have an affliction—his poor vision—but it was not one for which his peers thought less of him, as it came upon many men with age. He arranged for a pair of eyes to accompany him during his tenure as dictator, a young officer with eyesight rivaling the keen stare of a hawk: the former consul's son, Publius Scipio.

As his first act in office, Fabius pronounced that the Trasimene disaster had been the result of Flaminius' impiety and disregard for religious formality. Had nobody around him paused to notice that he began his pursuit of Hannibal on a *dies nefastus,* an inauspicious day, when no work should take place, during an hour when the gods looked askance at those who commenced new projects? Fabius ordered study of the Sibylline Books, hoping that the prophetic sayings of the Cumaean Sibyl would provide some direction, as they had in times past. He consulted priests and called for the immediate commencement of the rites, games, dedications, and vows that they said the gods demanded. Next, he issued an edict that all country people should destroy their crops, their houses, and even their tools at the first sign of Hannibal's approach. He ordered the call-up of two new legions to protect Rome. He sent Lucius Postumius to Cisalpine Gaul with two full legions, with the responsibility of keeping the Boii and Insubres under pressure. At best, he hoped, their armies might desert Hannibal to protect their own. At worse, Postumius could prevent them from sending new reinforcements to join the Carthaginian.

And then, just before leaving to take over Geminus' legions, Fabius addressed the Senate and conveyed to them the surprising strategy he had developed to defeat the enemy. He said that his grand plan was actually marked by its simplicity. He would simply not fight the barbarian. An army that does not engage in battle cannot be beaten in battle, he said. When asked if he would then let the invaders ravish the countryside, Fabius answered that yes, he would.

"Let them crisscross the land as they wish," he said. "Let the land not be burned only in their wake but also let the fires precede them. Let weeks and months pass without a decisive battle. Let them die one by one from the various hazards of life: illness and injury, or even age if they hang on long enough. By these various measures we will reduce the enemy's limited number."

He explained that he would not be inactive meanwhile. His army would shadow Hannibal's, harassing them and making life difficult for them. He would make it hard for the Carthaginians to feed themselves or to replenish their arms. He would let fatigue and time wear the invaders down. Rome's strength was that she could replenish her losses, recruit new soldiers, plant new crops. Hannibal could do none of these things—not easily, at least. This would be his undoing.

Fabius' strategy troubled many in the Senate. One man, Terentuis Varro, rose in the silent chamber and asked, "What madness is this, Fabius? Are you so full of despair? Have we elected you only to learn that you believe us doomed?"

"Hannibal cannot be beaten on the field," Fabius said, "but he can be beaten. Think wisely on this and deeply, not with vanity but with reason. Was Cornelius a lesser general than any man in here? Was Sempronius? Flaminius? And has the Roman army a history of defeat? Has any nation stood against us and prevailed? No. What we face now is the greatest challenge to our Republic since its founding. I do not know what god breathes genius into the young Barca, but we must admit that for the moment he is our superior in the open clash of arms. Friends, you did not elect me for my wit.

You did not bestow this responsibility on me because my mind is so nimble as to dance around this Carthaginian. You elected me because you believed in my judgment. That is what I offer you today. By my policies we will defeat this invader. Carthage will have its day of sorrow. Be patient and trust in me. I am your dictator. Rome will be saved."

He walked from the hushed chamber, his attendants all around him, Publius at his elbow. "How do you think they received that?" he asked, once out on the streets.

"Sir," Publius said, "birds could have built nests in their mouths and raised young, such was their shock."

Fabius smiled and said, "Let us hope it strikes Hannibal the same."

After Trasimene, Hannibal turned the army east and marched through Umbria. It was not a campaign at all but a moving feast, the whole country one great market from which they plucked goods at will. In each precinct Hannibal kept his ears open for encouraging words, for any people or city wise enough to desert Rome and join the winning cause. But people of Latin blood were a stubborn, recalcitrant lot. Several towns rejected the Carthaginian offer of goodwill and paid for it. The city of Spoletium was somewhat more formidable. It repulsed the Carthaginian attack with disdain. Foolish, that. Had Hannibal the equipment and time to besiege the city properly he would have done so, but there were other matters to see to.

In the first week of July, he settled the army in along the Picene coast and had them lay down their burdens, rest their bodies, and assess the booty they had amassed thus far. Despite their triumphs the men were in pitiable shape, wounded from battle, malnourished from the winter, tired from the march, and plagued by bouts of diarrhea. The animals were no better off. So Hannibal gave them time to recover beside the ocean. They bathed in the warm waters, baked in the sun, and put well behind them the hardships of the winter. They slaughtered the locals' fat lambs and cattle, ate fresh bread, and munched fruit pulled ripe from the trees.

The weeks of recovery were not spent in idle pleasure alone.

Hannibal had the Libyans rearmed with the best of the captured Roman weapons. They drilled with them and soon came to favor them and to better understand the Roman technique and how to counter it. He sent the Numidians out on far-ranging raids that brought back new horses, the best of which were put into training in their style. Hannibal also sent messengers to Carthage, carrying word of his victories and asking for reinforcements. He knew even as he composed these words that some within the Council would argue against acceding to his requests. But he had to make them.

The defiance on the faces of the peasants they had despoiled had surprised him. Why had they not dropped to their knees and praised him? Why had they not even lied for the moment and claimed to support him? He knew well the manner in which most people behave in the hour of their defeat; these Italians had not followed any model he had previously encountered. And Rome, it seemed, had yet to whisper a word about coming to terms. Through Bostar, he managed to keep a steady flow of spies back and forth to the capital. None reported any mention of appeasement within the city. None even suggested that this thought occupied the senators' private minds, much less played a hand in public policy. Instead, it seemed that Rome gave thought only to the next stage of the war.

At a meeting of his generals, Hannibal asked, "What does this mean, this dictatorship?"

They had gathered in a long-abandoned cottage that served as a makeshift headquarters. The door stood open, casting a square of the brilliant daylight across the room. It was stiflingly hot beneath the sun, so that the stools had been positioned to make the best use of the shade. Above them, lizards slid through the roof, rattling the sun-parched thatch of hay.

"It means they are afraid," Bomilcar said.

"As they should be. But how does a dictator change the struggle before us?"

"We should strike soon and hard," Maharbal said.

Monomachus sucked his cheeks and spoke through the dry pucker that was his mouth. "I care not for delay," he said. "Our men are rested. Let us strike at the Roman heart now, while our men still remember how easy it is to split Roman flesh."

Bostar listened to this with a pained expression. He had formed the habit of stroking the ice-scarred tissue of his cheeks while he thought. He did this now, rhythmically, and said, "To the commander's question . . . The Senate approves the call for a dictator only after a great disaster. In this way, we know they acknowledge the carnage we've inflicted on them. Instead of their usual two consuls, each of whom controls two legions, they put in place a single, ultimate commander. This dictator controls four legions at once, for a term of six months. His power is total. Last year, as you will recall, the Romans put six legions in the field, but they never fought as a combined force. They still won't, but with a dictator we can reasonably assume we'll meet a larger single force than we have thus far."

"So they have adopted a king?" Mago asked. "This means they are changing everything."

"Not so," Bostar said. "Romans fear monarchs more even than Athenians do. They will bear this dictator only so long as he is useful. Then they demand that he step down. The Senate chose Fabius because they believe him a prudent, humble man. They would not give this power to anyone but. If you will recall Cincinnatus—"

"Do not start repeating the Greek's tales!" Bomilcar said. "We all know this Cincinnatus. Picked his plow out of the field and struck the enemy about the head with it, then returned the plow to the ground and carried on. Are we to fight farmers, then?"

"One might say that, yes. Romans like to think of themselves as humble people of the land. My point in mentioning Cincinnatus is that he is the model of a Roman dictator. He was a man they could turn to in crisis, one who could be trusted completely to act with the greatest wisdom, a different sort of man than Sempronius or Flaminius."

"Fabius will be no fool, then?" Hannibal asked.

Bostar nodded in such a way as to indicate that the commander had stated the matter succinctly. "He will be no fool, which leaves you with this question: How will a wiser leader confront you?"

Bomilcar snorted. "If he were truly wise, he would not confront us at all!"

A few of the others laughed, but Monomachus considered the statement as if it had been offered in seriousness. "There are ways that we can assure that they fight us," he said. He leaned toward the commander and pitched his words low enough so that the others had to be still to hear him. "Let us order the men to kill everyone in our path. Not just men, but women and children, too. How could the dictator answer that except by battle? They would rush to fight us faster even than Flaminius. Anyway, I do not see the good in leaving children to grow into men, women to push out new soldiers. This is not sound strategy. We should slay them all until they beg us on their knees to stop."

"Monomachus, I sometimes wonder if you would halt even at that point," Hannibal said. "As ever, there is potent logic in your suggestion. As ever, I take your words seriously. But it need not come to that. I've not changed my opinion in the slightest. The only way to defeat Rome is to alienate her from her allies. The people of Italy must see that we are strong, but I would not have them think us monsters. We cannot win this war if all of Italy abhors us."

"But if we kill them they will be dead!" Monomachus said, spitting the last word out with the weight and resonance of a shout. "I fear not the anger of dead men. Ghosts are vapors. Never has one wielded a sword against living flesh."

An uneasy silence followed this. Eventually, Mago said, "I second my brother on this." He spoke forcefully, but having done so he seemed at a loss for anything more to say. Monomachus turned his gaze on him slowly, the lower lids of his eyes rimmed with condescension bordering on malice. Mago did not meet the older general's eyes, and he was visibly relieved when Hannibal spoke again.

"We know nothing of what Fabius will do just yet," he said. "Let us be direct. We will offer battle whenever we can. Perhaps Fabius will accept. One more victory should loosen Rome from her allies. This is how we will proceed. But we do not yet need to kill women and children."

The frivolity with which small-minded people spent money always amazed Silenus. Diodorus' chambers were lavish in the style of one new to affluence—in the manner, actually, of a public servant spending the wealth of others on trinkets: ostrich feathers, vases modeled on Eastern designs, cushions encrusted with glass bits meant to pass as precious stones, a few pieces of gold-inlaid furniture. It had been some time since the Greek had witnessed such an attempt at urban splendor. He did not miss it, and, despite the show of luxury, Silenus noted just enough signs of imperfect workmanship and garish design to indicate that the magistrate was not quite as prosperous as he wished to pretend.

Fresh from disembarking at Emporiae and on land for the first time in a week, Silenus had yet to accustom himself to the immobility of life on solid ground. His head swayed on his shoulders, still keeping the rhythm of the waves. Dried seawater crusted his face. He had formed the habit of absently drawing his fingers across his cheeks and down to the tip of his tongue, where he tasted the tang of salt. He was doing this when Diodorus finally appeared.

Silenus had only met the magistrate once, and that was years ago in Syracuse—when Diodorus became engaged to his sister—but he recognized in an instant that he had put on weight, around the torso and in the thighs, as a woman might in her mature years. His mouth was as wide as Silenus remembered and his eyes, conversely, as close together. The least appealing aspect of his appearance was that he wore a garment resembling a toga, not quite the genuine article but close enough to betray his aspirations.

"Silenus," he said, "my brother, I did not believe my ears when they told me you were here. By the favor of the gods, you look in good health! If I did not know better I would think you a warrior."

The two men embraced, quickly, and then drew apart. "And if I did not know better I would think you a Roman," Silenus said.

"Oh, not yet, but who knows how the gods will order things in the future? Sit. Sit and drink with me."

Silenus did so, and for a few minutes the two shared pleasantries. Silenus asked after his sister. Diodorus admitted that she made an adequate wife. Although, he explained, he much preferred the pleasures to be had from virgins. It was unfortunate that they were so hard to come by and expensive to purchase. Such pleasures were a constant strain on his resources. Silenus nodded at this, smiling despite himself.

Diodorus was also willing to speak at length of the tumultuous

path of his political life. Through the luck of others' misfortunes—
a few fevers, a tribal war, and a rapidly advancing dementia had
cleared a path for his ascent—he had moved up from a petty official of the city to one of its leading magistrates in just a few years.
Unfortunately, just as quickly he had seen his stature reduced by
the machinations of his peers. The only difficulty was that he was
never sure which god favored or despised him. To be safe he offered tribute to them all—a time-consuming task.

Eventually, when Diodorus seemed to have talked himself out,
Silenus addressed his true purpose directly, thinking to be most
forceful thus. "I come with a message from Hannibal Barca," he
said, "the commander of the Carthaginian army of Iberia and Italy."

Diodorus nearly choked on his wine. He spat a portion of it back
into his goblet, rose from the couch, and through his coughing managed to say, "You what? Hannibal, did you say?"

Silenus fought a smile. "He bade me speak with you of a prisoner
you hold here. You will know of whom I speak: his brother, Hanno
Barca. Emporiae was not wise to let the Romans keep him here.
Hannibal never called you an enemy and begs that you not name
yourself as one."

"Wait one moment," Diodorus said. "You come to me as a representative of Carthage? You, a Syracusan? When did you throw in with
the Africans? And now you come here into my home to demand—"

"Please," Silenus said. "This is a serious business; speak calmly
with me, as my kinsman."

Diodorus cast his eyes about the room, checking that nobody was
lingering to hear. "The truth is I've no quarrel with Hannibal," he
said. "I want him neither as an enemy nor as a friend. This business
of keeping his brother is no pleasure to me, but some things are unavoidable."

"Nothing is unavoidable except death, Diodorus. Is Hanno in
good health?"

One corner of the magistrate's lips twitched nervously at the
question. "You could say that," he said. "I mean . . . I believe so, but
I've only seen him a few times."

"Have you considered your fate when Hannibal wins this war?"

"When? Has it been ordained by the gods already?"

Silenus did not dignify this with anything except a smirk. He leaned forward and set his hand on the other's hairy wrist for a moment. "Diodorus, I did not join Hannibal's campaign because I believed he would win, nor because I cared either way. It was a form of employment, an adventure, a tale I could spend the rest of my life telling. And it has been all of these things. But I cannot deny what my own eyes have witnessed. I've never seen a man better suited to command. Everything Hannibal wants, he achieves; everyone he opposes, he defeats. That is the simple truth. I pray you will not make an enemy of him."

Diodorus pulled his arm away. He sat back, somewhat smugly, and studied Silenus as if noticing him for the first time. "Has he so won you over? Tell me, does he share your bed as well? They say that Hasdrubal Barca has a stallion's shaft. Is the same true of the eldest?"

Silenus did not dignify this with a response. He reached down into his traveling satchel, fished out a small leather pouch, and tilted it onto the table. Gold coins.

"What?" Diodorus asked. "Do you think me poor? Perhaps you have not looked around . . ."

"You are not poor, I know, but nor are you as rich as you would like. This gift is just a token. The riches he promises you for this favor will exceed your wildest dreams. This is why I know it is safe to show this to you. Accept it, and much more will come to you. Deny it, and you deny much more than you can imagine."

Diodorus, for the first time, forgot his look of haughty refusal. His eyes lingered on the coins. "But the reach of Rome . . ."

"By next year, Rome's reach will be no longer than the space from your shoulder to your fingertips."

"Do you really believe that? That this African . . ."

"If you knew him you would not doubt him," Silenus said. "Think with all of your wisdom on this. When the war is concluded, Hannibal will control the Mediterranean. He will not forget those who aided him. How would you, Diodorus, like to rule Emporiae as your own domain? Hannibal will call you his governor; you, of course, may think yourself more like a king, with access to as many virgins as your penis can service, among other pleasures. This is what Hannibal offers you."

"But what you wish I cannot deliver. I am only one magistrate among many, and the Romans do not bow to our wishes, anyway. Their guards answer only to their leaders—"

Silenus interrupted. "My mind is devious, brother. Say yes to this in principle and together we will think of a way to achieve it."

Diodorus thought for a long time. "How can it be," he finally said, "that you sit before me speaking of these things? It's madness, and my answer is no. I cannot do what you ask."

Imco had hardly thought about the Saguntine girl for months before the dreams started, but once they began they were a constant torment. He saw her as she had been on the day Saguntum fell. He would relive the few moments after he had found her wedged up into a fireplace. Again and again he agonized over her fate, wishing he could turn away and flee but never able to do so. Before long, she began to appear in camp, in his tent, at his feet as he slept, becoming more solid with each encounter until she seemed to be flesh and blood and she began to speak to him. She had walked this far, she said, to ask him what right he had had. Was he a god? Who had given him dominion over her?

He tried to explain that he had slit her throat not as a punishment, not out of cruelty or malice, but just the opposite. A gift, considering the circumstances in which he had found her. He had saved her from greater suffering. At this, the girl just rolled her eyes, rolled them and then set her gaze back on him again and pinned him. Then she would show him the scar and ask him whether it looked like a present she should be grateful for. She became bolder with the passage of time, grew to know him better and despise him more—which seemed a twisted progression to him, for surely the opposite should be true. He had killed her out of mercy, but the thanks he got was ghostly torment. Just his luck.

Perhaps because of her presence, the respite by the coast passed almost unnoticed, certainly unappreciated. When the word came that the army would be marching to intercept the new dictator, Imco groaned. He had just thrown down his burdens! Barely caught his breath. His vision had only recently returned to normal. His teeth had settled down in their gums once more, and his arms and belly were fleshed out a little better each day, but he was still a wisp of his former self and he told his squadron leader as much. He also noted that he still carried a chest full of phlegm, that his genital lice tortured him incessantly, and that his feet were tender with a rot from the marshes that had yet to heal. He also mentioned that his vision was impaired and that he was not sure he would be able to tell friend from foe on the battlefield—a small lie in the scheme of things. It might have been the one that saved him.

Much to his surprise, his squadron leader waved him away, telling him to stay, then, and join the guards watching over the occupied town and the stores of booty. After he had watched the tail of the army disappear over the horizon a few days later, it occurred to Imco that he was actually one of a relatively small company, made up partly of camp followers and slaves, charged with protecting a rather large treasure, surrounded by countless unseen natives who were naturally disgruntled at having been ousted from their homes. The first few days passed in tense appraisal of every puff of dust in the distance and every vessel appearing on the sea. Throughout the day, Imco stewed beneath the unrelenting summer sun, nagged by the growing suspicion that he was not fortunate at all to have won this duty. He was expendable—that was more like it. He even spent an anxious evening turning over the idea that the army might never return. This new dictator might, in fact, defeat them. And if that happened it would be only a matter of time before the Romans found them out and made captives of them all.

But the next morning dawned as quiet as the one that preceded it. Cavalry units came and went, scouring the neighboring countryside and depositing their gains at the camp. The soldiers kept watch through a rota system. One day passed into the next with little change and no news of a major battle. Sitting in the sparse shade of a stone pine on the shore side of camp, Imco found in the quiet sights a peace that he had not known for some time. The smell of the salt air, the thrum of waves collapsing on the shore, the view of fishing boats pulled up against the sand, the nimble movements of the shorebirds darting along the tide line: it was almost too tranquil to believe, in light of the more violent scenes he had been part of over the last few years. His situation verged on bliss, except that with fewer people around, the girl completed her emergence into the physical world. She escaped the confines of his dreams, visited him in the full light of day, and now felt free to pester him about a variety of topics.

He first discovered this one afternoon. He had noticed a stray dog patrolling the camp in wary fits and starts. He moved around cottages and shacks as if he knew the place well, but his gaze suggested that nothing was as he remembered anymore. The dog had one ear chewed off. He was dusty, his hair rubbed down to the flesh in spots. His pink tongue lolled constantly from the left side of his jaws. Imco found something humorously endearing in the dog's nervous movements about the camp. He called after him and tried to wave him over with benign gestures. But when the dog would come nowhere near him, he had a change of heart and threw a stone at it instead. "Pathetic creature."

Just after he mumbled this, a voice beside him asked, "Who are you to call another being pathetic?"

It was the girl, squatting beside him in the shade. She pointed out that he had chosen not to march with the others out of simple fear. Did not that make him more pitiable even than a dog? He went from moment to moment complaining about his fate in life, always fearing the next battle, the next injury or illness. If he hated war so much, why did he not take his own life as he had taken hers? She told him she would rather have been pierced by the lust of a warrior than spared by the trembling hand of a half-man. He had not allowed her that choice, had he? She had never known a man more hypocritical than he, she claimed. He could kill when the killing was easy, but really any act of valor he could claim was simply an act of cowardice turned on its head. Did they not call him the Hero of Arbocala?

"What a farce," she said.

By the end of the first week she was even following him through the midday sun, accosting him in view of other soldiers, who ignored her out of respect for him and, perhaps, empathy with his situation. It was most disconcerting, listening to her. She seemed to know his innermost thoughts. She understood him, in fact, with a clarity that baffled him. How had she come to know so many details of his life? To act as if she had spoken with his sisters and mother back in Carthage? He shot these questions back at her, but she answered that the dead have ways unknown to the living. Cryptic nonsense, he thought.

One afternoon the girl so harassed him that he lost his way while walking to the river he had grown accustomed to bathing in. Bathing was the only way to escape the stifling heat, and he preferred the fresh water to that of the sea. He cursed her for distracting him with a whole litany of questions about how various family members would view his cowardice throughout the campaign. The day was oppressively hot. The sun beat down like burning fingers massaging his flesh. He stripped off his tunic and walked naked with the garment flung over his shoulder. He spent some time struggling through the undergrowth before he finally reached the riverbank. But the point at which he reached it was all wrong. He was looking down upon a bend in the river from high above. He would have to walk a good distance upstream to find a route down. Resigned to this, telling himself that the sweat he would work up in the effort would make the swim that much more enjoyable, he turned to walk on. That was when he saw her.

She squatted on the pebbles of the far bank, scrubbing garments in the water. At first Imco took her for an adolescent, maybe one of the displaced townspeople camped on the outskirts of their former home. A little distance away, a donkey munched quietly on the sparse grass. Imco found the sight of the donkey strangely disturbing, but he did not wish to address this at that moment. He turned his eyes back to the young woman. He could make out no more of her features, huddled and low as she was.

He was about to move on when she rose and stood, stretching her neck, rolling her shoulders, and stretching out her arms to either side. Her tunic was thin and worn to begin with, but it had also been splashed with water so it clung to her chest and belly. The sight of this was like a divine revelation. Imco felt the air sucked out of his lungs, such was the impact of the contours of her body upon his. He had been weeks without sex, and he felt his penis stiffen. Imco patted it down and inched forward a little through the underbrush.

She was no girl at all, but a young woman. And by the gods, she was beautiful! As if toying with him, she stripped off her tunic and waded into the stream. Imco pressed forward, feeling his way through the vegetation with quiet toes. The woman walked out into midstream and sank down into the water. This made her no less exciting however, as the water was perfectly clear, revealing her body through pale blue highlights. She rolled over, dunked her head, and came up with her curls pressed to her scalp, and then dove forward so that her backside broke the surface for a fleeting moment.

It was all too much for Imco. His penis throbbed. Its scream for attention was not to be ignored. Imco obliged. Perhaps he should not have touched it, for in doing so he took his hand away from a grip among the bushes and took hold of a less useful anchorage. His attention was not on his footing, as it should have been. On the first stroke he gasped. On the second his eyes rolled back in his head. On the third his left foot slipped from beneath him. His body twisted just enough to dislodge his other foot. He reached out vaguely with his free hand, not yet realizing what was happening. His fingers touched only dry leaves and slender branches unable to hold him. He slid forward, grinding his bottom along the ground for a moment, fast reaching the edge of the embankment. He burst into midair amidst a rain of dust and debris.

He landed on a small beach along the near shore. The impact on his backside was painful enough, but his erection smacked against the sand with the full force of his fall. He would have doubled over in agony, but the woman stood up. She did not flee from him. Instead she strode directly toward him, kicking up a spray of water before her. She halted just a few paces away and spouted a fount of verbal abuse. As she stood berating him in a language he could not understand, he realized that her beauty, from up close, was even more astonishing than he had imagined. It radiated from her very skin. It floated off her like a fragrant oil. It reached out toward him as if her spirit contained arms separate from the thrashing limbs that threatened him. Her beauty was not simply a collection of parts placed favorably beside each other, although he did not fail to notice these parts in great detail. Her hair fell over her face as if it had a mind of its own and meant to toy with her. Her breasts jiggled wildly with her harangue. The muscles of her torso stretched and flexed with each step. Her upper thighs were as firm and smooth as an adolescent boy's, and the triangle of hair at her midpoint was dripping wet. Even in that moment of pain and outright trepidation, despite the immediacy of the confrontation and his embarrassingly excited nudity: still the image came to him fully formed of his mouth against the woman's sex, drinking the moisture dripping there as if from a sacred spring.

New images might have followed upon this one, but the woman closed her discourse by pointing at his own sex, spitting, and tossing her head with complete scorn. Then she turned, snatched up her clothes, and strode away. The image of her naked bottom would haunt him afterward. Somehow, the behind of the donkey following her only made his pain more acute. The creature fell into step a few paces after her, as if he were an ungrateful and unworthy husband, a four-legged barrier between her and a truly devoted suitor. They disappeared between a crease in the landscape, leaving him alone in the gurgling quiet of the afternoon.

Imco managed to rise. Once upright, however, he reconsidered. He placed a knee on the ground, then the other knee, then he lowered himself to all fours. This was not quite enough, either. Eventually, he lay on his side in the sand, his knees pulled up to his chest, his arms wrapped around them. In this posture he came to grips with the stomach-churning agony of his groin injury. This could not have been a chance encounter, he told himself. The hand of a gentle god had propelled him here. He did not question whether it was the same hand that had shoved him into midair at Saguntum, for the point seemed irrelevant. He had found a new purpose in life. A new destiny. He had to learn her name. He was—true to the unacknowledged poet inside him—in love.

Before long, he heard the approach of familiar footsteps. The Saguntine girl squatted in the sand a little distance away and said, "Have I used the word 'pathetic' already? You give new meaning to it."

How strange, Imco thought, that in such a short space of time two women should enter his life, each a torment of a different sort. Nothing was ever easy.

Fabius Maximus held his troops back like leashed hounds baying for blood. He stood with a hand on Publius Scipio's shoulder, listening to the soldier's description of the land below them and the punishments Hannibal had inflicted upon it. Publius had an even, measured voice, intelligent and thorough. He knew what the dictator wished to learn before Fabius even asked the questions and he always laid out the most pertinent features of the landscape first. With his aid, Fabius layered his mind's created images on top of the evidence of his eyes. The merging of the two developed a picture he believed to be clearer than one rendered through sight alone, nuanced with more detail and depth.

Perhaps the delay caused by this careful elucidation served as the foundation for the dictator's famous patience. He rejected the Carthaginian's offer for battle, first at Aecae, and then again each day afterward. He had the army trail the enemy through Apulia, keeping to the high ground so as to avoid the Numidian cavalry. He harassed them with quick raids, making small war, allowing atrocity after atrocity by the foe but evading open battle at all costs. Fabius' men were well provisioned, so he destroyed any supplies he suspected to be within his enemy's reach. He put special effort into picking off parties of foragers, staying ever vigilant, always near enough to spot the parties and send detachments to rout them. Even news of a single Massylii unhorsed was pleasant to his ears. Two Balearic slingers captured as they took target practice on a herd of sheep, a Gaul left behind due to a gangrenous leg, summarily tortured and nailed to the gnarled trunk of an olive tree: each of these came as an additional verification that his strategy was sound and would succeed over time.

Terentius Varro, his master of horse, chomped and foamed at the bit, muttering that Hannibal had arrived before them and they should vanquish him without delay. They could not keep to this policy of inaction! Perhaps it had sounded reasonable when he had dreamed it up in the safety of Rome, but here in Apulia they could see that it was not working. Italy was burning. Their allies killed and raped daily. What sort of policy was this? It rejected the long history of Roman warfare. Rome had not risen to power by letting an enemy run wild in their country. Rome had always attacked first, promptly, directly, decisively.

Fabius listened to his ranting and answered with all the dignity he could muster. Varro had not been his choice for his main lieutenant. Actually, the Senate had appointed him because he had spoken out against the Fabian policy. This rankled him—that even as they appointed him dictator they burdened him with a high-ranking officer who did not share his views. Varro was a man of the people. His father had been a butcher, successful enough financially to set the stage for his son's career. Fabius always found men of such new blood to be of questionable character too. Despite the young man's early achievements, he seemed better suited to the work of a laborer, to alleyway brawls, to taking orders, not giving them. He was, actually, something of a nuisance. Fabius restated his chosen tactics, held to them, and reminded Varro which of them had been given the title of dictator. Varro could not answer this except by fuming.

By Fabius' orders, they followed the Carthaginian army up and over the Apennines into the territory of the Hirpini, a land of rolling uplands interrupted by great, slanting slabs of limestone, a beautiful country planted with wide fields. Hannibal turned his army this way and that. He broke camp in the middle of the night and tried to outflank Fabius, or to surprise him with sudden proximity, or to vanish from sight.

Fabius watched anxiously as the city of Beneventum repulsed the Carthaginian attack. He sent a messenger to them with the promise that they would be rewarded for their loyalty later. On the other hand, he failed to anticipate Hannibal's strike at Telesia. He took the town with ease and found vast stores of grain hidden hastily within it. Again, Varro shouted in his superior's ear, as if his hearing were in doubt as well as his sight. But the dictator was as determined as the invader. He held to his chosen course.

One evening as Fabius returned to his tent from relieving himself, Publius spoke out of the darkness. He said that he could not sleep for thinking about the suffering Hannibal was inflicting upon the people. Fabius searched out his cot with his foot and lowered himself to it. Once comfortably situated, he gave the young Scipio a moment's thought. He had thus far not voiced a personal opinion of the campaign. Unlike Varro, he had been raised well, by a revered family and by a father who took his son's upbringing seriously. Considering this, he decided to dignify Publius with a brief response.

"Our charge requires that we must sleep," he said, "so that we may better work to free them on the morrow."

"You are right, of course," Publius said, "but do you not think of them at all? Do you not see them in your dreams?"

"No, I do not." Fabius spoke firmly, in a tone meant to end the conversation.

But the younger man said, "Their suffering is like a scene painted upon a thin curtain through which I see the world. I still see beyond them, but I cannot forget their present turmoil for even a moment. I see faces of individual men and women, of children, so clear it seems they are people known to me, even though they are not. They ask me to remember them, to realize fully that each of them has only one life, like fragile glass crushed beneath Hannibal's foot."

Fabius rolled irritably to his side. "You dream of poets, not of peasants."

"At times, simple people seem much the same."

"Such dreams do not serve you well. You should stop having them. It is not for a leader to think in specific terms: neither of strangers, nor of his own family. This is what the young do not understand. I consider a larger vision than you are capable of. Now go to sleep. You are my eyes, not my mouth!"

A few days later, the Carthaginian made another daring move. Hannibal departed Telesia. He snaked his army through the mountains not far from Samnium, crossed the Volturnus, and descended onto the plains of Campania. This country was in the full bloom of summer, as rich as the Nile delta, so far unscathed by the war and unprepared for its sudden arrival. Fabius did his best to send messengers ahead in warning, but he knew this effort was largely in vain. Hannibal had the whole of the Falernian plain at his mercy. If that were not bad enough, this move put him for the first time within striking distance of Rome itself.

Varro raged yet again, but still Fabius stood upon the hills staring out, firm in his resolve, ears attuned to the youth speaking softly beside him. It was Publius who casually mentioned that Hannibal's forces were now within a natural boundary, and that that could be used against them. Fabius pulled in his blurred gaze and focused on the soldier standing beside him, almost as if seeing him for the first time, though they had now been inseparable for weeks. He asked Publius to explain this notion. And the young soldier did, much to the older one's interest.

The situation became clear to Hannibal well before the body of his joyous army paused to consider it. They were afoot and unbeaten on Italian soil, enjoying the bounty of Campania, elated by their victories, fat from fine food, and sated from conquerors' sex. Most of the army had slaves they called their own in the train behind them, and these were laden with all they could carry and more: weapons and jewels; coins and tools and sacred items. Behind them followed hundreds of cattle, some newly slaughtered each evening, the scent of their roasting adding a pleasant air to camp. While they were constantly aware of the army following their every move, the Roman cowards did not dare engage with them. Hannibal several times set the army on a field perfect for battle and invited Fabius to engage, but the Roman sat on his hands and did nothing. None of the army of Carthage had ever imagined their lot could be this good. Campania had been a blessing to them; this Fabius had been less a foe than an escort. But Hannibal saw a problem stalking them, as gradual and inevitable as the change of seasons.

He called a meeting of his generals and opened it by asking them to study the charts of their current position, paying close attention to his notes detailing the best information he had on the Roman positions. They had entered the plain through the narrow pass of Callicula. Fabius took this pass shortly after, leaving a detachment of four thousand men sitting tight within it. The dictator then sent his master of horse to the defile of Terracina, where the mountains came down to the sea and the Via Appia could be easily held. He strengthened the garrison at Casilinum and lined the hills hemming in the plain with troops awaiting any weakness, easily called to arms, with a daylight view of all the Carthaginians might undertake.

"In short," Hannibal said, "we are trapped. This plain is a joy for summer raiding, but it will not sustain us through a winter. Nor would it be wise to stay here with nearby cities like Capua and Nola still hostile to us. Fabius knows it. That is partly why he watched us and did not engage, so that we might confine ourselves to winter in a depleted land. What thoughts have you each?"

As was their custom each general spoke in turn, each espousing a different course of action, if not from conviction then from custom, for Hannibal always asked to hear all reasonable alternatives before settling on the best. Bomilcar argued in favor of fighting through the pass; Maharbal suggested a dash toward the Via Appia, double time, to beat the season and reach someplace more favorable; Bostar suggested, though doubtfully, that they might ford the Volturnus; Monomachus was adamant that they could easily survive the winter, for they carried with them more than just cattle to eat.

Hannibal was silent. If he disagreed with any proposal he did not say so at once; nor did he have to, for Mago found the faults of each. The Romans held all the positions of advantage. The toll the Carthaginians would suffer in dead if they tried to fight up through the pass would leave them fatally weak. They would be no wiser than the Persians at Thermopylae, and unlike the Persians, they did not have thousands of lives to waste. They could run for the south, but this would spread them dangerously thin. The men would have to abandon their booty; this would damage morale, cost them much of what they had gained thus far, and betray a measure of fear that would give the Romans heart. The river itself posed a formidable barrier, hard to cross at any time and certainly no favorable route with an army ready to pounce on them.

Mago tossed the dagger he had been using as a pointer down upon the table. "Trapped! Fabius has all of Latium and Samnium and Beneventum to call upon for supplies. They will get fat while we starve. This plain of bounty will be the death of us."

Hannibal spoke lightheartedly, looking at Mago with a crooked grin on his lips. "My brother has a soldier's fire in his soul," he said. "And yet there's still some of the poet in him. It is my joy to see him grow this way."

Mago snapped his head up and stared at his brother, searching for sarcasm. Instead he saw a wry humor written on his face, like one who has thought of a joke and is about to share it. Mago had seen this look before. He smiled and shook his head at his own outburst. "Tell us, then," he said.

On that prompting, Hannibal explained how they were to proceed.

In the days that followed, the sprawling army marched back toward the ridge of mountains barring entry into Apulia. The plain they crossed stretched right up to the base of the mountains, and the peaks rose in one thrust. They could make out the dispositions of Fabius' army, clinging to the heights, waiting, watching. The glow of their fires stood out in the night, showing by their size the various routes through the mountains. The widest pass had the largest contingent of soldiers, but Fabius left no possible route unguarded. Small units held the smaller openings against spies or messengers or any who might seek solitary escape. Though many among the army groaned at their situation, Hannibal saw only the conditions he had anticipated.

The men ate quickly that evening. They made tight bundles of their weapons and supplies. They secured what supplies they could to the backs of horses and donkeys and even cattle. Men rushed out under the dying light of day and gathered all the wood they could find: fallen branches and decaying trees and twigs of all sizes right down to finger thin. These they piled near the edge of camp. Beside it they collected a hundred select steers in one mass of uneasy bovine life. For this task, Hannibal wanted only the largest from the herd they had gathered over the summer, the ones with wide horns and the strength to endure the ordeal he planned for them.

Mindful of the gods and of his men's morale, Hannibal asked Mandarbal to sanctify the proceedings. The robed priest went to his task with a surly belligerence, uttering the sacred words that were his province. He explained little to the nervous eyes watching them, but moved among the beasts cutting nicks in their shoulders and necks. He grasped at invisible objects, snatching them down and pressing them into his heart and rubbing them along the shaft of his dagger. he slapped away the hands of any who were touching the steers so that none fouled them during his ritual. By the time he concluded, all believed the method of their hoped-for escape had somehow been married to a great offering: a religious sacrifice and their own deliverance, at once.

Once Mandarbal retired, Hannibal himself oversaw the next phase of preparations. With his own hands, he tugged one of the animals away from the rest and toward the woodpile. He picked pieces of wood and placed them between the creature's horns, balancing them carefully. He called for twine to secure them. Soon the creature wore a headdress of sticks and branches woven through and tied to its horns and smeared with the pitch used to fuel torches. Hannibal stepped back and studied the wary, dejected creature, head heavy beneath its load.

Standing beside his brother, Mago said, "This is a singularly strange undertaking."

Hannibal did not disagree. He ordered that all the steers be similarly dressed.

The moon was thin and cast little light as the army left camp. They crept toward the base of the mountains and then up across their toes. For now, they went by the light of a few torches only. Fast behind them, herders drove the cattle forward. The rest of the army followed, awkward beneath their burdens, prodded by the feet nipping their ankles. Camp followers scampered in the rear, nervous about this whole venture but seeing no means to avoid it.

The route led some distance up toward two of the passes, the main way and a lower, narrower gap that was a plausible enough choice for Fabius to have positioned a small company there. When he could see the Roman fires in both camps, Hannibal whispered the agreed-upon command. The bearers of the few torches turned and offered them to those waiting near with unlighted wands. First one and then another and then many new flames sprang to life. In an instant they gave up all notion of stealth and watched each other's faces and bodies appear in wavering, warm yellow light. And then, before the beasts had time to panic, they were set on fire. The torch carriers moved among them, touching flame to the fuel carried on their horns. A moment later the herders shouted them into motion.

The cattle, unsure what was happening to them, sprang forward and ran upward, ducking their heads and weaving around trees and shrubs as if they might escape the flames through speed and footwork. The army trailed behind them. Though the beasts bellowed and snorted and filled the night with frantic sounds, the men moved as quietly as they could, coughing into their hands and shading their eyes against the smoke and trying to breathe through their mouths.

The Roman guards looking down upon this weaving herd of lights were mystified. They had seen nothing like this and could make no sense of the size of the fires, or of the way they moved, or of the eerie sounds carried by the night air. They woke the tribune in charge of the pass. He sent a messenger to Fabius, but he knew that he would not receive a reply in time to avert whatever mischief was afoot. He had to act. For lack of a better explanation, the tribune concluded that the Carthaginians were making a rush on the lower pass. Of course they were. That was the type of bold maneuver this African would attempt, to attack the weaker camp and push through with brute force. The tribune ordered the bulk of his men to speed across and down and reinforce the small contingent there. This maneuver would not be easy in the dark, but he had been warned of Hannibal's underhandedness and had no desire to be made a fool of.

Hannibal had, of course, counted on just this move. When he saw Roman torchlight leaving the high pass, he gave the order for the main body of the army to follow him. They moved away from the flaming cattle and proceeded, stealthily, toward the high pass, the one now being hastily deserted.

By the time the animals reached the Romans in the other pass, they were wailing like monsters under the torture of hide and flesh aflame. They came at the Roman infantrymen, a horde of beasts sent forth by the will of Baal himself, stepping from the dark frenzied, driven by smoke and flame. They shook their heads and raked them on the ground and bumped into one another and climbed in this chaos. A few Romans loosed their spears. One or two raised their swords as if to do combat. Most retreated, calling to each other, each asking the one beside him to explain this sight. None understood that at that moment Hannibal and the better part of his army were taking the high pass nearly unchallenged.

A few hours later the sky lightened just enough to reveal their gray forms. Fabius, watching through the eyes of the young Publius Scipio, saw the last of the Carthaginian army disappear over the pass. The remaining guards pulled up from their posts and bid the plains of Campania farewell. The whole army slipped out of sight, like the tail of a serpent into its den.

Sapanibal flew into a silent rage each time she heard of the Council's refusals to aid Hannibal. It was intolerable that so much time was passing without his receiving a single token of support from the country for which he fought. Even now, with the commander so close to victory, they had no vision. The mood of the Council bore no resemblance to the unwavering enthusiasm of the populace. The common people knew Hannibal for the hero that he was. They sang songs to praise him. Poets crafted verses that dramatized his deeds. Children playacted the parts of him and his brothers in the streets. Even slaves, it seemed, took some pride in his accomplishments. He belonged to the entire nation and exemplified the best of them. At least, this was true of all except a powerful group of councillors, centered around the elected leader of the council, the Shophet Hadus, and fueled by the Hannons' old hatred. No matter what Hannibal achieved, they found fault with him. Out of necessity, they praised his accomplishments briefly, but it was clear the words withered and turned bitter on their tongues.

Sapanibal was above all a reasoning woman, tempered by long years of sacrifice, not inclined to show her emotions in the public sphere or behave in ways unsuited to her sex. She had never before felt inclined to voice her thoughts outside her familial home, but the men of Carthage were on so misguided a course that they might end up losing everything. She decided her brother's enemies needed to be challenged. She had no faith that her allies in the Council were doing this with the necessary force. So she would have to see to it herself, and she knew just the setting in which to address the subject, to make a scandal of it, and through that to get tongues wagging. She attacked them where they spent most of their lives: the councillors' baths.

Sapanibal strode past the attendants at the entrance before they could think to stop her, before they had fully even comprehended her presence. The room was warm, pungent with stewed herbs and thick with the haze of incense and pipe smoke. Special torches on the wall and small fires attended by nude boys dimly lighted the chamber. The room's high ceilings gave no feeling of lightness but instead intensified the gloom. Every inch of the walls had been painted with murals of war scenes and illustrations of carnal stories and images of black-faced gods, masks that added to the sinister air.

She found the men she was looking for lounging at their leisure. Hadus saw her from a distance and rolled his eyes. He did not adjust his position at all, but sat with his weak chest exposed, his genitals just barely covered by a fold of his gown.

"What are you doing here?" a councillor behind the Shophet asked. "This is not a place for women."

"Nor is it a place for cowards," Sapanibal said. She looked at Hadus. "Shall we leave together?"

Hadus furrowed his brow. He was a thin man given to wrinkles and this expression made his face almost unrecognizable. "What is this?" he asked. "You enter our place of leisure to offend me? Barca women are just as arrogant as the men."

"Why did you speak against Hannibal this afternoon? He would not request help unless he needed it, and unless he knew it would bring victory. Do you want him to fail so much that—"

"What do you know of these things, woman?"

"I know that my brothers are the greatest wealth our nation has. I know that Hannibal's brilliance has brought victory where none of you believed victory was possible. I know it was here in Carthage that this war was declared, but that you are too cowardly or envious to see it through. What do you fear that you tie my brother's hands?"

"Someone take this bitch away before I lose my head," Hadus said, looking around as if he were addressing someone in particular but could not find him. "I've half a mind to smack her down and give her a good humping. She is no beauty, but rather that than hear her rattle on."

"Not even you could get away with that," Sapanibal said, dry and as composed as ever.

Hadus glanced around at his companions, his face puckered into an expression of utter, dismissive contempt. He did not look at Sapanibal when he spoke. "For my own part," he said, "I grow tired of talk of Hannibal. Never has Carthage known a man more presumptuous and vain. With the exception, of course, of the father who came before him. Only he surpassed his son in greed."

"You are mad to say such things!" Sapanibal said. "Everything that Barcas do, we do for Carthage. Hearing you, I know that Carthage does not do likewise for Barcas."

"Is that so? Where, then, is the tribute of his successes? Why has he sent none home to us to prove his allegiance?"

Sapanibal's jaw hung in disbelief. "Allegiance? How could he send anything to us when he must pay and feed his troops? He has borne the entire—"

Hadus interrupted her. "You say that the Council declared this war, but in truth the Council had little choice. The Barca brood was already running wild. They stirred Rome from its slumber. Had we denied that Hannibal was ours, Rome would have grasped for him and robbed us of our possessions. You cannot be expected to understand this, but our acceptance of the war was a defensive action. Unfortunately, your brother set off on his mad march without consulting us. He has brought no end of trouble upon himself and upon us. That is the real truth of it."

The servants had been active at the margins of the chamber since she entered. Thin creatures, they seemed offended by Sapanibal's intrusion but afraid to approach her. They had obviously sent for help, however. Two eunuchs entered the room with a purposeful walk. Sapanibal did not follow them with her eyes, but she was aware of their progress along the far wall, out of her view and then approaching from behind her. She heard the pad of their bare feet pause.

"Be under no illusion, Sa-pa-ni-bal," Hadus said, stretching out the syllables with calm contempt. "If I had my way we would call

Hannibal home and strike that genius of a head from its body. That is how I would save Carthage and assure my sons a future. What a gesture that would be to Rome. As it is not within my power right now, I will just have to let him hang himself. And he will. He will. No man can reach for the sun without being burned."

Sensing the eunuchs moving closer, Sapanibal snapped, "Do not permit them to touch me!"

Her voice was so sharp that several of the men winced. The eunuchs froze, eyes on Hadus for direction.

"I will leave as I entered," Sapanibal said. "Hadus, hear me now and recall my words later. The time will come when my brother's deeds exceed all others in grandeur. The time will come when he returns to Carthage victorious. I would not wish to be you at that moment. You will need eyes in the back of your head, for you shall have no future before you but will only look back on the things that might have been."

She turned, yanked her elbow from the reach of one of the eunuchs, and exited the chamber with all of the straight-backed grace she could muster. She knew that she had spoken the truth, and she took some pleasure in cutting Hadus down as if she were an equal, but she also feared she had done nothing for her brother's cause. And there was something else. Though she had given no indication of it throughout the exchange, her quick glance had noticed another man among the company: Imago Messano. He sat, bare-chested, toward the wall at the far end of the room. Carthage was a den of enemies, each one of the cowards scheming a way to become a lion killer. Why had she never seen this fully before?

Silenus lived from week to week in Emporiae. Each day he sought out and met with Diodorus. He tried to speak wisdom to him, to convince him to shake loose of his Roman rulers and accept the future that Hannibal offered. All he had to do was help a single prisoner to escape. That was all, and for it he would become as wealthy as a minor king. Like a man who takes sexual pleasure in being denied gratification, Diodorus heard his brother-in-law out each day. He teetered in his loyalties but never swayed fully to either side. At times he visibly licked his lips at the riches Silenus described to him in luxurious detail, but he would not consummate with action. He could not afford to make Rome an enemy. So Hanno's imprisonment went on.

Silenus called upon his sister to ask her help, but quickly learned that she would offer little. In keeping with Greek custom, her authority was limited to the hidden world of the home. She would not even speak to her husband on the issue of Hanno's release. After a few weeks, Silenus had stopped visiting her. Looking in her round woman's face, he realized that they had little to unite them, only the memory of parents long dead. Of what significance was that in a world swirling with the currents of war?

Silenus, having no other mandate, simply persevered. As an anonymous Greek in a Greek settlement, he was as free as any in the occupied city. He walked among Romans in the streets and listened to their banter. He cocked his ear at news of their war in Iberia. He sat beside them in the baths, so close that he could have reached out a hand and touched their bare flesh. Thus he learned of Hasdrubal's defeats and small victories, of his marriage, and of Roman schemes to press the conflict conclusively during the coming year. More than once he found himself the object of hungry, unsubtle stares. Romans knew little about amorous decorum. Like any men, they lusted, but they rushed into sex like four-legged creatures, humping quickly as if the chore were beneath them. Silenus rejected their overtures with all the disdain he could get away with.

Fortunately, not everyone in the city was an enemy of Hannibal's or a friend to the Romans. Many among the Greeks found the haughty Roman attitudes unpleasant, their arrogance that of cowherds drunk on the strange whim of Fortune that had brought them success. Silenus never showed his hand, but he did move from one circle to another, seeking out individuals with the deepest antipathy to Rome. Thus he chanced upon a group of Turdetani living in the city, in the lowest rungs of society, each and every one of them roiling at the indignities done to Hanno, each of them wishing to see the Romans fail. Hannibal had attacked Saguntum to protect them, they believed, and they felt a loyalty to him unusual among Iberians. Silenus believed these men—coarse criminals that they were—might be just the actors for the play he had in mind. But Diodorus still denied him the fruits of his mission, even when he put forth a complete plan of action, argued with all his powers of persuasion.

"I have the men," he explained. "They will do the bloody work of dealing with the guards. All you have to do is plan the rescue with me, gain all the details of where and how he is detained, the best routes to him, the rotation of his guards. Provide us the key to unlock his cell and chains. These are not difficult things for a man in your position."

"We will be found out," Diodorus said. "You may fly away with Hanno, but I'll be left to suffer the Romans' wrath."

Silenus moved forward suddenly and grasped one of the man's hands between his. "Listen. Just before we spring our plan, I will announce to one of the Turdetani just which magistrate is aiding us. I'll give whatever name you give me. They will whisper of it to a few others. Think about that. An hour after the escape is known, the entire population will be tongue-wagging, and none of them will think to say your name. In the fury of rumor, you will be one of many to denounce that other man. He will take your punishment; you will, eventually, take the city. You are a creature of political life. Surely you have an enemy you'd like to see crucified."

Though this speech was forcefully made, Diodorus clung to his indecision. Silenus wished he could communicate his efforts to Hannibal, but he knew that any letter would doom him if it were intercepted. Instead he prayed for some change of fortune. He called on gods he did not even believe in, asking them to prove themselves by divine intervention, promising that he would withdraw his complaints if they only showed themselves and acted on his behalf.

One day in the early autumn, something just as improbable happened; it changed nothing in his thoughts about the gods, for Silenus could name a man as its author. He waited in the morning outside Diodorus' chambers, his head muddled from wine consumed the night before. He had drunk too much of it and it was too cheaply made, but the young student with whom he had shared it was more than worth the trouble. The night's events were a clouded jumble of images and snatches of conversation, but still he knew he had prosecuted his conquest with rare skill. Later in the day, he hoped, he might pick up where he had left off.

When finally called in, he found the magistrate seated as always, with scrolls and documents spread before him. Everything was as it had been many times before, except that when Diodorus glanced up he seemed instantly ill at ease. His eyes quivered with a timorous energy and his hands moved like nervous birds across the paperwork, shifting and sorting and then undoing what they had just done.

Silenus began for the hundredth time. He stated again the generosity of Hannibal's offer, the simplicity of his request. He recounted Hannibal's victories, one example after another that he was superior to Rome. Two of them so far and counting. He began to name them, but Diodorus stopped him.

"Two, you say?" he asked.

"Ticinus . . ."

"Ticinus? You name Ticinus?"

"Yes, I do. It's a small victory but not to be ignored. Along with it, the Trebia . . ."

Diodorus interrupted him. "Why toy with me? We both know that the world has changed and everything in it has been cast in doubt."

Silenus had not been aware of any such thing, but he answered coolly, as if he were in fact toying with the man. "Yes . . . and how was that achieved?"

"You know full well how it was achieved. That madman you call master . . . He's made a butcher's block of all Italy. I know you rejoice over Trasimene, but don't treat me as a fool."

"Trasimene?"

Diodorus stared at him. At first he fixed him with a slack-jawed expression of loathing. But the longer he stared, the more this faded into incredulity. Silenus could not hide his confusion completely and the politician's eyes homed in on this. "You truly are ignorant of Trasimene?"

Silenus barely knew the name of the place, but he did not like to be found wanting by this man. "I'm ignorant of few things that pass in the world, my brother by marriage, but some things come to me slowly." He hesitated a moment. "Perhaps you have details that I do not."

"What do details matter? Either you know of it or you don't. Granted, it is hard to believe what I've been told. Somehow, your commander made a trap out of the land itself. He slaughtered Flaminius and his entire army like hens gathered together in a pen. I never imagined I'd live to hear of this."

The magistrate rose and fetched a jug of wine and a glass. It was early in the day, yes, but Silenus found himself thirsty as well. He motioned for the jug and drank directly from it, deeply enough that he would feel the effects. Diodorus took the jug from him and re-filled his glass. A few moments passed like this, the two of them shuttling the jug back and forth, each captured by thoughts of his own.

Diodorus was the first to raise his eyes. "Does your commander's offer stand?"

Four days later, in the afternoon, the two men walked quickly through corridors in the lower reaches of the fortress. Diodorus had at last found his motivation. He went at the task with a nervous, jerky intensity that surprised Silenus, but it proved a fine thing. The plan had unfolded just as Silenus had imagined, although he witnessed the aftermath rather than the event. The assassins had done their work, and they had suffered for it. Judging by the carnage in the hallway, the five Roman guards had each killed at least three Turdetani. The surviving Iberians were nowhere to be seen, having slunk away into hiding.

Stepping over and around the bodies, careful on the blood-slicked floor, Diodorus warned Silenus to prepare himself for the sight of the prisoner. The Romans had treated him harshly. Diodorus described the tortures they had used, and Silenus winced as he heard them. They had had a thousand questions for Hanno. He had answered none of them.

"So they abused him," Diodorus said. He stood before the door of Hanno's cell and fumbled to find the correct key, his hand jerking at the wrist, making the simple task difficult. Each jingle of the keys echoed down the hallway. "They did no permanent damage. He still has all his limbs and digits, but he has suffered. Have no illusion about that."

Silenus touched Diodorus' shoulder. "You say he did not answer their questions?"

"Not one word of betrayal escaped his lips," Diodorus whispered. "They threatened him with things to make a man's penis shrivel and his hair go white on the spot, but he uttered not a single word they wished for. He lives up to his family name."

The magistrate found the right key and rammed it home. He leaned to twist it around and then shouldered the iron-framed door open. Silenus followed him into the cell reluctantly. Diodorus' wide torso blocked out the view. Silenus conjured images of disfigurement, of nudity, of the various postures they might have bound Hanno in, but when he finally laid eyes on the second eldest Barca brother it was not at all what he had imagined.

Hanno sat on the floor in the corner, like a child suffering some long punishment. He was wrapped in a long cloak, hooded. His head drooped toward the stone floor. He did not move at all upon their entering. Silenus, thinking he must imagine them to be his tormentors returning, struggled for the words to greet him. He stepped forward reluctantly, one arm outstretched to touch the prisoner's knee. "Hanno Barca," he whispered in Carthaginian. "Hanno, I've come with the blessing of—"

Diodorus pushed past him. He scooped his hands under one of Hanno's arms and indicated that Silenus should do the same. Seeing the alarm on Silenus' face, he said, "Make your speeches later. Come, let's do this without delay."

They dragged the warrior's body between them, laid him in a wagon, covered it, and negotiated the back lanes of the city. Diodorus parted company with them near the docks, pressing upon Silenus all forms of praise for Hannibal, pledges of secret friendship, asking again and again for confirmation of the wealth coming to him. He walked away muttering under his breath, testing the inflection with which to answer the questions soon to be put to him, trying to find which lies best flowed from his tongue.

Silenus and his charge fled the city that evening, aboard a small vessel that cut through the waves with dangerous speed. Silenus, after so much waiting, found himself suddenly free of the land and in motion. The wind behind them some might have called a gale, but he considered it a blessing. The poor trader who captained the ship knew without asking that their mission was covert and perilous. He kept the sail unfurled and rode the back of the sea as one might sit atop a raging bull.

In the boat's small shelter, the two men huddled against the night chill and sea spray. Hanno awoke with the rocking of the waves. He fixed his eyes on the Greek and studied him earnestly, as if searching for him in some dim portion of his memory. Silenus tried several times to bring him into conversation, but Hanno chose his own time.

Eventually, in the darkness of full night, Hanno said, "Out of the clutches of one Greek . . ."

Silenus filled in the pause. ". . . and into the hands of an old friend. By the gods, you must have fared all right if you leave that chamber with humor on your tongue. Are you hungry? I brought food, for I feared they'd starved you."

Hanno shook his head. "Romans believe meat and rich food make a man soft. So they gave me meat instead of the plain food they favor." A fit of coughing choked out his words. He was silent for a moment and then whispered, "They fed me so that I would be stronger for their questions."

"Think no more about it," Silenus said. "It's over. Done. You've left that dungeon and none need speak of what went on there. I'll never betray you, as you never betrayed your country. That's all anybody need know."

Hanno looked as if he might try a weak smile but he did not. He just gazed into the other man's eyes with an intensity that was statement and question and silence all.

Silenus had to turn away. "And to think," he said, "at one time I thought we were just a few words away from becoming lovers."

Hanno closed his eyes as if this thought pained him.

The air above Rome hummed with a wild, bickering energy, with resentment and anger, with possibility and passion, with fear of the gods, and with the fervent hope that divine forces would soon smile on the Roman people. In alleyways and baths and markets, Romans spoke of nothing save the situation they found themselves in and how to remedy it. Few opinions sat easily next to one another, but the tone of the discourse had shifted. The shock of the Trebia now lay a distant memory; gone was the desperation following Trasimene; forgotten the notion of Hannibal's invincibility. In place of these, the Roman people stoked the fires of indignant rage. Under Fabius' leadership they had wasted an entire season pretending to be cowards. They had suffered humiliation after humiliation. When the old man finally seemed to have the African within his grasp he let him escape by a cheap, cowardly ruse. Things had to change, at all levels, decisively and soon.

The dictator received a cold reception on his return to Rome. He walked the streets with the decorum he had long nurtured, with his faithful around him. He showed not the slightest diffidence, gave no hint that he viewed his strange campaign with regret. He handed his dictatorship back into the trust of the Senate without a word of apology. This apparent indifference to public criticism united the people against him. A senator's wife dubbed him Fabius the Delayer. The name took. Children taunted him in the streets. They threw out insults that were rarely intelligible—spoken as they were on the run, with fear and laughter both garbling the words—but the sight of young ones darting to and fro through the dictator's entourage had a detrimental effect on his stature. Enough so that a street player could get away with depicting the dictator as completely blind, a feeble creature who complained that his testicles had somehow fallen out of the sacks that held them. By the end of the performance—to the hilarity of ever-growing crowds—the actor was down upon his knees, searching with his hands for the missing baubles. The audience laughed all the harder because mirth had been absent from the capital so long. With its return, however, a new future seemed possible. The elections only verified this.

Terentius Varro stepped first into the fringed toga of consul. He who had so chafed against the dictator's delaying tactics easily became the popular choice. He wrapped the garment around his thick torso and walked with one arm clenched at an angle that highlighted the bulge of his bicep. Though he was not exactly of the people, he knew how to play to a crowd, boasting with an earthy bravado that his family had once been butchers. He knew that citizens both rich and poor wanted action. It was not simply a matter of honor, of national pride, or even of revenge for lives lost. The fact was that people were going hungry. Food was in short supply. Goods normally transported across the country had been long held up. Italy, so rightly the object of Roman hegemony, was out of balance. Varro pledged to right all this by the age-old method of the Roman people—war on the open field. In his speech accepting the consulship he reminded the Senate that he had once before looked into Hannibal's foul face, some years back, in his city of New Carthage. He swore that the next time he caught sight of him would be the African's last day in command. He would do battle that very hour and bring this matter to a close.

The people greeted all this with enthusiasm. But Romans had embedded deep within them a cautious core, a twin who always wished to calm the passions of his brother. Thus the second consul elected was Aemilius Paullus, already a veteran of the office: He had commanded previously in Illyria. The family line of this more seasoned choice nowhere converged with that of butchers. He was a friend to the brothers Scipio and had apprenticed under Fabius himself. Indeed, it was rumored that on the evening after the election Aemilius supped at the former dictator's house, listening to the older man's counsel and taking within himself a portion of his views. But if this was true, he was prudent enough not to admit it.

The Senate, having appointed these two men with a war mission, did not fail to support them. In addition to the four legions already in the field, they called up four more. They increased the number of men in each to five thousand, and they demanded that their allies provide matching forces. More than one hundred senators left the Senate to serve in the coming year's army. Though they were going to war, the people felt propelled by an almost euphoric wave of enthusiasm. They would field an army such as the world had never known—a full eighty thousand soldiers for Rome. The destiny of their people was again within reach. They had only to remember themselves and seize it. They were Romans, after all.

Another point of interest in the new year's elections—an event hardly noticed in the consular turmoil—was the rise of Publius Scipio to the position of tribune. He was thereby entrusted with protecting the lives, property, and well-being of the people. The young man, son of the former consul, savior of his father at the Ticinus, whisperer in the dictator's ear, held to a path of quiet ascendance.

Hasdrubal found the Scipio brothers a constant nuisance, a two-headed viper that threatened to stir the whole of Iberia into rebellion. Word of Trasimene must have reached the Scipios quickly, for their tactics changed somewhat late in the summer. They became cautious. They turned their talents to political intrigue. The two sides played a game of strategic moves, one pressing around the side of the other, flanking and counterflanking, skirmishing at the fringes of their might but not clashing head-on. Both sides courted the various tribes, each vying to play the native people against each other, or against other Iberians, whichever seemed more expedient. It was an intricate game that ill suited the young Barca. He could barely keep track of who was loyal to whom, who an enemy of whom, and why, or which double or triple betrayal was in the works at any one time. Had it not been for Noba, with his labyrinthine memory, he would have overturned the game board in frustration long ago.

In the autumn, frustrated by the lack of direct action and warily feeling that the contest was turning against him, Hasdrubal pushed for a decisive military clash. His army was divided—half of his forces patrolled the far south, staying vigilant lest any portion of the empire grow rebellious—but he drew upon a fresh reserve of troops gathered from the Tagus region, mostly of the Carpetani. They were raw recruits, numerous but not entirely happy with their lot in life since Hannibal's rout of them a few years before. They might not want to fight, but like all men they would do so for their lives. If they were flanked on either side by the best of his troops, the Africans, then simple self-preservation would transform them into something useful.

When the opportunity came to surprise the Scipios, at an unremarkable spot near Dertosa, Hasdrubal snatched at it. At least, he thought he was surprising them. They drew up into their orderly ranks with amazing efficiency, and with the first volley thrown from the Roman velites his Carpetani troops broke ranks. Many of them grumbled against being pressed into the fight, and they all found the sight of Rome's ordered butchers too much to bear. They shifted in confusion, one line inching nervously back into the next and that pushing still further ranks into disorder. A tumult of confusion passed from man to man. The African troops held solid, briefly. They watched as the Roman front flowed in on the Iberians like a river pressing against an untried dam. They might have fallen upon the enemy's side to great effect, but such was not the mood of the day. Instead they turned and executed a quick retreat. Just like that the battle was decided.

Hasdrubal shouted orders that his signalers conveyed to the troops as well as they could. But fear can drench men faster than a downpour of rain. Hasdrubal had heard of such things but never witnessed them. The Romans that day did not so much fight as slaughter. The Africans, though retreating, had not actually panicked, so most of the Roman fury focused on the Iberians. They dashed forward, hacking and stabbing at the backs of the panicked conscripts, slicing at the tendons in their calves, stabbing into the soft tissue at the back of their knees.

More than ten thousand Iberians died at Dertosa. Only a few hundred Africans perished, but this small good fortune was as nothing compared to the ill will it inspired throughout Iberia. The Ilergetes of northern Iberia shrugged off any pretense of impartiality. They went over to Rome completely, sealing the alliance with the severed heads of the Carthaginian delegates in their midst. The Vaccaei—distant though they were, to the northwest—announced their defection to Rome. Even the Turdetani, for whom Hannibal had attacked Saguntum, were known to be corresponding with the Scipios. Andobales pledged that the agreements between Carthage and the Oretani still held, but Hasdrubal heard Bayala's cautioning words behind everything the man said, and did not trust him. Unfortunately, he had no choice but to go on as if he did.

Word came of another rebellion too symbolically important to ignore. The Carpetani, hearing of their losses at Dertosa, rose again, declaring their independence from both Carthage and Rome. Hasdrubal remembered the conversations he had with Hannibal as they marched toward these same people just a few years earlier. The memory was almost painful to him: the two of them mounted and conversing, a whole army behind them. At that time, Hasdrubal had not yet fully imagined the burdens of leadership. Even considering the bloody violence of the work, it was a memory of innocence.

But remembrances are of no use unless they inform the present. With that in mind, Hasdrubal acted—not in passion this time, but with cold determination. His southern troops had just returned from their duties. He stirred them from their short rest, met them at a double-time march, and in consultation with Noba planned to meet the Iberians' treachery with an even greater one.

The Carpetani greeted the approaching army in their usual form: as a raucous swarm propelled more by courage than by strategy. Hasdrubal timed the approach of his army in such a way that they came within sight of the horde toward the close of the day. They made camp, apparently to await the next day's coming battle. As Hannibal had done during their last encounter, Hasdrubal put his men into motion in the dead of night. But this time he had the bulk of his infantry back several miles, far enough to ensure that the Iberians would not be able to press battle the next day. At the same time he sent the full force of his cavalry on a mission under Noba's direction. He knew a good deal about this area, and he put that knowledge to use in navigating through the night.

At dawn, the cavalry swept down not upon the Carpetani horde but upon their unprotected wives and children some miles away. They breached the main town's defenses with ease and poured through the humble streets, slaughtering men of dangerous age. Hasdrubal had ordered the capture of all females of childbearing age. Quite a number this made. They were bound and sent on their own feet toward New Carthage, captives to seal the Carpetani to a new loyalty.

All this was a day's work. The men on the battlefield did not learn of the situation until the close of the day, at which point they could not vent their fury. Instead they spent the night in anguished confusion. Many, desperate to learn of their families' fates, slipped away during the night, hoping to find their wives and daughters safe. Meanwhile, Hasdrubal moved his infantry forward into position again. With the next dawn he fell on the disheartened remnants of the Carpetani. The butchery was fast and easy. That evening he accepted an invitation to parley with the Carpetani chieftain, Gamboles. In fact there was little parleying. Hasdrubal's diatribe was made more vicious by his fatigue and resentment and distaste for his own tactics. The women, he said, would not be harmed so long as the two peoples were friends. But should Carthage find itself betrayed, then each and every one of them would be pumped full of Carthaginian seed, to bear a half-breed army of the future.

"Do you understand me?" he asked. "The Carpetani must never rise again. You have been beaten beyond hope of future victory. Do not be a fool. Do not harbor plans for vengeance in your hearts. Do not walk from here with malice. Instead, understand that I've been more generous than you deserve. Tell this to your people. Speak plainly so that they may understand and hear your voice one last time before you come with me to be my guest in New Carthage. Do exactly as I say, because I promise you, Gamboles, if I hear one whisper of stirring, your women will suffer for it. As will you. I'll sever your head from your shoulders and shove it nose-first up your ass. Thereafter, your people will each and every one of them eat a diet of shit."

Hasdrubal rode away with all the promises he asked for. Not terribly satisfying, but certainly the best he could manage under the circumstances. He had never thought of cruelty like this before. He had no wish to see any of these punishments come to pass, but neither could he allow his father's empire to crumble on his watch. All things considered it was one of his more successful ventures, though he felt little pride in it and had no true faith that Fortune had joined his cause.

With the work done, he headed for New Carthage. The ten days it took to reach the capital passed in a blur, a tumult of motion and fretting and gut-deep longing to see his wife again and to feel her legs straddled around his hips. On arriving, he attended no business but went straight to his private chambers. Entering the outer room he called out, "Wife, come to me now! I need to pierce you!"

He dropped his sword unceremoniously on the stone floor, cast his cloak over a chair, and snatched up a waiting pitcher of wine. He did all this at a brisk walk and was therefore well into the room before he saw the two figures lounging on his couches. He stared at them for a long moment, openmouthed, with all the mystification he would have shown upon seeing ghosts. He held the pitcher halfway to his mouth, dripping wine upon the floor.

Silenus glanced at Hanno and said, "That's a strange greeting."

It was almost too much to bear thinking about, but Imilce could not help but do so again and again each day. She was ever being reminded that young Hamilcar was approaching his fourth birthday and that it had been three long years since his father had last seen him. She remembered how the two of them had looked the day before he departed. Hannibal had stood holding the boy in his muscled arms, looking down on him and whispering close to his face, telling him things he said were for the child's ears only. The boy's legs dangled beneath his father's grip, plump and lovely; his features were still rounded, his fingers chubby. The boy had listened to the man patiently, for a few moments at least. Then he squirmed free and ran off to play. Hannibal looked up at her, shrugged and smiled and said something she could not now remember, though she always imagined him with his mouth moving and wished that she could move closer to the recollection and place her ear against his lips and feel them brush against her.

It pained her to think how changed they both were now, how days and months and years had pushed in between that moment and this one. She knew her husband had suffered injuries that would mark him for life. She knew he had lost the sight in one eye and endured hardships she could barely imagine. He might be a different man entirely the next time she saw him. Likewise, Little Hammer would be almost unrecognizable to Hannibal. He had sprouted like a vine reaching for the sky. He no longer teetered on wobbly legs, but darted through their chambers like a cheetah. She realized her son thought of Carthage as his first home. He reached for Sapanibal and Sophonisba with complete comfort and unquestioning love. They luxuriated in this, even as they joked that they must treasure the few years the boy had left to spend in the company of women. Even Didobal softened in the boy's company.

Imilce had spoken to him over the years of his father, as had many others. The child was constantly reminded whose son he was and how much was expected of him. But lately she had begun to fear that her words found no purchase in his memory. As she spoke he stared absently into the distance. When she concluded, he moved away from her, always polite enough, always nodding when he was supposed to, speaking when asked to—but she knew the boy had a blank space in his center. Hannibal had actually been present just one year of the boy's four: no time at all. In the child's mind, his father could only be a creature built of words, a fancy like a character from old stories. Not so removed from the gods: like them, a part of every day, unseen and believed in mostly without evidence.

She was pondering these things one afternoon when Sophonisba called on her. Imilce reclined on the sofa at the edge of her chamber, looking out over the gardens. As usual she had nothing to occupy her, no responsibilities. Hamilcar was engaged in some activity that did not require her supervision. Sophonisba came in behind the maid who escorted her. She did not wait as the servant announced her with the usual formality of Carthaginian households, but pushed past the woman and plopped down on the sofa beside her sister-in-law. The maid tried a moment to continue the introduction, but then gave up. She withdrew, annoyance flashing on her face. Seeing this Imilce nearly chastised her on the spot. No servant should ever comment upon the actions of her masters. But Sophonisba was too eager to talk.

"If you are good to me," she said, "I will tell you a secret. You must promise to keep it, though. If you betray me, I'll never forgive you. You'll have an undying enemy for the rest of your life. Do you promise?"

Imilce looked at her with more seriousness than she intended. The proposition struck her with an unreasonable amount of fear. She could not survive in this place with Sophonisba as an enemy. The introduction of secrets brought with it both camaraderie and the awareness that somebody else was being excluded. Her heart beat a little faster, even though she knew it was silly to find anything ominous in this. The young woman's face was all mirth and welcome. Her threat was nothing but banter between two friends.

Imilce said, "Of course. Tell me."

"I spent the night in the wilds with Masinissa," the young woman said. She paused for dramatic effect, her lips pursed, eyes mischievous and painfully beautiful. She explained that she and her fiancé had stolen away from the city the previous evening, with her sitting before the prince on the bare back of his stallion. They rode out through a side gate, cut through the peasants' town, out past the fields, and on into the rolling orchards. The sky was clear from horizon to horizon. It was a screen of the darkest blue, alive with numberless stars. The land itself seemed endless, thrown out in ripples stretching deep into the heart of the continent. They sometimes passed campfires of field workers, or saw the signal fires of soldiers, but mostly the night was theirs alone.

Imilce chided her for the rash danger—not to mention the damage she might have done to her reputation and to the very union. They had only just become engaged, after all, and it was meant to be some time before they were wed. But Sophonisba laughed at both these points. As for the danger, when she said she rode alone with Masinissa, she meant "alone" in princely terms. A guard of fifty horsemen shadowed them.

As for reputation, nothing mattered to her mother more than the power of her familial connections; and nothing mattered to Gaia, Masinissa's father, more than the security of his kingdom. Everyone wanted them wed. So, she was sure, anything could be overlooked. And, anyway, there were stories that Didobal herself had been as mischievous as a jackal in her youth. She had a few secrets to pressure her with, things she had not even divulged to Imilce, sister though she was.

"Should I tell you what happened then?" Sophonisba asked. "Or need I find a different confidante?"

Imilce shut her lips in a tight line, keeping up the look of reproach for as long as she could. But her façade masked very different feelings. She was always amazed at how Sophonisba occupied and acted in the world. It was not just that she flouted tradition and decorum on occasion; it was the casual confidence with which she accomplished this. Imilce, staring at her, wished for a portion of this young woman's strength; with it perhaps she, too, would find a way to act boldly to answer the things that troubled her.

Eventually Sophonisba overcame the unanswered question and proceeded. Though he rode fast to impress her, and seemed to dash from feature to feature on the landscape at whim, he did have a destination in mind. They stopped at a strange structure set at the top of a gentle crest, with views of the country to either side. They dismounted and walked past a crumbling wall that squared a courtyard, no larger than a pen for a few horses. A tower rose from one corner, although it too was damaged at what must have been its midpoint. Blocks littered the ground.

"This is Balatur's watchtower," Masinissa had said. "Many times I've come here and thought about my future, about the world I will shape and the woman who will stand beside me as I do."

Sophonisba could tell she was supposed to be impressed, curious. So she showed neither sentiment. "Where is this Balatur?" she asked. "He should be chided for the state of this place."

Masinissa said that Balatur no longer was. He had died many years ago. The tale went that he had been an officer of much repute. While on a campaign against a tribe to the south, he had met a princess of the dark people there. He fell in love with her so completely that his life as a mercenary for Carthage seemed of little value anymore. He believed that she loved him as well, and yet he would not desert the army. He returned to Carthage after the campaign, but he never forgot her. He thought of her always, day and night, and with such hunger that he felt a portion of flesh had been ripped from him. He came to believe that she had bewitched him and that his failure to forget her meant she wanted him just as much. Eventually, he had himself assigned to this watchtower. He sent word to her that if she would come and meet him here, they could be together. If she, too, pledged her love they could flee together and find a life elsewhere. He swore that he would be mercenary or beggar, fisherman or a carpenter: anything and anywhere, so long as he could be with her. From the tower he looked day and night to the south, waiting for a messenger from his princess. He did this for a full forty years. She never came; he died in waiting.

"Such is the tale of Balatur," Masinissa had said, finishing his story with somber theatricality.

Sophonisba burst into laughter and admonished him to speak no more nonsense. "Of course she did not come to him," she said. "What princess would abandon her people to join a man who wished to be a beggar? Such devotion is not at all attractive. Anyway, never was there born a Massylii that loved one single woman."

The prince took exception to all of this. He dropped to his knees and said that he was another Balatur, a man possessed of a love so complete it eclipsed all others, as the sun does the stars. When they were joined, their love would be a tale for the ages. After he helped Carthage to defeat Rome, he would become king. Sophonisba would be his queen and together they would rule an empire second only to Carthage in its glory. He reminded her that he was no mere boy. He was the son of King Gaia and he would prove himself worthy of the Barca family very soon. He promised this with his very life.

Sophonisba's voice had taken on a passionate urgency as she recalled the prince's words. She breathed them in and out so that they had a husky quality, as if heated with desire. But when she finished this portion of her story, she laughed and let the emotion drop from her face, like a mask lowered by the hand that held it.

"Can you imagine such a show?" she asked. "I almost burst into tears right there at that moment. Tears of laughter, that is."

"Sophonisba!" Imilce said. "Are you so cruel? Never has a man spoken to me thus. Not even my husband!"

"And in that is a measure of my brother's truthfulness," she answered. "You see, I did not tell you that during all of this poetry the young prince managed to move next to me and take me in his arms. He bade me look out at the sky and the land and wonder at it—as if he'd created it all for me! And all the time he was trying to rub himself against me. He pretended that he was not, but I could feel his stiffness. He is truly a man of two parts: one of them a poet and the other a serpent with searching tongue. Yes, his words were fine, but fast upon them he was breathing in my ear, begging me for a taste of our wedding night, saying I cannot possibly keep him waiting till then. I told him I could do just that, and that I'd have him hunted down and quartered if he took me against my will."

"Sophonisba!"

The girl laughed. "That is just what he said. *'Sophonisba!'* He looked ready to cry. He would have, I am sure, except that I did him a small favor."

She let this statement linger, waiting for Imilce to rise to it. "What sort of favor?"

"I touched it," Sophonisba said, showing with an outstretched finger how gentle and innocent the gesture had been. "I asked him to show me the length of his love, and when he did I gave it a touch. Just a fingertip and he shot his praise to the gods."

Imilce did not know how to configure her face. It wavered between amusement and incredulity and outright reproach. Eventually, she said, "Sophonisba, hear me and believe me: You cannot play with men's affections this way."

"You should not fear, Imilce, he is only a boy, not yet a man. Though enthusiastic, yes. And handsomely gifted, if you understand me . . . Think of it, sister! The future king of Numidia, brave Masinissa, who says he's going to join Hasdrubal in Iberia this spring—conquered by the touch of a finger! Boys are such strange creatures."

"Boys grow to men quickly," Imilce said. "As do girls to women."

"Yes, yes." Sophonisba poured herself a drink of lemon-flavored water. She drained the glass in a few long drafts, as quickly as any thirsty worker. But when she glanced up, her face was again a beguiling conglomeration of features. Imilce realized that the trick of her beauty was that her face was always surprising. Somehow, each time one saw her she seemed newly created, as if her features were still wet from the touch of a sculptor's fingers. It took Imilce's breath away and filled her with warmth just because of their proximity. Masinissa did not stand a chance.

On a morning early in the spring, Hannibal found the letter waiting for him like any other piece of mail. It lay upon his desk among several other scrolls: dispatches from Carthage; inventories and figures compiled by Bostar; noncommittal missives from several Roman ally states, whose chiefs were willing to speak secretly with him but as yet gave him nothing; and a document from the king of Macedon. Compared to these, it had the least authority on a commander's desk, but his eyes settled on it alone out of all the rest. He recognized the size of the papyrus and the emblem on the seal. His own.

Hannibal dismissed his secretaries with instructions that he not be disturbed. Alone in the small cottage, he took a seat, plucked up the scroll, and wiped the others to the side with his forearm. He dug under the seal with his fingernail and rolled out the brittle material. It crackled under his fingers, ridged and imperfect, an ancient fabric born of the most aged of lands.

The words had been written upon it by a passionless hand, precise, formal, looking as official as any correspondence from the Council itself. But the words were Imilce's. They drew him with all the force of a witch's incantation. He heard her greeting as if she were whispering in his ear. He mumbled aloud in response to her questions of his safety, reassuring her of his health. Just the mention of his homeland's names brought forth a host of memories, images not dimmed by time. The mention of perfidy in the Council touched him with anger, reminded him that he never had to hide his emotions completely from this woman. Had she been with him he would have cursed the old men, the misers, those jealous of him and thwarting their own success because of it. How he would have liked to speak of these things with her, naked, in bed, sated and moist from being inside her.

The reading was over all too quickly. The space of minutes it took to finish the document was painfully insufficient, and the letter left too much unanswered. There was no mention of Little Hammer, not a word of how he grew, whether he spoke now, whether he remembered his father and still looked so much like him. And who was this Sophonisba? His sister, yes, but a person wholly unknown to him. He could not imagine her at all. He had lived apart from her almost all of her life, a strange thought now that she was nearly an adult. Stranger still that he wished to protect her, to meet this young prince, Masinissa, for himself and judge him as men do each other. And no, he was not sure of the wisdom of his decision to send Imilce to Carthage. Of course he wanted her with him, but how could he be the man he must be with her near at hand, drawing emotions out of him that he would have no other man witness? Surely, separation was the best course.

Not yet ready to roll the papyrus away, he lifted it, absently, to his nose and inhaled. The scents were faint at first, reluctant and shy. The longer he breathed in, the more he found traces of fragrances beyond the papyrus's dry flavor. Something of his mother's fragrant oils came to him. Something of Carthaginian palms. A taste of sea air and of dust blown high and far-traveled on desert winds. And there was Imilce. Her scent was the last to come to him. When it finally revealed itself it was the most potent. It filled him with a longing so painful that he pulled himself forcibly from it. He threw the letter on the table and stared at it as if he expected it to rise and attack him. He had searched for her scent, but having found it he knew that such passions had no place in a commander's chambers. They were more dangerous than Roman steel or cunning.

He called Gemel and ordered the letter rolled and stored away. "Put it somewhere safe," he said. "Safe and distant."

This done, he sorted through the other scrolls with an absent hand. Nowhere among them was the one he wished for, the one from Rome itself. Such obstinate fools they were. Other races would have conceded the war already. They could have come to terms, as strong peoples always had. Though he knew Romans were shaping themselves into a different sort of nation—that was why this war was necessary, after all—it still confounded him that they did not behave in accordance with age-old practice. He tried to imagine the men of Rome, the senators in the chamber, the citizens in their homes throughout the city, the allies in all their various forms. He even spoke inside himself in their language, trying to divine what their hearts told them. Over the years he had done this time and again with different races, sometimes with his focus on individual persons. It was a technique his father had schooled him in. To know the mind of the enemy was to defeat him, Hamilcar had said. Many times this wisdom had proved to be true. With the Romans, however, he was never at ease with what he imagined.

He paced the room absently. He moved to the doorway and looked out over the fields, just beginning to bud in the strengthening sun. Something in the smell of the air reminded him of riding through the Carthaginian spring with his father, surveying the family's lands. He had believed, in his early years, that his father was chief among the men of the world, wiser than any, stronger, braver. Almost as early, he understood that with these traits came responsibilities. That was why his father was called upon to put down the mercenary revolt so harshly. That was why he went to Iberia to carve out an empire. That was why he could never forgive Rome for its crimes against Carthage. This had all been completely right to him, undeniable certainties.

He thought of an incident he had not recalled for some time. It was in his ninth year. He had just learned that his father was to leave Africa for Iberia for a long campaign. Perhaps because Hamilcar had been absent for so much of his childhood, hearing this cut him with new agony. He accosted his father in the public square and begged to be taken with him. He grasped at his legs and swore that he was man enough for it. He was strong and could throw a spear and knew no fear of war.

Hamilcar had at first swatted him away, but the more the boy spoke the bolder his claims became and more the man began to listen. Eventually, he grabbed the boy by the wrist and dragged him to the temple of Baal, shouting as he entered that the priest should prepare a sacrifice. In Carthage the custom of infanticide was an ancient one, rarely practiced at that time but prevalent a little earlier. Hannibal, staring at the altar of the god for a few stunned moments, believed his father had had enough of him and was about to offer him up.

But then he heard the baying of the goat led in by the priests. The animal was solid white, its eyes pinkish in hue and horns so pale they seemed almost translucent. They had brought a fine animal, unblemished and likely to please the god. The priests were like all such that he had seen since, often deformed men, men strange in one way or another from birth and suited to the priesthood because of this.

His father knelt next to him. He felt the gnarled strength of his hand clasped over his, the skin of his palm like rough stone. "Listen to me," Hamilcar said. "I am not a priest, but you are my son. I hold the right to tell you the history of our gods. In a time long ago the father of gods, El, mistakenly decided to place Yam, the Sea-River, above all other gods. Yam reveled in this and became a tyrant and imposed his will upon all others. No other god had the courage to fight him. All thought him too mighty, even El who had blessed him. To appease him, Asherah, the wife of El, offered herself to Yam, so that he might learn joy and treat them all more kindly. When Baal heard this he was furious. He, alone among the gods, knew that Yam was an impostor who would never treat them justly. He made two great weapons—Yagrush, the chaser, and Aymur, the driver. With them, he strode toward Yam. He struck him in the chest with Yagrush, but this did not slay the god. So he smote him on the forehead with Aymur. Yam fell to the earth. So balance was restored to the world, with Baal as the supreme, yet just, deity."

Hamilcar turned his son to face the goat. He knelt close behind him and with one arm pulled the boy against his chest. "Understand me now. Carthage is the servant of Baal; Rome is like those who followed Yam. Rome has been placed above us now by a mistake of Fortune, but it will not remain so. You and I, we can be Yagrush and Aymur, the chaser and the driver. I do not claim that we are divine. This is a human affair, based more on justice than on the gods' favor. I do not ask you to hate without reason. I do not condemn Rome simply because it is full of Romans. It is Rome's actions I hate. It is the way Rome seeks to make slaves of all the world. So, I ask you now, will you swear your life to avenge the wrongs done us by Rome? Will you stand beside me as I take justice to them? Will you devote your life to seeing them brought down, as Baal brought down Yam?"

To all these questions the boy answered, simply, "Yes, I will do that, Father."

The priest handed Hamilcar the sacrificial knife. This the father slipped into the boy's hand. Together they pressed the curved blade against the trembling creature's neck and sank it home, the young hand and the old acting in one motion. So the sacrifice was made; Hannibal consecrated and bound with Baal. Days later, he set out for Iberia, and he had known no life but war ever since.

How far he had come since that day. . . . How much he had seen. . . . The trajectory of his life surprised him sometimes—not often, for usually his mind was actively engaged in shaping the future, and the art of war at which he excelled seemed the natural way of the world. But there were rare, quiet moments when melancholy pulled more heavily on him. He sometimes woke from visions of battle and felt—in the foggy moments of transition to waking—joy at the notion that it was all a dream, that he was not truly in so deeply, that the years might not have passed as he believed they had. This was always a short-lived notion, however. His single eye always opened upon scenes of men in armor, his ears filled with the noises of camp: constant reminders that his dreams were no more than mirrors projecting back the world he had created.

He turned and withdrew to his desk. He did not savor these moments of weakness. This was not the best of him. He would return to himself soon and plan a victory for the coming season like none in history. But he had one more indulgence he wished to allow himself. He thought of calling Mago to write for him, but he decided that the emotions, the truths and deceptions he was to write were too personal, too full of portents, better left unrevealed to others. He prepared a pallet and lifted the stylus himself. He could not help himself, even if the letter was destined to go unread, to end in glowing red embers as his earlier efforts had.

"Dearest Imilce," he wrote, "how I wish you here with me so that you could tell me of yourself and of our son, of my present and our future . . ."

For the soldiers of Hannibal's army, the spring and early summer of their third year at war passed in a haze of almost idyllic tranquillity. Instead of marching into action with the first warm weather, they planted crops under the direction of captured locals. The soldiers tended the herd animals, watched new calves born and nursed, and put themselves to practical trades such as leather working and iron smelting. They sent occasional, almost recreational, foraging parties to secure other goods from neighboring communities, but in general they were well fed on their own provisions. Their bodies returned to states of health they had not known since leaving Iberia. Late in the spring, as they pulled in the early harvest, more than one soldier joked that the commander must have taken a liking to the country and chosen to stay, content with the blooming weather and salt-tinged breeze off the ocean. But just as many voices argued that the commander had lost none of his hunger for war. Each action was calculated—even the duration of inaction. Who really doubted that the great man was concocting yet another unbeatable strategy?

Not Imco Vaca. If this was the best way to win a war, then he was all for it. Actually, though he followed orders that came to him and even on occasion delegated tasks to others, his attentions were more acutely focused on matters of a carnal nature. He had never truly recovered from the previous summer's meeting with the naked, swimming beauty. The Saguntine girl also continued to haunt him. She sat at a distance and watched his actions disapprovingly and sometimes shouted at him so loudly he was sure others would hear her. But she was nothing more than a buzzing fly compared to the torment the woman and her donkey inflicted upon him.

For months he found no trace of her. It seemed she had disappeared from the earth. Knowing this was not possible, he worried even more about what might have befallen her. He roamed the neighboring camp villages, meandered through the Gallic settlement, and even tried to win the trust of the camp followers. But it was difficult to search for someone he had seen for only a few moments, whom he knew nothing about and whom he would not describe in true detail because he did not want anyone else to know she existed. He knew many would call this search a folly unbefitting a veteran soldier, but Imco no longer knew how to separate reasonable behavior from obsession. Perhaps the insanity of war had damaged him. He thought this was likely, but so be it. He just wanted to find that girl again.

But then, as unexpectedly as the first time, she appeared. He had not even begun the day looking for her. He had accompanied a band of Numidian scouts, and as he did not know how to ride he sat behind one of the horsemen. Imco was thoroughly jarred and shaken by the experience. He would never have guessed that a horse's back was so hard, with such an array of knobs to prod at his legs and backside. Partway through the return journey he begged off the horse and set to walking.

Thus he came upon a cluster of dwellings belonging to some camp followers, a community he probably would not have noticed from the back of a galloping horse. Not having known there were camp followers living here, he thought he had come upon locals displaced by the army. But a few moments observing them marked them as foreigners from a variety of nationalities. They seemed to have a life of bare subsistence. The settlement huddled between the saddle of two hills, on a slope dotted with small trees. In this stood a humble conglomeration of tents and skin shelters. On the far hills, a herd of thin goats cropped the grass. In the center, a large cook fire burned in preparation for the evening meal. An old woman sat weaving. Two men debated the best way to erect a sun shelter. A baby cried briefly and then hushed. A young woman bent to fasten a rope around the back legs of a recently slaughtered goat—

Imco's head turned as if to move on to the next object, but his eyes stayed anchored to the woman. For a moment his pupils seemed to stretch and contract: into focus and then out and back in, as if something had gone wrong with his eyes. He felt a part of himself fly out of his sockets and hiss across the distance and touch the girl's backside. He darted behind a tree for fear that she could feel this touch physically. But she just kept at her work.

She ran the rope from the goat's bound legs up over the crook of a branch and back to the ground again. Using her body weight, she tugged until the creature swung, dripping blood. She worked up close to it, slashing at the hide with practiced strokes of what must have been a very sharp tool, spinning the corpse this way and that, each gesture cool and practiced. Next, she slipped her fingers beneath the goat's skin and began to peel it free. She pulled so hard that the creature hung taut for a moment, at an angle to her, before finally relinquishing its hide and dangling, naked now, utterly defeated.

It was brutal work, and there was no mistaking the butcher's identity. Her legs were just as slim and muscular as he remembered. Her calves stood out with an almost masculine definition. The thin summer shift followed the curve of her hips and even revealed the depression that split her backside into two round portions. Her arms were bare to the shoulder and her hair had grown considerably. It flowed down her back in a black tumult of curls.

And if all this was not enough, there was the donkey, standing a few yards from the woman, somewhat dejected, neither watching her nor eating nor doing anything save supporting itself on the four feeble posts of its legs.

The woman spun on her bare heel and moved away from the carcass. He pressed himself against the prickly ground and followed her with his eyes. She first spoke to the old woman, then shouted something to the men, and set off climbing into the hills. Imco was on his feet a moment later. He backed away from the camp and then circled it widely and walked quietly through a stand of pine trees. He lost the woman for a few moments and grew frantic. He tried to divine her destination from the lay of the land so that he could follow her from hiding, but no sooner had he begun this than he lost faith in the strategy. He dashed a short distance and then froze, tilting his head to catch any betraying sound, but he heard nothing except the wind shouldering its way through the trees. He ran on again, along the near side of a long ridge, through a confused jumble of boulders, then over the rise and down the pine-covered slope at a headlong run.

He burst into the open in a panting explosion, realizing too late that he had bounded out onto a path a few strides in front of the woman and the donkey, which trailed behind her. The woman pulled up in mid-step. She froze and stared at him for a shocked few breaths. But her surprise did not last long. With the fingers of one hand she grasped a handful of hair from high on her head and raked it forward, covering her face. She said something to him in a Celtiberian dialect. She parted the screen of black curls wide enough to spit, and then began to scramble up the embankment from which he had descended.

Imco saw the spit fan out on the air and shift away on the breeze. Before his gaze had even shifted to follow her, the donkey was occupying the space she had vacated. How the creature got there so quickly, he could not say, for it now stood completely still. It was a pitiful animal to look upon, ragged of coat, with ears tattered as if shredded by the teeth of some carnivore. Though it was faithful to the woman, she seemed to pay it no heed whatsoever.

"Do not forget your ass!" Imco called.

The woman paused in her tracks. She slowly turned around and took a few tentative steps down toward him. "What?" she asked. Her Carthaginian was heavily accented, but he could not from the single word guess what her first language might be.

"Do not forget your ass," Imco repeated. "Your donkey, I mean."

The woman cocked her head to the side and studied him. He could just barely make out her features through her hair. He thought he saw something written on them that was other than anger. It was a deep bafflement, but this was something he believed he could build upon. When she spoke, however, her voice was venomous and resolute. Unfortunately, she had reverted to the Iberian dialect and Imco could not understand a word of it.

She must have known this, for she concluded by making her point visually concrete. Her hands grasped something like an imaginary twig, snapped it, and tossed the two ends in different directions. Having made herself clear, the woman turned and scrambled up the bank and away. Imco stood for a moment staring at the spot over which she had vanished. Half of him wanted to chase after her, but what would he do upon reaching her again? He did not have the cold heart of a rapist. And anyway, he had accomplished something with the encounter. He knew that she lived safely in the arms of a small community. As he turned back to the camp, he realized that the donkey was no longer in sight. It had not scrambled up the bank, but must have found some other route by which to follow the girl. Would that he were as fortunate.

But he was not. Instead, he marched out with the body of the army a week later. He could find no valid reason to exclude himself and, it seemed, Hannibal wanted each and every able body. They marched at half-speed, angling to the south of the old consuls' forces, crossed the river Aufidus, and—with barely a grumble of protest—seized a Roman grain depot near an old settlement called Cannae.

It did not take long for rumors of the Roman approach to spread. First a few long-riders brought word of a great mass of men on the march, an army innumerable to the human eye, like a horde of Persia spilling across the land. And then spies brought in further details. The two new consuls were marching toward them at full speed. They whipped before them a massive army, thousands upon thousands of well-armed soldiers, both Roman citizens and legions from the allied cities. If the Carthaginians stayed where they were and met this force, they would not just be fighting the arrogant men of Rome; they would be clashing with all Italy.

Imco had many times before questioned Hannibal's wisdom only to see the commander's judgments proven right. But this did not stop him from doubting once more. No one man can harness Fortune indefinitely. So prolonged a war could not have been what he wanted, and now, perhaps, the winds of fate had shifted to blow the Romans forward to victory. Imco, in his foreboding at the coming conflict, could not help but ask for news and opinions from any man near at hand. It was because of this that he first met a young soldier who claimed to have overheard a conversation between the commander and his brother.

The soldier swore his tale was true, and he told it as he shared Imco's supper beside the fire. He had stood within listening distance, he said, assigned as a guard to the storehouse that the commander happened to check on personally. He had stood as unobtrusively as he could, straight-backed and still as a pillar. The two paid him no mind whatsoever. When Mago voiced anxiety about the Roman contingent's size, Hannibal said it was as it should be. He said he had recently heard voices inside his head. No, not as a madman does, for he understood that the voices came not from without but were born inside him. Sometimes the voice was recognizable as his own; at other times it was his father's, or the low grumble he believed to be the language of the gods. But they all told him the same thing. They all came to him with a single message. . . .

The young soldier paused here and contemplated the fire, seeming for all the world to have nothing more to say. Imco nudged him on.

"It is coming."

"What?" Imco asked. "What is coming? It is no secret they are coming. Is this—"

The soldier, forgetting the silent drama of a moment before, raised his voice. "That is what he said. 'It is coming.' He said, 'The coming battle determines everything. We look upon a space of hours that lead up to the moment I was born for.' That is what the voices tell the commander is coming: the moment he was born for. And you and I will witness it."

The soldier resumed his portentous air, but Imco clicked his tongue on the roof of his mouth and turned away. What sort of tale was this? One of the teller's own invention, probably. He would not flatter the fellow with questions. So he thought, but instead he found within himself a chorus of questions and answers. What *is* the moment he was born for? So vague a statement, like something an oracle would say. Did it indicate a day of glory? But was not the most obvious sense always the wrong sense when interpreting oracles? Perhaps the day he was born for meant the day of his death. Was that not the only certainty in all beings' lives? Had the commander seen his own demise? If so, why did he not flee it? For a moment this thought gave Imco comfort, but then he recalled how stubborn a character Hannibal was. Perhaps he planned to defy death, to spit in its eye and push it out of the way.

When Imco lay down that evening, sleep eluded him completely, like a creature that knows it is being tracked. He tried to think only of his beautiful camp follower, but when she looked at him he heard her voice repeating the message he wished to avoid.

"It is coming. It is coming. . . ."

During the first two weeks of the march from Rome, the consuls shared a single intention. They had to cover the distance quickly, make contact with Hannibal, and find the right occasion on which to bring him to battle. There was no debate on this much, at least. But as they came nearer, the strains of their dueling commands began to show. Varro believed that they should pour forth over the Carthaginians in one great wave, unstoppable. He argued that the location and terrain had no strategic importance, considering the overwhelming shock the enemy would feel on the first sight of them. He imagined their wide-eyed horror, the slack mouths, and the thumping in their chests as they beheld their doom striding toward them in a cloud of dust. That was the true strength of the army they commanded. They should use it to best effect, wherever they found the invader hiding.

Paullus held a different view. If they were to learn but one thing from the lessons of the Ticinus, of Trebia, of Trasimene, it must be caution. They were marching toward Hannibal; and he appeared to be simply waiting for them. Paullus found something disquieting in this. They should approach slowly. They should carefully assess just what the enemy might have planned for them. They should learn beforehand everything they could as to the lay of the land and Hannibal's current numbers and the morale of his troops and their state of health and supply. All of these things should weigh in their decisions. War was not as straightforward as Varro seemed to think it was.

In keeping with this, on Paullus' days in command he slowed the pace of the march and sent out scouts and surveyors to detail the features of the land around Cannae. What he learned troubled him. He was sure Hannibal's chosen spot was not a favorable place for battle. The land was too open. Apart from the rise atop which Cannae sat, the land stretched for flat miles in all directions, dotted sparsely with brush and stunted trees and cut by shallow, easily fordable rivers. It favored the African cavalry in every way. He spoke cautiously of this with his fellow consul, for it was hard for a Roman horseman to acknowledge the supremacy of any other. But Paullus believed they had to do just that. The last few years had proven that the Africans, especially the Numidians, were superior to them when astride a horse. He proposed that they move elsewhere.

"Listen to me," he said. He sat facing Varro in the war tent, between them the tribunes and officers of the horse and various others. Paullus had called the meeting toward the end of one of his days in command. He had opened it with his now familiar arguments and listened to the equally well-known rebuttals. But as he was giving up power on the morn he wished to do all he could to sway his fellow consul's opinion. They were so close to the Carthaginians now that any mistake could doom them.

He said, "Let us turn the column and march for more broken ground to the west, with hills enough to hamper the enemy's horsemen. We need someplace not of Hannibal's choosing but of our own instead."

Varro could barely contain his loathing of this line of thinking. "If Hannibal is so brilliant," he said, "how do we know that he is not hoping for just such a move? Perhaps he anticipates such cow-ardice. If we do as you say, we might simply be turning into another of his traps."

"I do not think so," Paullus said. He spoke gravely, with the fin-gers of both hands massaging his temples. "Varro, I beg you to temper your vigor with wisdom. Fabius fought hard to avoid situa-tions that—"

"Fabius fought?" Varro asked, cutting in with a raised voice. He cocked his head at an angle, as if his hearing troubled him. *"Fought?* Never has that word been so misused. I was there beside Fabius and I can tell you that he never raised a hand against the enemy. Fight-ing is not in that man's nature. And now you, Paullus, would do the same as he. You're nothing more than the old man's puppet. You think not for yourself but do his bidding—just as he does Hannibal's. Do you really believe Rome could survive another year like the one Fabius inflicted upon us? He made us out to be fools, cowards, sheep trembling at the sight of an approaching wolf. Perhaps you are those things, but I am none of them. We have let half the summer pass already. Believe me, if we do not strike now we will start losing allies. It will take just one defector for them all to crumble. But why am I telling you these things? You know them already. You only lack the heart or courage to grasp them and act!"

Paullus had gone red under this barrage of insults. He glanced at the officers around the chamber, all of whom shifted uncomfortably, eyes lowered to suggest no particular allegiance, faces as expres-sionless as possible. "We should speak privately," Paullus said. "It is not seemly for—"

"I don't care what is seemly!" Varro shouted.

"And I will not commit our troops to disaster!" Paullus roared back at him, his anger bursting out so suddenly that several of the officers started. "Truly, Terentius Varro, you're worthy of the butch-ers from whom you're descended. Would that your people had kept to their labors and left important matters to those suited to them!"

Varro shot to his feet; Paullus mirrored the motion. They stepped toward each other, first tentatively, and then, as if at some choreo-graphed signal, they fell toward each other like two rams in the sea-son of rut. The room was a flurry of motion. Some jumped back against the tent walls. A few sat frozen. More than one cowered as if the consuls' anger was meant for them. Only one person wedged himself between the two.

Publius Scipio was faster on his feet than either consul. He stepped forward and took the full brunt of the impact, Varro at his back, Paullus against his chest. He shouted to them to find reason. He batted their arms down and twirled to separate them with his shoulders. Heartened, others grappled the men and tried to calm them. Publius managed to get a hand to either consul's chest and push them to the full length of his outstretched arms.

"If you two were not the most important Romans in all of Italy right now I would sit and watch one of you overman the other," he said. "But there is no place for dueling now. Rome depends on you; be worthy of her. By the gods, find your senses! Our enemy lies outside this tent, not within."

Publius' fellow tribunes looked between him and the two senior officers, unsure just how his outburst would be received and therefore unsure how they would comment on it. He was the youngest among them and had up until that moment been the quietest. Varro seemed to be deciding just how best to take off Publius' head, but when Paullus withdrew a half-step he did likewise.

"The young tribune is imprudent, but he speaks some truth," Varro said. "You call me rash, but will you hear my plan?"

"You have a plan?"

"I am not a fool, Paullus."

"Tell me, then. I'd love to hear sensible words from your mouth."

Varro glared at him a moment, then motioned that they should all sit again. "We command the largest army Rome has ever fielded," he said, "perhaps the largest ever mustered by any civilized nation. This is our strength, and Hannibal will know it. We should show him from his first sighting of us that we are a hammer, and he the nail that we will drive into the soil of Cannae. We must use the full overwhelming grandeur of our numbers to best effect. To do this, we reduce the frontage of each maniple by a third and shrink the intervals between them. This will stretch the line so that the enemy will look out at an unending river heading toward him. Hannibal's men will shake at the sight of us, and some will run. Imagine it, Paullus. Remember that this is the first time we will meet them face-to-face and in the full light of day. You and I will command the cavalry on either wing. This is the weak point, but we need not defeat our counterparts. All we have to do is hold them for a time, keep them from flanking long enough to let the body of our infantry drive through. By then it will be too late for their horse to matter. We'll punch right through their center, divide them into two smaller forces, and attack each at will."

Paullus stared at his fellow consul with an intensity that made the edges of his eyes quiver. "You may be right," he said, "but I do not know that it is wise to modify our formations like this without first practicing it."

"Impossible," Varro said. "We are engaged already. And this plan works precisely because the troops are raw. Just as the enemy will see their uncountable numbers, so the troops in the front will take heart from the lines of men behind them. They will see that they are undefeatable. As a whole, they will become braver than they could be in thin ranks. This formation makes it impossible for cowardice to sway the battle. A man in the middle of this river will have nowhere to flee but forward, over the bodies of the enemy. Paullus, refrain from finding fault and be one with me."

"I am unsure," Paullus said, sincerely and without a trace of malice. Though they talked late into the night, he could offer no more than that.

As the day dawned the consuls were not exactly at odds, but neither were they of a single mind. Varro—in control—broke camp and moved even closer to Hannibal, so close, in fact, that it would be impossible for Paullus to retreat even if he wished to. He set up camp on the near side of the river Aufidus and ordered a small deployment to claim a spot on the far bank. He sent out units to harass the Carthaginian foragers, but ended the day more exasperated than vindicated. Numidian raiders ambushed the Roman water carriers instead, launching their spears at them so that the workers had to drop their jugs and run. And yet Varro had accomplished his main objective. He was locked in the preliminary stages of the struggle. The following day Paullus received word that the enemy was moving as if to offer battle, but he did not answer them. He shifted troops from one place to another, hesitating, trying to think of a way to better their position, knowing that on the morrow control went back to Varro. Wriggle as he might, he was pinned to the spot as surely as if his fellow consul had speared him through the foot. There was nothing to be done. The clash would come with the rising sun. Their fate was in Varro's hands.

Mago had already been up for hours by the time he met with Hannibal and a mounted contingent of his generals atop the rise of Cannae. Together they watched the armies assemble upon the wide plain. The sight approaching them was like nothing any of them had ever imagined. Mago had learned from his brother to approximate numbers of men by visual clues, to weigh on internal scales the density of troops and the area of land they covered, and to account for the receding scale of distance. But the number of Romans now before him was beyond his reckoning. Eighty thousand? Ninety? One hundred thousand? He could not possibly count them, and the exact number would have seemed arbitrary. What mattered was that the Romans' front line stretched to fill the entire field, so wide it would have daunted even the best of runners to sprint from one edge to the other. It was completely uniform, no portion lagging behind or preceding the others. This was all formidable enough, but it was the depth of the ranks that truly stunned him: they came row upon row with no end in sight, fading into the dust and distance so that it seemed they were marching out of the haze, an army born of the landscape itself.

"They have the wind in their eyes," Hannibal said. A simple statement, acknowledged with nods and a few grunts. "And more of the sun's glare than we do. I like this advantage."

Mago never ceased to be amazed by his brother's calm. Looking at him, he felt buoyed by his confidence. If Hannibal believed they would win this conflict, then who was he to doubt it? The day previous, the commander had presented his multiple strategies with calm, reasoned assurance. Even when he proposed the most improbable of maneuvers they sounded like testimony given after the events and not a plan suggested before. He had traced the bowed line the first ranks were meant to form, a convex front made up entirely of Gauls, headed by Mago and Hannibal himself. With this he intended to meet the first lines of the enemy. "We must keep this crescent from breaking," he had said. "Let it not snap but instead slowly manage a retreat. So carefully that the Romans are fooled into feeling themselves winning. So gradually that the Gauls are not frightened into fleeing."

When Mago questioned whether the Gauls would rebel against setting themselves up for slaughter, Hannibal answered, "You do not understand the Celtic mind, brother. These people do not conceive of the world as you and I do. Consider that they believe creation to be a balance between two worlds. Death in this one means rebirth in the other. Thus they mourn at a newborn's birth and celebrate upon that man's eventual demise. They have no fear of dying tomorrow; they run to death, headlong."

Mago had sworn that he would do everything Hannibal instructed, but after a sleepless night the immensity of the day's challenges left him staring in awe. Even the cloud of dust stirred by the Romans' feet filled him with dread. It was a great brown shadow that rose up into the heavens and stretched so far as to all but obscure the horizon.

"Look at them," he said. There was a tight quaver in his voice, as that of a man who has been punched in the abdomen but is trying to speak through the pain of the blow. "I never imagined there were so many of them."

Hannibal straightened in his saddle. He spoke without a hint of irony. "Yes, they are many, but not one among them is my brother. Not one is named Mago."

The others laughed, but it took a moment for this cool statement to roll over in Mago's mind, revealing its humor.

Monomachus was the first to respond, dry of voice, giving no indication that he spoke in jest. "They have among them few who would eat human flesh."

"What is more," Maharbal added, "they are not commanded by a man named Hannibal. I am sure this fact troubles them."

"And, unless I am mistaken," Bostar said, "nowhere among them is there a Bomilcar or a Himilco or even a Gisgo, not a single Barca, not one of them who prays to Baal or Melkart, none who were pushed through the thighs of an African mother. Truly, never have I seen so many unfortunate men gathered in a single place."

Hannibal's stern expression gave way to a grin. "I see your amazement, Mago, and I understand your point: we should have issued the men with two swords each, one for either hand to make the killing faster."

Mago ducked his head and ran the palm of his hand over his horse's neck and then looked up again. Just listening to them humbled him. Who had ever been as fortunate as he, to learn warfare from men such as these? He searched for a jest of his own to add to theirs, but jesting before battle was not a skill he had learned yet.

Soon the generals parted company, each riding off to lead different contingents of the troops, each with a different purpose in the coming battle. Mago stayed a little longer with Hannibal. They were to command quite near each other and did not need to separate until the battle was well begun. Even with the armies facing each other—paused with a wide gap between them—there were maneuvers to go through before the bulk of them met in earnest. The enemy's forward line glistened in the glare of the sun, armor reflecting the light in thousands of tiny bursts. At first their shields seemed as tightly wedged together as the scales on a snake's belly, but there were gaps enough between them to allow their skirmishers forward. These poured through onto the field. This battle would open in the manner that suited the Roman style, just as Hannibal had predicted.

"Velites," Hannibal said. "Let us see whether these pups have teeth."

The young soldiers moved not like men but like half-beasts, agile. They wove through each other, barking courage and yelling curses at the Carthaginians. They wore helmets draped in animal skins: the heads of wolves mostly, some bears, and a few mountain cats. At first, they were frightening to look upon, as if the animal world had united with humans and fought on the Romans' side. They came armed with several javelins each, which they hurled with all the strength their bodies could muster, sending them high into the air in deadly arcs. So it seemed to Mago, but Hannibal saw them differently.

"They are tentative," he said. "Afraid. Look, Mago, they seem to step forward boldly, but they come only near enough to loose their weapons. Then they retreat to gather up courage to repeat the maneuver. They have taken on the skins of warriors but not the hearts."

Mago had not realized this at first, but soon he saw that Hannibal was right. The velites were not so impressive after all. Their inexperience left them no match for veteran skirmishers. Balearic slingers swirled their tiny missiles into the air almost casually, picking out velites at will, breaking arms and ribs and occasionally dropping one when a stone broke a velite's head.

This went on for an hour or so, until Hannibal signaled that the slingers should be called back. They pulled up, shouted last taunts at the Romans, and withdrew into the body of the infantry. The Romans did the same. The velites vanished through the snake scales so that within a few minutes all motion stopped, save for the struggles of the wounded left on the field.

At about the same time, both sides began to move forward toward each other. The Romans accelerated to a trot and held it. Watching them, Mago found his insides knotted so intensely that he almost pitched forward in the saddle. He knew to look past the tricks of visual intimidation: the swirls and patterns and animal features painted on their shields, the high feathered plumes that rose up from their helmets to make them seem taller, the layered wall of shields and upright pila and glinting metal and legs beneath, shifting steadily forward so that from a distance they seemed not individuals at all but rather a single force eating up the land. Knowing these tricks did not make it any easier to watch the advance. The Romans moved in more skillful unison than even the Libyans, and there was no trickery in the amazing mass of them.

More than any of the visual drama, what struck the young Barca was the silence, the awful, unearthly hush of the oncoming enemy. They spoke not a word, no chant or instructions or shouts of rage. No sound came from them at all but the rhythmic pounding of their feet and the thrum of their swords upon their shields. This was noise, yes, but devoid of emotion. Mechanical. Frightening, for it seemed to be the beat of death. The various contingents within the Carthaginian army yelled and chanted and spurred themselves to fury by releasing deep-bellied roars. The Gauls sent forth a tremendous racket through their horns, the tall, animal-shaped heads of these stretching high into the air above them. It should have been ferocious cacophony, but the answering silence proved even more unnerving. It was as if Carthage had thrown a punch at a visible target but missed it and cleaved only the air. If the Romans felt any fear they did not show it, and the best the Carthaginian troops could do was to scream louder.

Mago knew what came next, but still it was a shock when it happened. The Roman vanguard—at some signal or position known only to them—all hefted their pila up and hurled them in the same instant. Two, three thousand missiles suddenly flew through the air. Several hundred soldiers went down, twisting, shouting in pain or silenced. From where Mago sat beside his brother, he saw whole portions of the front ranks buckle forward and disappear.

"As it should be," Hannibal said. "There will be a second wave. And then a third, remember that. This is what we've come for. We've prevailed previously through good fortune and Roman foolishness. Today we face them on their own terms. This is all as I would have it be. Take your position and remember everything I've taught you. Go now. And do not forget your name!"

With that, Hannibal slipped from his horse and joined the lieutenants and messengers and guards who would be around him throughout the battle. They headed off through the ranks down corridors left clear for them. Mago heard a soldier call to him, telling him they were awaiting him. He dismounted and handed his horse to a keeper and joined with the contingent of men sworn to protect his life. Something happened in him as he felt the earth beneath him and his feet moving him across it. He stopped trying to fight the passing of time, stopped wishing for more moments to process and think through the things he faced. He stepped into the present and felt an enormous rush of energy push him forward. He was about to fight as he never had before. The forces at play in the world had finally converged. He strode forward behind his lieutenants, growing more into his skin at every step. He was a Barca, after all.

————

The two cavalry units—one composed of Numidians, the other a mixed company of Carthaginians, Iberians, and Gauls—took up positions on either wing of the infantry. Their general orders were clear: Attack the opposing Roman horse. Hit them, hard and fast. Break them in the first moments of the struggle, wipe them from the field, and strip the main body of the Roman infantry naked on either flank. A good part of Hannibal's strategy depended on this. But not only on this. He also chose to fracture and confuse the enemy in smaller ways. That is why Tusselo and four hundred other Numidians went out on a specific mission. They understood that there was a danger in it greater than that of straightforward combat. It required both military prowess and cunning. They took up the arms customary to them, but each also carried an extra sword hidden beneath his tunic, wrapped in oddments of cloth to protect its wielder from the honed blades.

They rode in the wake created by Maharbal's cavalry, which was quite a trail to follow. They moved in a great, trilling herd at full gallop, launching their spears once, twice, and yet again before they even reached the enemy. By the time they collided with them, many of the Romans had already dropped, impaled by cool iron, and then pummeled beneath a barrage of hooves. Other horses wheeled and darted in confusion, their riders suddenly gone limp. Tusselo watched Maharbal sword-stab a wounded Roman under the arm and pull a spear from the man's thigh in something like a single motion. He planted this new spear in another's throat. He stabbed the weapon forward and back. The pierced Roman grabbed it desperately, jerked this way and that by a playful hand, recognition of his coming death splattered across his face with the stain of his own blood. Maharbal finally yanked the spear free and left the man slumped over his horse's neck. Without another thought, he surged toward a new target.

Tusselo lost sight of their captain, but he was only one among many. All the others were similarly engaged. That was the way it was with Numidians. They should have made easy targets, unarmored as they were, with only hide shields and no saddles to secure them to their mounts. Instead they moved without fear, so swiftly that it seemed there was no interval between their thoughts and the movements of their horse. The Romans had to yank on reins and fight with their mounts to control them before they could attempt a strike. They might have been skilled by their own standards, but that was not enough to help them here. The Numidians anticipated the spears to be thrown at them before they were even launched. They batted away the sword points aimed at close quarters, because they saw the preparations a Roman had to go through to ready himself for the thrust, and they always managed to be exactly where the Romans wished they were not because they recognized the flow of this mounted dance before the Italians ever could. They functioned on an entirely different scale of speed and dexterity.

The Romans pulled back, re-formed, and charged again. A repeat of the initial slaughter met them. They dismounted in an attempt to make the battle into an infantry contest. To their surprise, the Africans did not join them on the dirt but rode among them, darting them with even greater ease. Moments later all the Romans who could scrambled up into their saddles again, before any order to do this had been issued. And in this remounting was the first seed of panic. Such a seed germinates in an instant, grows, and flowers. The Romans turned and fled. The Numidians paused long enough to retrieve spears and to wipe their bloodstained palms. A few grabbed up pieces of treasure too appealing to leave behind. Then they set out after their quarry, smiling and joking with each other, like huntsmen on the trail of their favorite prey.

The time had come to make real the plan Tusselo had set forth to Hannibal several days earlier. Hannibal had initially found it improbable that the Romans would believe the deception it depended on, but Tusselo knew them better. He pointed out that the Romans far back in the army's rear would know little of how their cavalry fared against the Africans. They would have no true picture of the whole of the battle and would—in their arrogance—find it easy to accept what he proposed. And it would work because no Roman could conceive of such a deception; therefore neither would they recognize it in the actions of others. Having won the commander's trust, Tusselo set out to deserve it. He reminded the others to follow his lead and have faith.

With that, he and the four hundred pressed north. They rode

parallel to the rows and rows of Roman legions, out at a distance beyond missile range. They progressed largely unhindered. There were few horsemen left to confront them, and the legions ignored them, so focused were they on their advance. When he saw open space behind the army, Tusselo turned toward the Romans. Once he was sure the Numidians had been sighted, he spoke the first order loudly. His comrades obeyed. They slung their shields behind their backs. A little farther on he shouted again. They each tossed their spears out upon the ground, swords and daggers also, small darts. They advanced as unarmed men, with arms held out to either side, professing harmlessness.

Alarmed by their approach, a company of soldiers held in reserve fanned out to meet them. Tusselo took his position and ran over the words he would soon utter in the language he had not used in years now. He rode at the vanguard of the group and was therefore the first to be unhorsed. A legionary reached up for his outstretched hand, grabbed it, and nearly yanked his shoulder from its socket. He hit the ground on his back, hard enough to knock the air out of him. The soldier stood him up and punched him square in the mouth. He unsheathed his sword and made as if to run him through, but a nearby officer strode in, took the weapon from him, and pressed the point up under Tusselo's chin with enough pressure that the iron pierced his flesh and released a thin stream of blood that ran down the blade.

"Why do you come to us?" he demanded. "Give me reason not to kill you all right now!"

Poised atop the sword, Tusselo did not know if he could speak. He bit back the pain of the iron point grinding into his jawbone and managed to say, "You will win this day. Our gods . . . gave us signs of this. Hannibal ignored them. He walks toward death. We want no part of it anymore. You are the greater power."

The officer stared at him a moment in surprise. He had not expected an African to speak perfect Latin. Judging by his face this seemed to unnerve him. "How do you come to speak Latin?"

"I am an educated man," Tusselo said.

The Roman seemed unsure what to make of this. His face held

firm, but the point of the sword drooped. Tusselo, feeling an opening, carried on. "Spare us," he said. "We are not cowards. I am a prince among our people. By my word, the Massylii will desert Carthage in your favor. You, master, can bring Rome the Numidian people. And we can bring all of Africa."

"You do not look royal to me," the Roman said, his eyes on Tusselo's knotted mass of hair.

"Our people are different from yours, but I am as I've said. Ask any of the men who follow me."

For the first time the Roman wavered visibly. He looked up and found in the solemn faces of the mounted warriors enough to stay his death threat. He released Tusselo and stepped back. "You are wise to realize our superiority," he said. "Perhaps cowardly as well, but you will live at least a little longer for it." The legionary who had hit Tusselo began to object, but the officer spoke over him. "The Roman army still takes prisoners! We are not barbarians who kill men who come to us in defeat. Captured is just as good as dead, in some ways even better. Think what good slaves these will make."

Though he spoke this forcefully he seemed to doubt it a moment later. He muttered, "I would not want to act mistakenly here, would you? Find a tribune, at least. But in the meantime get them off their horses and keep them under guard."

They forced the Numidians to dismount and march between a company of armored guards who smacked them with the flats of swords, poked them with the butts of spears, taunted and threatened them, insulted the bitch creatures that had birthed them, and ridiculed the commander who had led them to their enslavement. Finally—collected in a tight group on a flat stretch of barren, sun-baked ground—they were told to sit on their black asses and not to move.

Few of them spoke. They looked at each other with their somber eyes, and this sufficed as communication. The man in front of Tusselo looked over his shoulder and offered him a strip of dried meat. Tusselo nodded in affirmation of the man's calm, but refused the food. He still tasted the Roman legionary's sweat on his sore lips. This reminded him of things he wished to forget, and yet something in him wanted to *remember* what he wished to forget. He thought that if ever a race of people shared an identity it was the Romans, even down to the consistency and taste of their sweat.

Tusselo alone among his countrymen spoke the enemy's language. He listened as reports came in, each more optimistic than the last. Word passed from man to man that Varro believed victory was theirs. Apparently, they were punching right through the Gallic center. They were a moving point of iron that Hannibal was powerless to stop. The plan was progressing so perfectly that Varro ordered men pulled from the wings to the center, to make them narrower yet and to drive the wedge further into the Carthaginians.

The man beside Tusselo nudged him, ribbed him, and then hissed in his ear, asking what the Romans were saying. Tusselo slammed him with his elbow and spoke from the side of his mouth. "They say the hour of their death approaches," he said.

This was spoken with cold force and fully convincing, but in truth the Roman news filled him with dread. Yes, he knew Hannibal had said as much would happen, but what if he was wrong? Despite all his faith in the commander, it did seem impossible that they could combat the Roman numbers. If only a quarter of the enemy managed to kill or wound an opponent, Hannibal's cause was lost. He realized that—strange as it seemed—he alone among the army at that moment was balanced between allegiances. To betray Hannibal, he need do nothing but sit where he was. He gazed out at the distant rear of the Roman army, all those many backs turned toward him. Nearer, before and behind them, swarmed the noncombatants, camp followers, horse boys, and slaves, all engaged in various tasks in support of the army. So many slaves. What people on the earth had ever so thrived, or ever would, on the suffering of others?

Tusselo chose his moment at random. Deserting was no real possibility. His loyalty was not simply to Hannibal, not even simply to his people. His loyalty was first to himself, and he knew his enemy better than anyone. He rose to his feet. He dusted himself off and stretched his neck from side to side. One of the guards shouted something at him and walked toward him, hand on the hilt of his gladius in threat. Tusselo uttered a single word, a clipped syllable that let loose a flurry of motion.

An African seated near the passing Roman pulled a sword from beneath his tunic. He struck the man with a swinging blow to the back of his knees. By the time the Roman fell to the dust the whole four hundred were on their feet: first a commotion of brown skin and tribal garments; then a bristling flurry of cloth-covered blades. They cut down all the guards, hacking them to death with the advantage of surprise and pure numbers. They then stood staring at the various noncombatants, some of whom just gawked, most of whom turned and fled in all directions.

Tusselo, knowing he needed to keep the men focused on combat instead of plunder, clucked his tongue and began walking. The others followed him. As they walked they stripped the remaining stray bits of material from their weapons and dropped them to flap and skitter across the ground, propelled by a dry wind. A little ways on they came to their shields and picked them up, and most of them managed to regain their horses, which had been hastily abandoned by the boys handling them.

So it was that, four hundred strong, they fell upon the Romans' rear. Not one of the Romans turned to look at them. Not one expected the attack about to come. Tusselo was only a few feet away from his target when that Roman soldier turned his young face around in sudden, short-lived terror.

Before the battle commenced, the commander had sent out a message, in every possible language and to each quadrant of his army, to all the men of his army's many nations. He said, "We are the enemies of Rome, all of us from races beleaguered by the men of the Tiber. Today Hannibal asks you to honor your ancestors with offerings of Roman blood. Follow his call and you cannot help but prevail. When the Gallic horns blast, know that in them is the voice of your commander shouting to you. When you hear cries of anger from any tongue, recognize Hannibal's roar within them. Know that the clamor of arms clashing is Hannibal's will transmitted through iron. Even when an enemy opens his mouth, it is our commander who you will hear. If he yells at you in threat, he is reminding you of your duty. If you twist an enemy on the point of your sword, it is

Hannibal's praise that spurts from his mouth. It is his joy at your deed and his order that you step over the corpse and carry on. Hear the Lion of Carthage in everything, and this day will be ours. Whenever men speak of war in the future, they will speak of today. Let it be your names they utter in awe."

Fine words, Imco thought, but bravery is more easily spoken of than demonstrated. Perhaps Hannibal contained within himself such brutal confidence, but Imco cared more that morning about saving a life—his own, that is. The years in the army had shaped him into a skilled warrior, often against his will and without his consent. His hands and body and mind moved nimbly during combat, faster than his thinking mind, with instincts of their own. His eyes found weaknesses to press home attacks. Only he knew that he fought simply for self-preservation, so that he might live while some other died in his place. He knew this was not entirely noble. Was it not better to kill for the pure joy of it, fearlessly? That was the type of man the gods rewarded and bred in abundance.

Imco gazed at the veteran killers milling around him. Already the bowed front ranks of the center of the army were engaged with the enemy, but these soldiers stood about cool and seemingly unconcerned with the chaos soon to descend upon them. They chatted among themselves and calmly stretched. They tested the fit of their armor, scratched absently at their scruffy beards. One man urinated where he stood; another pulled up his garments and squatted to defecate. A few kicks and jibes discouraged him from this. He stood and cursed them, but then agreed to wait and crap on a Latin corpse instead. Many of them were outfitted as Roman legionaries, from captured gear that made them a grotesque parody of their enemies. Some ran their hands up and down their tall spears; a few hefted these and practiced the overhand thrust with which they struck; still others tested the feel of the Roman swords in their hands. Imco felt as he had high up in the Alps: as if some mistake had been made a long time back and never corrected. He did not belong in this company. He was sure that the world never had created a more reluctant soldier than he. Never had Fortune played so mischievously with an individual, time and time again placing him in the maw of human folly.

The din grew as the minutes passed. Carthalo's horsemen galloped past on their way to meet the eastern wing of the Roman horse, a confusion of hooves and battle cries that soon faded into the haze. Still Imco's company waited. It was nearing the noon hour and the heat of the late-summer sun pressed down upon the heavy air. Clouds of dust blew over them, propelled by blistering gusts, foul-scented like breaths from some giant, tooth-rotted mouth. Sweat poured first from Imco's armpits, soon after from his forehead, his groin, his feet and hands. The moisture found its way into his eyes and they, in turn, dripped salty tears. From somewhere behind, a shout came for them to tighten up. They did so, each man measuring the small space around him, fitting himself in close to the man beside him, testing the position of their shields. Few spoke now; none stretched or joked; but still they waited.

When the shout came, Imco could not quite make out the order. He felt a press at his back and saw the man before him shift forward. He stepped into the space thus vacated. For a moment, that was all there was to it. He stared at the dented iron of the man's helmet and saw in it his own reflection. It was too dim to provide details, just a shadow in human form. Then a series of horn blasts finished their orders, driving them into a forward march. Still he did not fully understand. There was nothing in front of them, just a flat stretch off to the side of the main battle, but the horns were insistent. Like the others, he took short, shuffling steps, barely lifting his feet. Forward into nothing. For five minutes and then nearing ten. Forward farther.

Then the horns spoke once more, some turning maneuver. Again, Imco did not know how to interpret it. Fortunately, others did. The whole block of men, thousands strong, careened around a slow pivot, one side stationary, the other in full motion, as if swinging on the hinges of a great door. The man behind Imco savaged his heels, stepping on them every few moments. Imco was about to turn and curse him when a horn blasted a halt.

They all stopped in a single breath. Armor clattered to silence. Only then, peering around the man in front of him, did Imco see their goal. They had completed the turn. Before them, less than a hundred strides away, ran the long, exposed flank of the enemy army. By their dress it appeared they were not actually Roman's but an allied legion. They were tightly packed, part of one tremendous body. Not one of them was turned outward. All had eyes forward. They had no idea they had suddenly become targets of Hannibal's finest infantrymen. The next order was easy enough to understand. They charged.

Few of the Roman allies seemed to notice the approaching Africans until the last moments. The ones most exposed tried to re-form, but the soldiers next to them were pieces of a much larger formation and they held to their positions. Imco did not know what people these were but he would always remember the sunlike emblem embossed in red upon their white shields. The Carthaginians hit them not at a dead run, but at a slow jog, with a weight of impact that sent shock waves echoing through the close-packed men.

With the moment of first contact all ordered movements ceased. From then on it was pure blood work, different even from what they had trained for. Instead of the phalanx formation—shields locked, thrusting overhand in a deadly bristle of spears—they instantly spread out. Everyone already seemed to understand that this was no ordinary battle. The Latins almost refused to turn and face them, leaving open vulnerable spots at the side of the neck, down the arm, on the outer thigh, portions of the face. There were so many spots to strike and so many targets to choose from that the attackers fanned out in ravenous chaos, each man searching for the best place to enter the fray. Thus Imco was presented with his first enemy more quickly than he might have been otherwise.

There were men all around him, but he and a Latin spotted each other and both knew destiny asked them to contest their lives. Imco—not yet in full possession of his courage—let his spear fly. The man batted it down with his shield and stepped over it. It would not be that easy. Imco's early swordplay was tentative. He found it hard to find a place to strike. The Latin's shield was heavy and tall, the sunburst on it most distracting. It covered almost all his body. The high crown of his helmet looked impenetrable. Imco struck small blows, aiming at the face, at the man's sword arm, at the sword itself, trying to knock it free of his hand. For each attack he made he had to parry one in return, staying close behind his shield, taking a blow that nearly knocked his helmet off, receiving a thrust that just nicked his shoulder blade. He could not help but notice that the man's cheeks trembled spasmodically and that he closed his eyes each time he struck and that he seemed to suck in more air than he ever expelled. He realized that he might well be dueling with the single soldier more frightened by all of this than he.

At that moment something so strange and questionable happened that Imco would never afterward tell it to anyone, not even when they praised his murderous prowess. Hot air seemed to gather in a swirl beneath his legs, sweep up under his tunic, and enter him through his ass. His chest billowed, his head hummed, his arms and legs trembled with the power of it. He would later believe that it was a breath of fury sent to him by the beautiful woman, a blessing for poor Imco, a command to prove himself worthy and to live, to live.

Almost by accident—as his own body convulsed away from a thrust—the point of his sword sliced up from the tip of the man's chin, through both his lips, and on to split his nose into two equal portions. The man howled in anguish, spraying blood over Imco's head. He ducked beneath it and drove his sword up under the Roman soldier's chin. He felt it catch in the vertebra at the base of the head and he felt the snap as this gave way and let the blade drive up into the lower portion of the man's brain. Imco yanked the sword free and watched the man collapse, stunned that he had prevailed, amazed at the way a body lost all dignity in a single instant. The man hit the dirt, eyes opened but staring at the worst of possible views. But Imco was not to contemplate him for long.

Another Latin came at him, shield-smacked him, and sliced at his head. Imco punched him with his own shield, slammed a heel down on his foot, and struck until his blade bit the man at the neck. He then struck several more times just out of rage, until the soldier's helmet slipped up over his head and Imco's blade split the man's skull. Two deaths down and he had warmed to the work. The next one died even faster.

An hour later his arms felt like ropes of molten lead and his legs only supported him by finding footing among the dead below, wedged into the crook of an arm or jammed under someone's crotch. He had no idea how many he had killed. Nor could he gauge which side was winning the battle. For him the contest was smaller than that, decided moment by moment between him and one other. He kept reminding himself that he was still alive. He knew he could respectably retreat. Part of him almost wished to go on, but he could barely lift his sword. He stepped backward and shouted over his shoulder and another man stepped into his place. A few moments later he knelt in the filth with others from the front, panting, gasping for breath, spitting blood, calling for water. In this way, he found a few moments of rest, although no water appeared.

Imco might have stayed there indefinitely except that the giant named Bomilcar fell upon the resting men with orders that they rejoin the mêlée. "Rome dies this day!" he yelled. "Right now, this moment! This moment!" He roared through them, kicking men to their feet and slamming others with the flat of his hand and even knocking a few across the helmet with his sword. He was a strange sight, simultaneously furious and joyful. "Keep your blades wet! Let none of your weapons go thirsty!"

He picked Imco out from the group at random. He clapped his hands down on his shoulders and lifted him to his feet in one heave. He demanded to know Imco's name. On hearing it he asked, "Is your sword dry?" Imco turned to check, but the giant grabbed him by the chin. "A man does not have to check. He knows. A dry sword is like a limp penis. A limp penis never fucks. If you never fuck you are like a woman: you get fucked instead. Understand me?"

Imco barely followed a word the man said, but he nodded.

Bomilcar grinned wide enough for two men. "Imco Vaca, we are winning this. Live through the day and Hannibal will hear of your bravery." He turned Imco around, shoved him toward the battle, and carried on yelling.

When Imco returned to the front line something had changed. He felt little fear. His body did not jerk and bounce in defensive maneuvers. He carried a new calm within him, and he knew he was not the only one. The men on either side of him possessed it too. They moved not so much like skirmishing soldiers as like a slow tide enveloping the enemy. Perhaps they *were* winning. His blade increasingly found its way into the bellies and necks and through the arms of the men facing him. He thought less about each action. He wondered if his beauty would approve of this. Maybe he could find her a gift among the dead, a ring or medallion, perhaps a jewel-encrusted helmet. He could tell when he hit bone and stuck on it, or when the blade slipped between two ribs. He could capture her by surprise, wrap his arm around her belly, and drape her head in soft loops of rope. He began to feel he could sense just which organs he was slicing through by their different textures, by the way the tissues parted before or resisted his blade. Maybe he would buy her something someday, perhaps a string of pearls, in a place far from here, different altogether. His weapon became an extension of his hand, a sharp finger that shredded all that it touched. A quiet island, a single great rock rising up from an azure sea, a tree-covered home to sheep and goats, fig trees and olive groves . . .

At some point his exhaustion bypassed even this merging of gore and fantasy. His head pounded with tight-wrapped pain that appeared from nowhere. He did not retreat to rest this time. He just sat down on the tangle of the dead and half-dead before him, ignoring the stench of blood and viscera and feces. Without knowing he was going to—or that such a thing was even possible on a battlefield—Imco drifted off into a short slumber. He awoke with his face pressed against that of a Latin, their lips linked as if in passion. Of all the sensations he felt that day, the one that would linger with him the longest and haunt him most was the rough scratch of the man's beard against his cheek and the taste of the man's saliva on the tip of his tongue, the knowledge that he could name the very foods this stranger had breakfasted on.

The fighting still raged somewhere. He could hear it, but he had not the strength to seek it out. The world moved. The haze above shifted and thickened and dispersed. Cries broke the air occasionally, although a lower, more muffled anguish hung beneath them now. Looking down at his body he could not tell where his parts ended and another man's began. He was entwined with all of them. Together they created a new organism, an enormous being composed of dead and dying flesh, a thing that shifted with a million tiny, almost imperceptible motions. Squelching, sliding, settling, liquids pooling, eyes glazing. The struggles of wounded men translated through hundreds of bodies, all touching as they were, interwoven into some ghastly stitch, part of the carpet of Cannae.

And still he could not say who would win the day. Indeed, he found it quite possible that they had all lost, living and dead of whatever nation. He did not know whether he should be proud or disgraced, whether he had fought well or like a coward. It all seemed the same, a single nightmare named differently by different men but the same in substance. He wanted badly, very badly, to see his beauty again.

How surprised he was when she eventually appeared.

On the Roman side, the signs should have been obvious from the start. Usually the manipular formation of the legions allowed them amazing fluidity. They held together like a weave of men at just the right distance apart, with spaces enough for fatigued soldiers to retreat and allow the waiting replacements to come forward into the fray. But from the moment Varro ordered the maniples drawn together this give-and-flow vanished. The momentum of the army was so great and the soldiers packed together so tightly that anyone who sank down beneath injury was soon trodden on, first by a single foot and then another and then countless others. They died a suffocating death, feet grinding against the backs of their ankles, up their legs, and over their torsos, the flesh and bone of them pounded into the soil they were defending.

Publius Scipio would never forgive himself for not realizing sooner that the whole conflict was a choreographed sacrifice of massive proportions. He spent the early parts of the battle mounted, shouting courage to his infantrymen, himself taking strength from the resolute expressions on their innumerable faces. At some point his horse went lame from an unseen injury, refusing to move farther and shifting from foot to foot as if standing on a giant, red-hot skillet. Publius dismounted. To his surprise, the horse bolted, churning through the mass of men in a crazed effort to flee.

From then on, the tribune was one with his men. His legion was near the center of the Roman army. He took up a position near the rear of the soldiers entrusted to him, from which he could follow the flow of events and issue orders if necessary. With each passing hour, he found himself nearer and nearer to the front. The forward progress of the army continued, but instead of pressing through the foe they increasingly seemed to disappear into them. By the middle hours of the afternoon, the whole legion ahead of his had vanished. His men became the front and, unable to retreat, they fought like wild animals with their backs to a wall.

The fighting was beyond all norms. There seemed to be no pauses in the enemy's attack. The blond giants came at them like the demons of the bitter north that they were. They were all motion, roaring, white skin splattered with blood, their swords swinging in wild arcs. His men—compact, tight, disciplined—cut them down in great numbers. But where the Romans were packed tight, the Gauls were just the opposite. They were a mob as tumultuous as the sea in storm, always throwing new waves of men and sucking back others to rest. Against this, his men could only fight until they fell from pure exhaustion.

Caught up in the conflict, shouting orders and rallying his men, Publius forgot about the danger he himself was in and how his position required more caution. He fought in the ranks as he had been taught in boyhood, so savagely for so long that he could not lift his eyes to the bigger picture for some time. Publius might have died in the fray if his companion, Laelius, had not jammed his fingers down the rim of his breastplate and yanked him back. For a moment he stumbled backward, arms grasping the air before him. A most undignified display. When he finally regained his footing, he turned to give Laelius a tongue-lashing, but the man would have none of it. He pulled Publius up onto a hillock surrounding an old tree stump. He clamped his fingers across the tribune's jaw and indicated that he should look forward, above the mêlée, at a figure in the middle distance, among the enemy.

This man was raised above the rest by almost his full height, standing perhaps on a pile of bodies or an overturned cart. Several guards ringed him, lower than he but each with a shield and spear at the ready. For a few moments he surveyed the scene before him. Then, unexpectedly, he burst out with a barrage of words. Publius could not make them out, but he almost thought he heard the boom of them cut through the din. A moment later, his vision lifted again and took in the whole scene before him. Publius knew without a doubt that this was Hannibal.

"A pilum!" the tribune yelled. "Give me a pilum!"

"Do not be stupid!" Laelius said. "You're not Achilles; you'd never reach him. Don't look at him, Publius; look instead at what he sees!"

Publius did as requested, first looking again at the commander, then trying to follow his gaze back over the Romans, out on either side. Doing this, he realized almost instantly what Laelius must already have gathered. The near edge of the army showed it clearly, and, though he could not make out the other edge, the signs he could see indicated that the situation there was just the same. They were hemmed in on at least three sides. The struggle now was not one for ultimate victory. It was a fight to survive.

The next few hours passed in a singular effort at odds with the collective mind of the army. Publius tried to turn as many men as he could toward the wings, to have them punch a hole out the side of the column instead of through the front. Hannibal's troops could not be that deep. The tribune could not find a signaler to issue orders by horn, so instead he yelled himself hoarse. He elbowed his way through the throng, shoving soldiers, punching them to get their attention. He grasped men by the shoulders and shouted right into their faces.

With Laelius at his side, echoing his orders, Publius did manage to lead a turn among the troops. He slowly began to feel a shift in the collective body. The late hours of the afternoon found him at the head of the new movement, cutting a bloody path through a line of Iberians three deep. For a moment in the fighting Publius was taken by a vision of beauty—that of the splashes of blood on the Iberians' white tunics, every possible variety of swirl and slash, a million variations on red and brown and dark almost to black. He had a notion that he would like to keep one of these tunics as a souvenir, a wall hanging to be viewed at leisure, a story to be read through close study.

They poured forward, slashing and screaming, for a good distance thinking they were still fighting the enemy, only slowly realizing that their way was clogged not by enemy warriors but by dead bodies piled three and four deep. It was such an overwhelming relief to be freed that Publius believed the whole of the army would gush out after him. He found rising ground in the distance and set out for it. He tried to sheathe his sword but found he could not do so. It was bent twice along its length, in different directions, no straighter than any stick he might have snatched up from the ground. He ran with it in hand.

Small bands and lone Numidians plagued them much of the way, tormenting them for the pleasure of it. When he reached the slope, Publius turned around and viewed the chaos he had fled. He had not drained the center, as he had hoped to do. Indeed, the breach his men had created was all but sealed now. The entirety of it was finally clear to him, painfully, tragically obvious. Hannibal had planned it all. Each and every thing the Roman forces strove to do had played into his hands. As they had planned, they punched through the Gauls and Iberians in the middle; but Hannibal had wished for just that move. He had cleared the cavalry from either side of them so that as the wedge pushed forward his most veteran troops swung in upon either side. Then, once the Carthaginian cavalry had vanquished their counterparts, they returned and fell upon the Roman rear. And that was it. After that it was just butchery. A series of masterstrokes. An army of ninety thousand had been completely surrounded by a lesser force in the space of a few hours. They were immobile, the vast mass of them stuck in the middle, able to do nothing but await the moment when their lives were cut out of them.

Varro rode toward him at a canter, his closest attendants mounted and close behind him, many of them glancing again and again over their shoulders, as if they feared the whole of the enemy's army would turn to follow them. The consul gave no indication that he planned to speak to the tribune, but Publius darted in front of him, snatched his horse's reins, and stopped him.

"What news of Paullus?" he asked. "Where is the other consul?"

Varro fixed on him a momentary gaze of utter loathing. "Where do you think? He's back on that field. Dead. As is Rome's future. Out of my way!"

Publius jumped back as the consul swatted at him. He let the man ride away, shocked as much by his words and attitude as by anything he had seen that day. He looked back at the battlefield and, amazingly, all was as it had been before. Men still died in their hundreds and thousands. It took all of his discipline to move him on into action. Nothing could be done for the men trapped in the death circle, though he would have given his life to save them. He shouted to those who had escaped with him and those who trailed behind. He directed them toward Canusium.

They reached the town late that evening, finding it alight with torches and open to them. The guards native to the place stood nervously, looking out beyond the straggling line of soldiers in the clear-eyed dread they all felt—fear of Hannibal's pursuit. Battered soldiers occupied every available inch. Laelius went off to locate other officers. Publius never even paused to catch his breath from the long march. He moved straight in among the men, speaking to them with what cheer he could muster, commending them for surviving the day, asking after their leaders.

He did all this in a fog, however. He barely heard the soldiers' responses. He functioned as if another being altogether propelled him, something intelligent enough to move his body and form words with his mouth. But the true Publius Scipio occupied a more confused space. He saw again images of the day's bloodshed superimposed on the world before him. He heard in the din the voice of his father and remembered the many lessons his father had tried to teach him in preparation for his manly duties. To think of those quiet moments now cut him with a pain more acute than any of the numb aches of his body. What a child he had been! Up until this very morning he had known nothing! Even now he knew nothing! The great awakening that hammered at his head was the simple knowledge of his ignorance; the awesome possibility that the world might never be as he imagined and that he could never again occupy it with a child's vain authority.

Barely had the tribune dropped for a moment of rest when he was called again, with news that woke him from his stupor.

Laelius ran to him panting. "They're talking of abandoning the country."

"Who?"

"The younger Fabius Maximus, Lucius Bibulus, Appius Pulcher . . . All the tribunes I could find. They're talking of turning to the sea and seeking refuge—"

Before he could finish, Publius jumped to his feet. "Take me to them."

The officers had gathered in a hall used for public debates. Publius strode into it without a plan. In his first glance at the gathered officers he saw the defeat in their faces, the shame of conspiring men. He still carried his battered sword unsheathed. With the weapon upraised, he shouldered through the company toward the center. The former dictator's son was speaking, but Publius silenced him by shouting his name. The words that followed came out of him before thought, propelled by a strange mixture of fury and calm. Despite all the defeat and death he had seen that day, he felt a throbbing serenity inside him. In seeing these men's faces he was reminded that nothing mattered now save the certainty of honor. There was so little else that one could rely on in the world.

"Fabius Maximus!" he said. "I worked under your father. I know his greatness despite all those who malign him. Do you think he would ever consider the plan you here devise? Have you all forgotten yourselves? If so, then Rome truly died today. We are no more than the corpse; your words, the first stink of decay."

The younger Fabius began to explain himself, but Publius brought his sword hand down and punched him square on the mouth. The man dropped like a deadweight, unconscious.

"I swear to you all," Publius said, "that I will allow no man to abandon our country, nor will I betray it myself! I swear a dying oath to Rome. If ever I fail it, may Jupiter bring down upon me a shameful death. May he destroy my family honor and cast all I possess into the hungry mouths of my enemies. I swear this; who among you swear with me? And who among you die on my sword?"

Having spoken, he stood surrounded by a room full of mutinous officers, his single blade raised against them. Laelius flanked him, his hand in a white-knuckled grip around the hilt of his sword. But the others did not attack. Instead they each and all lowered their eyes. As he listened to first one man and then another take the oath,

Publius told himself that this was not the end, not of the war, not of his nation. The sun would rise tomorrow. The war would carry on. Publius Scipio had not died at Cannae as he might. Instead he recognized his life's greatest challenge. He would meet Hannibal again. He was sure of it.

Aradna would have forgotten about the young Carthaginian soldier if she had not stumbled upon him in the festering, open-air graveyard of Cannae. She and her band and other bands of camp followers rose before the dawn and greeted the sun at the edge of the battlefield. Usually, they would have swarmed through the dead at the first tentative light, but the sight before them was an unusual horror. The carnage of the day before was past belief. Looking upon the great, jutting, tangled, shadowed devastation, none of them dared enter. Moans filled the air with a low, unnatural tone of anguish. Even the least superstitious among the camp followers feared to tread carelessly among so many soulless creatures. The various afterworlds to which these men hurtled headlong could only hold so many new souls. Surely many of them lingered on this plain, angry at their lot and dangerous to the living.

Aradna, standing to the east of the field, felt the heat of the sun touch the back of her head and slant down her shoulders. She watched as the first touches of gold illuminated portions of the dead and crept down into crevices and gashes, across faces and private parts alike. The human form lost all reason in the jumble. Arms and legs twisted at angles impossible for the living, reaching up from the piles of bodies three, four, and sometimes even more bodies deep. Wounds lay open to flies. Slivers of bone jutted into the air. Flesh had taken on infinite coloration: shades of blue and purple, white as bright ivory, yellow and brown and sometimes strangely crimson. On several occasions Aradna's eyes tricked her into believing that among the human forms were the half-roasted carcasses of swine. But this was, of course, not the case. It was just that some men, in death, failed to look human. The view was no better in the light than before, save that now the carnage was betrayed for what it was—nothing ghostly, just the barbarous work of men on a scale never seen before. This, at least, was something the camp followers understood. They began their labor.

Why she stopped above the young soldier she could not later say, except to explain that she often had to pause that day and steady herself and take shallow breaths. He was buried to mid-torso in the arms and limbs of others. They propped him up so that he was almost vertical, with his head tilted back. Grime caked his face, sweat and blood and dirt commingled into a mask all men shared alike. His mouth gaped open to the air like so many others. A fly buzzed about the cavity, landing on his teeth, crawling over his lips and around the rim of his nostrils. Recognition crept into her slowly. She stared at his face so long that the strange, naked soldier she had met twice and still thought about occasionally emerged from beneath the mask. His features slowly aligned themselves into shapes and contours she recognized. She bent close to him, thinking him dead and feeling no threat from a dead man, touched by curiosity and the slightest notion of sadness.

The soldier grunted, stirred a little, and raised an arm partway up from the muck. That was the first indication she had that he lived. She set down the sack she had already stuffed full with items of jewelry and coins and sacred tokens, jeweled daggers and gilded bits pried from helmets and armor, anything that struck her as valuable in relation to its weight and size. She sat on top of her treasure and reached out a hand toward the man. The flesh at his neck was warm to the touch. She found a pulse and felt it beat beneath her fingers. He might have been unconscious, but the life inside him still seemed strong. She pulled her hand away and sat a while longer, studying him. Already she felt a strange intimacy between them. She had touched his flesh. She stared at him now as he really was, unconscious of her. What, she asked herself, could she learn of this man from his sleeping face?

She did not have time to consider this for too long. The surviving soldiers were up now, moving in small groups across the battlefield. They scavenged also, but they went armed. Judging by the occasional cries of pain, she knew they were dispatching the wounded:

the enemy certainly, but also some of their own if they believed them beyond mending. What might they make of the soldier before her?

Aware that she could only do what she wanted to if she did not think about it fully, Aradna put the consequences out of her mind and searched out the men of her band. With their bewildered aid, she wrenched the soldier free from the rest and dragged him to their camp. They did not question her; each in his own way loved her. In this they were more like family than anyone she had known since childhood. She thanked them and said no more and with her gestures warned them to be still if they wished to stay near the light of her favor.

That evening she sat beside the soldier beneath her hide shelter. He still slept soundly, snoring now that he was on his back.

"Never has a man been so tired," she muttered. "Only men can sleep so deeply."

She unbuckled his armor, lifted it from him, and set it to the side. She peeled his tunic away from his flesh. The fabric was stiff with dried sweat and grime, with blood, though she did not know whether it was his or other men's. She probed him with her fingers, searching for wounds. And there were many: cuts all over his arms and legs, a piercing wound under his collarbone, a gash in one of his nostrils. Bruises bloomed over every inch of him. These blood wounds must have drained his soul force terribly, but to her eyes none seemed fatal.

The soldier stirred.

Aradna snatched the torch up and held it between them. His eyes cracked open and seemed to focus on the hide above him. She believed she saw conscious thought in his gaze, but perhaps this was not so. He closed his eyes again and the rhythm of his slumber returned.

She carried on with her work. She dipped a cloth in herbed water and gently touched it to his face. She held the fabric there for a moment. When he did not react, she drew it across his forehead, wiping away the grime to reveal the rich, sun-browned skin beneath. As she peeled away the concealing layers, the soldier's face emerged. He had a small mouth, a somewhat wide forehead, and a perfectly formed nose, evenly placed and uniform, save for the scab of the small cut. His eyes pressed against the thin skin of their lids in such a way that she believed she could make out their character. She had to lean close to verify her impression, near enough that she held her breath for fear that he would feel it brushing against his moist skin. Still she saw the same thing. His eyes, they were gentle.

During this process the old woman, Atneh, had come over to the shelter and peered in several times. On each occasion she turned away without speaking and sat by the fire. Aradna knew Atneh had asked that the men stay near in case the soldier woke up in a rage. She fed them a soup she cooked on occasion, made from ingredients she did not name and about which they did not ask. They all sat quietly and talked over their departure on the coming morning. They were loaded beyond their capacity; best to make for the coast and on to whatever destination they chose after that. Eventually, Atneh squatted beside the younger woman and watched her for some time in silence.

"I never thought I would see that look on your face," Atneh said.

"What?" Aradna asked. She felt her cheeks flush and she turned her face away.

"We women are all fools in our youth. I was. My mother was before me. The gods wish it, so that they may sport with us. Men are fools as well, but that is different. . . . Women more often grow to wisdom. I had hoped that was true of you. I see I was mistaken."

"I don't know what you speak of."

"Yes, you do. Don't lie to me. It's useless and insults us both."

Aradna said, "Aunt, it's just that his face isn't like other men's. In sleep he looks like a boy I would choose as a son, as a brother."

This did not move the old woman. "Leave him," she said. "Tomorrow we go; he doesn't. Who can judge a man by his face? Better to judge him by his genitals and be wary of what hangs there. This one will bring you nothing but trouble. Do you hear? Leave him and carry on toward your goal. What is it you want of life?"

"Very little," Aradna said.

"But say it to me. What do you want? What are the things you told me in confidence? Say them again."

Aradna shook her head. "Very little," she repeated. "I want to go home to Father's island. I want to herd goats on the hills and watch boats pass at a distance. I want a quiet corner of the world away from all of this. Every day I want a little less. . . . Aunt, I just want peace."

The old woman nodded through this, solemn, her eyes fixed on the young woman and full of sadness. "Tell me, then: What place has this murderer on that island? Hmm? Do you truly think this killer of Romans, this African, would allow you the peace you have earned? Be no fool, dear one. Leave this man. He lives. That's more than he deserves."

Aradna could not dispute any of this. She knew Atneh was right, and yet she could not help making one last protest. "Aunt, several times already I have met this man. Twice before and now yet again. What does it mean that I found him a third time?"

The old woman answered quickly, struggling to her feet in the process. "It means you should have no doubt. He's more devious than he looks. Perhaps he's entrapped you in a spell. Either way, leave him."

And so she did. The next morning, she dragged away everything that she could from Cannae on a sledge harnessed to her back. They were to return to the coast, where, she believed, she would arrange passage across the sea to Greece. She was going home. Only a fool would do otherwise. It wasn't until late that day that she realized she did not know the man's name. Three times now, Fortune had brought them together, but she could not think of him by name.

Hannibal made sure that the body was tended in a manner commensurate with the quality of the man. He helped the attendants lay him out on the beam. He wound ribbons of white cloth around his ankles and across the groin, over the arms at the elbows and across his forehead, securing him into a rigid, disciplined posture. An officer's body should not be seen to flop about like others. He deserved better than that. That was why his innards had been scooped up from where they had escaped him, cleaned, replaced, and sewn into the cavity that housed them. Hannibal watched as the priests anointed his flesh with fragrant oils and tucked a small charm bag beneath the fold of cloth near his hands. Mandarbal entered once all this had been concluded and spoke his strange words over the corpse. He dotted the man's forehead and shoulders, hands and feet with his warm blood, drawn just moments before from a slit in the priest's wrist.

After Mandarbal departed, the commander dropped to his knees and rested his forehead against his friend's chest and murmured the man's name. Bostar. He repeated it softly, over and over again, a single word made into a prayer and a speech, a confession and an apology. He spoke as if he were alone with his deceased secretary, but his remaining officers rimmed the walls of the council tent. The last twenty-four hours had been filled with revelry at their victory, but the aftermath of the battle provided no respite from toil. There had been, and still were, a thousand different matters to attend to. This pause to mourn the passing of one of their own provided for most of them the first hushed moment for reflection.

Each of them had been wounded in some way. Maharbal had been hacked down to the bone of his lower leg with a dullish sword. He could barely stand, but claimed that he did not notice the injury when mounted. Bomilcar bore a gash across his forehead where a passing spear point had carried away a strip of flesh. He would wear the scar of it ever after, the first point on his massive visage that any newcomer's eyes settled on. He joked that he could tap the bone of his skull directly to clear his muddled head. Monomachus' arms were battered with bruised, oozing wounds, and he wore a cloth wrapped around his left hand, the material tainted a reddish brown where he had received the point of a dart thrown at close range. Carthalo lay on a cot in his tent, a spear wound in his thigh. Several lesser officers stood or sat about the chamber as their injuries allowed.

Mago watched his brother with a pained expression that had nothing to do with the physical. By the grace of Baal, he had survived the battle largely unscathed. He and his handful of attendants had fought near the front ranks of Gauls. His voice was still raw from all the yelling, from his crazed attempt to manage the wild energy of barbarians, to control their retreat and stay alive and watch Hannibal close the jaws of his trap. In the hours of battle, moment after chaotic moment passed as if it might be his last, each instant laced with a hundred ways for him to die. He had personally killed more men than he could count. He had stepped back, always at the edge of the retreat, receding before the Roman line as it trod over his soldier's bodies.

One of his guards had been impaled beneath the chin by a Roman spear. The weapon struck so hard that Mago, standing just beside him, heard the vertebrae snap under the pressure and saw how strangely the man's head hung from the spear point, attached to the body by tendrils of flesh but no longer connected to the framework hidden beneath. He still carried the sickening image in his head, ready to impose itself on any person walking past, any face he looked at. Nor was it the only disturbing image. He tried to flush these out with reasoned thought and celebration, but as ever he hid within himself the strange duality of character he had always found in battle. He was both inordinately skilled at it and absurdly haunted by it afterward. Strangely, it was he and Hannibal—the two most slightly injured—who seemed most troubled.

Hannibal was still whispering the dead man's name when Gemel stepped into the tent. He had assisted the commander for some years now, but he seemed nervous in his new role as Bostar's replacement, clumsy in it and hesitant in his speech. He lowered his head and stood in silence.

But Hannibal must have sensed his presence. Without lifting his head he asked, "What do we know for certain?"

Gemel glanced around at the others, but they all knew whom the commander addressed and with what question. "We can be sure of little, sir," he began. "The Gauls suffered most. They are still counting, but they may have lost more than four thousand. We cannot account for two thousand Iberians and African troops, and we lost at least two hundred from the combined cavalry. Commander, I am sure of none of these figures. This is just the best we could gather throughout the day."

"And of the enemy?"

"Your estimate, sir, would surpass mine in accuracy. We've captured a full twenty thousand—many of them wounded and dying—and taken both their camps. Some hid in Cannae itself. We are still rounding them up. A few escaped to Canusium and Venusia—"

Hannibal lifted his head. "Just give me numbers, Gemel, a simple tally."

"The best figure I can give this morning comes from the Romans themselves. They say they were ninety thousand strong. Twenty thousand of these we captured. Perhaps another ten thousand escaped us. So . . . This field may well be the death of sixty thousand of them."

Maharbal could not help but speak up. "Do you hear that, Hannibal? Think of it—sixty thousand! And the figure may be higher than that! Let me do what I proposed earlier. My men could ride before the dawn. Do not consider me injured—"

"I've already answered you, Maharbal," Hannibal said. He touched on the horseman with his one-eyed gaze, briefly. "I rejoice that you are so hungry to sack Rome. But he is a fool who does not place himself within a framework of other men's actions. We are not the first to conquer Roman legions on their own land. The Gauls sacked the city of Rome and had their way with her as if she were a whore. They left loaded with plunder and stories of their own greatness. But what did it come to? Rome went on. The Romans crept back into their city and built it again and spread their power and now have little to fear from the Gauls except annoyance."

"We are not barbarians," Maharbal said. "Their story is not the same as ours."

"Pyrrhus of Epirus did battle here—"

"Nor are you Pyrrhus!" Maharbal cut in. "He knew how to win a victory, but not how to use one. Do not make a different form of the same mistake."

Hannibal glanced up at him again, studying him as he might a stranger who had spoken out of turn. But after a moment he seemed to find the man he recognized and spoke to him with tired patience. "Pyrrhus defeated Rome on the battlefield," he said, "a deed that earns him my respect. Again and again he emerged victorious, but still he gained no foothold. Though he won, he lost. Rome replaced its soldiers like the Hydra replacing heads. That's what Pyrrhus never understood. Rome always has more men. Not because their women push them out of the womb any faster, but because they use the wombs of others. If they run low, they call upon their municipal cities, upon the colonies, and, beyond that, upon the allied states. It is that that gives them power. Sever *those* heads,

337

and the picture is much different. That is something Pyrrhus never succeeded at. He never isolated the Romans. That is the key, to cut them off from the outside world, hack at her bonds with her neighbors. This done, Rome is just a city like any other. And then any city—not only Carthage—may deal with her as she deserves. Rome will find herself the most hated creature the world has known. This, Maharbal, is as true today as when I first explained it to you. I know my mind on this. I will strike Rome not with the greatest force, but with just the right blows to find vulnerable flesh."

He indicated this with the edge of his hand, cutting the air before him. Then, remembering the body of his friend, he pulled his hand back. "This talk is pounding my head to pain. Gemel, have they found the slain consul yet?"

"No. He may've been stripped by camp followers already."

"Keep looking for him. He deserves an honorable burial, even if he was a fool. And see to it that the allied prisoners aren't mistreated tonight. I'll speak to them tomorrow morning. I want to send them home to their people friends instead of enemies. Have special presents sent to the Gauls, along with wine and heaps of praise and the cuts of meat they most favor. And Gemel, have careful counts for me before the dawn."

As the secretary withdrew, Monomachus said, "The gods, too, deserve praise for our victory. We should offer sacrifice. With your permission, I'll select a hundred Romans from the prisoners. We should torture them in the old ways, and offer sacrifices—"

"No. We offered enough sacrifices yesterday. And what is this man lying before me if not a sacrifice?"

This did not move Monomachus. "You know I'm sworn to Moloch. I can feel his hunger. This battle did not sate him."

"Don't talk to me of this."

"In your father's time, we—"

"Stop!" Hannibal snapped to his feet. "Have all my generals gone mad? There will be no sacrifice! We will not march on Rome and this is not my father's time! You are my councillor only as long as I tolerate you and that may not be much longer. Leave me now. All of you. Go!"

Monomachus turned away without comment and filed out with

the others. Mago started to leave also, but Hannibal stayed him with a glance.

Alone with his brother, the commander asked, "Why is my heart so troubled? I should rejoice, but instead I feel a new weight draped over my shoulders. I should honor my generals with praise; instead, I only find fault with them. I craved Roman blood for so many years; yet I do not want another victory like this. Mago, when I looked upon Bostar's face it was as if I were looking at yours, or at my own."

"I know," Mago said, "or I upon yours."

"This victory was not worth his life. I would undo it all to have him back. How strange, my brother, that a man like me, who wants only to defeat his enemy . . . How strange that in mourning I would trade everything that this companion might live."

"No good can come from talking so," Mago said. "You will not have to look upon a field like Cannae again. You will not have to bury your brothers. Surely, this is the end of war. Never will the world see another day like this. That is what you have accomplished. Bostar would reverse nothing that happened here."

Hannibal placed his fingers on the wood of the funeral table and pressed till his fingertips went white. "I know nothing of what Bostar thinks now. By the gods, I want to win this! It is all the work of my own hands, but at moments I look down and realize that I'm seated on a monster fouler than anything I could have conceived. Sixty thousand of them dead? Sometimes I wonder who is more bound to Moloch—Monomachus, or myself."

Hannibal dismissed the thought with a tic that upset and then released the muscles of one side of his face. Mago had noticed this tic several times in the past few weeks. He did not care for it, for during it Hannibal's face was briefly not his own. It was an ugly mask, similar to his, but different in disturbing ways. One of the torches began sputtering, a few loud bursts of oil combusting. Mago turned and watched it, wary lest an accidental blaze disturb the solemnity of the chamber. "You surprise me, brother," he said. "Do you pity yourself now, at the moment of your greatest glory?"

"I do not pity myself," the commander said. "I know no pity. Neither do I yet have the word for what I feel. Even the gods in whose names we fight remind us not to think of war always. Think of Anath.

After the defeat of Yam she hosted a feast in Baal's honor. When the gods were all assembled, she slammed the doors closed and began to slay everyone. She would have killed them all, for they had all betrayed Baal in the earlier war. You remember who stopped her?"

"Baal himself. He convinced her that the bloodshed had gone on long enough and that a time of peace and forgiveness was needed."

"Just so . . ." The tic disfigured Hannibal's face again. He closed his eyes and for some time seemed to focus only on his breathing. Watching his visage grow calm, Mago was reminded of the clay masks street players wore during the winter months. They were vague, almost featureless faces that hinted at human attributes without rendering the details. They betrayed no emotion, and one could tell the tenor of the play only by listening and watching that much more carefully. Even as a child he had found it strange that the same mask could at one moment indicate mirth, and in the very next embody sorrow. He was, then, both surprised and not surprised by what his brother said next.

"Let us forget this conversation," Hannibal said, opening his eyes and straightening to his full height. "It does nobody any good and we've much to attend to. Here is what we do, brother. You must go to Carthage on my behalf. . . ."

Never before had Rome endured so dreadful an hour. Each of the previous battles had struck its blow, but Cannae beggared belief. For days after the first news of the disaster trickled in, the people had no clear understanding of any of it. Just who had been killed, who captured, and who spared? Was there an army left? Was Hannibal already beating a path toward them with gleaming eyes? Was he truly, truly unstoppable? Questions multiplied with few answers rising to match them. Rome's people knew only that every aspect of their lives had been altered; now everything was at risk of imminent destruction. The streets and the Forum became roiling sluiceways of despair. The living and the dead were mourned simultaneously, in a jumble, for there seemed no way of separating the two.

On the suggestion of Fabius Maximus, horsemen rode out along the Via Appia and Via Latina to gather what news they could from the battered survivors—if any could be found. The gates to the city slammed shut behind them. All believed that Hannibal would come for them now. What object could there be but the destruction of Rome itself? The death of her men, the despoiling of her women, the theft of her riches: what greater temptation for the monsters of Carthage? For a people so buoyed by their enslavement of others, it was easy to imagine the trials ahead for them should the barbarians breach the gates. Masters crouched beside servants and wept with them and made declarations never heard before and whispered apologies previously inconceivable. All awaited the coming tempest.

Amazing, then, barely believable, mysterious . . . that Hannibal did not appear on the horizon. Yes, the details that reached them were horrendous, the death toll shocking, no portion of the news fair or welcome . . . but Hannibal did not come. He did not come. And with the passing of days into weeks and more weeks, people's thoughts turned from impending doom to other matters. Amid the fervor of war and hope in the city as Paullus and Varro marched out, none had taken note that prodigies had been occurring with unusual frequency. In the sealed, waiting city these events were recalled.

There had been lightning strikes at the Atrium Publicum in the Capitol, as also upon the shrine of Vulcan and the temple of Vacuna and upon the stones of the road in the Sabine district. This latter had left a gaping hole at the center of a crossroads, inside which a child found the handle of an ancient's dagger. There had been other strikes on lonely spots that set the hills on fire. In a village in the far south, a flaming goat ran through the street calling out, "Hurrah, hurrah!" It was assumed that the creature had likewise been the victim of a malicious lightning strike, though there were no witnesses to this.

All of this had taken place the previous year. As the new year dawned, the land seemed rife with signs. The earth split and peeled and offered up amazements that proved time and again that the natural order had been reversed. At Mantua there was a swamp that captured and held the overflow from the river Mincius. It was a foul place even in the best of times, damp and smelling of decay, rich in substance and yet somehow rank with death as well. All this was of nature's own design. But a man chanced upon the place one twilight to find that the waters had turned to blood: not just in color but also in substance, thick and congealed and metallic in his nostrils, as if the earth itself bled like humans.

At Spoletium, a woman awoke one day changed into a man. At Hadria, white forms were seen floating in the sky. Great numbers of dead fish washed ashore near Brundisium. And some said that the tunic on the statue of Mars at Praeneste protruded each sunset under pressure from the god's great, granite erection. Rumors to explain this flew as fast and chaotic as bats in the night sky. Some said the god was instructing them to procreate. Still others suggested that they should look to a leader endowed with a similar length and regularity. Before long the notion took hold that the local whores had sold themselves into the employ of Carthage. They had taken to servicing the god to distract him from the war effort. Reliable persons, however, never confirmed this, so this tale was best considered with skepticism.

For augury it was an abundant season, and the results fueled the deepening suspicion that the gods abhorred the Roman cause. The city had forgotten to honor them properly. That was why this Carthaginian conqueror prevailed so easily against them. The people responded according to the advice of the magistrates and priests. An edict was issued for a period of prayer to all the gods of Rome, lest one go neglected and feel slighted. Lambs were sacrificed, fat ones with fine coats and handsome faces. Their blood ran freely to appease the gods. Their entrails betrayed more omens too bleakly numerous to detail, so the priests looked to still darker measures. Two Gallic slaves were publicly beheaded in an elaborate offering to Apollo. It was rumored that even older rites were enacted across the Tiber at night, but what went on over there had no place in the public record. Some people even turned to soothsayers—unusual for a Roman as such a practice was more Greek in nature—and these questionable persons produced all sort of varied and contradictory advice. Some people hammered nails into sacred objects and offered them at the gods' temples; others left food outside their houses for certain animals or washed with a single hand only, refrained from saying certain words, or pricked their skin with needles and licked the blood clean.

Though some believed that these practices improved their fortunes, others found that unnatural incidents proceeded unabated. It was truly a volatile time, in which reason was hard to come by and quiet voices seldom heard. Two of the Vestal Virgins were discovered in unchaste acts. One killed herself with a dagger; the other had not the courage to take her own life but was instead buried alive by a raging mob. Gangs of youths swarmed the streets, flagellating beggars and rooting out poor souls they named as spies for Carthage. For weeks after the news from Cannae, the soldiers' widows walked the streets in tears, dragging their fingernails across their faces and arms and chests. Their mourning was so disruptive that the Senate roused itself to action. They banned any display of sorrow, calling it treasonous and un-Roman, and conscripted the raucous youths to police the ban.

And yet through all this turmoil and distress not a single voice of prominence suggested settlement. Rome sent no envoys to treat with the Carthaginian, nor did the city receive his messengers with anything but scorn. Without even discussing the matter, the citizens of Rome chose ultimate war over a compromised peace. They would live by their own rules, or they would perish.

FOUR

Dance for the Gods

Despite the almost fatal circumstances of his early years, Masinissa was a young man full of certainty. In infancy he had been threatened by an unnamed illness. A few years later, a smallpox outbreak took away his elder brother, several cousins, and many of his childhood companions: this was his earliest memory. A year later he fell sick with yet another contagion. Headaches and rashes plagued him. Stomach cramps doubled him over. He vomited whatever he swallowed, and other substances that came from deep inside him. Eventually, he lay unable to rise, feverish, his sheets stained pink by the blood escaping through his skin. Priests and physicians alike labored over him. Around them he watched the play of other creatures, small, half-human things that only he could see. These demons set their tiny hands on him and tugged, trying to lift him from his pallet and drag him off to some foul place. It took all of his will to fight them back. He was never sure just how he prevailed over them, but he emerged from his ailment with a quiet conviction in his own destiny. The illness had been a test; he had passed.

He was not tall, but his father had always told him that the best men were compact, hard as close-grained wood. There were so many possible substances from which a man could be made, but quality was hard to come by. His line, King Gaia had told him, was of unblemished mahogany. Looking at his reflection in polished iron, Masinissa found the comparison apt enough. His body was such that each muscled portion of it clung to his frame in just the right place. There was no fat; a lean coating of skin wrapped him like wet leather dried to form by the sun.

He had been a horseman since before his memory began, and he could do everything as well mounted as on foot. He smoked his pipe on horseback, ate many a meal, even pissed off to the side occasionally, joking with his companions about the strength of his hose. He sometimes dreamed of mounted sexual conquests, although this art did not come as easily in the waking hours. As for combat, he could hurl missiles at full gallop, pierce birds in flight, squirrels at dead runs. Larger creatures just made easier targets, none more so than the wide breasts of men.

When he sailed for Iberia, he promised Sophonisba he would return to her a hero. He meant it, and it pained him that she looked at him with such amusement, as if his words were no more than bluster. He hungered for her. It was not so much pleasure that she gave him as it was the awareness of the richness of pleasure denied him. She was exquisite and cruel: the combination was irresistible. After his father's death, he would make her the queen of his empire, and then he would extend his domain in new directions. Even as Carthage ruled the Mediterranean, the Massylii would extend their dominion to the west and bring the Gaetulians and the Moors into submission, not to mention the Libyans. He would squash Syphax beneath the heel of his right foot, and then he would turn southward. He would forge new bonds with Audagost and Kumbi, cities he knew little of except that they belonged to rich and prosperous, ancient cultures. With them as partners, he would control the flow of trade between inland Africa and the Mediterranean. What a world he would create then! He would heap treasures of gold and ivory, beads and cloth and dyes upon his bride. She would see in the years to come that he was no boy to be laughed at, but a man to be remembered by the ages. Of all this, he was certain. He had only to make it happen.

With the first few months on the ground in Iberia he proved himself the warrior he claimed to be. He knew that the best way to wage war changed with circumstance. Romans were slow to understand this, but Numidians were at their best when their minds and strategies shifted and darted as quickly as their mounts. His men once surprised a Roman reconnaissance mission as it was returning northward. He knew not what they had learned, but whatever it was died within their throats, each and every one of the fifty of them. He led raiding parties far up into Catalonia, blazing into villages with torches in hand, leaving them flaming pyres of despair.

He had no personal ill will toward these people, but they were traitors to Carthage, friends to his enemies. He tried to make the Scipios feel that they had no control over their territory, could offer no protection to their allies. He could strike at will, wherever he pleased. As far as he was concerned, he could keep this up indefinitely. He was new to war, yes, but he already felt a mastery of it pumping in his veins. With his aid, the Barca brothers must prevail. He reminded them of his skills often. They laughed to hear his boasting, but clearly it pleased them. They clapped him on the back and hugged him roughly and pulled on his hair and called him younger brother. Hasdrubal once shot back, "True enough, prince, may you never be an enemy. May Fortune never betray us so completely!" Even Hanno, who he knew had suffered at Roman hands and who was generally a taciturn man, warmed to him.

Late in the summer of his first season in Iberia, both of the Carthaginian armies were in the field. It so happened that Hasdrubal's movements brought him near to the Scipio brothers at Amtorgis. Hanno, who had resumed command of an army, was nearby but separated by miles of hilly terrain. The Romans had apparently tired of skirmishing and wished for a real battle before the season's end. They were on the offensive, just as they believed their countrymen were in Italy. For a moment the situation looked dire for Hasdrubal's army, separated as he was from his brother. But instead of attacking him with their full force, the Romans split into two armies. Gnaeus marched north to hedge off Hanno, while Cornelius set himself right next to Hasdrubal, separated from him by little more than a river.

At first glance, both of the Roman forces were considerable, each numbering some thirty thousand. But from his wide-ranging scouts, Masinissa learned that Cornelius' numbers were made up predominately of Celtiberians. Only a third were Romans. In answering this news he spoke a gibe against the Celtiberians, but a moment later he stopped in his tracks, stunned by what he had uttered. It was a simple idea, but it had a certain sublime beauty. When the generals met at the midpoint between their armies for a hastily called council Masinissa could not help but begin the meeting with his idea.

"Listen to me," he said, speaking with his customary rapidity, starting before the group was completely settled. "Those Iberians have no joy in their hearts. They don't look forward to this battle, nor do they love Rome. We have silver. Why don't we just pay them?"

Hasdrubal dropped onto his stool, shaking his head. "They won't fight against Rome. They're too bound to them; and they've been too foul to us to expect our friendship."

"I didn't say they should fight against Rome," Masinissa said. "There need be no question of that. Pay them, but not to fight for us. Just pay them *not* to fight."

"*Not* to?"

Masinissa searched for the words to explain himself further, but then realized he had stated his position well. He just nodded.

Gnaeus Scipio had had more than enough of Masinissa. From the moment he started his northerly march, the whelp plagued his every move, barking at his heels, darting in again and again with attacks so rapid his men had barely time to muster into formations to face them. Masinissa's force would appear just long enough to hurl their spears, to slice a few baggage handlers in the neck or upraised forearm, to drop a flaming torch into a wagon, or to spook horses into revolt. Then they would vanish, crouched low, galloping at breakneck speed beneath the branches of the pine trees. These were a coward's tactics, but each raid cost him dearly in lives, supplies, and pride.

That was why Gnaeus ordered the silent march to commence at midnight. He knew that Indibilis and his Tartesians—Carthaginian allies—were afoot only a few miles to the east. Masinissa's harassment might be a ruse to keep him distracted as the Iberians marched to join forces with Hanno. He decided on an action to stir the matter, praying that when the dust settled he would find himself to have gained advantage. He left a lagging corps of men to man the campfires and sound the passing of the night's quarters and generally make themselves out to be more numerous than they were; then he and the bulk of his force slipped away unmolested, no mean feat for an army of twenty-five thousand. If this went as he envisioned, he would make quick work of the Tartesians and then turn back to face the greater threat. He was quite sure that Indibilis would pull up his red-fringed tunic and crap stones when he realized the numbers marshaled against him.

The march commenced perfectly, the men keeping good order, making almost the time they would have in the daylight. Dawn found them within sight of the Iberians, just as his scouts had foretold. He forced them into battle, a loose affair spread throughout the rolling, wooded hills. His men had to fight singly, like so many gladiators in a great contest. This would have proved difficult for most legions, but Gnaeus had trained them for just such a possibility. From the start, he gained the upper hand. The Iberians stepped backward with each thrust or parry.

But when he heard the first shrill, stammering Numidian calls, his blood went cold. A moment later Masinissa's horsemen carved into them from both sides, African furies let loose like an army one of the Numidian gods might have spat out of its great, rotten mouth. But even this did not decide the matter. The blood that was icy one moment burned red hot the next. Gnaeus shouted for his men to tighten up their formations. The horn beside him bellowed out instructions, turning the men at either flank out to the side to meet the marauders, halting the advance into the Tartesians and alerting each man to take a managed defensive position. Once some amount of order had been achieved, the Roman forces began to retreat.

All this was skillfully done, but other powers conspired against him that day. A horseman churned up to him with the last ill blow of Fortune: Hanno fast approached. The Romans had been so distracted that they had not noticed their advance until they saw them walking in great columns through the dappled light beneath the pines. The general's gaze flew out toward the tree-lined ridges the scout indicated. It might only have been an illusion caused by the wind up there, but the spires of the pines trembled and swayed as if buffeted by the soldiers shouldering through them. He told the horseman to gather a small band and ride for Cornelius' camp to beg whatever aid he could provide. As his messenger spurred his horse away, Gnaeus knew the effort was in vain.

Message dispatched, he issued new orders. The Roman soldiers stopped in their tracks and set about building fortifications. They ignored the normal order of a defensive camp. Gnaeus rode from point to point, throwing out instructions as suited the landscape. Velites and camp staff dug trenches in the crumbly soil. Men hacked down trees and set them falling in a pattern that knitted one into the next to form a perimeter just behind the trenches. They strung the wall between elephant-sized boulders and tried to use the land's contours to their advantage.

All the while missiles fell among them. The signaler beside Gnaeus went down in twisted, silent anguish. A javelin punctured his chest at the lung and pierced him, emerging on the far side. He seemed to have no idea how to respond to such an injury, so he just lay down. Moments later, five Numidians jumped clear over the trunk of a fallen tree and engaged at close quarters with the general's staff. Gnaeus himself drew his sword and struggled to get close enough to split one of them open at the skull. But they were gone before he even swung a blow.

Then Hanno's army arrived. There was no way to count them in the broken, tree-covered terrain, but they numbered in the tens of thousands. Hanno's forces fanned out in an encircling maneuver. They intermingled with the Tartesians, who greeted them with cheers and horn blasts. They surrounded the Romans both bodily and with a wall of sound and wide-eyed, bloody lust. Gnaeus shouted courage to his men, although he could not quite keep his voice from betraying the nearness of death. He took some pride in the next few moments. His men fought with complete devotion. He saw not a crack of panic in any of them. He asked Jupiter to allow someone to live through this and tell the tale. After this prayer he did not think anymore. He got down from his mount and waded into his troops. Beside them he met the horde pouring over the fallen trees.

Four days after his brother began his northerly march, the Suessetani with Cornelius Scipio awoke and broke camp hurriedly. They tore down their tents and piled supplies onto their pack animals' backs. When Cornelius sent a translator to ask what they were doing, they answered flatly that a disturbance in their own country demanded their presence. Hearing this, the proconsul went to their chief men himself and tried to reason with them. He implored them to stay on, hinting vaguely that they would be rewarded for doing so. He was only a hair's breadth from actually offering them pay, but his pride cut off the words before he uttered them. Finally, he rebuked them for their treachery and accused them of scheming with the enemy. He reached forcefully for one of their chieftains and found himself poised between two bristling fronts of spears: the Celtiberians before him and his own behind. He almost shouted for the capture of their leaders, then he realized that he had no such power. The Suessetani outnumbered them two to one.

The sight of them strolling away in a loose, casual herd let loose a shiver of fear low in his back. Cornelius knew he had been betrayed. He turned around and started to count his men with his eyes, but stopped himself. He knew the numbers and what they meant. He called for his officers and with them decided to fly in pursuit of his brother's force. There were four days between them, yes, but if they sent out swift messengers immediately and strode out at all haste they might manage to converge in less than a week. Their smaller number would speed them, anyway.

Hasdrubal's force crossed the river behind them and shadowed about a day's march behind. Occasionally over the first two days, skirmishers from the Carthaginians harassed the Roman baggage train. On the morning of the third day, one of the original messengers rode into camp on a lathered horse, a creature dead on its feet from the moment it stopped moving. The man himself had nearly lost his left hand from a sword blow to the wrist. His horse's side and his own leg were spattered with blood. Streaks of brown cut across his face where he had tried to wipe away sweat. Cornelius had received fair news from worse-looking messengers before, but the first words out of the man's mouth proved such was not the case in this instance.

The route north was alive with Numidians, he explained. They were everywhere, roaming at will. The others of his party had been lost. He had escaped only because his horse took him down a sliding gravelly slope so steep nobody would follow. They had better prepare, because the Numidians would be on them any moment.

Cornelius bent close to the man, who was now seated, having his injured arm dressed and gulping down water between sentences. "Are you sure of what you saw?" he asked. "Is it not just that the Numidians trailed behind my brother's army? If they are so close, then Gnaeus is close as well. Perhaps they are pinned between us."

The messenger shook his head. "Sir, when we met them they weren't in pursuit of your brother. They faced south. They're coming for us."

The land to the east was barren and, to the Romans, largely unknown. There were no important settlements, so the area had been largely ignored. But it was not very wide a stretch. In five days they could be at the coast; another two and they would be among allies. This was no easy choice to make. Cornelius did not know whether some catastrophe had befallen his brother. He could not tell whether pressing forward would reunite them or lead him into annihilation. All he could do was make decisions based on what he knew. His ten thousand were no match for the Carthaginian forces now. There was an army behind him, and marauding Africans in front of him. He ordered the dash for the coast.

They left behind their wagons and the camp supplies that needed to be dragged by pack animals, keeping only enough food to get them through a week. They made good time that day. They did not halt until after dark and were up again before the dawn. Cornelius demanded the strict rationing of water, but the second day took them through a terrain so parched it seemed to suck fluids mischievously from their skins and gourds. The sun perched in a cloudless sky, blistering from above, scalding as the fury of it bounced up from the sand. The heavens gave no sign that they remembered the approaching autumn and the rains the season always brought.

The third afternoon they passed through an area of cave dwellers. They were a strange people with no military might who watched the Romans from gaping black mouths in the rock. They seemed to know who was in danger here, for they showed little fear. Children clustered about the adults' legs, staring, chatting, pointing at the strange sight of a Roman army in full flight. Cornelius ordered water requisitioned from the peasants, but not a drop of the stuff could be found. How they scraped out an existence in that craggy land was a complete mystery.

On the fourth day, the Numidian cavalry attacks—which had been sporadic and light—picked up. The horsemen appeared at their sides. By midday they began to attack before the Romans. As the sun finally tilted toward the horizon, scouts brought Cornelius the worst possible news: They believed Masinissa himself directed the cavalry attacks. And to the west they had seen a cloud of dust rising from the ground, catching the red fire of the setting sun: It could only indicate a large host. Hasdrubal's troops alone could not account for such a sign. The Barca brothers' armies must have joined.

If this were so, Cornelius knew, Gnaeus might well have perished. He spent the night wrapped around this possibility and rose not having slept at all. The Numidians allowed them no peace from the moment the sun rose. They found no water that day. Instead they stumbled across dry riverbeds. In resting moments he saw men clutching their heads, their lips dry and cracking, their eyes receding into their skulls. Some of the horses refused to walk. A few collapsed from exhaustion, toppling their riders to the ground. They only needed another day, Cornelius believed. Only another day of running. But he knew as the sun fell for the fifth time that they must live through a long night before then, and the territory they had to do it in was so barren as to beggar belief.

They paused on the only feature of note on the land around them, a bald hill that fell gently in all directions, nothing more than a pimple on the landscape. The full ten thousand men barely fit on its slope. It offered none of the many things needed to build a fortified camp. There was no timber for stakes. No turf to slice and peel up to build walls. They could not even pierce the stony soil to dig a trench. The proconsul hesitated only long enough to confirm all this for himself. He looked ahead and verified that the land offered only more of the same everywhere he could see.

He formed the infantry into a circle around the hill with orders to beat off the enemy's cavalry charges, which started even as he uttered the words. Inside this barrier of men, all the others stripped saddles from mounts, packs from supply animals, gear of any and all sorts. These they tossed into a heap that formed a second line of defense. They hefted stones into place. They slaughtered fifty mules and hefted their bodies up onto the wall of debris. Soon after, they dispatched the rest as well, for what use would they be to dead men on the morrow?

By the time this was accomplished, the Carthaginian forces had appeared in their full might. They spread across the land like a river of congealing blood, their armor a hardened skin that pearled the fading glow of the carmine sky. The Numidians drew back to consult with them and Cornelius ordered his infantry inside the strange fortress. They sealed the entry. Cornelius set sentries all around the ring and had lookouts climb to vantage points to keep watch on the enemy. This having been done, a silence settled over the army. There was nothing more to do. They stood panting, grimy, so dehydrated that many of them could no longer sweat. Cornelius instructed them to rest, to share water if they had any, to keep weapons close at hand, and to remember their gods and the nation they served. They were here for noble reasons and not one of them need regret it. Not one of them need meet what was to come with anything but bravery.

The night blackened and then grew lighter as the moon rose and the stars fired to brightness. Around them was nothing but silence. Occasional wisps of African words carried on the breeze, but they gave no true indication of the sea of animosity that surrounded them. Cornelius sat on a simple stool, ringed by his officers. They spoke quietly around him. They recounted aspects of the day, pondered the night ahead, and optimistically proposed strategies for defense. But to the elder man at their center their words were children's chatter. Alone inside himself, he prayed that the Carthaginians would wait the night out. They will delay, he said silently to himself. They will rest. No army presses an attack at night. He wanted to stand on the mound and yell this to them in case they did not know it. Night maneuvers were folly. Wait till the dawn. Wait till the dawn! But even as he wished for this, he recognized that the Carthaginians would be fools not to finish them that night. And Barcas were not fools.

Cornelius tried to find some reason why the gods would have blessed the enemy so suddenly. The night marked the Nones of the Wild Fig. The day was meant to honor serving women for once defending Rome. There was nothing at all portentous in it. He had never understood the reasons behind the teetering rise and fall of Fortune, and his age had only made this stranger to him. No matter that others could always explain away success or failure. To him it had never seemed that people understood even a portion of the gods' inclinations. He had never wavered in worship, never failed to offer tribute, never let his vigilance in service wane for even a moment. So why had Fortune not been as constant toward him?

Though he had expected it, the shout when it came jarred him so much that he visibly flinched.

"There!" a sentry called. "They're coming!"

The white walls of Carthage simmered under the sun's glare, glorious, blinding, like structures cast in silver and polished to brilliance. Mago remembered how much he adored this place. He set foot once more on African ground, inhaled African air, and looked upon his countrymen. News of his arrival had preceded him. People accosted him on the street as he made his way up from the harbor. He was hugged and kissed by women, grasped and patted by men, praised and questioned by both. But he would not speak of the rumors they had heard, not just yet. The Council summoned him a few hours after his arrival, but he delayed them some time and ordered a series of crates brought up from the ship.

He sped home to his mother. In public she received him with all the dignity of her position, but inside the privacy of their grounds she hugged him to her in the manner of a mother. He did not fight against her. He told her everything he could. She heard it all, smiled and frowned as appropriate, and passed her reasoned judgment on the campaign with all the authority of an old warrior. Like Hannibal, she accepted the victories as natural enough and looked past them to how to end the war. Mago found it strange listening to her. There was a cadence in her voice that reminded him of his father. He had not noticed this before.

Sapanibal greeted him with more enthusiasm than usual. She pressed close to him and touched his face with her fingers and began to ask him details of where the campaign stood, how damaged they had been by the lack of reinforcements, what Hannibal thought of marching on Rome. . . . If Didobal was an old warrior, Sapanibal was the younger equivalent, a roiling cauldron of schemes and ideas.

Sophonisba rescued him from her. She launched herself at him as if she were still a girl, landing on him with her legs wrapped round him, pecking his face with kisses. He was as shocked by her as he was pleased. Astarte had been hard at work on this one; or was she the creation of the Greek goddess Aphrodite? She was no longer a girl, even if she played at being one. Though her brother, he recognized the stunning beauty of her face and form. His awareness of this made him instantly uneasy. Pray that war never comes to this land, he murmured on his breath.

This thought was still in his mind as he met Imilce. She alone approached him with the reserve demanded by Carthaginian decorum. She bowed before him and greeted him with praise and rose only when he begged her to do so. She asked after Hannibal demurely, matter-of-factly, as she might have inquired about the weather. He answered only in the vaguest of terms, speaking not of her husband but of the victorious commander. He certainly had no desire to speak of the damage to his brother's body, of the trials they had seen and the changes Fate had sculpted in the man. Only Hannibal himself should convey such things. Mago did slip her the scroll that his brother had entrusted to him. Of all the documents he had arrived with, this alone he hand delivered. He could see by the urgency in Imilce's eyes that she wished desperately to read it. But she did not. She only nodded acceptance of it and handed it to a servant.

When he finally presented himself to the Council, the clamor of their questions rang through the dark, smoky chamber, which was lit by the rippling, orange glow of torches. Mago did his best to quiet the men with his upraised hands. He said he had come to them bearing proof of the greatness of Hannibal's exploits, proof that he would lay before them in just a moment. First, though, he wished to recite his brother's accomplishments to make sure that all understood their magnitude. He described the geographic obstacles they had overcome. He named the battles they had fought and numbered the enemy dead from each. He said that so far Hannibal had been responsible for the death of nearly two hundred thousand Roman soldiers. He had captured and ransomed over forty thousand more, and sent countless Roman allies home to their people to sing the praises of a just Carthage. He spoke at length, saying nothing openly disparaging to the Council but letting them know that all these things had been accomplished with the most limited of resources.

He went on to outline Hannibal's plan for the continuation of the war. Let it be a multi-pronged strategy. Send reinforcements to Italy, yes, but also redouble efforts to hold Iberia, attack Sicily and win back the old allies, and send aid and support to Philip as he strove to end Roman influence in Illyria. If Carthage could keep Rome stretched thin and struggling in the outer circle, Hannibal would drive home his attack in the inner circle. He would strip the Romans of her allies one by one until she stood alone and naked among enemies. Carthage, in a year's time, would be the first nation of the world, the single greatest power, with no impediment to expanding beyond all far horizons.

When he concluded his address, one councillor, Gisgo, shouted above the others who had started to question him. Mago could not help looking to the ceiling with mild annoyance. Gisgo had been his father's enemy of old, and by the look on his thick face he was still an enemy to all things Barca.

"You talk grandly of your brother's victories," Gisgo said, "but you speak with a double tongue. If Hannibal has won such great victories, why has he not sacked Rome already? If you are to be believed, not a single man of fighting age is left in all of Italy. Does Hannibal need help in fighting women and children, then? Is it old men he's afraid of? You name victories, and then you ask for more, more, more. Explain this to me, for I am confused."

Mago's face lost none of its cool composure, although he was taken aback. He had expected some resentment in this chamber, but it amazed him that the first questions posed were so openly hostile. Hannibal was right again. They were responding just as he had assured him they would, almost as if his brother had put the words in their mouths. So many years distant, but still he knew his people perfectly.

Mago let his surprise take on the outward expression of humor. "Councillor," he said, "I'm not sure that any amount of explaining could cure your particular confusion."

"Do not insult me!" Gisgo shouted. He struggled to his feet, a difficult task for him as he was quite heavy and he bore the weakness of old injuries. "You are not a prince standing before us. Your brother is no king. Answer me with answers, not with wit. Or I will see your wit nailed to a cross!"

Other voices murmured vague approval, although few seemed pleased by the outright threat. Somebody said in a more reasonable voice that it did seem strange that a victorious general was constantly begging for assistance. Another voice, one of the younger Hannons', added, "Your brother did not ask our guidance when he began this war; why now seek our help to finish it? This war is not truly even Carthage's doing. This is Hannibal's fight, and the outcome rests on his head alone."

"Does all the glory go to him in victory then?" Mago asked.

The answer came from another section of the chamber. Hadus did not rise. He spoke softly, but somehow his voice carried all the authority it needed. "Hannibal will get what's Hannibal's," he said. "But let us not speak out of turn. You said you brought proof, young man. Show it to us."

Mago seemed to debate this a moment, but then nodded that the time was right enough. He tilted his head and projected his words high. "Honorable sirs. You are quite right. I will show you what I've brought. I'll do just that. I bring you a present from my brother, Hannibal Barca, son of Hamilcar, pride of Carthage!"

His voice rose toward the end of the sentence so that he shouted these words. This was obviously a signal, for a moment later there was a commotion in the foyer just outside the Council courtyard. Several men, slaves naked from the waist up and each of them lean and well-formed, pushed and tugged a heavily laden cart into the center of the Council. It was covered in a thick cloth that hid the contents, hinting only that it was piled high with some sort of booty. Mago paced around the cart a moment, running a hand over the cloth.

"When we report to you the greatness of our victory at Cannae I hear many questions. Some doubt the facts as have been relayed to them. Some ask for numbers, for proof, for some way that you here in the safety of Carthage can understand what Hannibal's army has accomplished in your name. But how to bring the reality of our victories from the field to this chamber? And how to name with certainty the number of enemy dead? Who but Baal knows the exact number? I've yet to count them myself, but honorable men, if you would know the number, feel free to count these, taken each from the hand of a dead Roman citizen! A gift from Hannibal and the field of Cannae!"

With theatrical grandeur Mago yanked the sheet from the wagon. Almost simultaneously, the slaves tilted it from the back. The contents poured onto the stone slabs in a clattering avalanche. At first it was hard to tell what the objects were in the unsteady light. They shimmered and bounced on the stones, rolling, skipping, and sliding. Strangely enough, it was a single item out of all those thousands that made it clear. It rolled forward away from the others, an erratic path that took it near to the councillors' benches before it turned ever so slightly and arced back. Mago, with quick fingers, snatched it up and held it aloft. It was a gold ring. One of thousands. Roman rings, so many that the sight was unbelievable.

The councillors were silent. The hush was strangely pronounced after the clattering of the rings. Mago stood beaming, watching the surprise and awe and dawning understanding on the men's faces. He forgot the sense of reserve his brother so often exemplified. He could not help himself. He grinned from ear to ear.

Nor did he stop smiling for several days, not until the Council ordered him to return to the field with a new army. But, despite all that he had revealed to them, they refused to let him return to Hannibal in Italy. Instead, they sent him to Iberia, where he could build on his brothers' successes. Hannibal, they told him, would manage without him for a little longer.

The autumn after Cannae passed in a strange, gluttonous haze, as if the battle had been some enormous festival and each living participant was left spent and reeling. The Carthaginian forces floated on a tide of euphoria, fed each week by new bits of good news. The first major Latin municipality to declare for them was Capua. Long a rival to Rome, the Campanian city had chafed in its subordination. The city turned on Rome by popular consent, but not without a certain amount of subterfuge. Given a warning that the people were turning against them, Roman officials and their supporters were tricked into gathering in the baths for security. The doors were barred and the whole lot of them were steamed to a blistered and bloated death. Afterward, their families were dragged from their homes and stoned. Thus did the people of Capua seal their union with Carthage in blood.

The terms they set out for peace with Carthage declared them the preeminent city in Italy, no longer a subject of Rome, but also outside Carthaginian jurisdiction. These were strong terms, which perhaps overreached the reasonable, but Hannibal was not inclined to look unkindly on the gift.

Other cities followed. Calatia and Atelia came over to his side. The tribes of the south revolted: the Hirpini and Lucani and Bruttii. Ligurians from the northwest agreed to fight for pay. Unlike their Gallic neighbors, these men were slight of build, quick foot soldiers and fine skirmishers who fought without armor, in woolen tunics that they wore regardless of the season. In addition to this, news issued from the north, a strange tale that was a joy to hear.

Members of the Boii tribe of Gauls had flown north from the battlefield of Cannae on triumphant wings. They had finally seen clear proof that Hannibal would deliver on his promises. They took this news to their countrymen, along with trinkets from the Roman dead, jewelry and weapons, knucklebones and teeth. It was not hard to convince the populace to rise in earnest against the Romans, who still patrolled their territory, slapping them down at every opportunity. Though the Boii were a strong, proud, and warlike tribal people they were not known for tactical insight and coordination. But they had among them an enemy they now knew could be beaten. For once, they conceived a plan of organized attack that seemed to each man so inspired as to deserve his complete devotion.

They knew that a mass of the enemy was to march on a route through a stretch of forest they called Litana. The Gauls chose a thickly wooded section for their trap. Ancient pines lined the narrow route, trees of great girth and height. The Boii went to work with axes and toothed saws. Before the Romans reached the area, hundreds of trees had been left balancing on the barest remainder of uncut wood. They looked, to the passing eye, like a forest in full growth. The Gauls set their long swords down at their feet and crouched in the ferns beside the wounded trees and waited.

Lucius Postumius led his Roman force unknowingly into this wood. He had two legions under his control, and beyond that allied troops drawn from the coast. They numbered some twenty thousand of them, so they were a long time winding their way into the wood. Once they were all in, the Gauls rose from hiding and pushed over the trees farthest from the path. They had levers prepared for this purpose and ropes attached to some, while others they just sent over with a push. One tree fell against its neighbor. Both fell against their neighbors and so on, until the two forests of falling timber met in a crosshatched confusion, the Romans caught in the center of it. Columns of wood blocked out the sky. Beams cut down men and horses and shattered wagons. The air was a wild stir of sound and leaves and dust, through which birds tried frantically to rise.

Some men managed to elude that horror and flee, but not one of these escaped alive. The Boii stood waiting. The bewildered soldiers stumbled upon them and were cut down like stuffed figures set up for their amusement. The Gauls wielded their great swords in sweeping, grandiose arcs that sliced more than one Roman head clean from the shoulders that carried it. Postumius himself was stripped and humiliated. The Boii then severed his head and peeled away the skin. They liquefied the brain and drained it out. They gilded this shell and made a ghastly drinking cup to offer libations to their gods.

Hannibal sent the Boii messengers who told this story home with new gifts and praise. Soon after, he moved the army to Capua to winter in comfort none of the men had seen in years—with luxuries that some had never experienced in all their lives: rich food pulled from the sea, flowing wine, warm beds, and women happy to pleasure them in return for portions of their battle-won riches. He released his men to roam the alleys and dens of the city, and then he withdrew to his host's villa and tried to focus on the coming year.

It was there, surrounded by sprawling opulence, that he received the news of the Scipios' demise in Iberia. And, just days later, yet another welcome envoy arrived.

Lysenthus entered the room at a brisk walk. His hair hung long and dark and his features were all as Hannibal remembered, hawk-like, strong. At seeing the commander, he stopped in his tracks and called out, "By the gods, Hannibal, you are a man of ages! Your name will not soon be forgotten. Let me not call you a man: You are a deity in the making! I bow to you and to your children and your children's children."

The Macedonian bent from the waist, then touched one knee to the ground as if he would prostrate himself. Hannibal grabbed him, pulled him upright, and embraced him. He had not planned the gesture, but the man's enthusiasm infected him instantly. The sight of him brought back memories of their last meeting—so long ago, it seemed, in the innocent days when this whole venture was just a plan, when his brothers were all around him and Bostar still among the living.

"So you are impressed, then?" he asked, grinning.

"I am, but more important, my king is. Philip hangs on any phrase that begins or ends with the name Hannibal. He believes that any such utterance is guaranteed to sound the death knell of Rome. Someone could say to him, 'Hannibal pricked his finger on a thorn,' and he would shout for joy! He would say, 'Did you hear that? Hannibal pricked his finger on a thorn; Rome is doomed!' I will tell you all the many things my king has planned, but give me drink. Commander, you would not believe the trials I've been through to reach you. Water me, and I will tell the tale."

By "water," of course, the Macedonian meant wine. Hannibal rarely drank it, but Lysenthus' thirst seemed to inspire his own. He seemed to feel completely at home in the Greek's company and sat listening to his tale with a merry glimmer in his eye.

A storm had come upon them off the Picene coast, Lysenthus said. The vessel was near to sinking, the rim of the deck sometimes dipping beneath the surface, the whole craft waterlogged. They survived only to be boarded by a patrol off Salapia, and held in that city for five days as the local magistrate tried to figure out what to make of them. Fortunately, they carried with them papers expressing Philip's sympathy for Rome's plight and his desire to be of aid. Pure nonsense, of course, but the documents reassured the magistrate and he let them go. Shortly thereafter, their ship began to take on water. In trying to get to land they ripped the hull apart on a reef and were literally tossed to shore.

"That was truly a black night," Lysenthus said. He paused to spill a bowl of wine into himself. Some of it trickled into his beard and splattered on his breastplate, but this seemed almost intentional, as if he considered a certain amount of disarray necessary to heighten enjoyment. He went on to tell of the land voyage they then embarked on, breaking up into smaller parties, wearing disguises, twice stealing horses, and once riding in the back of a merchant's wagon, often walking from sundown to dawn to get to where he now sat.

"All this to bring me here to you," Lysenthus said. "As I've said, my king is impressed. You have placed yourself in the company of the great."

"You honor me, Lysenthus of Macedon."

Lysenthus waved this away. He was only speaking the truth, he indicated. He then grew somewhat more somber, looking from his own scarred hands up at the commander's face and down again. "I see the tale I heard was true," he said. "This war has taken a piece of you. I understand such losses, friend. May Rome take nothing further . . ."

Hannibal nodded.

"To business now. I come with a proposal for a treaty between our nations. Philip wants the scourge of Roman domination removed from the Adriatic. Macedon will unite with you to defeat Rome. He will fight mostly in Greece, but he will bring the battle here also. In the spring of next year, he promises to appear on the Roman shore with two hundred ships, enough to make the Romans piss themselves."

For a moment after he took this news in, Hannibal was too pleased to respond. He saw the warships clearly in his mind's eye, and the sight quickened his pulse. The pieces of his plan were truly coming together.

Ever since she had spied Imago Messano in the conspiratorial, bare-chested company of Hadus and several of the Hannons, Sapanibal had shunned him as a traitor. He, in turn, campaigned to convince her that he was true to her and to the Barca cause. By custom, Sapanibal had almost no choice but to receive him when he called on her, which he did often, making his case with all the passion of a man arguing before the Council. Of course he spent time in the company of those base creatures! he explained. How could he not? They were of the same class. Apart from war matters, he had to conduct a whole variety of business dealings with them. A man such as he was invited to functions. More than once, he had swayed entrenched opinions while returning from a hunt or overseeing some religious ceremony. He was often at his most convincing during the late hours of the night, with his tongue loose from wine and entertainment. Imago found leverage in being on close terms with Hadus, an access to information denied those he thought of as staunch enemies. None of this changed his heart. Nor did it sacrifice any of his dignity.

Sapanibal listened to all this with narrowed eyes. He could do what he liked with whomever he liked, she responded, but he could no longer expect to receive her full trust. She could tell this indifference hurt him more than her anger. He recoiled as if from a red-hot poker. This she liked, for through such romantic torture she might just gain valued information. This was exactly what happened in the summer after the year of Cannae. Imago confided in Sapanibal a piece of clandestine news: something not yet public, and sensitive, for it undermined the newfound enthusiasm for Hannibal at home. And also, he saved the family from what she believed could have been a grave error of judgment.

They met as they had ever since Imago's alleged betrayal, not in the inner garden but on the couches in the exterior welcoming chamber, a dim, solemn place. The room had a stifling heaviness. The tall pillars stood like so many silent soldiers, the play of torchlight shifting over them, creating shadows that were ever in motion. Imago chafed at the formality with which they now met, but he accepted it with a resigned expression that yet seemed to say he would not put up with it indefinitely.

"I heard some troubling news this morning," he said. "News from Rome . . . It seems that your brother sent the cavalry officer Carthalo to the city, along with representatives of the Roman prisoners from Cannae. He was to set a price for their ransom and organize the transfer. The Senate barely deigned to receive him. When they did, they rejected all payment outright. They even forbade the men's families from buying them free themselves."

Sapanibal thought about this. She wore her hair pulled back from her face so tightly that the skin of her forehead was a smooth, taut sheet. It made her features more rigid than usual. "Clever," she finally said. "And foolish at the same time."

Imago nodded his agreement, although he seemed unsure just what she meant. "But no disgrace marks those soldiers except that they had a foolish leader who took them to slaughter. In Carthaginian tradition it's the generals who are nailed to a cross for failure, not their men. But Rome doesn't see it that way. So they deny themselves thousands of soldiers out of pure spite. They are a strange people. When Hadus hears of this he'll claim it proves Hannibal has not been very successful."

"What does he know of anything?" Sapanibal snapped. "He says black is white one moment, and white is black the next. It's his doing that Mago must go to Iberia instead of returning to Hannibal. If

I were to write my brother, I'd tell him to ask the Council for the opposite of what he desires; only then might they, in their spite, be tricked into acting reasonably."

Imago absently bit a hanging flare of fingernail and ripped it free. It was a rough gesture for a normally gentle man. He seemed to notice this. He flicked the bit of nail away and covered the offending hand with the other. "Strange that you don't pile rage on the Romans as you do upon your own."

"There's nothing I can do to affect the Roman Senate; I save my spite for targets closer to home. Is there anything else, or are we finished?"

"There's another matter, also. Perhaps more urgent . . ."

Imago inched forward until his bottom rested on the edge of the couch, his heels bouncing as if he were a boy anxious to be somewhere else. He stretched his arms out, palms upward, as if indicating that the matter in question was best transferred to a woman's hands. "It concerns your family. Your sister, to be precise . . ."

Imago hesitated, but Sapanibal said, "Proceed."

As he did, she listened from behind her tense façade, showing no sign that the story affected her except perhaps in her eyes, which seemed to want to recede into her skull. It was hard to believe what he said, but—despite her show of indifference—she knew that he would not lie to her about things that mattered.

A short time later the two moved toward the front door. Imago stepped slowly, speaking in faster time. "Sapanibal, one day I will call you *my dear Sapanibal.* I want that very badly, and I know you are too wise for me to disguise my longing. I do wish that you were not so cold to me. I am a mature man with many choices. If I choose you, it is because I find in our conversations a depth of life I've never experienced with a woman. Don't shun me forever, Sapanibal."

The two stopped walking at the edge of the courtyard. A servant stepped out of the wall—not actually, but with such a complete appearance of this as to make it a fact—and stood waiting to let the guest out. Sapanibal gave no indication that she had heard his speech. She only said, "Thank you for the news you've brought me. I'll act on it in a manner that aids the nation. Farewell."

Imago said his parting words, rehearsed phrases spoken with

emotion befitting a poet. Sapanibal's face did not crack. Nothing about her suggested the least concession to his ardor. And yet, as he moved away, she brushed her fingers across his upper arm. He turned as if to question this, but she had already begun to walk away, cursing herself for the gesture.

It was no easy work verifying Imago's story. State law and custom provided no excuse for an aristocratic woman to traffic with merchants and seamen. But she had no choice. She was not willing to allow Imago any further role in this. Nor could she entrust the task to a servant. And yet still it had to be done. She went hooded, with a bare-chested guard trailing behind her, a eunuch naked from the waist up and burdened by heavy muscles that hung loosely from his frame. She made her way down to the docks, through the crush of naked slaves, around beasts of burden hauling crates. Woven sacks sat on the stone, swelled to bursting with their burden of fish, the smell of them thick in the air.

Imago had given the time scheduled for the voyage to Capua. He named the vessel, and the captain who had accepted the unusual passengers. She asked several freedmen about the captain and finally found him. He was not an altogether unsavory sort; in fact, he had a councillor's confident bearing, a strong jaw, and a smile set off by several missing teeth. Sapanibal met him before a steaming warehouse. She did not disclose her identity, but she was confident her stature would speak for itself. She told him that the journey would not be going forward with the special passengers. She would double the price he had already received, so that his troubles would not go without reward. But for this she demanded one thing.

The ship itself was a modest vessel. Its wood glinted bone white, silvered by the cloudless days and salt spray. It was a sailing craft but also had slots for oars and rows of benches, well worn, the impression of the unfortunate rowers' backsides cut in the wood. The single chamber used to carry passengers sat at the rear of the deck, a small hut that seemed an afterthought, built of different wood, secured by large wooden pegs nailed through the planks into the deck. The captain had to jerk the door several times to open it. Inside was a tiny, dank chamber, full of stained wood, a pile of rope, and unrecognizable debris.

Seeing the look of revulsion on Sapanibal's face, the captain said, "She did not ask for much. Nor did I promise it. Stay as long as you like." He grinned, gap-toothed, and said, "But not too long. I put out in the morning. So unless you wish to find a new life at sea . . . ."

Sapanibal did not dignify that with an answer. She and the eunuch climbed inside the small chamber. She took a seat on the benchlike structure and he stood off to the side, stooped, for the roof was low. And that was it. She waited.

It was hot, stifling like the baths but foul-smelling instead of pleasant. It was clear that livestock had recently been transported aboard the ship. As her eyes adjusted she began to make out pictures drawn on the rough boards, the coarse work of men of many nations. There were several sexual images, simple drawings that differentiated male from female by exaggerating their sex organs, by their postures of submission or aggression. Why did men's minds always turn to such crudities when left ungoverned? Was a single one of them worth the power and faith women bestowed upon them?

She thought of her husband. Following so fast upon her observation, the recollection hit her with surprising force. It struck low in the abdomen, a longing akin to nostalgia. Hasdrubal the Handsome was so very different from Imago. His physical beauty was much more obvious than the councillor's: features bold and yet sharp, like shapes cut with quick swipes of a blade through smooth clay. His gifts: a quick and sinuous tongue, a smile that melted the unwary of both sexes, a mind for intrigue, a memory that stored minute facts like scrolls in a library. She had been a fool for him entirely. He could suck the very breath from her lungs with a wink.

At least, so it had been to begin with. Once their marriage was official he gave up all pretense of ardor. It was a business transaction concluded favorably. He was wed to the Barcas; that was all it meant to him. The words with which he had wooed her were barely off his lips before he turned from her. He rarely came to her at all, and when he did he fucked her quickly, with his face far from hers, as if he found her very smell repugnant. And yet she had seen him with other women many times, pleasuring in them in more ways than she could have imagined. These were far from being chance encounters: he made her watch him. He brought others to her chambers at night and woke her to laughter and moans and lewd incantations. At times he frolicked with men as well. He had all the qualities of a degenerate, but he managed to keep these entirely separate from his public responsibilities. He was ever within Hamilcar's favor. After Hamilcar's death, he carried out the revenge raids with great skill and then managed Iberia with a silver touch. Through all the petty tortures he inflicted upon Sapanibal, he kept a hold over her and never quite let go—had not let go even now, so many years after his death.

Imago Messano would never treat her as Hasdrubal had. Sapanibal knew it, and the knowledge pained her the more because she wanted badly to answer his declarations with her own. But she did not know whether she could stretch her emotions between two such different men. Try as she might, the girl inside her had yet to fall out of love with that dead lecher. She still carried the pain he caused her draped over her neck like a necklace made of a slave's chains. How could she ever look at Imago except with fear? He might carry the keys to unlock her and set her free; or he might simply wish to add more links to her burden.

She was still staring vacantly at the obscene pictures when she heard noise outside the door. She snapped upright, hands folded across her lap, legs crossed. The door opened roughly, lifted first and then swung back on its leather hinges. Blinding light flooded in. Sapanibal fought the urge to block the sun with her hand until a shape stepped into the portal and cut the glare. Imilce. Her son stood at her hip, peering in at his aunt in complete bewilderment.

Sapanibal rose and stared into the young mother's shocked face. She had had words in mind for this moment, but they sat like stones inside her. She held Imilce's gaze, conveying as much as she felt she needed to, and then she said, "Let us go now. There's nothing in this ship for us."

As she brushed past Imilce she slipped an arm over Little Hammer's shoulder and placed her palm against the flat area at the bottom of his neck. She turned him with a slight pressure and led him away, bending low to prattle with him. She felt the coldness of all this: Imilce's awful silence, the way her face drained of color, the brevity of her own words, and the fraction of time it took to pull Imilce's plans out from under her. She felt something like satisfaction. And something that was very much the opposite: the bitter joy that is the pain of seeing loved ones hurt, of knowing they suffer just as much as you.

Still, some things were necessary. Some things were for the greater good. Imilce would see her husband again after the war, but not until then, on his terms and not on hers. A wife could not go to her husband during war; he could only return or not return to her. Imilce would accept this eventually.

Publius Scipio first heard the announcement of his father's and uncle's deaths in the Senate, surrounded by hundreds of eyes that turned to study him. There had been such confusion in Iberia and so much preoccupation in Rome that the news took many months to reach them. He wanted to jump from his bench and grab the messenger by the throat, call him a liar, and demand that he prove the death he had just proclaimed. But he would have disgraced his father with such a show. He had no choice but to set his jaw and listen unflinchingly. He fought to make sure his face betrayed no inkling of his emotions, and then to stand and lead the chamber in remembering the two men.

Later, alone in his father's home, he dropped to his knees in the center of the atrium and clasped his head in his hands and wept. Waxen images of his prominent ancestors hung on the walls around him. The faces were hidden behind the façades of miniature temples, each etched with inscriptions detailing their achievements: offices held, honors won. The last time he had seen his father they met in just this spot. Cornelius, for some reason, had spoken of Publius' mother, who had been dead for as many years as her son had lived. Cornelius said that that woman was still precious to him. His love for her had been undignified, far beyond the terms of their marriage contract. He had adored her like some Greek poet his muse. Should she have lived, he might well have become an absurd creature. Senators would have called him effeminate, too much a slave to a woman's love. And they would have been right. Perhaps that was why Fortune took her from him on the day she gave him a son.

"But don't look at me like that," Cornelius had said. "You're too old to despair over such things. Your mother wanted you born, so much so that when the birth went wrong she begged the surgeon to cut her open and bring you forth. Our lives are only passing events. The things we do or fail to do are not ours to own; they belong to the honor of the family. Perhaps the gods will see fit to allow me to return to this home again. But perhaps not. This is not for me to say. So I must remind you that all I am, all I have accomplished, I pass on to you. In your turn, you must add to our glory and pass the spirit of the Scipios on to your sons. We are all links in a chain. Be as strong a link as I know you can be, and raise your sons to be even stronger."

To think of this speech now troubled Publius. His father had been speaking to him as if from beyond the grave, and from now on he always would. He could not find fault with the sentiments Cornelius had spoken. Indeed, it gave him pride to remember them. They lodged at his center beside his unshakable faith in the right of Rome. And yet something about the sincerity of his father's declarations shamed him. He did not know whether he could live up to them. He did not know that he was yet worthy of the man who had been his father. He could not say for certain that his path in life had thus far proved the man's faith well founded.

Recruiting and training new troops kept him in Rome, though he had pleaded to return to the field. All day long he focused his mind on war. He marched the new soldiers—farmers and slaves, tradesmen and merchants—through the midday swelter. He pored over chronicles of earlier wars. He interviewed those who had already suffered from Hannibal's cunning stratagems, absorbing what he heard, taking it in and reworking it, digesting it, making it part of the fabric of his consciousness. He largely kept his opinions to himself as yet, but he inquired much of others and listened to any man with a mouth willing to use it. He set about studying Carthage itself. And he meditated long and hard on the man: Hannibal. No man could be unbeatable, Publius believed. No man. Not even the gods were without weaknesses. He was fond of things Greek, had been since he first bloomed into early manhood. He thought of Homer's aged tale of Achilles. Splendid, beautiful, peerless warrior that he was, even he possessed a weakness. Hannibal must, as well. He must.

Submerged so fully in martial matters, he often drilled his men well past the ninth hour without knowing it. He would find the midafternoon sun slanting into remission, shadows lengthening, men staring at him with veiled questions behind their eyes. More than once his lieutenant had to pull him aside and remind him of the time of day. Even in wartime, he was reminded, a Roman must still be a Roman. He should not forget the day's divisions: the portions of the day set aside for work, and those for leisure.

Waking from the world of his thoughts, Publius was always surprised that the normal workings of Roman life went on undisturbed. Strolling into the Forum in the early evening, head full of military violence, he would look up to find his countrymen's faces turned congenial. Though he invariably wore his toga, the people of the night dressed in bright tunics, reds and yellows and blues, garments embroidered with gold, the hooded cloaks that were the fashion that summer. Perhaps it was the freedwomen who took the most pleasure from these pageants, widows who eyed the limbs and torsos and backsides of young men and giggled like girls with their servants. The air was alive with sounds of merriment, with storytellers plying their trade, with the smells of roasted sausages and fragrant honey cakes. And after all this, the evening meal, the cena, tempted everyone to give in to food and wine and rest.

Most evenings Publius ate reclining, talking quietly with his companion, Laelius. He took joy in these moments, but it was a strange joy. Laelius was the only person he could confide his sadness to. He found it hard to understand how people could go on seeking small pleasures. Were they so forgetful? Were they deceived or overly proud? Or was there a testament to the Roman spirit in this? People had no choice but to live until they died. So it always had been. Perhaps the children of Rome, the prostitutes and lusty matrons and wine-soaked senators, knew this better than he. Perhaps there was wisdom in what seemed like folly.

Even if this were true, there were other moves afoot that Publius could not find virtue in. Terentius Varro still commanded the Senate's respect. No man in history was responsible for the death of more brave Romans than he, and yet few seemed to notice this. Publius bore him no unfair ill will, but he did fear that Rome would not learn from the man's blunders unless they recognized them as such and said so publicly.

On the other hand, aspersion after insult after curse was thrown upon the thousands who had surrendered to Hannibal at Cannae. They were seen as so disgraced that the Senate refused the ransom Hannibal demanded and forbade the men's relatives from paying the sum themselves. Better that they should languish in the enemy's hands. Publius—who had only just escaped disgrace himself—bridled at the insult to those men. Never before had so many soldiers been abandoned by the state.

Eventually, most of them trickled home. Hannibal gained nothing from them monetarily, so he released them and set them walking through a country that no longer wished to claim them. Many considered it an insane gesture, but Publius saw reason in it in terms of striking blows at the nation's heart. On the other hand, he despised the Senate's reaction. They sent the bulk of the men to Sicily, to serve Rome's cause on foreign soil, where the sight of them need not offend the eye. Surely this was madness. Publius, imagining the men's shame, knew that they would make valiant fighters yet. Who more than they had cause to prove themselves? And Publius knew that any survivor of Cannae had stared a particular horror in the face, a vision of hell unlike anything in living memory. This bound them together and made them special, even if other men's petty understandings suggested otherwise.

In the Senate, on the Ides of the new year, he rose to speak. He invoked his father's presence and asked for his blessing on what he was about to propose. And then he said out loud, "My countrymen, if ever you valued my father and called him and his brother heroes of the nation, then give me what I ask of you now. Let me go to Iberia and take up my father's command. The Scipios left their task unfinished there, and I would dearly love to see it through."

The chamber was silent for some time. Then, gradually, various senators posed questions. A few debated the issue of Publius' youth. Still others suggested that he need not sacrifice himself out of mourning. The truth was that with several enemy armies roaming Iberia some in the Senate were whispering that they should write the place off for the time being. But this was just talk. In the end, the senators, knowing that no one else wanted the assignment, acquiesced to the young man's wishes. He would not have a great army. He would not have the full resources of the state. And the task was formidable. But if he wanted it . . .

Sapanibal never spoke a word to Imilce about her attempt to sail to Italy. She never explained how she found out about her plan, never chastised her for the foolishness of it. To Imilce, this silence became an even greater admonishment. Hers had been too absurd an idea even to merit reproach. She could not explain it herself. It had just come upon her suddenly: the knowledge that Hannibal wintered near Capua, the desire to fly to him. What might she have found, arriving unannounced in some foreign port? Would Hannibal have welcomed her? Would he even have recognized her, or she him? And what if she had been captured by the enemy?

She still believed Sapanibal a coldhearted creature, but with each passing day Imilce felt herself more and more in her sister-in-law's debt. One of the strange things about the family she had married into was that there was something about each of them that made Imilce crave their approval. This was not usual for her. Most people, she had learned long ago, are not worthy to judge others. She had found that many wore their avarice in the motion of their hands, their lust in the pout of their lips, their insecurities on their tongues, their petty minds behind the flutter of their eyelids. Not so with Barcas. Each was an island of stillness to her. Sapanibal had taken inside herself the discipline of her family name and demonstrated it in the only ways possible for a woman of their class. Even Sophonisba—for all her chatter and gossiping—contained strength unusual for her age. And Didobal awed Imilce with every motion: every word said or not said, each gesture, the placement of her gaze and the tilt of her head and the flare of her nostrils in breathing. Their encounters were tense affairs, during which the matriarch rarely uttered more than the polite minimum.

In the mild, damp weather of early spring, Imilce earned the honor of braiding the older woman's hair. She had been in training for this throughout her time in Carthage. The intricacy of Carthaginian headdresses was wholly new to her, influenced, she heard, by the ways of people far to the south. On odd days of the week, she met Didobal in her quarters, in a small chamber whose walls were hung with layer upon layer of colorful cloth. The room was always warm, heady with incense and full of threat. Oil lamps stood on stands all around the floor: tiny flames, but so many that they gave off an almost even light. Imilce once singed her gown negotiating them. Another time she knocked two over with a single misstep. Servants dashed in with wet blankets to squelch the fire. Didobal did not comment on either incident.

One morning, weeks after her aborted journey, Imilce ran her fingers from the top of the woman's head down through her tresses. Didobal's hair was thick in her fingers, dark and heavy. It did not fall limply around her, but had a wavy, tensile strength in each strand. Imilce combed the hair into strips measured by fingers. With the aid of an assistant, she began to treat them separately. Some she sprinkled with an oil fragrant with cinnamon. Into others she combed dust flecks of silver. Still others she bound in ribbons of seaweed. Today she was to fashion her mother-in-law's hair in imitation of a certain bust of Elissa, a design of tight plaits low across the back of the head, building a platform into which to set the gold headpiece that would anchor two great curving horns of hair.

As happened too often, Imilce found herself speaking to fill the nervous silence. Words issued from her mouth of their own accord: an observation about the rising level of water in the cisterns, a recollection of her dream from the previous evening, a question—which went unanswered—about the fate of Tanit's veil, that holy relic so beloved of the goddess. And then, without knowing she was about to say it, she commented on the pain of being separated from her husband for so long. It was unfair, she said, that he fought so far away that he could not return for the winter as most soldiers had throughout history.

Didobal cleared her throat. She touched her assistant with her eyes. The girl stepped back, turned, and moved away. The other servants followed suit. They retreated into the folds of fabric on the walls; their faces went blank, eyes glazed and unfocused, still as statues. All this, Didobal accomplished with a single look. Imilce feared the woman was about to dismiss her, but instead she asked, "You feel a great passion for my son?"

"Yes," Imilce said.

"Such as few women feel for their husbands?"

"I don't know what other women feel, but I think of him always."

"By your tone, you suggest that I know nothing of this. Do you think you are the only one who has loved her husband almost to foolishness?"

"No. No, I did not mean . . ."

"I did not know what to make of you when we first met," Didobal said. "I did not trust you. Forgive me, but it's hard for a mother to watch his son give his affection to another woman. A mother always feels that she came first: the first womb, the first breast between their teeth, the first unreasoning love . . ."

The woman turned her head slowly, tugging the thick braids from Imilce's hands. Her eyes were large, the whites slightly yellowed, deep-veined and very dark in the iris, a brown that at the moment looked solid black. She said, "I'm sure you understand this."

She turned back and again showed the younger woman her face in profile. "Because of this I couldn't help but receive you warily," she continued. "I had you watched. It's shameful—but, Imilce, you have hardly done a thing while in Carthage that I did not know of minutes later. Why did I do this? Because a person proves who they are not with their mouth but through the accumulation of actions over time. Were you in my household purely for our riches? Did you care for the fate of your husband, and did you honor his people's traditions in your secret moments? Did you partake in the diversions this city offers even to women of our class? Did you simper and smile beneath the gazes of powerful men? Forgive me, but I had many anxieties."

Throughout this discourse Imilce attempted to carry on with her work. She set pins to keep the lower plaits in place. Then she picked up an ivory comb to work on the mass of higher hair, somewhat wild now, chaotic compared to the close weave at the back of the neck. But she slowed down as Didobal spoke and, eventually, stood with the comb in hand, held out to the side, inlaid pearls pressed tight between her white fingers. What a set of questions, Imilce thought. For all the world at that moment she could not imagine the answers the woman might have received. She had been watched! All this time . . . In a strange way it made sense. It explained much of her discomfiture. All this time . . .

"Hamilcar was as hard not to love as Hannibal now is," Didobal said. "They are of the same mold, those two. We who live near to their fire are as blessed as we are cursed. It seems also that you and I are not so different as we seem. During the Mercenary War, I couldn't bear to be separated from my husband. I did what you— with greater wisdom—did not do. I followed him into the desert when he chased the mercenaries away. I caught up with him two days after the battle at Leptis Minor. He was victorious, but never had I seen him so, caked in blood and filth, eyes reddened and skin peeling from him as if he'd been burned. I expected him to be angry, and I was afraid, but he said not a word of reproach. Instead he took me as he never had before, like a lion, growling at me. His passion was beyond words and he did not speak to me through the act at all. He did me no kindness, left me red with the stains of war.

"It was horrible, Imilce, but I thought, that night, that if this was my husband's ardor on campaign, then it was well I should be there, for who but me should receive him like that? The next day he took me by the hand and led me over the ridge and down into the valley where they had fought. He showed me the battlefield. He walked me through the high-piled mounds of bodies. Imilce, it was a sight you should never wish to see. Three days in the heat, and the bloated bodies belched gases and shivered as if life still resided in them and came to them in spasms. Some burst as if boiled too long. They sent up the foulest of scents. Scavenging birds blackened the sky, long-necked creatures that flew in from all directions, bald demons.

"And that was just the beginning. I spent the week at my husband's side. He made me watch everything. They spent days tilting up crosses to crucify the captured leaders. Other prisoners they set free without their hands. Some had their feet severed at the ankles and were left to fight off the hyenas. Others they blinded and sliced out their tongues, cut off their manhood, fed live to captured lions. The war had been brutal beyond imagining, and Hamilcar—my husband—answered earlier barbarities in kind. All these years later, these sights are as alive in me as they are real somewhere. Somewhere in this war such scenes are being repeated. The men we love are their architects, or their victims. That is why I chose never to trouble my husband again. I left him to his work, not as a sacrifice, but because I hated the way it made me look at him. I hated—and never understood—how such a man could perform such horrors. Because of this I spent the larger part of my married life away from him. I loved him; and therefore I could barely stand to be with him.

"I'm not sure if this makes sense to you, but do not seek the ways of war, Imilce. Do not wish to understand it. Take your husband in his quiet moments, when he's in your arms and when he looks upon your child with love. You must do this, for if you know too much of a warrior's work you'll grow to hate him. And I would never have you doubt my son."

"Nor would I," Imilce whispered.

"Then hold on to your ignorance. Men's follies are better left as mysteries to us."

"Do you think it is all for nothing?"

"All for nothing?" Didobal pursed her lips. "No, I wouldn't say that. The world thrives on the strife of those living in it. As food nourishes the body, so does turmoil feed the gods. One creature must prevail over another. I would not wish our country to be used like a slave woman, so I pray daily for our victory. What else can we do? On the day this war ends, a new one will begin. It's dreadful, but so it always has been. There is no reason to believe it will change."

"So we can never live at peace?"

Didobal answered flatly, "Not until the gods are dead. And as we both know, they are immortal. The gods will ever make us dance for them. That is what it means to be born of flesh. In truth, Imilce, I feel the gods are restless with this war. I do not know what will happen, but it's coming quickly, like a storm from the north. Like a tempest blown down from the heavens. Let us keep all of my sons in our prayers."

Didobal lifted her arm and held her hand out to her daughter-in-law. Imilce took it and felt the woman squeeze her fingers, her regal hand heavy with rings. Something in the pressure made her feel like a child holding a giant's hand. "Forgive my earlier deception," Didobal said. "I like you very much, daughter."

Publius sailed from Ostia at the head of a fleet, carrying ten thousand infantrymen and another thousand cavalry, the full measure that Rome allowed him for the year. Barely had his men's feet touched solid ground at Emporiae when he had them exercising to regain the strength the journey had sapped from them. He gathered the battered remnants of the existing army and with them left behind the distractions of the Greek city. They marched to Tarraco, where Publius set up his headquarters and began interviewing anyone and everyone with knowledge he considered useful. He had never been busier. He had never directed so many men, faced such challenges, held such complete responsibility. He knew Rome was too far away to rely on for any guidance, so Iberia was his to win or lose. Only the constant motion kept him from pausing long enough to weigh the staggering gravity of this.

Within seven days, he had sent out invitations to all the tribes aligned with Rome already, and even to a few still with Carthage. The delegations came to him with varying degrees of enthusiasm, with more complaints than promises, with wary eyes that took in this youthful new leader skeptically. Was this truly the best Rome could do, to send a boy with barely a hair on his chest? What could he hope to achieve that his father and uncle had not, especially now that the situation was even worse? Cornelius and Gnaeus had been skilled commanders with years of experience, two armies, and a force of allies it had taken years to win. But they had been destroyed. Now, with Mago Barca having arrived over the winter, the Carthaginians had three armies in Iberia. They roiled across the land, storm clouds hurling down bolts of retribution for earlier betrayals. Hanno had hammered the chieftain of the Vaccaei to a cross and sent five hundred of his people's daughters to New Carthage as prisoners. Hasdrubal burned a scorched path along the river Tagus all the way to the Great Sea, enslaving whole tribes, burning villages, twisting their leaders on the burning spit of fright as only Carthaginians knew how to do. Mago laid new levies on the southern tribes and daily built his army into a great horde clamoring to become the second wave to march for Rome. Considering all this, more than one envoy asked, what assurance could Publius give that Rome's cause was not dead and rotten like the corpses of his predecessors?

Strangely, Publius found something calming about staring into these belligerent eyes. As the translators conveyed their messages he took in their foreign features, their varying dress and demeanor. The more disrespect the Iberians showed him, the stronger the set of his jaw, the more steady his gaze, the more fluid the motions of his hands. He promised nothing in exact detail, he said, for no one individual ever decided such complex matters. But he did pledge to fight the Carthaginians as they had never been fought before. He reminded them that never yet had Rome uttered one conciliatory word to the Africans; such was their certainty that the long war would eventually swing their way. They had made mistakes. They had been hasty when they should have been patient, honest when they should have been devious, restrained when they should have exploded with fury. In many ways, they had fought the war unwisely up to this point. Yes, he admitted, even his father had made errors of judgment, but none of these need be repeated.

These speeches met with mixed receptions, but each time he spoke them Publius believed his words a little more. He was discovering traits in himself that he had not known before, but he had little time to pause and consider these things. Laelius, like a twin beside him, did not speak a thought not directly related to the war, so he did not do so either. He trusted no other officer as completely as he did his companion. With him alone, he laid out all the charts and information he had about Iberia. On their hands and knees, they crawled across the marble floor, talking through each piece of information, from the obvious to the most complex. They both believed that they must strike, and soon. They could rely on no reinforcements from Italy and, for all they knew, Hannibal might soon strike another great blow there that would further complicate matters for them. They could win the confidence of old allies and secure new ones only through a victory. A winner always had company.

Such was Publius' thinking on an afternoon two months after his arrival, well into the dry heat of early summer. His period of grace with his men was short. Already he felt them murmuring their doubts. Each passing day suggested hesitation. Had this new commander any plan at all? The truth was that he did not, but he woke and slept and ate and shat with the belief that he was at the verge of revelation, that the key to unlocking Iberia was within his grasp if he just knew how to reach for it.

He entered his war room to find Laelius stretched out atop the charts, writing notes directly onto the parchment. His body covered the circles that marked the three Carthaginian armies. His left ankle hid Hasdrubal's base at the mouth of the Tagus; his right foot lay flat across the Pillars of Hercules, where Mago resided; his torso entirely covered the center of the peninsula, where Hanno based his operations. The single marked spot of importance that was visible fell in another area entirely, one that suddenly appeared to Publius as what it was: completely isolated, lightly protected, vulnerable.

"We've been thinking only of the hounds, but not of the sheep they guard," Publius said. "Laelius, what do you see when you look at this from on high?"

Laelius stood and peered about. He began by restating his earlier argument that they should seek out Hanno's force first, as he was reportedly having trouble managing his Celtiberian troops. "We could gather at—"

Publius touched him at the wrist. "Friend, think. Remember when you saved me at Cannae? You raised my outlook so that I saw with my enemy's eyes. I learned from you that day, and I'm alive because of it. Now you must use such foresight as a matter of course, each day that passes, each moment until this is concluded. The Barcas don't fight like normal men, and neither will we. Look at these charts and answer me. What is the weak point? What holds all of this together and yet lies exposed?"

It took Laelius only a moment to grasp Publius' meaning. His face shifted from perplexity to mute understanding, and then the left corner of his lips lifted.

When they departed for the south a fortnight later, they traveled in haste, troops marching double time, Laelius and the ships shadowing them offshore, cavalry riding out in small units, hunting any who might betray their movements. Publius had yet to reveal their goal to any but a select few, no more than the fingers on a hand. He was so intent on secrecy that he refused to tell the twenty thousand men of his army anything more than necessary to get them through the day. If his plans for Iberia were to succeed, this first effort must not fail. He left nothing to chance, but this did not stop him from mingling with the men daily. He rode up beside his troops during marches and harangued them from the saddle. Everything was about to change, he declared. The gods themselves had told him so. Never again would they make small war in Iberia. Never would they fight skirmishes for no real gain. Never would they divide their forces and rely so heavily on Iberian honor. They would strike only decisive blows, well timed, perfectly placed, and so effective that the brothers Barca could not recover even from the first attack. Hannibal might have rewritten the rules of warfare; now it was their turn to take up the stylus and inscribe the rest of this history.

They marched around Acra Leuce without a sideways glance, forded the river Segura, and strode out onto the cape of Palus. There were seven days like this, but still they were each of them stunned when they caught their first glimpse of the city. None of them believed it a reasonable destination, so they sought some other explanation for why their route took them close to it. More than one of them sat down to behold the madness that had brought them to the teeth of the enemy's maw. They had marched to New Carthage.

Their arrival caught the inhabitants by complete surprise. Shepherds rose up from drowsing no more than a stone's throw from the advance guard. It took them only a glance to know that these troops were not their own. They ran, but not one of them escaped the cavalry's darts. Slaves looked up from the near fields and dropped their work where they stood. Soon the watchtower sounded a great horn that drew everyone into the city like rabbits scurrying to their burrows. Just before the gates slammed shut, a band of six horsemen galloped out. Messengers. Each curved off in a different direction, gone to cry warning to the Barcas. Publius quietly ordered patrols to fly out after them, with simple orders:

"Hunt and kill them," he said. "Let none of them get through."

That evening they camped at the base of the isthmus and Publius spoke to his assembled troops. "The city behind us stands as the greatest monument to the rule of the Carthaginians in Iberia," he said. "Out of it flows all the wealth of the continent; into it, the desires of its far-reaching masters. Inside are whole chambers piled high with silver, with amber and gold, storerooms of weapons and siege engines, warehouses of raw iron and the great furnaces that fire it into tools of war. Inside stretch palaces worked by servants, fountains that flow with wine on festival days, temples where they sacrifice to their dark gods, and an ancient wood filled with exotic animals imported from Africa. There are many thousands locked within those walls, but there are merchants and sailors and aristocrats, priests and magistrates, Iberian prisoners, slaves, the old, the young—not fighting men. And there are women, a great many of them. Isn't Hasdrubal himself rumored to keep a court of a thousand beauties?"

Publius had made up this last detail on the spot but enjoyed the effect it caused and spoke into the building enthusiasm. "All this inside that city," he said. "But who protects it? I'll tell you—a scant thousand soldiers. Yes, one thousand alone. This may seem impossible to you, but consider their thinking. They'd never have imagined that we'd aim for this target, just as many of you never did. They've been safe here and taken their destruction elsewhere for so long that they do not see their vulnerability. They're like Achilles, who had only a single weakness but went to war with it exposed to his enemy's arrows. Where is the wisdom in that? Why not fashion greaves to cover the spot, and therefore become invincible? There is, of course, one reason. We're not alone in our struggles here but act on the small stage overseen by the gods, and the gods have never yet allowed any single people perfection. I believe that Apollo offers us this city as a gift. Tell me this is not so. Tell me you do not care to dine!"

Laelius later commented that Publius had a growing gift for oratory. To which the commander smiled and said that Laelius had a growing knack for noting the obvious.

They were two days at planning and shifting troops and reconnoitering the land and outer bay, the reefs in the shallow water, and the breathing of the tides into and out of the inner harbor. Publius spent the whole of the second day alone with a fisherman who had once called New Carthage home but had fallen foul of a few important people and been cast out. He had reason to despise the city, and an intimate knowledge of details Publius was very interested in.

The attack began on the fourth morning, much as any might have guessed. The bulk of the Roman troops rose early and clamored out onto the isthmus, laden with tall ladders. They walked forward flanked by archers who set up a steady barrage of arrows, many of these set aflame and aimed far beyond the walls themselves. A detachment from the city poured out the front gate to meet them, but pulled back just as quickly, no match for what they saw coming toward them. Publius strode with the front ranks of soldiers, protected by three shield bearers and to all appearances completely unafraid. He urged his men on from right in among them. He shouted reminders of their duty, but also fed their desire for revenge. It was in this city that Hannibal had grown into a man. Here he planned the murder of Roman men, the rape of Roman women, the conquest of their homeland . . . it was inside these very walls that he had dreamed of making them all into slaves!

The citizens of the city, however, had no intentions of making this easy. What they lacked in soldiers they made up for by enlisting all able bodies. Over the walls they tilted giant logs that wiped whole ladders clean. They dropped rocks the size of ostrich eggs, heavy enough to dent helmets, knock men unconscious, crush fingers, snap limbs, and dislocate shoulders so that men clung to the ladder one-armed, howling with pain and able neither to ascend nor to retreat. The walls themselves were smooth and in many places taller than the ladders placed against them, a fact that some of the anxious soldiers only discovered at their upper reaches. Other ladders snapped under the attackers' weight and crashed down in a jumble of fractured wood and broken bodies.

The defense of New Carthage was furious. If not for Publius' presence, his men might well have broken. Few of them believed they could win the city this way—but that was not their young commander's intention. What none of them knew was that as soon as the frontal attack began, Laelius with several ships had entered the harbor. The transports maneuvered as close as they could to the shallow shelf of rock and coral that distinguished the bay from the open current of the sea. The boats perched on the vast blue water, but next to it the men could see the stones they were meant to walk upon, clearly visible and solid, but submerged almost to a man's height in water. Laelius shouted his orders, but for some moments the soldiers did not understand the apparent madness of what was being asked of them. They knew they were meant to be the first inside the city, but they knew no more than that.

As the boats pitched on the swells, the captains added their voices to Laelius' and got the men off quickly, for the rocks threatened to gouge in the hull and end this for all of them at any moment. Few of them could swim, so it was an act of faith or courage or—for some—resignation to step from the boat, falling through the stilled oars, splashing down into the water, heavy in their armor. They fought to keep their heads above the surface. Some fell into depressions and dropped their weapons and clawed at the feet of their companions until they were lifted up. Two of their number were unfortunate, jumping at the wrong moment in the boat's pitch and missing the rocks. They slipped into the depths, clawing for purchase on the water, fading into the blue until they were swallowed by the color and lost. More than one imagined the jaws of some beast rising up from the depths beneath the boat and clamping down on them, and many would say afterward that the hardest part of the day had been that first hour of waiting.

The last objects off the boats were a few ladders, tossed atop the men's heads by the anxious crew. What they were supposed to scale with these, they could not say. They were not near the city at all. It sat some distance away, protected by a long stretch of water, most of it too deep to walk. Somebody whispered that perhaps Publius had placed them here as an offering to Poseidon. He said it as a joke, but none of those who heard him laughed.

When the change came it was with a shift of the wind, so that it seemed a divine force was involved. Gusts of air whipped across the water, blowing spray into the soldiers' faces, causing them to turn away and shade their eyes. They looked up only in short glances but these put together created an accelerated version of events. They felt the water draining from around them, the tug hard enough that they had to lean forward to maintain their balance. The tide was shifting. Rocks soon projected into the air, round heads of coral draped in translucent sea grass. Soon whole stretches lay bare to the sun, a path bridging the distance to the city, dotted with shallow pools alive with crabs and tiny fish that the men kicked out of the way as they scrambled forward, slipping and unsure but growing confident with each step.

Laelius mounted the wall at the top of the first ladder and stood gazing at the city before him. No one opposed them. No one even imagined them. Men clambered by him on either side. They finally understood it all and moved with grunting hunger, with a thirst for vengeance they had not felt just moments before.

The city was theirs within a bloody hour.

Hannibal's spies in Rome kept him remarkably well apprised of events in the city's distant chambers. There was a delay of a few weeks as the news traveled to him, but he learned quickly enough that the consular elections had brought Tiberius Gracchus and Claudius Marcellus to power. Because he was a veteran warrior known for his steadfast martial outlook, many believed Marcellus to be the coming man of this war. But Fabius Maximus, a greater power than ever now that his whole philosophy of avoidance had been justified, disagreed. He found a technical error in the elections and had Marcellus dismissed. Fabius was then kind enough to step into the post himself and proceed to restore reason and purpose to the populace.

Under him the course was set for the coming year. Of generals in command of their own armies there would be several: Tiberius Gracchus, of course, alongside Claudius Marcellus, Quintus Crispinus, Livius Salinator, and Claudius Nero. The Senate doubled the war tax. Call-ups went into effect with the goal of creating twenty-five legions in the coming years. Rome's leaders strove to make every available man into a warrior. They told boy-children to early put away knucklebones; they should pick up sword and shield instead. The age of enlistment was lowered to seventeen years, but many even younger than that found their way into the newly formed legions. The city bought eight thousand slaves from their owners at public expense. They were armed and set to training. Temples and private homes were stripped of ornamental weapons, of souvenirs from past wars; these trinkets returned to their original function. Nothing would be the same in Rome again, the spies reported. Cannae had changed everything in an afternoon.

Hannibal heard this news with a mixture of pride and reservation. He imagined the delight his father would have felt to know that his son's victory had set the people of Rome trembling. Such had been his aim, and now it was achieved. On the other hand, he could not help but wonder what lay behind the Romans' strategy. He had thought they might revert to avoiding combat as under Fabius, but instead they were investing in an even more colossal army. He still welcomed this, but it was disconcerting to hear that they could produce such numbers so quickly. They had set a goal that meant they believed they could create one hundred and twenty-five thousand fighting men from nothing, just like that. If this was true, then slaughter was not as effective against them as one would think.

And how were they managing to pay for this? Hannibal knew that the death of so many citizens must have cut Rome's wealth significantly. The destruction of field after field, farms and supplies and surpluses, would have brought lesser nations to their knees. Husbandless families surely struggled to keep their farms and businesses going; their daily lives must be a misery in a variety of ways. He listened for signs that a heavier tax burden was being levied on the allies, but if it was, they accepted it and did not think of revolt. Though Hannibal struggled with doubts upon waking each morning, he held fast to his belief that he had been correct in his actions after Cannae. The Romans' continued stubbornness proved that they would not have surrendered the city if he had marched on it.

As the new year began it took some effort to drag the men away from the gluttonous bounty of Capua. He prodded them on with promises of even greater things to come. He sent Bomilcar with ten thousand men to patrol the southern cities, to recruit troops and generally solidify the Carthaginian presence there. Then he turned the rest of the army west and moved into Campania, hoping to press his advantage further by bringing more cities to his side early. He chose as his first target Neapolis, important enough that her defection would do much to influence others along the coast. And she had a beautiful harbor, well situated to serve as a funnel through which to bring in reinforcements from Carthage. He approached her with a thronging army of veterans at his back, but he had every intention of offering the city peace on fair terms. Why should they fight, he would ask, when they were not enemies? Indeed, the truth was that they had a common foe: Rome. Hannibal planned to point out to the Neapolitans that nothing in his actions so far belied this. Had he ever attacked a city that welcomed him? Had he not spared allied prisoners and released them time and again to fly home to their cities? Had Rome ever treated them with the mildness that Carthage displayed?

The Neapolitans, in their pride, did not even bend an ear to hear him pose these questions. They sent the full power of their cavalry out on the offensive. A foolish move. Maharbal ambushed, routed, and massacred them in a single day. But still, when Hannibal set his gaze upon the city, its gates were locked. The towers and walls bristled with defenders. They would not hear the envoys he sent bearing terms for peace. Instead they threw down all manner of missiles, tossed stones, and even slung bags of rotten fish.

Monomachus argued that an all-out siege was in order, a punishing, rapacious slaughter to answer this haughty belligerence. Hannibal dismissed the suggestion with a gesture. Taking the city by force was no way to endear the people to them, he said. It would unify others against them. Better to let time do the work. The Neapolitans simply needed to let the meaning of Cannae sink in. They were in shock and had yet to sort out the new order of things. Also, the Carthaginians had no siege equipment.

Monomachus said that such things could be constructed. Adherbal was still on hand, with no projects to test his skill. Within a few weeks they could be pounding Neapolis' walls to rubble. But these arguments did not convince the commander. They controlled Italy through mobility, he said. To tie themselves to a siege made them a sitting target. Instead he ordered a withdrawal and marched on Puteoli. He had some success with securing a large part of the city, but he failed to take the port—his whole objective—and gave up the attempt for the time being. He sent Monomachus before the main body of the army to ravage the territory around Neapolis. Then he darted quickly toward Nola, whence he heard rumors that he might be warmly received.

On his arrival, however, he learned that the proconsul Claudius Marcellus had beaten him to the city. Hannibal knew Claudius' name well enough, although this was their first encounter. As a young officer, Marcellus had fought against Hamilcar in Iberia. Later he commanded campaigns in Gaul. His record was as varied as that of any man at the mercy of fate, but as a soldier he seemed steadfast and resourceful enough. Like Fabius, he was no fool; unlike Fabius, he was a man of the blade, as Hannibal soon learned.

Even with the Roman legion garrisoning the town, an embassy from citizens friendly to Hannibal still managed to slip out of the city, bearing messages of continued support. Grimulus, the leader of the group, even came up with a plan: They would bar the gates of the city behind the Roman army if ever the bulk of it could be enticed out to battle. Then, trapped against the walls, they could be butchered at Hannibal's leisure, with no retreat or source of support. It was a simple plan, base and devious, the kind of plot the Romans had never mastered. Grimulus—standing beside Hannibal, narrow-shouldered, with eyes shadowed beneath a gnarled outcrop of brow—positively salivated at the proposal and the turn of fortune he believed it would offer him. Hannibal did not care for the man, who took too much pleasure in betraying his city. But the plan had its merits.

For several days after coming to agreement with Grimulus, Hannibal arrayed his army and offered Marcellus battle. He simply drew his forces up into ranks and announced via his horns that he would happily wait while the Romans came out and formed up. It was a traditional enough gesture, an enticement that often proved too great for an ambitious general to pass up. But the gates stood dumb, immobile, like a child who purses his lips to keep from revealing a secret. The soldiers clung to their posts on the towers, looking down but not tempted to action.

Two days passed in this standoff. On the morning of the third day, Hannibal decided to press the issue, stir the reluctant soldiers into motion, goad them to act in some way, any way. He ordered Mono-machus to advance behind a screen of light troops. The Balearic slingers in particular seemed to view this assignment as sport. They unwrapped their mid-range slings from their foreheads and set them with stones. This load was heavy and unwieldy, but given room the men managed to whirl their weapons into motion. They picked out individual targets as they approached and set the stones hurling through the air as hard and fast as from a light catapult. The whole army could tell when they successfully dislodged a defender from the walls. The entire body of them would shout, joke, or ap-plaud or brag.

Behind the cover of the slingers, Monomachus marched with his sword drawn—a purely symbolic gesture, for the enemy was not yet around. The men around him carried makeshift ladders, hastily constructed but sufficient for the city's modest walls. They wore full helmets jammed down tight on their heads, and each bore a heavy shield to deflect the missiles that would likely fall on them.

The foremost ladders had just touched the walls when the doors moved. They rocked once as if struck by a stone. All eyes turned. All motion ceased. The soldiers standing before the doors had little time to consider and act on what this might mean. A moment later the doors swung open, propelled by a hundred hands, and behind those, thousands of warriors. Romans rushed out with a roar, so loud that even horses at the rear of Hannibal's forces started and skittered nervously. They poured out at a full run, shields wedged close together. They hit the surprised Carthaginians with their shields, knocking men from their feet, tipping them off balance, and then stabbing at whatever exposed skin their swords could find. From behind the vanguard a barrage of javelins sailed, cast high, cutting arches that ended far back in the Carthaginian force.

Initially, men flew past Monomachus in stumbling retreat, but the general held his ground and steeled the others by striding for-ward toward the enemy, his face like an ancient's mask, mouth gap-ing, eyes in black shadow beneath his brow and helmet. He spoke not at all but dove into the fray, so conspicuous that others could not help but remember themselves and their skills.

Nor was Hannibal himself slow to respond. He assessed the situation and spoke his orders rapidly. The message went out through the horns, and with them the soldiers were visibly buoyed. The commander spoke to them. They should not fear battle. This was what they were here for. He had just arranged the body of the troops into orderly formations when gates far to either side of the main one broke open. From these issued two rivers of cavalry, many with velites riding partnered behind. They moved at a full gallop, dropped the infantrymen near the fray, and then plowed into the ranks. This new strike changed the whole balance. Hannibal was hard pressed to keep his troops from panicking.

It was a quick engagement, over in a couple of hours. Only afterward did all the pieces come together. Marcellus had learned of the plot, captured the rebels, and conceived a scheme of his own. The troops on the walls were not the prime soldiers they appeared to be. Instead, they were the injured and old, boys not yet of fighting age, and even some women disguised as men. Now all of the able-bodied males were freed to fight. The great noise when the gates swung open had been produced by each and every voice of Nola, not just the warriors': a ploy to make the fighting men's numbers seem enormous. It worked. And Marcellus had placed some of his best troops at the side gates. When they fell on the flanks they inflicted serious damage and achieved the most for their efforts.

In a final gesture, once the fighting had stopped, Marcellus hung a line of bodies from the wall by their feet, a ghastly decoration but one most effective on all who beheld it. Grimulus, standing not far from the commander, let out a low groan. There was a single gap left in the line of almost fifty bodies. Grimulus recognized that space as his own.

For the first time in the war, Hannibal had been duped and beaten. He muttered to Gemel that he felt like a boy-child given the switch by a tutor. All in all, the battle had been masterfully orchestrated—the more so because Marcellus was wise enough not to press his luck. The gates closed once more behind his troops. He sat in the towers and enjoyed his success, but could not be provoked to try his luck a second time. Hannibal, considering his options, turned toward a new objective. He had all of Italy at his mercy, why waste time on one recalcitrant polis? There were others, many others.

A small jewel of a city, Casilinum perched on a narrow finger at a bend in the river Volturnus, surrounded on three sides by water. Here also there had been talk of breaking with Rome. A whole faction of the council advocated this publicly. A misstep, for they were seized by a rival party and executed for treason. Once again Hannibal arrived to find closed gates. This time, however, he was in no mood for benevolence. Nor was there a Marcellus to toy with him. His overtures rejected, he sent against them Isalca, a Gaetulian from the territories south of the Massylii who had lately risen to the post of captain. The plucky townsfolk repulsed him, taking a heavy toll in African blood. Next Hannibal had Maharbal try to scheme a way inside the city, but his reconnaissance missions fell into preset traps that took several of their number and lamed even more horses.

The evening Monomachus brought him this news, Hannibal sat at a folding field table set up at a distance from the city, with a panoramic view that took in a great swath of country. It was lovely to behold. The grass had long since baked dry beneath the midsummer sun. It covered the land like a blanket woven from a Gaul's blond hair, a stark contrast to the dark green blooms of trees that dotted the landscape, the slabs of gray stone. Insects swarmed in the near distance. They must have had silver in their wings, for they sparkled like metallic dust blown into whirling clouds. Hannibal sent out a corps of scouts to capture some of the insects and bring them back to him, a strange request that he had to repeat several times to make himself understood.

Though he did not want to admit it, he felt the weight of his old melancholy returning. His limbs hung heavy; his thoughts moved more slowly than usual, more often tending toward recollection, anchored to things from the past instead of actively shaping the future. Staring out at the lands of his wartime exile, he acknowledged how dim the memory of his homeland had become. He tried to recall the plantations to the south of Carthage, the desert leading out toward the Numidian country, the scraggly hills of the Gaetulians' land, which he had seen in passing on his boyhood voyage to Iberia, as he marched the whole stretch of North Africa with his father. He felt that these scenes resided in him still, but it was hard to call them forth. They faded in and out and mingled with the wide, dry stretches of Iberia and the mountain pastures of the Pyrenees and the Alpine lakes that dotted the mountains. No scene from the dim reaches of his memory held steady. It was as if these were not real landscapes at all but imaginary ones, formed from the bits and pieces of other lands. He suddenly thought of his brothers and how he missed them and craved word of them. He knew that Hanno lived, that both he and Mago had been ushered to Iberia, and that Hasdrubal struggled to hold the country, but otherwise his information was patchy, creating more questions than answers.

Monomachus came upon him as he contemplated all of this. He stood just off to the left, in the blank space created by the commander's blind eye. Hannibal remembered his father once saying that Monomachus had been like a rabid wolf when he first appeared in the army. It had taken considerable molding to shape him into a soldier. He had first to be tamed. Tamed enough, at least, that his ferocity could be managed. And Maharbal had once told him that Monomachus claimed never to let a day pass without killing someone. Hannibal had not probed into whether this was true, but he had no reason to doubt it.

"What do you think, then?" Hannibal asked.

"We should go no further than this city until our swords are sated," Monomachus said. "We'll look fools otherwise. If I commanded this army I would lay waste to this city."

"You do not command this army. Answer me as what you are, not what you would like to be."

The officer grunted low in his throat. "As a warrior, I give the same advice. Offer their children to Moloch. The god is hungry and we have not honored him fully."

"These people are of no use to us dead," Hannibal said. "Whatever we do here must speak our cause to other people."

"Blood also speaks."

Hannibal fought the urge to turn his head and bring the man into better view, but there was something strategic in his placement, something to be lost by responding to it. He knew what Monomachus looked like, anyway. "All right, you have my permission," he said.

"Besiege them. Blockade them. Starve them. Drop rotten corpses in the river upstream of them. Build what machines we need. Do whatever you must, but make this town ours."

Monomachus did not speak. He did not nod or show emotion in any way. And yet Hannibal knew that he was pleased. Never in his life had he met a man more drawn to blood. This man gnawed at the bone of suffering like no other. He was indeed a wolf, Hannibal thought as he watched him move off, turning, at last, to study him. But his father had been mistaken. Such creatures can never truly be tamed.

Imco Vaca was confused. He had been since the aftermath of Cannae, and the months since had done nothing to order his mind. In some portion of his consciousness that day's slaughter never actually ended. It went on in a place just behind his left ear, as if he saw out of a rent in his skull that looked back to that field of slicing and stabbing and trodden gore. In his dreams, he found himself swimming in a shallow sea of bodies, pushing through arms and legs and torsos. It seemed that he might never truly end that day, never forget it, never see the world without a stain across it, never take a breath without sensing the fetid taint that clung to the hairs high up in his nostrils. How was it possible that such a day could somehow be entwined with his memory of a creature of sublime beauty?

He dreamed daily of the camp follower. She seemed less a real person now and more a divine being, a goddess or nymph, a healing deity who had pulled him out of that putrid carnage and nursed life back into him. He saw no sign of her in the days after he awoke and could learn nothing of her whatsoever. He took to whispering prayers in her behalf. He called her Picene because that was where he had first set eyes on her. He made offerings at each meal, a portion of his food, a sip of his water. He pleaded with the gods to lead the girl back to him, to offer some explanation so that he might find satisfaction. He yearned only for enough anonymity to allow him to slip away to some other life altogether. What if he just abandoned the military life and went in search of Picene? He was not a poor man. He had distinguished himself. His faraway family was actually prospering! Not that he had yet reaped the rewards of his efforts. If he could find Picene and convince her to live quietly with him, a life of the simple things: farming, food, warm bedding at night, and sex, definitely sex . . . In a field under the white sun, in a shed with hay caught in her hair, from behind as she cooked for them, his face buried between her legs at the day's end, the perfect fit and give of her breast held between his thumb and forefinger . . . It nearly drove him insane thinking about it, even more so because he was so uncomfortably surrounded by men. He feared that somehow they might discover his secret thoughts and foul them. He tried not to think about her, but only did so with even more urgency.

The girl from Saguntum found this more than a little amusing. "You've barely got the sense of that ass of hers," she said. She was ever present now, beside him even during intimate moments. Should his hand in thinking about Picene reach down to stroke his penis, he would hear her chuckle and offer some gibe. What was that he was going to scratch? she would ask. Had a scorpion stung him down there, or did his thing often swell so? He had of late concluded that nobody else could see or hear the girl. This suited him fine. He redoubled his attempts to ignore her, but she was as persistent as she was sarcastic.

For all the torment these two women caused him, they were only at the fringes of his daily hardships. He was so constantly in motion that he felt himself propelled forward by an unseen hand. The troop numbers shrank and swelled with a rhythm he could not comprehend. Last he had heard they numbered just over forty thousand, but this included new recruits from Samnium and Capua, the same type they had slaughtered so completely the year before. Hardly the sort to cement one's confidence, a strange bunch with their Latin customs, their absurd language and superstitions.

It only took a quick glance around to verify that he was in the company of the vilest men. The army was entirely different from what it had been in the early days. That period now resided in his memory cloaked in a heavy nostalgia. Whatever happened to the one named Gantho, who always slapped him on the back and called him the Hero of Arbocala? He disappeared after the Trebia, dead probably, though none could confirm it. What about the one called

Mouse? He had been quite a character, perhaps not completely sound of mind, but who was? He had carried a pet—his namesake—in a bag he wore over his shoulder. He fed the pink-nosed creature from his own rations, and was known to converse with it freely. He was head-addled, but Imco liked him well enough, until Mouse was speared in the groin at Trasimene and died slowly, writhing in agony. One of the units' cooks had been kind enough to often allow Imco extra rations, saying he needed it more than most. And a Libyan named Orissun had always been good company. He had a hose as long and wrinkled as a stallion's, a fact that he made clear each time he lifted his tunic. All of these men were long gone now. Viewed through the haze of distance, they seemed venerable creatures, far better than the new rabble that surrounded him, with their Latin customs and dress.

The attrition of the original army had effects on more than just his melancholy. Each day that he survived, he rose to greater prominence. Bomilcar had not forgotten him after Cannae. It took him a week to find him, but after Imco reported back to his captain the giant sought him out. He came upon him when Imco was huddled over a bowl of beef stew. He had barely touched it, steaming hot as it was, but he knew the broth would be tasteless and the meat stringy, without passion or zest. Food was plentiful for once, but the preparation still painfully primitive. He was still sore, every inch of him, from the fighting. That was why he yelled out so when the general clamped his massive hands down on his shoulders. It felt as if some great eagle had pierced his flesh and was about to carry him aloft. The next moment it felt as if a hyena had clamped down on his genitals—but this was an effect of his own stew, which he had spilled in its entirety onto his lap. He screamed in agony, and for this Bomilcar took to calling him Imco the Howler.

For his bravery at Cannae, the general had Imco's rank raised to captain and put him in charge of a unit of five hundred men. He instructed him to manage their circuitous march south, as Bomilcar was taking his ten thousand to hold the lower reaches of the peninsula. Imco tried to talk his way out of this, but Bomilcar laughed off all his complaints as if they were jokes. It was clear that the man only heard what he wanted to and that for some reason he wanted to make Imco into a fool in the public eye. He was sure this would be obvious to all, but strangely enough when he gave an order the men generally followed it. Despite his doubts, he did know how to imitate authority. When he needed to utter a command, the words came to him. He knew the proper order of march and could measure distance with surprising accuracy.

He got his first taste of battle command against Tiberius Gracchus at Beneventum. The fighting was savage, especially because Gracchus' army was made up of debtors and slaves who had been promised freedom in exchange for victory. They had been instructed to prove themselves by retrieving the heads of the men they killed. This they did, to gruesome effect. Bomilcar conceded defeat and withdrew, quickly, not even pausing to break camp but backing right through it and on. Brave and powerful as he was, the big man was no Hannibal, not even a lesser Barca. To make things worse, Imco was quite sure that the Romans had decided to fight only where Hannibal was *not*.

Hence he felt a certain amount of relief when late in the summer the commander himself met them outside Tarentum. They desperately wanted the city as an ally, with its marvelous port and protected inner harbor, its Spartan origins and position of leadership among the Greek cities of the south. As a captain Imco now sat at the fringes of councils with the great man, listening to him discourse on the value of a jewel like Tarentum. He spent many hours near enough to study his leader's features and comportment. Hannibal had certainly changed. Aged much faster than the years in passing. Imco still envisioned Hannibal as he had seen him long ago outside Arbocala, in the full bloom of youthful strength, unblemished, confident, with eyes of such glimmering intelligence that he seemed all-knowing, undefeatable. What had the years done to him?

The answer was not obvious. In fact, it was contradictory. To a person who remembered him from years before, Hannibal showed many signs of physical privation. His brows seemed to have lost their grip on his forehead. They slid down and hung like twin black cornices over his eye sockets. His blind orb sucked the vision of others into it. The clouded, scarred tissue seemed to possess a hunger fueled by its inability to look outward anymore. A welt ran from under his breastplate diagonally up his neck, and all manner of nicks, cuts, and lesions peppered his forearms and hands. Occasionally his tunic shifted far enough up his thigh to expose the edge of the ragged spear wound he had received at Saguntum.

If such injuries caught Imco's eye immediately, they also faded in consequence with each following moment. He had heard through some of his lieutenants that portions of the troops—the newest, in fact—grumbled at the slow pace of the summer, suggesting Hannibal had fallen foul of the victorious wind that had earlier propelled him. But these men did not sit so close to him. In truth, the man's single eye glinted with enough energy for two. He sat straight-backed, the muscles of his arms and shoulders taut under his skin. Though he was motionless, it was hard not to stare at him. He looked as if he might snap to his feet at any moment, draw his sword, and slice someone's head off. But this was not to say he seemed angry. He did not. He sat in complete composure. He simply seemed capable of anything, at any moment. No, Imco thought, Hannibal was still formidable. He was battered and worn by the campaign, but the mind behind the man's features had lost none of its sharpness, as he demonstrated in his assault on Tarentum.

He had been sitting outside its gates barely a week when two young men, Philemenus and Nicon, ventured from the city and swore that there was a large contingent intent on switching allegiances. Imco sat with the other officers off to one side, able to hear all that transpired. They said that the Romans had recently treated their countrymen roughly and unfairly. A group of Tarentines had been held in Rome since after Cannae. They were meant to ensure their city's fidelity, but in the previous month some of the group had escaped and made their way home. Whether there was treachery in this was unclear, but the Senate, perhaps showing its nervousness and frustration, accused them of fleeing to the enemy. They ordered the remaining prisoners scourged and then tossed them to their deaths from atop the Tarpeian Rock. The news of this act greatly stirred the Tarentines' anger. The city was still officially a fortress locked against the Carthaginians and guarded by a Roman garrison, but the two men believed that many would like to see this reversed. They wished to gain promises of Carthaginian goodwill toward them and their people. This guaranteed, they would do what they could to open the city.

Hannibal did not answer their proposal directly. He spoke through his translator, although Imco knew he did this primarily for the benefit of the monolinguals among his officers. "Just how did you escape the city, considering that it's the locked fortress that you call it?" he asked.

Philemenus, the shorter of the two and the more talkative, said, "That's easy. The Roman guards know us well. They let us out to hunt boar. Every now and then we bring them a—"

"You say you leave and enter the city often?"

"Of course. At all hours. Sometimes our hunts—"

Hannibal cut off the man's speech with a single raised hand. He let the silence linger a moment while he thought, and then said, "Friends, you were wise to come to me. Ambitious. And you've planted in me the seed of a plan . . ."

For the next two weeks, Philemenus became quite the hunter. He left the city almost daily, often returning late at night laden with deer and the occasional wild swine. As the Romans grew accustomed to this, and to gifts of fresh meat, Hannibal also let the rumor circulate that he was ill with a fever, bed-bound and in fear for his life. He then sent out a select force of ten thousand infantrymen with four days' rations and orders to march at night and hide themselves away in a ravine very near the city. On the chosen evening, Hannibal met the troops and approached one of the side gates. Inside, Nicon dispatched the unwary guards with a dagger and then let Hannibal through. The army streamed in behind him, as quietly as possible.

This much Imco saw with his own eyes, but at the city's far gate Philemenus—shadowed by a thousand Libyans—served as does the smaller of a crab's two pincers. He shouted up to the guards to let him in and quickly, for he was burdened with an enormous boar. They admitted him through the wicket gate, along with three soldiers disguised as herdsmen aiding him with the corpse. The guards had bent to gawk at the beast, and this became the last thing they ever did as living beings. Soon the main gate was opened and the Libyans strolled in.

Only then, with twelve thousand soldiers inside the city, did Hannibal order the men to draw their weapons. They poured through the night streets unencumbered, stumbling on the stones in their enthusiasm, barely able to contain the joy of it, whispering for the townspeople to hide in their homes. Their blades were bared against Rome. The two conspirators set up shouts of alarm near the Roman barracks. As the groggy-eyed soldiers emerged, they were cut down with ease.

All things considered, the devious ploy saved more lives on both sides than a full onslaught would have. The only Romans left alive were those sequestered in the citadel. Given its strong position far out on the peninsula, Hannibal quickly deemed it too formidable an obstacle to besiege. Instead he dug a trench, threw up a wall between it and the city, and left the soldiers to contemplate their fate. He knew that they could be reinforced from the sea and that the Tarentine fleet was trapped in the inner harbor. In fact, the city itself would have more difficulty receiving aid from a distance than the Romans would. But even this Hannibal overcame.

He simply lifted the fleet out of the harbor, set the ships atop wagons and sledges, pushed them through the city streets, and eased them to float again in the sea. The townspeople had never seen so strange a thing as the masts of ships traversing their narrow alleyways. Just like that, a problem other men would have written off as insoluble Hannibal solved to his advantage in days.

Within weeks, Metapontum and Thurii came over. Soon after, all the other Greek cities in the south did likewise, except for Rhegium. This brought port after port into Hannibal's hands. He could now call on Carthage to send reinforcements in through established channels. Amazing, Imco thought, that a single night's work could bear such fruit. The commander had lost none of his genius. Perhaps he was only tempering it into a finer material.

The great waves crashed along the Atlantic coast with a bulk that dwarfed anything seen in the sheltered Mediterranean. Since he had arrived at the mouth of the Tagus the previous winter, Hasdrubal had never tired of staring out at the seething expanse. It spoke to him in each plume of spray, with each rolling, slate-black ridge of water. During the winter storms he heard low grumblings that the locals told him were muffled roars of giants fighting beneath the waves. Silenus—who had accompanied him after learning that he would not be able to rejoin Hannibal soon—argued that he had heard of such noise before and believed it to be the grinding of boulders rolling forward and back on the seabed. The locals laughed at this and pulled his long ears and imitated his bowlegged gait, as if these gestures refuted any theories he might propose. Silenus, in turn, spurned their tales of deep-sea monstrosities. They told tales of creatures with jaws so great they could snap a quinquereme at its midpoint, with a hundred arms to snatch up the unfortunate crew and drag them under.

One evening—drunken, late, over a low fire in the smoky hall these people entertained in—Silenus told what he knew of a land far to the south of Carthage, well past the rolling bushland and the arid hinterland. Past the nations of Nubia and Ethiopia and Axum. Far, far to the south there lived a white-skinned people who burned so quickly beneath the sun that they never ventured out in the day. They lived in subterranean caverns that connected to others and spread all across the known world. They ate only the raw bone marrow of normal men. It was feared by many who knew of these people that they might one day take over the earth, emerging from crevices and cave mouths to wage one massive surprise attack.

His tale was met with dull, black eyes, glazed expressions of anxiety. Several of the courtesans covered their heads with snatches of triangular cloth, and a few men whispered prayers and poured droplets of wine on the floor and peered out into the dark with newfound trepidation. Only later, after several knowledgeable men had confirmed portions of his tale and one even claimed to have met such an African in Gades one night and another asked which gods one should appease to keep these creatures at bay . . . only then did Silenus double over in laughter. He had made the whole thing up! he yelled. Every word of it. Did they see now how easy it was to deceive a feeble mind? He asked them, had they heard about the blue people who live on hammocks slung between the stars? Or the race of men who urinated through the big toe of their left foot? Or the unfortunate tribe whose colorful, bulbous backsides attracted the attentions of amorous baboons?

The Greek made no friends that evening. But, truth be known, Hasdrubal began to enjoy the company of these strange people. Also, Silenus was a constant amusement who somehow brought out the humor in any situation. Life, for the first time in ages, had something of joy about it. He missed Bayala daily and sorely, but there was a sweetness even to this. He knew that she awaited him and would be his again before long. His seed had stuck inside her last autumn. Making offerings daily to Astarte, he asked for a boy child, a cousin to grow beside Little Hammer in the days after the war. Hanno and Mago roamed the country, still elated with victory, beating lessons into the Iberians that they would not soon forget. They were far-flung, yes, but the end seemed nearer than ever before.

For all of these reasons, the first news to reach him of Publius Scipio sucked the air from his lungs and left him a deflated skin of a man. In a few sentences, the messenger made reality of all the pressures and burdens and trepidations that the arrival of his brothers had so recently relieved. New Carthage gone! The heart of all their operations ripped out of them! His home, his brother-in-law's palace, his father's dream, the capital that Hannibal had entrusted to him, the wealth of his nation, hundreds of merchants, captives, aristocrats: all stolen in a single day. The Whore's Wood set ablaze; the streets stained with the blood of those who once called out to him in adulation. It was staggering.

He thanked the gods—both his and his wife's people's—that Bayala had been at her father's Oretani stronghold attending her sister's wedding when New Carthage fell. This, at least, was a blessing. The possibility that she could have been captured, defiled, possessed by Roman soldiers pressed on his head at the temples, set his heart thumping in his chest, and made his fingers tingle. Even though he knew it had not come to pass, the possibility filled him with a greater fear than he had ever known. It cast warfare in an entirely new light, made it foul in ways he had not imagined before. He realized that a husband fights differently than a bachelor. And perhaps, he thought, a father fights differently yet again. It was not a realization he had expected, but these new perspectives produced a gnawing humility. He understood something of what lay behind the faces of the men whose lives he destroyed, whose wives he ordered imprisoned and children enslaved. For the first few days of his mourning, it was almost too much to bear.

But, like so many leaders, Hasdrubal was blessed with an aide who grew stronger at the times he most needed him. Noba never acknowledged his general's grief. He never mentioned Bayala except to write Hasdrubal's correspondence to her. He spoke only of the strategic setback caused by the loss of New Carthage. Also, he served as a funnel through which reports about the Romans' new proconsul came to him. Not only was Publius Scipio's taking of the city masterful, but when dealing with prisoners he showed an astuteness of yet another sort. The Carthaginians and Libyans and Numidians he enslaved and quickly sold onward for profit. But he freed almost all of the Iberians. He protected the diplomatic hostages: children and wives of Iberian chieftains. He bade them return to their people with no animosity from Rome.

In the weeks after his victory the proconsul made allies of Edeco, Indibilis, and Mandonius, three of the most powerful chieftains of the peninsula. Once again the various tribes of Iberia were like so many balls thrown in the air. Hasdrubal could not possibly catch them all, so which should he grasp for and which let fall? With Noba's calm voice speaking in his ear, Hasdrubal pulled his army up by the roots and headed inland. They had to stanch the bleeding away of allies without delay. They sent riders ahead with orders for several tribes to gather at Oretani. This also meant Hasdrubal would see Bayala again.

The army moved quickly, without hostile incident, although not without discomfiture. On the third day, they came upon a town that none had heard of before. The place was a conglomeration of stone huts spread out across a wide valley, huts that from a distance looked inhabited. Some even claimed to have seen smoke drifting up from cook fires. But as Hasdrubal's force marched by the settlement, they saw the tattered roofs of the buildings, the tumbling decay, the silent interiors, the fire pits so long undisturbed that the charred scars had been washed clean long ago. Not a person to be seen among the structures, no animal or fresh food or any sign of life save that left there by the ancients. It was a strange place that all were relieved to see recede into the distance. From then on Hasdrubal saw messages written everywhere on the land: in the wavering rusty stains dripping down from rock faces; in the form of a great boulder the size of a fortress, cracked into four equal parts, as if some giant had dropped it to the earth; in the strange cloud formation that appeared above them one evening, a fish scale pattern complete in its perfection from one horizon to the other. But these were not signs he could interpret, only greater mysteries that filled him with a rising dread.

As he neared the lands of the Oretani, a messenger approached him with instructions he claimed to have received from Bayala. Hasdrubal was not to enter Oretani land. Instead, he should meet his wife in Baecula, to the southeast. Hasdrubal exchanged glances with Noba. The Ethiopian sucked his cheeks and muttered that he did not favor this. He asked the messenger to explain himself. And where was Andobales? Their business was that of men. This army did not turn at the whim of any woman, even Bayala. Did the other tribes not await them?

The messenger said that everything would be explained at Baecula. It was only three days' march away. Noba still had questions and he framed them one after another, so intensely that the messenger finally looked away from him and addressed Hasdrubal simply. "Bayala calls for you, Commander," he said. "You know Baecula is loyal to you and has been since your father's time. Bayala is there and she begs you to make haste to her. You will understand the rest when you see her."

But at the gates of Baecula the messenger approached Hasdrubal again, stopped him, and said he had one last message to convey. "It is meant for your ears alone," he said. Once Hasdrubal had sent the others onward and had his guards back up a few steps, the messenger said, "Andobales says you are no longer his son."

Hasdrubal stared at him dumbly a moment. Then scowled. Then grinned and then scowled again. "How? How? Did I not marry his daughter? Does she not have my child in her? He hasn't turned to embrace this Scipio, has he? Andobales is not such a fool! Go back and tell him to be no pawn to Rome. I am his family, now and forever. We are wed by blood."

The messenger took this barrage silently. Like all the Oretani, he wore a leather band around his forehead, into which he slipped the feathers of certain birds. Hasdrubal, in his sudden exasperation, ripped this from the man's head. This insult got no response. When Hasdrubal concluded, the man said, "Sit with this news and you will come to understand it. But—have no doubt—you are Andobales' son no more." Without waiting for dismissal, the man mounted and galloped back along the marching army. Hasdrubal watched him for a few moments, confounded, filled now to the crown of his head with unease.

This grew worse as he walked into the city. A band of ten mounted Oretani surged past him without so much as a glance. And inside the palace reserved for the Barcas, he did not receive the usual welcome but found only a chattering confusion among the servants and city officials. He heard Noba yelling. Guards of the Sacred Band rushed past him in a clatter of armor and unsheathed weapons and black cloaks. Silenus, who had entered early to summon Bayala, met him with outstretched arms. He grasped the commander and repeated something over and over again, though Hasdrubal did not listen to him. He threw the Greek off. Moments later he had to elbow through his men, who for some reason barred him from Bayala's chambers.

A crowd of women servants sprung from their hunched grouping around the central bed and scattered. Bayala lay supine on the platform, her arms cast out to either side, her shift high on one thigh. For a moment he was mystified—why would she lie in such a position in a crowded room? The thought had not fully matured before it was silenced. He moved nearer, calling her name, even though he knew already that she could not answer. Again he knew the Greek was at his side, trying to pull him away. He could have swatted the bowlegged man to the far side of the room. But one glimpse of the gaping crescent carved in Bayala's neck stole all anger from him. He crumpled and crawled forward across the floor and clawed his way up onto the blood-drenched bed. She was still warm. She was still warm! He yelled this as if somehow it was the key to everything. Then he felt himself enveloped, first by Silenus' arms, soon after by Noba's. He knew both men were speaking to him. Did neither of them realize that she was still warm?

To say Hasdrubal mourned his wife's death puts a complex thing too simply. He beat his chest and pounded his fists against his eyes and shouted curses into the night sky. He wished he had listened to her and never trusted her father. He wished he had cut Andobales' head from his shoulders when he had the chance. He wished that he had never met her, that he had no memories of her, that he was not cursed to recall a thousand different pleasures now turned around and revealed as tortures.

His first impulse was to fall on the Oretani. Although the messenger who had led him to Baecula escaped, the Sacred Band did catch the fleeing assassins. Only three of the ten survived to become prisoners. One of these proved impervious to torture, but the other two spoke before they died. They swore that Bayala had been murdered on her father's orders. It was meant to be an irreversible declaration: Andobales severed all bonds with Carthage. He was an ally to the young Roman now. Hasdrubal hated the chieftain with blinding ferocity. It seemed he had always loathed Andobales but only now understood how completely. He was a waste of the life breathed into him. He was vermin. He was a murderer. He had killed his future and killed beauty and killed a child as yet unseen by human eyes. He had slit a most perfect neck. He had split flesh that should never have known pain. He had coldly ordered the blood drained from her body. The shock she must have felt . . . The fear in those last moments . . . Andobales deserved the worst possible of deaths and Hasdrubal ached to bring it to him.

Noba, however, convinced him that Romans were too near for him to risk engaging with Iberians. The council he had called would never come. Everyone, it seemed, was anxious to befriend this Publius. To attack when fueled by passion would surely be to blunder; it must have been what Andobales hoped for. So he could not give it to them. The two men argued long about this. At times they even came to blows, each man leaning into the other and pounding his frustrations into the other's torso, jolts that would have doubled lesser men over in pain.

In the end they moved the army to a wide plateau near Baecula, a high tilted table atop two terraced steps that rose out of the plains below. Hasdrubal watched as Publius' army approached and offered battle. The Carthaginian held fast, not venturing out to meet them. He did not budge for a week. Perhaps, vaguely, he was awaiting his brothers, hoping they would converge on the Roman force. But he did not send messengers to speed this along. The world around him and the threats it offered paled next to the storm inside. This is why he did not think twice about the troops skirmishing on the lower terrace. His forces had just met the climbing soldiers when another force emerged on the right. He sensed the peril in this, but he was slow to understand.

Noba awakened him from his stupor. He strode up from the second terrace and, without a word, slapped Hasdrubal openhanded across the cheek and temple. He was a strong man and the blow nearly knocked the general off his feet. Silenus, who had been standing just beside him, had to catch the commander by the arm to stay him from drawing his sword.

"Are you all mad?" Hasdrubal hissed, twisting from the Greek's grip. "Why do you touch me?"

"I may be mad," Noba said, "but I slap you like a woman because that's what you're acting like. Mourn your beloved some other time. You'll find another tight rump before long, but right now we're about to be destroyed. Wake up and do something about it!"

"I could kill you for speaking to me thus."

"You could," Silenus said, "but do it later. I think Noba speaks harsh wisdom."

"She meant more to me—"

Noba stepped close enough that his breath billowed off Hasdrubal's face. "I know. Tell me of her tomorrow. And then again next week. Then in the many years to come. But right now, call a retreat!"

And he did. These two men served him well. Under Noba's directions, the better part of the army fled. Elephants roared down the far side of the plateau, careening through the trees. The baggage train—wagons and laden pack animals and sledges—bumped down the slope to the relative flat. The army marched a semicontrolled retreat, the very rear brawling for every backward step. It was dangerously close to a rout, but Noba again acted quickly. He shouted orders that none considered questioning. He told the camp staff to abandon the wagons and sledges. These proved temptation enough to slow the Romans, one soldier anxious lest some other get booty meant for him.

By nightfall, Publius had pulled up. Hasdrubal pressed his troops on, putting all the distance he could between them under the light of a thin moon. He barely understood what had happened, neither why his strong position had been overturned so quickly nor what it meant to be running headlong into the night. But as motion and danger returned him to his senses, he decided one thing with certainty: He had had enough of Iberia. How many times had Iberians betrayed his people? How many times had they killed those he loved? His wife, his brother-in-law, his father . . . So many others. He cursed the land and spat on it. He could not stand the sight of it, not the feel of it brushing his toes nor the stench of it in his lungs. The next morning he sent messengers to both his brothers, begging their forgiveness, asking for their blessing. And he sent another that he hoped would eventually reach Carthage itself. He had decided; now they could only hear his will.

Hasdrubal Barca marched for Rome.

The boat pushed out from a small port north of Salapia just after sunrise on the planned day, signs having been provident and the winds northeasterly. They would sail through the morning and stop at the far spur of land pointing toward Greece. There they would rest, and the next dawn—conditions being favorable—they would shoot across the Adriatic in a single day. Considering the distances Aradna had traveled till now, this would not have been a very long journey. And it might have been her last, for it would have carried her and her modest wealth back to the territory of her birth, as she had so long wanted. Nevertheless, she was not aboard the vessel.

Instead she sat on the shore, watching the small craft plunge through the waves, rising and falling. Once it was past the breakers and onto the breathing swells, the oars lifted and flapped a moment in the air, like featherless wings. The captain moved about the deck, his silhouette gilded by the glare of the new sun. Some bit of his speech careened toward her, only to be snapped back by a current of air. The rowers laid the oars down along the deck and a single square sail unfurled and snapped taut against the wind. From then on the ship's progress was steady, the fate of the passengers aboard it no longer tied to hers.

Aradna dug her hands down into the sand and squeezed the coarse grains between her fingers. She had pulled her hair back from her face and fastened it with a strip of leather. Because she hated the things men and women saw when they looked at her she rarely exposed her face for the world to view. She had never thought of beauty as anything but a misfortune, but there was no one to see her at that moment and she needed to feel the movement of the air on her features. Her eyes shone with their accursed, startling blue; her wretched full lips tilted downward at their pouting edges. Tiny curls of dried skin clung to the curve of her nose, but these only served to verify that her face was that of an earthly being made of the same materials as all others.

Touching her hips at either side and just behind her lay all the possessions she had in the world. One sack held the coins she had traded her stores of booty for. Another contained the simple provisions of life: food and knives, herbs and bedding and pieces of fabric and needles. The third had not been hers until a few days ago but had been bequeathed to her. A little distance away lay a dead crab Aradna had not seen when she chose this spot. Its body was longer than it was wide, with two enormous claws that the indignity of death had flung out to either side. She tried not to look at the crustacean or think of it as a comment on the decision she had made in the dead hours of the previous night.

It had not been easy. It had not happened as she had wanted. If anything, she would have welcomed the certainty she needed to be aboard that vessel. Atneh had nearly succeeded in instilling this in her. When she had sought excuses for not leaving, the old woman shot them down like an archer pinning pigeons to the sky. "What fear of the sea?" she had asked. "As far as I can tell, you fear nothing. A little water beneath you? What is that compared with the trials life has already shown you? If the gods had wanted you dead, they would've taken you already." When she would not come to terms with the merchants who would translate her motley finds into coin, Atneh smacked her on the back of the head and named reasonable terms for her. When she complained that none of the vessels she had seen looked seaworthy, the old woman found one that was. And when she suggested one last scavenging mission, the woman shook her head at the foolishness of it.

"Casilinum?" Atneh had asked. "Forget it. What's one more city? You have enough already. Don't let me see you become a fool. I see what this is about, and it's nothing to do with a few more coins. You know, don't you, that the gods sometimes play us as toys? Think about that. Imagine yourself with a string pinned to your heart. If you feel that string tug you in one direction or another, know it for what it is—the whim of the foolish ones. It can do you no good. Remember my words. Anyway, I'm an old woman. You mustn't leave me to make this journey myself."

So Aradna had taken Atneh's certainty inside herself and set her sights across the sea. But just when she thought her path lay before her as clear as ever it had . . . just as she lifted her foot to step upon it with prayers that it was the right one and would lead her to the happiness she sought and the future Atneh assured her was awaiting them both . . . at just that moment the old woman fell ill. She could not name what had laid her on her back but she said she could feel it eating at her from the inside. It was a pain in her two breasts that radiated into her whole chest and interlocked its fingers in the gaps between her ribs. She found it difficult to breathe and within a few days she could only manage shallow inhalations. By the end of a moon's cycle she had developed a cough that tortured her. It came as regular as breathing, one painful shock after another.

In the middle of one night, Atneh awoke Aradna by tugging at her wrist. She wanted Aradna to promise that when she died she would not become a fool but would remember her words always. Aradna tried to tell her she was not dying, but the old one scorned her with a look that Aradna could feel through the darkness. She asked Aradna to describe again the quiet life they would have. For some time the old woman listened, rustling uncomfortably, shaken by her coughs.

Aradna thought her words might be soothing her somewhat, but then, unexpectedly, Atneh said, "I can't see anything!"

"That's because it's dark, Aunt. It's night."

The old woman was silent for a moment, then said, "That's what you think."

The next morning, Aradna and the rest of their band buried Atneh deep enough in the sandy dunes that no creatures would disturb her. They bought and sacrificed a goat and offered it up to Zeus and killed hens to fly to Artemis and poured out wine to ease her entry into the next world. The others had assumed she would either stay with them or continue on the journey she had planned with the old woman, but Aradna became unsure of either route. She had long dreamed of the soldier from Cannae, but in the light of day she had banished him into the mists. Now this became increasingly hard to do.

She sometimes awoke with the suspicion that he had visited her. She thought she could remember his smell, although this seemed improbable. He had been covered in filth, in blood and dirt and unnamed stink. How could she scent the essence of the man underneath all that? But then she awoke from another dream with the memory of washing his flesh clean with a cloth, kneeling forward and touching his skin with her nose, breathing him in. Whether this was done in dream alone or had actually happened, she was not sure. There was an intimacy in her thoughts of him that embarrassed her. It made no sense that she—who had avoided men for the plague they were, who had once snapped an erect penis between two stones and had often protected herself with knives and gnashing teeth—so longed for this man. She wanted to sit near him and maybe touch him and hear his voice and speak slowly so that they could understand each other. She had many questions for him. Why had their paths crossed three times in the midst of the chaos that was this war? Something like that is not simple chance. Perhaps the gods wished them together. She had never even stopped to hear the man out. Perhaps he brought her a message. . . . These lines of thinking left her breathless with the possibilities. This man might have an unimagined place in her life, and she might have been spurning the gods when she turned away from him.

Aradna was still sitting on the beach, watching the now empty sea, when something caught her eye. A shape cut the surface of the sea out in the middle distance, a solid object as dark as basalt against the water, moving to the south. It vanished and then appeared again, a little farther on. A moment later it appeared yet again, but farther out, and then the backbones of sea creatures broke into the air at a hundred different points. Aradna's toes clenched tight around the sand. She did not like this sighting. She took it as an omen, but as ever with such things she knew not how to interpret it. One of the men at the camp was skilled at such things, but she hated his stare and the way he touched her, as if he were a blind man who needed to feel to see, even though everyone knew his eyes were as keen as a child's. Instead she closed her eyes and tried to believe those passing beasts had import for someone else's life, not hers.

She found the spot in the dead of night. She could barely see at all under the light of a thin moon. At first she dug with a pointed stick to loosen the soil. She squatted down on her knees and reached in with her hands. Eventually, she lay down with the rim cutting into her abdomen, knees dug in as anchors, her backside tilted to the sky, scooping up dirt and pebbles with a flat clamshell, yanking at roots and fighting with the debris that sought again and again to slide back into the hole.

She did not so much decide she was satisfied with the hole as just give up on going any deeper. Her arms were only so long, anyway. She placed the various parcels in it, making sure their wrappings stayed in place. She refilled the hole quickly, then spent some time shifting stones and tugging at fallen branches and arranging pine needles to hide her work.

She did not finish until the thin light of morning. She gazed around her long enough to verify her solitude and register the landmarks in her mind, and then she walked away without looking back. She no longer led the donkey with a tether. In her own silent way she turned her back on the creature and offered him the possibility of a life without her. But he fell in behind her.

A little time later she stepped over the back of the near hills and saw the land rise up to meet her, the whole breadth of it: the farm-lands on the plain below, the jagged serrations that rose in the distance, like the backs of those sea beasts but captured in rock. She did remember the old woman's words. She thought of them with every stride she took, and she spoke her respect to the woman. At-neh was wise, but no single person held all inside them. Aradna fol-lowed her nose. No matter that reason said otherwise; she could smell that soldier over the distance and she had no choice except to find him and see this through.

Where had childhood gone? Mago asked himself this one swelter-ing afternoon a few weeks after Hasdrubal's defeat at Baecula. He walked solitary along a low ridgeline. Guards shadowed him at a dis-tance, but he ordered them to stay out of his sight. He needed a few moments alone. He longed for even a short break from the inces-sant maneuvering of war. The question about childhood came to him fully formed when he looked up into great pine trees sur-rounding him. Their branches did not start till high above the ground, but they were so straight and strong that they interwove with those of other trees, like men standing with their arms locked over each other's shoulders. Had he seen such a sight as a child, he would have called to have a rope brought to him. He would have climbed up into those branches, pushing through the needles, sap gumming his palms. He would have sought the highest point he could reach and looked for the creatures that lived there and gazed out at the world from that vantage, imagining himself an owl or a hawk or a great eagle.

How strange to think that there was a time in his life when he had wished for turmoil instead of study, noise and clash of arms instead of quiet conversation with his tutors, sparring with his companions, the embraces of his mother and sisters. He had once spent whole days listening to the epic tales in Greek, lost in the adventures of men who had lived centuries before, who had communed with the gods and touched greatness time and again. His study of war had once been an exercise of the mind, played out with carved granite soldiers that patrolled miniature battlefields. They were silent, emotionless, bloodless figures, animated only by his fingers or knocked off balance by the pebbles he tossed at them in their mock battles. There was a time when such boyish games comprised the sum total of his experience of war. And yet he had yearned to grow up in an instant so he could experience mayhem for real. He had wanted to be the hand that drove home spear points, that slashed heads from shoulders, that ordered this man killed and that spared. What boy upon the earth has not dreamed of such things?

But those times were long gone now. No longer had he playmates to set up pieces against. Instead he spent his days walking among a throng of killers, men of many nations who were united only by the hunger for slaughter and spoils. It was not exactly that he bemoaned the change or could imagine what other lot in life to yearn for. It was just that he did not understand how he could contain within himself both that child and the soldier he now was. At Hannibal's side, he managed to maintain his faith in the grandeur of war. Their feats had seemed to be the very essence of legend; their victories, majestic moments smiled upon by the gods. For a while his work with Hanno and Hasdrubal had also filled him with joy. They had been touched by the same greatness, it seemed. Finally, they could all believe they had a place beside Hannibal's brilliance.

But that was before Publius Scipio. One man, a few months, two battles: everything changed. It was not just the strategic realities that troubled Mago. In Hannibal's absence, the first shifting winds of defeat blew away a mask that he had not even realized he was wearing. It had been like a helmet that blocked portions of his vision and limited the world he perceived. He had acknowledged only the things that confirmed the realization of his childhood fantasies. The last few weeks, however—with the mask removed—the unacknowledged images bombarded him unhindered. He could not help but recall the faces of orphan children, the suffering in the eyes of captured women, the sight of burning homes, the cold glances of people being robbed of grain and horses and, indirectly, of their lives. He heard their wailing in some place beyond sound, high to the right and back of his head. Everywhere were signs of the barbarous nature of conflict, ugly to behold. Nowhere was it possible to avoid these things. It suddenly seemed to him that such scenes were the full and true face of war. What place had nobility in this? Where was the joy of heroes? Why could he no longer recite the lines with which epic poets enshrined the greatness of clashing men? It was weak of him to think this way. He knew it, but he could not shake free of the mood. He thought briefly of the melancholy that sometimes took hold of Hannibal. He never explained it. . . . But, no, it could not be the doubt that he now felt. Hannibal was as certain of his place in the world as if he had created it himself.

Hanno trudged up toward him, quietly, for the pine leaves cushioned his steps. He wore a shimmering garment of scale armor, silvered metal that caught the speckled light like the moving skin of fish. Glancing at his face, Mago saw his mother in his features. He winced to think of her and the high spirits he had last shared with her in Carthage. How foolish to be joyful at one moment, forgetting that the wheel of life turns, so that he who looks at the sun at one moment soon finds himself crushed against the hard earth.

Hanno stood beside him for a time, not speaking, looking out through the trees toward the plain in which their army fidgeted in nervous expectancy. The branches were so thick that he could not possibly see through them any more than Mago could, but still he waited a long time before he spoke. When he did, Mago heard a quality that again reminded him of their mother. The part of Didobal in him seemed to be the strongest portion, the firmest in its resolve to confront the future.

"Come," Hanno said, "we can wait no longer. It will be at Ilipa."

Having said this, the older sibling retraced his steps beneath the trees, just as silently as before. When he faded out of view, Mago heard the rapping of a woodpecker, a loud barrage of thuds and then silence, a loud barrage and then silence. There was no way back to that other time; there was only forward through the world he now inhabited. Only onward into the clash that had to come. His brother had named the place. Mago followed him down toward it.

Two days later, the armies came in sight of each other. For the three days after that, they assembled. Both forces marched down out of the tree-dotted ridges on which they camped and approached almost to within shouting distance of each other. There the troops waited, the generals taking stock of the opposition, skirmishers exchanging volleys. They sweated under the sun and chewed strips of dried meat and swatted at flies, but otherwise rested as well as they could. Neither side broke this strange truce, and in the evening the Carthaginians withdrew first.

Mago and Hanno spent each night talking through what this might mean, trying to learn something new for the following day. Having assembled a force of all their remaining allies, they outnumbered the enemy, numbering fifty thousand to the Romans' forty. Perhaps this was working on the Roman consciousness, paralyzing them with fear, softening them for the onslaught they knew was coming soon. Publius positioned his various units in the same formation each time: legions in the center, Iberian mercenaries on either wing. Each time the Carthaginians met this in kind, with their Libyans in the center, their strongest soldiers to oppose his. They divided their twenty elephants evenly on both wings, hoping to use them as giant stabilizers to hold the army in formation. The two brothers considered changing the arrangement, but no matter how they thought it through, the deployment seemed sound. Publius might have been looking for a weakness, but each day Mago believed a little more that all they presented was strength.

But in the first gray light of the morning of the fourth day, the Roman cavalry pounced on the forward Carthaginian outposts. A few riders managed to escape to sound the alarm. But just afterward the entire Roman force slipped into view like a slow river in flood, through the trees and out onto the flat plain. The Carthaginians had no choice but to rise groggy from bed and grab up arms and rush to form up ranks. Mago shouted all the things he knew the men expected of him. "This is the day!" he said. "The enemy is trying to surprise us, but early rising alone will not win this battle." None could say that he had not learned from his brothers' example, but inwardly he realized something was happening over which he had no control, something he still could not predict. For the first time he understood how an enemy must feel facing Hannibal across a battlefield.

The approaching army was still some way out, but Publius' deployment had changed. Skirmishers trotted in a weaving crisscross of confusion, like so many ants. His Roman legions now made up the wings; the Iberians held the center. The Barcas worked frantically through what this might mean and how to combat it, but there was no time for them to order a change in their own lines. The men were in enough confusion just trying to form up. Why had Publius put his weakest fighters against their strongest, and vice versa?

As soon as they were into the flat the Romans picked up their pace. A little farther on, they fell into a trot. As they drew nearer still, the Roman wings—hearing the horn signal—kicked their pace into a wolf-lope. Mago thought that at that rate they would be out of breath by the time the two armies met. Their armor must have weighed heavily on them. But as he watched, he realized they had trained for such a run. Their lungs billowed to meet the demand and nothing about them suggested fatigue. Their legs moved them forward, sure of step, determined. Meanwhile, the Iberians in the center kept to their slower pace and soon fell behind. After launching their fistfuls of missiles, javelins, and darts, the skirmishers withdrew through the ranks. They slipped out of sight and emerged behind the legionaries, regrouped, and fell into step behind them. They pulled swords from sheaths secured to their backs, drew daggers from their belts, or snatched up pikes that the rear infantrymen dropped for them. With so many of their helmets covered in animal skins, they looked like an unnatural pack of hunters—lions beside wolves beside bears and foxes—chasing the army forward, nipping at their heels.

When the two sides finally met, the Roman front line looked like a horseshoe. The two prongs of the veteran legions smashed into the Carthaginians' Iberian allies and from the first moments made quick work of them. The skirmishers fanned out and around and swept in on the Carthaginian flanks. Meanwhile the Libyans stood in confusion, glancing from side to side, waiting for orders, their spears to hand but useless. The front line of Iberians that should have met them did not do so. On a single horn-blasted order they all stopped. They hovered out a distance, just too far to engage, but near enough so that the Libyans could not turn away from them for fear of being pounced on. The Libyans could neither aid their dying allies nor rush forward, because to do so would break formation and lead to all manner of chaos. They just waited, panting and impatient, as men near them fell to the Romans' cut and thrust.

Publius had orchestrated the impossible. He had encircled an army larger than his own, simply by moving his various troops about in unexpected ways. The Libyans in the center were as dead on their feet as all of the Romans trapped shoulder to shoulder at Cannae.

Yet the matter was decided not by men but by four-legged creatures. The elephants—which had been stung again and again by the skirmishers' javelins—spun and careened in toward the center of the army. In pain and fury, the creatures moved heedless of which men they trampled, which they swatted out of the way with tusks and trunks. The drivers atop them smashed them about the head and yanked their ears and roared at them to change course. But it was no good. The elephants turned as if by common agreement and each cut a swath of grisly death toward the Carthaginian heart. With this, the battle collapsed. From then on Publius commanded a rout.

Mago stared and stared at what he saw, so long and intensely that he was saved only when one of his guards jabbed his horse in the rear with a spear. As he hurtled off on his bucking horse he called for a retreat to be sounded. With that the troops gave up all semblance of discipline. They turned and fled, Romans fast behind them. The sky opened above them in a sudden outburst of rain. This slowed the Roman advance. Mago fought to keep the army moving through the night, but the distance they covered in the stumbling dark was not enough. In the morning the Romans followed on their heels, leaving corpses like waypoints marking their path. Despite all Mago's dismay at the fact, eventually he, Hanno, and five thousand mounted soldiers—Massylii and Libyans mostly—dashed before the body of the army in undisguised flight.

For much of the long summer, Imco found himself standing just behind Hannibal's shoulder, watching as Fortune favored one side and then the other. Marcellus became the sharpest thorn in Hannibal's side, single-handedly trying to undo all he had accomplished. Only a fortnight after Hannibal left Casilinum, he had retaken it through siege and treachery. Capuans had garrisoned the city—not the best of troops but, considering its natural defenses, even they should have held it. But they lost their nerve, scared, no doubt, by Marcellus' growing reputation. They struck a deal with the Roman for their surrender, in return for which they would be allowed to return to their city unmolested. But when they strolled through the gates the waiting Romans pounced on them and hacked them beyond recognition, punishment for crimes that they believed predated this betrayal.

Casilinum was not the only setback: Fabius Maximus retook Tarentum, Claudius Nero mauled a band of five hundred Numidians, Livius Salinator surprised a Carthaginian admiral off the coast near Neapolis, frightening the cautious sailor back to Sicily. But more often the Roman foolishness flared so brightly that it left Imco shaking his head in amazement. There was Tiberius Gracchus, for example. Overconfident after his rout of Bomilcar's forces, Gracchus marched too close to Hannibal. His guides, perhaps having mistaken their route in all innocence, abandoned him the moment they spotted Numidian riders. This set the slave army in turmoil, a situation easily exploited. Watching this from the height where his troops stood in reserve, Imco was struck by the thought that battles were won or lost on the basis of a single factor that each and every soldier controlled. Not the hand of any god, not the cunning of any one leader, not superiority in arms or training: none of these mattered as much as the bravery of individual men. Perhaps slaves could be expected to understand that least of all. They panicked, all at the same moment. The matter was decided, and Tiberius Gracchus perished in the ensuing rout.

Soon after Gracchus' death, the Romans fell under the spell of a centurion named Centenius Paenula. Some recalled that on the day of his birth considerable prodigies had occurred. Another scholar connected clues from several of the ancient texts and announced that the young soldier's name was destined to sound in glory throughout the ages. Striking in appearance, tall and fine-featured, he did not have to do much to convince the Senate that he was just the one chosen by the gods to strike a blow at Hannibal. With the remnants of Gracchus' army and a horde of enthusiastic volunteers, he marched into Lucania, met Hannibal, and promptly offered up all eight thousand of his force for sacrifice. They were slaughtered down to the last man. Centenius Paenula, it turned out, was not a name that would ring down through the ages.

Imco was in the very room at Herdonea when Hannibal met with a foolish magistrate who dared to drink his wine and accept his gifts, but begged more time to decide whether he could deliver his people to Hannibal's side. The commander nodded at all of this and spoke graciously. Of course, he said, more time was reasonable. He was, after all, only prosecuting the greatest war the Mediterranean had ever seen. If the magistrate needed to think this over, he could do so, by all means. Hannibal and his entire army would wait on him. The magistrate might or might not have recognized the irony in the commander's voice, but when he stood to leave Hannibal made all clear. The magistrate could have as long as he needed to decide, except that he must do so before the wine he had just drunk escaped his body. The man looked at him in mystification.

"You see," Hannibal said, "I happily give wine to my friends, but a man who drinks my wine and then rejects my friendship is a thief. I'd like to know which you are before you piss my goodwill onto the ground. Take as long as you want, but before you loose your bladder I must know what you are to me. Perhaps you should sit down again."

Herdonea was soon his. As was Caulonia. For a time that city's magistrates and officers held out in the citadel with their families, refusing to surrender: They were well provisioned and believed that Nero—with yet another Roman army—would soon come to their aid. Hannibal, however, conceived of a way to stir them from the nest. Some bored Balearics had come across a shallow cave teeming with snakes, hundreds or thousands of them. Hannibal had the creatures gathered up and placed in large urns. In the gray light just before dawn one morning, he had these hurled into the citadel with catapults. Most of the urns smashed against the walls, but several landed atop the structure. They exploded into jagged shards of writhing, slithering life.

The Caulonians, waking to this commotion, cried out that Hannibal's gods had called upon them a plague of serpents. Women took up the shout, and children wailed with fright. Stumbling and running through the half-light inside the cramped citadel, the people panicked. Guards jumped from the top of the tower, thudding dully against the dew-licked turf. One leaped in a different direction than the rest and fell in straight-legged horror, so stiff that his legs anchored him in a mound of dirt thrown up by the diggers. His ankles snapped at the impact, but he sank to the thighs and stood trapped there, howling. The Balearics, arguing that this was all their doing and that therefore to them went the sport, used the man for target games. They slung their tiny pellets at the swaying figure, battering his chest, knocking out his teeth, and bashing in an eye and tearing chunks of flesh from his biceps. The man died shortly after they began betting on who could shoot into his scrotum in a way that left the missiles sitting in the sacs, twins to the balls naturally at home there.

The magistrates, after receiving assurances of fair treatment, gave up the citadel. Reasonable behavior, Imco thought. If Hannibal could make the sky rain vipers, what chance did they have against him?

Not even Marcellus could last forever. He and Crispinus both perished near Venusia in an episode surprising only in its anticlimactic result. The two generals had each encamped on the far side of a growth of knobby hills. Hannibal, on approaching them, noticed the hills and sent Numidians out in the night to secure them. This they managed, while also keeping their presence secret. The Romans, however, soon noticed the same feature. The two generals, believing themselves safe, rode out to inspect the territory personally. The Numidians recognized them at once and sprang a trap that killed Marcellus on the spot. Crispinus died days later from his spear wounds.

Regardless of all he had witnessed at Hannibal's side, or perhaps because of it, Imco was surprised almost to fright when the commander invited him to sleep out with him on the ridge of hills to the east of camp. He said they would slumber on the open ground, like boys, and talk beneath a canopy of stars. Just why Hannibal chose him for this honor, Imco could not say. They had sat together often enough at meetings throughout the summer, but they had not yet spoken on such intimate terms. In fact, whenever Imco opened his mouth in council he had the feeling that the commander was gazing at him with a certain amount of mirth. He was not even sure that the other remembered their first meeting, back at Arbocala, when Imco had begun the great deception that was his military career.

As they climbed up from the camp, Hannibal carried nothing except his cloak and a small sack. Imco slipped his somewhat more elaborate bedroll under his arm, embarrassed, for suddenly it seemed like a luxury out of character with Hannibal's invitation. Atop the ridge, the glorious burning colors of sunset were just starting to dim. The rim of earth that cut the sun's passing went a deeper and deeper red, bloody and congealed, as if the roof of the sky would be tacky to the fingers, if one could reach so high. The country below hulked off in all directions. Imco thought the hills looked like a hundred shoulders shrugging their way into the distance, curves of muscle and bone captured in the soil itself. He could have studied the view for some time. Though it struck him as beautiful, there was also something ominous in the creeping shadows that he half thought he should keep an eye on.

And these were not the only shifting forms that kept him ill at ease. The guards of the Sacred Band flanked them on all sides. They formed an eight-pronged star, each of them black-cloaked and solemn. They never spoke or looked at their master directly, and yet they followed every move and kept their formation as much as the lay of the land allowed. Though they carried various daggers in their belts, their main arm was a spear in the Spartan style. They planted the staff of the weapon like a third leg each time they halted, and then stood so still as to be made of stone.

This, for Imco, was a troubling illusion. He could not help but look askance at them. Of course he had seen them before and noted their fierce aspect, but he had never stayed so long at the center of their focus. He also realized that the Saguntine girl was nowhere to be seen. Perhaps these men unnerved her as well.

"My lord," he said, "must they follow you everywhere and never speak a word?"

"Why should they speak?" Hannibal asked. "I never talk to them or they to me. They each know how they are to serve me, and they do it. It's strange that you mention them. Myself, I barely notice them. From the day I first set out for Iberia with my father, the Sacred Band has shadowed me."

Hannibal tossed out his cloak and dropped onto it. From a pocket in his cloak he produced a handful of apricots. He spread them out beside him and motioned that Imco could help himself. After a time, he said, "Look at this country, Imco. Sometimes I understand why Romans fight so stubbornly for it, though I doubt many of them notice its beauty. Some men look upon such things and see only trees and earth, the bare materials only. Are you one such as this?"

"No," Imco said, "I see rocks as well. Some shrubs . . ."

Thankfully, the commander laughed at this. He seemed in a jovial mood. Perhaps it was the warm light, but his face held little of the brooding solemnity with which he oversaw meetings. Even his blind eye did not look so awful. It moved now like the other, still filmed over but lively enough that Imco almost suspected the commander could actually see out of it once more. But he might only have grown used to it. He no longer kept the eye closed and it did not ooze the yellow liquid that had so long plagued him.

Hannibal spoke of his boyhood, of his early years in Iberia. "By the gods, it was a time of marvels," he said. His father and brother-in-law still alive, the whole peninsula before them, one nation after another against which to test themselves. They were so far from the meddling hand of the Council that they wielded the power of kings. And yet it was the simple things from that time that he remembered most fondly. Long discussions with his father came foremost. He thought happily of his life among the soldiers. He was younger than any of them, but known by all. He was gifted with thousands of uncles. He would wander out each night and toss himself down anywhere among the thronging army and talk late into the night with whoever he landed near. It was there that he learned of different men's customs, of their gods and the things they ate and their desires. He could greet men of a hundred nations in their native tongues, with the gestures of respect they would each recognize. Truly, that time was the foundation of his education.

He was silent for a few minutes, chewing the golden fruit. The grin at the side of his lips indicated that he was remembering something fondly. He said that as a youth he had not been so soft as he was now. He had slept without a bedroll at all. He had simply cast himself down and accepted the contours of the earth. There had been a time when he had even made a project of sleeping on bare rock. He learned to find comfort within the hardness, the cracks and crevices and irregularities. "Stone is much like the human body," he said, "but it took some training to discover this."

Imco pursed his lips and almost admitted that he preferred the soft beds of Capua to anything he had otherwise experienced, but he deemed this best kept to himself.

"We told many stories in those days," Hannibal said. "The histories of the gods."

"Do you remember them still?" Imco asked.

"Of course. I could speak tales all night if asked. Do you remember El? You will recall that he went out to sea on a reed boat in the early moments of the world—"

"Why?"

Hannibal had fallen into the cadence of a storyteller. Imco's interruption brought him up short. "What?"

"Why did El go to sea? As a fisherman? A merchant?"

"Do you know nothing of the gods?"

Imco said that he knew something, but still the tales he had heard thus far called up more questions than they gave answers.

"Imco, at times you are like a child," Hannibal said. "I like this about you. Talking to you is like speaking to some grown version of the man I imagine my son might become. But it doesn't matter why El went to sea. The god went to sea. That's all there is to it. Would you ask whether he rowed his boat or sailed? Whether he went alone or had a crew? Would you ask how he could have a boat in the time before the world was fully created? Don't answer me, Imco— I'm sure you would ask all those questions. But don't. There are some things you ask questions about. What is for breakfast? Is it raining or snowing? But when I'm telling a story of El, you don't ask; you listen."

The captain held his tongue. His head still rang at the magnitude of the casual compliment the commander had just uttered. This, more than anything, quieted him.

Hannibal began at the beginning, reminding Imco that El was the Father of the Gods, the Creator of Created Things. He was called the Kindly, and he loved the quiet of peace above all else.

When he was young, he decided for some unknown reason to go to sea. Far out on the water he met two beautiful women, Asherah and Rohmaya. Taken with them, El killed a bird flying overhead with his spear. He roasted it and—blocking it from the women's view—sprinkled the flesh with drops of his semen. When he fed the flesh to them, they took his seed inside them and were charmed by it. He asked them whether they would stay with him, and whether they would rather be his wives or his daughters. They chose to wed him, just as he had hoped. They bore him two children, Shachar and Shalim, the dawn and the dusk, and so the world began to take the form we now know, measured by the passage of days, shared between the old one's children. In the ages to follow, Asherah became the more prolific mother of the two women, giving birth to more than seventy offspring, all of the many divine ones who live in the world beyond human awareness.

After Hannibal fell silent, Imco asked, "Do you think, then, that El is the greatest of gods?"

"No. No, I don't believe that."

"But without him all that came after wouldn't have been possible."

"Perhaps. Or perhaps someone else would've achieved the things he did in his place. You cannot say that without El there's nothing; in truth, without El there's something else. As to his greatness . . . Just as with a man, there are aspects of his character to admire; others not to. In his love of peace, he was at times a coward. His own son Yam had the old one trembling with fear. Through threats alone, he forced El to assign him a position over Baal. I would never pattern myself on him. Baal laughed at him for his fearfulness. I would've done the same. Peace is blessed; but first comes the sword; and then the sword must be held aloft to slay any who would take advantage of the calm. This is simply the true way of life."

"But Moloch of the Fire defeated Baal in battle."

Hannibal looked at Imco and grinned, as if the young soldier had just betrayed something about himself that he found pleasing. "The greatest do not always prevail. Often the strongest is defeated. Moloch is not all-powerful; Anath tracked Moloch across the desert and cracked his skull with a staff."

"Then Anath is the greatest? A woman!"

"Imco, things are not as simple as you would like," Hannibal said. The edge in his voice suggested an end to the conversation, but another question appeared in Imco's head and he could not help but ask it.

"Why do you think the gods are so quiet now?"

"They're not," Hannibal said. "It's just that not all of us can hear them."

This kept the younger soldier silent for some time. He wondered whether Hannibal was referring to the priests. Just a few days before, the commander had stood beside Mandarbal as he carved up a yellow bull and read the signs written in its guts. He knew that the man had often predicted the future correctly, but he thought it unfortunate that the intermediaries to the gods were always such unpleasant creatures. Mandarbal's breath was so rank it seemed to fall from his mouth and slink across the ground in search of prey. His jutting teeth and leather gloves and the strange shape of his lips . . . With all the beauty to be found in the world, why did the gods so often depend on the likes of Mandarbal to make their will known?

Thinking that the commander had drifted to sleep, Imco said, "Sometimes, Commander, I question whether this warrior's life suits me."

To his surprise, Hannibal turned and studied him. Incredulity etched his forehead in thin, moonlit lines. "Why would you say such a thing? You are a blessed man, Imco Vaca, a natural warrior. Otherwise you wouldn't have lived through the things you have. You won honor way back at Arbocala. I haven't forgotten that. And Bomilcar—who is a good judge of fighting men—says you have a gift. Perhaps you're beloved of a god who wards off the arrows meant for you, blocks sword swings and spear thrusts. If this is so, then who are you to question it?"

Imco thought about the time he had caught an arrow in the palm of his hand, but this was a small wound that would hardly refute the commander's statements. "Bomilcar thinks too much of me."

"I, too, am a good judge of men," Hannibal said. "There is something in you that I much admire, though I cannot name it. Stay the course until you discover your destiny. It will come to you when the time is right."

"Have you truly never known doubt?"

Hannibal settled himself back against the earth and closed his eyes. "My father in his later years had many doubts. He questioned everything about the life he'd led. He wondered why the gods had ever created the world we know. He marveled at the chaos that seemed to reign just behind it all. In some ways, I believe he wished he'd lived an entirely different life. But at the same time he pushed forward with the many things entrusted to his care. He could not be other than he was. As they say, a lion cannot shed its skin and take on another's."

Imco waited a moment in silence, until it was clear Hannibal was finished speaking. "But, my lord," he returned, "it was you I asked about."

"Why should I know doubt now? The season is matured and closing for winter. We have both won and lost this summer, but for us that is ultimate victory. Think of it this way: We may have suffered in Iberia, but perhaps now the Council will change its ways. They'll bemoan their riches lost, but they'll finally reinforce me, the only hope of finishing off the war. The Romans, believe me, will harness this young Scipio and set him against me here in Italy. And this is what I want more than anything. I hope they are as confident in him as they were in Varro before Cannae. My brother is on his way to us. Surely, you've heard this report as I have. Perhaps Mago and Hanno will soon do the same. Would you bet against the four of us, free to finally end this conflict? In one set of defeats we've been freed for a greater victory. Afterward all that was lost can be gained again. And I hope that the spring will see the fleet of Macedon lining the Adriatic. Carthalo will return with them. I'll finally see Lysenthus in battle. . . . These are the many reasons I look favorably on the future. What place has doubt, considering these things? Now, Imco, let us be silent. As ever, there are many things I must think over, and there is noise enough in my head without your questions."

And that was that. Imco lay beside the commander for some time, unable to sleep, worrying about the things he had said and how the man might interpret them, listening to his breathing and knowing that he was not asleep either. He felt uncomfortable for some time. And then he did not, although this may have just been the calm of approaching slumber.

It happened three days later. He had just eaten a breakfast of boiled eggs and smoked fish and roasted squash, a meal prepared for him by the Tarentine boy assigned to him as a servant. As he rose from the meal, stretching and scratching his groin, his eyes touched on the creature. He had turned and begun rolling his bedding before the image ordered itself in his mind and slowed the work of his hands. It could not be.

He spun around. The spot where he had seen the creature was now empty but for a dilapidated hut and a bit of fencing that had been once a pen. Imco, however, was quite sure his eyes had not deceived him. He let his gaze travel slowly, up along the narrow road, out toward the fringes of camp, and then up along a goat track to the crest of a narrow ridge. There the donkey stood, big-eared and potbellied and knock-kneed. Pathetic in its worn coat, glazed in expression, tail drooping. It could be no other.

Imco looked around for the Saguntine girl. She must be playing a trick on him. This could not be the animal he thought it was. He had been so long at war, so far from home, so tormented by longing and the slow gnawing of dread that he had simply lost his senses. He should be careful, or he would soon be one of those lunatics raving along city streets. If Hannibal knew even a fraction of the absurdities that went on in his mind, he would have him flogged and sold as a slave.

He paced so fast that his feet stirred up dust. A passing group of old Italian women looked at him with more than the usual distaste. They muttered something in their language, an insult surely. The Tarentine boy wrinkled his brow and pretended not to notice him.

Something in the boy's dismissive look broke his resolve. Damn reason. Damn sanity! Both were overrated and daily trumped by the world. If he was insane, perhaps he could be happily so. When would he again have the chance to follow a figment of his imagination in pursuit of the great love of his life? Such moments come rarely and are best seized at once. So Imco told himself as he gathered up a minimum of supplies and walked casually away, nodding to the men in his charge as if he were just going off on some mundane errand. But once he was well away, he picked up his pace and turned to follow the ass's arse.

It would have been inappropriate to offer such a young leader as Publius Scipio an official triumph. After all, he had never held the office of consul. The blood of his battles was barely dry. The news of Ilipa preceded him by only a few weeks and had yet to be considered in detail. Despite his string of victories the great peninsula of Iberia was far from pacified. Some thought him foolish to leave his post before his assignment was completed. Considering all this, the Senate decided that on his return to Rome Publius Scipio should pause outside the city, at the Temple of Bellona on the far bank of the Tiber. There, beneath a chill drizzle from a slate-gray winter sky, he made sacrifices in praise of the gods. He humbled himself before the divine forces and gave a full account of his campaign to the gathered senators, many of whom sat with their arms crossed, searching the proconsul's face for the first signs of hubris.

Publius did not try to justify himself too boldly, but he did suggest that his return was only a product of his continuing duty to Rome. He believed he had accomplished most of what he could in Iberia. As the first Roman general to defeat Carthaginian forces so far, he thought he should bring news of his tactics home and aid in planning future moves. They needed a new thrust to end the war for good, a strike like his move on New Carthage, an attack that bypassed Hannibal's armor and struck at his weakness instead of at his strengths.

Having said only this much, he entered the city to a roar of welcome from the people made more impressive by the lack of an official celebration. Men shouted their support on the street, from windows and rooftops and bridges. Women tossed trinkets of affection at him, reached to touch him, called him their savior, their hero. Girls pouted with painted lips and smiled and swooned as he passed. Children greeted him wearing headdresses meant to suggest a Numidian's curly locks. Some wore shifts like the red-rimmed Iberian tunics or sported tufts of donkey hair stuck to their chins to look like Hannibal's guards. They ran from the proconsul in mock panic, looking over their shoulders, never truly disappearing but instead looping back toward him again and again so that they could renew their cries.

The people believed his Iberian victories to be a sign of things to come. Some said that Publius conversed in person with Apollo and had thus devised his ingenious tactics for success. Others, thinking of champions from the past, pored over their records, concluding that Publius had accomplished more than they had at his age. Priests—never far from the current of public opinion—found in their augury sign after sign that favored Publius. Mass opinion was so clearly in his favor that he was voted into the coming consulship, making him the youngest person ever to hold such an honor.

But if rumor and enthusiastic chatter helped buoy him into office, so, too, did they stir the ire of his peers. Someone had heard him declare that his consulship bestowed upon him a mandate to prosecute the war to completion, as he saw fit, calling on no counsel save that of his own inclination. Others said that he had already begun preparations for a mission so secret even the Senate had no say in it. Or that he had dismissed his fellow consul, Licinius Crassus, as irrelevant. And a few swore that he had offered to meet Hannibal himself in individual combat and so decide the issue with his own blood.

Publius heard these tales with a smile. He had said none of those things. He did have a plan, but he kept it sealed within the close circle of those he trusted most. Once, Laelius' body had pointed out New Carthage as a target; this idea, too, came to Publius through his companion. Shortly before they left for Rome, as they shared wine and hashed over recently arrived details of Hannibal's campaigns in Italy, Laelius said that they should offer thanks to the elders of Carthage.

When asked to explain himself, Laelius said, "They alone may save us from Hannibal. If they'd once given Hannibal the support he needed, we'd be finished. He's won and won again for them, but they send supplies and men everywhere but to him. Hannibal fights like a lion, never realizing that behind him a pack of hyenas salivates to bite him in the ass. He sheds his blood for them, but what do they—"

Laelius froze mid-sentence. "What?" he asked. "What's wrong with you? You've gone white as a barbarian."

And so he had. Publius had just heard in his companion's words the key to the war. In fact, he must have known the answer for some time. It was not even a completely new idea, but now Laelius had banged him on the forehead with it. Hannibal's weakness, his Achilles' heel, the force that drained him month after month but never offered him a thing . . . It had been right there before them all the time. Carthage itself. Carthage. Carthage. Publius had said the word a thousand times that first day and was still uttering it inside his head, a prayer composed of a single word.

Though he tried to keep the idea quiet until the right moment, rumors of it spread, as if bits of his own thoughts were slipping out of his skull and whispered in the ears of his enemies. Success and ambition—he was fast learning—change everything. No thought is truly secret, no conversation truly safe from someone's keen ears. And rivals spring up in the most unlikely of places. Fabius Maximus—the same man to whom Publius had loaned his eyes only a few years ago—brought the issue up in the Senate before Publius had yet done so himself. The venerable senator rose with care and indicated that he would speak on a grave matter. He could not see the other side of the chamber, but he spoke with his gaze moving from place to place, as if he were making eye contact with the entire room. He was stooped with age and seemed to have deteriorated disproportionately fast since his dictatorship, yet this frail look and his graying hair gave him an air of wise authority that had come to serve as a weapon in a world populated by younger men.

"Considering the points I am about to make," Fabius began, "I might need to preface my remarks by making it clear that I hold no ill will toward young Scipio. Some will say I am jealous of his accomplishments, but this is nonsense. What rivalry can there be between one of my age and history, and another younger even than my sons? Perhaps I would have some of his youthful vigor to please my wife, but such things fade in accordance with the will of the gods. Consider, if you will, that I was called upon to serve as dictator in Rome's hour of greatest need . . ."

Publius exhaled loudly and impatiently, enough so that all near him heard the slight. Fabius may have heard it himself, but it was hard to be certain as the old man's hearing was fading just as his vision already had. Laelius guffawed. A few others chuckled behind their hands. Some turned stern gazes on the young men. But all present knew, as Laelius and Publius did, that they were in for a long ramble. Fabius had often recounted his past deeds on even slimmer pretexts. This time he spoke at length, trying to erase any notion that his record could possibly be matched by anyone, assuring all that any criticisms he had to make of Publius' plans were offered only for the good of Rome and in a spirit of sober, mature thought. Publius thought that with each extra phrase and qualification the aged senator undermined himself, but he was content to let the speech run its course.

"Let me point out," Fabius said, after having spun out the full measure of his own accomplishments, "that neither the Senate nor the people have yet decreed that Africa be the young Scipio's province, much less a target of campaign. If the consul is to be understood to have usurped the Senate's authority, then I, for one, take offense at this. Do not my fellow senators agree?"

Some obviously did, judging by the murmurs of affirmation. Fabius, heartened, went on to ask why the consul did not apply himself to a straightforward conduct of war. Why not attack Hannibal where he lay, on Italian soil? Why go to a distant nation of which he knew little, to fight on land with which he was not familiar, with no harbors open to him, no foothold prepared for him, opposed by a numberless army? Would all this truly force Hannibal to return? Not likely, Fabius suggested. If anything, the enemy might march on Rome itself. That was the true threat. And if Hannibal were somehow convinced to leave his entrenched second home, how could the young consul possibly hope to defeat him on his own soil when none of his predecessors had yet done so in Italy?

"Consider how fickle the inclinations of our children are," Fabius said. "Cornelius Scipio, that venerated personage, turned back from his quest to Iberia in order to save his homeland. Now we've before us his son, who wants to leave his homeland in order to win glory for himself. Countrymen, regard this plan for what it is—the scheme of a youth misled by early success, a boy on the verge of a great mistake. Be wiser than this, friends, and do not make the child's error the death knell of the nation."

Fabius sat down to considerable applause. Not enough, however, to convince Publius that his cause was lost. He rose to answer the old man. He stood firm and straight, letting his gaze move around the room just as the aged senator's had, except that Publius made it clear that he truly saw each face he looked upon.

"I extend my heartfelt appreciation to Fabius," he said. "What an introduction he's given me! He's been kind enough to argue against my proposal before I've even offered it. Also, I had no idea he cared so much for my well-being. It is surprising, in fact, because I do not recall him protesting when only I among all this company volunteered to take upon myself the war in Iberia. Back then, when my father and uncle were slain, when three Carthaginian armies roamed that land unvanquished . . . well, back then it seems no one deemed me unfit to lead a military venture. Was my age then more advanced than it is now? Did I know more of the conduct of war then? Are the armies of Africa larger than those I met in Iberia? Did Carthage keep all of her finest generals home?"

Fabius muttered that the young one was right to have so many questions. "He asks them in jest, but perhaps they should be considered—"

"Fabius, the floor is mine!" Publius snapped. Having spoken harshly, the consul inhaled, measured a few breaths, let calm ease through the stilled chamber. "The choice you have before you, Senators, has thus far been written in the blood of our nation. You might continue on the path that has seen us suffer year after year of war and that has led to defeats whose names I will not even utter here. You may choose to carry on like that until Hannibal is truly at the gates, or you may choose to boldly finish the matter. Do not be misled by the doubts spawned in timid minds. Ignore the fears of the fearful, the protestations of hand-wringers. Hear my words now and understand what I promise. Granted your permission, I will speed at once to Africa. You will almost immediately hear that the country is aflame with war. And, as soon as you hear that, prepare for the next news: that Hannibal has been recalled to protect his homeland. This is the one and only strategy that can achieve success. The one thing Hannibal will not expect but will most fear. There is no more to my proposal than this. Judge it and weigh it by merit, and merit alone."

Debate raged for some time after this, until someone remembered that the two consuls had still not drawn their provinces. Nothing could be decided until it was determined whether Publius would be limited to the European or the African theater. This was only a temporary obstacle, however. Publius drew Africa, and a good many senators saw the hand of Fortune in this. It was decided that Publius could plan his attack on Carthage, if he must. But, the senators said, as such a venture was outside the more pressing protection of Rome the consul could not levy new troops for this purpose. He could go, but not with his normal count of two legions. Instead, he could make his war with the disgraced veterans of Cannae who had been banished to Sicily and with whatever volunteers chose to follow him.

As they left the meeting, Laelius rolled his eyes. "So much for gratitude."

FIVE

Sons of Fortune

I t was a harsh country they wintered in, cold beyond reason. The Cavares welcomed them in their simple manner, but the rough customs by which they lived provided little in the way of comforts. When it was not snowing it was sleeting; when it was not sleeting, a chill rain fell, perhaps worse than the frozen stuff. It seemed to seep deeper into the skin and settle in the bones, in the chest cavity, under the eyes. Days of clear brilliance occasionally scattered the clouds, but the nights after such days were colder still, all the heat rushing up into the heavens.

Silenus caught a cough while crossing the higher reaches of the Pyrenees. He nursed it throughout the long season along the Rhône. He spat up bile that changed color from one day to the next. For a time his body burned with fever. He lay sweating, head spinning; at the mercy of a Cavaris mystic who draped his naked body with shreds of animal fur drenched in various unguents. At first Silenus tried to swat the hooded creature away, especially when he saw the sores festering on his hands and caught a glimpse of the conglomeration of features from behind which he viewed the world, a face as wrinkled and bulbous as if it had been baked of

435

lumpy dough. Later, he grew too weak to move. He closed his eyes and cursed the man in long Greek diatribes that went wholly ignored. Nor did he thank the mystic when he regained his health. Of course he was going to recover, he said. He would have done so sooner if that ogre had not harassed him so.

From then on Silenus ventured out only rarely. When he did, he found the frozen world a strange place indeed. He spent a portion of each day writing down his observations. The bare branches of trees that dipped down into the frigid stream currents fascinated him. The water flowed by in its liquid form, but it clung to knuckles of wood in knobs of ice. He had noticed that men sent to reconnoiter the mountains during clear spells came back with faces and hands as sunburned as they would have been in Africa. And he found certain fishes frozen in chunks of ice. Testing an assertion of the local children, he set them to thaw in a bowl beside his cot and found they returned to life as they warmed, flapping a tail or fin as each came free, rolling their eyes. These northern lands made no sense. He would have rather stayed with Hanno, whom he thought of often. But such a decision was not his to make, and the priority was for him to get back to Hannibal.

The state of Hasdrubal's health began to worry him. He suffered no physical infirmity, but his spirits sank so low that he sometimes received no visitors at all for a day or two at a time. When Silenus did gain the man's tent, he invariably found him in the same position, hunched at the edge of his cot, a black bear fur draped over his shoulders. The upper skull and jaw of the beast rested on Hasdrubal's head. The creature's teeth pressed against his forehead. He had even gone so far as to run the bear's legs down his arms and secure the paws to the back of his hands. He spent the day scratching figures into the dry dirt of the floor, wiping them clean, and then drawing again on some other inspiration. Silenus never figured out just what he was doing. He thought the pictures might be charts, battle plans, a map of the territory they were entering. Sometimes he caught suggestions in the lines that reminded him of parts of the human form—an eye, a lock of hair draped over a forehead, contours that could have etched a chin. But Hasdrubal always scratched through the images before he could really make sense of them.

When asked about his health, his thoughts on the situation they found themselves in, the coming year, the state of the men's morale, the best way to communicate with Hannibal, the prospect of negotiating the Alps in early spring—when asked anything—Hasdrubal, if he responded at all, answered with the same phrase.

"Bears sleep in winter," he said.

Silenus found no comfort at all in this answer, even apart from the wild smile that accompanied it, the great bulbous swell of his eyes, and the way he chewed on one corner of his lips with teeth that—in the dim light—seemed inordinately large. Asked to explain the statement, Hasdrubal merely repeated it. Then he grunted a few times, as the creature might. Silenus stopped asking questions. Instead, he reminisced about the things he had seen with Hannibal and conjectured with willed optimism about what the future held for them all. He tried to remind Hasdrubal that a world of possibility lay beyond this Gallic hell: people and places and joys yet to be discovered.

He was not sure whether he succeeded in these attempts, but with the first thawings of spring the bear stirred into motion. Hasdrubal gathered together the ragged remainder of the troops he had escaped Baecula with. All told, just over eleven thousand of them had survived the winter, far fewer than Hannibal had at his command at the same geographical point. None of them looked eager to fight, but all wanted out of that cold place and they knew they had mountains to cross no matter what. So they accepted their general's lead.

Hasdrubal pushed the army across the upper Rhône, where the river was narrow and posed only a moderate obstacle. He moved ready for trouble, his lookouts vigilant and his soldiers marching with spears at hand. Silenus had sworn that he could be of no aid in negotiating the Alps, but this was mostly because he wanted no responsibility for errors. In actuality, he managed to have an opinion every step of the way. For some time Hasdrubal joked with him that his only aim was to avoid any route that even remotely resembled the one he had taken with Hannibal. Silenus did not dispute it. Actually, he was happy to see the Barca find humor again. Perhaps his winter-long concern had been unnecessary.

The Gauls, remembering the first passing horde, greeted this new one with curiosity instead of fear. And perhaps with a measure of pity, for Hasdrubal's men looked none too impressive. Even the wild people who perched on the crags offered little trouble: stolen livestock, a camp follower snatched here and there, an occasional trap set more for amusement than to do real damage. The Allobroges would undoubtedly have proved more menacing, but the Carthaginians avoided them.

And they had chosen their route well. The crossing was—by Silenus' reckoning—blissfully uneventful. Much happened, certainly. Avalanches; days spent trekking into dead-end valleys. A blizzard howled over them for three days straight, then vanished. Stores of grain were ruined by damp; a pack of wolves that had a taste for human flesh attacked stragglers. But there was nothing to match the epic struggles he remembered from Hannibal's venture. They just progressed. Up and up. And then, at some point subtle enough that Silenus failed to notice it, they began their descent, at a moderate incline, via a different pass altogether. Before he dared to believed it they were out of the mountains and onto blessedly even terrain.

On arriving in the region of the Padus River, Hasdrubal sought to correspond with Hannibal. He did not know exactly where his brother was, or in what condition, but above all he wanted to unite their forces. He dictated a longer letter than Silenus would have expected. It seemed, actually, that he had more to discuss than just the logistics of war. He had been so long without his brother that he wished to explain everything that had passed in the years that separated them. So he did. Silenus transcribed it faithfully for him.

This completed, Hasdrubal gave orders for the dispatch of a group of skilled riders. They were to ride south at all haste, to weave their way secretly through the long stretch of Italy, through Apulia, and on into the region of Tarentum, where they hoped to find Hannibal. As soon as the riders thundered out of camp—their horses throwing up divots of soil—Hasdrubal ordered the march commenced.

They approached Placentia as if to lay siege to the place, but as they had no siege equipment the display was really for show. Instead they sat outside the city, taunting the Romans, who refused to climb down from the battlements and fight them. The greater show he made of spoiling for a fight, the more the local Gauls felt the call of war in their blood. Representatives trickled in at first, testing the possibilities for new alliances with the Carthaginians, new promises. Hasdrubal made grand projections about the coming year. He had left Iberia, he said, to join his brother and finish this war. In the ports to the south, he would be joined by tens of thousands of reinforcements from Carthage. He would unite with Hannibal to crush Rome itself. He would drench the streets in blood, a hundred killed for each wrong he could recall: each soldier unjustly killed, each woman raped, each treaty disregarded, every pompous Latin word. He would see the city in flames, loot the place, and drag Roman women through the streets by fistfuls of their hair.

By the time he left, fifteen days after he had arrived, a horde of thirty thousand Cisalpine Gauls trailed behind him. Apparently, they liked what they heard. Outside Mutina, they picked up guides who claimed to know all the best routes south and how to connect one to another for maximum devious effect. With them in the fore, they marched south. At first, the guides hardly seemed worth their pay: The army simply trotted down the Via Flaminia, a road like none any of them had ever beheld. So wide and flat, the stones set with such precision. Initially, they made almost double their normal time, so enthused were the men by their progress, by the fact that the enemy's own handiwork was helping them on. They passed Ariminum undisturbed. The townspeople gathered on the fortifications and watched their progress. The soldiers of the garrison held their positions, pikes jutting up into the sky. But they stayed shut behind the town's gates, so Hasdrubal carried on toward his goal. They followed the coastal road past Fanum Fortunae. The guides had them cross the Metaurus River and proceed along the relatively open ground toward Sena Gallica.

It was here, finally, that they discovered the Romans were not going to let them stroll on indefinitely. An army under Livius Salinator waited for them, encamped in a wide valley mostly cultivated with grain. For four days the two armies sat assessing each other. Cavalry units skirmished on a couple of occasions. The Romans shifted the position of their camp, although it was unclear what advantage this offered them. By his assessment, Hasdrubal's forces slightly outnumbered the enemy's. With so much of his force composed of unruly Gauls, however, he hesitated to engage on such open terrain. He tried to find traps hidden in the land, but the position was not one suited to wily tactics. It favored open battle. Noba volunteered to lead the Libyans on a night march to circumnavigate the Romans and surprise them from the rear at an agreed-upon moment. But as they debated this an individual arrived who changed everything with the news he bore.

This spy had barely escaped the Roman camp with his life. Indeed, a sentry had noted his solitary departure. Before he had made contact with Carthaginian forces he had found himself running from a band of Roman cavalry. He was bashed about his helmeted head with a sword, cut on the shoulder. He swatted away a flying javelin with one hand, gashing his palm in the process. He escaped by plunging down a ravine too steep for his mounted pursuers. The fall was nearly vertical. He bounced from rock to rock, ricocheted off the trunks of trees, and ended his flight suspended in a clump of shrubs so thick that he only broke free of them with some difficulty. For all this, the Roman cavalry was still chasing him when he sprinted into sight of the Carthaginian outposts. The Romans drew up at the last moment, considered the view of the amused Carthaginians and of the Numidians riding out from the main camp. And then they bolted, suddenly recalling that there was a more substantial threat to their safety than anything that lone man might represent.

When all this was reported to Hasdrubal he had the bound man brought to him. He studied the pox-scarred olive skin, the squat build, the wide forehead, and the simple garments that marked him as a legionary. He turned and waved Silenus nearer, as a translator. One of the guards standing at the man's side said that was not necessary: The man spoke their tongue. Hasdrubal's forehead creased at this, four jagged lines that did not relax until he asked, simply, "What have you to say?"

The man bowed his head and kissed his fingertips in the way of the Theveste people. He spoke perfect Carthaginian, laced with rich tones that matched his greeting. He offered himself as a servant of Baal and praised all those who were likewise. He said that though he was of Roman blood and could speak Latin he had been loyal to Carthage since his father had been captured in the first great war. He was born of an African mother in the same region as Didobal, wife of Hamilcar. He had trained from birth in the ways of his father's people so that he might eventually be of some service to his adopted nation. In the second year of this war he had found his way into the Roman ranks, having received instructions that issued from Bostar himself. But since that man's tragic death, he had been orphaned inside the enemy host with no connection to Hannibal and no one to report to. He bided his time and stayed true to the gods they shared and waited for the right moment to break free. He had found that now, and the news he brought was grave beyond any he had held before.

"And what is that?"

The man bowed his head again, kissed his fingertips. Then he pushed his hand out to either side in a gesture that meant he pushed away deceit and now spoke pure truth. "You are sitting in a trap," he said. "The messengers you sent did not reach Hannibal. Nero captured them near Tarentum and found the correspondence meant for your brother. He knows everything. I am a soldier in his army, one of the six thousand he selected. He left the south seven days ago, claiming to march on Lucania, but he turned north once out of your brother's sight. He marched us like a madman and two days ago joined our forces with those of Livius Salinator."

"Six thousand men?" Hasdrubal asked.

The man nodded. "And a thousand cavalry."

"I saw no such thing," Noba said.

"We arrived at night. Not all of us have mustered on the field. Many stay among the camp followers. We sleep cramped in the other men's tents or on the open ground. We await only Lucius Licinius. He's shadowed you down from Placentia and now blocks the Via Flaminia. When he arrives with his ten thousand, all will be in place."

"They'll outnumber us by fifteen thousand," Hasdrubal said quietly, his voice tinged with disbelief.

"What Nero is this?" Silenus asked. "If you speak of Claudius

Nero, I don't believe you. He has a long record and none of it as bold as what you describe."

The man regarded the scribe, then turned back to Hasdrubal to answer. "The Greek speaks the truth. But so do I. I cannot explain it, but please believe me, my lord."

"And Hannibal knows nothing of this?" Noba asked.

The man shook his head. "Not from the mouths of the men you sent. They talk no more."

Hasdrubal received this last statement with the slightest shake of his head. He looked up at Noba, at which sign the Ethiopian stepped close to interrogate the man further. To each question the man had a reasonable answer. And each answer boomed like a mighty drum struck in the distance, moving closer with each blow. If he spoke truly, they found themselves in an even graver situation than Baecula. For now they were in the enemy's land, Hannibal still far away, unaware of them. . . . But only if the spy spoke truly.

"We don't know him," Noba said, after the man had been taken away. "He says he reported to Bostar, but I've never heard of him before. Perhaps this is a ploy."

"To what purpose?" Hasdrubal asked.

"To confuse us. To make us flee. To lead us into some error."

The creases of Hasdrubal's brow fixed in a way that Silenus found uncomfortable just to look at. He bit one corner of his lips, chewed on it, gnawed like a mongrel at a scrap of sinew. "He knew of my message," he said. "He knew the number of men and where I sent them. His speech was accented with the tongue of the Theveste."

"There are numberless means of deceit," Noba said. "Can he not be made to prove himself? What thing could we ask him—"

"No," Hasdrubal snapped. "If he's been coached in how to lie to us, how can we prove it for sure? Do we torture him? If he tells the truth, then he can only tell the truth. If he lies, he can only keep on lying, because he'll know the worth of his life if he confesses. I cannot see my way clear of this. Why is nothing straightforward? Not one thing happens as it should. Not one thing . . ."

He bit off his words, bit his lip again, turned, and fixed the scribe in his glare. "Silenus, what does your heart tell you?"

The Greek raised his hands, palm upward, and groaned at being brought into the discussion. He looked between the frame created by his hands and shook his head. "These things are not for me—"

"What does your heart tell you? Just say it!"

"I believe the man," Silenus said.

"Noba?"

The Ethiopian said, "We must be cautious. Send scouts—"

"The same question I asked the Greek! Answer it."

"If I must . . . The spy is true. I believe him."

"I do, as well," Hasdrubal said. "So we withdraw. Noba, send your scouts to prove or deny the man's story, but unless they do so conclusively we withdraw this very night. That's my decision."

At the first call to march, the guides slunk away into the dimness, never to be heard from again. Hasdrubal damned them, but then said it did not matter. They would follow the Metaurus River through the night, then chart a better course in the light of the next day and ascend into the Apennines to find cover in the rougher terrain. But from its first moments the retreat went foul. Even in the full light of day the river's course would have been difficult to follow. The channel cut a deep meandering confusion of a trench through the plain; the ground was thickly wooded, with sloping banks, with stones tilted at strange angles and roots that looped up from the earth and grabbed men's feet. In the pitch dark the forest came alive with malicious intent. Men could barely take a step without stumbling under the packs, spilling food and weapons around them, cursing. The river became a giant serpent, flexing and squirming, never where it should be. Groups lost their way and shouted to one another, but the uneven landscape played tricks with their voices and led them into greater confusion.

The Gauls did not fear the woods as much as the Africans did, but they grew frustrated and lit torches to see by. Others yelled for them to douse the lights, complaining that the patches of wavering brilliance just made the dark more frightening, distorting the land even more, casting shapes about so that some yelled that the Romans were upon them. Then someone dropped a torch and failed to pick it up fast enough. The flame scorched through the pine needles, to the dry bark of several trees, and up them as quickly as a squirrel fleeing. Within moments the forest was afire above their heads. Horses went wild with fear beneath them. Cattle yanked free of the tenders and searched out dark places and then grew frightened there and ran back toward the light.

For much of the night, Silenus walked slowly, paused often, held his hands either out in front of him to ward off branches or to his temples to calm himself. This was all wrong. They should have kept to the open ground, away from the river. Even if they had marched without direction they would have made better time than they were now. He knew this, and he knew that Hasdrubal must know it. That was why the general worked so hard. His voice rang through the trees, pulling lost men in, redirecting their course. Several times he rode splashing through the river itself, urging men on, keeping sanity with the power of his voice alone.

Hasdrubal did not sleep at all that night. He should have been exhausted, drained, senseless from the continuous labor. But the next morning he shone with vigor Silenus had never seen in him. He seemed to feed on the direness of the situation they found themselves in and showed no sign of the melancholy that had plagued him through the winter. When Silenus commented lightly on this, Hasdrubal answered seriously. He said, "I suffer. I wish Rome to suffer with me."

In the first light of the new day, Hasdrubal explained to all the men just what was going to happen. The Romans were upon them. They would fight that day. If they did not, they would be slaughtered as they ran, and he had no desire to run anymore. He led them away from the river and onto the clearer, undulating ground upon which the day would be decided. As soon as they were out of the trees they could see the waiting mass of the joined Roman forces. The great numbers testified to the truth of the spy's information. They were already in position, drawing up into battle formation.

Hasdrubal called for his forces to do the same. Before long he strode before the front ranks with his sword unsheathed. He seemed taller than ever he had, hardened from his normal physical perfection into something still more statuesque. He wore no leg or shoulder armor, but walked with his chiseled arms and legs bare; they flexed and quivered and jerked with energy. Even the muscles of his neck snapped into and out of view as he lifted his chin and called out his instructions over the masses. He ordered a narrower front line than usual, as the terrain would hamper the wings.

Hasdrubal's gaze met Silenus', but before the Greek could acknowledge him with a gesture the general turned away and the battle commenced. Silenus stood some distance behind Hasdrubal's command position, but the view he got of things to come was much the same. The two forces collided as if each were nothing but a barbarian horde. The Romans hurled their mighty timed volleys, but Hasdrubal had his men rush through these opening maneuvers and draw in to close quarters quickly. Order broke from the early moments and there was nothing of art in the combat. Nothing resembling finesse or strategy. Nothing except for the pure slashing panic of men trying to kill before they were killed. The Gauls bellowed their war cries and blew their animal-headed horns and swung with such force that their braids snapped about them like whips. The Libyans worked with their spears, thrusting overhand like the quiet killers they were, piercing a face here and a shoulder there, twisting the prongs as they withdrew so that Roman flesh tore free of the tendons and bones that held it. The Iberians worked with their double-bladed swords, cutting arms and legs to the bone, and then through the bone, slitting unprotected bellies, spilling loops of guts about the ground. To all of this, the Romans gave as good as they received.

And so it might have carried on until one side gradually tipped the balance in its favor. But Nero, Silenus saw, played one move that changed the balance in an instant. He must have realized that the troops of his right wing, nearer to the river, were tangled in the broken ground there and could find no one to fight. Nor could they progress and keep formation. He had several of these cohorts withdraw, turn, and march behind the bulk of the army to the far end. They then turned again, moved forward, and fell upon the opposite Carthaginian side. In a few moments they caused so much mayhem that the whole battlefield shimmied away from them, rocked by a wave of confusion that must have meant little to those fighting in the center. The move, it was clear, had decided the battle. The Romans seemed to recognize that the advantage was theirs, and they fought the harder for it.

Silenus drew his eyes in nearer and searched out Hasdrubal. For some time he could not see him, but then he saw his standard and picked out his form and that of Noba beside him, both rushing to join the mêlée. His throat tightened so much that he could barely breathe. For the first time in his life, Silenus called upon the gods to intervene. He asked them to prove themselves just this once, to save Hasdrubal Barca from that pack of wolves. He wanted to look away. He wanted to avert his gaze so that the gods might work their magic with subtlety. And also he wanted to grasp up what he could of his scrolls and records and run with them clutched to his chest and put all the distance his bowed legs could between him and this scene.

But he did not. He could not move except with his eyes, which followed that lion standard and Hasdrubal's helmet so near it. He saw him join the thick of the fighting and saw how quickly he became the center of the battle. The Romans must have recognized him for who he was. They swarmed toward him. Silenus saw him fall, engulfed in a mass of enemy soldiers. Ten and then twenty and then more of them surrounded the spot into which he had disappeared, all of them stabbing, thrusting, shoulders and elbows popping into and out of view, reaching over each other to pierce Barca flesh over and over, as if they so feared that he would rise again that they could not stop.

Hanno had visited Cirta, the Libyan capital, as a child. Now, as his quinquereme rowed into its harbor, the city seemed smaller than it had back then. It sat low on the horizon, not so imposing as Carthage, nor as breathtaking in its situation as many of the Iberian fortresses. It was the same dull color as the soil around it, with few embellishments other than inlaid shells outlining certain portions of the walls, and bright red and orange tapestries hanging to seal out the heat of the sun. The Libyans might have grown powerful in recent years, but to Hanno's eyes they were not yet completely committed to abandoning their nomadic traditions in favor of city-building.

There was something about the place that he despised from the start, although this may well have been a product of the circumstances that brought him here. Both he and Mago had been beaten by Publius, deserted by allies, expelled from Iberia, and forced to abandon the expanse that their father had once called his empire. At least they were persevering; none could fault them for that. They had not given up. Despite their fatigue, both of them had embarked on new missions. When he left Iberia, Mago and Masinissa had been preparing for a voyage to the Balearic Islands. They hoped to recruit soldiers there, to inspire them with tales of Hannibal's victories, and then to land a force on the Italian mainland. To Hanno fell this return to Africa. First, he was to call on Syphax, the Libyan king, and find some way to bring him and his thronging army into the conflict. Libyan mercenaries had long been the backbone of the Carthaginian army, but Hanno intended to push for more—not just soldiers, but a true allegiance that would commit Syphax to their cause completely. After this, he intended to go home to Carthage, to report all to the Council. If they did not crucify or behead him, he would do everything he could to sail another army toward Rome. Now more than ever he craved victory. They had lost so much; they had no choice but to fight on.

He did not notice the Roman ships until his feet were on the stones of the dock and he had begun a brisk walk toward the city. The sight of the two vessels stopped him in his tracks. Roman galleys, one flying the flag of a consul, moored and at rest in an African harbor. Never had he expected such a thing. For a moment he considered dashing back to his ship and sailing for Carthage. Before he could decide to do this, he saw the dignitaries walking out to meet him. They moved in grand formality, a small, tight pack of men surrounded by all manner of servants, clearing the way for them, fanning their every step with palm fronds. They gave no sign that things were amiss, so Hanno carried on toward them, behind a procession of his own—men bearing presents to honor the king. He had allocated all he thought he could spare from the treasures he had managed to leave Iberia with, but already he wished he had more.

In the hours to come he found himself in a stranger situation then he could have imagined. At the main meal, where he was to meet Syphax for the first time, he found himself introduced to a man whose face he had many times tried to imagine, a nebulous visage ever changing in his mind, that he had found a thousand ways to hate. Now before him was the real face: thin-lipped, with a crooked nose, and eyes that were intelligent if slightly uneven. Dark hair framed the features in a manner that made the whole more handsome than the parts might have indicated separately. Hanno stared at the man until he opened his mouth and spoke, in Latin.

"Believe me, General," Publius Scipio said, "I am as surprised by this as you. My mission here is diplomatic, as I'm sure yours is. Let us be statesmen just now, warriors later."

Hanno looked around the room. Syphax was nowhere to be seen. Cats roamed the chamber at their ease. They were large specimens, well fed and not too far removed from their feral ancestors. They wore bells on their necks, which tinkled as they moved or preened themselves or snapped bits of meat from the table. There were other guests, but these hung off at a distance, propping up the walls, speaking in whispers and with shifting eyes. Hanno ignored them and spoke, knowing that his voice would carry around the room.

"Fine," he said.

He sat down on the other side of the low table and studied the bowls of dates and grapes set there. His mind reeled from one thought to the next, one question to another. He knew Publius had returned to Rome and been elected consul, but what, what, what was the consul doing in Africa? Had something happened to Hannibal, so that he was no longer a threat? Had Syphax already struck a deal with Rome? Was he dining in the enemy's lair? Would he ever get out of it? Did Rome now have designs on Africa?

"You have affection for Greek things, don't you?" Publius said, his tone familiar and conversational. "I recognize this in your eyes."

As if seeking to refute this, Hanno lifted his gaze and stared straight at him. "I might have once, but no longer. Now I take little joy from life except that which comes from slaying my people's enemies."

The consul laughed. "Then you must be an unhappy—" But even before finishing the sentence, Publius raised a hand in apology.

Syphax entered then, flanked by attendants, men of various ages, some armed and some cloaked as civilian advisers. Hanno turned and solemnly faced the king. He was not a tall man, but his shoulders were wide and the thin fabric of his gown highlighted the strength of his chest. His skin and eyes were of the same grainy brown as the walls of the city, as if he were made of the same stuff. Knobs of curled locks reached up out of the tight weave of his hair. He wore a beard of sorts, made up of tiny balls of hair tied with string, running down his jawline to under his chin.

"Please, sit," he said, grinning and speaking his native tongue. Over his shoulders he wore a necklace of beads, cheetah fur, and gold, an indicator of his rank. He touched this as he said, "We are all equals here. We should speak as such. Perhaps Syphax will one day be famed for mediating the peace between Carthage and Rome."

Neither visitor smiled at this, as Syphax obviously wished them to do. Publius, after hearing a translation, cordially managed to say that the differences he had with Carthage were not such as could be talked through on this occasion. Hanno did not dispute this, and Syphax, clearly amused by the position he found himself in, sat them down and commenced the banquet.

Throughout the meal Publius managed to keep the conversation lively, always complimentary to the host, but amusing also, quick to find humor, tactful in steering clear of the matter of war. Amazingly—despite everything—Hanno found himself enjoying the man's company for the brief moments during which he forgot just who he was and what suffering he had caused.

The king, on the other hand, was somewhat less engaging. As he drank more of the thick malt he favored, he grew loquacious, self-congratulatory, almost maudlin. He had tattoos on the backs of his hands. They were stylized drawings that looked familiar, but Hanno could not quite place them. He rubbed each with the fingers of the other hand, changing hands occasionally, with something feline in his gestures. Though neither guest spoke openly about seeking his alliance, he seemed to believe himself on the verge of a great advance in fortune and spoke as if his past were fading into history.

"Do you know that I was always ambitious?" he asked. "Even as a boy, I tested myself against other boys. There was one in particular who always bested me and my peers at games. He was the fastest afoot, the nimblest with a staff. He had a man's hand and feet even before he sprouted hair on his groin. You know the pure hate one boy can feel for another?"

The two guests nodded.

"Such was the hate I felt for him. One day I had an idea, yes? A small cruelty. I could've been no more than six, seven years of age. I saw Marcor walking toward me across a courtyard. It was crowded with men, and I saw a chance to embarrass him greatly. As our paths crossed I stuck out my foot to trip him. I thought to catch him unawares and spill him flat on the stones. But his foot was better rooted than mine. It was as if I'd kicked a tree stump. I went tumbling instead, landed like a fool, sprawled out and ashamed. Marcor turned and stared at me as if he thought me mad. He knew my intentions and yet was amazed that I was foolish enough to believe I could upset him. He stuck out his hand and helped me rise."

When the king paused, Publius asked, "And what became of this Marcor? Did he grow into as strong a man as he was a boy? I sense some moral soon to be revealed."

Syphax studied on the question. He twirled a massive ring around his thumb, tugged on it, and twirled it again. "Yes. He was my superior in many ways. In most things, really, all but one very important thing. He wasn't my father's son. So on the day that I stepped in to rule my people I had Marcor beheaded. I impaled his body on a stake and set it to rot outside the city. Vultures pecked at him and then hyenas and jackals, and within a few days there was not even flesh left for maggots to eat. So I would say that in the end I tripped him after all."

"I'm sure there is a lesson in this," the consul said.

"Moral?" Syphax asked. "Lesson? Perhaps. Perhaps not. It's just something that happened. Many things happen, don't they?" He dropped the subject and turned to Hanno. "How's that sister of yours? I trust she grows in health?"

"Sapanibal?"

The king laughed through his nose. "No, not that one. The beauty, Sophonisba. Why am I asking you, though? You've not been home in years." The king leaned forward. He motioned Hanno closer with his fingers, his hand like a cat's paw. "I caught a glimpse of her the last time I visited your homeland. Several years ago, this was. She was just a girl, really, but she wore a woman's gown. Her breasts were firm like fruit just about to ripen. Her face . . . Her face was like . . . It was something you could stare at and stare at. I mean no offense to your family, but had I the chance I'd fuck that one till her legs bowed. A mystery of beauty like that should be possessed."

Syphax broke off and flopped back against his cushions. He seemed drunker now than he had just a moment before. Without a thought to his guests he scratched his groin, lingered a moment on the stirring there. He looked up and fixed his gaze on Hanno, the first time that evening that he had looked at him with particular import. "Truly, Sophonisba could drive a sane man crazy. Remember that I mean no disrespect, friend. But she's been in my dreams, waking and sleeping. I've seen bits and pieces of her in other women, but never the whole. Never has a bitch stirred me like she does. I'd even marry her if that's what it took."

Out of the corner of his eye Hanno could tell that Publius, just having gotten the translation of the king's words, was shifting his gaze between the two of them. He knew that the artery on his forehead was beating visibly. There flashed before him the sudden image of him clamping one hand around Syphax' neck and bashing his face in with the other. He wanted to look away, but he held the man's bloodshot gaze for as long as he had to.

Syphax broke away. He moved his chin to the side, toward Publius. The rest of his face seemed to follow a moment after. "But he wouldn't know about this, would he?" he asked the Roman. "She is his sister. He's not an Egyptian, after all. . . ."

Syphax cupped his large hands over his knees. At the gesture, Hanno realized that the tattoos were a stylized rendering of lion's claws, the pattern they made on wet soil. The king rose, saying he needed a woman. They would talk more on the morrow, he promised. They would talk much more.

But in his three days in Cirta, Hanno never had more than a few moments alone with the king. They met briefly in the mornings and in passing in the afternoons; both he and Publius shared the man's table for the main meal, required to sit across from each other, to speak politely, neither one wanting to show his hand or to flare up in frustration. He was not sure whether the consul managed any more genuine discussion himself, but still he could barely contain the simmering anger this kindled in him. Syphax, a petty king, was exploiting the situation to feed his own pride. He seemed to have forgotten the strength of Carthage and to be ignoring the old history of Roman treachery, living in the short glow of his own self-importance. He was a fool, Hanno thought, but he kept this opinion decidedly to himself.

By the time Syphax escorted the two guests out toward the harbor to depart, Hanno still was not sure where his nation stood in relation to Libya. Were they allies or not? It seemed that both sides had tacitly agreed not to press the issue while in each other's company, and as far as he could tell, neither had either of them gained anything certain. Syphax seemed as he had when they arrived—an amused, neutral party. Not wanting to discourage the Roman's departure, Hanno decided to pretend to leave, and then to circle back as soon as he could. He hoped the consul would not attempt the same.

"We have concluded our business, then?" Syphax asked.

Hanno nodded. "As ever, you have the best wishes of Carthage," he said. "May we always be brothers."

Syphax smirked at this. "Fine. Fine. Take my blessings to your countrymen, and to the women of your family."

Hanno half-turned, one arm vaguely pointing toward the docks. It was an invitation for Scipio to precede him, but the other did not do so. The consul scanned his face quickly, and then stepped close to Syphax. He spoke softly, but with no real attempt at secrecy.

"Good king," he said in the Libyan tongue, "since your business with Carthage is now concluded, I would speak to you of a few more matters. Just a few moments of your time in private. You will find interest in what I have to say."

Hanno, fuming, watched the men ascend toward the palace, the Roman close beside the Libyan, their heads bent in toward each other. He almost set out after them, but he had already been beaten, in diplomacy as in the field. Before he sailed, though, he composed a letter to the king. He stated his wishes in the clearest of terms and alluded to all manner of grand rewards for his friendship. He admitted that he had no power to agree to anything on his own, but he assured Syphax that his nation valued his friendship above all others. Staying true to it could only serve Syphax' people, and make the king rich beyond his present imaginings, and as powerful as he had the capacity to become. Carthage would give him anything he asked. Anything it was within the city's power to give. He wrote that he would dock near Hippo Regius.

Only a few days later, a messenger brought word of the possibility that—despite the generous overtures Rome had made to him—Syphax would become an ally to Carthage once more. Little was needed to secure the bond, because they were two nations with roots deep in the same land. Theirs was a partnership to be nurtured, to be enlarged, to be sanctified. They were old friends, but they could be more. There were just two things he must have in return. First, he wanted a guarantee that Carthage would recognize his dominion over the Massylii. King Gaia was ill and sure to die soon. Syphax wanted his nation as his own, and Carthage must acknowledge him over Masinissa.

This was bad enough, but as he read the second demand Hanno felt his pulse through the fingers that touched the parchment. There was one sure way to unite them, Syphax wrote. One way that they could truly merge their two peoples forever.

Each morning, Imco awoke with a start. As soon as his eyes fluttered the world into existence and his conscious mind recalled the dream of a life he had been living for some weeks now, he flung himself upright. He cast around, searching for the woman to confirm that she was real. If she lay nearby he would stare at her in awe. He would move closer, trying not to wake her, his gaze roaming over her long, muscular legs, over the gentle curve described by her hip; he would imagine the weight of her breast so innocently resting on the soft skin of her inner arm. He would study the fall of her dark hair over her golden skin, the intake and exhalation of her breathing, the flecks of sunburned skin on her nose, the tiny ridges of her lips. Then, as her stillness always made him nervous, he would jab her with a finger until her eyes opened, slowly, clear in their opal grandeur from the first moment, as if she had never truly slept but had simply rested in imitation of slumber. If—as on several occasions already—she was not inside his tent, he was on his feet in an instant. He charged outside—clothed or naked, it did not matter—calling the name she had mouthed for him with her own precious lips. Aradna. Aradna!

The simple truth was that he did not fully believe in her. Did not trust that he had actually found her or that she was anything other than a phantom created in his own wandering mind. It had all come from his walk behind the donkey. The creature took him up onto a ridge of wooded hills, down along a lentil field. For a time they walked one each in the two ruts of a wagon road, and then they crossed a flat, fallow field. At times it seemed the donkey stood just near him; at other moments he realized the creature was far away, hurrying him on. He lost sight of it several times, only to find it again. When he stopped at the edge of a settlement and could not see the donkey he had the feeling that he had reached whatever it was the creature was leading him to.

He entered the settlement nervously. The hair on the back of his neck flexed and quivered. He felt himself walking into an ambush, although he knew this did not make sense. What bandits employ donkeys to lure their prey? He slid a hand down his side and fingered the hilt of his sword. It was a group of camp followers. A poor lot of mixed race. There were tents in the Carthaginian style, but there were also skin structures, hovels made of sticks, lean-tos covered over in hides. The place smelled of human waste, of dogs and unwashed people. Smoke from numerous low fires drifted up in the still air like columns stretching to the sky. From around the fires hostile faces glared. A group of men stood and watched him, a few of them picking up sticks and axes. A woman snatched up a running child by the hair and then slapped him as he began to cry. Others went about their work without seeming to have noticed him, but he still suspected devious intention in their erstwhile endeavors.

In his alertness to danger he must have looked everywhere except just in front of him, for suddenly a woman stood and her torso rose into view. Just then noticing him, she spun around and froze facing him, holding in her arms the sticks she had just gathered. Just like that. She stood before him, near enough that if they had both stretched out their arms they could have touched. Her face drained of color as she stared at him.

She was exactly as he remembered. Well, not exactly. Her hair jutted up from her head in several matted plaits. Black lines of dirt clung to the creases of her forehead and under her chin. A sore glistened red and painful at the corner of her lips. The simple gown she wore had no shape whatsoever. It was caked in mud and spotted with oil stains and with a thousand shades of brown. Imco took all of this in but none of it mattered. Behind the disguise he recognized her as clearly as if she stood before him naked and dripping with cold, fresh water. Picene.

He almost called her by the name he had given her, but he had not taken leave of his senses completely. Not knowing what else to do, he motioned for her to take a seat. The only spot available in their immediate vicinity was the mangled stump of a felled tree. Realizing this, Imco flushed with embarrassment. He looked about for another seat, but as he was doing so the woman sat on the stump and watched him, sticks balanced on her knees. It then took him a few moments to decide to sit on the bare ground. Having done this, he was again at a loss. He heard himself speaking before he really knew what he was saying. He told her his name, his rank in the army, and the unit he ran. He suspected vaguely that this was an absurd way to begin but he could not stop himself and went on blabbering until the woman shook her head. She said something in a language he found familiar, but he did not catch her meaning.

"I can't understand you," he said, shocked by this realization, and by the unexamined difficulties it signified.

The woman smiled, and Imco saw the humor as well. They had both said that they did not understand the other in languages that the other could not understand. Imco thought this a serious problem, but the woman's smile hinted that it might not be. She said something else to him. It seemed friendly enough, but he had no idea of her meaning, and his bewildered face showed it. The woman seemed to find further amusement in this. She spoke on. From the stream of words he at least gleaned that she was speaking Greek. As the Carthaginian army used Greek for battle commands he knew a few words of the language, but hardly enough for this type of conversation. The woman solved this temporarily.

Motioning that he should stay where he was, she set down her bundle of sticks and moved off quickly. A few moments later she returned, accompanied by a girl of no more than ten years. She was thin as a stick, and blond. To Imco's surprise, however, she spoke Carthaginian. From the flashes of quick anger in her eyes, it seemed best not to ask how she came by this language.

She sat between the two of them and translated. Her interpretations were rough, presumably inexact, but they both listened as if every word mattered. Imco did not have the earlier difficulty of stating the irrelevant. Instead he said the things he actually meant. He said that he had thought of her ever since he first saw her. He meant her no harm, but he had dreamed of her often. He had been plagued with anxiety for her, wondering where in the world she was, how she fared amid the turmoil of a land at war. A woman should not be alone in a place like this. She was alone, right? She was not bound to a man, for example?

In answer to all of this, the woman said she fared just fine. A cold answer, Imco thought, although this might have been a product more of the translator than the speaker. She did not address the issue of whether she was bound to anyone, but she admitted that she had not forgotten him either. She wanted to understand why their paths had crossed three, and now four times. This was more than chance, she believed. Was he hunting her? Imco swore that he was not. He never had. Not, at least, until the donkey came and got him. It was the donkey that led him to—

"What?" the girl asked, for herself and with no prompting from the woman.

Imco went on: He had been living his soldier's existence with no real aim except to survive. It had come as pure shock to him each time they bumped into each other. The fact that she found him on the battlefield of Cannae stunned him with disbelief every day. Nor did the way he found her this time seem any more probable. He had followed the donkey he recognized as hers and here he was. He knew this would sound strange, but it was not the strangest true thing that he could disclose. The dead Saguntine girl who had been following him, for example. She had been no end of annoyance—

This was the last straw for the girl translating. She stood up abruptly. Forces were at work here that she did not understand, and she thought them better kept at a distance. She warned them not to bother her again and she stalked off.

Again, in the silence after her departure, Imco thought the whole venture in danger of failing, which would be so much more terrible now, unthinkable, tragic. Nothing in the world mattered more than the proximity of this beautiful woman. He was still amazed by her presence, her nearness, the radiance that lay under the grime and that knotted hair. He gazed at her as she drew a little nearer, watched her place a hand to her chest, and studied her lips as they pushed out these syllables: "A-rad-na."

"Aradna?" he asked. When she smiled and nodded, he went through the same motions to tell her his name. For a time the two of them sat near each other, each intoning the other's name, testing it as if searching for answers in the sounds themselves. A little later, Aradna took coal from a neighbor's fire and started her own. She did not tell Imco to leave, and he did not offer to. She roasted a squash by burying it at the edge of the flames, reaching in occasionally and spinning it with her bare hands. Imco brought strips of dried beef out of his satchel, along with heavily watered wine. The two ate in the dying glow of the autumn day. It grew cool quickly, but Imco welcomed this because it brought them nearer to the fire, to each other. Aradna talked freely, conversationally, without the slightest regard for the fact that he could not understand her. She made it seem that the most complicated sentences were understood between them. It was only the simple things that called for gestures and grunts: offering more food, reaching for the wine jug, pointing to a wolf-skin blanket.

He did not notice at just what moment they had moved close enough to touch. At some point they were simply side by side, sharing warmth from the hide, Aradna speaking up into the night sky. He fell asleep watching her profile and woke later to the amazing revelation that the woman's body was curled just next to his and that her hand had slid up under his tunic and was touching his sex. Noticing that he had woken, Aradna drew her hand back. He lay for a long time considering this, and then, nervously, he let his own hand crawl toward her. He touched her at the knee and then slid his fingers up the crease between her thighs. He paused there and might have proceeded no further except that one leg lifted to allow him in. She was both wet and hot and the sensation of her pubic hairs against his fingertips was the most erotic thing he had ever experienced.

He was still in awe of this when she moved, so quickly that he started. She climbed on top of him. He gasped as if in pain. Her warmth as she slid down onto him was overwhelming, complete, the center of his world, and just as hot as if he were pinned to a sun. He could not believe this was happening. She pressed him to the ground and grabbed his lower lip between her teeth and would not let go. He simply could not believe that his life had led to such an utterly, completely exquisite moment.

The next morning he awoke to the smell of her sex on his fingertips. If he had not known what the scent was he would have thought it unpleasant, but because it was proof of their intimacy he inhaled it with pleasure. He could not get enough of it. It did not linger long enough in his nostrils, so throughout the day he again and again placed the back of his nails under his nose. He returned to the camp followers' settlement as often as he could over the next week, until he convinced her to go with him back to the main camp. Though they still could barely speak to each other, neither one considered parting. The army was to be largely stationary for the winter, and no one thought twice about Aradna's presence. Most of them had slaves or servants or captives to keep them warm, if not wives. They simply thought of Aradna as one of these, and Imco kept the truth to himself. She was not a sideline to his daily life; she was the center of it and all else revolved around her. He found that he could say things to her that he had never considered saying to another person. He sometimes feared the Saguntine girl would overhear him, but since Aradna's arrival he had neither seen nor heard from the girl.

One evening, Aradna met him outside his tent. She stalked up to him proudly and, through an enormous smile, spoke a single sentence in Carthaginian. "You are handsome." She grinned at herself, proud as a cat, and Imco knew for a divine certainty that he had never seen anything more beautiful. The only flaw in all this was that he worried constantly that she would leave him, or that he would die in the next battle, or that her beauty would draw trouble. It astonished him that her disguises fooled anyone, but she rarely attracted the type of attention Imco feared. When the next blow— the first great blow—fell, it had nothing to do with their love affair. It was completely unexpected, and it woke him to the unpredictable world they both still inhabited.

He heard the commotion while in his tent. He was watching Aradna's fingers as they plucked strips of goat meat from the hot stones lining their fire pit. Outside the horns sounded a call he could make no sense of. Feet tramped by; people yelled unintelligible things to each other. Imco was up in a moment. He spoke over his shoulder to Aradna, saying that he would just be gone a moment, and then he joined the growing crowd moving toward the command tent. Eventually, he had to shove and claw his way through, frantic now, for something evil was in the air and he could make no sense of the bits and pieces and exclamations he heard.

When he finally broke through the circle around the front of Hannibal's tent he saw the commander on his knees, a shocking sight in itself. His arms hung limp at the sides, palms out, fingers quivering. Before him lay a round object that at first made no sense. It seemed to be a head, clasped between two hands held in place with twine. Imco stepped closer, blinking. It *was* a head clasped between two hands held in place with twine. The man's face was barely visible, bruised and battered, rotten, bluish and reddish and brown all at once. Ghastly. And yet Hannibal had no difficulty recognizing who the person had been.

"What have they done to you?" he asked. "Hasdrubal, what have they done?" He bent closer to the head, but his attention focused on the hands. He touched the knuckles with his fingers. "These are not his hands!" he said, drawn in like a madman clutching at a tendril of fantastic possibility. "They are not his!"

If these are not his hands, Imco saw him thinking, perhaps this is not his head. Maybe it is all a lie. Several of the other officers drew closer. Gemel reached out as if to touch Hannibal's back, but he did not do so. He studied the severed limbs, and then he whispered in the commander's ear. The news he gave sapped all hope from the man. Hannibal, as if angry at whatever Gemel had said, scooped the head up and cradled it against his torso. He strode silently into his tent. The flap fell shut and all who remained stared about in dumb silence.

Gemel whispered something to a few of the other officers, and then, seeing Imco, he approached him. "We must all meet at once," he said. "There is much to discuss. What you see is true. That was the head of Hasdrubal Barca, thrown down outside of camp by a band of Roman horsemen."

"And the hands?"

"We cannot know for sure, but the horsemen, as they left, shouted the name of the scribe Silenus."

Hannibal wanted to rage. From the moment he recognized Hasdrubal's features, wrath stirred within him. He felt it twisting him. He heard the roar of it in his ears, a force such as one hears facing into a fierce wind, a noise that takes from the world the variations that differentiate sounds and leaves only the pure cry that is noise and silence at the same instant. He wanted to rampage. He felt Monomachus clutching his elbow, clawing at him, begging to be allowed free rein to spread his terror a thousandfold in retribution. He knew that he muttered consent to the man, but he did not do so with the full measure of his sorrow. He did not know where to direct his anger. Rome was the obvious target. He would never say otherwise in his life. But a man has quieter demons to contend with and these spoke more softly than the wraiths. They asked who was truly to blame. From whose hand dripped the most blood? And also they answered: Hannibal's. Hannibal's.

Trapped between these feuding choruses, he could barely move for days after receiving the terrible gift. Like a man punched so hard in the gut that he cannot respond, cannot speak, cannot strike back, Hannibal doubled over the head that had once been atop his brother's marvelous shoulders and he simply held it. He did not care that the stench thickened the air in his tent. He ignored the decay. Yes, it sickened him so much that he heaved dryly, convulsively, trying to expel whatever was in him. Skin peeled roughly off the skull and the very touch of it on any object left a malignant stain that he could feel as much as see and smell. All this was true, but still this was his brother. These were the eyes he had once used to see; the mouth he had spoken with; the ears through which he had heard the world. He rubbed away the grime crusting his dry orbs and tried to look inside. It was impossible that Hasdrubal no longer resided somewhere behind those eyes. He placed his lips against the rotten flesh and whispered to him. Words tumbled from him, never long thoughts, but simple sentences like those spoken to a child. He told him that it was all right. It was fine. It would be all right. Oh, but his mother loved him. His mother thought him the handsomest. All women thought so. His father knew him to be the bravest, the strongest. He would take him home, he promised. Home to Carthage. He would leave that very day. Come. Together they would see the city jutting up from the Byrsa hill and they would smell the lemon trees and watch sparrows darting overhead in the fading light of evening. They would run out to the obelisk on the point overlooking the sea and they would stand with their chests pressed to the marble, gazing up at the long stretch of stone piercing the sky, awed that the clouds above slid by untouched.

He had been so young when he left Carthage, but now the place called to him somberly, offering him the past reborn, assuring him that what had been might be again. By going back they would find a new way forward, a different future wherein Hasdrubal lived on. And Imilce was there. His son lived in that place. Hanno and Mago could be called home. Mistakes could be undone. What madness was it that he was not with them at that very moment, all together, in health, beneath an African sun, sheltering within palm groves, walking the innermost gardens of his family's palace?

Hannibal's stunned sorrow and longing did not leave him in the days and weeks that followed. He did not, of course, bear Hasdrubal home to Africa; he had no choice but to sow him in Italian soil. Mandarbal undertook the monumental task of sending his soul on into the underworld despite the damaged vessel that he was. The smoke of incense clouded the air; bells tolled for days; priests called out their sacred words unremittingly into the day and night, uttering rites that none understood but that all cowered before, walking nervously, living quietly, afraid lest some new horror be released by all of this. Eventually, Mandarbal answered the lack of a body by beheading a Roman prisoner whom he deemed suitable to provide Hasdrubal's double. With this man's limbs and organs acting as his own, the general finally lay down to search for peace. Hannibal took no joy in any of this. It provided little comfort, but it had to be done. As so much else did.

He had a war to prosecute. In meeting with his generals, he acted as if nothing of personal significance had happened. Hasdrubal's death mattered only because a skilled leader had been eliminated. An army had been routed and scattered, leaving Hannibal's force once again alone on the peninsula. None of the news his generals brought was good. He learned, finally, detailed versions of all that happened the previous year in Iberia. The loss of New Carthage was tremendous, but Baecula, Ilipa, and now Scipio's preparations to attack Carthage . . . The defeats themselves meant staggering losses. And, what was most important, he saw in the young soldier's actions signs of military genius previously absent from the Roman side. No Roman's mind had yet moved so nimbly, with such cunning, using brilliance tempered with humility. He wondered if this, too, was his fault. Perhaps in taking so long to win this war he had allowed for the maturing of a student, a protégé who was unfortunately aligned against him. He wished that he could somehow draw Publius to stay in Italy, but the news of his intentions reached him too late for that.

He had more to contend with. The Macedonians sent to secure a treaty with King Philip had been captured at sea months ago. Lysenthus and Carthalo had been executed, the other officers kept as prisoners, and the staff sold as slaves. A Roman force under Valerius had sailed to raise other Greek cities into rebellion. Valerius had surprised the Macedonians at Apollonia, routed the army, and burned most of the fleet. As the documents had never reached Philip, there was no treaty, and instead of playing a part in winning Carthage's war, Philip was fighting for his very survival.

Such news might once have been dumbfounding, but events were now moving so swiftly that Hannibal put it behind him. Bomilcar died suddenly in his winter quarters. He was taken not by any war injury but by a swelling in his groin that grew over the space of weeks and seemed to sap the life from him. A work of witchcraft, undoubtedly, and yet another massive blow to Hannibal, for they had been friends since adolescence. Mighty Bomilcar gone; it barely seemed possible. He should have died in the thick of battle, with a sword in one hand and a spear in the other. Why had he been denied that?

Livius Salinator skulked nearby, not offering battle but intent on keeping the Carthaginians pinned down in the south. That was all he really had to do. Even without major battles Hannibal's numbers dwindled slowly, from the attrition natural to the passage of time, fatigue, injury and illness, and occasional desertions. Carthage continued to deny him reinforcements. The city's councillors had already begun to worry about their own skins.

Perhaps most directly pressing for him, however, was that Capua was suffering under a new siege. Three Roman armies had the city surrounded and they looked intent on pushing through to the end. They had even sent a message to the city leaders advising them not to waste their time considering under what terms they would surrender. Rome alone would name the conditions, and they could be sure these would be harsh. Representatives of the city had managed to escape and were begging Hannibal to come to their aid. The other generals advised it too. There was no real choice. Capua could not be abandoned: It had been the first city to join their cause willingly. If it fell, more tentative alliances would fall away like leaves in an autumn breeze.

Hannibal agreed that he must take action, but he dismissed the council, saying he needed the night to consider the situation. Back in his tent he tried to do this, but he found his thoughts drifting. They would not stay on one thing but moved from Capua to Rome, Hasdrubal to Publius, Iberia to Carthage. For a time he slept, and on waking he knew he had dreamed of his father and a conversation they had years before. He lay on his cot remembering the look of Hamilcar, the cadence of his voice, the stern intelligence in his eyes. He was not sure whether he remembered things as they actually had been, or whether he had composed and woven his own words into the memory. Perhaps this did not matter. The memory felt real.

It occupied a part of him, thoughts and concerns that were real. It was from near the end of his father's life, a decade earlier. They were camped in Iberia, near a hostile tribe to their west. Hannibal had called early upon his father—as was his custom—during the hour before dawn. They spoke briefly of the day to come, but just as he was turning to leave Hamilcar stopped him.

"Hannibal, stay with me a moment as I prepare for this day," he said.

"Gladly," Hannibal said. "Should I help you with your armor?"

"That would please me."

Hamilcar waved away his attendant. The servant ducked out of the tent, though they both knew he was within earshot. Hannibal picked up where the other had left off, bent below his father to lace his sandals. He left the bands of leather loose around the joint of the ankle for mobility, but a little higher up he tugged the hide snug against the flesh like a second, thicker skin.

Hamilcar was an old warrior, past his fortieth year. Every part of his body bore the damage to prove it. A livid scar dripped from his left eye, a curving incision made during the mercenary revolt, as if the artist who drew it had wished to place a permanent tear on the man's cheek. His right hand had been shattered beneath a chariot wheel his first year in Iberia. He thought the injury fortunate, as he favored his left. Ribs cracked the year previous had healed at an off angle and had left his chest cavity asymmetrical when seen without armor.

When he spoke, he almost seemed to have been spurred by a musing on his injuries. "Do you know why I chose this life?"

Hannibal almost responded glibly, thinking for a moment that his father might be leading into a joke. But looking up, he saw the distant look on the older man's face. The wrong word might silence Hamilcar even before he answered his own question, so he pursed his lips and carried on with his work.

"I did not have to make war my life," Hamilcar said. "My father fought, but I could have chosen another pursuit. I could have taken our riches and built upon them in truly Carthaginian style. I could have lived a soft and luxurious existence and never known the danger of battle or the pain of being far from the ones who complete you. There is some good to be had in such a life, but I could not honestly have chosen it."

Hannibal finished with the sandals and began to fit greaves over his father's shins, pounded iron infused with a red dust that gave them a color akin to blood. "We are richer now than your father could ever have imagined," the young man said. "Is that not true?"

Hamilcar considered the point, cocked his head, and looked off again. "Yes. I rule a vast empire now. I bend hundreds of thousands to labor for my benefit. My father would not have imagined that. But as to my earlier question, I chose the sword because it seemed the only honest pursuit available to me. Only with the blade, through a contest of wills in which one measures gains and losses against the value of one's own life . . . only this have I found to be truly honest. Do you understand what I mean? That I can be honest and yet lie time and again to achieve my aims? The honesty is in the simple fact that any and all who treat with me know the lengths to which I will go to achieve my goals. If I tell one of these Iberian chiefs that I will have his allegiance and his tribute by his permission or over his mutilated body, he knows I am a man of my word. To fulfill that word I may kill innocents or bribe his friends. I may fight on the open field or set a trap for him. I may not fight with him at all, but might find a willing slave close to him to slit his neck in sleep. I may, to prove a point, unleash an orgy of bloodletting and lust that erases his people from existence. All this I may use to achieve my ends. Do you think that I can still call this an honest profession?"

"Yes. You are honest in your goals. You deceive no man about them."

"And what right have I to demand anything of another?"

"The right of capacity. Does the rain ask our permission to fall upon us? Or the seas to drown ships? You do because you can. All of nature is the same."

"But the seas and rains are elements controlled by the gods. They are beyond our question, beyond our justice."

Hannibal paused in his work and looked up, a smile at the edge of his lips. "Father, are we not tools of the gods as well?"

"Yes, yes," Hamilcar conceded, waving his son away as he tested the fit of his sandals and shin guards. "Blessed be Baal, perhaps I am only a sword in his hand. Simple vanity makes me sometimes believe I am the hand instead. I say I choose this life, but who is to say it was not chosen for me?"

Hannibal rose from his knees and found his father's breastplate. It was a heavy piece of iron, intricately molded. The portion that protected the abdomen bore an image of Elissa, she who had founded Carthage in the dim past. She had fine, strong features, even lips, and a headdress. This was a crown of sorts, and yet it had a martial appearance, as if she might wear it into battle. Her hair curled upward in two thick braids, like the curved horns of a ram. But—a strangely intimate detail—locks of hair escaped at her temples and fell down in wavering ribbons that framed her face. It was an ancient piece, artwork melded with the needs of war. He had always admired it. The only fault was in the hollow orbs of her large eyes. As beautiful as it was, this blind stare always troubled him. Why had the artist not gifted her with sight?

Hamilcar let his son drape the armor over his shoulders. "Another day coming on outside this tent," he said, "another opportunity for the fates to side with or against us. It is strange to remember that all men do not likewise gamble their lives each day. Do you recall the councillor Maganthus? His estate is in the rolling hills and pastureland south of the city. Do you know how he passes his days out there? He has thousands of slaves who work the fields surrounding him. But he has one special slave, a Thracian, I think he was. This slave's task is to search among the fields each morning and bring to him a young woman or girl. Maganthus sits naked on his patio, looking out over his workers while the woman takes his penis in her mouth and stimulates him to climax. The Thracian stands to the side, sword unsheathed and at the ready, should the woman try to damage their master. The combination of the girl's mouth upon him and the slaves in the field and the young Thracian with his sword unsheathed . . . the danger and the power of it all, that is where he finds his pleasure. He told me this himself, as if he were proud of it. What do you make of him?"

"He's a slave himself," Hannibal said, "to his body's desires."

"That was never a difficulty for you, was it?"

"You have always shown me how a man controls his desires."

"I've tried, yes, but this control has come more easily to you." The old soldier paused a moment as Hannibal clipped the buckles snug around his battered chest. It must have pained him, for he closed his eyes and drew his breath in slowly. The muscles beneath his tear-shaped scar twitched a few times, then settled.

"Maganthus is a perverse wretch," Hamilcar said, "but it's not his desires that interest me. It's the delusion he lives under. He told me that each girl who services him gives him proof of her loyalty to him. Any one of them could clamp down and end his pleasure forever. The fact that they don't proves to him that they love him. He disregards the sword in the Thracian's hand. That to him is no honest deterrent. If her life were miserable, she would give it up. So the fact that she neither harms him nor gives away her own life proves to him that all is as it should be."

Hannibal had finished with the breastplate and now stood with his father's helmet in his hands. "Maganthus forgets that the gods created us to love life without reason, even in the face of torture."

Hamilcar motioned that he would not have the helmet on yet. "That makes it seem as if the gods destined us to be slaves," he said. "Slaves to life, at least."

Hannibal smiled. "That's how it has to be, but a true man is a slave to nothing else, right? Not a slave to another man. Nor to desires for sex or fear or drink or riches . . ."

"What about to the bondage of marriage? You have no idea, my young son, how much of my time is spent in silent conversation with your mother. She has been a splendid wife to me, given me strong children, and raised them in health. But she doesn't approve of what I—of what we—do. You'll never hear her say so, but I know this to be true. I did something once that I always regretted afterward. I showed her my work. I let her see my bloody masterpiece— a battlefield piled high with mercenary dead. I wanted to shock her with it. I wanted her to see my work, to understand the wrath of Hamilcar Barca and see that I—a lone man—could dominate many others. I should never have done this."

"Why? Did she not understand what she saw?"

"No," Hamilcar said, "just the opposite. She understood it completely. She's loathed me ever since."

"You're joking," Hannibal said. "Mother never once spoke ill of you."

"What do you know of it? You were nine years old when we left Carthage. Do you think she would've spoken of such things to you? Didobal did not stop loving me; but she loathes me at the same time."

"If that's how she feels, she is wrong," Hannibal said. "Honor comes from battle with formidable opponents. The mercenaries had Carthage on its knees. Only you could save them. No woman can know what that means. So she shouldn't judge."

Hamilcar placed a hand on his son's shoulder. There was gentleness in the touch, though the hand was callused and misshapen by years of violence. "Don't speak with that tone when you speak of your mother. You believe you have all the answers, I know. But this is a sickness of youth. We get other illnesses in old age, but in youth, when our bodies are strong, we suffer from one thing only—certainty. When I was younger I too had few doubts about my purpose."

"Do you now?"

"No. You know my goal. I've never wavered from it. I still don't. Despite all my old man's dithering, few know their calling as clearly as I do. I don't truly question the rightness of my deeds in the world. Your mother is a creator; I am a destroyer. There is balance in this."

The old warrior stepped away and tested the fit of his breastplate again. Resigning himself to the armor, he dropped his arms and looked again at his son. He said, "I do, however, question the rightness of the world itself."

Hannibal, lying on his cot in his tent of grief, realized he was just now learning to understand the man. How was it possible that conversations of years before could speak to him now in such a different way? He wished he could ask his father what wisdom the intervening years had provided him for his own old questions. But one cannot make new queries of the dead. If there were answers to be found, they must be in the scripts already written. "The rightness of the world itself," the old man had said. That was what he doubted. Ten years on, Hannibal was beginning to understand Hamilcar. In some ways, he was becoming him.

But the next morning, when he spoke to his assembled generals, he focused on one portion of his father's words and pushed aside this last proclamation. It might have been true, but what use was doubt to those who still breathed air and lived? Doubt undermined; it offered no help to those still slaves to life. When he issued his decision on their opening move of the season, the entire council looked at him in disbelief. Gemel asked him to repeat himself. Hannibal did. There was one way to tie all of these disparate problems together in a single action. They were to strike camp by the end of the week and march north.

"But not to Capua," he said. "Our target is Rome."

Word of Hasdrubal's death preceded Hanno's arrival by a scant few days. The Barca family was still in mourning, though they did so in a strange way that angered Sapanibal. The priests, with their fickle wisdom, deemed that Hasdrubal's death should not be marked in the normal manner. They decreed that he had done something to invoke the ill will of Moloch. His failures in Iberia, his flight toward Italy, and his defeat proved it. Because of this the family could show no grief. They could not wail or cut their hair. They could not go veiled. They could not utter his name without speaking it down toward the ground. They could not prick their fingers with pins or cut their veins at the wrist to bleed until they were weak and faint. Instead, the priest forbade them to eat meat for the month. They could make their own offerings to the gods throughout the day, but in the evening all the Barca women were made to bow their heads as the priests offered sacrifices to cleanse the nation of Hasdrubal's sins.

This galled Sapanibal. They should be praising the man and easing his way into the afterworld. In typical Carthaginian fashion, they betrayed him instead. Hers were a petty people, she thought, who neither reward a man for his successes in life nor honor him in death. Sapanibal raged against this in her private chambers, with only her servants to hear her. In public, she kept her thoughts to herself. Neither Sophonisba nor Imilce showed anything on her face but the fear she expected from them. Even Didobal seemed to accept the advice of the priests. She swore to herself that if one of them looked at her with an inkling of rebellion in her eyes she would rise up and decry the priests' orders. But they did not. Not that she could see, at least.

She wondered if any of them would rouse from stupor if the city one day disrespected Hannibal in a similar manner. She could not imagine that they would not, although this should be no different. A brother was a brother. A husband a husband. Why did only she understand this? She felt, as she often did before, that the male energy inside her was rendered futile by her female body. If she had been born a son instead of a daughter she would have wrung those priests by their necks.

Thinking these things, she rejoiced to hear that Hanno had returned. Wonderful enough that he was alive, but better yet if he arrived in holy anger and cut out the corrupt heart that beat at the center of the city's institutions. He was a warrior, after all. How the soft men of the Council would wither before him!

But in this, too, she was disappointed. Before he had even returned to the family compound, he stopped at the Temple of Baal and there made offerings and underwent a cleansing, to remove the stains of war. The next day he still did not come home but met with the Council instead. From what Sapanibal could gather through her sources, the magistrates grilled him on every aspect of the Iberian wars. Hannon railed against all the Barcas: against Hannibal for starting the war with Rome, against Hasdrubal for abandoning the peninsula without permission, against Hanno and Mago for losing it all through their military ineptitude. Equally reprehensible, they had left alive this Publius Scipio, who reportedly had found killing Carthaginian soldiers so pleasurable that he was now planning to attack Carthage itself. Hadus proposed crucifixion as a just punishment for Hanno's being foolish enough to return. Another peace party member suggested offering Hanno's head as a present to the Romans, along with entreaties to end the conflict. Perhaps Carthage should add his entire family as slaves, Hannibal included.

But even in their foul mood, most councillors balked at this. Many of them had lost fortunes in Iberia and knew that giving in to Rome ruled out ever regaining this source of wealth. And they knew Rome had already been too terrified for too long to settle for an amicable peace. With the exception of the staunchest peace advocates, the others—after chastising Hanno in every manner, over the space of three full days—asked him what he proposed to do next. And he answered, although he gave this portion of his testimony exclusively to the Council of One Hundred Elders. His proposals were best made in secret, so he met with the elders deep in the Temple of Moloch, in a chamber protected by the god himself. There were, therefore, a few aspects of his dealings with the councillors that Sapanibal had yet to learn.

When she did lay eyes upon him, she stood beside the other women of the household in the Chamber of the Palms. He paused just inside the reed outer door, blinking in the dim light, waiting for his eyes to adjust. His face was ashen from his ordeal. He seemed to walk in a daze. The thick scent of incense clung to him still, Moloch's powerful aroma. It seemed he brought something of the hungry god into the room with him. He gazed at his family, behind whom towered the pillars meant to look like an ancient forest. Among these clustered the house servants, officials, eunuch guards: all seeking their first glimpse of the returning son.

Hanno bent his knee and lowered his head and explained that his safe arrival was not his doing alone. It was allowed by the gods, and so he acknowledged the power of Baal, who blew the wind across the sea that bore him home; the kindness of Tanit, who protected Carthage and blessed her crops; the blood rage of Moloch, which took lives other than his own; Astarte, from whose fertility he issued, without whom his homeland would be a barren wound; Eshmun, by whose power his many injuries were healed; Ares, who had filled him with fury in battle. . . . He had always been devout, and he did not forget any of the Carthaginian pantheon for the role they had played in any good fortune he had experienced. His prayers took some time but he completed them without rushing. Only then did he bridge the few steps between them and fall into the women's embraces. Up close, Sapanibal could smell more than the initial aroma of the incense. With her nose close to his ear she smelled the essence shared by all Barca men. It nearly brought tears to her eyes.

Finally, late that night when the household was quiet and the fires burned low and the lyre player in the garden had stopped her plucking and lain down beside the instrument, Hanno came to Sapanibal in her room. She embraced him again, hanging from his neck like a lover. They sat on the terrace overlooking the olive groves. Hanno sipped a heavy red wine, so thick it tinted his teeth a brownish color in the torchlight. And he told her everything. He spoke with a voice both dull and honest, describing the life that he had seen these few years. He spoke with the complete honesty he saved for her among all people. He even described the tortures the Romans had inflicted upon him, the things they promised him if he would turn on his brothers. It was not that he had ever been close to Sapanibal or loved her overly. But he had never been able to lie to her. She had been an older sister who had always seen through him. She judged him, yes, but he ever sought her for confession. Their relationship was no different now. At first, it warmed Sapanibal to fill this role again.

But at the first mention of Syphax she felt a tightness in her throat. She realized that the sensation mirrored a constriction that had gripped Hanno's own voice. He spoke more slowly and kept his eyes pointed out toward the darkness beyond the orchards. He explained that the Roman consul, as part of his plan for attacking Carthage, had made overtures to the Libyan king. This could not be allowed. It would have spelled their death in and of itself. King Gaia was ill and powerless; some said he was already dead but that it was being kept secret until word could reach his son, Masinissa. In any event the Massylii were about to be swallowed into Syphax' empire. This was certain. This was happening no matter what. Carthage, drained by the other theaters of war, was powerless to stop it. Masinissa was a brilliant young man, of whom Hanno was personally fond. He had been a great soldier in the Iberian campaign. They had parted as the best of friends, but Fortune thinks little of such emotions.

"Masinissa has been outmaneuvered without even knowing he

was in a game," Hanno said. "This is tragic for him, but if Syphax joined with Rome and turned against Carthage it would be the end of everything we have ever worked for. It would mean the destruction of the nation. Barcas nailed to crosses. Amazing punishments. Unthinkable things . . ."

"I understand the picture you paint," Sapanibal said. "What did you do about it?"

"I saved our nation," Hanno said. "I made an arrangement with Syphax that won him to us. I promised that we would not contest his actions against the Massylii. And I gave him Sophonisba for his wife."

Sapanibal had been looking intently at her brother and went on doing so for a few moments. But then the meaning of his words drew all of her attention as a dry sponge sucks up water. Her vision blurred. Hanno went out of focus. She had to blink to bring him back again. Her response was first a simple refutation. He had not done that. "Sophonisba is betrothed to Masinissa," she explained. "She's been promised."

Hanno pursed his lips. "I'm sorry. I like Masinissa well, but their marriage is not to be. It is unfortunate . . ."

Sapanibal's look of complete disbelief hushed him. "Who gave you the authority?"

Hanno pressed his chin to his chest and held it like that for a moment. Then he looked out again into the night. "The Council sanctified it," he said. "Didobal agreed. They've already annulled the engagement. It doesn't exist. It never did. To speak of it will be a crime punishable by death."

"You are not telling the truth."

"Why would I lie?"

"But she loves him. Do you understand? She *wants* to marry him. Is this how you save your neck? By trading your sister into slavery? Have Barca men fallen so low? When she hears of this she will die inside—"

"She already knows," Hanno said. He waited for his sister's response to this, but she only stared at him. He sighed and tried to regain a calmer tone. "Sapanibal, if the gods one day ordain that I may split Syphax on my sword and watch the life escape him, I will do so. At present, I cannot."

"So instead you'll call him brother? What's happened to you? I thought war made men, not turned them back into children."

For the first time Hanno's voice rose, heated, quick of tongue. "Sister, look at me. I return defeated, without an army. I have nothing but my life, and that's worth very little. The Council was half a breath away from nailing me to a cross. Hadus would have disemboweled me himself and eaten my entrails while they were still warm. Do you understand? I am alive because I could promise those fat men that an army of sixty thousand Libyans wouldn't be banging on the gates of our city. Instead they'll fight for us. I've hardly saved my neck, sister—not considering the plan I've devised and the risks of it. None of our necks are yet safe. Sophonisba understood this better than you appear to. You surprise me. You are wise in so many ways, but you have a woman's blind spots in your vision."

Sapanibal stood and moved near to her brother. She placed her hands to either side of his chair and, looking close into his face, she said, "I see more clearly than you imagine, but if I could turn my eyes into stones and rip them out to throw at you I would. You don't know what you've done to her. Syphax? Syphax?"

She had spoken calmly, but something changed with her proximity to him. Hanno began to remind her that Syphax was no demon. He was a king, who would treat Sophonisba well—

Before either of them knew it was going to happen, Sapanibal slapped her brother. "Was Hasdrubal the Handsome a demon?" she asked. "Was he? Was he? Was he?" She slapped him again, with the right and then with the left hand, and then with a mad barrage from both. He sat taking it, his features smudged and reddened; then she dropped on him and hugged him in a strange embrace, her fingers digging into his shoulder blades.

Later still, Sapanibal walked barefoot down the hall toward her sister's quarters. She stood between the eunuchs who guarded the entry, which was open to them but hidden around a corner. The two men each straightened when she approached. They did not speak, did not ask after her business or even set their eyes upon her for more than the instant it took to recognize her. She just stood, not sure what she would say to Sophonisba, or that she would even enter. She told herself that it was her duty to soothe her sister while also reminding her of the union's importance to their nation. Of course, this was what her reasoning mind believed. Her outburst against Hanno was a confused thing, the product of prolonged worry, of her own weakness. Fortune spins like a top and one never knows on what symbol it may land.

The soft, round notes of a pipe chime came to her, pushed by an evening breeze. For a moment she had the strange thought that some spirit had brushed past the chimes as it rushed to confront her, to grab her by the neck and squeeze all that nonsense out of her throat. She did not believe any of it. Maybe she never had. Maybe that was why this pained her so, because her whole life in duty had been an empty torture, a slow, prolonged strangulation. She heard movement inside, the murmur of a voice, and then a short, clipped sound that could have been either laughter or crying. This prompted her to move, although she did not know what she would say.

Rounding the corner into the soft lamplight she noticed Imilce first, leaning on Sophonisba's makeup table. Once, Sapanibal would have felt a pang of jealousy. She was no great friend to her sister, but Imilce had become one. She had taken the place in Sophonisba's life that Sapanibal might have occupied, if she had not been so cold to Sophonisba, if she had not envied her beauty and disdained the joys she took from life. She got no farther than the entrance, and then stood, elbows tucked into her sides.

Her younger sister sat on a stool before the small desk in which she kept her makeup and jewelry. Sapanibal caught her breath, frightened by how beautiful she was. She wore her hair pulled back and her face in profile was a twin to the goddess Tanit's. The curve at the ball of her nose, the full richness of her lips: all glistened as if they were molded anew each morning. She seemed ever to step out of a sculptor's workshop, unblemished, not even a grain of imperfection in the marble of her skin. Her gown fell off one knee, exposing the weight of her calf, a single foot, five toes, the smallest of which wore a tiny gold ring. Perfection. Tragic perfection.

She was about to withdraw when Sophonisba jerked her head around. Viewed straight on, her face struck Sapanibal with the force of a ceremonial mask. The dark makeup with which she etched the edges of her eyelids had run. Black lines streaked down her cheeks in the trails that dipped into the corners of her mouth. She stared at Sapanibal for a moment, then twisted her lips and asked, "Why do you look at me that way? I am not the first woman to wed for the sake of Carthage. Is that what you're going to tell me? Remind me of your own marriage and all the good it did our family? Say it, if you like. You must've waited many years to."

Sapanibal closed her eyes. When she opened them a moment later tears burst from them. The harsh expression fell from her face completely, replaced by a trembling chin, flushed red cheeks, a ridged and quivering forehead. Several times she tried to say something, but the words bumbled around behind her teeth and nothing came out but sobs of hot air. That was not what she was going to say. Not at all.

Sophonisba stood and moved forward, lifted her arms, and pulled her sobbing sister into her embrace. "What's becoming of us?" she asked.

It was a day that Masinissa would always remember, a moment of decision that shaped everything in the life that was to follow. He began that fateful day trying to find a way to convince Mago not to quit Iberia. They need not be beaten yet, he argued to himself. He could send to his country for more horsemen. Carthage might provide another installment of infantry. Up to that moment, he had found it inordinately easy to kill Romans. He still believed he could accomplish all the tasks set before him and return to Numidia on his own terms. Though he had not mentioned it to the Barcas, he had even rejected envoys from Scipio the previous summer. The Roman had offered him friendship in return for his abandoning the Carthaginian cause. Scipio promised him Carthaginian lands as his own, with gifts from the wealth of their treasury, with numberless slaves, and with permission to rule Africa as he saw fit. It was a lot for a single agent of Rome to offer; this Scipio was bolder than his father. But still, it was of little importance. He rejected the offer with contempt and went on killing them. Who were the Romans to offer him anything other than their blood to wash his spear?

It all changed in a single moment, when a messenger whispered in his ear. What he heard stopped his breathing, blocking his throat so that for some moments his lips opened and closed uselessly, neither speaking nor drawing in air. This happened just after first light of the morning. Before the sun had reached a quarter height he arrived at Mago's camp. He entered at full stride, speeding past the two surprised guards and kicking the tent flap open with his foot.

"How long have you known?"

Mago looked up from the correspondence he had been reading. His first answer was a frown, his eyes nervous and—the Numidian thought—deceitful. "What news have you heard?"

"You know what I've heard. I've been told the sky is falling and my head is uncovered."

This seemed to confuse the Barca. His frown deepened for a moment; then he dropped the pretense. "The news comes to me just this day as well. By the gods, Masinissa, I had no part in this. Syphax saw an opportunity and he grasped for it. But do not be rash. We can yet mend this."

"How? How, when everything has been taken from me? My father is dead! I am no longer a son, and I am not a father. Now another man takes my Sophonisba to his bed and fucks her full of my enemies. Instead of my children she will push out Libyans, beasts that will bark for my blood. How can this be mended? Things done cannot be undone. There is only one way forward. I resign my command in your army; I leave Iberia—"

"You cannot!" Mago said, up on his feet now and coming toward him. "Don't be a fool, Masinissa. I know your blood is hot. I'm sorry they have done this. It was done without my knowledge. Nor would Hanno betray you, or Sophonisba herself. This is the work of the Council. Fight on with me, brother, and we will one day set things right again."

"Again I ask you, *how?* Would you have me fight for you still, when you are allied to the man who has grasped my kingdom as his own? Have you not understood?" Masinissa blinked his eyes furiously. The conflicted reality of the situation flashed across his face in bursts, as if he were still being pelted by new realizations, continuously putting together how one thing rebounded against another.

"All along I've been played for a fool. Sophonisba . . . Sophonisba herself trapped me. She made me a dog, leashed by Carthage. . . ."

"No, that's not so. I know my sister's heart is true to you. I saw her with you. I saw the flush of her cheeks and the joy you kindled in her. If she betrays you, it's with a knife to her throat and no other choice. Tell me you believe me, and we can make anything possible."

The emotion in his heart was too much for Masinissa to bear showing another man. He gripped Mago and pulled him in so forcefully that the solid impact of their chests took away his breath. He pressed his cheek against the rough grain of Mago's neck. "I wish I could believe you," he said, "but this morning a veil has been lifted from my eyes and I see everything differently."

"I cannot be your enemy," Mago said.

"And I cannot be your brother," Masinissa whispered. "I loved you, but think of my position. I am a king without a kingdom and a husband without a bride. I don't know about the bride, but I must at least claim my nation back."

As he walked away he counted each step toward his horse, listening for the call, the shout for him to halt, the order for the soldiers of the Sacred Band to rise up and grapple him to the ground. But the shout never came. Perhaps this was a last act of brotherly affection; perhaps it was a sign of weakness. Either way, he was soon up on a high ridge, riding with his guards around him. With the wind in his face and his horse beneath him he thought most clearly. He sent a messenger to the Romans the next day. He swore allegiance to them on the terms Publius had earlier offered, with the new condition that Rome would help restore his kingdom to him and help him make war against Syphax. It was strange to make promises to Romans. It meant, of course, that he was now at war with Carthage, but it could be no other way. He was a Massylii. With his father's death he had become a king. Strange that he had not heard of this for several weeks. Strange that someone had to whisper in his ear for him to know the whole world had changed.

Telling the Romans that he was returning to his country to raise an army, Masinissa departed Iberia with two hundred of his most loyal horsemen. He could have pulled more of his men if he had the time or ships to aid him, but he did not. Only his friendship with

Moorish traders made his flight possible. He considered sending word to Maharbal in Italy, asking him to forsake Hannibal and return to Numidia, but he had not the resources to do this. Not yet, at least. Perhaps he also feared the answer he might receive. Maharbal did not know him. Who was to say he would even acknowledge him as his king? He had first to make sure any of his people would.

The events that unfolded from the moment his feet touched African soil came so fast and furious that the prince barely rested. He slept no more than a quarter of the night's cycle and yet still the waking moments were so full of shifting providence that he felt a lifetime passing in what should have been weeks. He landed on a barren stretch of beach east of Hippo Regius. His men disembarked beneath the light of a waxing moon, the world cast in bone highlights, full of shadow and light, with little gradation in between. They rode their horses right from the transports into the water. They churned up onto the shore in a froth of spray, propelled by bubbling rows of waves. The mounts neighed and tossed their heads and kicked sand into the wind. Not a soul moved on this lip of the continent except for them. This was as it should have been. Masinissa hoped to arrive home unannounced.

But Syphax, he soon learned, had anticipated him. As soon as he received confirmation from Carthage, he had shouted his men to arms. He called in soldiers from throughout his vast empire, making the usual promises: riches and women and the rule of all North Africa. He sent multiple armies marching into Massylii territory, a many-pronged attack that took the city of Thugga with barely a fight and stormed Zama with great violence and cast a net of terror over the plains of the upper Tell. He had King Gaia's grave identified and dug up. He set his corpse aflame and erased all monuments to the ruler's reign and set about placing his own name on all that had been Gaia's. The Massylii were a brave people but without a unifying leader they could not withstand such onslaught; without Carthage's blanket of protection they suddenly seemed a small nation. Syphax pressed them beneath his heel and took joy in it, for to do so had been his hunger all his life long. The summer was not yet half over, but he retired to Cirta to await his new wife and the pleasures he was sure she would provide him.

Masinissa had landed in a country in turmoil. He was branded a bandit from the moment he arrived, a wanted man, treasure to the killer who severed his head and offered it to Syphax, a greater fortune to the man who brought him in alive for the king's amusement. Scouts roamed the shoreline in competing bands. Though he missed him by a day, a Libyan captain named Bucar spotted signs of Masinissa's arrival and set out after him. He ambushed the young king's men a few days later, on the flatlands outside Clupea; he swept down on their riverside camp, trapping the small band between a force of two thousand horsemen and four thousand foot soldiers. There could be no contest between such numbers, so Masinissa's men simply struggled to escape the tightening vise. They fled the horsemen but everywhere found pikes aimed at them from the ground, javelins flung at them in numbers and thickness like a school of barracudas.

By the time they sprung clear of the foot soldiers they numbered less than fifty. In the daylong running skirmish they killed three times as many as they lost, but this was a losing equation. To their honor, his men protected Masinissa with their own lives. That was why there were only four of them alive when Masinissa led them at a full gallop into the river Bagradas. The current lifted them and tumbled them in the brown, silt-laden water. They slid obliquely past their pursuers, at a steady speed faster than the horsemen could make over the irregular terrain, gnarled and choked as it was with bushes. Some of Bucar's men plunged in after them, but three of these went under and disappeared. Seeing the same happen to at least two of Masinissa's men, Bucar pulled up the chase. The prince learned later that he had declared him dead and ridden for Cirta to bring Syphax the news.

But Masinissa did not die. The river spat him to shore at a constriction in its great girth, on a patch of sand so fine and soft that it reminded him of otter fur. His two remaining men found him and together they sat contemplating the desolation that had overtaken them. They had been no great force that morning, but now they had only two horses to share between them, and one of those was lame. How could this have happened? Masinissa asked himself silently, again and again as if the answer would come with dogged persistence. He had accomplished nothing, nothing at all, and now he feared he could not.

One of his companions tugged at his elbow and urged flight. Villagers from a nearby settlement had spotted them and were suspiciously watching from the opposite bank. They could sail for Rome, his companion proposed. They would enlist in the Roman army and return later to set these matters to rights. But these men, brave and true as they were, were not leaders of nations. Masinissa knew that if he arrived in this condition in Rome his life would be worth no more than the price of his skin, the value of his bones and of the jewelry that clung to them.

Instead, he turned from the plains and ascended into the Naragara highlands of his father's territory. He traded his tattered royal garments for a humble disguise. He wore no emblem of sovereignty and shared the two horses fairly with his guards, taking his turn afoot when it came. They dressed the same as he and, to onlookers, occupied no different station in life. In the guise of a holy pilgrim, he sheltered with the peasants of Mount Bellus and made offerings there to the Egyptian god Bes, hoping for some of his mischievous power. He ate the meat of goats roasted on open fires and stole fruit where he could find it. Throughout this time his companions looked on with troubled eyes, for he seemed to have no direction. He did not speak to them of strategy, of tactics to regain his throne. He kept his thoughts to himself and appeared miserably content to roam the land without direction, from the mountain back down to the plains and then through the orchard lands south of Zama and from there into the scraggly hills south of Sicca, a land of mountain goats and of people who walked as if on cloven hooves themselves. They went high enough that they looked down on the flight paths of eagles and condors, creatures that could only take flight by jumping from heights onto columns of heated air rising from the plains.

To aid him his companions spoke casually with the people they met, testing their opinions. Did they mourn King Gaia's death? Did they welcome Syphax, or loathe him as he deserved? They brought Masinissa reports of all they heard. The people were afraid, they said. They despaired, but they still loved the line of Gaia.

Sometimes, huddled beside the campfire or mounted on a ridge or plucking the feathers from a rainbow-throated dove—anytime, really, for it came unannounced by an external impetus—the prince muttered aloud things strange for the men to hear. Words of praise, evocations of beauty, whole speeches of bottomless longing, Sophonisba's name pronounced so slowly that it seemed a new word added to the language, something expressing the tortured love of a man stripped of the skin of artifice: all this embarrassed his men and made them nervous.

When he spoke of his father they understood him somewhat better. He had always claimed that his father had no vision, no ambition. He was a kind man, wise and strong enough to hold together the disparate Massylii people, but Masinissa admitted to his companions that he had always been an ungrateful son, sure he could do better. He could not remember a time when he did not count the days until his father stepped from power and let him stride on to greatness. He had just woken to the fact that he knew nothing of how to be a king. He knew only what it took to be the spoiled son of one.

To this one of his companions offered, "That cannot be so. Our fathers teach us whether we listen or not."

"A crocodile is born of an egg and never knows his parents after hatching," the other added. "And yet he grows to be a crocodile; he cannot be anything else."

Masinissa turned to the two men and stared at them for a long time, unsure that he even recognized them.

When they arrived at the remote council of Massylii elders a few weeks later, it seemed nothing more than a chance happening, as if they had been blown there by a random wind. The council took place at an ancient site known only to the tribal leaders and outside the range of any one elder's base of power. Masinissa was fortunate in his timing, although as yet he took no comfort from this. The council seldom needed to be held more than once in a generation, always in times of turmoil. This was such a time.

There was no structure large enough for the men to gather in so they met in the open. If they noticed Masinissa at all, they thought him one of the local herdsmen. His clothing was poor and bedraggled and his hair hung in knotted locks that obscured his features.

He listened as the men—some of whom he had known from birth—spoke of the troubled times they lived in. They couched their words cautiously. It was obvious they wanted to speak frankly to each other, but none knew who among them might have turned to Syphax. They might speak their minds tonight, only to find themselves skewered tomorrow. So the conversation was roundabout and seemed to be heading for no definite conclusion. It was clear that Syphax had grabbed them all by the balls. They hated him for this and spoke with fondness of their dead king. But it was not until one of them offered a prayer of remembrance for Masinissa himself that the prince decided his time had come. It would have been unnatural to hear one's own death lamented and not speak up.

Masinissa stood and pushed his way into the group of men. They turned and looked at him. One elbowed him and another asked his business. He held his tongue until he had centered himself in their circle, and then he kept silent a little longer. He drew his hair back from his face and fastened it with a thong made of lion's hide. And then he dropped his arms, raised his chin, and met the men with his gaze. His fingers twitched as he stood there, ready to draw his dagger and take all the lives he could before he was killed, if it came to that.

He said, "Do not mourn me. The king's son lives."

Landing on Sicily in the spring, Publius found the island simmering like a pot of boiling water just taken from the fire. The cities of Syracuse, Agrigentum, and Lilybaeum had not watched the war indifferently. Throughout it they had swayed in their allegiance, tipped here and there by the machinations of their ambitious leaders. Many of their residents—the Greeks especially—remembered the fine times they had enjoyed under Carthaginian rule and had not found Roman dominion to their liking. They had rebelled, although with only mixed, temporary success. At the time of Publius' arrival, however, the island had returned to Roman hands. All active revolt and political ploys had been quashed by the forces stationed there, thanks, in part, to the irresolute support Carthage had provided those declaring for them. The Greek rebels in Syracuse found themselves being stripped of their wealth. Many had been kicked onto the streets, where Latin children pelted them with stones and women spat on them and men used any pretense to lash out at them.

Publius, looking at this, reckoned it hardly a stable base from which to launch the greatest military action of his life. So he set about to right things from the first day. Citing his authority as consul, he ordered Greek property returned and demanded that the people of the city live together once more as they had in the years before this recent conflagration. In as short a space of time as he could manage, he circumnavigated the island, bringing this message to all the cities. Then he called the disgraced legions from Cannae to muster. He merged them with the seven thousand volunteers he had secured before leaving Italy. Together, this formed an army of just under twelve thousand, the vast majority of them infantry.

He drilled them mercilessly. He had learned a great deal in Iberia and he tried to convey it to his men and build upon it further. Each day brought more supplies in from the stores kept throughout the island, saw new weapons crafted and honed, filled the harbors of Sicily with the sails of more vessels. The seafaring cities of Etruria laid the keels of some thirty warships, preparing them in the remarkable time of forty-five days from the moment the trees were felled until the hour they sailed for Sicily. Laelius led scouting missions along the African coastline, looking for a place to land, surveying the cities there, getting an idea of their defenses, and making contacts with likely spies. He did not go near Carthage itself, for Publius had another target in mind. The intelligence that Laelius brought him revealed that all the pieces were in place.

The morning of their departure dawned gloriously clear, pleasantly warm, with just enough breeze to buffet the forty warships and hundreds of transports that bobbed in the harbor of Agrigentum. Publius himself called for silence on the ships. When this message had been passed on to all the vessels he invoked the presence of all the gods and goddesses of land and sea. He spoke the words he had practiced for this occasion, with nothing kind in them, but a plainspoken demand that the divine forces aid them in bringing to Carthage all of the terror and suffering Carthage had unloosed on Rome. And he asked that they further be allowed to press the matter to a conclusion, so that the men of Rome and all those allied with her could return to their countries laden with treasure, with plunder enough that they could bury their chins in the bosom of it and forget the strife that had been inflicted on them. He sacrificed a cream-colored bull with a star splash of white on its forehead, slung the entrails into the sea, and watched how they floated on the surface. Finding the picture to his liking, he gave a signal to this effect. A rolling, irregular roar traveled from ship to ship, a great cacophony of voices and horns and bells that some swore must have carried all the way across the water and set the Africans trembling.

They sailed through that day on a middling wind and made slow progress through the night as a thick fog blanketed the sea. Even so, first light brought the shoreline of Africa into hazy view. So near as that, Publius thought. So near to us as that. The first point of land, the captain called the Promontory of Mercury. Publius liked this well enough, but ordered that they carry on to the west. The next morning the captain called out that he had sighted the Cape of the Beautiful One. This, the consul believed, was just the place for them, not far at all from Cirta, but at a good enough distance for him to get his troops to land and into order.

At the sight of them the peasants along the shore ran in fear, grabbing up everything they could carry and kicking their children and livestock before them. Laelius asked if they should chase them down and stop them from sounding the alarm. Publius answered in the negative. In fact, he quite wanted the alarm sounded. Let it ring all the way to Carthage, all the way across the plains of Libya, to the Atlas Mountains and back. The farther away they heard the call, the better.

With the entire army on land, they at once began to march on Cirta. Most of the troops under Publius' command now had not been with him in Iberia, and many of them grumbled at this first move. They were heading in the wrong direction! Why go west when Carthage was to the east and stood undefended? But, as had proved prudent in the past, Publius kept his own counsel.

Some distance outside the city, a delegation from Syphax approached under a banner of parley. Publius agreed to hear them. The message they brought was that the king himself wished to meet with Publius. He believed they had spoken once as reasonable men and could do so again now. Publius sent back saying that the situation was much altered from their last meeting. He came not to talk now but with an army actively at war with Carthage. He said that he knew of Syphax' marriage into the Barca family, and he knew that Hanno Barca was at that very moment raising troops among the Libyans, while several Barca women resided in Cirta. He had every reason to believe that the state of war now stretched to include Syphax' people. Unless the Libyan king renounced his allegiance with Carthage immediately and completely, he faced an imminent clash of arms.

To this Syphax responded with his sincerest hope that it need not come to that. True, he was married into the house of Barca and therefore to the fate of Carthage. Hannibal's wife and elder sister had accompanied his new bride and were in his care at present, but he was still a ruler of his people and capable of making his own decisions. Indeed, this situation placed him in a special position that might benefit them all. Before he need consider breaking with his beloved wife, he again proposed that he mediate between Rome and Carthage. This conflict had gone on too long, too many had died, enough had been destroyed, and both sides had been shown to be great powers evenly met. Hanno, as a commander on African soil, had authority to make arrangements by which his brother in Italy would have to abide. Let them here work out a peace wherein Hannibal withdrew from Italy and Scipio sailed home. Do not answer rashly, but consider that the bloodshed could end with words instead of the sword. Did this not promise benefits to Rome so great that they deserved considering?

When the two of them stepped away from the delegation to ponder this, Laelius asked Publius, "Do you believe he is sincere?"

"He is a jackal," Publius answered.

Laelius considered this for a moment. "But a sincere jackal?"

In answer, Publius told Syphax that he owed it to his people and to the brave men of his army to explore the possibility of ending this conflagration peaceably. He would consent to a meeting with the king, but only after they had corresponded on enough details to verify that such a conference would yield results. Syphax agreed.

While this got under way, Publius had his army camp on the plains, about a half-day's ride from the city. An equal distance away lay the enemy's camp, a site that had long been used by the Libyans to house troops in training and keep armies of raucous men outside the city itself. Through informers whom Laelius had recruited on his early reconnaissance missions along the coast, Publius knew a great deal about the army he was to face. Syphax had a core of well-trained soldiers, some who fought as spearmen in the manner of the Greek phalanx, others whose primary weapon was the sword. These fought standing side by side, with the edges of their feet touching, slicing like so many butchers at whatever came near them. They carried wooden, hide-covered shields, but their work was more suited to attack than defense.

These men posed as serious a threat as any trained by Hannibal, but much of Syphax' army comprised troops newly called to service from throughout his empire. He had no system for training and for-mation to match that of the Roman legion, and therefore aimed to prevail through sheer quantity of fighting men alone. Soldiers drifted in like hyenas drawn to a kill. They came singly and in tribal bands, lone creatures who looked after themselves foremost. They were clad in leopard and cheetah and lion skins, burly-armed and long-legged, some with enormous locks of hair like a hundred snakes, others with shaved heads tattooed in imitation of their spirit animals. They carried a wild variety of weapons, many ghastly in ap-pearance: spears of differing sizes and functions, pikes with many-pronged heads, flails that ripped divots of skin loose with each strike, harpoons attached to cords so that a pierced man could be yanked off his feet. One group had chosen the ax as their favored weapon and each of these wore the shriveled remainder of their en-emies' severed limbs to attest to their weapons' utility. A band from a seashore people to the west appeared with small round shields en-crusted with coral, carrying tridents so heavy that a man once pen-etrated by their points was thereafter anchored to the spot and could be dispatched with a small shell knife.

The ranks of the African army swelled from one day to the next. Clearly, this was just what Syphax hoped for, and Laelius again and again asked Publius when they were going to act. He feared the enemy would number thirty thousand soon. Forty or fifty thousand before long. Who knew how many sand-colored men would eventually step out of the landscape? Their own troops were only twelve thousand strong. How long could they wait? Each day their number grew, and each day Hanno had more time to shape them into a more cohesive—

"How many died at Cannae?" Publius interrupted.

"You know the number," Laelius replied.

"Yes, I do," Publius said, as if this were answer enough to the whole line of questioning.

A week into the slow negotiations, Publius commented that the Libyans had not expanded the boundaries of their camp. No doubt in a desire to conceal their numbers, they contained their growing bulk behind the original perimeter. This structure was formidable, built as it was of stout, gnarled hardwood, woven into a tight wall bristling with thorns as long as a man's finger. It was not a new kind of defense, but had been improved over the years. It was formidable, Publius pointed out, but it was also wooden. For that matter, the huts in the Libyan camp were built mostly of reed and thatch. The Carthaginian contingent, following its custom, built in earth and dried wood. What the camp now presented was a wealth of fuel, contained in a smallish area, crammed with men and animals, supplies and clothing and foodstuffs. The only things not vulnerable to fire were metal objects, and rings or cups, spears or axes, which had never harmed anyone of their own volition.

His companion, as ever, searched in this observation for the course Publius was formulating and then began to see it, unclearly, in outline.

Still the negotiations went on. Syphax had first to convince Publius that Hanno was committed to the possibility of peace. Then Publius needed proof that Hanno had the authority to conclude an agreement. After that, they began a back-and-forth on basic conditions that had to be agreed upon before they went any further. Some among Publius' own staff grumbled that they were playing into Syphax' hands. Though this was never said within his hearing, Publius learned that some of his men believed he had been stricken with fear and wanted to conclude a peace without further risk so that his previous successes would not be overshadowed by a failure. This opinion was hard to refute, for his plan needed to mature. He let them talk.

To Laelius, he noted the tendency of the wind to rise after sunset and gust for some hours as the earth adjusted to the change of day into night.

Nine days into the negotiations, Masinissa arrived at the head of nearly two thousand mounted Massylii. Publius could not help but comment to Laelius on the strangeness of watching the African horsemen ride calmly into his camp. The last time he had beheld such a sight he was looking on his sworn enemy; this time, however, he did his best to put their previous relationship behind them, to dismiss it as a historical detail, not something to trouble them with suspicions now. At least, so he declared publicly, in his opening remarks. Masinissa's people introduced him using the title of king. Publius did not hesitate to take up the term. Why not? Either it would become true in practice, or the young man would die in the effort. That much was clear.

Masinissa, at their first meeting, reiterated the other officers' nervous views on the swelling army of Libyans. Although he spoke no Latin, he could make himself understood in Greek, which pleased the consul almost as much. Publius calmed him, saying that when the time came his men would be in a position to slaughter as many of them as they could hold pebbles in their hand. Publius noted that the young man looked often in the direction of Cirta. He knew why, but for the time being he said nothing.

By the eleventh day, it seemed they had corresponded through messengers for as long as they could. In the final few days Syphax and Hanno increasingly set out demands that proved them scoundrels. In return for ending hostilities and pulling Hannibal back from Italy, they not only wanted Publius' withdrawal from Africa, they also required that Iberia be largely returned to Carthaginian hands and that ports captured by Hannibal in Italy be traded for the Roman-controlled ports on Sicily. They proposed that neither side actually admit defeat at the other's hand; thus

Carthage would not be required to pay a war indemnity to make amends for the damage done to the Roman people. And they wanted Masinissa handed over into Syphax' custody.

None of these terms were acceptable. Publius believed that Hanno well understood this, but perhaps his hand was forced by representatives of his council. Or, perhaps, with the fifty-some-thousand men in their camp, they believed they held the advantage. In any event, the consul put aside whatever compunction he might have had about his plans and sent back his reply. It was agreed. They would meet in person in two days' time, on the neutral ground between their camps, just after first light. Hanno and Syphax should both be present. And they, like Publius himself, should have spent the preceding evening in prayer and purification, so that all they said the following day would be kindly looked upon by the gods.

Only on the morning before the arranged meeting did Publius call his generals together and lay before them the complete situation as he saw it, answering all their questions in a single meeting. Of course he was not considering the terms of the enemy's offer. He had never intended to. He had put Carthage to their backs deliberately, not to avoid the issue but to win it more conclusively. The simple fact was that Carthage had no army inside its walls. There were riches in there, fat men and beautiful women and slaves enough for a city twice as large, but there were few fighting men. Carthage had never been a nation of citizen soldiers, and this was their great weakness. They preferred to elevate men of genius to military leadership and then buy temporary armies as required. Hannibal had changed this, to some extent, but Hannibal was not in Africa. The people of Carthage believed themselves safe inside their city's massive fortifications. They could easily hold out for months; they had done so in the past. As they could all see, Hanno Barca and King Syphax had gathered for themselves a sizable force here beside Cirta. Why so?

"Is it not clear that the Carthaginians had hoped that we would attack Carthage?" Publius asked. "Once we had done that and were entrenched, committed, limited to the grounds that the enemy had for generations shaped for its defenses, then and only then would their massive army attack us, not from the city itself but from behind our backs. They would have chosen the spot, the time, the circumstances. They'd have marched in with one unified force under their best commanders, numbering the exact maximum they could muster. This, at least, is what they wished. But something very different will take place.

"This war began with deceit and trickery," Publius said. "Now it will end by the same."

There was some debate about what Publius then proposed, but it was halfhearted. The generals all saw its deadly efficiency and knew that any other course might mean their doom. Accordingly, the evening before the scheduled meeting, the various generals led their men out and into positions near the Libyan camp. They waited until dark and, letting their men's eyes adjust, marched with no torchlight to give them away. Each corps carried a red-hot ember in an earthenware jar, wrapped in leather to insulate it and pierced with air holes to feed the coal.

When Publius judged the hour right, he took a reed whistle and played a wistful melody. Others picked it up and passed it on, as had been arranged. With this, the keepers of the coals in four different areas tipped them onto the dry timbers they had prepared. Men huddled close around each of these, protecting the infant flame from the wind that had begun to blow. As soon as the red glow flared into gold tongues, men came forward with torch after torch.

Publius, from where he stood at a distance to take in the whole scene, saw the lights multiply from a few small points into many moving flames. He watched as four fires became hundreds, carried by men in sweeping movements that fanned out all around the camp. He knew the moment the first torches touched the thorny perimeter wall. And he saw how moments later the torches leaped in somersaulting arcs, landing among the reed-and-wood structures. With the evening wind buffeting across it all, it was a matter of a few breaths before the whole place was aflame. The dry wood and reeds went up as quickly as lamp oil.

The Africans woke and at first none understood the horror that was afoot. A few guards shouted alarms, but they were unheeded. Men ran out of the camp's few exits in disarray, bleary-eyed, often weaponless. They stumbled, pushing each other, in a frenzy, some of them swatting at their burning garments. Then they were cut down by what to them seemed to be soldiers the shape and color and consistency of flame, who stepped out of the gloom with sword and spear. Within moments there were so many bodies piled by the entrances that the Romans had trouble planting their feet. Or perhaps it was fear that made them clumsy, for the scene before them soon became a vision of hellish agony. By the time the third and fourth contingents of soldiers had replaced those stationed at the exits, they were not soldiers but angels of mercy, cutting down the flaming, maddened, humanlike figures that ran howling out into their last escape.

In the full light of the following day the army took in the scene with hushed amazement. The camp was a blackened wasteland. Demons of smoke drifted through the charred remains, bodies in every imaginable contortion, man and beast likewise reduced to black, shriveled versions of their former selves. The charred poles and skins that had been shelters could have been carcasses too. Syphax had, of course, been in the camp to perform the purification rites. Publius had required these especially for this purpose—to keep him out of the city and away from his new bride. He had been captured during the night and now sat bound by the arms and legs. He stared with unreasoning eyes at the scene around him and yelled curses at Publius, at Rome and the gods of Rome. He called them all liars and scoundrels and said that history would know their perfidy. A day would come when all of their sins returned to plague them manyfold.

So he harangued them for some time, but Publius soon got the gist and stopped having his diatribes translated. Later, the king hung his head and blubbered into his chest, looking as dejected as a mutilated veteran of some forgotten war. Thus was Fortune fickle, even for kings of men. Hanno had not been found, but nothing in the world suggested that he had done anything except ascend toward the heavens in ash and flame. He had gone the way of the army of Africa, leaving Carthage undefended and, finally, conquerable.

Still looking upon the scene and thinking thoughts such as this, Publius saw the approaching messenger and the banner under which he rode. The message had been five days in transit, not such a short space, really, but short enough for Publius to feel some urgency. He thought he saw Fabius' trembling hand in the document, but even that did not lessen its impact. Hannibal was marching on Rome, the dispatch said. The Carthaginian made no secret of this but instead rolled across the land announcing his movements with drums and horns like some traveling entertainment. He was sweeping in new allies along the way and had also unleashed a hitherto unseen degree of barbarity directed by his general Monomachus, who worshipped the Child Eater and was at that very moment devouring Italy's young. The Senate chastised Publius for the grave danger he had placed them in, saying that he had promised Hannibal would quit Italy on word of his arrival in Africa. Instead, the invader had used the consul's absence to strike his final blow. Rome now found herself in the greatest peril she had ever faced. The burden of this rested upon Publius' young shoulders. He was, therefore, recalled to protect Rome. Immediately. There must be no delay.

Looking south from the terrace adjacent to her rooms at Cirta, Imilce thought it ominous how little of consequence happened in the whole great swath of country she could see. It was true that laborers worked the fields; a flock of birds rose, swooped, and landed, flying from one field to the next and on again, dodging stones thrown by children employed for the purpose; a breeze stirred the palms lining the river and set them rattling; a cart trundled along beneath her, two men talking in Libyan atop it; the dry hint of smoke drifted in from the continent, a scent mixed with the smell of the vast stretches of farmland. Yes, much was happening as she stood there, but all of it seemed false, an imitation of life in denial of the larger movements afoot. She was sure of this and found it most disconcerting that the world was such a resourceful deceiver. From the moment she placed her fingers on the smooth mud of the wall she felt that she must not move until the mystery hanging in the air had been revealed. As it turned out, she did not have to wait past mid-morning.

She first saw them as a ripple on the horizon, a dark line that for some time appeared and disappeared. She thought it might be a trick of the light, the play of heat demons out on the plains. And then the strange thought came to her that a mighty flock of ostriches was rushing toward them. But this impression vanished almost as quickly as it came and she knew what it was that she looked upon: an approaching horde of mounted men.

"Is it my husband returning?" a voice asked, flat and emotionless.

Imilce did not turn to meet Sophonisba. She smelled her sister's perfume, and that was enough to increase her melancholy. The fragrance was just slightly musky, masculine in its richness of tone. It struck the back of the nose, so that by the time one scented her she was already deep inside. Imilce felt the younger woman's hand slip over hers. She reached up with her thumb and acknowledged her by clasping her little finger for a moment. They had been together every day now for weeks, ever since both she and Sapanibal had insisted on traveling with Sophonisba to Cirta. Such an escort was customary when a young woman journeyed to wed in a foreign nation, and the two older women would accept none of Sophonisba's protests. Indeed, Imilce found the resolution with which the girl accepted her fate almost unnatural. She kept reminding herself that Sophonisba was a Barca. That was where her strength came from. She had said as much before. "I am not like most girls," she had said, long ago. "I do not pray for childish things. I pray that I will somehow serve Carthage." And so she was doing. Imilce wondered whether she, too, was serving Carthage when she held Sophonisba as she sobbed, in the hour before dawn when she sometimes slipped away from Syphax' bed. How cruel the things nations ask of their women.

"I cannot tell," Imilce finally answered. "They're horsemen, but—"

"They will have been victorious. I should prepare myself. The king will want me."

So she spoke, but Sophonisba did not lift her hand or move away. Imilce felt the film of sweat where they touched. She almost thought she could count the rhythm of the girl's heartbeat through her palm, but it might have been her own pulse. She was thinking about this, and had been for some time, when Sophonisba whispered:

"They are not Libyan. They ride under King Gaia's banner."

The young woman possessed keen eyes. Just a moment later the guards must have reached the same conclusion. A shout. And then the great drum beat the alarm. Men and women and children all knew the sound and responded. Soldiers sprang up from rest and yelled instructions to each other. Those outside the city dropped their work. Women of the fields lifted their garments above their knees and ran for the gates, which started to close, the loud clicking of their works yet another signal of distress.

Imilce looked around from one tower to the next and then out to the horizon, waiting for someone to end the alert, to explain away the banner as a prank or a misunderstanding. It had to be, for no enemy army should be approaching them now. Hanno had assured her they had everything in hand. Either the Romans would make a peace, he said, or the Libyans would rout them with their superior numbers. She tried to think of some way that either possibility could lead to this new development. Perhaps the peace had been concluded, and the approaching force was friendly—

Sophonisba whispered again. "The gods are punishing me still. It's him."

It took Imilce a moment to pick him out amid the throng of men, but there he was. Masinissa. Imilce glanced at her sister-in-law but could read nothing in her profile. It was stony and cold and distant: all strange words to describe such rich features. Sophonisba's lips parted. "Let us go closer."

It took a few moments to leave their quarters, walk through the palace, and cross the courtyard. The men might have barred them from scaling the gate tower, but none yet knew what to make of Sophonisba. She might be only a girl, or she might be a tyrant queen with the power of life and death over them: they were not sure which. They parted before her, and the two women soon found a vantage point overlooking the city's main entrance.

"Look at him," Sophonisba said. "Just look . . ."

Indeed he was something to behold. Gone was the lithe adolescent figure Imilce had last seen frolicking with his friends after a lion hunt, gone the roundness of his boyish features and the handsome innocence of his eyes. Masinissa rode as a man at the head of a mass of men. He wore a royal garment, a vibrant sweep of indigo cloth wrapped around his body and up into his hair to form a headdress. He approached the gates of the city with utter confidence, his legs and feet bare. The vibrancy of his dress made him the center of attention outside the walls. Those behind him seemed a dusty, sunbaked manifestation of the continent itself: dressed in many hues but all beginning and ending in shades of brown, clothed in animal hides, tattooed, with knotted manes of hair, lion teeth dangling around their necks, spears clenched in knotted fists.

Masinissa shouted that the gates had best be opened. The city's new monarch had arrived; he was thirsty and hungry, for meat and for the pleasures of his office.

The magistrate in charge in Syphax' absence answered that he opened the gate for no man but his king. He joked that the young prince had been sent to the wrong destination. The city was sealed against him, he said. That was plain to see. Perhaps the prince was ignorant of the army awaiting him on the plains. If he wished to win the city, he must first turn and face its king.

Masinissa grinned wide enough to show the ivory of his teeth. Alas, the magistrate was mistaken in many ways. First, he was no longer a prince. And second, the battle on the plain had already been fought, and won by the Roman-Massylii alliance. Syphax' army was in ruins. Dead and burned already. As this was so, debate was of no use. Simply open the gates and all inside would be treated fairly.

"The battle is concluded," he said. "Let us shed no more blood today. We are all of Africa here. Now open!"

At a shout from an officer, the spearmen along the entire wall facing him lifted their weapons up to the ready. Masinissa was within spear range and could easily have found himself a cushion stuck by a hundred points. His soldiers called for him to retreat somewhat, but he lifted his fingers and snapped them—one loud pop—in the air above his head. A moment later, in answer, two mounted guards led a bound man forward. He sat straight-backed atop a silver horse, his hands chained behind his back, his head bare to the heat of the sun, dressed like the simple prisoner he now was.

"Behold your former king," Masinissa said.

Sophonisba inhaled sharply, a breath like a child who has just stopped crying. She must have recognized her husband immediately. The magistrate, however, did not. He shouted down that never had this man been his king. The Massylii laughed at this. A guard at one side of the man in question shoved him savagely with the butt of his spear. The man gripped the horse with his legs, but not tightly enough. He tumbled off, landing hard upon his shoulder. His cheek pressed against the parched soil, and his neck bent dangerously. The horse did not move. It simply blew air through its nostrils and waited for its rider to fall completely free. Having done so, the man stayed curled on his side, in a fetal pose, deaf to Masinissa's calls that he rise.

For a moment, the scene grew chaotic. Masinissa's men wrestled the man up from the ground, kicking and cuffing him and demanding that he stand. He made himself deadweight, then bared his teeth and nipped the flesh of one guard's cheek. At Masinissa's direction, one of the Massylii clamped his hands around the man's head and tilted it toward the sun, showing first one profile and then the other. They ripped his tunic down the chest, as if this would identify him. And then they held his hands up for inspection, pointing at the lion track tattooed there. The magistrate could have no question now. It was Syphax.

Masinissa dismounted and strolled near enough to the wall that he hardly even had to raise his voice. "Fortune has turned," he said. "I wouldn't be here before you now, except that your king seized my father's domains a few months ago. We who were blameless he dishonored. We who were proud were made to bow before him. But all has been set right again. I'm not here to harm you. Why would I, when you are now my servants? All that Syphax took from us I reclaim; and all that was previously Syphax' I now call mine. You will find me a kinder master than he. So open!"

But still the magistrate hesitated. He argued with his advisers and thought up new questions to ask the young king, who grew more and more annoyed. What had become of the Carthaginian leader? Hanno Barca was dead, flown into the air as ashes. He was a memory. If they knew Publius Scipio, Masinissa said, they would not doubt him. The consul had lost barely any men in the battle, such as it was. Publius had sent him to pacify the city through offers of peace, as a brother, but if the gates stayed closed then Cirta—with no army in all of Africa to call on—would find herself besieged by the might of Rome.

One of the officers saw a chance to throw a gibe and did so: Was

Masinissa truly a king? He sounded more like a bed partner to the Roman. The laughter along the walls flared and died quickly, nervously. In answer to it Masinissa kissed his hands and pushed the air in front of him out with the palms of his hands. He swore that his offer of mercy ended in the next few moments. "If the gates do not open now I will commit myself to the slaughter or imprisonment of the entire population, the mutilation and torture of the magistrates . . ."

He began to detail the methods he would use, but Imilce did not hear him. Sophonisba grabbed her by the arm and dragged her through the soldiers, pushing and cursing her way down off the battlements and into the crowd below. The young woman's grip was bruising, but Imilce did not care. She was hardly aware of the people around her. She was not thinking about what was to happen to her next, or about the turn of fortune in the war, or about Hanno's death, or how she might survive the next few hours. Instead, she thought of her son. Ideas came at her like darts zipping in from unseen attackers. Hamilcar was safe in Carthage! What a joy that he was safe in Carthage! But the next moment, Imilce realized she might never see him again, might not know what became of him. He might forget her in the coming years and call some other woman mother. She thought of Didobal caring for him, and this struck her as both a relief and as a sadness. She had a momentary fantasy that Tanit would feel her distress and lift her up and fly her home to Carthage. She closed her eyes, even as she stumbled forward, asking the goddess to let her touch him again, let her cradle that boy in her arms and kiss him and kiss him and kiss him . . .

Even in this state she recognized the grinding clink of the main gate. The decision had been made. She opened her eyes and realized that they had not gotten very far at all, just to the edge of the central courtyard, which they would have to cross to get back to their quarters. She could see the gate shifting heavily. Sophonisba ignored it and kept on. They pressed their way slowly through the mass of tightly packed bodies, the scent and heat and sweaty proximity almost overwhelming. Imilce's head swam and for a moment she feared she would faint.

Then Sapanibal was with them, solid, head-clearing, determined. She grasped both women around the neck and pulled them in to her and began explaining their means of escape. She already sent a servant to gather peasants' clothes for them. They would meet her near the northeastern gatehouse, which had a secret door that she had arranged to have opened. From there they would make their way to the docks. Perhaps one of them would ride a donkey. They would look like servants sent by their master on some task. None would question them, as long as they beat Masinissa's men to the harbor. She believed they could do that, but they must leave immediately. The captain of the vessel that brought them would wait for them. She was sure he would, and after that it was only a matter of navigating home through the Roman sea patrols. It would not be easy, but they must . . .

Even as she spoke the drama just behind them played on. Some of the horsemen came in so fast upon the gates that their horses reared, seeming to kick the doors wide. They poured forth in a tumult of mounted fury, propelled by a wind that roared through the new opening, bringing a cloud of dust and the scent of smoke. The horsemen trilled their tongues and carved circles with their mounts. They waved their spears in threat and cuffed at those who approached too close, many already begging for mercy, promising to lead them to treasure, to act as guides to the palace, to show them in whose homes the greatest fortunes could be found. Amazing how fast allegiances turn.

"Let's go now," Sapanibal said. "Before—"

Masinissa came into view. Imilce's eyes flew toward him and she knew Sophonisba's did the same. He dismounted and sauntered with his hands resting on his hips and his elbows cutting angles out to either side. His blue garments flapped and snapped in the wind. The magistrates were before him in an instant. They dropped first to their knees, and then to all fours, and, finally, flat to their bellies. They were awaiting the king's attention, but his gaze stayed above them, searching for something he knew none of them offered.

"Enough," Sapanibal hissed. "We must go now!"

This seemed to wake Sophonisba from her stupor. Her eyes flashed over to Sapanibal, wide and intense, full of purpose. "Yes, sisters," she said. "Do that! Do that this very minute! Whatever happens, go, and do not wait for me."

With that, she twisted from Sapanibal's grip and flung herself into the crowd. Both women called after her, but she made furious progress. Moments later she stepped out of the circle of the townspeople and stood alone. She straightened her garments and walked forward. A Massylii horseman almost ran her through, but thought better of it and froze with spear upraised. Sophonisba strode past him, toward Masinissa.

Lawlessness flourishes in uncertainty. Sapanibal and Imilce struggled through the growing tangle of it as they raced down toward the harbor. Already young men had found occasion to snatch food from stalls. A Libyan trader went down, slashed across the forehead for an insult that had not existed a moment before. He rolled in the dust and reached for Imilce's legs. They passed a moneylender's table as it was overturned, coins spinning in the air, hands grasping for them. A boy of ten shoved past Sapanibal, nearly knocking her from her feet with the ostrich leg slung over his shoulder. Through all of this the two women walked forward. They wore servants' dress and watched the ground before them, making themselves smaller than they were.

The ship's crew did not recognize them when they tried to board. Sapanibal slapped the sailor who barred her way. She spat at him and spoke her name with her teeth so near his nose it seemed she might bite him. This did the trick. The captain had only to hear the barest of explanation before ordering his men to cast off. The first hordes of Libyan horsemen had rounded the city and started toward the harbor as the crew bent their backs to row out into open water. The vessel was a merchant vessel, not designed for quick initial maneuvers although nimble when under full sail.

Sapanibal, who had been so resolute, collapsed on the deck near the boat's stern. Everything was spinning into madness. There was too much to take in: Hanno's death, Syphax' defeat, Cirta's surrender, Masinissa's appearance, Sophonisba's actions. All of this piled on the earlier shocks of Hasdrubal's death and the defeat in Iberia and Sophonisba's marriage. The boat's rocking made it worse. Everything within her—mind and guts alike—churned with the rise and fall, the tilt and lift and fall and rise. For a time she felt her body to be a cauldron in which a massive stew bubbled. When they pulled free of the harbor and met the chop of the shifting currents she knew they were beyond Masinissa's reach, but she could not contain herself any longer. She stuck her head through a gap in the railing, and she heaved up everything inside her. Heaved and heaved, watching droplets of matter slip away on the slick backs of the waves. She was at this for some time, long after she had gone empty and could only convulse dryly.

Afterward she balled up in exhaustion. She folded in on herself and tried to separate the threads of narrative in a manner that made sense. She had no idea what would befall Sophonisba. She had seen her sister drop to her knees before the king, seen that Sophonisba was speaking and he listening, but that was all she knew. They could not have stayed a moment longer. Massylii soldiers were working toward them through the crowd, battering people about the heads and upraised arms, jerking them up to their feet and shoving them into groups by sex and rank. At any moment, they would have been noticed. It took a massive effort of cold determination to tug Imilce into motion, but she did it. Sophonisba had made her decision; she and Imilce had to do the same.

And Hanno. What of her brother? Masinissa had named his method of death. She tried to curse him as a liar, but his very presence suggested he spoke the truth. She could not imagine what Masinissa and the Romans had done, but it must have been something devious. Hanno had gone out to cleanse himself for the meeting with the consul, full of hope. Just a few days ago when they had parted, he had been more alive than she had ever seen him. He stood before her in a corselet of orange, protected by bronze plates that scaled over each other like the skin of some armored fish. He held a helmet clamped under one arm and looked at her with a grave intensity that was, silently, a form of speech.

"Are you going to make war or peace?" she asked.

"Let us pray that it be peace," he said. "We've all had enough of war."

Sapanibal had nodded then and said she hoped the Romans felt the same way, but as they were a more warlike people she did not put too much stock in the wish. "At least," she said, "you've built for your-self a strong position here. You have African brothers, as you wished."

Hanno closed his eyes at this, first one and then the other, and then he opened them in the same order, as if they registered a wave of fatigue passing through him. "Sapanibal, for all my days I will grieve that bargain. The union only need last until the war is done. Then, on my word, I'll personally free her—if that's what she wishes."

"You make that promise to *me*?" Sapanibal asked. "Why not make it to Sophonisba?"

"You'll take the message to her. It's hard for me to look at her now. She utters not a single word of complaint, but that only makes this marriage seem a greater crime."

Sapanibal had been surprised at what he said next. The words did not seem to fit the image she had of him standing there, an armored warrior ready to ride toward the enemy. He did not soften his erect posture or come any nearer to her, but he had made a confession to her. He said that for all the years he could remember, he had feared Hannibal, feared and envied him. Hannibal had made his life a mis-ery just by being so gifted, so beloved by all who witnessed his deadly grace. But recently this had not mattered to Hanno as much. He had come to believe that they are all put on the earth to be who they are, not to aspire to be anyone else, not to be measured against others at all, but rather weighed on a scale calibrated each to one's own special trials. And if he could make peace with the consul on the terms they had already set forth, then he would have achieved something great of his own.

"Hannibal makes war better than anyone," he had said, "but per-haps Hanno will find a gift for making peace."

That was what he had said, what he had thought, felt, hoped. It was madness that a man aspiring to such things died with them un-done. He was gone, and she had nothing to take home to present her mother. Nothing that had come from his dead body, no trinket taken from his neck, no locket of hair, no ring.

When she finally looked up—ashen, cheeks sunk, and lips still trembling—Imilce was sitting near at hand. She cradled her legs up to her chest, hugging them into her, with her chin resting on one knee. Sapanibal did not speak to her, but it filled her with affection just to know Imilce was near and that she was not yet totally alone in the world.

They did not travel far that night, just out of sight of Cirta, really; then they cut in and anchored off a fishing village. That evening the crew stripped all distinguishing trappings from the vessel. They furled both the flag of Carthage and the Barca lion. They tossed watered-down excrement onto the sail, for it was far too white to go unnoticed. They pried the golden eyeballs of Yam off the prow and scratched at the face painted there with hooks to make it look old and ill maintained, and they piled fishing nets into heaps at visible points on the deck.

In the dead of night, they lifted anchor and moved on. They tried to go slowly, for the coast was not without dangerous shoals, but they were passing the Roman landing point and had no wish to dally either. Indeed, at first light they spotted an entire fleet of Roman vessels beached along the shore. Hundreds of them. And there were more coming. The captain had thought to pass at half-sail, but spotting several ships moving in from the north, he gave the order to bend all the sails and fly behind the wind. Fortunately, the gods favored them again. They passed unnoticed, or at least without piquing the enemy's interest.

Later that day a Roman quinquereme came upon them at an angle heading toward the shore. The warship passed within shouting distance, a lean craft four times their length. Oars, stacked five rows high and numbering almost three hundred, dipped into the water, sliced up into the air, and splashed back down, all to the beat of a great drum that even from a distance thudded against Sapanibal's temples. The vessel dwarfed theirs completely. It cut the sea into two foaming curls, interrupted by the lifting and submerging of the prow through the waves, an armored prong that looked like the head of an angry whale each time it broke the surface. Had it rammed them it would have splintered their boat into pieces and plowed through them without losing the slightest momentum. But the quinquereme did not turn toward them. It just rowed on, some of the crew peering over long enough to inspect them in passing, uninterested, on other business they deemed more important.

They sailed on into the night, turned the point of Cape Farina

the next morning, and steered straight for Carthage across a frothy
sea, the glass-clear water whipped into foam by the same wind that
carried them home. That afternoon, the captain approached the
two women where they sat behind a shelter toward the rear of the
boat. He walked steadily, even though the boat heaved with their
progress, and he stood before them, body swaying to adjust to the
boat's pitching. He did not look at them at first, but just remained
nearby, kneading the coarse hairs of his beard with his thick fingers.

"It's ill news that we carry home with us," he said finally. "It's
likely we'll be the first back with word of Hanno's defeat. The Council won't look on this kindly at all. Perhaps you should report the
news in your brother's name."

"You fear they'll kill the messenger?"

He squatted and looked at Sapanibal. His eyes were a remarkable
blue, as if they held the sea. "They wouldn't harm you, but me or one
of my men?" He pinched the air and flicked his fingers, as if tossing
sand into the wind. "Tell them to call Hannibal back, if they haven't
done so already. Nothing else can save us now. Without him, Rome
will grind us like wheat beneath a millstone . . ."

"Is this the state of Carthaginian manhood?" Sapanibal asked,
scornfully. "You ask a woman to do your work, and then despair of
the nation in same breath. Have you no pride?"

Under his sunburn the captain flushed, but he answered calmly,
so firm in his reasoning that anger was not necessary. "If I speak out
of turn, please silence me before I offend. But think of Troy, my
lady. Think of Thebes. And there are other cities whose names are
no longer spoken. If Rome seeks a pretext to wipe us off the earth
they have only to look into the past. Only a fool believes that a victor knows mercy."

"So you know the future as well as the past? No one yet wears the
crown of victory in this war."

"Just so," the captain said. "This is why the Council must call
Hannibal home. I pray they already have."

Once the captain rose and moved off Imilce said, "Carthage will
not perish. My son's life will never turn on such catastrophe. I must
believe this, or lie down and die of grief right now."

Imilce stopped short, glancing sideways, inhaling through her nose to indicate that perhaps she was being foolish. But in a few moments she lifted her eyes. "Do you love no one, sister?" she asked. "No one who makes you imagine the best of the coming world?"

Sapanibal's first impulse was to answer scornfully. Did the question suggest that she was unlovable? But looking into Imilce's eyes she knew otherwise. They were a wonderfully light gray, flecked with streaks of metallic brilliance, set against a white background almost clear of blemish. They stared at her with such naked kindness that she wanted to reach out and kiss each orb. Why was her instinct always to calculate her place in the world as if in combat? She had to put such thoughts behind her. And how could she have thought herself superior to this woman? Sapanibal knew nothing more than Imilce did. She was no wiser. No stronger. She answered honestly.

"There is a man," she said.

"Is there? And do you love him truly?"

"I've never told him so," Sapanibal said, "but perhaps I do. He fills me with fear, but it's not only fear . . ."

"Such is the one cruelty of Tanit," Imilce said. "She binds together love and loss so that one always lies beneath the skin of the other. But you must tell him. Go to him at the first opportunity. We have so little, Sapanibal. All around us things come and go. People live and die. We kill each other for petty things. We make such a great noise across the world, and why? Who is ever happy because of any of this? Who? Have you ever been happy?"

One of the sailors shouted that he had spotted Carthage. The two women rose and looked out over the water.

"There were times when I thought I was," Sapanibal said, "but those were delusions."

Sapanibal felt the other woman's thin fingers grip her wrist. "No! No, those moments were the truth. It's all the confusion we make that's the delusion. I know this for sure. I asked Hannibal to bring me the world. I wanted to be queen over all that I could, but that was the fancy of a child. If he delivered the world to me now, I would hand it back. I would ask, At what cost, this? What I want most now is to make new memories like the old ones that I cherish. Like birthing Little Hammer and putting him to my breast the first time. Like lying cradled in the hollow of my husband's back. Hannibal once fed me grapes by putting them first into his mouth so that I took them from his lips to mine. That was truth. Sister . . . why do you cry?"

Sapanibal shook her head fiercely, and then swiped at the tears with her fingers. "The salt water stings my eyes. That's all." And a moment later—as she found herself thinking of Imago Messano and the best route from the harbor up to his villa—she said, "Please continue, Imilce. Tell me more of what you've found to be truth."

For several days after arriving in Cirta, Masinissa felt near to bursting with bliss. He had solved the two great problems of his life: his enemy was defeated; his love his to possess. And not only had Syphax been crushed; he was virtually forgotten. That first afternoon in the courtyard, Sophonisba had dropped to her knees and looked up at him from behind the amazing beauty that was her face. Tears hung at the rims of both her eyes. Her lips glistened from the moisture of her tongue. Two maroon swipes of color flushed across her cheeks. She swore to him that she had never stopped being true to him. She said she loved him and only him, and would love only him her entire life. Each time Syphax touched her, she had cursed the fact that she had skin. Each time he pushed inside her, she felt pain and revulsion instead of pleasure and love. She asked the gods to change her from a woman into some other creature. She said she would rather be a vulture, a frog, or a crocodile or a scorpion. She said that each night she would break a vase of Grecian clay and hold the jagged shards to her skin and pray for the power to sink them home and cut her face to shreds. She wanted him to know—no matter what fate held for her—that she had only ever wanted to be his wife. That was why it saddened her so to know that instead she would be ravaged by Roman soldiers. In a few days they would shove her onto a ship and sail her into slavery. They would take everything that she had wanted to give him and twist it into torturous retribution.

By all the gods, she was a revelation. The fascination he had felt for her in his youth was simply boyish infatuation compared with the ardor that gripped him as he looked down on her. And she spoke the truth! Clearly, she spoke the truth, both about her feelings for him and about the danger she now faced. And as this was so . . . Well, he could not let it be so. He did not have to. He was the king of all Numidia. Nothing that he wished to see done was impossible.

He lifted her to her feet and before the magistrates of the city, before even the eyes of the former king, with the hasty blessings of Syphax' own priests, as his army continued to pour in through the gates, without asking her views, in the space of a few moments . . . he married her. And then began his bliss. For the next few days, he barely left their private chambers at all. He made love to and with her again and again on the bed that had once been Syphax'. She laughed at him as they took pleasure in each other, and this was sweeter still. When her body was close to his, he wanted to possess every inch of her being. He could not stop his hands moving all over her, his fingers kneading, feeling the smoothness of her skin, the weight and contours of her. He wanted to consume her, to bury his face in the cleft between her breasts and cry with a joy so complete it felt akin to pain.

The weight of doubt so long on him lifted. He had his throne, his wife, his world. With Publius recalled to Rome, he could get on with carving his name across Africa. Maybe, he even ventured to think, Carthage would sue for peace. He could make overtures of friendship to them once more. Perhaps he had been wrong. Things done can sometimes be undone. . . . Sophonisba said it herself. When Hannibal returned, Carthage would again see reason. Perhaps Masinissa would find them an ally still. Their old friendship was worth more than this new dalliance with Rome. Sophonisba made things seem amazingly clear.

So he thought for a few precious days. Then Publius arrived, fresh from overseeing the aftermath of the fiery massacre, already having squelched several other Libyan towns and taken their leaders prisoner.

From the first glimpse of him striding into the room—strong-arming his guard to the side—Masinissa felt the substance behind the façade of his world crumbling. Publius yelled at him in Greek, cursed him, and asked him the same questions over and over again. It was so shocking an entrance that Masinissa could only stare at him, openmouthed, trying to make sense of his words and yet yearning not to. The Roman asked: Was he mad? A fool? Had he lost his reason? Publius repeated these questions until they became accusations. Did he really think he could wed her? It was pure madness. Sophonisba was a prisoner of Rome, as a member of the Barca family and as Syphax' wife. That's who she was, and that's why she would have to be sent to Rome. Had he forgotten that they were at war?

"I let you take the city as a gift," Publius said, "so that you might know I was true to my word, but do you believe you can play me for a fool? Why would you do this?"

"What do you mean, why?" Masinissa asked.

"Why would you do this?"

"Have you never loved? Ask me why I breathe; the reason is the same."

"Are you bewitched?" Publius asked.

Masinissa stuttered that he might be. He stared into the other man's eyes and nodded. Maybe he had been bewitched. But it did not matter: They were married already. Sophonisba was his wife, and no harm could come to her now. He had slipped into speaking Massylii, but the consul brought him back to Greek.

"Foolish boy," Publius said. His anger seemed to fade. "My foolish boy. You thought this would save her? Listen, let us sit down and speak like brothers. Speak plainly to me and I will do the same to you."

What passed between the two men after that, Masinissa would only remember in a fragmented jumble that could not possibly have comprised an entire day, but did, apparently—spanned all the hours from the sun's rising to its setting. Publius asked him about Sophonisba and listened as the Numidian told him everything. He went all the way back to the first time he saw her. He told him about the time they had ridden out from Carthage under the cover of night. He had told her all the things that could be and she had laughed at him. So cruel she sometimes was. But she had also brought him to ecstasy with a single touch of her fingers. And cruelty was a useful trait. She would make a fine queen. She was a woman—not a girl—who made anything possible.

The consul paced through most of this, but he did not interrupt.

He did not frown or joke or shout. But finally he stepped close and slipped a hand over the Numidian's shoulder. He caressed the back of his neck and pulled him in. With his forehead touching Masinissa's temple, Publius' words brushed his face like the hot breaths of a lover. "Masinissa, do not think I'm deaf to your love. But what you wish cannot be. We are fighting for the world together. Why would you risk this for the pleasures of a woman? If you are to be worthy of a partnership with Rome, you must prove yourself—not just with your skill atop a horse but with your reason, with your wisdom in thought and action. Sophonisba can never be your wife. I'm sorry I did not make this clearer to you before you came here. She has a strong pull and men such as you feel emotion deeply. I understand this. But the promise of union you shared with her as a youth is no more. It's gone with the past and will never be again. There is something more. . . ."

The consul brushed his lips against the man's cheek. He ran his hand up into the African's locks and clamped his fingers there. "Do you think this is easy for me?" he whispered. "Think about it. My nation has been humiliated, my family destroyed. I am here trying to save the world as my people know it. In Iberia, some of the tribes declared me a living god. Even some among my own troops believe I walk blessed by Jupiter's hand. But you and I know the truth of these things, don't we? The gods are silent in me; are they the same in you? It may be that I lose everything tomorrow. I simply don't know. I have nothing but these hands and this mind. . . . These are the things with which I try to save my people. That is why I need you with me. The hour soon comes when I will meet Hannibal himself. You must be there."

Publius loosed his fingers and drew back a little, but still he spoke in hushed tones. "I'll tell you this, and you'll become the first to know: I'm not returning to Rome yet. My work here isn't complete, and it must be made so. You will understand, then, how strange a position I am in. On one hand, I disobey the orders of my Senate; on the other I force you to heed them. Do not question the equity in this. Just hear me and do as I say. Be the left hand to my right. Pull with me on the rope that will drag Hannibal back to Africa. Do as I say and you'll become one of Africa's greatest kings. Give up the girl. She is a Roman prisoner: the wife of one enemy and the sister of another. It's not in your power to change this. It's a certainty that Sophonisba will go to Rome as a prisoner. If she is ever free again it will only be after Carthage's complete defeat, and she may never be free, Masinissa. Her life is not hers to direct anymore; nor is it yours. If you spurn us in this, you have no future. The Senate will tell me to crush you and flick you away like an insect and find another man to call my favored king; and if they ask me to do that, I will. But it need not be. Sacrifice this one thing and everything else is yours."

Publius stood erect again and paced away a few steps. "I will hear your answer now."

"I cannot live without her," Masinissa said.

"Of course you can. Does a single heart beat for both of you?"

"But I cannot—"

"That is not your answer!" Publius snapped. "Who will know you for a king if you cannot be strong?"

The Numidian started to shake his head, but something in the question struck him in a different place and pressed home. In an instant he was reminded of weeks during which he roamed Massylii lands in hiding, exiled in his own country. He had learned so many things during that time, and one of them was that he was no different from other men. Though he wore the crown of a king inside his heart, no man recognized him. He ate stringy meat beside fires and rode beside merchants and slept on the open ground with dogs and beggars. Who knew him for a king then? His own people did not recognize him. They saw a man before them of flesh and bone, with hair on his chin, a person who ate and peed and shat like any other. But they did not see a king.

"You ask who will know me for a king?"

"That's what I ask."

"And you want me to know that I can be replaced. Masinissa gone and some other on my throne."

"As you are now on Syphax'. And in his quarters, even in his bed . . ."

Masinissa spoke before he knew he was going to. One thing was as impossible as another, so he said, "I will do as you wish."

"Good," Publius said. "You've assured your future. You may send the girl a note of condolence, but do not see her again. Tell her that she cannot be your wife, and that she is a prisoner of Rome."

Quick as that, the consul turned and walked away.

Once he was gone, Masinissa flung himself onto the bed. Sophonisba's scent flooded him and twisted his insides into knots. What had he just said? Was he mad? He could not live without her. He could not. He simply could not. He said so over and over again. He would always wonder where in the world she was, and with whom. He would eat at his own heart in fear that she was being abused. Or—worse yet—was she giving her love to someone else? He could not possibly live with this hanging over him. So he would take his own life. That was it—he would take his own life!

He called for a servant of the house and asked the startled man if his old master had had any poison. He had, of course, and this was duly fetched. A few moments later he held within his hand a tiny vial, ornately worked. But looking at the vial he knew he could not do it. He was not a normal man. He was king. He had promised a whole nation of people that he would lead them into the future. He had rescued them from tyranny. He could not abandon them; what would become of them? Would not Rome turn against them in rage at his betrayal? And what of all the greatness he wanted to achieve in honor of his father? This had become the new duty of his life. He had to make up for all the years that he had been youthfully ignorant of his father's wisdom. He simply had to live.

And with that thought he decided. He called to his manservant. When he appeared, he spoke calmly. "Take this to my wife. Tell her that I'm keeping my promise to her. She will not fall into Roman hands, but I cannot be her husband. Ask her to drink this."

The man took the vial without comment. Once he was gone, Masinissa tried to shift his attention to something else. He thought of Maharbal and hoped that he was still the commander of Hannibal's cavalry. He would have to speak to Publius about him, for he had of late conceived a plan that might aid them greatly, if Maharbal was still loyal to the Massylii. He began to rehearse what he would say. With this victory he could raise another ten or fifteen thousand men from his own people. For that matter, he could probably recruit from the Libyans—those not burned to cinders . . .

And just like that, the manservant was back. No time at all had passed. Masinissa was sure that the vial had not been delivered. The Romans had turned him around; the servant could not find her; he came to ask Masinissa to reconsider.

The man said, "She has received the gift, my king."

"What said she? Tell me exactly. Exactly!"

"She said that she accepted it, but that it saddened her. She said that she would have died a better death if she had not married the same week as her funeral. She said to remind you of the tale of Balatur. She'd wanted to believe it, but truth was as she had said, wasn't it? No Massylii was ever true to a single woman. She said to tell you that she only ever loved you . . . only you, singly out of anyone in the entire world. And she drank the poison. She drank all of it without hesitation, and then she handed the vial back."

The man held it out for the king to take. Masinissa had already been in tears, but seeing the bottle he crumpled to the floor. The servant left him writhing on the marble, as if he sought to melt into the surface and become one with the stone, to go as cold and hard as it was and to feel no more.

It was glorious to behold. Hannibal calculated every move of their new campaign. For the first few weeks it seemed he pulled the strings to which the workings of the entire world were tethered. He put melancholy behind him. He yoked his sorrow so that it might pull him forward behind it. He marched from Tarentum to Metapontum, picked up the bulk of Bomilcar's former soldiers—who brought their numbers to just above thirty-four thousand troops—and then turned north, following the river into Apulia. The army of Livius Salinator shadowed them, but they were no more trouble than a swarm of gnats. They crossed the spine of the peninsula through the valley of the Aufidus and caused great panic as they threaded between Nola and Beneventum. They moved at a leisurely pace, scouring the country to both sides with an almost festive attitude. It was early summer and the land bloomed all about them. As ever, it was a joy to pluck from it at will. He knew that Monomachus was stealing children from the locals and sacrificing them to Moloch. This troubled him more than he would admit, but for the first time he gave way to another's certainty. Perhaps Moloch did want a greater share of the blood they were spilling. So be it.

Joining the Via Appia they trudged through daylong waves of showers, drenched one minute and dry the next, chilled by the rain and then warmed by the sun, then chilled again. Hannibal asked his men how they liked this ritual purification. It was a blessing offered by the gods themselves to anoint the campaign to follow, he said. Approaching Capua, they slowed just enough for Hannibal to gather intelligence as to the situation there. Three armies held the city pinned down—those of Claudius Nero, Appius Claudius, and Fulvius Flaccus, nearly sixty-five thousand men in all. They had completed the circumvallation of the city and built outer fortifications. Any attack on them would be a siege in and of itself. Hannibal hesitated for a moment. His brother's killer was close, and his desire to avenge Hasdrubal burned within him, but he held to plan.

He marched the army in a hooked route that brought them up to their old camp on the slope of Mount Tifata. From there, they swept down toward the city. They clashed throughout the afternoon with Fulvius, and then pulled back as if to prepare for another engagement the next day. They did not, in fact, prepare a full camp, but only went through the motions until the light faded. In the darkness, Hannibal dispatched a messenger sure he could get inside the city, telling them not to fear his sudden disappearance, because it was part of a greater scheme.

The whole army shouldered their burdens and marched north, past Casilinum, across the Volturnus, around Cales and Teanum. They came to the Via Latina and followed it toward Rome. They burned bridges behind them, set fire to growing crops, fanned the country into a state of terror like that after Cannae. This was all as Hannibal wished, for his intentions were twofold: through terror in the capital, he hoped to see the blockade of Capua abandoned, and—knowing the shallowness of support for the consul's actions—he prayed that the Senate might recall Publius from Africa. Surely, the Rome he had thus far encountered would look to its own interests firsts. Of course it would.

They cut across to the Anio River and camped there, Rome just a morning's march away. Hannibal waited another day, letting the Numidians range within sight of the city; each passing day, he believed, would fill the enemy with more anxiety. Indeed, he learned that the city was in greater turmoil than ever. Though forbidden to disturb the peace, people poured out into the streets and into the shrines of the gods, wailing at their impending doom, convinced that their tormentor had finally come to settle this long dispute. Women loosed their hair and swept it across sacred altars and beseeched the gods with upraised hands, growing louder in the process as each tried to project her call with a force that would get her heard. A slave of African origin seen running through the streets early one morning caused a nervous citizen to declare that the enemy had entered the city, setting off a tumult that took the greater part of the day to dispel. Guards shot out to every possible post: along every section of the walls, in the citadel, on the Capitol. Men went armed even to the baths, and sentries around the city waited to sound the alarm. The panic was so great that all former consuls and dictators were summarily reinstated to their posts, an undertaking that must in itself have been a grand confusion. And then a report came in that Fulvius had pulled up from Capua and made for Rome on the Via Appia, just as Hannibal had hoped. With the news of Fulvius' move, Hannibal believed one of his objectives might well have been met, but he could not come so close to Rome without offering up a challenge.

He addressed the troops early the following morning. The trees and grass dripped with dew, but the sky was so clear as to be a brilliant white. He strode through the gathered throng with a chicken under one arm and a fistful of grain in the other, his voice booming out as he went. He asked how many among them had come with him across the Alps four years before? How many had seen the Ticinus, Trebia, Trasimene, and Cannae? Surely there were a few left among them who had been beside him the whole time. He clambered up onto the bulk of a felled tree, half of which had been sawed into sections for chopping. Enthusiastic soldiers jostled each other to hear him; a few jumped up onto nearby portions of the tree and fought to keep their balance as their fellows shoved and yanked them. He said that they would use a Roman method to determine the favors of the day. So saying, he tossed out the handful of grain. Men had to jump back to clear a space for it. He grasped the fluttering chicken with both hands and released it. The bird flapped its wings frantically for a moment, but then, seeing the mass of men all around, thought better of a long flight. It dropped down into the circle of bare ground and began strutting the space with nervous head bobs.

As he watched the bird, Hannibal said, "You've slaughtered Romans until your swords bent and dulled on the flesh and bone of them. You've seen them run before us like children fleeing before monsters of the night. You've looked in the face of the impossible a hundred times and laughed. Haven't you?"

They answered that they had.

"And so you'll be rewarded for it. By the gods, you'll be rewarded for it. What army on earth ever deserved victory more than ours? This will not go unnoticed—"

"The bird eats!" a man cried. "The Persian fowl eats!"

As this message fanned out through the crowd, Hannibal said, "Through the bird, the gods tell us the day will be ours. We, too, will feed upon our prey. This very day you'll set eyes upon the hated place itself. I know all of you have been impatient for this from the start. Now the time has come. Let's go call on Rome!"

He mounted one of the last surviving elephants from the shipment they had received after Cannae, seeming to take great pleasure in the vantage it provided him. Around him men and animals moved across the countryside, through fields and farms, leaping across irrigation ditches, ducking beneath trees, rising and falling with the slow undulations of the land. The Numidians rode out in front. Some soldiers, taken with enthusiasm, jogged before the main force like children anxious to behold something long promised them. Hannibal called for a sack of dates and munched on them as he rode, rocking with the elephant's slow gait.

Hannibal caught his first glimpse of the city as he rode through the saddle between two hills. If he had been on his own feet instead of mounted, he might well have stopped in his tracks, such was the way he drew up. For a moment the expression of mirth faded from his face and his single good eye became the center of his being. It was most dramatic, complete, and undeniable, the way the hilly farmland and pastoral view ended abruptly at the capital's mighty walls. Compared with the green landscape around it, the city was a raised scar inflicted on the land by the hands of men. The walls stood ten times a man's height and stretched in a strong, curving line, towers evenly spaced, the stone so smooth it almost glowed in the bright light. Even from a distance, it was clear that the populace crowded the walls. The upper rim was lined with staring people, with the bristle of soldiers' spears, the curve of archers' bows. And behind them hulked the city itself. All the famous hills, the Quirinal and Viminal, the Esquiline and Caelian and Palatine and Aventine, the Capitoline: Hannibal found himself ordering them in his mind. Stone structures crowded every space, temples beside palaces, the reddish roofs scaled like fishes' backs, steaming as the last of the night's moisture evaporated beneath the sun. Narrow lanes cut between the buildings; tufts of trees crowned some rises; the mixed scent of sewage and food, feces and incense—the stink of humanity—just touched them as the breeze blew into their faces. The writhing line of the Tiber shimmered as if it flowed liquid silver.

Rome. Finally, Rome.

The soldiers catching their first glimpse of the place slowed and hesitated, bumped into each other as they stared. They might have stopped completely except that Hannibal, on his elephant, carried on. After a few moments of hush, generals, captains, and bold men remembered themselves. Numidians trilled and surged forward on their mounts. Gauls bellowed that they had returned to finish the sacking they had started years before. They and Iberians blew on their horns, a ruckus like a thousand stags in rut. And the Latin contingents strode forward singing. Thus Hannibal led the enemies of Rome to the city's very walls.

He halted the advance on the clear ground an arrow's shot from the walls. Here he turned the elephant and progressed along the walls, commenting on the craftwork and calling out to the enemy.

Just who was in charge here? Might one in authority announce himself? Was Fulvius in there, the cunning creature? To whom should he direct his terms? Or would they come out and settle this dispute like warriors? His own men were outnumbered, but they were not against a hard day's work. No? If not today, then on the morrow, perhaps? As an aside he offered fair prices on plots of land in the Forum, if any of them were interested in getting in on the transaction early. He did not discriminate. He would even accept Roman coins as fair tender.

He had surveyed the entire distance between the Colline and Esquiline gates when a sudden barrage of arrows sailed into the air. They did not quite reach Hannibal, but sank squelching into the ground nearby. The commander seemed to find humor in this. He pointed at an individual on the wall, blinked his good eye, and grinned at him, as if the two of them had shared a joke and Hannibal was weighing his rebuttal. A few moments later a missile ripped through the men not far from the commander, shot from a ballista, a mechanically strung bow of great strength. The bolt pierced straight through the soft of one man's neck, severing the artery in an expulsion of blood. It ricocheted off a Bruttian's round shield and caught a Capuan with an upward trajectory that pinned him by the torso to the flank of a mule. The man was dead on the spot, but the beast set up a wheezing cry and threw a series of lopsided kicks. Men laughed at this and commented on Roman spite, asking what the mule had ever done to offend them. They made light of it to demonstrate their fearlessness, but nevertheless they withdrew a short distance.

And so the day passed. Hannibal seemed content to sit on his elephant, munching dates, spitting seeds to the ground like a boy, and chatting with whatever men were near him. The soldiers had come by now to know that half of war is in the waiting. And so they took their lead from their commander's mood; they stoked their fires and roasted animals newly snatched from the local farmers. Those who had musical instruments brought them out and played into the night, so that surely the Romans huddled inside their walls heard a strange chorus of festivity: bone whistles and hand rattles and bells played on the fingers of camp followers or slave women. The complicated rhythms of African drums went on the longest, like the heart of the army beating so loud so that all inside the city would know that Hannibal's army lived, prospered, waited for them.

The next day Hannibal marshaled the army in the wide field east of the city. The sky was heavy with cloud, the light dim beneath it, the ground moist enough that the men's feet stirred no dust. To the commander's joy, Fulvius and the consuls did not shy from meeting him. They emerged from the Esquiline gate to great fanfare, rank after rank of men stepping in unison, bearing tall shields of yellow or red, emblazoned with boars or wolves. People lined the walls, jostling for views, shouting their support like spectators at the Circus. The troops moved with synchronicity, answering the calls of the lituus and tuba promptly, despite the combined clamor of the spectators and Hannibal's soldiers. The velites—wolf, lion, bear-head—prowled forward of the others, creating the usual distractions. Many of them howled or roared like the beasts that adorned them. A few came forward far enough to launch their missiles, and their taunts.

Hannibal waited patiently throughout. He did not orate to the troops—his voice was hoarse from the previous day—but he did make casual comments that passed from one man to the next. He checked the sky as much as he did the enemy army and remarked, "The heavens promise a bath for the first man to draw blood." Counting the various standards of the consul, the former consuls, and the former dictators, he turned to Gemel and asked, "How many heads does this beast have? They should be careful one doesn't bite the other in the ass." A little later, having watched a velite stumble and sprawl on top of his shield: "There goes a cub in bear's clothing."

The sky had grown even darker by the time the Romans were assembled. Both sides seemed anxious to ignore it, but this became impossible. The clouds dropped their load just as the skirmishers stepped forward to start the contest in earnest. But it was not the cleansing shower Hannibal joked about. Rain fell steady for a few moments, and then dropped down in a series of buffeting blankets. A sudden wind whipped the water sideways and snapped and twisted the points of the nearby trees. Scarcely had the men covered their eyes before they looked up again to an entirely different scene. The very air before them had turned to water. Water fell from the sky and jumped up from the turf in a great confusion, so thick that the line of soldiers in the distance faded out of view. As if this were not enough, pellets of ice dashed them, pinging off helmets and shoulders and snapping punishments on bare knuckles, driving the horses to run in circles, looking for escape. Hannibal gave no orders for the men to break ranks, but in the confusion and noise many believed he had. Some units turned and withdrew, others dropped to their knees in the sudden muck and whispered prayers, grasping idols draped around their chests: Divine forces were at work here. There would be no battle that day.

For that matter, it took all of the commander's persuasiveness to convince the men to resume the field the following day. He walked through camp that night, speaking with groups of soldiers privately, joking with them, and belittling the timorous quavers in their eyes. Had they not seen greater storms than that throughout this war? Had they not traversed ice and mountain snow and pushed through tempests? As a child he used to laugh at such storms and run out into them, tilt his face up, and catch the ice stones in his jaws. Let the Romans fear the heavens! For Hannibal's men, it was a blessing. They must remember that Baal was a god of storm. In the downpour he was just announcing his presence.

But his efforts proved to be in vain. His troops drew up in battle formation again, but the enemy did not. They stayed secure behind their walls and, over three consecutive days, would not be baited out. Perhaps their priest deemed the storm a sign. In any event, Rome shut its gates, held its soldiers in its bosom, and watched.

At council, Hannibal listened to his generals' opinions. Isalca, the Gaetulian who had of late risen to prominence, still thought they could lure the enemy out. He proposed starting a rumor that Hannibal was sick. Or they could concoct an ill omen that the Romans would read favorably. Perhaps the commander could fall from his horse near the temple of Hercules and sprain his ankle. . . . Monomachus heard this with disdain. They should crucify some of the prisoners captured as they marched—on open ground for the entire city to see. They would have to answer that. Maharbal and

Tusselo proposed a ploy to lure them into opening one of the gates. Imco Vaca was of another mind. They could settle down and proceed with building siege engines. The land around them provided all the necessary supplies. Adherbal had done little more these past years than exercise his legs. Why not call upon the engineer at last? They could build structures such as Rome had never seen and bash their way in. Even if it took eight months, the way Saguntum had, still it would be worth the effort. So argued Imco. Gemel seemed to agree. Hannibal listened to even more voices as he sat there. He heard snatches of earlier opinions uttered by Hasdrubal, by Bostar and Bomilcar. He wondered what Mago would say and what insight Silenus would have shared.

Eventually, Hannibal heard the engineer's report. He sat with his head cradled in his hands and listened as Adherbal rattled off the details in his monotone. The walls were at least as formidable as they looked: nine feet thick at the thinnest points, with a core of packed earth lined on either side by stones connected with metal clamps. Such a construction was not easily knocked down. The inner portion of the wall rose high enough to make firing into the city difficult, especially as the troops could not get very close without coming under attack from above. Nor would tunneling be an easy feat, as the outer wall was sunk down some distance under the soil. There were few weaknesses, and any method that required concentrated work on the outside could be countered with efforts from inside. Adherbal concluded that perhaps the best attack would be one using great towers, built to the height of the wall, that could be wheeled forward to a chosen point. The lumber would need to be gathered from quite a distance, and the construction—

"Enough," Hannibal said. "Why not just throw a rope around the moon and swing in?"

Adherbal considered this, but Hannibal waved him away and ended the council. His mood had blackened suddenly, and he did not want his men to see it. They would not win Rome by siege. He had always known it; now it was clearer than ever. Certainly he could not lay siege to her with the army he had now. Not without siege engines. Not without reinforcements. Not when Rome had thousands upon thousands of soldiers to flow toward him. Their numbers were such that if he built siege walls around the entire city they might do the same around him. His army would be trapped with walls of Romans on both sides. Perhaps, he thought, after Cannae we might have . . . The situation was different then. Perhaps Maharbal was right. . . . But he did not say this aloud, and fought himself just for thinking it. He spent the rest of the evening in the monumental effort of pushing bleak thoughts from his mind. Nothing was lost yet. He had only to await the news that Capua was free, or that Publius had landed. Either of these things would mean a success of sorts.

Barely had he awoken with this fresh mind-set when a Capuan arrived to reverse it. When Fulvius left Capua he did so with only about fifteen thousand men; at least fifty thousand surrounded the city, showing no intention of going anywhere and stating their demands more forcefully. Capua was still in peril. And a spy who had managed to get out of Rome confirmed that there was no word yet from Publius, nothing to confirm that he had received his summons or had any intention of responding to it. The spy also said that the mood of the capital had changed. The panic had eased. People murmured that they had nothing to fear. Each passing day convinced more of them that Hannibal was powerless against them. Someone had even sold the land on which the Carthaginians were encamped. It had been on the market before their arrival and sold at the asking price. The new owner planned to erect a monument to their victory against Hannibal, surrounded by housing for the city's expanding population.

Ten days after he arrived before the capital, Hannibal sat atop the rise on a small stool, Sacred Band nearby. The evening sky was clearing. Patches of turquoise and crimson peeked from behind the thinning clouds. Rome sprawled before him. Studying it beneath the changing light, he confirmed to himself that he was not in awe of this city. This comforted him in a small way. Some portion of him had always feared that he would look upon this city and know himself inferior to it. He would realize too late that his father's dream had been mistaken and both their lives pursuits of tragic folly. But this was not how he felt. The city was not enormous. It did not look vastly wealthy. It did not, like Carthage, perch majestically above a great port. It was not a diamond embedded in the landscape, like New Carthage. Its leaders were men like other men, but no better. He had almost defeated them. He was sure of it. One more misstep, and they would have been his. Why—with all the effort he had put into it—was that single misstep denied him?

He spotted the Numidian approaching him and tried to wipe any melancholy off his face. But as the man reached him and he saw the strong weight of his features and the long locks that gave him a head like a lion, he forgot pretense. He motioned for the man to sit beside him and take in the view. He spoke to him in Massylii, pronouncing the words slowly, with the slight hesitation that marks internal translation.

"Tusselo, you lived in the city for a long time. This is so?"

"Too many years, my lord," the Numidian said. He did not actually sit, but squatted in the Massylii way, on one heel, with the other leg straight out to the side. When Hannibal did not follow up on the question he added, "I've been a prisoner here my whole lifetime."

"Is it so memorable to you as that? You were born in Africa. You became a man there. And you've been free some years now. So how can you have spent a lifetime here?"

"You are a free man, my lord, freer than anyone alive in this age. You have tomorrow." Tusselo seemed content to leave it at that, but Hannibal prodded him, thinking that he had missed a double meaning. Tusselo explained, "The sunrise that Tusselo sees tomorrow is already claimed by Rome. As my eyes open, I think first of Rome, never first of Tusselo. I feel sometimes that they've tattooed their words inside my skull."

"Why not take a chisel and destroy their words? Their words don't belong in you. Expel them."

Tusselo nodded, but the set of his face indicated that he did so out of respect. He did not accept that such an action was possible, but he did not choose to refute it. "You have the promise of immortality. Hannibal may not live forever, but the force inside him may yet walk this earth in a thousand years. In two thousand . . . This is not true for Tusselo. Believe me, I am still their prisoner."

"Does it trouble you to look upon this place again?"

"No. I look upon it every time I close my eyes."

"Perhaps you joined me solely to return here," Hannibal said. "Anyway, you know the city well. I want you to speak truly to me. Will the people give in to a siege, as Imco hopes?"

"No, they will not give in," Tusselo said.

Hannibal sighed at this, casually, as if he had heard an unfortunate report of the coming weather. "Of course they won't," he said, turning and gazing back over the seven hills. "Do you realize that I've never once been beaten in a major battle? Not in Iberia. Not here in Italy. Never once has an enemy army slain men under my command with abandon and celebrated it afterward."

"I know that, Commander."

"Tusselo, I fear Rome will win this war out of pure stubbornness. How do you defeat a people who won't admit defeat? It's as if you stab a corpse a thousand times and then step back and, to your horror, the body rises to fight on. You slice off its arm and it picks its sword up with the other arm. You slice that one off, only to discover that the first has grown back. You cut off its head, but then the thing rises and slashes blindly at you. . . . How do you defeat a creature like that?"

The Numidian cocked his head and then straightened it.

Hannibal looked at him for some time, as if he had forgotten something and expected it to soon appear on the man's features. "I've killed them by the tens of thousands, scoured their countryside at will, pried their allies away, and humiliated them day after day. I have burned their crops and looted their wealth. I've sent a whole generation of their generals into the afterworld. All the grief and rage . . . Have I changed nothing? They are stronger now than before. They are more than before. They fight more sensibly than before. They win when they used to lose . . ."

"If that's so," Tusselo said, "you have changed them very greatly."

The following morning the troops heard Hannibal's order to withdraw with a hushed silence that included both relief and shock. In the coming weeks they were to make haste along the Via Valeria, around Lake Fucinus, and then down through Samnium and into Apulia. When he reached Tarentum a few weeks later, he would learn that Capua had surrendered, from hunger and in fear that Hannibal had abandoned them. And only two days after this, an envoy from Carthage found him, bearing clear orders supported by the full membership of the Council and sealed with the mark of the One Hundred.

Watching him, Tusselo realized that his commander, who excelled in all things, carried also a burden of sorrows such as most other men could only ever imagine. He was sharing a simple meal with Hannibal on the evening when he revealed his recall to Carthage. On a sign from the commander, Gemel reluctantly read the letter aloud to the small company of remaining generals. Sparely worded, it described the situation, named the participants, and concluded that Carthage was under threat. Just as his father had been summoned home years before to quell the mercenaries, Hannibal was called upon to save the city of his birth from invaders both foreign and African. No, he was commanded to do so. He could delay not at all, but must journey home at once, with all the soldiers he could muster. They would send boats to meet him at Croton Metaontum, but only to speed his return. The same demand had, apparently, been sent to Mago, who was either on the Balearic Islands or in northern Italy.

Isalca used the silence after this announcement to spit vitriol on the Council. As a Gaetulian fighting for Carthage by choice, he owed them no blood allegiance. In this order he found an opportunity to condemn all of the Council's earlier failures, the broken promises, the troops not sent, the support not given. If they had not been petty fools, the war would have been won; instead, it was ruined. He was not sure that he would obey. He would have to speak to his men, but he knew that many would feel as he did: that the best battles of this war had already been fought, and that it had been won or lost at some point that was now behind them.

"There are not so many of us left, anyway," he added, glancing at the commander.

Hannibal heard all this with his eyes closed, just breathing. Nor did he comment when Maharbal asked to have the messenger brought in and interviewed. The Numidian was particularly interested in the power struggle between the Massylii and the Libyans. What, exactly, had happened? The messenger explained. The blood drained from Maharbal's face. He asked no more. Imco Vaca was in attendance as well. But, like Tusselo, he kept his thoughts hidden.

For some time, the men sat in silence, none touching their food; the only noises were Isalca clearing his throat, Gemel rubbing his fingers over his chin beard, Imco shifting uncomfortably and then settling again. Tusselo realized that at some point the commander had opened his eyes.

When Hannibal spoke, it was a comfort just to hear his voice, for that was the same as ever it had been, only gentler, softer, there being no need to project his words in this small chamber. "The One Hundred," he said, "did not even mention sadness at my brother's death. They tell me Hanno Barca is dead, but they spare not a word to admit that I might be grieved by this. He's only another failed general, best forgotten. I've always loathed this about my nation. If dead generals are all failed generals, then what is the Carthaginian legacy except a catalog of failures? We are all dust eventually. Nations should have memories. Even if people forget, a nation should not."

Isalca asked, "Will you obey them?"

Hannibal fixed him with his gaze and stared, just stared until the Gaetulian lowered his eyes. "First I'll pray for my brother. And then, yes, I will go home to save my country. What kind of man would I be if I did not?"

Later that night, Tusselo packed his few things and rode out of camp, thinking parting words and wishing them out to the sleeping men, asking the commander for forgiveness and offering thanks for the gift of time they had spent together. It had not been easy to decide to leave, but neither was the decision a sudden one. He had suspected for some time that his journey might not end the way he had imagined when he first joined Hannibal's army, years before, still fresh from winning his freedom and trying to find his place in the world. He had seen so much. He had watched genius at work and witnessed a mighty, hated nation being humbled. He had had some joy. But none of this had changed who he was, or healed the scars, or returned to him the most precious things that had been stripped from him. So he framed a new vision of the statement he might make, and now he determined to see it made real.

Not far out of camp, he sat his horse atop a shallow hill and looked north across the heaving knots pushed up in the landscape. The month had just passed the Nones by the Roman calendar. The moon hung in a cloudless sky, so clear that he could see the weathered skin of it, cracked and pitted and pale like an old Gaul. It would flesh to fullness in a handful of days, on the day called the Ides in the Roman tongue. It was already bright enough that he could make out fields and huts and the ruts of roads. He could even distinguish a few thin streams of smoke that rose from fires. The signs of man were all across the land. It would be no easy task to map his way through it, alone over much the same territory he had just traversed as one among a great host. But so be it. This was his journey. He aimed to reach Campania under the full moon and work his way steadily north through the rest of the month. By the Kalends he would be at the heart of his goal. He would announce the new month in his own special way. The Kalends, the Nones, the Ides . . . he knew too many of their words. They came too often to his head. He had tried to expel them, but this was not as easy as Hannibal believed. No matter. It would all be undone soon enough. He touched his mount on the neck. She stepped forward and the two of them began the slow descent, toward the north, back toward Rome.

At first he backtracked down the wide, barren road Hannibal's withdrawing army had made. He covered as many miles as he could at night and rested in secluded spots through the daylight hours. Twice he roused packs of dogs that chased him to the outskirts of their towns. Once he had to call on all his skills as a horseman to outrun a Roman patrol. And another time he had to chase, capture, and subdue a Campanian boy who stumbled across his daytime hiding place. The boy could not have been more than ten, but Tusselo had to beat him soundly to shut him up. He even explained to the boy in Latin that he meant him no harm. The wide-eyed, frightened youth did not seem to understand a word he said, although the language should have been familiar enough to him.

Two days away from the capital he released his horse and walked away from her. She followed him for some time, until he threw stones at her and frightened her with upraised arms and shouts. That evening he sheltered beneath an overhang of rock, in a moist hollow dripping with springwater. He squatted over the thin stream and, taking a knife he had honed especially for this task, he hacked at the long locks of his hair. The stuff came away in great clumps. He measured the tangled weight in his palms, surprised by it. The knots bound within them moments of his history. He felt them floating free into the air with each new cut. It seemed each day of the last five years had somehow been trapped in there: the essences of different countries, the scent of horses, of flowers budding and leaves bursting with the change of seasons, drying and crumbling. He smelled pine forest in there, the dust of Saguntum, the water of the Rhône, the residue of melting ice, tiny drops of other men's blood flung into the air during battle. He thought of eating fried fish with the old man on the seashore in Iberia. He recalled the frozen morning near the Trebia River when he spat insults at the Roman camp to wake them for the day's conflict. He remembered the Arno swamps, the mists pulling back from Lake Trasimene, the great cloud of dust the Romans sent up as they approached Cannae. There was so much to remember.

It had been good to own his hair again and feel it growing thick around him. But it was good to be free of it also. He pressed the blade against his flesh and slid it carefully across the contours created by his skull, drawing blood here and there, once getting the angle wrong and slicing up a ribbon of flesh. But these were tiny wounds compared to others he had suffered. He had never known that the air had fingers. He felt them that night, gentle pressure against the new skin of his scalp, like the spirits of his ancestors reaching out to caress him. Strange as it was, he felt comforted by the touch.

The next day he traded a large Tarentine gold coin for a farmer's old mule. And the following day he bought a fresh-killed boar, a female and no great burden strapped to the mule's back. He secured his spear beneath the load in such a way as to make it look more like a tool and less like a weapon. He gave his other meager possessions to any field workers who acknowledged him as he passed: a few more coins to this one, his dagger to another, random articles of booty to still others. By the time he reached the city he carried nothing on his person but a long cloak that fell back off his shoulders. He had long ago learned that much of one's identity as a slave was revealed in the eyes. He cast them down in the manner he remembered as he entered the Colline gate. If the guards noticed him at all they kept it to themselves.

Again he was within Rome. It was as it had ever been. The bustle and stench were the same; the noise and clatter of wagons and confusion of tongues had not changed in the slightest. He remembered the route to his old master's home, but he did not take it. This mission was less personal than that. He wound through the cramped streets, down the ridge of the Esquiline hill. He led the mule behind him, lowering his eyes whenever he noticed someone watching him. He did not need to look up often, for he knew this city as if he had never left. There was nothing he needed to see again.

He did not even truly look up when he reached the edge of the Forum. He hung back near the wall of an adjacent building, as if waiting for his master. People thronged the place. He heard their talk and smelled their perfumes and the bodies the fragrances disguised. He even felt the heat radiating off their skin and the cool seeping up from the marble of the flooring and out of the pillars and statues adorning the place. He still did not look up. He did not need to study people's faces to know the expressions they would bear. He could see the wrinkled faces of the old women in his mind as clearly as any around him, the prominent noses of senators, held high. He knew he would catch glimpses of matrons' thighs, of young men's hairy torsos, of children at play in a world of their own.

He placed his fingers on the clasp that held his cloak fastened at the neck. He did not loosen it immediately, for to do so was to change everything that could be changed in his life. He did not feel the fear he might have expected. Neither did he feel the hatred that he had harbored for so many years. Instead, each passing breath filled him with a new portion of something like euphoria. For the first time in his adult life, he felt he had complete control of his place in the world. He understood that the crimes Rome had done to him could never be escaped, never mended, never made right or forgotten; they could only be faced and cleansed through blood and oblivion, and through release from memory. There was no defeat in this. Instead, it was the ultimate revelation, a complete refutation of the single thing that had bound him to slavery—the fact that his own mortality had trapped him. Free of that, he would be free of all the chains that weighed him down.

It was a religious moment, one that must be sanctified with an offering. With that in mind, he loosened his spear and tugged it free of the mule. He smacked the creature on the bottom and watched it trot away. Still, nobody paused to note him, but that was about to change. He unclipped the clasp and yanked the robe from his shoulders. He tossed it high into the air with a snap of his wrist and strode toward the center of the crowd.

"Rome!" he yelled, speaking Latin. "How do you live without my black heart to beat for you?"

He punctuated this by thumping his knuckles against his chest. For a moment all around him he watched images of the world slowing from motion to stillness: the tail end of words spoken fluttered away on the breeze, laughter fell to silence, his cloak rumpled onto the stones, a hundred Roman faces turned and stared at him. He swung his spear into a two-handed grip, squatted slightly, stretched his eyes open wide and frantic, quick as those of a hunting leopard. Already he saw soldiers converging on him from several directions.

Good, he thought. Good. Tusselo will be a slave no longer.

To his amazement, Mago discovered that the sun had turned black. That was why he paused on his mount, turned sideways, and stared at it. He could not take his eyes off it. The black orb pulled at him as if it were a deep well and he were tumbling toward it. It did not matter that battle raged around him. The Romans who had boxed them in for days now had sprung their trap and the full brute force of three legions slammed into him from as many sides. His face was wet with blood that had sprayed up from a man some distance from him whose head had been severed from his standing body, making him a momentary fountain. His lieutenant was screaming that they must withdraw, but for a few seconds none of this mattered as much as the fact that the sun had gone black.

He heard a voice call his name. It was urgent, moist, and close to his ear, a whisper that somehow penetrated the din. As if injured by the impact of the voice, Mago's horse shuddered. He felt its forelegs buckle and thought he was going to fly over its head. He was still staring at the sun, however, and instead of toppling forward the mount kicked out twistingly and tilted to the side. Mago saw the sun flare and thought the orb smiled maliciously. Then the horse smashed against the ground. The impact drew his complete attention. He saw the pilum jutting out of the mare's chest, and saw her kicking and struggling to rise, and realized that his leg was trapped all the way up to his groin. It amazed him that he had not been injured; he felt no pain, although he was aware that the animal's weight was grinding him against an exposed rib of gray rock.

"Mago? General, you must wake for a moment. . . ."

He snapped at the speaker, saying he was not asleep. He was trapped! Help him! But the man would not and Mago had to twist and squirm and shove at the horse. The mount looked back at him, neck bent unnaturally, her eyes like those of a mistreated dog, offended, disappointed. Mago kicked her off with his free leg and rose to survey the scene. But what was this? There was no sign of his army at all, not even of the speaker. Instead he was alone among the enemy host. They encircled him, approaching from all directions, stepping slowly, menacingly, pila pointed at him like thousands of erect, deadly penises. Their helmets caught and reflected the black glow of the sun. He realized that his mouth was awash with wine. It was an evil taste. He exhaled it on each breath and had the momentary thought that blood was the same as wine. Perhaps he had already been pierced. He looked down to find the wound and in the anxiety of the moment his vision blurred and darkened. He realized that his eyes were closed and he pried them open.

One view of the world peeled over another. He looked up into the face of a man named Gadeer, a Moor, one of his captains. Gadeer tilted the mouth of a skin to his lips and tried to pour more wine into him. Mago twisted his head away, cursing.

"I'm sorry," the Moor said, "but we have found nothing better for you. The physician was lost, perhaps captured. If possible we will get some unction from one of the other boats."

As the man's mouth moved, the world around them took greater form and substance. Gadeer crouched below wood beams and the slight to-and-fro of his head in contrast to the beams betrayed the rocking of the sea. Mago could feel that more men stood nearby, but he did not wish to address them. One face was enough to focus on. There was a growing sensation spreading over his body that he would have disdained as well, but the swell of it was inescapable, pulsing.

"Where am I?" Mago asked. He knew that he had asked the question before, received an answer, and should remember it still, but he did not.

"Bound for Carthage," Gadeer said. "It is night. The watch reported passing Aleria on Corsica while you were sleeping. They saw the lights. We are now in open water. I'm sorry to wake you, but we must decide. We have no physician, but all who have seen you believe that we cannot wait any longer. By the gods, we wish we could get you to Carthage first, but in truth we cannot."

Despite the growing pressure that clenched and released his entire body, Mago understood the words the man spoke. He just did not know what they meant. They had no context. "What are you talking about?"

Gadeer drew back. His wide nose flared and relaxed. He had smooth brown skin untroubled by the passing years, freckled about the nose and forehead. "It's your leg. . . . My friend, your leg must come off."

This was an even less substantial statement. "Speak truth! I don't understand you."

It saddened Gadeer to hear this. "Near Genua," he said, "the Romans pressed us into battle. They repelled our elephants. Your leg was broken in a fall—"

"Genua?"

"In the north of Italy. Our plan was bold, General, but we failed. . . ."

Gadeer went on speaking, but Mago's mind caught on those last two words. With them the horror of it all came back to him. He remembered the last few months in one complete burst. He had left Iberia for the Balearics and on landing heard the first rumor of Hasdrubal's demise. This shocked him almost to immobility, but it also made action that much more urgent. He spent a few hard weeks trying to convince any of the islanders to join his fight. He assured them that Hannibal was on the verge of destroying Roman power. He explained how the landing of one more force in the north would clinch it all. The Ligurians and Gauls would join them and they would sweep down from one direction while Hannibal roared up from the other. They would trap Rome between the two of them and squeeze it like a fat pimple between two sharp nails. Fine hyperbole, but what finally swayed them was his promise that in addition to the normal pay for the season he personally promised them an extra payment of wine and women, just as their ancestors had accepted in days of old.

Midwinter, boatloads of Moors belatedly answered his entreaties and landed on the island, offering themselves as mercenaries. They were a blessing from the gods of Africa, the obverse of Gallic grandeur: big men, lean and tall, with long-fingered hands, bulbous knuckles, and skin as dark and smooth as oiled mahogany. As Mago set about training them he tried to believe his own rhetoric and held on to a daydream in which Hasdrubal had not been killed. He was alive and fooling everyone, perhaps playing out some ploy of Hannibal's.

But like so many bursts of enthusiasm throughout the war, this one proved short-lived. Arriving in Ligurian territory, Mago found that Ligurians and Gauls alike treated him coolly, with a dismissive air verging on outright insult. It turned out that both peoples had of late suffered Roman retribution for their support of Carthage. Two legions operated from well-fortified camps throughout the spring and early summer, hammering at the tribal powers at will. The Ligurians and Gauls had grown bitter toward the Carthaginian cause: angry with Hasdrubal for dying, with Hannibal for failing to aid them, with Mago for letting so much of the summer pass before he arrived.

Again Mago found himself calling on all his powers of persuasion, a task made more difficult when the Romans made him the focus of their campaigns. They shadowed his every move, hemmed him in, blocked his chosen routes, and struck at him during any moment of weakness. They pounced on whatever people he had last visited with such fury that soon no tribe would even consent to meet him. They had him at every disadvantage, and still no word came from Hannibal. Instead he saw only confirmation of Hasdrubal's demise.

Reluctantly, he decided to retreat. Maybe, he thought, they could risk sailing south and land nearer to Hannibal.

Before he could break for the sea, a third Roman army appeared. How the Romans could still field new armies confounded him, as did the bold vigor with which they attacked and the underlying events that made the attack possible. That was why he finally came to do battle with all three of them. He was near enough that he could smell the sea, but he had no choice but to turn and fight. His fifteen thousand were vastly outnumbered, low in morale. Mago was caught in the center of this, shouting what direction he could from horseback, and his mount had indeed caught a thrown pilum in her chest. The horse had reared just as in the dream. He had been pinned beneath her on a sharp ridge of rock. But that was where any resemblance to his dream ended. The impact snapped his femur and the pain exploded out of him in a howl of animal intensity. His men rallied around him and pried the horse up using pikes. Someone tugged on him too quickly, before his ankle was free. The thick muscles of his thigh contracted and the leg bone folded. As they dragged him from the field the jagged end of his femur seemed to snag on anything and everything. All manner of debris caught in the wound, dirt and filth, bits of leaves and other men's blood. Each contact sent him into convulsions of pain.

He had sweltered for two evil days in a hut along the shore before a messenger found them with the recall from the Council. He was carried aboard a vessel and had been in its hull since, feverish, in physical anguish, awash in the wine they poured down him and the urine and sweat that drenched the bed, only vaguely understanding that Hannibal too must have been ordered to leave Italy and that the dreaded Publius Scipio was on African soil.

All of this came back to him with Gadeer's admission of their failure. He remembered his wound too vividly to look down at it again, but the pain of it had come back to him fully. It was the center of his being. It was from his left thigh that his heart beat, and each contraction propelled pain through him.

He realized that Gadeer had left him sometime during these musings and was just now returning. Another man followed him, also a Moor. This man carried a sword he had sometimes seen

Moors wield. It was similar to the Iberians' curving falcata, except heavier, thicker. It was a weapon to be swung in sweeping arcs with the intention of doing lethal damage with a single blow. Seeing the direction of Mago's eyes, the man carrying it seemed embarrassed and moved the sword out of view.

Gadeer held out a halved gourd. "Drink this. It's an infusion from my people. It won't stop you from feeling pain, but it will prevent you from caring about it. A man jumped across from one of the other boats to bring it. We all want very much for you to be well."

Mago took the cup between both his quivering hands and craned his neck forward. He managed to get most of the liquid in his mouth, although some poured down into the creases below his chin. The concoction was bitter, grainy, and filled with floating bits of leaf that stuck in his teeth and to the roof of his mouth. But it was cool. It was other than wine. From the moment his head flopped back against the bunk he believed it might help him. If he could only breathe through the pain and pass on to someplace else. . . . Then everything would be better. He felt the promise of someplace else dissolving into the room around him, fizzing in the air like bubbles in water. He closed his eyes and tried to listen to air and think only of breathing, but Gadeer would not let him be.

"This is Kalif," the Moor said. "He is a strong man. He'll cut clean, with all his force. Two or three strokes at the most and he'll be through. His blade is very sharp . . ."

"Don't do it," Mago said, eyes shut tight, shaking his head.

"There is no other way."

"I said don't do it."

"We clamped your artery to stop the bleeding. The leaking was killing you. Instead you live, but your lower leg is already dead. It's rotten, Mago. It's eating up into you. Let us do what we must. I cannot arrive in Carthage with you dead, not without having done everything to save you."

"But I said no. You must obey . . ." Mago did not finish the sentence. The effort sapped his energy. "The sun was black," he said. He knew this would sound strange, but he felt a need to explain it while he could.

"That may have been," Gadeer said cautiously. "I did not notice that, but it may well have been so."

"Like the eye of a beast before it kills," Mago said. Having said that, he felt some amount of completion. The world fizzed around him and the pain was not so important now and he thought he might just fall asleep. He heard Gadeer talking with the others. They were debating whether to bow to his wishes or to treat him. He was no longer a part of the discussion. He was curious and tried to follow them, but his mind would not stay put. He thought of an old man who used to sweep the steps leading into the Council chambers in Carthage. For all he knew, the man was dead. He had hardly ever shared words with him in life, but as a youth he sometimes tossed him coins for his trouble and listened to his toothless mouth give profuse thanks. Why did he think of a man he hardly knew? Why not have visions of Hannibal? Of Hasdrubal and Hanno, of his sisters, of his mother? He could not remember the details of what the man said to him. The old one might have claimed to be a veteran. He might have had wisdom to ease him through this transition. Might have, but he could not remember now.

And then he thought of the Roman senators' rings from Cannae clattering on the floor of the Carthaginian Council chamber. Perhaps the old veteran had commented on this. He had been so proud at that moment, so gleeful at the great killing that Cannae had been. He remembered the way he had grinned as the circles rolled out across the stones, and he regretted his mirth. That grin seemed foul. Of all the things done and undone in his life, he wished he could take back that grin.

Eventually he heard Gadeer say, "All right, let us do it now as he fades."

He sensed the other man step forward and felt several hands on his body, moving him this way and that. He knew, without looking, at just what moment Kalif raised his sword and he understood why and it saddened him beyond comment. When the blade struck the first time it felt as if a club had hit him. How could the blade be so dull? The second blow was the same. The third and fourth as well. Really, he thought, they were not very good at this. And it was useless, anyway. He felt death coming toward him, no matter these men's efforts.

Most generals would have considered the task of withdrawing an army entrenched throughout southern Italy to be a deadly difficult operation, the kind of test presented to a leader once in his career, a chore for an entire summer, requiring careful planning, fraught with risks equal to those of any offensive campaign. To accomplish it successfully within a month, as Carthage demanded, was impossible, as Hannibal's generals warned him. But if it was, it was simply the latest of many such impossibilities to challenge his leadership.

The commander was, of course, tired now in a way he had never been before: suffering the physical ills of campaign, mentally drained by years of constant leadership, spiritually wrecked by the deaths of his brothers and friends, by the slipping away of a dream so nearly realized. He felt as if the world pulled him toward the ground with twice the normal force. The old falarica injury from Saguntum plagued him with phantom pains, as if the wound were still raw and new, the spear point still probing his flesh. His thoughts came more slowly than they once had. Each idea was somewhat unwieldy now. It had to be rotated in his mind, turned over and identified and set in place. Rest did little to refresh him. Indeed, he dreamed of fatigue, of constant motion, unending hikes. He planned routes in countries far from this one, fought segments of old battles, merging one conflict with another so that they all raged on in him at once, a grand confusion that never came any nearer to an end.

But even in this state he moved through the world looking every bit the commander he had always been. He still managed to accomplish the impossible. Hemmed in as he was in the southern regions of the peninsula, he bade the whole long stretch of Italy farewell in a style befitting his long dominance. He backed his troops in swift, orderly formations, directing his generals to march at night, to move unexpectedly, to survey the land they traversed so that no Roman army might catch them in a trap. He took everything he could from the region, stripped the land of grain and vegetables, beans and livestock. He did not hold these in reserve but instructed his men to feed themselves heartily. He told them to put on weight if they could, to sate themselves now, because they might never see this land again and because they needed strength for the fight to come.

He was not sure what sort of troops he would find waiting for him in Africa. He stirred the Gauls by painting pictures in their minds of the riches to be granted by his grateful nation. On the other hand, he pointed out, if they remained in Italy they would be far from home and with no ship to remove their feet from hostile land. And they would be at the mercy of the vengeful legions. He reminded the Campanians still with him that concluding the war successfully would benefit their people in the long run. He harangued the Lucanian and Bruttian towns about the requirements of friendships; he lured peasants with promises, dragged some from their homes forcibly. He needed men, even if only to stand before his veterans and blunt Roman swords. He drained the foot of Italy of everything he could. At Croton he met the ships dispatched from Carthage, and he put Italy behind him.

It was already late in the season when he landed at Leptis Minor, as the Council had arranged. Apparently, Carthage wanted him near but did not actually favor inviting the whole army inside the city's defenses. Awaiting him were mahouts with seventy-eight elephants. This would have been a welcome sight, except that from his first inspection of them it was obvious that most of the beasts were young, many of them untrained, all of them novices at battle. Vandicar stared at them with tight lips and eventually said he would need three months to train them, at the very least. Hannibal gave him three days, after which they marched to Hadrumetum. He picked up the twelve thousand troops who had served Mago. He knew that there was a well of sorrow possible in contemplating yet another brother's death, but he did not pause to explore it. He put the anguish of it in a compartment of his mind that he would return to later.

Upon receiving detailed reports from the Council, he learned what the enemy had been up to. After securing Cirta and the surrounding area, Publius and Masinissa had turned east and ranged across the flatlands to Hippo Regius, which they took without difficulty. It seemed that Publius had paused there for a week and sent reconnaissance missions into the hills of Naragara, perhaps gathering further troops among the Massylii. Then the whole army marched on Utica, besieged it by land and sea. The Council sent out an army from the city's garrisons, believing they might attack the enemy from the rear while they were engaged with the siege. A mistake. Masinissa outflanked them as if he had dreamed the whole maneuver up in his spare time. Carthage lost nearly four thousand men, many of them from aristocratic families. In pursuing them in retreat toward Carthage, the Romans captured Tunis, which had been abandoned by its garrison. From here the consul could literally gaze across the bay at the target of his enmity. Such was the unease in Carthage that envoys opened peace talks with him, although these were cut short on word of Hannibal's arrival.

Publius did not waste time trying to haggle with the councillors. Neither did he attack Carthage itself. Instead, he turned his army to the south and had them ravage their way down the broad valley of the Bagradas River. Every field they passed was left a blackened inferno, every village and town, every storehouse of grain, every orchard. They took town after town by storm, enslaving everyone with a value as a slave, dispatching the rest. At Thugga they tossed the bodies into the river and let them float toward the ocean, like a great vein bleeding out the life of the continent. When the town of Abba sent out envoys to discuss terms of surrender Publius had the men's hands cut off and spun them around with the message that there were no terms except the complete surrender of Carthage itself. At Kemis he repeated the atrocity of the plains, burning alive an entire village of thatched huts, the young and the old alike, capturing those lucky enough to escape and enslaving them.

The people did not understand who this demon was and why he had dropped down on them with such fury, but Publius was as calculated in his cruelty as he had been in his generosity in Iberia. Hannibal knew exactly what the Roman was doing, for he had used the same tactics himself. The consul bore those poor people no malice, just as Hannibal had not thought of the Latin tribes as naturally inimical to him. But by abusing them Publius prodded the Council to swift action. They, in turn, pressured Hannibal to give chase before he had truly gained his footing in Africa, leaving him little time to raise new troops and none to properly train them.

At first, Hannibal balked at being ordered about in this fashion. He did not move immediately. Instead, he came to terms with the Libyan Tychaeus, who was a relation of Syphax and hungry for revenge. He brought three thousand Libyan veterans into the army, a great gain. But in the days it took him to arrange this, new orders came from Carthage. Hannibal was to track the Romans down and annihilate them while they were still far from the city itself. Should he have any question about following these orders, he should remember that his family still lived in Carthage, by the grace of the Council. They were sure, they said, that Hannibal would not want anything unfortunate to befall them, especially his wife and young son.

As he closed his eyes after reading this Hannibal entertained a vision of turning his army on his own city. He had always believed that he knew the Carthaginian mind intimately. Now he wondered whether Carthage was viler than he had yet imagined, deserving of harsher punishments than he had ever visited on his enemies. Did not his men love him more than Carthage itself? They would rally behind him. He would find no difficulty reminding them of all the many ways the city had neglected them over the years. He would make them believe that together they could reach into the capital and rip out its foul heart and replace it with something to be proud of, something that would enrich them all with treasure beyond booty, beyond gold and slaves. He would build a new Carthage on the foundations of the old. And that city—his creation—could then turn its full resources to anything, even back to the defeat of Rome.

But this was only a fancy, and Hannibal was not one to entertain fancies. Ever since retreating from the walls of Rome he had known that this war would not lead to victory. Rome had taken the worst he could give it, and had lived. He would spend the rest of his life trying to understand just how that had happened, for he still did not fully comprehend it and could not order the events in a way that added up to the outcome Rome achieved. And in a more intimate way it baffled him. For all the years of his remembered life, he had believed that it was his destiny to defeat Rome. The knowledge that he had been mistaken cast everything in doubt. He was not even confident that he could rid Carthage of Publius Scipio, not considering the way Fortune's wind blew in his favor. He would have argued against the Council if he had known what to say, but the words eluded him. So he bowed to their wishes and began his pursuit.

It seemed that nothing in the world alarmed the animals of Africa more than the spectacle of an army of men on the march. As Hannibal pushed southward down the Bagradas valley, he drove herds of gazelle bounding before them across the scarred, smoldering landscape. Ostriches crisscrossed in front of the tide of men with their great, long-legged strides, occasionally becoming so disconcerted as to flap their useless wings in a desire to gain the air like other birds. Hyenas protested their progress each step of the way, retreating just so far before the approaching army, then spinning to challenge them with a chattering cacophony of yelps, only to spin again into bare-bottomed retreat. One evening Hannibal awoke to the calls of a lion, a tortured sound that seemed to warp the very fabric of the air through which it issued. The commander thought his tent fabric shook with each blast of sound, but in the dim light he could not be sure of this. It felt like the beast was communicating with him, but if this were so he knew not the language that it spoke.

As they were not themselves bent on destruction, the army rapidly gained on the Romans. From outside the pit of misery that had once been the trading center of Sicca, Hannibal sent out spies. They returned several days later and told a strange story. Several of them had been captured. When they were brought before Publius, one of his generals, Laelius, unsheathed his sword. They expected the customary fate of captured spies: to have their hands and tongues cut out and then to be released. But the consul laughed and waved for Laelius to sheath his sword. With another motion, he ordered their hands unbound. He called them guests and said that if Hannibal wished to know the state of his army all he had to do was ask. He personally escorted them throughout the camp, showing them everything, pausing long enough so that the men's nervous eyes could count and gauge the numbers they were seeing. This they did.

After they ended their report, the spies stood nervously about, with something more to say although they feared to do so.

"What else?" Hannibal asked.

One of the Libyans answered, "Commander, forgive me, but Publius told us to ask you whether his spies might survey your camp under the same conditions."

Hannibal sent the same man back with a negative answer. He did say, however, that he would be pleased to meet Publius to discuss the terms of a peace. Without waiting for an answer, he kept to his tasks as he saw them. Maharbal's scouts surveyed the land between the two armies, and the commander maneuvered his troops according to their reports. It soon became clear that Publius had chosen the wide plain east of Zama as the stage for their encounter. A strong decision. The land was perfect for an open engagement, with nothing to favor either side, no traps to spring or avoid, no reason not to judge the ground a fair venue for combat. It was a spot, in fact, that Hannibal could find no excuse to avoid.

Strangely enough, he wished he could. He felt the fingers of another man's hands pushing him this way and that, and he did not like it. In the past he would have found some way to snatch control, but he could see no way to do this now. The consul held all the advantages he had had in Italy. For that reason, Hannibal meant his offer of discourse seriously. The Council wanted him to destroy the Romans, but if they believed that only he was capable of this, they must accept his word if he chose a negotiated peace. That might be just the thing they all needed, to talk peace, and then to go home and be citizens again. He sent a second envoy to the consul.

On the afternoon that he approached Hannibal with the news of Publius' acceptance of his proposal, Gemel found him asleep on his stool. He sat upright, with one hand stretched out before him on his thigh, as if he were reaching to accept an object into his palm. The officer almost commenced speaking, but then he noticed the slump of his head and the labored steadiness of his breathing.

"Hannibal?"

The commander opened his eyes. He did not start or jerk, or give any sign that he had been surprised. He simply straightened his head and turned his gaze on the officer and studied him for a quiet moment. "I was just thinking," he said, "of how I used to kiss the drool away from my son's chin. There's nothing so soft as a baby's cheek, just there at the corner of their lips. I would like to do this again, but if I ever see young Hamilcar I probably won't even recognize him."

"Of course you will," Gemel said. "He is your son. My first son had a Turdetani mother, but still he came out my double."

Hannibal frowned. "You have young?"

Gemel nodded. "I have three, Hannibal. Two by that Turdetani woman. I do not know their fate, but she was resourceful. They may yet live in Iberia. My youngest is by a Bruttian woman who still travels with me. This child is a girl. Unfortunately for her, she looks like me as well."

Hannibal's gaze drifted away, moving from one thing to the next but obviously seeing only the thoughts inside him. "I did not know," he said. "How can it be that I never spoke to you of this before?"

"When we speak it's of other things, Commander. More important things. That's why I'm here now. Scipio has agreed to speak with you. Tomorrow, on the field between the two armies."

"So he agrees that we may end this with words?"

Gemel looked uncomfortable. "That I cannot say. Commander, are you well? If you wish I will propose a delay."

Hannibal stood and stepped closer to his secretary. He placed a hand on his shoulder and rocked him gently back and forth, humor on his fatigued features. "You ask whether I am well. . . . You have come very far with me, Gemel, and you have become as dear to me as Bostar was. I remember the morning after Cannae, when you stepped in to fill his position. You had nervous eyes then. You stood very erect and spoke clipped words, such as would make any drill officer proud."

"Some people have said that I still speak that way."

"Yes, yes, you do. But I've grown so accustomed to it. I am sorry that we haven't spoken more as friends. This was a mistake on my part. Do you accept my apology?"

Gemel, embarrassed suddenly, nodded crookedly, in a way that both affirmed his acceptance and denied that any slight had been done.

"Good. Send Scipio my word; we will meet on the morrow. There is no need for delay."

Hannibal slept like the dead that night. He woke in the predawn and automatically began to go over the speech he had to make. But he soon found that the words he meant to use did not need practicing. He felt like speaking the truth, and the truth is never rehearsed. Deciding so, he stilled his mind, stepped out of his tent, and watched the dawn.

Hannibal's forces marched down the slope from the northern boundary of the field of Zama and paused halfway, before them a great stretch of land as flat as a rough-cut paving stone. The Roman army occupied the southern area of this great space. They had drawn up in battle formation, in the checkerboard pattern of cohorts. Behind them rose the dim shapes of hills galloping off into the continent. Hannibal stepped forward before his army and walked toward the enemy without a weapon on his person. No guards—not even the Sacred Band—accompanied him. Only a translator trailed behind, also unarmed, a man of Egyptian blood and fluent in all tongues of consequence. Hannibal had no intention of using him, but it was the arrangement he had agreed to.

Publius likewise emerged as a single figure before the mass of men. His translator walked beside him. For a time he seemed very small, but as they neared the stools set up for them in the middle of the barren field, the man's proportions came into order. Lately, Hannibal had felt the vision of his good eye played tricks with him, especially in bright light. Because of this he opened their discourse abruptly, before either man had even sat down.

"We cannot speak sensibly in such a glare," he said in Latin. "Would you mind if I called for shade? A single slave. On my word, he'd bear no weapon."

Publius had clearly not expected this, neither the tone of it, its content or language. It took him a moment to recover. Call whomever you wish."

Hannibal dispatched his translator to fetch a slave, and the two men sat on the stools, facing at slight angles away from each other. No more than three strides separated them. Publius bore the uniform of his office well. The bronze of his muscled breastplate glinted with fresh polishing, almost to the hue of gold. His empty sheath was attached to his body by a crimson band tight across his torso, and from his helmet rose a great horsehair plume dyed the same color. Hannibal could not help but notice his opponent's youth. By the gods, he was only a boy! His eyes set widely on his face, a sharp nose cutting between them, with thin lips closed and waiting. Not exactly a handsome face, not fierce as Marcellus' had been even in death, not spiteful like the faces of so many Roman prisoners, but even silently and in stillness he conveyed his intelligence.

Hannibal knew it was upon him to open the discourse. And so he did. He simply opened his mouth and let the thoughts within him out. He spoke in Latin.

"It is strange to finally look upon you," he said. "I fought your father and knew much of your uncle, but never sat as close to them as I now do to you. Nor had I as much to fear from them. Publius Scipio, the conqueror of Iberia . . . the victor of the plains . . . I've heard so much of your exploits that in meeting you I expected to see either a man kissed by the gods or some demon, with the touch of death in his eyes. You are neither of these. You are younger-looking than I expected."

Hannibal turned to watch the interpreter returning, beside him a slave with two large palm-leaf shades. The slave was clearly an Umbrian, naturally pale, although tanned by the African sun. He stood near them, completely naked, and perched the bases of the two palm fronds between the crooks of his arms and his back. Somehow he managed to cast shadows on both the men. Hannibal regretted that they had sent a Latin, both because of the unnecessary insult it suggested and because the man would have to be killed afterward for being able to understand them.

Shade in place, Hannibal continued. "Fortune has been my fickle mistress for several years now," he said. "When I raged down into your land, winning battle after battle, Fortune always asked for pieces of me in return. She took my eye. She took first friends and comrades, and then my brothers one by one. I lost never a single open battle, but still she held ultimate victory just beyond my arm's reach. Now, when Fortune has decreed that I must come to meet a Roman consul and sue for peace, she does me the kindness that it be you to whom I come. At least by that I am honored. Strange, isn't it? The first battle I fought was with the father; now the last may be with the son."

The commander paused a moment. Publius—intentionally or not—nodded: Yes, this was indeed a strange way for events to play out. He waited passively, but with a set of his jaw that showed his formal reserve undiminished. Hannibal smiled. Publius could speak of his own losses, but he rejected the invitation to admit common ground between them. Hannibal noted this and silently commended it.

"I'll speak honestly to you. And I'd have you do the same to me. Nobody listens to us now. The rabble of rich men who rule our countries are not now in attendance. This matter is for us to decide. Let us discard pride and instead rely on reason. This is not hard for me to do. I have little pride left, but I fear from the eyes you set upon me that you have yet to learn many of the things war has taught me. You are like me after the Trebia, after Trasimene and Cannae. Young men often long for victory instead of peace. I know this well. Such is the difference between the old and the young. But if we clash tomorrow neither you nor I will decide the victor. We are the twin sons of Fortune. Who can say which of us will prevail? You might even lose your own life. At this point—when you've come so far—that would be tragic. Hear this wisdom and let us end this today, without the loss of many thousands more. Far too many have died already, and the brave men who stand behind us desire life—not death on this field tomorrow.

"Here is the peace that I propose. It's a way to end the war this very day, and I'm sure I can persuade my city's Council to honor it. You may keep everything for which I began this war. Sicily is yours. Sardinia. All the islands between our two nations. In addition, I release all claims to our possessions in Iberia. That rich country, which we tamed, is ours no longer. My people will remain on African soil. We will not rebuild our navy. We will not attack any Roman possession. Nor will we challenge what I now believe is inevitable—that Rome will reach into new provinces and grow stronger yet. Carthage is chastened, Publius. Leave us to live simply, as we were, looking only away from you and no longer causing Rome grief. That is what I can offer you."

The Roman consul received all this without giving the slightest outward sign as to his thoughts. When Hannibal concluded, Publius studied him a little longer. Beads of moisture had swelled to fullness on his forehead. A few trickled into others and slipped along his hairline and down under his jaw.

"You are mistaken about my character," Publius said. "I don't think I'm unbeatable. If ever a man was unbeatable, you were; and here as I look at you I see defeat draped over you like a shawl. You are a lesson to me. But I cannot accept these terms. I am not a king standing before you, but a representative of my people. And I know they would not accept the peace you offer. Before you arrived in Africa, I began talks with your Council. Then, perhaps, I could've accepted the terms you propose. But not now, not after your Council backed out and sent you to do their work for them."

"If the terms were fair then, they are so now," Hannibal said. "The world has not changed so much in these few weeks."

Publius cocked his head questioningly. "You asked me to speak plainly. Hannibal, I believe that if our armies meet I will defeat you."

"Others have thought that also," Hannibal said.

"Nevertheless, this is what I believe. I also believe that your people cannot be trusted to honor any terms. If Carthage kept control of Africa, she would grow rich again by the morrow, war-hungry again the day after that. I'm in allegiance with Masinissa of the Massylii. It was with his help that I fought Syphax and came to know this country. He is now the king of all of Numidia and a friend of Rome. So you see, the very forces that brought me here demand that I present you with these terms: You are allowed to remain in Carthage, with your customs and laws. But you will abandon all possessions outside of the immediate surroundings of your capitol. To Masinissa, you return all territories that once belonged to him or to his ancestors. You may never make war—either inside or outside Africa—without Rome's permission. We will have all your warships, military transports, and elephants, and you are forbidden to train more. There will be a fine as well. I don't know the amount, but it will be considerable, paid out, perhaps, over fifty years or so. You must return all prisoners, slaves, and deserters—"

"Are you making this up as you go along?" Hannibal asked.

"And I will personally pick one hundred hostages from your people's children. From any group, councillors, generals, even from among the Barcas."

The Umbrian slave adjusted his position slightly, whether from fatigue or as an inadvertent comment on what he had just heard, it was hard to tell. Beads of sweat dotted the man's entire chest now. Occasionally—set loose by his minute movements in steadying the parasols—droplets ran freely down his form, some falling from him to splat on the sand. Hannibal watched the spot where they landed for a few moments, stilling himself. Although he gave no outward sign of it, the import of the last demand froze the air in his lungs. He had to consciously draw a fresh breath and blow it out before he could answer.

"What you propose is not acceptable. The Council would kill me for bearing them such terms, and it wouldn't accomplish your wish. Their hatred for Rome would burn undiminished. That would not be a peace at all, just a pretext for . . ." Hannibal let whatever he was going to say drop. He blinked it away and resumed: "But this isn't about terms. Don't be so foolish as to take personal revenge. Revenge doesn't bring back those who've been lost; it only taints their memories. Must we risk everything in a clash of arms?"

Publius grinned, not a joyful expression but one that suggested somber humor. "Can it be that Hannibal now disdains war? None in my country would believe this. Of course this is personal! It was personal from the moment you set foot on Roman lands. You should know by now that no Roman fights alone. Be an enemy to one and you are an enemy to all of us. I would happily die tomorrow in battle with you; as I fell, another would step into my place. Can you say the same?"

Hannibal did not answer.

"We are all the walking dead," Publius said. "It's illusion to think otherwise. If I did not know better, I'd think that you've misjudged the situation you find yourself in. The outcome of this war has already been decided. No wind can blow Rome back from victory.

You know that. We fight tomorrow only to determine the terms of your surrender: fair or less than. But either way, Rome has won."

The commander brought a hand to his face and gripped his chin. He let his fingers slide up far enough to press against the closed lid of his bad eye. "Then we have failed the men behind us."

The consul rose to his feet. "One of us has," he said.

Hannibal did not address the army collectively the next morning. He could not conjure any words to encourage them that he had not already used and that did not sound hollow to his ears. If he could have spoken honestly to them, he would have told them to fight with all their courage for no other reward than the continuation of their own lives. Fight so that they might stop fighting. Fight so that they could throw down their arms and trudge back to wherever their homes were. Fight so that Hannibal would not see his family made prisoner to Rome. This seemed as important a factor as any. Publius was right. This was all personal. But he had no desire to admit as much to his army.

Indeed, as Hannibal set up his command on the slope behind and above the field of battle, he was not sure that the army he commanded was, in fact, his. His mind stuck on the unfortunate thought that he had few trusted comrades left. A man named Hasdrubal led his first line of Gauls and Balearics and Ligurians, but this was an imposter bearing his brother's name. In the second line—the Libyans, Moors, and Balearics of Mago's army, along with other newly recruited Africans—he recognized the color and feel of the men, but he barely recalled their officers' names. And the third line, his veterans, composed of Carthaginians and Libyans who had been with him all up and down Italy . . . well, they were fewer than he would have liked. True, Monomachus commanded there, as did Isalca and Imco Vaca; he was thankful for them, but even more aware of those not present. He could not look to one of his brothers and know that their fates were bound by blood, that they had shared a womb, entered the world the same way, and suckled first from the same breast. There was no Bomilcar among them, no model of unwavering strength. No Bostar, with his nimble mind for details. On his right there mustered a contingent of Carthaginian cavalry, but the man who led it was not Carthalo. And where was Silenus, the Greek who had so often murmured mischief in his ear? He could not even call upon Mandarbal's dark arts, for the priest had left him at Hadrumetum to conduct holy rites in Carthage. He felt almost completely alone, set apart from the many brave soldiers readying themselves to fight under his direction, privy to a vision of what might come that was very different from theirs.

But fading into melancholy served no one on this day. He wrested his focus back and studied the enemy deployment, searching in it for anything that required a change in his own tactics. The Roman formation was plain enough: a wide front line of infantry, three maniples deep, with a further line of veteran triarii held in reserve. On his western wing was the Italian cavalry, led, he knew, by Laelius, the consul's trusted friend. An even stronger contingent of Numidians composed the eastern wing, directed by Masinissa. There was something strange about the quincunx, the checkerboard pattern of their infantry, but Hannibal registered this without addressing it.

Surveying the enemy helped straighten his spine. As the skirmishers began to exchange missile fire, there was a comforting familiarity with the scene before him. He had watched such mass movements before, and every time he had pulled strings and moved men at his will. Perhaps he could do so one more time. The two forces were of nearly equal number, about forty thousand troops each. Many of his men were raw, some only marginally loyal, but they all knew what was at stake. And it was not as if he had no strategy in his deployment. The lines were spaced with distance between them for a reason, each with a role he had secretly assigned. And the elephants, all of which he had placed along the front line—with a small breath of Fortune they would open the battle marvelously.

Motion caught the corner of his eye and drew his complete attention. Into the general skirmishing, the cavalry on the right flank, under Maharbal, streamed forward at a full gallop. Hannibal, surprised, yelled for them to halt. He snapped around and shouted for the confused signaler to raise his horn and stop them. But even as he spoke, he knew it would not work. He changed his order to one that would steady the rest of the army, just tell them that nothing had changed, not to break ranks or move. Looking back again he still could not understand. He thought the flamboyant general might have a plan in mind, but could not imagine what it was, why they had not discussed it.

From the Roman side, Masinissa's Numidians rode out to meet them. They flew toward each other as if they would collide at a full gallop and rip each other to shreds. But at the last moment—just before the crash of men and horses, teeth and hooves and spears—the two sides turned. They carried their speed into a coordinated movement that brought them together, riding side by side, not engaging at all but merging like two rivers mixing currents. Even from the distance at which he watched, Hannibal heard their trilling flying up from tilted chins. And then he understood completely. Maharbal and the bulk of his men had just deserted to Masinissa, their tribal king. Of course they had! They were Massylii.

Hannibal issued new orders. He pulled a portion of the left-flank Carthaginian cavalry out, had them traverse behind the army and position themselves in the vacated position. It was the correct response, but even as he oversaw it he breathed hard to recover from the shock. The fact that he had not seen this coming stunned him. He had fought so long with Maharbal at his side that he had not paused to consider whether the arrival in Africa would change his sympathies. It was a shocking oversight, one that he never would have made before. But he had no time to ponder it. The Romans had begun their forward march.

To answer them, Hannibal ordered the pachyderms to advance. As they shuffled forward, he gave the order for the front line to ready their spears. These soldiers were hard to direct from a distance, but he hoped to get them to launch at least one unified volley of missiles to further fracture whatever the elephants did not break of the Roman ranks. But just after he spoke, Hannibal received his second shock of the morning.

Halfway across the field a number of the elephants stopped dead in their tracks. A few others trembled and tossed their heads and changed direction. The sound reached him later than the sight, so it took him a moment to hear the blast of noise that had met the elephants. The Romans, all at once, had unleashed a barrage of sound. Nearly all the men of the front line carried war horns. These they blew on. Behind them the others shouted in unison, on signals given to various cohorts, so that the sound pulsed, first from one place and the another. All the men banged their swords or spears on their shields, on their breastplates, on their helmets. The elephants, especially the young ones, had never heard anything like it. They must have wondered what sort of beast they were approaching and why.

As soon as the first of the elephants neared pilum range, hundreds of missiles flew at them, piercing the creatures between the eyes or in the ears, catching them in their open mouths, dangling from their chests as they ran. For many of them, this was too much. They turned and retreated, adding their maddened trumpeting to the tumult. The thirty or so that did manage to enter the enemy ranks found the troops drawn into an alternating pattern of tightly wedged men or wide, open avenues. This was what had been strange about the quincunx. They had been positioned in such a way that the troops could step out of the elephants' path and slot into each other. Faced with the path of least resistance, the elephants, no matter what their mahouts tried to convince them, hurtled down through the open stretches as if racing to exit the far end. Few of them made it, however, for the Romans turned and pelted them in passing. Pila and stones, javelins and smaller missiles: all so great in number that the creatures stumbled and fell beneath them, roaring, crying, tears dripping from their long lashes, their hides stuck like pincushions. Some soldiers even began to approach them, stick a foot up, and yank out the missiles to see if they could be used again.

As all this took place on the Roman side, the Carthaginian side suffered conversely. Several of the elephants stampeded straight back and through the infantry, cutting a path through the men like four-legged boulders. To the left, four elephants in close formation drove a wedge through the cavalry, sending them into complete chaos, a situation which Masinissa soon exploited, appearing among them out of the elephants' dusty wake. He drove the confused horsemen from the field. Before long Maharbal and Laelius set the right wing to flight as well. They rushed up the slope at an angle off

David Anthony Durham

to the north, and for the next hour the horsemen were to play no part in the main conflict.

The Romans resumed their march toward Hannibal's first line. They did not have many missiles left, but Hannibal could not get his troops to take advantage of this. They did not launch the volley he had hoped for, but tried to pick out singular targets and met with little success. The Romans stepped up to them slowly and began the cut, block, and thrust, cut, block, and thrust that they were so efficient at, using their shields to knock their opponents off their guard or even off their feet. The mixed troops trying to fight them in a variety of styles had no chance against the relentless uniformity of the Roman advance. As the Gauls jostled for room to swing their long swords, the Romans jabbed at their naked torsos, slit their trouser legs open, and sent them to their knees. The slight Ligurians fought well at close quarters, quick with short swords, standing up and squatting, striking high and low, whirlwinds of movement, but rarely landing fatal blows. Many of the Africans fought with spears, but they struggled as individuals trying to fight their way into an impenetrable wall.

Hannibal was not surprised when they began to crumble. First one soldier and then several and then large groups from the first line retreated toward the second. They thought they would sink into their masses. As they approached they discovered the second line would not accept them, no matter how they tried to push through, cursing and indignant. Spears and swords and grim faces met them, held them in place until the Romans caught them up again and they had to turn and fight once more. This was just as he had ordered. Treacherous, yes, but the circumstances left little room for anything else.

Before long the Romans fought standing on the corpses of the first line. The Libyans, Moors, and Balearics of Mago's army fought with fresh vigor. They had a higher level of discipline and during the first moments they stopped the Roman advance dead. But as a river builds slowly to protest a new dam, so the Romans' collective weight began to move them forward again. When the second line broke they were not prepared for the shock they faced on their retreat. The third line would not allow them refuge, just as they had

552

spurned the first. They were cut down fighting, their backs pricked by a wall of their troops' spears.

As the Romans made contact with his veterans, Hannibal thought he might have them. The legionaries would be exhausted by now. The front ranks, facing the fresh veterans, would fall in great numbers. His officers would pull back slowly, leading them on, making them climb, slip, stumble over the bodies of the dead to reach them. They might at least maul them badly enough in the first few minutes as to work a change in the collective psychology of the soldiers.

But Publius must have seen these possibilities as well as Hannibal. He pulled his men back. Even with the blood fury on them, he spoke a command; it translated through the horns; the men listened. They withdrew in semiorderly manner, treading backward in high, careful steps over bodies and weapons and viscera. They regrouped, speaking to each other, finding their places in line, and forming up tightly, panting, wiping sweat from their eyes, spitting blood.

By the time they marched forward again they looked as orderly as if the battle had just begun. The two sides collided, shield to shield, the veterans meeting them in kind, with much the same equipment and technique. The impact sent an echoing clap fanning out in all directions, like the thud of a hundred mountain rams all colliding at once. From then on it was butchery, both sides equally matched, each man dancing with one malignant partner after another, the armies eating into each other. Hannibal could not see as much as he wished. Dust clouded the scene, and the spray of blood above the field seemed a dark rain falling on that one spot in all the world. But he could tell from the general steadiness of the mass of men and from the noise that the issue was not yet decided against him. Somewhere in there Monomachus led the killing. Isalca rallied his woolly-haired Gaetulians. Imco Vaca worked his magic. Perhaps the gods would bless the fresh-faced Vaca again and raise him up as the hero of this battle. Maybe, if they could just hold long enough, the consul would pull his men back, afraid to find himself stranded deep in Africa with only a few shattered men to protect him. Each passing breath increased the chance that they would both concede this contest as a draw. Then, surely, he and the consul would reach a peace agreement. He would even give a little more if he had to. This seemed so possible that the commander began to plan how best to retract the veterans.

But then, from off to the west, he heard a familiar thunder. Because of the slope he could see nothing for a few moments. The sound grew and grew and seemed to engulf him from the opposite side as well. At almost the same moment, cavalry crested the rise to the west and emerged from the scoop of a gentle ravine to the east. Hannibal needed no more than a glance at their speed and vigor and numbers to know that both forces belonged to the enemy. His horsemen had obviously been vanquished. And with this the battle was decided. Masinissa first, but then Laelius and Maharbal rode in with their thousands of soldiers, attacking the veterans from all available sides. The infantry faced about to meet them, but it was a losing effort. The Numidians must have gathered up fallen spears before they returned. They carried extras that they flung at leisure, looking from a distance as if they were betting with each other, telling jokes, laughing. They never got close enough for the foot soldiers to injure them. They just whirled and darted, trilled and darted.

When a few of them caught sight of him and turned their horses toward him, Hannibal knew there was no need to stay a moment longer. Part of him wanted to throw himself into it and meet his end. There before him were thousands of men who hungered to spill his blood. For a moment, he almost gave it to them. But even in his fatigue, even in defeat, he could not help but remember his duty, both to his nation and to his family. It would be cowardly to die now, irresponsible. So he agreed to the Sacred Band's entreaty that they fly. As their horses were rested, they soon outstripped their pursuers and ate up Africa toward the northern horizon.

He was four days on the journey to Hadrumetum. He paused there only long enough to dispatch a seaborne messenger to Carthage, stating his defeat simply, warning the Council that he was on the way and that he brought with him the end of the war. They must concede and accept any terms offered, he wrote. They had to prepare themselves.

Then he set out again. For some reason that he could not explain even to himself, he chose to walk the final days to Carthage. No matter what Publius might have planned, he would be delayed for weeks by the aftermath of such a success and by the need to move an entire army. Hannibal, for this last journey, did not have to rush. He walked with the Sacred Band trailing behind him. At first they were a party of fifteen, but as they passed people gathered to watch them, whispering to themselves.

Someone quickly named him as Hannibal, swearing that he recognized his likeness from a coin. But many protested that this could not be Hannibal. His beard was wild and unkempt. He stumbled as he walked and the sole of one sandal had begun to flap with each step. He looked like some terrible beggar, a veteran of an ancient war, a man lost in the southern desert and surely insane.

But what of his eye? others asked. He has sight in a single eye, just like Hannibal. And does not he wear the garb of a commander? Is he not guarded by the Sacred Band? They threw question after question at his guards, who refused to answer and for some time chased them away. Eventually the numbers grew large enough that they chose instead to ignore them.

Across fields and orchards and pastureland, Hannibal walked at the vanguard of an ever-increasing horde. They were sure now that he was indeed the famous commander, coming home, bearing news to shape the future of the nation. This news, to judge by the look of him, could not be good. He stopped eating on the second day and drank water only from the streams he passed over or waded through. He was emaciated, and beneath the thinness of his skin the muscles of his arms stood out, the striations in his legs. He did not stop to sleep. He walked on through the night and lost many of his followers, but by the middle of the third day they had caught him up again. He walked through the next night, and again the same thing happened. He was so near to Carthage now that curious pilgrims from the city came out to meet him. They shouted greetings to him, prayers, questions. What was their fate to be? Was the wrath of Rome upon them?

Monomachus rode up beside him just after he had come in sight of Carthage. He had yet to wash or clean his armor. He was coated in dust and grime that had dried into the blood over every inch of him. He looked like a corpse moving in imitation of life. The general offered a report on the last moments of the battle. He named specific officers and described their fate, explained how he and a small contingent had cut their way out through the Romans and escaped. Few others had been so lucky. "Only the ones blessed to kill another day," he said. He understood that the Romans had begun the northerly march once more, although they showed no haste and might take a couple of weeks to reach Carthage.

When he was done, Hannibal said nothing. Indeed, he had hardly listened at all. He kept walking. Monomachus rode along beside the commander for some time, and then, as if it had just occurred to him, he asked if Hannibal had need of a horse.

"The way would be much quicker mounted," he said. "If we are to fight on perhaps we should make haste."

"The war is over," Hannibal said, uttering the first words to escape his parched lips in days. "The only fight left in me is the fight for peace."

"Moloch abhors peace," Monomachus said.

"And I abhor Moloch," Hannibal snapped. "He's your god; not mine. Not anymore."

Monomachus—stunned, angered, frightened by the blasphemy, all of these—yanked his horse to a halt and sat on the creature immobile as the crowd issued around him.

Hannibal walked on.

Late in the morning, he paused to stare at the full grandeur of his native city, its great walls, the thick foundations, the hill of Byrsa upon which Elissa had first laid claim to this blessed and accursed portion of Africa. Had that beautiful Phoenician queen known what she was starting when she landed here?

By midday he walked down an avenue hemmed in by throngs from the city: young men jostling for position, laborers who had dropped their tasks, women of the lower classes who managed to watch every move he made while simultaneously keeping their eyes lowered, priests looking on from beneath the hoods that hid them from the light of day, slaves and children, aged crones who greeted him in the old way, kneeling on the ground with their wrinkled foreheads against the dust. Vendors sold food, offered water from gourds. Even dogs peered out between legs, curious in their own way.

It was both wonderful and sad to see their many faces, so different in features and skin tone, persons born in this land and those drawn here, some with black curls tight to their scalps, or locks flowing in waves, or hair straight and fine as silk. These were his people. They were the embodiment of all the nations of the world.

Several times councillors stepped out of the crowd and approached him with an air of importance, wearing the robes and the stern faces of their rank. He passed them by, but not out of malice. He would speak to them soon, but first he had other business.

He saw the figures standing on the walls from a long way out, and those gathered at the top of the main ramp leading into the city. He was calm until the moment he saw his family banner hoisted. The Barca lion. It marked the place where his family stood. At the foot of the granite incline he paused and squinted his single eye. He squeezed the figures up there into better focus. There stood his mother, cloaked in a purple robe, her hair bound up into an intricate crown rising above her head. Beside her Sapanibal, touching at the shoulder with a man whom Hannibal could not name just then, an old friend of his father's. It took him a moment to pick out Imilce from among the numerous household servants. But she was there, and before her stood a boy. Her hands rested on his shoulders and though he bore no resemblance to the two-year-old he had left five years ago, Hannibal knew who the boy must be. He hesitated for a few moments, and then he turned to one of the Sacred Band. He sent the man up with a message.

As he stood waiting his heart beat at an ever more furious pace. He called for water and someone brought him some. He drank deeply, but felt bloated suddenly, decided he hated water, and tossed the gourd to the ground. When he looked up again, the guard was leading the boy down the slope toward him. Hannibal could only stare. They seemed to approach so quickly. In an instant they were in front of him. The guard presented him, saying, "Commander, here is your son, Hamilcar." The man stepped away and then the father stood, weak-kneed, before the child.

Hamilcar was not as he had been before. He was tall, lean, and as finely formed as a father could have wished. He wore a gown of Eastern silk, light green, upon which a bird had been embroidered with blue thread, its wings flecked with gold. He stood with his arms pressed down to either side, a posture that accentuated the lines of his collarbones and the thinness of his shoulders. Hannibal could see the contours beneath the fabric and he wanted to place his hands atop them. His ears jutted out from his head, visible even though his hair hung in loose curls around his face, ringlets just the size to slip around a finger. Most of his features were entirely unfamiliar, nothing like they had been. They needed to be memorized anew. All except his eyes . . . His two large, bright eyes contained both the mother and the father in them: brown at the center, grayish along the outer rim. They sheltered beneath a strong brow line, like his, and yet the shape of them was all Imilce. He was magnificent.

Thinking so, Hannibal was completely unprepared for what happened next. The child's lower lip began to quiver. His chin flexed and convulsed as if tiny creatures writhed below the skin. His nostrils flared, his eyebrows twitched, and it began: the boy cried. Hannibal realized all of sudden what the boy must see. While he was looking on the child's beauty the boy was gazing at a beast. A gape-mouthed ogre with a single eye, with blistered skin and cracked lips, with great hands scarred by battle, pockmarks in the flesh of his knuckles, his hair wild about him like the mane of a dying lion, his beard unkempt, bearing bits of debris in it. The blood of millions tainted him and he must have smelled of it, a stench of such magnitude that no bathing would ever cleanse him completely. He loomed over the boy, casting him in shadow, worse than any demon of Moloch. He reached for him, wanting to bring his goodness close to him, but the boy flinched and took a half-step back.

"No, no, don't cry, Little Hammer. Don't cry. I . . . I am your father returned to you. It's all over."

The boy's face twisted into a mask of misery at this. Tears poured down his cheeks. Hannibal scooped him up in one arm and tried to comfort him with the other. He felt the boy go stiff against him, tense and sobbing even more, twisting as if he would reach out to someone for salvation but feared to. Hannibal began to ascend the ramp. He supported the child with a single arm, the other swaying at his side as a countermeasure to his careful steps. He murmured as softly as he could to ease the child's fear, asking him not to cry, saying that he was not the monster he seemed. "There is no need to cry," he said, over and over again, speaking the truth and lying at the same time, unsure which was which anymore.

All the while his eye stared fixedly at his wife. He watched the distance between them close and inside, silently, he asked for forgiveness.

Aradna had many gifts to thank the goddesses for. She had escaped war. Scenes of death haunted her dreams, but they were no longer the fabric of every waking moment. She had found her way to the island she had known only by name, and on landing she discovered the remnants of her father's family, an uncle who barely remembered his brother, several cousins, and a sister-in-law who—magically—welcomed her without question. Boys from the village laughed at the strange accent she spoke Greek with, but clearly they liked her company. They helped her build a hut of stone and clay, with a wood-framed roof of clay tiles. In a pen beside it she raised Persian fowl. She helped her reclaimed family harvest their olives and tend their pistachio trees and repair fishing nets for the village fleet. She helped an old man from the town raise edible dormice. This particularly gave her joy, for the squirrel-like creatures were shy and quiet, with trembling noses and bulbous black eyes and fur so soft she marveled. True, they all eventually went into pots to fatten and were sold live at the weekly market, but still it was a gift to watch them born, to hold them in hairless infancy and see them grow. Nobody hungered to rob or rape her. Her small fortune was hardly even necessary, and yet was a comfort buried deep beneath the earth floor of her dwelling. She set her donkey loose to roam the nearby hills, though the creature never wandered far from her. Was this not happiness?

Not quite. That was why every day since her arrival Aradna had climbed up to the old ruin at its summit. The first few times, she followed a goat trail part of the way, but she soon found this course too circuitous for her liking. By the late autumn she had carved her own path straight up a gully, out of which she rose so abruptly that she scrambled for a time on all fours, and then onto a ridge that took her the rest of the way. Considering the distances she had covered during her life as a camp follower this hike was a small exercise that hardly even broke a sweat on her, no matter how hot the day. The goats watched her with skepticism, standing big-bellied and recalcitrant, flicking their ears as if to comment on her disregard for protocol. She sometimes told them what she thought of them, but in fact she enjoyed the company of peaceful beings and she knew that her compulsion to gain the hill daily did actually verge on absurd.

Once into the labyrinth of aged white walls she found a certain peace. The ruin had once been the rambling estate of an Athenian exiled to the island for reasons of political intrigue. It had been abandoned many years ago, although just why Aradna never learned. As no single flat space existed to serve as the base of the house, it meandered through several terraced levels, stone walls blending in and out of the vegetation, as if the designer had bent to nature's plans and constructed the buildings not to offend it. In this regard it was strangely modest, despite its size and wonderful placement.

Aradna's destination was always the same. She climbed to the very peak of the island, which was a lumpy rise within the estate's crumbling walls. There, beneath the ancient olive trees, with the grainy soil crackling beneath her sandals, she would turn and take in the panoramic, circular view of the sea as it stretched out in all directions. On a clear day, of which there were many, she believed she could see everything that floated within a day's sail. And it was for just this that she came, day after day. She waited through the slow dying of autumn and even through the winter, when ship traffic slowed. She would just sit on the blustery heights and watch the hand of the wind drag its fingertips across the waves. She would think of the first time she saw the soldier, naked and aroused, falling from midair down to the sandy riverbank near the Picene coast. She would marvel at how they had met again and again in the chaos of a war-torn country. She would recall bathing his naked body beside a great battlefield and think of his strange claims that he conversed with a slain Saguntine girl. She would remember that he had a gentle mouth. For a few moments she would feel ashamed that she had parted with him angrily, calling him a fool for journeying back to Africa with his commander. But she did not chastise herself too much. He *was* a fool. There was no disputing that.

But he also had a destiny that she knew would not be decided on a battlefield. That was why she climbed here every day, because she would eventually see the sails of the ship bearing him home. One way or another, Imco Vaca would find her again. She was sure of this. Of course he would. It was only with this possibility that any of her life made any sense. So she chose to believe it.

Following the close of Hannibal's war, the treaty between Carthage and Rome formally held for fifty years. The Carthaginians paid the yearly indemnities on time or early, and before long the city began to prosper once more. Hannibal was elected Shophet (or Suffete) in 200 B.C., largely with the support of the populace against the power held by the oligarchy. Holding supreme power for five years, he implemented a number of democratic and financial reforms. But his old enemies within the Council conspired against him. They sent word to Rome that he was planning new hostilities against them. He was forced to flee the city to avoid capture by the Romans and spent the rest of his life as a mercenary general in largely unsuccessful wars against Rome's eastward expansion, first for the Syrian king Antiochus III and later for Prusias I of Bithynia (northern Turkey). It was in Bithynia, at the age of sixty-four, that Hannibal decided to stop fighting and to stop running. He committed suicide by taking poison. His last words are reported to have been "Let us now put an end to the anxiety of the Romans who could not wait for the death of this hated old man."

Even with Hannibal dead, Rome feared Carthage's power. By

191 B.C., the Council offered to pay off all the tribute scheduled for the next forty years. Such wealth may have been as alarming as any military prowess. In 149 B.C., Rome declared war once again, this time on a pretext stemming from a dispute between Carthage and the aged, prospering King Masinissa. Carthage fell after a three-year siege and her citizens were killed. A door-to-door slaughter left only fifty thousand survivors out of an estimated seven hundred thousand. Buildings were knocked down, burned, obliterated. Carthaginian culture, literature, art, and customs were systematically erased from the world's historical legacy. Having destroyed its greatest rival, Rome went on to build a vast empire.

ACKNOWLEDGMENTS

For their kindness in reading early portions of this work I would like to thank Laughton and Patricia Johnston, Nick Armstrong, Beth Johnston, Jim Rankin, Gordon Eldrett, Helen Harper, Jamie Johnston, Sorley Johnston, and Jane Stevenson. Everything in these pages had to survive the prior scrutiny of my wife, Gudrun—and this was a good thing. I thank my children for filling the workdays with joyful interruptions. Especially, I am indebted to my son, Sage, for inspiring one of the novel's characters. You will know the one I mean. Thanks to Sloan Harris for continuing to represent. And thanks to all the folks at Doubleday and Anchor for their faith, especially Gerry Howard, Bill Thomas, Steve Rubin, and Alice Van Straalen. Special acknowledgment must go to Deborah Cowell, my first editor and the undeniable reason that this book is in your hands right now. I also appreciate it that the folks at the Birnam Institute in Birnam, Scotland, provided me the luxury of a chair with a view and good coffee. Much of this novel was written in that corner, looking over the gardens.

This book is a work of fiction and should only be read as a novel. It was inspired by real figures and events, but I have taken many liberties to arrange the material into a workable narrative. For those interested in a historian's take, there are many sources to consult, beginning with the ancients themselves: Polybius and Livy. Among the many more recent texts I considered, I wore a few thin and ragged: Lesley and Roy A. Adkins' *Handbook to Life in Ancient Rome;* Nigel Bagnall's *The Punic Wars;* Ernle Bradford's *Hannibal;* Brian Caven's *The Punic Wars;* Leonard Cottrell's *Hannibal: Enemy of Rome;* Gregory Daly's *Cannae;* Theodore Ayrault Dodge's *Hannibal;* Florence Dupont's *Daily Life in Ancient Rome;* Peter Berresford Ellis' *The Celtic Empire;* Gustave Flaubert's *Salammbô;* Adrian Goldsworthy's *Cannae;* Victor Hanson's *Carnage and Culture;* B. H. Liddell Hart's *Scipio Africanus;* Serge Lancel's *Hannibal;* J. F. Lazenby's *The First Punic War* and *Hannibal's War: A Military History of the Second Punic War;* John Peddie's *Hannibal's War;* John Prevas' *Hannibal Crosses the Alps;* Frank M. Snowden's *Blacks in Antiquity;* John Gibson Warry's *Warfare in the Classical World;* and Terrence Wise's *Armies of the Carthaginian Wars, 265–146 B.C.*

I, CLAUDIUS

From the Autobiography of Tiberius Claudius

by Robert Graves

Tiberius Claudius Drusus Nero Germanicus lived from 10 B.C. to 54 A.D. Despised as a weakling and dismissed as an idiot because of his physical infirmities, Claudius survived the intrigues and poisonings that marked the reigns of Augustus, Tiberius, and the mad Caligula to become emperor of Rome in 41 A.D. *I, Claudius*, the first part of Robert Graves's two-part account of the life of Tiberius Claudius, is written as Claudius's autobiography and stands as one of the modern classics of historical fiction.

Fiction/Literature/0-679-72477-X

THE KING MUST DIE

by Mary Renault

The King Must Die is the story of the mythical hero Theseus, slayer of monsters, abductor of princesses, and king of Athens. In Renault's thrilling historical re-creation he emerges from his myth as a clearly defined personality: brave and aggressive, tough and quick, highly sexed and touchily proud. Renault retells Theseus's Cretan adventure, during his epic slaying of the Minotaur and ends with his fateful and bittersweet return to Athens.

Fiction/0-394-75104-3

AUGUSTUS

by John Williams

A mere eighteen years of age when his uncle, Julius Caesar, is murdered, Octavius Caesar prematurely inherits rule of the Roman Republic. Surrounded by men who are jockeying for power—Cicero, Brutus, Cassius, and Mark Antony—young Octavius must work against the powerful Roman political machinations to claim his destiny as first Roman emperor. Sprung from meticulous research and the pen of a true poet and winner of the National Book Award, *Augustus* tells the story of one man's dream to liberate a corrupt Rome from the fancy of the capriciously crooked and the wildly wealthy.

Fiction/Literature/1-4000-7673-0

THE PTOLEMIES
by Duncan Sprott

They were the last pharaohs to rule Egypt. Ptolemy Soter begins it all when he takes the kingdom of the Nile as his share of the empire and brings along Alexander the Great's carefully embalmed corpse for luck. Soon enough, Ptolemy becomes pharaoh, the living god of Egypt. Scheming priests, conniving wives, errant sons and daughters, and an epic's worth of battles and intrigue make for a tale so rich in upheaval and mayhem that perhaps only our narrator, the irreverent and disapproving Thoth, Egyptian god of Wisdom and Patron of Scribes, could do it justice.

Historical Fiction/1-4000-7510-6

THE DRUID KING
by Norman Spinrad

Vercingetorix was both a man of myth and a real historical figure—he managed, where others had failed, to unite the tribes of Gaul and lead them against the might of the Roman empire. After watching his father's harrowing death, young Vercingetorix retreats to the forest where he learns the ways of the druids. Soon he must return to civilization to reclaim his birthright and his father's honor and confront the greatest military power the world has even known—the Roman legions of Julius Caesar.

Historical Fiction/0-375-72496-6

JULIAN
by Gore Vidal

Julian the Apostate, nephew of Constantine the Great, was a military genius on par with Julius Caesar and Alexander the Great, a graceful and persuasive essayist, and a philosopher devoted to worshipping the gods of Hellenism. He became embroiled in a fierce intellectual war with Christianity that provoked his murder at the age of thirty-two, only four years into his brilliantly humane and compassionate reign.

Fiction/Literature/0-375-72706-X

VINTAGE AND ANCHOR BOOKS
Available at your local bookstore, or call toll-free to order:
1-800-793-2665 (credit cards only).